THE NEVER PARADOX

THE CHRONICLES OF JONATHAN TIBBS

VOLUME 2

T. ELLERY HODGES

Cover design by Damon Za www.damonza.com

Library of Congress Control Number: 2017904872

Foggy Night Publishing, Seattle, WA

ISBN-13: 978-0-9907746-4-8

ISBN-10: 0-9907746-4-3

Dedicated to those who wished Marty McFly had asked a few follow up questions when Doc claimed that The Flux Capacitor made time travel possible.

PROLOGUE

DATE | TIME: UNKNOWN | FEROXIAN PLANE

HEYER'S FEDORA CAST a shadow over his eyes as the sun began to set on the Feroxian plane. He crouched at the edge of a ravine, watching members of his brother's adopted species gathering below. They would take no notice of his presence. He was high above, his dark clothes blended with the terrain, and their white eyes were set on the gateway humming at the ravine's center.

A short time earlier, the vibrations had been imperceivable, but as they accelerated, their familiar sound had called to the tribe, telling them that one of their sons was returning. They approached in quiet humility, and the space within the ravine grew crowded as each entered and knelt. They bowed their heads, and pressed their right fists into the dirt.

Long ago, the ancestors of the Ferox gathering below Heyer had been told a story. A race designed with certain limits on their imagination, they could make little distinction between creator and god. So, when this story was told to them, it came from the mouths of their gods. These gods had said that this story was not like any other story—it was not a story at all, but the truth. The story had told the Ferox how and why they came to be, it gave them their roles, but most importantly—it told them who they served.

In this story, the gateway was an instrument of their gods' will, placed on their world so that the Ferox could fulfill the purpose for which they had been created.

The generation gathering below were distant descendants of those who had first heard the story. To the Ferox who lived today, these gateways were more sacred than they could have ever been to their ancestors, as the eldest among them were not so far removed from a time when their gods had abandoned them—when extinction had seemed an inevitability. It was believed that those distant ancestors had insulted their gods, and that their kind had been punished with fear. Fear, that took the form of watching helplessly as their population plummeted. This had taught them a lesson never to be forgotten.

The news of their gods' return came from *Ends the Storm,* the eldest Alpha leader among them.

"Our gods have returned and they speak through me. The thrum of the gates is restored. We have endured our punishment and we have learned its lesson. They grant our people their mercy. Their will powers the gates—their will is our purpose. Their will is our life," *Ends the Storm* had said.

Any question of the truth he spoke ended when the first of their sons was chosen. *Ends the Storm* placed a stone in the son's palm, and it had glowed red with the power of their gods' will. The youth had swallowed, and stepped through a gateway that had slumbered all their lives. When he returned, he had reached fertility and carried his trophy. That was the day that all the Feroxian tribes believed. *Ends the Storm* was more than a leader, but something they only understood from their spoken legends. Those they had looked to for leadership beforehand pledged obedience to his divine decrees. *Ends the Storm* was their prophet—his words were the path to the promised land.

Heyer knew the story as one of the many shameful chapters in his species' history. No gods had ever abandoned the Ferox, but it was true that the last living ancestors of the Ferox's creators had returned to save them. No prophet had been chosen to speak the will of their returning gods—his brother had simply taken their most respected leader's body in order to play the role. The Ferox below had no concept that alien technologies, as opposed to divine forces, were at work. In fairness, the smooth circular surface of the gateways appeared to be what the story had taught them. It looked like an ancient artifact, sculpted from the stone found within the ravine. It gave no sign that it was a complex machine, but took a simple shape, reminiscent of a sundial large enough for one of their kind to stand at its center.

As the vibrations intensified below, granular black dust that had been swept onto the platform by the planet's wind seemed to levitate off its surface. The turbulent red and black globe of the portal took shape. Currents of excess electricity arced across the sphere's liquid surface and the smell of ozone filled the ravine. When the light came, Heyer and those gathered below turned away to protect their eyes.

The vibrations stopped. Their hum becoming an echo rolling off into the distance as the Ferox turned back to the gateway. The corpse of the slain son now lay before them on the platform. *Rakes the Claw* had been a Red. One of a small handful of the tribe's mid-ranking males that Heyer could recognize by sight. Injuries covered his lifeless form, but it was the gaping hole in *Rakes the Claw's* torso that had ended his battle with the abomination on the other side—the challenger had won.

Under the circumstances, time was a relative thing, but to the Ferox present now, *Rakes the Claw* appeared to have been killed quite recently. Blood still ran from his wounds—it drained out of him and pooled on the gateway's surface. He had been brought to the threshold of fertility before he was slain. His neck was still swollen and his dead eyes were black. They shined, now, in the light of the setting sun.

The tribe hung their heads in a moment of respect for their fallen brother, and Heyer joined them in the gesture of silence. Though relieved Jonathan had survived another confrontation, he'd learned of this victory on the wrong side of the gateway. Seeing the toll his survival had on the Ferox tribe who called *Rakes the Claw* one of their sons made celebration a distant thought.

Eventually, the Ferox rose and began to disperse. As was their custom, those they called the Carriers of the Dead stayed behind. Before entering the gates, the deceased had chosen them. Should he not survive, they would remove his remains from the platform. They would wash his blood away, and take his body on a different path than the rest of the tribe. Their path would take them to a lake of exposed molten rock where the body would sink below the surface and slowly melt away. Much like the pallbearers of mankind, the request to carry the dead was given as an honor.

By the time the ravine's last occupant had gone, the glossy black pillars in the distance cast long shadows on the planet's surface. Heyer stood and, slowly, began descending from ledge to ledge with an effortless stealth. It was not long before he landed quietly on the ravine floor.

His brother's vessel, similar to his earthbound equivalent, hid in plain sight by mimicking the terrain of its surroundings. Had Heyer not known where the entry was, it would have appeared as though he approached one of the many unremarkable surfaces on the ravine's perimeter. Beneath his feet, there was a network of tunnels—caves formed during a period of the planet's geologic history when gases had been escaping its core. These caves were where the Ferox took shelter. A male of the species spent a majority of his waking hours on the planet's surface, but instincts lead him underground in moments of vulnerability. They slept, bred, and healed from injuries beneath the surface.

When the species had thrived, the females had often stayed below for long stretches after the birth of a child, the young needing the safety of the surrounding caverns and a community of watchful eyes until they reached a level of maturity. In the past few generations, Feroxian males had found fewer and fewer opportunities to achieve fertility, and as a result, the female's long stretches below were far less frequent. They now occupied the surface nearly as often as the males.

Heyer could not enter the caves through the same surface openings as the tribe, especially this close to the sun setting. He may as well stroll into a wolf den. In order to avoid alarming the entire tribe to an intruder, his brother's vessel allowed for an entrance only Heyer could open. Of the two, Heyer made the journey across dimensions when communication was required. This was a matter of practicality. Malkier's role in the Feroxian leadership meant he could not be absent for long periods without attracting notice.

Heyer pressed his hand to the glassy rock and the surface rippled as though he had disturbed the reflection of a pond. Once the entrance finished altering its molecular structure, he stepped through, and the rock returned to a solid state behind him. The interior of Malkier's vessel mimicked the natural caverns in the same manner as the outer ravine. The Ferox who entered these tunnels were never aware of crossing a boundary between true rock and the vessel's projections. Heyer's entrance appeared to be a small tunnel leading to a dead-end. Its narrow, restrictive size made it uncomfortable to the Ferox, but not a man. As such, it was seldom traveled by anyone but himself.

As he made his way to his brother's quarters, he was thankful he had a last moment of solitude before undertaking the task that had brought him back to this planet. He had never hoped to outrun the corpse of *Dams the Gate* back to the Feroxian plane. Any chance of hiding the body was long past, leaving him no other option but to triage his brother's reaction.

There were moments that Heyer fell victim to the delusion that time was a sentient being—an opponent whose agenda was usually counter to his own. Often, he could almost hear that being whispering to him: "*I understand, really, I do, but this was never meant to go your way.*" The actions of *Dams the Gate*, the rebellion that had brought about the adolescent Ferox's death at the hands of Jonathan—these were not whispers. Rather, Heyer got the sense that time saw his efforts as a joke and could not stop laughing.

As he arrived at the familiar drop-off at the end of the corridor, he waited a moment, peering down and listening for any sign that his brother was not alone before dropping into the main chamber.

A light within the room illuminated a rectangular platform raised out of the floor's center. His brother often used it as a table, but tonight, *Dams the Gate*'s body lay there as though the stone were an autopsy table. The corpse's black blood had run, hardened into tar-like lines down the sides, and pooled where the edges met the floor. Heyer's brother sat close by, staring into the remains as if seeing something that wasn't really there.

The light illuminating the platform was coming from a window recessed into the wall behind his brother. The opening projected a visual persona where the artificial intelligence of Malkier's vessel could be addressed. Her name was Cede, though, in reality, she had no gender.

She was humanoid, to the degree that she possessed a head, arms, a torso, and legs, but her appearance was made in the image of a Borealis, the brothers' birth-race.

When the brothers had been born into their natural bodies, they possessed translucent skin, and one could see their bodily fluids pumping, and the movements of their internal organs, muscle, and skeleton. Though it would seem an unsightly lifeform to gaze on in a mirror, their biology had been more like staring at precious metals. Cede's skin was similar. Looking at her, Heyer could see the mercury-like fluid and the tissues like polished silver beneath the skin.

Cede's face was not chosen at random, but had belonged to a woman named Sayira, their mother. Heyer had no memory of her, and felt no emotional attachment to the face or the name outside of a regret that told him he should. When the brothers were young men, he had been jealous that Malkier had been alive to know their mother. Over the centuries, seeing the pain her absence brought him, Heyer had grown to suspect Malkier envied him for just the opposite, Heyer having been spared from knowing the misery of losing her.

Cede's projection was no mere avatar displayed on a monitor. Instead, she appeared to look in on them from her own chamber within the wall. Her room was brightly lit, and the walls a milky white with seamless contours, all a stark contrast to the bleak caverns that made up his brother's home. The illusion was so real it seemed that Heyer could reach through the window and touch her if he wished.

Heyer felt it ironic that whenever he interacted with Cede, she felt more alien to him than mankind. It was a strange thing when one's own species was so foreign that one could hardly tell individuals apart. Heyer knew the face of his mother. He would recognize his original face, and his brother's, but when he saw historical records of his own species, he could scarcely tell one Borealis from the next.

After all this time, and despite all of his brother's animosity for his own species, Malkier had never asked the A.I. to change her projection. Cede didn't have the character, or perhaps programming, that Heyer's own vessel possessed. She never displayed a sense of self, almost as if she'd been created to think the concept narcissistic. Perhaps, though, Cede had the capacity to see herself however she wished, and simply lacked the desire to be anything more than his brother's tool—a means to an end.

Heyer heard his brother's voice, then: "Thank you. That will be all, Cede."

The computer nodded as her chamber disappeared, taking the light with it, a stone wall forming where her window had been.

"I know you are there, brother," Malkier whispered.

Heyer closed his eyes, then exhaled slowly. The quiet flap of his coat and the muffled contact of his shoes' soles touching the floor confirmed his presence. He bowed his head in empathy before Malkier, and the gesture required no false sentiment. He could loathe everything his brother had become, but could not abandon compassion in the face of this tragedy.

Malkier did not move, but sat, unblinking. The white slits of his eyes might have hid from the Ferox how lost his brother now was. The subtle manifestations of a Borealis' suffering beneath a Feroxian shell were nearly imperceivable to his brother's adopted species. But Heyer saw grief stewing in Malkier's disbelief, as though a part of his brother was not ready to comprehend what was lying in front of him. Heyer understood—once he accepted what he saw, there would be nowhere left for Malkier to hide. He would have to take responsibility for the part he'd played in it.

Dams the Gate's eyes, black and empty, stared lifelessly at the chamber's ceiling. Closing the eyes was not a Feroxian practice, nor was grieving over the dead in such long duration. Heyer wondered if his brother had taken the remains under some false pretense, abused his role as prophet to keep the body from being cast into the molten burial grounds. *Dams the Gate* had been forbidden access to Earth, so it was unlikely he had chosen carriers of the dead. How ever the events had played out upon the body's return, Heyer hoped his brother's private grief remained unknown to the Ferox. Though unlikely, alien frailties within Malkier could give the few Ferox who questioned his leadership more reason to mistrust him.

Malkier looked away from the body as Heyer stepped closer. Now, he saw more clearly the injuries the corpse had endured. As Heyer's eyes traveled down the face of the dead Ferox, he saw the faint reflections of light caught by broken links of chain. Shards of metal were embedded like shrapnel in the jaw and neck. When his eyes fell lower, mental alarms went off, and Heyer had to turn his face away from his brother to hide the storm of thought passing through him.

Jonathan had said he'd thrown *Dams the Gate* from the rooftop of an unfinished skyscraper. When Heyer had learned the Ferox's name, he should have asked for the specifics. He had failed to imagine they may prove so dangerous.

He reached for the chain. There was no chance Malkier had missed so glaring a detail, but Heyer could take it from sight, try to keep his brother from fixating on it.

The sound of metal links moving against one another caused Malkier's face to turn to him in anger.

"Leave it!"

Heyer let the chain fall against the stone table, the links shattering into hundreds of brittle metallic shards as they hit the surface.

"I am sorry," Heyer said. "I… I only wanted to remove it for you." Heyer trailed off, but his expression remained one of shared sorrow. Malkier's abrupt rage quickly burned through its fuel, and his brother retreated back into grief after he realized Heyer's intentions had been to protect him from a sight they both knew he didn't want to see.

When his brother's gaze left him, Heyer quietly swept some of the shards off the stone, palming them into his jacket pocket. An analysis would give him the specifics, but the steel's deterioration would give him an idea of how long ago it was that *Dams the Gate's* body had returned to the Feroxian plane.

"You've never believed in Karma," Malkier said.

Heyer found Malkier's gaze now lingered at the line on the floor—where the blood had pooled beside the table. "No." Heyer said. "If I recall, you thought it an overly human sentiment yourself."

His brother nodded slowly. "Eyes watching? Tallying our trespasses? Singling us out for…" Malkier paused, grimacing as though the words he'd thought to say had stabbed him, and he could not yet speak through the pain. "The death of one man? Could fate care so much?"

Heyer approached slowly and gently placed his small, human hand on his brother's monstrous shoulder. "Sometimes chance is simply cruel. Trust me, you only do yourself harm looking for justice in it."

Malkier's head shook, shivering in a show of his unwillingness to accept coincidence. He needed causality, needed there to be a meaning. "He entered the same gate. He knew…" Malkier said. "And the weapon, it is—"

"I know," Heyer whispered.

A moment passed, and Malkier turned his eyes questioningly to Heyer. "You have spoken to the man responsible?" Malkier asked. "You could not have known to come so quickly if it were otherwise."

Heyer nodded, knowing there was no point in denying what his brother had reasoned out.

"Does he think himself a warrior?" Malkier asked. "Having murdered a child?"

"Please, Brother, you know he was given no choice. Do not go looking for a villain," Heyer said. "There is no justice to pursue on Earth. You must look for answers here. We must know how he entered the gate without our knowledge."

Malkier grew quiet, seeming to ponder his brother's words. As time passed in silence, Heyer sat beside him, hoping that his presence might somehow help to dull what pain it could.

"This man," Malkier finally said. "Was he named?"

Heyer drew in a long breath after the question, and made no attempt to hide that he was not sure if it was wise to answer. His brother was not asking that he reveal the man's birth name, his Earth identity. Malkier sought to know the honorific *Dams the Gate* had granted Jonathan. The Ferox often gave those they respected in combat a name. Malkier only hoped to learn what *Dams the Gate* had thought of his opponent before he fell.

"*Brings the Rain*," Heyer said.

JULY 1990

FIFTEEN YEARS EARLIER

CHAPTER ONE

JULY 1990 | FIFTEEN YEARS EARLIER

TEARS RAN DOWN the swell under Grant's eye as he cowered in the shadows. He was still in pajamas, a child, gripping his knees with his arms as he stared down at the floorboards. He shivered, trying to hear if his aunt's footsteps were coming closer or heading away.

Just go, he prayed. *You'll just be later if you keep looking. I'm not worth it.*

He had crawled to the center of the space beneath the antique pool table his uncle had left behind. If he stayed precisely where he was, his aunt couldn't see him unless she went to the trouble of getting down on her hands and knees. He feared the day she bothered, the day when she gave him the ultimatum of coming out on his own or her crawling in and pulling him out.

Having hidden here many times, he'd discovered that the underside of the table had been neglected the same detailed attention lavished on the exterior. The outside shined with smooth, oiled wood, but beneath, the surfaces were coarse and splintery to the touch. Whoever built the table must have felt there was nothing to be gained spending time on the interior when the exterior was all anyone saw.

Finally, Grant heard the spring on their back door as it stretched and then pulled the door shut, followed by the clicks of his aunt's heels receding up the driveway. When her car's engine started, he realized he'd been holding his breath. He exhaled and shut his eyes, gasping air in hungrily now that she was gone. He began to whimper. When the engine sounded far enough away, he crawled out from under the table and walked to the window to watch her car turn the corner.

He was on borrowed time now. When she was late for work, it would be his fault. He'd been what slowed her down. She wouldn't forget—this morning's terror was only on pause until his aunt came home that evening.

He stepped away from the window and sat on the couch, staring emptily at his bare feet. He thought over what had led to the swollen spot beneath his eye. He'd forgotten to put his toys away, left them out on the floor of the hallway. She had snapped the heel of her shoe when she'd stepped awkwardly on one of the action figures.

He'd woken up in pain when his aunt struck him in the cheek with the same toy. It had taken him a while to understand, but she'd been screaming at him. Grant was a selfish and worthless drain, she said—the reason for everything wrong in her life. He was why her husband had left them, why her sister had died in childbirth. She despised him when strangers thought he was her bastard child. His only value was when they knew that he wasn't hers, when she could brag about her selfless adoption of her sister's poor orphaned child. His only value was as a symbol of her charity.

Grant heard the clock ticking then, the only sound in the empty house. Seeing the time, he bit his lip and reached for the television remote, a hopeful smile growing on his face as he flipped stations and finally heard the theme of his favorite cartoon.

"*He-Man and the Masters of the Universe*," said the television.

He leaned forward on the couch and watched Prince Adam of Eternia in yet another life-and-death struggle with the evil Skeletor. Grant waited for his favorite part, when all seemed lost and the good guys brought out the real weapon. He was transfixed as Prince Adam reached for the Sword of Power sheathed across his back and raised it into the air.

Then came the words that flipped the switch: "*By the power of Greyskull!*"

Lightning and magic funneled into Adam through the sword, transforming him. His clothing was stripped away to reveal a battle harness and chest plate with its insignia of the red iron cross.

"*I have the power!*" He-Man roared.

The events of the morning were forgotten for a half-hour as cartoon images danced across Grant's eyes. The story quieted his fears. No one knew who Prince Adam had been destined to become. One day, a wise and mystical being had come along and given him limitless strength, and every powerless moment that had come before was finally given meaning.

OCTOBER 2005

NOW

CHAPTER TWO

THURSDAY | OCTOBER 6, 2005 | 2:00 AM | SEATTLE

JONATHAN STOOD IN front of the mirror, gold lines of light radiating out from beneath his skin. He'd been alone in his bedroom when the twitch in his chest told him the enemy had opened the gates. The absence of the searing pain that normally accompanied activation had been enough to make him suspect he was dreaming. The two figures on either side of him in the reflection confirmed it.

His father's expression was grim but certain. Opposite him stood the little girl in the pink hoodie. Jonathan didn't know her name, but most nights, her dead eyes waited for him in the reflection. Whenever he gazed back, all he could feel was the guilt of abandoning her. Most nights, he didn't meet the child's eyes, but tried to look at his father's. Douglas placed a hand on his shoulder. He couldn't feel the reassuring weight of it—he could only see the gesture in the mirror before his father gave him a nod.

Jonathan hardened his expression and returned it—the time for standing in front of mirrors was over.

He didn't remember gathering his gear, pulling Excali-bar out of its concealment, or starting the engine on his bike. Time played its tricks as it always did in dreams, and soon he was speeding down a street, tracking the enemy with alien instincts. Knowing that he was only off to fight a dream didn't change anything.

He was later than he preferred, the gateway having already delivered its passenger. He could feel the Ferox on the move near the east end of the city. A moment later, he was on the outskirts of downtown, amongst the older brick buildings. No longer on the roads, he ran along the city's roof tops, tracking the signal as it moved between the buildings on the streets below.

He leaped, quiet and efficient, from one roof to the next. The Ferox thundered its way forward in search of people to slaughter, unaware that the very *life* it sought to take was closing in from above. Something was off about this dream though, different, and Jonathan sensed it like a man who was approaching the wrong car in a parking lot. The make, model, and paint job may have all been correct, but he suspected he was approaching a vehicle that he didn't have the key to.

Jonathan didn't recognize this part of the city, wasn't sure if he'd ever been here. Regardless, the dream carried him forward. He pushed himself to come into striking distance and threw himself from the safety of the roof tops. He began a hard descent toward his enemy's back. Its skin was blood red, covered in the chaotic web-like exterior of black tar. The Ferox's biological armor was a warning not to underestimate it. Tonight's enemy was older, more experienced, more controlled. It would not easily lose its patience, not be as quick to give into instinctual rage like one of the species' frog-skinned adolescents.

He tucked his knees toward his chest as he plunged out of the skyline, readying against the coming impact. This maneuver… it seemed as if he'd practiced it tirelessly, to the point of thoughtless execution, but that familiarity was strange. He wasn't merely starting the fight with a surprise attack, but a devastating combination of strikes. Yet, what followed was a mystery to him the moment it began.

When they connected, the Ferox's feet lost contact with the ground, its body slamming into the street as he pressed his knee into its lower back and grabbed hold of its shoulders. He rode the momentum aboard his enemy's back while its face bore through the asphalt, tearing a gouge into the street beneath them.

This wasn't going to stop it—the Ferox could take a lot of damage—but Jonathan knew the bastard was going to feel it. The friction from ripping through the street finally brought them to a stop, but he was two steps into the future before his enemy had a chance to shake its surprise. He realized that he expected the Red to plant a fist into the pavement, that it was beginning to push itself up out of the ground by putting the weight onto its right arm. He knew when the moment was right, and struck with precision into the side of its shoulder blade.

He understood what he'd done when a wail of agony screamed out beneath him.

In that brief instant, while the Red's arm was placed just so, a chink in its armor had presented itself. His fist had targeted it as though he'd exploited the weakness a hundred times before. He'd felt the soft give in the creature's exterior, thinner skin, when his strike slipped in past its rugged outer armor and hit a leathery patch that covered a joint in the creature's skeleton.

Jonathan jumped, back flipping off the Ferox to land on his feet behind it. He'd gotten clear right before the thrashing Ferox turned over and lashed out for him. Experience told him to push the advantage, that he should have kept the Red pinned, should have relentlessly hammered the back of the beast's skull into the asphalt while it was face down. Even though every neuron in his mind was screaming that this was a mistake, the dream gave no regard, refused to obey his sense of strategy. Unable to seize control of his actions, he could only watch as the Ferox rose back to its full height and set its empty white gaze on him. Yet, the menace that usually stared back at him was conflicted, hiding flinches of pain. The Ferox's right arm hung limp at its side, and the creature was trying to avoid moving it.

Jonathan's eyes grew wide as he realized it was injured. Feroxian bones were strong, near impossible to break, but they were malleable. From the look of the arm, Jonathan was betting that he'd put a bend in its skeleton, right at the joint, which had hindered its movement. He watched the Red slowly come to the same conclusion. Hesitation surfaced on its face and it took a step back instead of forward.

"It's called fear," Jonathan said. "Your entire species is going to feel it."

The moment was stolen from him without warning as pain shot down his left side.

Suddenly, knocked off his feet and spinning in the air, the building on the far side of the street came charging toward him. He was upside down when he hit, nearly punching through the brick and mortar of the building's exterior. The wall held, though with a man-sized dent left behind, and debris following him as he dropped back onto sidewalk. He reached for Excali-bar on instinct, already in motion, crouched onto his knees and ignored the many reports of pain from his body. He searched the street for what could have hit him, finding where he'd stood a moment earlier.

There was nothing, only a sudden, disturbing silence.

It was as though a Ferox had walked up behind him and backhanded him across the street. Yet, that was impossible. He hadn't taken his eyes from the beast, hadn't felt any movement within his mind. He fought down a sudden surge of adrenaline as he realized he no longer felt his enemy at all. The asphalt still lay torn apart in the street like a trail of destruction pointing to where the injured Red should still be standing, but it had vanished.

The sound of breaking glass and bending metal drew his attention. Turning toward the noise, he saw an overturned pickup truck barreling down on him. With no time, his reflexes thrust him forward, sending him rolling into the street and barely getting clear before the vehicle finished punching a hole through the wall.

Coming out of the roll onto his knees, Jonathan felt the rumbling thud of a massive body hitting the street behind him. A shadow crawled over him, the night seeming to grow darker as he knelt in the street with his back exposed. He spun, coming to his feet and fully committing as he swung Excali-bar at his attacker.

There was a thunderous clap as the demolition bar connected.

Jonathan's body jerked to a painful and unexpected halt after having struck an unmovable object. A massive black fist had closed around the end of his weapon. His gaze followed up its arm—charcoal, rhino-like, Feroxian skin covered with the crisscrossing black tar. When his eyes reached its face, where its empty white slits stared down at him, he saw it was waiting for his attention. The Ferox studied him with an almost human calmness he'd never seen in the species. Its stillness quickly began to drill holes in his mental armor.

"They will not follow you," the Black Ferox said. "You have no hope to offer them."

Its words did not translate in his mind. They came to him in English, though disturbed by the guttural tone of Feroxian vocal cords.

The words were followed by a short-lived quiet inside of him. He closed his eyes, and for a moment, he saw fractures forming across a brick wall, black smoke seeping through the cracks. He swallowed the urge to run, choked it down into a void within him. He could hear it, a pressure building, shaking the city around him, the asphalt breaking beneath his feet as his dream began to crumble.

When he spoke, his words betrayed a raw hatred for this monster who dared to speak his fears. "No, I can't give them hope," Jonathan said, then his voice dropped to a whisper, "but I can give them anger."

The Ferox studied him, pondering the reaction, its eyes taking in the shaking landscape of the dream with a demeaning curiosity. When Jonathan's stare failed to waiver, the beast spoke one last time. "Your anger," it said, "will never be enough."

With impossible speed and strength, the beast kicked into his chest. The grip Jonathan had on Excali-bar, the footing he had on the ground, and the air he had in his lungs was all lost in an instant. The pull of gravity seemed to shift violently, and he was airborne, watching the face of the monster and the crumbling streets rapidly shrinking below him. Yet he didn't feel as though he were shooting through the air, rather, as though he were falling.

He fought to breathe, though his lungs insisted that they had forgotten how. He finally gasped—air came in and his heart began to slow. He wiped the sweat off his forehead, sitting up to place his feet on the cool floorboards. His room was dark, but the moonlight from his bedroom window let him see the outline of his reflection in the mirror. Only Jonathan looked back at him. In time, the illusions of the nightmare resolved themselves with reality.

His dreams had always been relentless, but for weeks now, they had ended on the same theme. He felt he'd already gotten the message his subconscious seemed so adamant that he acknowledge. His self-doubt didn't seem to want to take any chance he might forget it.

The muffled sounds of the television downstairs told him he wasn't the only person up, and he knew it was Hayden again. There was no point mentioning that he had noticed his roommate's insomnia—Jonathan would have been the pot calling the kettle black. In truth, he had been grateful of the development. He didn't wish for his friend to have any issues sleeping, of course, but since Jonathan had last spoken to Heyer, he'd had more trouble sleeping through the night. His roommate being in the same boat gave him someone else to talk to.

Hayden waved as he came down the stairs. The volume on the TV was down low, so he wouldn't wake anyone else. When Jonathan looked at the screen to see what he had on, the film looked familiar, but wasn't his roommate's typical science-fiction-action-adventure nonsense.

"What's this?" Jonathan whispered.

"The Shawshank Redemption," Hayden said. "It's one of my favorites. I watch it once or twice a year."

Jonathan sat beside him on the couch; a moment later he remembered having seen the film at some point. It was the story of Andy Dufresne, sentenced to life in prison for a crime he didn't commit. Hayden was near the climax, and Andy was already making his escape to freedom through a sewer pipe, or "a river of shit," per the narration by Morgan Freeman. The symbolism was straight-forward enough that Hayden didn't feel the need to pause and explain it as he usually did. To reach freedom, Andy was literally crawling through a sewer pipe, the action a fitting metaphor for what his mind had been forced to endure while imprisoned.

Jonathan watched quietly as Andy pulled himself out of the pipe and into the open, plunging into a stream where the sewage emptied. Then Andy got to his feet and began to run, tearing off the prison uniform he'd been forced to wear. Rain beat down on him, but as Andy pulled off the filthy clothes, he reached into the air and let the water cleanse him, near rapture with the feeling of freedom he'd won.

A question came to mind, the type Jonathan knew his roommate would appreciate. "Why is it always raining?" Jonathan asked.

Hayden paused the film and turned to him, a small smirk on his face. "Writers and directors use rain a lot in film," Hayden said. "Mostly it heightens the drama of a scene."

"Right, but..." Jonathan paused. "Why?"

"You can see water a lot of ways," Hayden said. "It can be a cleansing, hence its use in sacraments like baptism. Sometimes, it's indicative of life, as most living things require water to survive. It's also a force, as the flow of water can break through about anything if given enough time. Rain itself is more specific. Some think rain drops are like tears, and they remind us of crying. But, I think it's more basic than any of that."

Jonathan turned to Hayden with a knowing grin. Now that he'd built up the drama with what he didn't believe, his real answer was ready for Jonathan's ears.

"Rain means change," Hayden said. "Change just gets associated with sorrow most of the time, because it's not human nature to embrace it."

Jonathan nodded, and Hayden thoughtfully started elaborating.

"You can't always predict what the change will be, but if the director of a film is going out of his way to capture a scene in the middle of a downfall, nine times out of ten, something big is about to change. In this case, Andy went from a prisoner to a free man. The change is a happy one."

"Not usually the case?" Jonathan asked.

"Depends on how you feel about it," Hayden said. "Take the finale of the Matrix trilogy, when Neo faces off with Agent Smith. Right about when Neo sees that he can never defeat Smith through violence, he realizes that the only way to save mankind is to do the one thing he thought would kill its last hope. So he sacrifices himself, lets Smith imprint onto him. You could say he must let his enemy become a part of him, because fighting evil as an external enemy is a battle that couldn't be won. He only has the means to destroy Smith's army by taking the darkness into himself.

"It's happy, sorta', in that Neo finds a solution. It's sad because that solution means he must sacrifice himself to the point of being consumed by his enemy. Still, the rain comes down in heaps throughout the entire battle, and when it stops, everything has changed. Mankind has been freed, but hundreds have died, including Neo himself. How it all shakes out—good and evil, darkness and light—those are all subjective." Hayden turned to Jonathan and smiled. "But change—that part is certain."

CHAPTER THREE

THURSDAY | OCTOBER 6, 2005 | 2:00 AM | PORTLAND

IN THE EARLY morning, long before the sun would be an obstacle to The Cell's activities, Olivia stood in a cemetery outside of Portland, Oregon. She was flanked on each side by men in suits, monitoring status updates from various locations around the perimeter. Extra precautions had been put in place to ensure that no civilians became aware of this evening's undertakings.

"The vehicle has arrived, ma'am," one of her men said.

Olivia nodded, and a moment later, a black sedan pulled up. A man dressed in a grey suit stepped out of the backseat. Agent Laurence Rivers studied his surroundings before walking across the lawn to where she was waiting for him. The dark skin of his face showed unperturbed professionalism, though Olivia imagined this was a mask hiding both jet lag and a curiosity that was spilling over at this point.

Agent Rivers had been pulled off his current assignment and flown here without explanation. He was about to interview for a position that he had never applied for, and if Olivia approved him, she had little doubt he'd accept.

"Good morning, ma'am," Rivers said, coming to stop a few feet from her. "I was instructed to report to you immediately. I apologize, but I've not been told much about what this is regarding."

"No apology required, Agent Rivers. I informed your superiors that I would brief you on arrival," Olivia replied, glancing into the graveyard. There was a group of bushes and trees not far off. They were currently surrounding an outpouring of artificial light. "Please, take a short walk with me?"

"Yes," Rivers said, then hesitated. "Pardon, but may I ask how I should address you, ma'am?"

"You may call me Olivia," she said as she nodded to one of the men behind her. He handed her a folder and Rivers fell in beside her as she began to walk, though neither of the men followed. "For the sake of this assignment, you will report to me. I have no official title or rank. You'll have realized by now that we are operating outside of standard channels."

"Yes," Rivers replied. "I've never been instructed to meet my commanding officer in a graveyard at two in the morning, for that matter."

"Efficiency, Rivers. Meeting here helps to kill more than a few birds with one stone." Olivia said. "Your CV shows an impeccable record for adherence to protocol and experience in conducting computer crime investigations. That, and an aptitude for lip reading. Your background shows no immediate family or other such attachments."

"That's all correct," he replied.

A moment of silence followed as Rivers continued beside her, the light in the trees growing closer.

"Our Cell is charged with investigating the activities of a perceived threat to Global Security. This threat, unfortunately, is in possession of technology superior to any at our disposal. As such, our methods are highly specialized.

"What I am about to tell you could easily be discussed over a telephone or sent in an email. However, we have no means of ensuring the protection of electronic transmissions against this threat, so we avoid them whenever possible. Exceptions are made, but sparingly."

She paused then for a moment, turning to look Rivers in the eye as he came to a stop beside her.

"When it comes to the methods developed to engage this threat, certain details are kept strictly off-book," Olivia said. "In other words, pay close attention to what I tell you throughout this discussion, as it is not written down anywhere other than in the minds of myself and the individuals I choose to work with."

Once Rivers nodded his understanding, she handed him the folder she'd been carrying. He accepted it politely before reaching into his pocket and retrieving a small flashlight he kept on a key chain. She studied him as he clicked on the light and became fully engrossed in the folder's contents.

Inside, Rivers found several photos, incident accounts, and a police report. If he was as sharp as she'd been assured, he would quickly see evidence from crime scenes that appeared to be murder investigations. She was curious to see how long it took him to notice that no homicides were mentioned in any of the reports. Once he'd realized this, he would notice that all but one of the sites listed appeared to be associated with military facilities. The last item he would find in the folder was a photo of a tall, blond man in a black hat and trench coat.

"What sticks out to you in the file, Agent Rivers?" she asked.

"This incident involving Jonathan Tibbs. He appears to be the only civilian victim, and he also appears to be the only individual whose whereabouts are currently known."

"Very quick," Olivia replied. "However, you have made one assumption."

Rivers' brow drew in as he went over his choice of words in his head. Olivia waited patiently until he shrugged.

"You referred to the individuals in the folder as victims," Olivia said.

Rivers blinked, then nodded slowly, conceding that he hadn't considered the angle. "If not as victims," he said, "how are they classified?"

"That is one of the many questions we are attempting to answer," Olivia said. "What else did you notice?"

"All male, in their early-to-mid-twenties. All reported seeing or being confronted by a tall, blond man before being..." Rivers trailed off, then flipped through the medical reports and frowned again. "In all these cases, no explanation is given for the condition they were found in," he said. "Have these details been excluded on purpose?"

"The reports are complete." Olivia replied. "No credible explanation was found for the blood loss or state of mind. Yet all evidence leading up to the events indicated that each man had no contact with any of the others, and that there were no grounds to believe they were being dishonest about their experiences."

"So, then," Rivers said. "Have any theories been proposed as to what's going on here?"

"Nothing solid," Olivia said. "Certainly nothing we can test."

"This file, does it contain all incidents on record?" Rivers asked.

Olivia looked at him but made a point of not answering the question. He took the hint and followed beside her as she continued toward the light in the bushes. Soon, the sound of heavy equipment began to reach them.

Rivers pulled out the picture of the blond man from the folder. "The man in the fedora," Rivers said. "He have a name?"

"We refer to him as 'The Mark'," Olivia replied.

"May I ask, in all due politeness…" Rivers said. "If you've been able to get close enough to photograph him, why hasn't he been brought into custody for interrogation?"

Olivia stopped, turning to face him once more. "We haven't been able to manage it."

Rivers frowned. "Why is that?"

"The Mark has been followed by a team of trained specialists into a boxed alley, only to disappear. Documents have been removed from buildings with the highest level of security, only to find that surveillance footage showed no sign of anyone entering or exiting the building, that any camera hooked up to a network during one of these incidents has been compromised, the footage irretrievable or untrustworthy."

"So what are we dealing with here, then?" Rivers asked. "A magician and a team of hackers?"

Olivia allowed a moment's pause before she spoke. "What would you say, Agent Rivers, if I told you I have seen this man disappear with my own eyes?" Olivia asked. "Blink away as though he'd ceased to exist?"

"I'd say you were talking science fiction," Rivers replied.

Olivia raised an eye brow. "You would be mistaken."

As they reached the stand of bushes, she led Rivers through an opening to where the activity was taking place. Two large sets of flood lights illuminated a burial site. A civilian contractor shut down a bulldozer as the rest of his team pulled a casket out of the hole that had been dug. Olivia watched Rivers' eyes fall on a pile of rolled grass the workers had stacked beside the site. His attention then moved to a new coffin sitting beside it. The moment that the original casket had been retrieved, the team set to work replacing it with the new one.

"You're exhuming this body and covering it up—replacing the ground cover with fresh grass and a decoy casket," he observed.

"Does this bother you, Agent Rivers?" Olivia asked.

He hesitated only briefly before shaking his head. "No, ma'am. This situation clearly requires the utmost discretion," he replied. "I am curious, though—what is it you hope to learn from the body?"

"If experience sets the precedent, then what we find in that casket will lead to more questions than it will answer," Olivia said as she stared at the muddy box being loaded into one of the Cell's vehicles. "You will find it necessary to be comfortable reacting to situations where you seldom know what it is you're dealing with, Rivers. That is, if you're brought on board."

"Understood," Rivers replied.

Olivia studied him a moment, but saw no doubt cross his features. "Good," she replied.

They watched the operation continue without speaking, making sure the team executed as instructed. Finally, Olivia nodded to one of her nearby agents and he began to give commands over his ear piece to remove any trace that The Cell had been present and prepare to clear out.

Olivia indicated for Rivers to follow her, and they walked back the way they had entered. She resumed their conversation once they were out of earshot.

"Originally, when a subject such as Mr. Tibbs was identified, a standard protocol was initiated. A surveillance team was dispatched to follow and observe. Police and medical records concerning the event, if they could not be removed entirely, were replaced with documents that disguised any suspicions. Local law enforcement was instructed that the event was outside their jurisdiction, any evidence retrieved turned over, and all investigations ceased immediately. Any media coverage was suppressed.

"Despite these efforts, my predecessors found that standard procedures were ineffective. Any surveillance information that was not gathered by a team using anything but their own eyes and ears was untrustworthy. Audio bugging of a domicile was useless. Monitoring the subject's email and online activity also proved to be fraught with misinformation.

"However, what repeatedly frustrated my predecessors' efforts was that, no matter what degree of diligence was made to keep the identities of our team from the subject's knowledge, these men repeatedly became aware of their tails and the deep cover agents installed in their lives. The effort became useless—one subject was so bold as to step onto his front porch and wave to everyone who'd been assigned to watch him."

"You've discovered how they were identifying their tails?"

"Not precisely," she said. "A method of observation was developed based on the theory of a civilian consultant. We refer to this as the secondary protocol. So far, it has remained effective. The subject, Jonathan Tibbs in this case, can be aware that he is under surveillance, but remains unable to identify members of our team or their locations."

"What was the theory?" Agent Rivers asked.

"It was proposed that these men were showing a form of precognition as a side effect of what The Mark had done to them. The secondary protocol required our team never engage The Mark under any circumstances. So far, it has been the stressing of 'any circumstances' that has made the difference. As long as our people can be trusted to do absolutely nothing outside of observe from a safe distance, they retain their anonymity."

"You'll have to forgive me—I mean no disrespect by asking this, but a superior has never, ever asked me to consider psychic abilities as a factor."

"What is your question, Rivers?" Olivia asked.

"Why would a no-engagement protocol limit a psychic precognition of our team members?"

Olivia nodded. "As far as *why* this has proven effective, the theory is that the subject's precognition is related to the intentions of others. If no intention of intervention is present in their instructions, no agents' identities become compromised."

Agent Rivers paced, puzzling over the explanation. "So, by removing any contingency in which the team could foreseeably interact with the subject in a manner that would reveal their true identities, they remained unknown to him."

Olivia nodded slowly, studying him for one last moment before coming to a decision. "I want to offer you a position, Agent Rivers," she said. "Return to the vehicle that brought you here. You will be taken to the airport, where you will be brought up to speed on the team's current efforts regarding Jonathan Tibbs. I will join you shortly, after tests on the body have concluded."

"Yes, ma'am," Agent Rivers nodded.

Leaving as he'd been instructed, he paused after a few steps and turned back to her.

"I probably shouldn't ask, but I'd like to be sure I'm clear on what is expected of me," Rivers said.

"Yes, Rivers?" Olivia asked.

"The decoy casket," Rivers said. "Does it also contain a corpse?"

"No," Olivia said.

"So, earlier, when you said you were killing a few birds with one stone…" Rivers said. "Am I to understand that if I, theoretically, had been less agreeable to your team exhuming Tibbs' father in this manner, that I'd have been wise to keep it to myself?"

She wanted to smile, but she didn't. "Rest assured, Agent River, that you would not be here if I had any doubts that you would not be compatible with our operation."

CHAPTER FOUR

THURSDAY | OCTOBER 6, 2005 | 9:00 PM | SEATTLE

JONATHAN HEARD PAIGE'S door shut on the floor above.

"That seemed..." He trailed off.

"Cold?" Collin asked. "Yeah, what's colder is that you're only now noticing. She's been pissed off at you for a few days now."

Jonathan frowned as he turned back to Hayden and Collin. The three had been sitting in the living room when their conversation had come to an awkward stop. Paige had walked in, politely greeted everyone but Jonathan, then brushed past him on her way to her room.

"What did I do?" Jonathan asked. "I've hardly seen her the last few days." When neither of his roommates immediately offered an explanation, he was forced to probe. "Collin, you two have been hanging out a lot," Jonathan said. "She didn't say anything?"

Collin grimaced slightly and turned his palms up. "Honestly, when I noticed that mentioning your name was followed by silence," Collin said, "I stopped mentioning your name."

"Great," Jonathan said. "Thanks for the heads up."

Collin shrugged apologetically. Meanwhile, Jonathan noticed that Hayden seemed to be trying a little too hard not to look at him. It wouldn't have been telling, except the film they had been watching had been paused since Paige came home and now Hayden seemed unwilling to break eye contact with the still image on the screen.

"Hayden?" Jonathan asked.

The bearded man's eyebrows lifted but he didn't turn to look at Jonathan. Finally, the silence drew out as Jonathan patiently stared at him and Hayden's face paled.

"Okay, I don't actually know," he said. "But she looked upset a few days ago, like she might have been crying. I asked her about it, but I think I just embarrassed her. She said it was nothing, went to her room, and closed the door."

Jonathan tongued the side of his teeth while he thought. "Maybe I should go talk..." He trailed off as he saw both roommates shaking their heads, their faces pinched into sardonic lemon-faced smiles.

"Tibbs, I find that having to ask what it is you're sorry about before apologizing has about a fifty-fifty chance of making things worse," Collin said. "I'd figure it out first."

Jonathan thought it over a bit longer before he nodded. "You're probably right."

With that behind them, Hayden unpaused the film, James Cameron's *The Terminator*, and the three continued watching. For a while, Jonathan failed to pay much attention, preoccupied with trying to remember the last time he'd spoken to Paige but coming up empty.

Maybe something to do with Lincoln? he wondered.

Paige had asked him to have his personal trainer over, and he'd eventually done so. The trainer had hit it off better with his roommates than with Paige, but the two had met up together at least once afterward. That had seemed to be the end of it, neither mentioning anything about the date to him. Jonathan figured it simply hadn't gone anywhere. He didn't see how that could turn around and get Paige mad at him, but he was grasping at straws.

"I didn't build the fucking thing," said Michael Biehn, the actor playing the part of Sergeant Kyle Reese.

"And pause," Collin said, pointing at the screen. "You see, there it is—so quick you hardly notice. They try to hide it in plain sight."

"Hide what?" Jonathan asked.

Before Collin could answer for himself, Hayden chimed in with a loud sigh. "Every story with time travel has some lame concession to make the plot work," Hayden said. "Collin here thinks it's the dirty secret of all time travel movies. At some point, the story throws up its hands and says 'because that's how it works.'"

"You don't agree?" Jonathan asked.

Hayden shrugged. "In the case of the Terminator movies," Hayden said, "yeah, there are logic gaps you could drive a semi through. Doesn't mean it couldn't be done. Stories like Terminator struggle because most of their logic concessions are really excuses for better action scenes."

Jonathan rubbed at his forehead with his index finger. Sadly, his roommates' overzealous consumption of science fiction actually made them the best authorities on time travel he had. "What… paradox?" Jonathan guessed. In the past, whenever his roommates were upset with time travel logic, they indefinitely brought up time paradox.

Hayden chuckled. "We haven't even gotten to that yet," he said. "Take this scene: the police ask the time traveler, sent back to save Sarah Conner from a killer cyborg, why he hasn't brought any weapons from the future along to help protect her."

"Yeah," Jonathan replied. "I've seen the movie."

"Well, what does he say?" Hayden asked rhetorically. "*'Only living tissue can go.'* Makes no sense. I mean if you can send a robot with skin surrounding it back in time, why not wrap a plasma gun in a skin bag and take it along with you?"

"Ahh," Jonathan nodded. "Because that would be a boring movie."

"Hence the logic starts to unravel, and you have to tell your brain to butt out if you want to enjoy the movie," Collin said. "When the rules are examined, the story has to admit it makes no sense, which is when lines like *'I didn't build the fucking thing'* rear their ugly head."

Jonathan nodded his agreement, though he was really thinking that he wished he could bring these two along as consultants whenever Heyer showed up. Though the movie's dialog was vulgar, it was almost precisely how the damn alien had replied when Jonathan asked him anything specific about how the device implanted in his chest worked.

"But back to what you said, 'paradox'," Hayden continued. "Say you send a machine back in time to kill someone. Okay, fine, but if the assassination is a success, then the future changes. So, when time catches up to the point you'd have hatched this master plan of yours, lo and behold, Sarah Connor was never around to motivate you to kill her in the first place."

"Is this supposed to hurt my head?" Jonathan asked. "Because it's working."

Hayden sighed.

"There wouldn't be a Sarah Conner to send a terminator back to kill," Collin said. "So you wouldn't send a terminator, so it wouldn't have happened, so she would have never died. Now, if she didn't die, then you do have a reason to send the terminator after her. Paradox. No matter how you try to kill her with time travel, it doesn't work."

"Right," Jonathan said. "So there is no point in going back in time to change the future, because you'd inevitably get rid of your reason for going in the first place."

Both roommates nodded.

Cautiously, Jonathan thought out a question for them to consider. "What about when you have a situation more like *Groundhog Day*?" Jonathan asked.

When he got empty expressions as a reply, he elaborated.

"Where one guy keeps experiencing certain portions of time twice. He goes through one version of events, but then gets sent back to the start, and experiences a completely different version."

Hayden's eyes twinkled before he grinned. "Tibbs, I honestly didn't think you had enough nerd in your lineage to ask such a question."

Jonathan shrugged. "I liked *Groundhog Day*."

There was not much of a safety concern getting his roommates' thoughts on the matter. Hayden loved having his expertise called on to answer questions that most would have thought of as mere mental masturbation. He enjoyed being the authority far too much to overthink Jonathan's sudden interest.

"So," Hayden said. "What exactly are you asking?

"If the first experiences on the first pass never actually occurred, how would it be possible that Bill Murray would remember what happened before starting his second pass?" Jonathan said. "I mean, if the first timeline no longer happened, how could he retain it?"

Hayden pondered this for a moment. "Technically, the movie wasn't really about time travel, but something more like alternative realities with a peculiar footnote of time travel. The logic would be, uh… squishier… and consistency would depend on the rules. Honestly, though, I never thought about it. *Groundhog Day* is a comedy. They didn't have to bother giving an explanation outside of 'because magic.'"

Knowing how to get what he wanted out of Hayden was a subtle art, so Jonathan smiled patiently.

"Okay," Jonathan said. "Let's say the movie had been legitimate science fiction, with logical rules. Bill Murray keeps his memories from all his different experiences of the timeline, but everyone else only experiences one final version. Any alternate reality that only Bill remembers ceases to be when he goes back to the beginning."

"The question is kind of a case in point with what Collin was saying," Hayden said. "Why would the alternate reality cease to exist? What happens to this alternate reality so that only Bill and his memories are immune to its disappearing? You're already making unexplained concessions."

Jonathan fell into thought. It wasn't that he didn't understand what his roommate was getting at, but Hayden had unintentionally boxed him into a corner. Jonathan knew this was the rule, or at least, he thought he did. Unfortunately, Heyer had never explained why, an excuse Jonathan couldn't feasibly bring up.

"Okay, so for the sake of discussion, can we assume there is a logical explanation? How would it be that everyone in the world experienced one reality," Jonathan asked, "but Bill had memories from another?"

Hayden's expression was growing slightly irritated. "I don't know, Tibbs," he said. "Let me write an email to Stephen Hawking and get his take on it."

"Ahhh, sarcasm…" Collin said, nodding, his grin becoming the very definition of shit-eating. "Has the student stumped the professor?"

"No one said that," Hayden replied. "Coming up with some explanation isn't all that hard, but Jonathan said it had to be logical."

Collin smiled. "Oh, my apologies, Jonathan. I jumped to conclusions. Apparently, he will be relying on semantics instead of sarcasm," Collin said. "The lawyer's escape route, then. I suspect that the defense will require a brief recess to review the case?"

Hayden chuckled. "Yeah," he replied. "Ass-face."

"Careful, Councilor," Collin said. "Insults will land you in contempt."

"My apologies," Hayden said. "I meant to say Your Honorable Ass-face."

CHAPTER FIVE

FRIDAY | OCTOBER 7, 2005 | 4:00 PM | SEATTLE

HE WAITED NEAR the opening of an alley, crouched in a corner between a wall and a dumpster. When folks on the sidewalk passed close enough to notice him, they faked polite smiles and held their noses.

Grant was young, healthy, and muscled. These things made the crazy homeless man costume he wore a challenge to pull off. He had on plastic sunglasses that may have been fashionable in the early nineties. His dirty blond hair was long enough to be hanging down from the sides of his baseball cap. He'd grown a month and a half of unkempt beard, and the rest of his face looked as if he'd washed it with gutter water. The layers of clothing on him grew exceedingly humbler the further away he'd placed them from his skin. A long, brown tweed coat that looked as if it had been used as a hand towel after an oil change hung off him. It all came together to make him invisible beside the dumpster.

From time to time, he took casual glances across the street. There was a car parked along the sidewalk next to his building. Two men sat inside, watching the entrance, waiting to follow when Grant left the building. Getting in and out of his downtown flat had been the first obstacle. It had taken patience and a perpetual changing of his routines. Regardless, it was a necessity, as he couldn't see enough of what he was dealing with from inside. Today had been informative—these two in the car were new.

By his count, that brought the tally of men he'd seen assigned to him up to eight. It was flattering, the amount of resources Olivia used to keep tabs on him. These two would rotate out soon, replaced with some of her other peons, ready to follow should they see him exit the building. Nowadays, they only caught Grant leaving when he wanted them to know. These two were growing tired. They hadn't noticed when he'd slipped out hours ago, but in their defense, he hadn't used the entrance.

Grant watched as the peon in the passenger seat answered a cell phone. The call was brief, and when the man put the phone away, he nodded to his partner. The two stepped out of the vehicle and began walking down the street, their eyes still focused on the front entrance to his building. Grant rose then, walking across the street himself and into a small restaurant at the corner.

Quickly, he removed the tattered coat before the management's attention was drawn to a dirty vagrant entering his establishment. Beneath the coat, Grant wore nondescript clothing, his appearance suddenly altered from that of a homeless man to merely a grungy one. He stuffed the coat into the backpack he'd hid beneath, removed his sunglasses and hat, and pulled up the hood of his sweatshirt.

When he'd first tried this, he was amazed how easily he'd managed to slip past the team watching him. Most of the trick to it was a matter of keeping Olivia's people convinced he'd never left the building. It helped that she'd always seen him as simple. She had never imagined he might have the wherewithal to slip past a highly-trained surveillance team.

But we all get sleepy eventually, don't we, Princess? He thought.

Still, their underestimation of him alone hadn't been enough. He'd been careful picking his environment. After all, they'd given him the money to afford whatever he needed.

Grant sat down at a table in the back. There wasn't any hurry, and he was hungry, so he ordered food and ate. He paid his bill in cash, then walked past the counter where, down a hallway and behind the kitchen, the restaurant provided restrooms. The woman who ran the register never said anything, as long as he'd paid for his food.

He kept walking past the restrooms, turned the corner, and made his way down a set of steps leading to a storage area. Awhile back, he'd found that the restaurant had a basement for shared storage connected to his own building. As far as he could tell, Olivia's peons hadn't become aware, and so, their eyes remained focused on the wrong entrance. He always took the stairs up to his loft on the ninth floor. When he reached the seventh floor of the stairwell, he removed what remained of his excess clothing and put each item into the backpack before stashing the bag in a maintenance closet. Then he continued up the last two flights.

It all might be overkill—it hadn't been lost on him that Olivia might very well be watching every move he was making and letting him go about it to lull him into a false sense of security. There were degrees of paranoia he had to accept. Thing was, even if that were true, he had called her bluff. Grant had come plenty close to Jonathan and his roommates since she had forbidden him. So close there were times he could have reached out and touched them. Olivia had either not been aware or done nothing about it. This meant that, the day he made his move, *Princess* might show up knowing everything, but she would also know he had not been afraid to defy her either.

When he stepped inside his flat, Grant started looking for signs of disturbance, anything that would tell him that they had known he left and used the opportunity to enter his home. It had taken him a while to realize that it was a matter of surplus attention to detail that would eventually give him his edge. They had practically explained to him that he would be watched, then slapped a pile of money into his hands and told him to get lost. Again, their first mistake had been funding him.

His loft had been step one. There was no way that Grant, who currently worked a part-time job as a parking lot attendant, could afford to live on the ninth floor of a new building in the middle of downtown if his bank account had not been padded by the recent payoff. When he had decided to move into the city, he'd gone looking for just such a building. The lofts were bare open spaces, meant to be decorated by their owners. He hadn't bothered adding pleasantries, and as a result, his home had the feeling of living in three interconnected cement rooms. This had been key. It didn't make it impossible for her team to bug his house with cameras and listening devices, but forced them to get creative if they actually wanted to hide them from him.

From the doorway, the largest of the rooms was connected to the kitchen in an open floor plan. The room was furnished with a wooden bench, two large flat screen TVs, a desk with two computers, a police scanner, and a weight bench. The TVs were both set to various news networks. One of the computers was attached to an internet line, the other completely removed from any external sources. He'd done away with plush furnishing; too many places to hide their devices in the fabric and cushions.

There was a cement room that made up his bathroom, and the third was a bedroom. His bed was the one luxury. He needed it, because he had to have a place to take the girls. No matter how cheap a prostitute she was, he didn't want to be crawling around on cement floors while he relieved himself. At first, he thought that sheets, pillows, a mattress, and a bed frame would be a perpetual nuisance. Nothing more than things he would have to reexamine every time he came and went to make sure that a new bug had not been planted. Then he changed his thinking.

He had a drawer full of The Cell's crap that he'd taken a hammer to since moving in. Small wireless microphones found sown into the mattress, GPS trackers in his bags and clothing, cameras in the ventilation, motion detectors in his hallway. When he'd first managed to give his tails the slip through a complicated series of clothing changes and overpopulated areas, he bought new clothes, leaving the trackers they'd hid on him in the back of a truck that was in line for a ferry crossing over The Puget Sound. He got a cheap chuckle imagining all the time and energy he had managed to waste of those keeping tabs on him, but never let it go to his head. He'd seen the extent Olivia had gone to watch Jonathan and he wasn't about to believe the woman had shown him all their tricks.

He'd used that first opportunity to slip off and purchase equipment, the kind of devices owned most often by extremely paranoid hobbyists. Radio frequency and camera lens detectors. Not as hard to come by as he'd imagined. There were local businesses completely devoted to this type of equipment, usually attached to the same places that sold firearms.

He used these things, but never let himself get too comfortable. He doubted that the U.S. government couldn't develop something that simple store-bought gear wouldn't be able to find. In the end, he went over every inch of his place looking for anything they could slip in. When he wasn't able to find anything new each day, he'd started to get more confident that he was giving her peons the slip.

When he finished sweeping the apartment, he kept some of the GPS trackers intact. Made a point of wearing them when he didn't care if The Cell knew where he was going. He purposely left a camera operational in his bedroom. It was located near the ceiling, behind a ventilation duct that looked down on his bed.

He pulled out a set of binoculars and stood at his window in the living room, looking down at the car parked outside his door. He recognized the two agents now relieving the men who had been watching when he was down on the street. While he stood at the window, he turned the binoculars to the windows facing his loft on adjacent buildings. Every few weeks, he'd notice the glass of a window he'd previously been able to see through had suddenly become opaque. It was important to keep an idea of the buildings they were likely using to watch from. Olivia might be standing behind one of them right now, looking back at him.

There you are, Princess.

Now, for good reason, he couldn't trust anyone, not since he'd headed down this road. There had been a few attempts, he suspected, to insert a mole into his private life. A pretty new girl calling herself Diana had shown up at work. She'd been a little too forward, a little too interested in coming home with him. He never allowed her in his home, only agreed to go back to her place and see how far she was willing to take the ruse. That had repeated itself a few times before, he assumed, Olivia realized she was wasting a highly-trained and educated government asset to save him the trouble of calling a prostitute.

Grant had been like a pig in shit playing with the girl as she tried to endear herself to him. What did Olivia think, that a pair of tits would get him to tell his whole life story? That he didn't know what she was after, that he hadn't seen her methods of getting that information? Fine, he would play that game, make up a few bullshit leads for them to follow. Grant was good at bullshit. What he couldn't believe was just how long Olivia had let it go on before Diana suddenly stopped coming to work, never to be heard from again. It just so happened that she disappeared the day after Grant had slipped, got her name wrong. He'd been leaving her apartment and said, "Thanks, Paige. I enjoyed that."

Oops. Sorry, Princess, I guess you know I'm on to you. Must be so deeply infuriating. That I knew who he was long before you'd even heard the name. Is it? Frustrating?

In the end, it was why he'd decided to leave the camera in his bedroom's ventilation. The day after Diana disappeared, he'd called an escort service and asked for a dark-skinned brunette in business attire and glasses. He'd instructed the operator that he wanted the girl to respond to the name *Olive*. He always made Olive keep the glasses on, made her face the foot of the bed so she was right in front of the camera. He wanted Olivia's whole surveillance team to see him pounding a carbon copy of their boss. He wished he could have been there, seen her face when she watched the footage.

Bet you lost that composure of yours? Tell the truth, Princess, Did you get excited?

Thinking about it, now, he was worked up enough to call and see if *Olive* was available this evening, but something on the television set caught his eye. Two news networks, both reporting an emergency broadcast.

CHAPTER SIX

FRIDAY | OCTOBER 7, 2005 | 4:45 PM | SEATTLE

THE DAY HAD begun to give way to evening as Jonathan stood, wearing an orange vest and hardhat, beside his foreman. Another employee of Mr. Donaldson's demolition crew operated the heavy yellow backhoe, digging out a ditch of broken up concrete and moving it into a trailer bed. The foreman was explaining where the materials were being taken while he pointed out the various safety procedures that came with operating heavy machinery.

Since being hired, Jonathan had yet to operate any equipment unsupervised, only watched and listened as those who were signed off on the machines trained him. Until recently, he had been assigned to small housing jobs in the suburbs. Either way, he was learning a lot and finally making enough money to keep his debts from increasing.

"Gotta keep your mind on what you're doing when you operate this..." His foreman's voice trailed off, or rather Jonathan stopped listening as he felt the twitch in his chest.

Damn, he thought.

His jobsites had already proved, on other occasions, to be one of the last places he wanted to lose control over his motor skills. During a previous activation, when his legs had stopped supporting him, he'd tumbled into a ditch much like the one currently being dug out by the backhoe. Unlike this ditch, he'd nearly been buried under the rubble a bulldozer had been pushing in. Luckily, the crew had stopped the driver before it had come to that.

Jonathan didn't know if he could die in the middle of the transition. For that matter, he didn't know what happened if he died before a Ferox got the chance to try and kill him. Would the time line simply stay in place? Would the Ferox get pushed back through the gates to its home world? Or would it be diverted to one of those alternate nodes that Heyer had mentioned? These were a few of the untold number of questions he lacked the answers to, because the alien still hadn't found time to stop in for over a month.

Jonathan used the few seconds he had before his body stopped obeying to look for a safe spot where he could fall to the ground. Hopefully somewhere that he wouldn't be found writhing in pain as the transition took control. Stepping away, he put as much distance between himself and the heavy equipment as he could, setting his eyes on a half-demolished cinder block wall a few strides away. His muscles quit responding just as he cleared the wall. He managed to land on his back, the hard hat protecting his head coming off and rolling to an awkward stop behind him.

There was nothing mission-critical in avoiding his coworkers, but he preferred not to have them see him in pain when there was nothing they could do. He had transitioned in front of them often enough to know he didn't want to see the helpless panic that always entered their eyes before his vision failed him, nor their confused expressions when he got to his feet. He had decided to stop wasting time giving explanations to people who were never going to remember.

When the activation had run its course, he felt control of his nervous system returning. He opened his eyes to the overcast sky and drew in a long breath. The brief moment, he found, helped to take the edge off his body's immediate adrenaline surge after feeling as though it were being burned from the inside out. He glanced down at the source of the horrible pain and saw the power surging through the lines running over his torso. The familiar orange glow was there, wisping out faintly from beneath his t-shirt. No matter how many times he experienced the shock, he would never get used to being a glow stick.

The Ferox's presence came to his attention then, and his face hardened as the compass in his mind pointed him south. He sprang to his feet and headed to where he had parked Eileen, his old motorcycle, on the street outside the demolition zone.

As he broke into a sprint, his foreman yelled to him. "Tibbs! There you are. Where the hell you going in such a damn hurry…?"

The man's voice had already receded into background noise. Jonathan filtered out the unimportant and focused on the task at hand. He pulled the work vest from his body as he ran, shredding through it as though it were newspaper before thrusting himself into the air. He cleared what remained of the construction zone and the fence separating it from the parking lot. When the ground absorbed his landing, a cracking thud shook the space immediately around him. Experience reminded him to put his hand out and grab Eileen's handle bars before the disturbance rocked her over. The motorcycle really didn't need another dent, even if said dent would only exist for the short time that the gates remained open.

Beneath a cargo net on the bike's rear he retrieved his jacket, careful not to let his strength tear the lining as he slipped into it, then tossed his helmet to the ground before hitting the ignition. He didn't bother with the headgear when he was activated anymore—it only got in the way. The first time he'd had to engage the enemy without getting the helmet off first, he had found it limited his vision. For that matter, the first clean punch the Ferox landed on his face had shattered the helmet to pieces.

Jonathan threw his leg over the bike, and checked that Excali-bar was safely locked into the carabiners welded to the side of the bike's frame. He'd coated the weapon in a black oxide to hide how the alien steel caught the light. He got enough questions as it was just for driving around with an oversized demolition bar. Luckily though, he didn't have to re-coat the weapon after each use. Whenever he sent a Ferox corpse back through the gates, the staff was like everything else in this time bubble outside of Jonathan's memory—completely untouched by the incident.

Small favors like this and a bit of sarcasm helped get him through the day. If he had to risk his life killing interdimensional trespassers while his friends and family continued to become more alienated by his increasing instability and off-putting behavior, well, at least the job came with free self-repairing gear and no clean up. For that matter, fuel was essentially covered while he was on the job. He'd set five or six different beasts on fire with the exact same gas can and flare this month. Jonathan often heard it was important to find the silver lining in things.

He gunned the engine and set off. Motorcycle safety was no longer much of a concern—his strength and balance allowed him to push the bike's limits, and once he hit the freeway the needle on his speedometer quickly bounced over the 100 miles per hour mark. At least, he assumed it had. Really, he no longer bothered looking down to check, but kept his attention on avoiding collisions.

Since the Ferox had started coming with regularity, there wasn't a definitive pattern he could identify, no time of day that was more regular for them to show up. They had increased in frequency until he seldom got more than a twenty-four hour break in between. These assaults had become too frequent for him to ever feel safe for long. Yet, a part of him he didn't think wise to indulge felt, for better or worse, satiated by it—almost addicted to it. He already felt that part of himself now, creeping up behind his eyes and whispering to him to push the throttle harder.

Cars blew past—humanity seeming an endless stream of obstacles for the moment. Had this been some other ride, his mind might have wandered. Jonathan might have found himself thinking how every person on this road believed that they were the good guy. That each of them got up every day and did the best they could with what was put in front of them. How each tried to improve their lot in life without consciously hurting anyone else's. If they could remember what Jonathan was about to do for them, they would probably have called him a hero.

The truth was, he was off to end the life of a creature that had come here because it had no other options. Sure, the Ferox were monsters—killers. But the person who might confuse him with a hero was just rooting for the killer who was on their team. The people he passed didn't have to give any thought to the likelihood that had they been born a Ferox, he would be their enemy.

Jonathan, at least the part of him that recognized the truth in the matter, had to simplify his moral dilemma: *One of us has to die, and I'm not ready to let it be me.*

He heard sirens then, and frowned as he saw the lights of a police car in his side mirror. *That was quicker than usual,* he thought. He sometimes wondered what got their attention first—the speeding or the helmet violation? Just as he noticed the cops, he felt the alien signal's location move in his mind. The Ferox was through the portal and heading away, toward the west, just as the freeway was about to lose its usefulness.

He turned for the off ramp, hit the brakes, and gripped the clutch, letting the drag of his tires slow his momentum. The tires screeched as he took the turn far too hard, and as the guardrail of the ramp drew near, he put his foot out between the wall and the bike. His leg took the force against the wall as he planted his other foot on the freeway and brought the bike to an abrupt stop.

He began shifting back down to first gear as he looked to the west, trying to get a visual sign of the Ferox. It felt close, maybe four or five blocks away, but there were too many buildings blocking his view. Turning his head back the way he came, he saw the flashing lights of his pursuers catching up to him. They weren't of much concern as long as he kept enough distance between them, but he didn't want them boxing him in once they figured out he had no intention of pulling over. It wouldn't stop him, but dealing with the obstacle would slow him down.

He dropped back into gear and sped down the ramp. Within seconds, he was in the city, running a red light and causing an accident in the intersection as several cars slammed on their brakes to keep from hitting him.

Five blocks became four, four became three, and then he heard its call.

Challenger!

The translated word forced its way into his consciousness, borrowing his own internal voice in sync with the Ferox's growl. It no longer unnerved him, more or less just helped bring his A-game to the surface.

Finally, he saw his enemy out in an intersection in front of him. A Red, its back to him as it raged to get at civilians trapped inside their car. The door gave the Ferox little trouble before tearing from its hinges. Jonathan poured on the throttle as he aimed Eileen's front tires for the creature's back, freeing his clutch hand and reaching down to grip Excali-bar.

He prepared to leap from the bike, leave the motorcycle on its path to rip into Red's back and give it a taste of the fight it had pick—

Something tugged at his consciousness, a sensation he'd never felt before causing momentary disorientation. It felt as though the compass in his mind had suddenly become unsure of where the signal was coming from, even though he had the Ferox in sight. Before he knew what to make of it, he was torn out of the moment entirely.

"Gotta keep your mind on what you're doing when you're operating this rig," the foreman explained.

Jonathan staggered forward for a moment, then halted suddenly, looking around the construction yard like a rabid animal with his fists still clenched. He couldn't sense anything the beast wasn't there in his mind, it had disappeared.

"Tibbs," the foreman said, looking back at him, "you all right, man?"

Jonathan's eyes were still circling the work yard, trying to get his bearings. When he looked to his foreman, he found he had his palm raised between them as though he were telling the man to be patient.

Then he realized his device wasn't activated.

Keep it together. Jonathan swallowed, pulling his hand back to his side.

He was safe, it seemed—back where he'd been activated—but Jonathan had grown accustomed to having a moment to prepare himself for return to normal life. Without it, he'd been thrust back to the moment of activation while still in the mindset that he was a split second from entering a death match.

"I don't know," Jonathan managed, noticing the concern on his foreman's face deepening. "Sorry, I… I just got dizzy for a sec."

The man gave him a suspicious look. "That happen often?" he asked.

"No," Jonathan said. "Never."

CHAPTER SEVEN

FRIDAY | OCTOBER 7, 2005 | 7:00 PM | SEATTLE

LEAH SAT AT the edge of Paige's bed while they talked about plans for the weekend. She'd tuned out of the conversation after hearing a motorcycle turning up the drive. It could have been Collin coming home from school, but the engine sounded like Jonathan's junker.

A girl wouldn't have to worry about you getting clingy or overly attached, if… if she were looking for someone who wouldn't get clingy, or overly attached.

The words had been repeating in her head for weeks now. She had been forced to leave the statement out of reports, as she couldn't have explained her thinking to The Cell. Her conscience, assisted by inebriation at the time, had stolen her good sense. Then her mouth had been dense enough to go along with it. Now, without fail, it seemed to Leah that those words were said at the worst possible time. Certain tactical complications had followed.

The Cell was pleased with her progress for the most part. She had managed to infiltrate Jonathan's social circle ahead of schedule. Perhaps this would have been more challenging if Leah actually fit The Cell's expectations—some fantasy from a Bond movie, an intelligence asset who had spent years training for undercover work. The reality was that she had *some* training, but that the role she was playing now was only a few fabricated documents and a fake name away from who she was anyway. What Olivia's team didn't know about her past had simply been filled in with assumptions that came with her clearance level—the less they knew, the grander said assumptions tended to be.

Unfortunately, editing her reports was no longer as easy as simple omission should she wish to keep The Cell in the dark about any particular interaction. There were no audio recordings, but within the last month, Olivia's team had managed to complete a full network of hidden surveillance cameras within Jonathan's home. If one of Olivia's team wanted to know exactly what Paige was saying right now, her recollection needed to be a close approximation to what the lip readers had transcribed. Attempting to lie would be dangerous.

However, though they forced more discretion in her actions, the cameras had proved a necessity. For Leah to do her job, she needed Jonathan's face to be an open book, had to feel what he felt, know him better than she knew herself. With Jonathan unaware of his every moment in the house being recorded, his behavior became something she could study without drawing unnecessary attention to herself. So she spent every moment she was able reviewing the footage, considering every expression, his body language, how he reacted to those around him.

Leah had always had an insight into people, the type that most found difficult to learn even through training, and Jonathan was the easiest sort to read. He was terrible at lying, so terrible he'd probably given up on it at an early age. When he had something to hide, he omitted it. If pressed, he retreated behind a wall of silence. That wall was Leah's challenge, and The Cell's newest solution to the failures of previous operations: a very indirect approach, which relied on her understanding of Jonathan and the trust she had built between them. Leah, in short, was the one who decided what the right questions were and when to ask them—when to push, and how much pressure to apply.

As getting into his head was her job, The Cell never thought twice about her repeatedly poring through Jonathan's footage. All they saw was the level of commitment to her task that was expected of her. What they didn't see was the guilt—she'd slipped, she had been protecting Jonathan from the very purpose that had put her in his life. What weighed on her about this now was that she suspected that she'd missed the opportunity she had been hoping for, and feared she might not get another. The situation had rapidly changed.

The Mark had not been spotted by any of the surveillance teams watching any of the subjects for over a month now. His last known sighting had been a conversation with Jonathan. That conversation had taken place before the cameras were in place, but The Cell kept detailed records of what was observed. The Mark had spoken with him, a discussion that had lasted for roughly forty-five minutes, before departing. After, Jonathan had sat, hardly moving, for hours.

In the weeks following, it seemed that The Mark's words had become a dark cloud around Jonathan. He was more withdrawn, seldom home during the day and always training if he was. When Leah had been able to force their paths to cross, she felt as though she were talking to a ghost. He seemed to play the part of Jonathan Tibbs, but nothing pulled the one she'd been watching for months beforehand back to the surface. His roommates hadn't sensed the change—not like she had, at least. Though, in fairness, pinning down who Jonathan was from one day to the next had become a fruitless endeavor to them before she'd really managed to get herself into the picture.

Studying him on the cameras, she'd begun to feel as though a different person was hiding under the same mask. The more confident she became that she wasn't imagining the change, the more she wondered what The Mark could have possibly said to cause it. Jonathan had already been exhibiting the signs of immense stress before the conversation.

When confronted with a burden one doesn't believe oneself able to carry, the average person looks to others for help. Jonathan didn't seem to see that as an option.

In Leah's experience, there were two types of people in these instances, but they only differed in the manner by which they gave up. The first type saw their limitations and admitted to themselves that they couldn't carry the weight. They gave up by simply dropping the burden and accepting the consequences. The second type gave up in an opposite manner. They decided they could never put the weight down, even if it meant they would be crushed under it.

There was never any doubt that Jonathan was the latter—everything she'd seen of him told her that his solution would be to "give up" on being a person who wasn't able to carry the weight. And again, the more she suspected this, the more she regretted her momentary lapse in priorities. Perhaps it was all in her head, and nothing she said or did would have made a difference, but she had this feeling that there had been a moment—in those first days after The Mark had spoken to him—when Jonathan might have looked for help. A moment where maybe, just maybe, he might have been desperate enough to see her as a safe place to go.

For a while, she feared that another opportunity wasn't going to present itself, but then, Jonathan had turned a corner. The reasons for his sudden improvement weren't completely clear to her, but when she studied the tapes for an explanation, only one other change was obvious. The fog had started lifting around Jonathan about the same time that Hayden started having symptoms of insomnia.

Most of their interactions were taking place between two and four in the morning and she couldn't listen in on what was said due to The Mark's known audio block. What the lip readers transcribed of the discussions hadn't given her much to go on, either, and frankly, they were pretty one sided, with Hayden doing the majority of the talking. Regardless, something far more useful had developed.

Jonathan missed her. When Leah was present, he lingered on her, stole glances when he knew she couldn't see him watching. He would stop sometimes, inside his garage, and peer through the window at her house. He wished her door was open to him.

"Leah!" Paige said. "Are you even listening to me?"

Leah looked up and found Paige's annoyed expression. "Sorry," She said, "I heard the motorcycle, thought it might..."

Paige's eyes fluttered almost mockingly, as though Leah's apparent fence-sitting about Jonathan had become a topic of boredom. "Would you two stop acting like 3rd graders and get on with it?" she said. "Just make it happen already."

Leah smiled politely.

Jonathan had never told anyone that she had already made it happen.

Her smile turned to a grimace as she reflected on her first act after their one night of intimacy—discussing the matter with the head of The Cell. By now, every detail she'd shared had likely been repeatedly analyzed by Olivia's team.

Leah thought it was time to tell Paige that something had, in fact, happened between them, but then she heard his footsteps on the stairs.

He'd come in through the garage, taken his practice staffs from the cabinet, and then pulled out the facade. He swapped out Excali-bar with the decoy, his original demolition bar that Heyer had modeled the weapon on, into the bike's clips. Jonathan had no illusions that this was fooling any of the investigators who watched him. They could have inspected his cabinet every time the house was empty and there was nothing he could do about it. He only took the precaution to keep his roommates from ever picking up the bar and noticing that not only was it no standard piece of steel, but that it had a name engraved on one of its flat surfaces. He had no interest in inviting unwanted questions.

Before he put the facade back in place, his eyes lingered on its backside. Shortly after his last visit from Heyer, he'd attached a chalk board. At the top of the board he'd written two names and then placed a dividing line between them down the center. On the left he'd written his initials, "J.T.," and on the right, "Universe."

There had been a time when he didn't expect to survive long enough to worry that he might lose track of the number of Ferox he'd dispatched. He'd been wrong. So he had started keeping a record. One night, on a whim, he had turned the tally into a scoreboard. The competition had become an ironic private joke—no matter how many points he scored, the *Universe* only needed one to win.

There were red and green hash marks under his initials, depending on the type of Ferox he'd slain. Among them, there was one that wasn't a simple tally mark, but a red "H." Jonathan lingered on the letter until memories he didn't want to revisit began to surface and he refocused himself. Picking up the red chalk, he added a question mark to his side of the scoreboard.

He looked at the mark and sighed. Until he saw Heyer, all he could do about today was put a question mark on a chalkboard. He'd never returned to his body without killing—he hadn't thought it possible to close the gates without destroying the stone the Ferox carried inside of them. Jonathan doubted that getting an explanation would mean anything good.

He put the facade back, closed the cupboard, and entered the house. At the top of the stairs, he heard talking from inside Paige's bedroom—Leah's voice behind the closed door. He lingered in the hallway for a moment, looking at the door opposite his bedroom and wishing he had a reason to knock. Paige didn't want to see him, though, and even if that weren't the case, Leah had asked him not to get attached.

More than anything, he wanted her to show up in his garage again, as she had before. Whenever he thought to approach her himself, he couldn't shake the feeling that whatever he said would be an obvious excuse, that he'd be as transparent to her as he always felt.

No matter what he said, his face would change the words into: *Please, say it is okay to touch you. Put your hands on my skin again.*

Maybe, if he didn't pursue her, if he did precisely what she had asked, then she would trust him. Maybe that trust would never extend more than to those moments she felt lonely and vulnerable. Still, if that was the most he could be to her, then he wouldn't risk it by pushing. Even if it had been a temporary escape, Leah was the only person he'd felt safe with since the night the device had been forced on him.

He threw his coat on his bed when he entered his room, then noticed something was off. His computer was on, as though someone had woken it from sleep the moment he entered. What was odd was that it appeared to be booted into DOS. As he stepped closer, he saw that wasn't the case—instead, a single line of white text was written at the top of a black screen.

Jonathan, be discreet. Pick up the computer. Take your desk chair to the southwest corner of your room. Sit, wear headphones.

For a moment, he figured he'd gotten a virus and reached out to press the escape key. That suspicion didn't last more than a moment. The thought of a virus using his name made his hand go still over the keyboard.

Would Heyer contact me this way? he wondered.

His friend in the fedora usually favored appearing out of nowhere without any warning. Maybe he couldn't risk being present, physically, with Leah and Paige in the house? Maybe he knew something had gone wrong today, and it was too important to wait for Jonathan to be alone? Why not? If he could jump through space and time, how much trouble could it be to bypass Windows security? Then again, what if it wasn't the alien? Couldn't The Cell be just as capable?

He was still considering this when the screen suddenly flashed and his desktop showed up as though all was normal. He frowned, his hand reaching out again for the keyboard, when he heard a knock behind him.

"Hi, Jonathan," Leah said. She was standing in his doorway.

"Hi," he managed.

With her eyes on his, Jonathan's priorities became confused. Investigating the strange message was more important. He knew this, and wished that he didn't, because he wanted to put it on hold for whatever had brought Leah to his bedroom.

She was about to say something, but paused, studying him a second before her expression turned into a frown. "Is this a bad time?" she asked. "You look like you're thinking of a polite way to ask me to leave."

"Yeah," he sighed. "It's not the best moment."

"It's okay." She shrugged. "I'll catch you tomorrow."

He nodded and she turned to leave, but he stopped her. "Hey, Leah."

"Yeah," she said, head leaning back into his doorway.

"Was it important?" he asked.

She grinned. "It can wait a day."

Then her face was gone, and he heard her footsteps receding down the hallway and the stairs. As he listened, watching the empty space where she had been, his laptop's display flickered at the corner of his vision. He turned to see the same white message on a black screen again.

The timing of it disturbed him. Whoever was manipulating his computer somehow knew when he wasn't alone.

CHAPTER EIGHT

HE LET OUT a sigh as he stared at the message. Ever since Heyer had come into his life, Jonathan was forced to make decisions with no idea of the consequences. The only choice he ever seemed to have was to go along and see where things took him. If he ignored the message, he'd never know what it meant.

He locked his bedroom door, then shuffled through the drawers of his desk for a set of earbuds. Once he figured out which corner of the room was southwest, he took a seat. Shortly after, the black and white display flickered and an unexpected face looked back at him—an animated cartoon of a bald man with big white eyebrows, blue eyes, a plain white T-shirt, and a gold earring. Jonathan blinked, recognizing the iconic face immediately.

"Mr. Clean?" he asked.

"Do not speak," said a masculine voice through the earbuds. "You will need to type your side of this conversation. I am monitoring the spyware installed on your computer and modifying the keystrokes it reports to your surveillance team."

Jonathan's eyebrows drew in. Of course, he'd figured his computer was being monitored—what was baffling was why a TV mascot for cleaning supplies was suddenly telling him about it.

"Heyer left instructions for me to contact you in the event that an unforeseen contingency occurred while he was off-world. I observed strange fluctuations within the gates today," Mr. Clean said. "I am hoping that your experience of events might shed some light on the oddities."

Jonathan hesitated. A hundred questions crashed through his mind, but some of them needed immediate answers if he was going to tell this cartoon anything.

Who are you? Jonathan typed.

"I am an Artificial Intelligence designed by Heyer's species."

Jonathan's eyebrows lifted at the answer, processing it. Heyer had mentioned that a computer assisted him in the past. Jonathan hadn't given it much thought—he never imagined he would find himself interacting with... it?

How do I know that is the truth? he wrote. *And why can't I speak?*

"Jonathan, I assure you that there is no other entity on Earth capable of monitoring the fluctuations within the gates. Heyer's own awareness requires my reporting of the activity," Mr. Clean said, and then one of his big, white cartoon eyebrows raised. "As far as you speaking, it is my understanding that humans who witness a man talking to himself find the action suspicious."

Jonathan bit his lips and typed, *I am still unsure.*

"A month and a half ago, Heyer noted that you requested a means to communicate with him when he could not be physically available. At that time, there was a question of where your loyalties ultimately stood. Within minutes of your last conversation, Heyer requested to be sent on an unscheduled trip to the Feroxian plane. He was in a rush, but before he left, Heyer activated certain fail-safes to ensure problems on Earth were not left unchecked, one of which was permission for me to contact you."

Why permission? Jonathan typed.

"I am not allowed to make decisions regarding such things for logical reasons. Heyer, being a biological entity such as yourself, is better suited to the subtleties of human interactions."

Mr. Clean's explanation fit with what Jonathan knew, enough that he felt he could trust this was not some clever ruse. He couldn't imagine a human being spinning such a tale. It was too strange, yet too accurate to have been guessed.

Why did he go to the Feroxian plane in such a hurry? he wrote.

"He only said that there was an emergency, and that he needed to reach his destination as quickly as possible," Mr. Clean said.

I mentioned the name of a Ferox I had slain. He asked me if I was sure of the translation. He only became rushed after I confirmed the name," Jonathan typed.

"The boundaries of my permissions do not allow me to provide any information you may request, except in the contingency that Heyer is incapacitated. His health has not been compromised and therefore this requirement has not been met," Mr. Clean said. "That said, I have detailed records on the Ferox who are permitted access to the gateways. If you provide the name, I will tell you what I can, provided the information is not off-limits."

Jonathan paused for a moment over the keyboard. If Heyer had wanted him to know, would he have left without telling him? He only hesitated over these thoughts for a moment. The time for wishing he'd remained in the dark was over—ignorance wasn't his ally.

Dams the Gate, Jonathan typed.

"Peculiar. Not a common Feroxian name. I see why Heyer asked you to confirm your certainty of the translation," the A.I. said. A moment passed. "I have no matching listing. However, we can make some assumptions based on the name's absence in the registry."

Like what? Jonathan typed.

"Malkier has not reported this Ferox as ever having been given authorization to access the gates," Mr. Clean said. "Therefore, you are either mistaken about the name, or it would appear that *Dams the Gate* came to Earth without approval."

Jonathan sighed.

He had a crude understanding of how the gateways functioned, but no real idea what entry looked like from the Ferox side. He'd only ever needed to know how to send them back, not through. It was news to him that only certain males were allowed entry.

I need to know more. About the gates, the Ferox, he wrote, and then after a moment, he added, *and Malkier.*

Slowly, the cartoon's head nodded. "I can only tell you what I am permitted. However, this is not the best use of our time now. The team watching you will eventually grow suspicious of why you've been sitting in that corner for so long. For now, it's best we focus on my inquiry. Specifically, what happened while the gates were open today?" Mr. Clean asked.

He was about to answer the computer's question, but something unspoken in Mr. Clean's previous statement had given him a disturbing pause.

Wait, Jonathan wrote after lingering over the keyboard. *Why would they grow suspicious? I thought the point of sitting in the corner was to get out of my window's line of site. How would they know I'm sitting in this corner?*

"The Cell was able to lock down the schedule of you and all the members of your household nearly four weeks ago. This allowed them to infiltrate your residence on a number of occasions. They now have a thorough network of surveillance cameras watching you at all times. Currently, you are sitting in the one corner of your bedroom where they do not have a camera facing the laptop display," Mr. Clean said. "I will show you, but I advise you not to display any emotional reaction."

An array of camera feeds filled the screen. Jonathan saw himself from multiple angles, Paige now alone in her bedroom, his roommates watching television in the living room, and the garage with a shot focused directly on his weapons cupboard, among other things.

"This, of course, complicates our communications. We have to take measures beyond that of simply disrupting their audio recording devices. If we abuse this knowledge too often, they will realize you've discovered the location of their cameras. It would be more advantageous for us if they believe you remain ignorant of their presence," said Mr. Clean. "I can disable their cameras in an emergency, but in doing so, they will know an external entity compromised their systems."

Jonathan struggled to process what the video feeds meant for him and everyone around him. He'd always suspected it might be possible, but seeing it confirmed turned paranoia into an impotent rage. All these people he cared about had had their lives invaded for no reason other than their proximity to him. He couldn't warn them, and he couldn't protect them.

"Jonathan, please, mind your emotions. Your face is beginning to show distress."

He took a breath, his face turning blank as he locked this anger behind a wall—let it take up residence with all the rest.

"Thank you," Mr. Clean said. "The Cell is monitoring the data coming and going through your internet feed as well. I have cloaked our current conversation as a streaming video file for now. Still, you can see we are pushing the amount of time that could lead to suspicion. I recommend you make it a routine to start sitting in this corner when you are doing ordinary activities."

Irritation hit him, but he kept it hidden from his face. It wasn't the breach of privacy alone; it was the time limits, again. Heyer nearly always showed up and rushed off, and Jonathan was constantly trying to keep up with the minutia of their conversations, only to berate himself for not having been quick enough to ask the right questions later. Now, when he thought he was finally going to get unfettered access to some answers, he was, yet again, being rushed.

He started typing again—faster.

Today, I returned to the moment of the breach without killing a Ferox. I was activated, went to intercept, but before I could engage it, I was back where I'd stood when the gates opened. I didn't destroy the portal stone.

"That is all?" Mr. Clean asked.

Yes, Jonathan typed. *Does it mean something to you?*

"For now, it appears that part of your memory has failed to carry over. There are scenarios where this could occur, but the conditions necessary to cause them should not have been in play. Unfortunately, I am not permitted to discuss said scenarios, but I will compare your perception of events against the activity in the gates."

Wait, Jonathan typed. *You mean I fought the thing, killed it, but didn't get my memory back?*

"Yes, that is the best answer I can give at this time."

CHAPTER NINE

SATURDAY | OCTOBER 8, 2005 | 8:00 AM | PORTLAND

OLIVIA SAT IN the sedan across the street from Evelyn Tibbs' Portland home, finding it to be what she imagined. It was an average-size house in a rather typical suburban neighborhood. The yard was well-kept, likely tended by landscapers. The family wasn't rich, but Tibbs' mother was far from poor. There was a rose garden around the outer fence, and Olivia wondered if Evelyn tended to this herself.

She'd been ready to interview the mother, had almost opened the car door to cross the street, when she'd received a call from the lab. The test results on the body had been completed.

The corpse her team had taken out of the ground was, as she'd suspected, another layer of mystery. She hadn't gone in with any expectation, not precisely. Rather, the results would either be exactly what they should—the body of Douglas Tibbs, father of Jonathan, killed in a car accident years prior—or something they'd never seen before, something alien. The body had proved to be neither. Completely human, and yet not belonging to Douglas Tibbs at all.

This left Olivia reconsidering the two files on the car seat beside her. One for Jonathan Tibbs, and one for Grant Morgan. There was a connection between the two and she was failing to see it. Her first thought had been that perhaps they were half-brothers—but DNA tests had not only confirmed that neither of the men shared parents, but further, that the body of the John Doe they had exhumed from Douglas Tibbs' grave was completely unrelated to either of the young men as well. This left her with a new cache of unanswered questions.

Her team had been in Seattle for barely a week before they had gotten the news they had been waiting on. A 9-1-1 call indicated that a man, a student at the university, had been found in a bloody mess in his home, reportedly attacked and sedated by an unidentified, blond male assailant, without any physical injuries to account for the blood loss.

When Jonathan Tibbs had been identified as The Mark's target, her team had gone into action, keeping the event out of the media, taking over jurisdiction of the investigation, and later, doctoring and removing the medical records. The general public was not to become aware of the strange circumstances surrounding the incident, if Jonathan was to be observed properly.

At the time, Grant had been romantically involved with Jonathan's roommate. It had seemed a fortuitous coincidence that an army specialist stationed at the nearby military base was already in position for her team to take advantage. Only later had it come to light that Grant was not there by any random chance, but was, in his own amateur way, investigating Jonathan as well. Grant had seemed convinced that Jonathan was a dire threat. What wasn't clear was why.

The only link she had been able to find between the two men were their fathers. Grant had been adopted by his aunt and uncle after his mother had died in childbirth. The father had been unknown, or so it was thought. Later, a private investigator uncovered that Grant's mother had been involved with a member of the same strike team sent to Libya under Douglas Tibbs' command. The name that the P.I. had given was of one Jeremy Holloway—and his involvement with Grant's mother took place in a suspicious nine-month period before Grant was born. The problem was, precious little could be uncovered about Mr. Holloway, almost as though every record of the man had purposely been removed. However, seeing as Grant had no one that would miss him should he disappear, the time she was willing to allow for passive observation to give answers was drawing to an end. Grant, she had no doubt, would not resist for long under interrogation.

Perhaps Grant's confession could provide her with some much needed answers concerning Douglas Tibbs. Jonathan's father was thought to have died stateside in a car crash when Jonathan was thirteen. The body had been beyond recognition, and the truck he'd been driving completely engulfed in flames after the gas tank had exploded. The body of the John Doe back at the lab was, in fact, horribly burned—still, DNA had been retrievable. What was interesting was that dental records had been a match. Someone had gone to some trouble to make it appear that Douglas Tibbs had died in that car crash.

It was easy to assume that the father had faked his own death. The problem was that the story didn't line up with anything The Cell knew about Douglas Tibbs. Before his death, if Olivia were to assume that he was, in fact, deceased, he'd been a responsible father and husband, the owner of a successful auto repair business, and a veteran discharged from duty twelve years earlier. Why would he fake his death, leave his wife and son grief stricken, and never show up anywhere on the grid for nearly ten years? Surely, given the body had been a decoy, she would have to give the command to start an investigation into his current possible whereabouts, but Olivia was highly doubtful that any trace would be found.

As Olivia watched the house now, she wondered: Did Evelyn know of it? Had the mother been a party to whatever cover up had occurred or was she completely in the dark? Given what she had just learned, Olivia's preparation for this interview now felt incomplete and she was not in the habit of letting things play out as they may. However, she was reluctant to reschedule. She'd come out here personally, and itched to be back in Seattle where she could control events should they get out of hand. So, she sighed and made her decision, reaching for the door handle and stepping out into the street.

Evelyn heard the knock at the door and was thankful for a distraction. She'd called Jonathan's cell phone again, only to hear the phone ring and go to a frustratingly full voicemail box.

She imagined Jonathan taking the phone out of his pocket, looking at the caller ID, and pressing the ignore button. That was an image that pissed her off to no end.

Kid, you must know you're only making it worse for yourself, she thought. Her son couldn't hide from her forever. She'd drive up to Seattle and camp on his lawn until he came home if he kept this up much longer.

Composing herself, she made an effort to withdraw from her righteous parental indignation, setting the phone back on the receiver to answer the door. She found a woman with immaculately pressed clothes, a handful of manila folders, and a professional smile standing on her doorstep.

"Thank you," Evelyn said, moving to shut the door as she did so, "but I've found Jesus."

"Ms. Tibbs?" the woman asked. "Evelyn Tibbs?"

The use of her name caused her to pause with the door half shut. "Yes."

With her free hand, the woman at her doorstep reached into a pocket, producing a business card and holding it out to her. "My name is Melissa Hart. I am here on behalf of the U.S. Army's Historical Records Department, and I was hoping I could ask for a few minutes of your time."

"In regards to what?" Evelyn asked, accepting the woman's card.

"We've had an unfortunate mismanagement of records and we are attempting to reconstruct them," Melissa said. "This is in regards to your late husband's time overseas in 1984."

She appraised Ms. Hart for a moment, taking in a deep breath. Evelyn wondered if this would actually prove a better use of her time than staring angrily at the phone. "If you are looking for details about conflicts he was engaged in, he never spoke about it," Evelyn said. "I respected his silence on the matter."

"I understand, but I was hoping that you might be able to assist us with names and faces. Perhaps provide some photos if it's not too much trouble," Ms. Hart said. "If it's a bad time, I could come back later."

After a moment, Evelyn shrugged, stepping out of the doorway. "I'll make coffee," she said.

CHAPTER TEN

SATURDAY | OCTOBER 8, 2005 | 8:00 AM | SEATTLE

THE HOUSE WAS quiet. This wasn't strange for a Saturday morning, but Jonathan had never completely outgrown a certain sensitivity to being alone in his home. It was more of a left-over tic these days than anything, but the absence of another human being was something he always seemed to notice.

As he made his way down the stairs, the loss of his memory the day before continued to concern him. He was being placed in yet another situation where control was out of his hands. He was left with no other option but to continue life as usual and hope Mr. Clean could fix the glitch before he was activated again.

Paranoia kept eating at him. Jonathan thought he had accepted that he had to trust the alien's choices, but the AI's inability to pass on information left him unable to ignore that he was, again, being manipulated. He couldn't shake a suspicion that the real reason Heyer had ordered Mr. Clean to withhold details was because Jonathan had learned something he shouldn't have in his last activation. Something he wasn't supposed to know.

Had his memory been kept from him intentionally?

He put the thought aside for the umpteenth time. He had to trust Heyer. Regardless, from what he understood, the only individual capable of remembering what played out within the gates was the survivor.

Clearly, that had been him. As far as he knew, there was no way for Heyer to know what Jonathan had witnessed before the gates closed. Of course, that whole chain of thought depended on Jonathan's altogether incomplete knowledge of how the gates worked.

He needed his memories.

If he continued to lose them when he closed the gates, he would be cut off from his greatest asset: the very knowledge and experience that kept him alive. He reminded himself that there wasn't anything he could do about it, and pushed the thoughts away. For now, the best thing for him was to focus on the things he could control.

"Stay diligent in your training," had been the alien's parting words to him.

He'd followed that advice. He had pushed himself, managing to add another ten pounds of muscle in the month that followed. With every Ferox slain, the truth in Heyer's words became more certain: he could be stronger than any opponent the Ferox had faced. Jonathan had begun to experience that edge—with every pound he gained, the space between maximum Ferox strength and his own grew wider. If he lived long enough to be the size of someone like Lincoln, his personal trainer, then any Ferox who entered the gates would be sent back to its people unrecognizable.

He overheard Collin speaking to someone in the driveway, and realized he'd been mistaken thinking the house empty. The voice that replied was unique, feminine, and foreign. He didn't recognize the owner, nor could he place the accent. He stopped next to the door, wondering if he would be intruding.

He couldn't remember Collin ever having a girl over to the house. His roommate had been hopelessly infatuated with Paige since she'd moved in. Usually he was all for rooting for the underdog. Unfortunately, neither Hayden nor Jonathan thought it wise for Collin to ever act on his feelings, both doubting that Paige would return them. Jonathan thought Paige was either well aware and pretending she didn't notice, or was simply blind to what she didn't want to be true. That said, if Collin had met someone, he might be doing them all a favor and saving them from an awkward living situation.

Still, Jonathan wasn't going to wait around to start the day. He figured he would only be interrupting long enough to say hello and be on his way. When he entered, he saw the garage door was up. Collin leaned over his bike in the driveway, fully engrossed in conversation with a woman, who was straddling a motorcycle of her own.

Her back was to Jonathan, her sports bike parked facing the street. She wore a heavy, leather-armored jacket, in the same style as the ones that Collin and Jonathan owned. Despite her covered arms, Jonathan could see she was an athlete. He'd learned to recognize the signs. It was her posture and the broad muscle of her shoulders. Her hair was straight, long, a natural black, and held in a tight braid that ran down her back such that it left the skin of her strong neck exposed.

"You should be ashamed," she said, "letting him buy that thing. It's a disaster."

Jonathan still couldn't place the strange accent. It sounded almost Italian to him, yet calmer, slower. Her voice made talking seem more like an amusing pastime than a necessity for communicating.

"Trust me, I tried to talk him out of it," Collin replied. "He named her Eileen, after the old woman who sold it to him."

The woman snorted. "Yeah, fits perfectly—thing has one foot in the grave."

Jonathan nodded to himself in understanding, then braced himself to be mocked as he stepped into the garage.

"Tibbs, where have you been hiding this girl?" Collin asked upon seeing him. "I thought I was your only cool friend."

"Uh…" Jonathan frowned. He'd been about to ask Collin a similar question.

The girl turned, pivoting gracefully as she dismounted the motorcycle and put her boots to the pavement. She was close to his age, her skin olive and face attractive. If Jonathan had known her, he wouldn't have forgotten. It caught him off guard for a moment and her dark brown eyes grew wide, her lips curling into a playful and pleasing smirk at seeing him. He felt a bit transparent, thinking her amusement must be because of the way he was reacting to her.

"Hello, Jonathan," she said.

He felt embarrassed immediately, at a complete loss for how the woman knew him by name. It still seemed impossible that he could forget such a face and voice, but he clearly knew her from somewhere. Perhaps they had shared a college class.

"Hi, um, I'm sorry," Jonathan said. "I'm having trouble remembering your name."

Her eyelids drew down, eyes seeming to fill with sass. She drew in close to him, close enough that he had to resist the urge to step back. He was unsure if it would be rude. She was clearly foreign by birth and some cultures simply had smaller personal space bubbles. He swallowed while politely trying to hide the discomfort of her standing so close.

"Games, Mr. Tibbs?" she asked, her dark eyes watching him with an intensifying gaze. "Why don't you think a bit harder? I don't have a lot of interest in playing games today."

Jonathan was going to apologize again, insist he wasn't playing at anything. However, her confidence, assertiveness, and the sudden formality of her words triggered an alarm in him.

He was sure he'd never met her. Yet she clearly recognized him—she knew his name, where he lived. It occurred to him that this woman could very well be a member of The Cell. Her words suddenly felt like a veiled warning to remove his friend from their conversation. Perhaps she was here to tell him that the surveillance was over, that no one had been fooled by his sitting in the corner of his room last night. His mind began to race, his eyes doing the same, scanning the streets out in front of them, looking for signs that she wasn't alone.

I'm a damn fool, he thought. *I should have planned for this.*

Now, all he wanted was to get Collin away from her. He had to protect his roommate from getting pulled into his problems. If she was giving him the chance to keep Collin from witnessing his arrest, he had to cooperate.

Jonathan cleared his throat and kept his expression calm, trying not to let his paranoia off the leash until he was certain this woman was what he suspected. "Collin, can I get a moment alone with my friend here?" he asked.

Collin looked disappointed, but he shrugged it off. "Sure," he said. "But if you're planning on taking the bikes out, come and get me?"

Jonathan nodded, returning his full attention to the woman as Collin walked into the house. His eyes hardening into a wall while he waited for his friend to be outside of earshot. When Collin shut the door behind him and they were safely alone, her face didn't turn serious, didn't reveal the monster he had feared. Instead, she suddenly seemed quite fragile, the strength she'd projected a moment ago drowned out by the relief she no longer felt necessary to hide. It was so contrary to what Jonathan had imagined that his face softened immediately in concern for her.

A second later, she had him in an embrace. She laid her face against his chest, wrapping her hands around him to draw him close. He could feel her warm, solid body pressed intimately against him. Flustered, he felt his face turning red in embarrassment for her.

He'd clearly misjudged the situation. Now, with no clue what was happening, he didn't know how to respond to the affection. He felt torn. Her behavior had passed inappropriate and he couldn't lead her on. At the same time, pushing her away felt hurtful and heartless. He found himself searching for a gentle median, a way to put space between them.

He heard her begin to laugh against his chest. "Why didn't you come to me?" she asked. "I worried. I thought something awful had happened."

He began to pull back slowly, but guilt hit him in a wave when he could see her face. She was so vulnerable; he didn't want to say he didn't know her, that she was confused.

"Please, ma'am," Jonathan said, placing his hands gently on her hip and shoulder to separate them. She resisted for a moment, but finally conceded and allowed him to break the contact between them. "I'm sorry, but you must have me confused with someone else."

Looking into her eyes, he saw her joy turn to hurt, relief turn to fear—but what followed was a state of confusion and anger.

"Stop it. You don't… It's not necess—" She stopped mid thought and pulled away from him harshly. His hands were left hanging in the air, no longer needed to keep her at arms' length. "You aren't playing," she said, and he could see that she was beginning to tremble.

Jonathan shook his head slowly and saw a tear forming in the corner of her eye.

"No," she whispered. "No, no, no." She repeated the denial over and over as she backed away.

"Please, ma'am," Jonathan said, "I don't—"

He cut off when he saw how she had shut her eyes tight, so upset by his use of the word "ma'am" that every word that followed seemed to be making it worse for her. She turned away, the grace she'd had a moment ago gone. She picked up her helmet and threw one leg over her motorcycle, shoving the helmet down over her head, in a hurry to be far away from here.

When the obvious occurred to him, her panic and embarrassment turned infectious.

My memory…

His certainty faltered—he hesitated. How? If she somehow remembered what happened within the gates, it couldn't explain her affections. They were too much; he couldn't have possibly lost enough time for this woman to feel so intimate with him.

Her engine had come to life, and her bike already in motion by the time he thought to stop her. She looked back at him once as she sped away. He couldn't see her eyes behind the reflective screen of her helmet. A moment later, she was gone, nothing more than the sound of a motorcycle engine fading away.

Jonathan hadn't moved, still standing in the driveway, dumbfounded, berating himself for having handled the situation so poorly and misjudging everything that had happened from the moment she had said his name. He couldn't understand how he had just caused so much pain to a complete stranger.

Slowly, he stepped back, knowing it wouldn't do any good for him to stand staring at his empty driveway any longer. When he turned, he was surprised to find he wasn't alone. Leah stood in her front yard, her face looking as confused as his own must have. He was startled when he caught her there. It dawned on him, then, how all of what had just played out must have looked. He heard the woman's retreating words repeating in his own thoughts:

No, no, no.

She wished she'd moved before he turned around. Now, Leah didn't know quite what to do with her face when he looked at her.

Should I leave? Should I say something?

She'd felt jealous and hurt seeing another woman hold on to him like that, a self-sabotaging little voice inside whispering that Jonathan had never avoided her—that he hadn't simply been respecting her wishes. He'd not been alone. Yet, she knew it was a ridiculous reaction. Jonathan having any relationship with the woman was impossible—Leah would have been briefed on such a thing had it ever developed, and that was the problem.

The "Leah" she let Jonathan see couldn't possibly know this. At the same time, after asking him not to get attached to her, what right did she have saying anything if he had started a relationship with another woman? The variables felt like they were boxing her into a corner.

He waved to her awkwardly, taking a step toward the picket fence that divided their property. Leah waved back, not knowing what else to do, but still glad that one of them had moved. So she met him halfway.

"I don't..." he managed, "know what just happened."

Leah tried to smile politely, shrugging as she did so. "She seemed upset," she said. "Was she a friend of yours?"

"No," Jonathan said as he looked back toward the empty street. "I've never met her. It was so odd. She knew my name, seemed to think—"

Jonathan didn't finish the sentence. She could see the increasing weight of his thoughts behind his eyes when he turned back to her. Leah knew that look. He got it whenever he was afraid and was trying to get control of it. She hadn't seen it on him in a while now.

"She was so confused," he said. "And hurt."

Leah studied him, and knew now that he was hiding something. His concern was genuine, though, and she found herself wanting to reassure him. "I'm sure she'll be okay," Leah said, reaching out over the fence to place her fingertips on his arm. "What about you? You seem rattled."

His eyes had become focused on the hand now touching his skin. He blinked a few times, and she almost pulled away, fearing she had misread the situation—but then he smiled, slowly reaching to put his hand over hers. He looked at her, studying her eyes, and the moment seemed to get away from her. When too much time had passed and no one spoke, she found herself failing to keep a grin off her face.

Jonathan cleared his throat. "What was it you wanted to talk to me about last night?" he asked.

Here we go, she thought, *changing the subject when he doesn't know how to answer.*

Leah played along, making sure her expression made it clear that he wasn't fooling her. "Last night?" Leah said, pretending to think about it. "You mean before the hot little Brazilian girls started jumping you in the driveway?"

"Was that the accent?" he asked. "I was wondering—couldn't place it."

Leah shook her head and waited. In a moment, if he knew what was good for him, he'd realize that now was not the time to fixate on the girl no longer standing in front of him.

He closed his eyes and smiled. "I meant, yeah," he said. "Before that."

Leah played with the sleeve of his T-shirt, caressing the fabric between her fingertips as she made him wait. "I wanted to ask if you'd come over for dinner," she said. "We haven't talked much. I never meant to scare you off."

Jonathan smiled slowly. "I'd like that."

Leah heard the sound of the door opening in the garage, and Collin reappeared a moment later.

He looked around the driveway and found the girl on the motorcycle missing. "Hey," Collin said, face disappointed. "Rylee take off?"

Olivia stood in the hallway, holding her small plate and coffee cup. Evelyn had decorated the walls on either side of her with family pictures. From inside one of the frames, Douglas Tibbs looked back at her. He was in uniform, a black beret on his head—standard issue for Army Rangers outside of a war zone.

Jonathan looked like his father, though Olivia had already known that. Studying the pictures, she wondered if Evelyn had any idea how much the boy from these photographs had changed. Not just physically, as Jonathan had put on at least thirty pounds since any of these photos were taken, but in his expression as well. The son looked more like the father now than he ever had in his childhood.

Evelyn returned holding a cardboard box, and watched Olivia as she studied her family photos.

"Your son. He has a lot of your husband in his features," Olivia said.

Evelyn nodded and smiled. "It didn't end with a handsome face. Kid takes after his father," Evelyn replied, walking past Olivia and back to the living room. She placed the box on the coffee table.

"How so?" Olivia asked as she followed.

"They hardly ever speak, for one thing. Happy to spend all day in their heads. Except when they were together. I think they brought it out of each other. Jonathan and I never got on quite like that. It was worse after his father passed. The kid was like Fort Knox if he didn't feel like talking."

Evelyn took the lid off the box and revealed a collection of memories: pieces of Douglas's time in the military, photos, keep sakes—all things she didn't want to be reminded of after he'd died.

"You said this soldier, Jeremy Holloway…" Evelyn said. "He was in Douglas's battalion?"

"Most of the records are lost, including all the pictures, but from what we could tell he served with your husband. He didn't make it back home with the rest of the battalion," Olivia said as she retrieved a digital camera from her briefcase. "Would you mind if I took some photos as we go through these?"

Evelyn shrugged.

Olivia began arranging the pictures and taking shots as they moved through the box.

"I see the name listed," Evelyn said, "but I can't honestly tell you which of these guys was him. I met some of his friends from the Army when he got back. If this Mr. Holloway fellow died over there, I wouldn't have met him."

"I understand. I have a few other individuals on my list to track down. Still, maybe by compiling what I have with what you've shown me, we can piece it together back at the Records Department."

Olivia's eyes fell on a framed photo. It showed Douglas with three fellow soldiers. There was a caption inscribed on the frame: *Staff Sergeant Douglas Tibbs, with the surviving members of his Army Ranger Strike Team, Libya, 1984.*

When Olivia looked at the faces of the men kneeling beside Douglas, she had to keep her eyes from going wide. Her thoughts began to race. Mainly, they screamed that she should be on the phone to her superior as soon as she was back in her sedan. She pushed the reaction down, knowing it would be a miscalculation to give Evelyn any reason to notice a change in her mood or to leave abruptly at the sight of any one of the photos.

Olivia took a last sip of coffee and calmly asked, "Do you mind if I remove this from the frame? I think the glass might create a reflection in the picture."

"My computer has a scanner, if you prefer I could make a copy," Evelyn said. "I'm terrible with technology but you could email it to yourself."

"That would be perfect," Olivia said. "But no need to email it out. I brought a drive with me."

CHAPTER ELEVEN

BETWEEN THE WOMAN in his driveway and Leah asking him to dinner, Jonathan had difficulty keeping his mind on training, a task that wasn't made any easier by Collin, who had been joining him to lift weights more and more often. His roommate's sense of curiosity—or perhaps suspicion was more accurate—refused to let the topic of the girl in the driveway drop. In fairness, Rylee had simply known too much about Jonathan for Collin to buy that he'd never met her.

"She asked for you by name," Collin said.

Jonathan shrugged.

"She said..." Collin paused. "You were expecting her? That you gave her our address?"

"I don't know what to tell you," Jonathan said. "If I did all that, I don't remember it."

Collin studied him skeptically. "Any history of sleep walking I should know about?"

"No." Jonathan grinned. "Not to my knowledge."

"Then…" Collin frowned. "Why did you ask me to leave you two alone?"

That was an excellent question, and Jonathan didn't have an answer for it. He laid under the weight bench and started a set of chest presses, trying to buy himself a moment to think of an excuse—but by the time he finished and Collin helped him put the bar back in place, he still hadn't come up with anything.

"Well?" Collin asked.

"I, uh…" Jonathan said. "Misread the situation."

His roommate rolled his eyes. "Yeah, obviously, but if you didn't know her, what did you—"

Collin paused, interrupted by the sound of Jonathan's phone vibrating on the other side of the room, a distraction that Jonathan eagerly used as an excuse to duck the unfinished question. When he reached it, the caller I.D. said Evelyn Tibbs.

Damn, Jonathan thought, sending the call to voice mail for the third time that day. His mother's attempts to get him on the phone were becoming more and more frequent. Answering a call from Evelyn Tibbs was a bit like dodging a bullet by jumping into a minefield. Still, it had given him an idea he would never have thought of otherwise.

"I thought my mother may have sent her," Jonathan said. "I never told her about the hospital. Ever since I told her I dropped out of school, she calls me about every day. I've been avoiding her."

Collin frowned. "Why would your mother send someone you didn't know to lecture you?" Collin asked.

"I told you," Jonathan said, "I misjudged the situation. Got paranoid."

Jonathan reminded himself that this was why he shouldn't lie. He was terrible at it, and if Collin kept pressing him, he was going to get his story screwed up. As he watched Collin think about it, Jonathan saw his roommate come around to the possibility that he was just an idiot.

"Not what I thought you were going to say," Collin said.

Jonathan gave his roommate a sideways glance. "What did you think?"

"Well, gee, Tibbs, I feel bad about it now," Collin admitted. "But, I thought you had a stalker ex-girlfriend and you were pretending not to know her so our neighbor wouldn't find out."

"No," Jonathan said, seeing the real motivation for Collin giving him the 3rd degree. "I guess I'm flattered you would assume I had so interesting a love life."

"Too bad. She knew her stuff as far as the motorcycle was concerned. I kinda hoped..." Collin paused to think his words over. "Well, I didn't think she was nuts, is all."

Jonathan grew troubled, and Collin didn't miss a beat picking up on it.

"It's none of my business, but you seem less sure than you're letting on," Collin said.

Jonathan took a long breath and gave Collin an appraising glance. He could seldom discuss his life—he always kept his friends at a distance. This didn't feel like it had to be just another moment where he stoically refused to comment.

"If I run something by you," Jonathan said, "can you keep it between the two of us?"

Collin frowned, his hands coming up as if pretending he was offended Jonathan needed to ask.

"Theoretically," Jonathan said. "Have you ever lost any time?"

"We talking, blacked out while drinking?" Collin asked. "Or alien abduction?"

Jonathan narrowed his eyes, but chuckled before responding. "Let's go with the drinking option."

"No, not really," Collin said. "I mean, I've had memories get foggy, but I've never completely forgotten say, meeting a girl, giving her my name and address, and asking her to visit me at my house."

"Right," Jonathan said. "I mean, all that couldn't have happened in some fleeting ten-minute window."

"Tibbs?" Collin's face had become a question mark. "You were home last night—when would you have drunk that much anyway?"

"I..." Jonathan said. "Hey, I said it was theoretical."

Collin held his palms up, indicating there was no need to get defensive. "Well, the last time I heard a blackout drunk story," he said, "it was my brother trying to explain to his girlfriend how he'd come to 'accidentally' cheat on her. You know, the old, 'I'm somehow not responsible for my actions because I don't remember them,' strategy."

Jonathan nodded. "How'd that turn out for him?"

"You know," Collin said. "Let's just say I don't recommend it."

When his roommate quit for the day, Jonathan changed over to weapons training. By mid-afternoon, he had finished running practice drills with the staff. He went up the stairs, drenched in sweat, looking for food and a shower and reminding himself that he now had the added chore of spending an hour in the southwest corner of his room pretending to read.

After the events of the morning, he was anxious to hear back from Mr. Clean, fairly certain that they couldn't wait for Heyer to figure out what had caused the glitch. Unless an attractive foreign exchange student who suffered from mental illness had become fixated on him, then happened to show up in his driveway the day after his memory became compromised, Occam's Razor pretty much confirmed that the girl had memories of that day that he didn't.

The more he thought it through, the more hindsight berated him—he should have recognized what was happening. The way Rylee had locked up reminded him of his own speechlessness at times. Circumstances often put him in situations he couldn't explain to someone else. And what did he do when someone pressed him on it? He either said nothing or found the fastest way out of the conversation that he could. He'd never fled the scene quite like Rylee had, but he'd never honestly had the option. Most of the people who pressed him were people he lived with. Outside of refusing to answer calls from his mother, he really didn't have any choice other than stubborn silence.

Seeing it now, he wished he could rewind, go back and ask her to explain, promise her that he would keep an open mind. Having failed to do this, he was growing increasingly sure that he was the clueless one and now had no way to find the only person who knew what was going on.

Tired and irritated with himself, he entered the kitchen. Collin and Hayden stood over the table, staring down at comic book panels and a mess of poorly-organized notes. They nodded to him as he entered, then continued staring at their mess as he pulled some food out of the refrigerator and tossed it into the microwave. Standing against the counter as he waited, he watched as his two roommates struggled with the continued arc of their comic book series. It was seldom that they were this quiet.

Collin and Hayden's first run at the digital marketing of their comic book—a rebooting of the Gospels that portrayed Jesus as a parody of Superman—had been more successful than they'd expected. Apparently, the two of them arguing on message boards—which, frankly, sounded exactly like when they bickered in real life—had garnered a larger internet following than either of them had anticipated. Their posts had an avid group of devoted fans who often dropped their two cents into the conversation. When they'd released the first three books and started notifying the boards that they were producing the comic as a team, a modest viral reaction to the series had occurred. Now, the two seemed stalled on the next three books, the success having sapped the fun out of writing it. They had difficulty agreeing on which direction they wanted Jesus and Damian, their antichrist villain, to go in.

"You guys still stuck?" Jonathan asked.

Both roommates nodded.

"We are still trying to decide on a trigger event," Collin said.

"There has to be something in their upbringing," Hayden said, "a moment that starts each of them down the road to savior or destroyer. The thing is, the villain's story isn't that different from the hero's. Something happens to each that molds their perspectives in different extremes."

"See, we want it to be the same event for both of them," Collin said. "Jesus has to walk away and begin the road to Christhood while Damian begins the road to antichristhood. It's just hard to create an event that would lead Damian to condone the suffering of others, while creating the polar opposite in Jesus."

Jonathan nodded somewhat blankly, seeing as he didn't have any insight on the matter.

Collin sighed. "Let's table it for now," he said. "I've got an idea that might work, but I need to flesh it out."

Hayden agreed, seeming all too happy to have an excuse to move on.

"Any thoughts on the final straw?" Collin asked. "When they officially acknowledge one another as enemies. What sets them irreparably at odds?"

"It's a tough spot, since Christianity's message is one of forgiveness of sins and loving your enemy and all that. You have to make a core exception in order for Jesus to be at odds with anyone, really," Hayden said.

Collin nodded. "But the antichrist doesn't have to fit into that box," he said. "The obvious angle for Damian would be that, upon learning that God banished his father to Hell—"

"Objection," Hayden said, interrupting. "The Bible doesn't actually say that Lucifer was cast into Hell. If anything, it depends on interpretation."

Collin gave it some thought, but seemed to shrug it off. "Our readers aren't biblical scholars. It's a comic book. We can get away with the pop culture assumptions of Christianity."

Jonathan shut his eyes, rubbing his forehead with his fingers as he fought to keep from smiling. These two never stopped baiting one another with passive-aggressive insults.

"Let me hear it," Hayden said.

"Damian goes all antichrist after learning that God imprisoned his father in Hell. But, since God is out of reach in Heaven, Jesus becomes the next best target. He can't exactly ransom Jesus for his father's release from Hell, but he can at least take his revenge on the Son."

"Why does that plot line sound painfully familiar?" Hayden said.

Collin's face grew smug. "Well, it's pretty much the story of General Zod," Collin said. "You know, the famous Superman villain. Which makes sense, because Superman and Jesus are the same char—"

"Objection," Hayden said. "Zod's son didn't come after Superman. Zod did it himself. I mean, if we are sticking strictly to the 'modern pop culture' Christopher Reeve version."

Collin glowered back at his roommate. "Technically, it is still revenge brought on by the actions of the father."

"Oh 'technically?'" Hayden said, pretending to push his glasses up from the end of his nose while using his best "nerd" voice. He snorted to complete the effect. "Overruled," he said. "You lose."

Jonathan found himself interrupting. "Is this what you guys do now? I mean the court room jokes—is that the thing now?"

Collin and Hayden ignored him, which was fine with Jonathan, because the microwave dinged.

"We both lose," Collin said. "Superman's father, Jor-El, was the one who cast Zod into the Phantom Zone, a perfect analogy for God casting

Lucifer into Hell. Remember what Zod says to Jor-El right before he banishes him?"

Hayden gave his friend a who-do-you-think-you're-talking-to expression, before going on to quote the line in-character: "*You will bow down before me Jor-El, both you*," Hayden said. "*And then one day, your heirs!*"

Collin nodded. "You're making my point," he said. "Picture a panel, somewhere toward the end of the story, where the antichrist stands over Christ and says, 'Jesus of Nazareth, Son of God, kneel before Damian!'"

Now holding his food, Jonathan watched in quiet fascination as Hayden at first stared blankly at Collin. Then, Hayden's foot began to tap the floor—accelerating excitedly with each passing second.

"Okay! Okay!" he finally said. "How do we make this work?" He looked at the linoleum, shaking his head as he tried to think of a way to bridge the stories. When the answer came to him, his face took on a calm, self-assured smile. "The Holy Trinity," he whispered.

As Jonathan watched, Collin's fired-up anticipation seemed to diminish into an unenthused blankness. "I don't get it," Collin said.

"Christians," Hayden said, "believe that Jesus, God, and the Holy Spirit are all the same being existing in different forms at the same—"

"No, I know *what* the Trinity is," Collin said. "I just don't see how it helps."

"If Lucifer's son is an evil reflection of Jesus, then it stands to reason that the antichrist would have an anti-Spirit," Hayden said.

"Anti-Spirit… sounds like a stick of deodorant."

"Fine, an Unholy Spirit, then," Hayden said.

"Okay, I'm listening."

"The point is that attacking Jesus could be the same as attacking God; meanwhile, Damian being the son doesn't matter either, because he, too, is both Lucifer and Damian at the same time."

Collin's expression became pained. "Oh, man, that is convoluted. I never understood this whole part of Christianity. I mean, God and Jesus, okay, one's a god and one's a man—but what's the difference between God and the Holy Spirit?" Collin asked.

Hayden started to respond, then frowned. "It's complicated," Hayden replied. “The Holy Ghost or Holy Spirit is sort of a metaphor for how God reaches out and asserts His will on Earth.”

“Hmm... Are you sure that isn’t the modern pop culture definition?”

Hayden squirmed a bit. “Maybe?”

Jonathan began to leave the room with his food, but slowed as he saw Collin’s smile growing smug again, something that didn’t go unnoticed by Hayden either.

“What?” Hayden asked.

“Would you say the Holy Spirit is kinda like God’s smart phone?” Collin asked.

Hayden glared at his roommate. “No,” he said. “I would say that is a pretty crap analogy.”

“I don’t know,” Collin said. “My phone is the tool I use to exert my will on the internet.”

As Jonathan shook his head and departed up the stairs, Hayden’s voice grew irritated: “The Holy Spirit isn’t a tool,” he said. “You, on the other hand…”

On the arrivals concourse of SeaTac airport, Olivia’s driver opened the sedan’s rear passenger door for her. Beside her empty seat, Olivia found Agent Rivers waiting for her.

“Welcome back,” Rivers said.

“Thank you,” she replied. “I assume you’ve been brought up to speed?”

“Yes. There was a development while you were in the air. I felt you would want to know as soon as you landed,” he said. He reached into his briefcase and produced a folder. “I’m still getting used to working with hard copies.”

He handed the folder over and Olivia found photos of an olive-skinned woman dismounting a motorcycle. The girl was in the parking lot of what appeared to be a motel outside of downtown Seattle.

“Who am I looking at?” she asked.

“A Miss Rylee Silva. She showed up at the household earlier this morning. She spoke briefly with one of the other male roommates, and then with Jonathan Tibbs. The surveillance team watching attempted a recording, but as you indicated would be the case, the audio was useless. From what I gathered, no one has seen this woman on the premises before."

"How was her identity confirmed?" Olivia asked.

"The license plate on the motorcycle was legit—New York based," he said. "Background information is still being researched, but we've confirmed she has relatives on the East Coast, and her family moved here from Brazil a little less than two decades ago. That was all we had uncovered before I left to meet you."

"You felt this could not wait until I returned to the office?" she asked.

"None of that was the strange part. I was able to partially read what Ms. Silva and Jonathan discussed via the surveillance camera in the garage. Jonathan was confused by the woman's presence; it was clear from his body language that he didn't know her. Ms. Silva, however, became quite emotional, and embraced him as though they were intimate friends. When he pushed her away, she seemed upset—left in a hurry. Given there is no record of them meeting, and Jonathan has been under constant surveillance for months, I thought you would want to be informed."

Olivia flipped to one of the pictures. It was taken with a long-range lens somewhere outside the residence. Ms. Silva was in the foreground, and Olivia could make out Jonathan, somewhat out of focus, behind her. Rylee was mounting her bike, about to pull her helmet down. A clear wet line shined down her cheek.

"If she was acting, then Ms. Silva has no trouble bringing herself to tears at will," Rivers said.

"Yes," she said. "I'll make a note to discuss this with my superior. He should be flying in, himself, shortly. In addition, our informant will need to be brought up to speed on whatever we can uncover about Ms. Silva. Was there anything else?"

"Yes," Agent Rivers said. He appeared to grow uncomfortable with what he was about to ask. "Does the name 'Mr. Clean' mean anything to you?"

CHAPTER TWELVE

JONATHAN LEFT HIS laptop on the bed beside him in the hopes that he would seem casual when he reached for it. He'd been pretending to read a paperback off his bookshelf for the last half hour while trying not to glance at the clock too frequently. When he felt he'd put on a decent enough performance, he tossed the book, grabbed the computer, and flipped up the monitor. The desktop loaded as he got the earbuds in and leaned back in the chair as far as he could without being obvious.

Nothing unusual happened immediately, and, unsure of what to do next, he opened a browser window. Heyer never showed up when he wanted him to, so why would Mr. Clean be any different? Still, there had to be some way to get the A.I.'s attention. Jonathan started typing, "Mr. Clean, Mr. Clean," into the search engine as he hummed the old commercial jingle.

The screen flickered then, and the cartoon's face appeared, wearing an unamused expression. "Not very subtle, Jonathan."

Sorry, but I'm rather concerned about my loss of memory, he typed. *Have you figured out the glitch?*

"I have a highly probable theory. Unfortunately, it's a contingency I cannot discuss with you."

That's it? Jonathan typed. *You know what's happened, but you aren't going to tell me?*

"Heyer would want to be present," Mr. Clean said. "Jonathan, it is a matter of discretion."

Can you at least tell me if it will happen again?

"Yes," Mr. Clean said. "It is highly probable that this event will repeat itself."

Jonathan closed his eyes and took a long breath to keep himself in check. He couldn't exactly raise his voice or yell. He doubted that typing in all caps would have any effect on the computer.

Can you tell me, Jonathan typed. *Is there any possibility that memories from my life, outside of what took place within the gates, are being lost?*

"No," Mr. Clean said. The cartoon avatar's expression became curious. "That is a peculiar question. Have you experienced additional memory gaps from which you drew this conclusion?"

Not exactly. Maybe, Jonathan typed. *A woman appeared in my driveway this morning claiming to know me, but I had no recollection of her. Which means she was either nuts or my memory of her was lost. The timing is too close to be a coincidence.*

A small window appeared in the corner of the display, and footage from The Cell's various cameras within the garage appeared. They were time-stamped for today's date, and Mr. Clean appeared to be fast-forwarding through one of the feeds facing Jonathan's driveway from within the garage. Eventually, Collin appeared, opening the door and pushing his motorcycle outside. A few minutes later, Rylee pulled in. The moment she removed her helmet, the footage froze.

"Facial recognition matches the female to a Rylee Silva. An analysis of her credit card transaction history and cellular GPS coordinates show she has been thousands of miles away from you for the majority of your life. It is therefore highly unlikely that you've crossed paths," Mr. Clean said. "This is sufficient evidence to conclude that your memories outside of the yesterday's incident do not need to be called into question."

Well, at least there's that, Jonathan thought.

Can you tell me, did the source of this glitch occur on the Feroxian side of the gates? Is it related to something one of the Ferox did on the other side? he typed.

"No, Jonathan, that is not the case," Mr. Clean said. "Even if there was a means to do so, the rules forbid any tampering with your memories."

The rules. Jonathan remembered that Heyer had once told him that there were rules that the brothers had agreed on. He had only been told of one of them, which said that outside of the implant, Heyer was not allowed to provide a human any assistance that was outside of earthly means. Jonathan had not yet had an opportunity to ask what other rules were in play, though he got the sense that the rules weren't necessarily something Heyer's integrity forbade him from bending. Rather, something he cheated for the benefit of mankind if he knew his brother would not be able to discover it. The thing was, Jonathan assumed that Malkier likely had the same attitude on behalf of the Ferox, which lead him to wonder if Mr. Clean was really telling him that his memory should not have been tampered with—not that it could not have been.

Are you allowed to tell me the rules? Jonathan asked.

"Yes," Mr. Clean said. "Most of them, at least."

Jonathan frowned. *How many are there?* he typed.

"A few hundred," Mr. Clean said.

When concern showed on Jonathan's face, Mr. Clean reminded him that he needed to keep his expression calm. "Understand, most of these rules have no bearing on the means by which man and Ferox engage. A majority are safety protocols concerned with the use of the gates themselves."

I once asked Heyer for a weapon, something from his species that I could use against the Ferox. Something a little deadlier than a fancy spear, Jonathan typed. *He said it wasn't allowed.*

"Yes, and as you would assume, this was, in part, to deny you an unfair advantage. However, even if Heyer had access to such things, he could not have left Borealis technology in your possession."

Borealis? Jonathan asked.

"A term we use for Heyer's ancestors," Mr. Clean said. "*Borealis* is the English translation most frequently heard by humans when a Ferox makes reference to their gods in battle. Of course, the Ferox do not realize that their gods and Heyer's ancestors are one and the same, and so the term is as good as any. But in regards to my original point, Heyer could not leave advanced technology where it would fall into the hands of your surveillance team."

But Excali-bar doesn't concern you? Jonathan asked.

"The staff is a crude tool. It doesn't give its holder any particular edge over a sharp stick, aside from being far more difficult to break. In addition, the weapon is not true Borealis steel. Excali-bar is made of materials harvested from Earth, but forged using a Borealis metallurgy process."

Thinking about it, Jonathan saw that the computer had a point. He could imagine numerous applications for the steel: it would certainly make for an innovative new building material, vehicle armor plating, a better bullet proof vest, or even a better bullet, for that matter. However, Excali-bar itself was just a piece of steel in the end. It wouldn't make much difference unless mankind could reverse-engineer it in large quantities.

"So what other rules can I know?" he typed.

Mr. Clean's face shrunk so that it was only filling half of the monitor, and on the other half, white text began to scroll on a black screen.

1. Neither Borealis will intervene in conflicts until one combatant remains
2. Arena environment restricted to Earth
3. Human survivors retain their memory
4. Humans who would possess a device compatibility exceeding 43% are disqualified
5. Ferox Alpha males are likewise ineligible for entry into the gates
6. No gateway will remain active beyond initial energy expenditure
7. Repeat human victors will not be targeted
8. Ferox males deemed genetically irrelevant are ineligible for entry into the gates
9. Proximity overlap…

Seeing that text was continuing to run across his screen faster and faster, and Jonathan wasn't sure if he understood a majority of what he was reading, he interrupted. *Stop, slow down,* Jonathan typed. *I don't understand half of these.*

"No," Mr. Clean said, "I imagine you wouldn't."

Why rule two—why is the Arena always Earth?

"Practicality and necessity. The gateway equipment already existed on the Feroxian plane—each gate only needed to be re-targeted to Earth. However, redundancy in time was the main factor. Human combatants experience their battle, followed by a mental reversal back to the moment prior to the gate's opening. However, the Ferox do not experience this redundancy, as this would eliminate the entire point of the exercise. In the event of a Ferox victory, their bodies must return to the Feroxian plane in the same state they were in upon leaving combat—injuries included. The directionality of the Feroxian gate opening to Earth is the only arrangement that can facilitate a redundancy in time for human victors and lack thereof for a Ferox victor."

Jonathan found that this answer left him with more questions than answers. "*What purpose does all that serve?*" he wrote.

"The male Ferox's physical state must be preserved after the engagement in order for them to achieve fertility. They must also bring their trophy—a human combatant's corpse, covered in their pheromone excretion—for offering and consumption by the female they wish to mate with," Mr. Clean replied. "If a Ferox male was returned to his home planet and only retained the memory of a battle, he would not achieve the physical state necessary for copulation, nor would the Ferox female achieve fertility without presentation of his offering."

Jonathan shook his head. He'd never heard the specifics about the Feroxian mating rituals, but the way that Mr. Clean described the process made it difficult to keep from being disgusted. The whole act sounded as if Ferox males came here to get turned on, aroused by violence.

"*Why is it a rule that Earth's survivors retain their memory at all, then?*" Jonathan asked. "*Seems counter to the goal of keeping the human race in the dark.*"

"Correct. It would be a simpler affair if humans never became aware of what was happening to them. Heyer found this strategically problematic if he wished to build any kind of a resistance army in the future. However, he could not demand human combatants keep their memories without providing a valid reason," Mr. Clean said.

Jonathan understood Heyer's angle in this instance. He wanted his army to have experience when the time came. Jonathan had only survived his first encounter with the Ferox out of sheer luck. If he had lost the memory of it ever having happened, he'd have entered his second confrontation blind to what he was facing. What he didn't understand was how Malkier didn't see this as a blatant foreshadowing of betrayal.

So, how did Heyer pull that off? Jonathan asked.

"With less difficulty than you might imagine. Heyer cannot feasibly attend every engagement, but he must always be present for a man's first conflict. This is so, in the event of a human victory, Heyer can train him to properly close the gates. If humans did not retain their memories, then Heyer would have to be present for every confrontation. Because of this, the implants are installed such that humans retain their memory. Modifying the device's settings once it has become part of a host's active biology is highly dangerous, so again, practicality requires that men continue to retain their memory for the duration of their survival," Mr. Clean said. "Now, that said, there are also potential uses for human memories to Malkier's people in the long run. These potential uses are symptoms of rules four and five," Mr. Clean said.

"Device compatibility of 43%?" Jonathan asked. *"And the Alphas?"*

Mr. Clean nodded, but as he did so, it almost seemed as though the cartoon's attention had suddenly become divided.

Explain the compatibility percentage, Jonathan typed faster.

"Yes, limits had to be set on what degree of power a human should be allowed during a confrontation," Mr. Clean said. "You have to remember, Jonathan: the expectation is that the human will put up a fight, but still lose."

Jonathan shook his head. The injustice of the whole arrangement—seeing how rigged the system was against the human combatants—was infuriating. *"Seems unlike the Ferox to want their opponents handicapped,"* Jonathan wrote. *"They are a lot of ugly things, but cowards never seemed to be one of them."*

"They have no awareness of these rules, nor do most human combatants. In addition, the Ferox possess an emotion akin to human fear, although the triggers are not identical to those of Man. Their sense of self-preservation is less tied to themselves as individuals, and more to their species as a whole. They fear mass extinction far more than personal injury. When a means to keep the Ferox from dying off presented itself, they were facing down their most innate fear. You can imagine that the Ferox leaders asked few questions about the fairness of the battles when their gods returned to open the gates."

Jonathan nodded. *So Malkier found a human compatibility max where the Ferox feels threatened enough to achieve fertility, but the human is still unlikely to win. Meanwhile, the Ferox don't know the fight is rigged for them.* Jonathan paused a moment, finding he still didn't understand something. *But, how does any of this mean Malkier eventually benefits from human combatants retaining their memories? You said it had something to do with the Alphas?*

He'd been looking at the keyboard as he typed, and when he came back to the screen, Mr. Clean's face was more distracted. "Jonathan, I am noticing that multiple terminals are now monitoring your internet line. The Cell has taken notice of how long you have spent in their blind spot. It is prudent that we continue this conversation at a later time."

Just quickly, answer this one question.

"There is no shortage of individuals with lower compatibilities. Malkier originally saw no advantage in keeping the outliers—that is, those with substantially lower compatibilities who had survived despite the odds being heavily stacked against them. He wanted them disposed of, so their devices could be retrieved and re-implanted in hosts more psychologically ideal to serve his goals. However, because of the compatibility max, finding a human capable of—"

Mr. Clean stopped speaking momentarily.

"I am sorry, Jonathan. We will finish this conversation at another time. Leave the corner immediately and do not initiate communication with me again. I will contact you at a more appropriate time."

The screen returned to his normal desktop.

Dammit! Hastily, Jonathan slammed the screen shut and threw the laptop back onto his bed.

He regretted the action, having forgotten that his behavior was being filmed, but the unanswered questions were infuriating. Why had the gates already existed on the Ferox world but not on Earth? Why was there a time redundancy on one side but not the other? But…

What purpose could human memories possibly serve for an Alpha Ferox? Jonathan wondered. Given the recent gaps in his own memory, this question bothered him more than the rest.

CHAPTER THIRTEEN

LEAH HELD A glass of wine she had yet to touch, an endearing grin on her face as she watched Jonathan.

"Again!" Jack said.

They sat in her dining room, the boys locking hands over their empty dinner plates in an epic battle of thumbs. Jonathan was playing a part for Jack, always allowing the little boy to win in the end, but only after putting on a performance of intense struggle. Her brother was a mixture of laughter and focus as the competition continued. She felt her grin waver for a moment when the reservations returned; those moments where her mind broke the spell and she remembered this wasn't real—that she was playing a part as well.

Jonathan pinned Jack's thumb and started to count down, letting the kid bring all his efforts to escape. Soon, Jack would have the upper hand, or thumb, as it were, and Jonathan would pretend to be shocked when the underdog somehow turned the tables on him. What Leah found so fascinating was that the boys never seemed to grow tired of seeing this story play itself out. Jack may have still been young enough that he believed they weren't following a script, but Leah was quietly studying Jonathan's every nuance. He clearly had something invested. He didn't want to break the little boy's illusion.

It played out the same each time. Jack let out a roar, as though he were Bruce Banner turning green, suddenly having the strength to break free of the bigger man's thumb as he became the Hulk. Meanwhile,

Jonathan would begin to struggle, losing his grip with wide-eyed disbelief. That was when she'd see what she found so fascinating. It was so important to him that the young boy believed he could call on something inside of himself, something with the power to change a losing situation.

She'd lost count of the number of times the two had played this out. When they started the countdown to another round, she looked at the clock and saw that it was approaching Jack's bedtime.

"You two think you can put the war on hold for dessert?" Leah asked.

Her little brother's eyes lit up with the promise of sugar. When she saw Jonathan's eyes turn to her, she gave the subtlest of tells, puckering her lips faintly enough that Jack would never catch the flirtation. The little boy wouldn't notice the unspoken words that the adults had shared with a glance. One look at each other being enough to replace an entire discussion and make them allies in orchestrating events that would expedite the child's bed time.

"Dessert is a pretty serious reason for a cease fire," Jonathan said. "Truce?"

Jack looked at him with narrowed eyes, as though he suspected Jonathan's thumb would pounce if he dropped his guard.

"If we keep going," Jonathan said, "my thumb might be too tired to hold a fork."

Jonathan had to agree that they would both let go on the count of three before Jack released his hand, and Leah returned from the kitchen with three slices of cheesecake.

Jonathan grinned at her like a co-conspirator as he ate his dessert, though the smile didn't hide an eagerness to be alone with her. She didn't let it show, but there was something subtly different about the willingness to let her see that in his eyes. He looked at her without wavering. There had been a time when he had lacked the courage to own the desire his gaze betrayed when they caught one another's stare. It had been as though the question of whether or not he had permission to look at her so candidly had finally been answered. That question had only ever existed in Jonathan's head. He'd always had her permission. It had just taken him a frustratingly long time to realize it.

Their looks across the table made it increasingly difficult to remember the child was there, made each bite of the rich dessert a struggle with patience; every moment, a tease.

"Time for bed, Jack," Leah said the moment the boy finished placing the last bite on his plate into his mouth.

"Awww—" Jack started to complain.

They were ten blocks away, standing in the basement of what had once been a neighborhood grocery store. When the business had gone under and the property foreclosed, the building had been scheduled to be demolished. Instead, Olivia's team had bought the space through an intermediary with no traceable link to any government entity funding their operations.

There had been an excessive amount of care put into the location, with every detail of its preparation overseen by Olivia herself. The walls were soundproofed to excess, with mesh metal wiring covering the inner surfaces to help block signals in or out. The only hard lines in were Internet and surveillance feeds. Olivia allowed herself no illusions—The Mark may have already been well aware of the location. Still, she'd gone out of her way to make sure that protection from any manner of eavesdropping humanity had at its disposal was in place. Every computer had been stripped of camera and microphone. Cellphones and radios were not allowed on the premises. She assumed, because there was no way to be sure, that The Mark may have had the means to know every detail of the information that came into the facility, but that didn't mean she would allow it to be any easier for him to know what her team had made of said information.

At the moment, Olivia watched the monitors intently with Agent Rivers beside her. He was doing his best to explain the minutia of Leah and Jonathan's dinner conversation from the surveillance camera feeds. His interpretation was limited, as lip reading wasn't an exact science. The art of it was complicated by cameras not being in the ideal position to see a speaker's face, or the simple act of a person's hand being in front of their mouth as they spoke. That, and it was hard to watch everyone's mouth at once. Rivers failed to make out every uttered line, but the conversation taking place in the presence of the child was unlikely to tell them much anyway, and he could review the tapes to get a better transcription later, when they weren't watching the screens in real time. Regardless, Olivia could read the situation fairly well from context.

She had become rather fascinated watching Leah work. She studied how their asset swayed the subject with her body language so naturally. Olivia could manipulate, and did so regularly, but she had no use of seduction in her day-to-day dealings.

Olivia followed Leah on the monitors when she left the table to retrieve dessert, waiting to see if she'd falter or fall out of character once out of sight.

Agent Rivers spoke then, breaking her concentration. "Wherever you found her, she was an excellent decision. I've never seen an agent this young able stay in character so..." He paused, seeming to search for the right word. "Convincingly."

Olivia nodded without taking her eyes off the monitor. "Wasn't my call. She is an outside contractor brought in from the private sector. A direct order from above. We call her by her assumed identity because we don't have a real one," she replied.

"I've never heard of an order so outside of normal procedures," Rivers said. "I mean, consultants on technical matter is fairly standard, but your main asset with direct access to the subject?"

"Yes. At the time, I put in a formal objection and was overruled," Olivia replied. "However, once I had more information, I came to see why her involvement was strategically wise."

"Is it within my pay grade to ask what changed your mind?" Rivers asked.

"Normally, no, it would not be." Olivia said. "Seeing as how it's a complete absence of information, I see no reason you can't be aware. Frankly, my commanding officer is rather proud of this asset."

"Absence of information?" Rivers said.

"Leah and the young child," Olivia said, pointing at Jack on the monitor. "They do not exist."

Rivers' gaze slipped off the monitors momentarily, and Olivia could feel his curiosity frowning at her.

"With approval, I was permitted to launch a full inquiry into the identity of both Leah and the child. I found out later permission was granted as an exploratory exercise."

"Intriguing," Rivers replied. "What did you find?"

"Almost nothing was uncovered, and what little there was led nowhere," Olivia replied.

He seemed to ponder this for a moment before drawing a conclusion. "Command went all out removing any possibility of her identity being discovered. He knew your record, that you had never failed to achieve results, and so he allowed you to launch an inquiry to see how successful the removal of their identities had been?" Rivers asked.

Olivia nodded. She was becoming increasingly pleased with Agent Rivers' ability to keep up. She would see to it that the man was given a promotion, possibly made lead on the next identified person of interest. For now, she considered him an ideal protégé.

"You said 'almost nothing'," Rivers replied.

"There was one hit. An image brought up by facial recognition software. It was a picture of Leah stepping out of a vehicle in Jefferson, New York a little over a year ago. The image was immediately removed once I reported it, but I was allowed to follow all leads that could be explored from confirming where she had been. No ties were found to the area or the nearby military base, and the vehicle was untraceable. My suspicion is that she received some type of training at the site."

"So, were they pleased or annoyed that you found something?" he asked.

"I imagine a little of both," Olivia replied. "But I do not consider the investigation closed."

Her attention returned to the monitors, as it appeared Leah had left Jonathan alone while she put the child in pajamas and made sure he brushed his teeth. Jonathan stood in the kitchen, placing plates in the dishwasher.

"What do you think about the recent peculiarities in Jonathan's behavior?" Olivia asked.

"Not a believer in coincidence. Ms. Silva's appearance, Jonathan starts sitting in the one corner we happen to be unable to monitor. This Mr. Clean," Agent Rivers said, "I have a hunch."

"I entertain all hunches."

"We monitored his internet feed today when he started using his laptop. It gave me some concerns," Rivers replied. "The activity on the net looked like a random combination of pornography searches while he listened to streaming music. Seemingly standard profile for a man his age, except Jonathan hasn't behaved like a standard profile since this investigation began."

Olivia nodded in agreement of the observation.

"Then, he abruptly became upset and walked away from the machine. We've reviewed the sites he visited—none of the material appeared particularly offensive. It got me thinking of Mr. Clean."

Finally, she turned away from the monitor; her curiosity now piqued enough to take her attention from Leah tucking Jack into bed.

"It's typical for hackers to use an alias. I searched the various government intelligence departments' computer crime records but was unable to find a substantial link to the alias 'Mr. Clean'. The team didn't believe there was a hacker out there skilled enough to fool our best analysts, but I am working off the assumption that they're wrong. That this alias is nowhere on record because he, or she, is that good. What if Jonathan is talking to someone technologically savvy enough to pull the wool over our eyes? An accomplishment for a man, sure, but a seemingly small one for an alien that can teleport all over the globe."

Olivia nodded again, though this time she appeared almost irritated to him.

"Like I said, it was only a hunch."

"And a fair one," Olivia said. "It troubles me because of the predicament it creates."

"Ma'am?" Rivers asked.

"We now have two options, Agent Rivers. If we remove the blind spot and cut off the possible contact, reason dictates that if your theoretical 'Mr. Clean' exists, he will notice that we've become aware of him. If Jonathan ceases to sit in that corner, we can also assume he is aware of the cameras. Alternatively, we can maintain the illusion that we are not suspicious of the activity, and see how it plays out. The question is, do we want Jonathan talking to this theoretical 'Mr. Clean' so we might observe the results, or do we want the communication to cease immediately?"

"Yeah," Agent Rivers said, "I see the predicament."

"For now, we'll let it play out," Olivia said. "Set our efforts to confirming this Mr. Clean is more than a hunch before making a move."

CHAPTER FOURTEEN

SATURDAY | OCTOBER 8, 2005 | 9:00 PM | SEATTLE

JONATHAN OCCUPIED HIMSELF with dishes as he waited for Leah to put Jack to bed. He heard her when she was at the child's door.

"Love you, Jack," she said. "Goodnight."

"Hall light?" Jack asked.

"Okay, 'til you fall asleep."

The exchange brought Jonathan back to childhood. He'd been afraid of the dark at Jack's age as well. Leah had told him she'd lost her parents. She'd had to step into the role of a mother. Jonathan had been an only child, but he didn't imagine that siblings could easily flip a switch and act another part. Leah seemed to manage, and he respected her for being what Jack needed her to be.

He wondered if he'd misunderstood that day in the garage, when she asked him not to get attached. Had he taken the comment too personally when it had nothing to do with him? She'd needed something for herself and hadn't pretended she could be anything else. Maybe she didn't want him getting attached because she was already stretched too thin?

Suddenly, he felt so shortsighted. Not because he'd ever thought badly of her, but because it took him so long to see such an obvious reason for putting a buffer between them. The thoughts dominoed, and he saw that there were a lot of good reasons to keep him at a distance.

Jonathan hadn't exactly been a pillar of stability, or even sanity, the last few months. Even if Leah had been an ordinary, single twenty-something with no responsibilities, Jonathan could see what he might look like—a glaringly bad decision. The shortcomings Leah knew about paled in comparison to the ones he could never tell her. He thought about the blank side of the scoreboard hidden in his garage. One bad day would be the last time Leah ever saw him. If he was being honest with himself, he was being selfish. He should have been the one telling her not to get attached.

The guilty thoughts evaporated when she returned. She had a look in her eyes that he'd seen once before. He reminded himself that he wasn't a saint as her fingers beckoned him to follow her into the living room, where they would be far enough away from the ears of the not-yet-sleeping child.

"What happened to you, Jonathan?" she asked as he followed her.

She asked it casually, as she always had in the past. When his roommates or his mother asked him a question like that, they were reminders that a wall had to remain between him and everyone else. Leah had always been different. When she asked him a question, she had a way of making it feel as though she'd meant to give him a gift, a chance for him to say something she sensed he desperately needed to say.

"I know. I could have left things... less vague," she said. "I did want to see you again, but for awhile you were never around, I mean, not just out, but—"

"I know," he said, stepping into the living room behind her.

"When I saw that girl putting her hands on you," Leah said as she turned to look at him, "I thought, maybe..."

"No," Jonathan said. "I couldn't…" He trailed off, not because he didn't know the words, but because he hated the idea of speaking them.

No matter how vague things had been left between them, the idea of looking for affection from another woman was a mistake he would only make in a nightmare. Yes, he was human, and, yes, he wanted someone, but doing something that could hurt the chance of being with the girl standing in front of him was a mistake he would never even imagine making.

He would fail at speaking the words because he wasn't ever going to deliver them the way he felt them. He would smile, or laugh, or be too vulnerable to look her in the eye—the words would be forced through a filter of cowardice, him trying to pretend he didn't take his own feelings seriously.

So he took a breath and looked at her with all his longing. He hoped that if she could just be Leah, the girl who always saw through him, then he wouldn't need to say anything at all. After a moment, he saw that she was the one who almost shied away, who was almost unable to hold his gaze. Then Leah bit her lip and stared right back, her eyes narrowed in a playful way.

"You think you can get away with looking at me like that forever," she said, "but someday I am gonna want you to use your big boy words."

He smiled. "Anyone ever accuse you of being overly perceptive?"

"I like how you look at me when I'm busy being perceptive," she said, and then added, "Subject changer."

He stepped closer, and her face became an invitation as she matched his steps.

Leah pushed against him, pinning him to the wall. Her lips pressed hard against him. Her mind raced ahead, impatient to lock him behind her bedroom door.

When he broke contact, it came without warning, left her gasping as suddenly Jonathan pushed her back, his arms bracing to keep her away. Being severed from him was startling, jolted her with confusion. She felt a moment of anger—until she saw his fear.

"Leah, step back," he whispered.

The look on his face froze her. Something was terribly wrong, but she couldn't escape the moment that had preceded the change so quickly. She couldn't bring her faculties back in line to understand the danger he seemed to suddenly see.

"Back up, Leah," Jonathan repeated, his voice urgent, forceful enough that she obeyed without thinking.

As soon as he didn't need his arms keeping her out of reach, he rolled away, using the wall to support his quaking legs. He was heading abruptly for the door, one hand reaching clumsily for the handle while the other held his chest.

Finally, Leah found her voice: "Jonathan?"

He stumbled out of the house and she followed, not knowing what else to do. He struggled through three more steps before he tried to turn, then collapsed, falling on his back onto her lawn. The disturbing manner in which it happened shot adrenaline though her, shattering the lingering myopia of lust and confusion. It was as though he had died, like his brain had unceremoniously disconnected from his body. She almost screamed, but caught the sound in her throat, only to hear a muffled cry escape her.

In the dark, she was seeing something impossible. Jonathan's blood—she could see it beneath his skin, lighting up in his veins as though it had caught fire, the orange glow pulsing stronger with each beat of his heart. Leah didn't remember moving, but found herself kneeling in the grass beside him. He was in agony, the visceral pain visible on his face. She was hypnotized as lines began to take form on his chest. The light was so concentrated there, unmistakable beneath the fabric of his shirt.

She knew she was finally seeing what Jonathan hid, but in that moment, she couldn't have cared less. He was in so much pain—all that surfaced in her was a desperate need to do something. Fear and helplessness drowned out her thoughts, a terrible question now at the forefront of her mind. *Was this how it would happen?* Was this the moment he'd be lost to her, where she'd be left staring at an empty patch of grass.

No, she'd seen it happen when Peter was taken. It hadn't been anything like what she was seeing now. She had to cling to that thought, use it to force down the rising helplessness. She had to do something. She had to see what was forming on his chest.

She forced herself to move, crawled over him, and pinned each of his shaking forearms under her knees to control his seizures. She grabbed hold of his shirt and pulled, breaking through the buttons. Light spilled out, no longer dampened by the thin layer of fabric, and she flinched as her eyes attempted to adjusted to the sudden brightness. A moment later, he suddenly went dead still, his limbs unmoving beneath her, his writhing gone. The light in his chest flickered out, disappearing. She blinked and felt herself shivering in near-silence, only to hear a sigh slip out of him as though his lungs had taken their final breath.

She was jolted when the glow returned, becoming solid, brighter, and constant.

With his face illuminated in the orange glow, Leah tentatively reached for his cheek, but her hand stilled as she saw movement beneath his eyelids. Finally, his eyes opened and looked back at her.

Resurfacing out of the fire of activation, Jonathan slowly came back to himself. It was a disorientation he had experienced enough times to know when something felt... different.

He could still sense that difference in the fog of his returning thoughts. There had been something at the onset, as though the push to initiate had been taking hold of more of him. The thing was, previously, he couldn't imagine that there was anything more for the device to burn through. He knew, somehow, that every time he'd been activated in the past, the device had been holding something back.

Not clear on where he was, he noticed the ground felt soft beneath him, the air cool, and that his hands were held down. His vision cleared, and Leah's face was the first thing to come into focus. She breathed heavily, her face illuminated, turned orange by the glow from his chest. He saw she'd been crying, though she didn't seem aware of the tears even as they ran down her cheeks. Not knowing what else to do, he smiled up at her. The concern on her face broke, her lips trembling when they smiled back. She breathed as though she had forgotten how and was just now remembering.

"You're still here," she whispered.

He realized, then, that she must have seen him go through the entirety of the change—he knew it appeared as though he'd been dying. "Where could I go? You're on top of me."

She gasped, smiled, and whimpered all at the same time—a sound one only makes when one believes they are on the brink of witnessing their worst fear, only to have that fear go unrealized. Her eyes travelled back to the inhuman energy beneath his skin. Her hand reached out, shaking and unsure, coming to rest over the exposed glow of his chest.

"Warm," she said.

He was about to tell her it was an understatement, that a moment ago he'd felt like a furnace, but when he looked down, his words caught. The lines—they were brighter, glowing stronger than they ever had. A development he'd have given more attention to had movement not then pinged like radar against the alien instincts in his mind. The position of a Ferox, not yet in focus, brought reality back down on him. The smile fell off his face. Leah must have noticed the change in him, because fear began returning to her expression.

"What is it?"

"I have to go," he replied.

Within a few seconds, he felt her putting weight on the hand touching his chest. "No. No way—not until you tell me what just happened," she replied.

"I need you to get off me, Leah," he said, as gently as he could.

"Not gonna happen."

"Leah," he said. "It's dangerous. I could hurt you by accident. Do not make me move you."

Defiance came over her face—a look that said, *I dare you to try.*

"People are going to start dying. I don't want to see that," Jonathan said.

Her defiant expression flinched at his tone and he could see that she believed him. She only hesitated a moment longer before easing off him. "What people?" she asked.

He waited until she was a step back before he stood. He looked down at his chest, and back into her eyes. She seemed to be struggling to keep from looking down, and under different circumstances, he'd have found the role reversal more entertaining. Instead, he found himself carefully pulling the shirt closed; embarrassed of the attention it drew off his face.

Standing, now, he realized he was having trouble telling exactly where the Ferox was, that the signal was taking longer to grow certain. He was only sure that it was somewhere in the city. He shut his eyes and moved his head slightly, as though it were an antenna and he was trying to get better reception. This was odd. He normally felt where the enemy was the moment he was fully conscious. Slowly, the signal began to clear, accelerating into focus swiftly as it did so. Jonathan's eyes shot open as the reason he'd had trouble resolving the location became absolute.

He turned in disbelief, taking a few steps toward the city as though he'd heard a bomb denoted in the distance.

"Jonathan, please," Leah said. "Tell me what's going on. What people?"

He spoke, though he knew she'd never understand, that she'd never remember. "There's two of them," he whispered.

This—it wasn't supposed to be possible. Hadn't Heyer said as much? He had to move, but after three steps toward the garage, he hesitated.

"Jonathan? What does that mean? Two of what?"

He heard her—she'd followed him, was standing right behind him now—but there was no point. He couldn't take the time to explain. If he died tonight, he would disappear right out of her arms. He should have listened to the guilt when it told him he was being selfish.

"Jonathan?"

He forced her voice out, brought his mind to focus on the signals. One wasn't far, but it was already on the move, headed away from him. The other was further away, but...

"It's not through yet," he said.

There was a chance, if he moved fast enough, that he could keep them isolated. He just had to hope he could take down the first quickly. If the second made it through and found him still fighting the first, he wouldn't stand a chance.

CHAPTER FIFTEEN

THE WIND RUSHED past as he closed the distance, pushing the bike as hard as he dared on the suburban streets. Leah had watched him, standing in the opening after he'd torn the garage door off its rails. She'd stared, her fear turning to anger the more her questions were returned with silence. He'd gotten into his gear, pulled Excali-bar from the closet, and dropped the decoy on the floor.

He'd been able to ignore her eyes on him until he'd gone to start the bike and found the key suddenly missing from the ignition. Then he'd had to look at her, standing with the keys in her fist a few steps away.

"Leah, give them to me," he'd said.

She was shaking, conflicted, trying to take control over the situation, trying to slow him down. "You've done this before," she'd said, and he heard her voice growing louder. "I can tell you have. You aren't even scared, doing things like you've done them a hundred times."

"Give me the keys, Leah."

"How is that possible?" she asked, her words coming out as though she were becoming unhinged. "How could you hide this from everyone?"

"Dammit, Leah!" he yelled.

She recoiled when he yelled, and it ate into him. He closed his eyes, got control of his voice. "You aren't going to remember any of this."

Leah swallowed, face contorting in confusion. "But you will?"

"Yes, only me—always me."

"How—"

"Leah!" The clock ticked in his eyes. "Please don't make me take them from you. Every second you keep me here is... killing me."

He put his hand out, and she walked to him slowly, stopping when the keys were hovering above his palm. She looked him in the eyes. "Tell me. What I can't remember," Leah said. "Make me believe you." She watched as his eyes raced between her and the keys, waiting for her hand to open. "Promise me?"

He let out a heavy sigh, wishing that time had not been so stacked against him, and said, "I'm sorry I yelled at you." He glanced at the keys again, and Leah shook with frustration—knew, even then, that he was refusing to promise her anything.

"I would have believed you," she'd said, letting the key drop into his palm.

He'd driven off then, as fast as he could. He'd never be able to tell Leah anything if he was dead, and now he needed her as far from his mind as possible.

He skidded through a turn, barely avoiding oncoming traffic as he hit the busier streets near the city. Maneuvering more and more dangerously as the roads grew wider, he finally came to a steep hill leading to a freeway overpass, one of the few ways to get over the I-5 freeway that ran through downtown Seattle. He gained speed, accelerating down the incline, weaving around cars until he was on the overpass. Unexpectedly, the Ferox that had been on the move changed directions—its signal suddenly rocketed toward him instead of away—headed for the freeway traffic underneath him.

His foot hit the brake and the bike swerved, back tires skidding around behind him, until he was perpendicular with the oncoming traffic. He took hold of Excali-bar, freeing it from the motorcycle as he brought his foot down and released the handlebars, allowing the bike to slip out from under him and become a spray of sparks headed down the overpass. The steel of the old bike shrieked—drivers slammed on their brakes and Jonathan ignored a cacophony of back-end collisions as he ran across the lanes and reached the overpass's narrow shoulder.

From above, the first Ferox's signal finally lined up with his eyes as the beast smashed into the freeway traffic below him. The monster slammed into an SUV, knocking the vehicle across three lanes and into the nearest divider, where the car crumpled in around it. What immediately struck Jonathan as strange was that the Ferox, a Green, had attacked the oncoming traffic by ramming into it ass-first.

The Ferox began to claw its way out of the SUV's collapsed remains just as Jonathan caught sight of a second figure shooting out over the freeway. The figure connected with the creature before it had time to plant its feet, a fist taking the Green on the jaw and spinning it back around. The Ferox tore through what remained of the SUV and broke through the divider.

The figure was smaller, human, female, and her face—Jonathan blinked—belonged to the woman from his driveway.

CHAPTER SIXTEEN

HE SHOULD HAVE moved, but Jonathan locked up when his mind started trying to connect the dots of the past few days with everything happening below him. Heyer had always made it seem as though these devices only functioned in men. Hadn't he...? Or had Jonathan projected his own assumptions? Shaking his head, Jonathan grabbed the safety rail, preparing to jump the barrier and drop into the fray, but took a final look to decide where to position himself. He paused, the way Rylee moved leaving him in a humbled trance.

She fought the enemy inside the rapidly-widening gap of traffic that had begun after the Ferox crashed through the divider into the northbound lanes. The drivers were being forced to slam on their brakes at dangerously high speeds—screeching tires, crunching impacts, and shattering glass became ubiquitous background noise all around him.

Rylee flowed around the Ferox as though gravity was not a force that governed her but was an ally, working for her. She used her hands and legs as if they were interchangeable, seeming as comfortable in a handstand as Jonathan would be with both feet on the ground. She never held a stationary stance—she was always in motion.

In a maneuver that could not have lasted the length of two complete seconds, Rylee put her boot between the Green's eyes just as her hands made contact with the freeway. Before the blow was delivered, it had appeared she was landing a handstand—yet she pushed back with her heel against the creature's forehead. She used the leverage as a means to flip herself so that she was standing toe-to-toe with the beast—but she never stopped flowing through the movements; the toes of her foot touched ground and she was already dropping backward before her heel had planted. What looked like a fall backwards became the means to shift her weight onto one hand behind her. That hand became the center around which she swiveled her legs full-circle, sweeping the Ferox's feet out from under it.

Rylee was already bounding away before the Ferox's skull cracked against the road.

None of it seemed like the well-practiced steps of a memorized routine, and only a high-speed camera could have captured her at a moment precise enough to label her position a handstand. Rylee attacked as though movement was thoughtless, transcending the notion of any strike so simple it could be named.

The tactics played havoc with the Green's instincts. Young and impatient, Rylee's style was forcing him to fight from the center of a constantly moving circle, perpetually making him pivot to keep his back from being open to attack. The Green's head bobbed in frantic motions to keep track of her, its tail whipping about in agitation, his patience becoming unhinged by a challenger that refused him a stationary target. She denied it the opportunity to launch an attack from a place of strength, keeping the creature off-balance and overextended with each attempt to hurt her. He swiped out at her with fists and tail, repeatedly finding that she was no longer there, and growing more and more reckless as she nickel-and-dimed its energy away.

The trance that had kept Jonathan watching her was shattered when a heavily loaded semi-truck transporting new cars joined the chorus of screeching tires in the southbound lanes. As the panicked driver tried to stop, his trailer swung out from behind the vehicle and jackknifed toward the divider. The tires left the ground, starting to tip over as it hit. Cargo broke free and dropped down over the divider, into the northbound lanes where Rylee's attention was focused on the Ferox. She must have felt the crash, because she rushed to get out of harm's way, but only had time to make a desperate dive past the Ferox as its tail swung for her. Though she managed to slip under the tail, the Ferox grabbed onto her ankle before she cleared its reach. Not wanting to be caught under the same falling car Rylee had been dodging, the Ferox spun away with Rylee's momentum pulling him along, turning her into a tether ball.

Jonathan had only just started swearing at himself for standing still as the Ferox brought her back around and let loose, sending Rylee straight back at the danger she'd been avoiding. She crashed through the roof of a brand new Toyota Prius as the car hit ground against its driver side. The windows exploded and the roof collapsed in on her just as Jonathan shot himself off the edge of the overpass.

The Green never saw him coming, never had a clue—and Excali-bar came down like a hammer. The shaft made contact on its shoulder and drove the Ferox's feet into the pavement like nails. Where it had stood, the road became rubble, and its knees crumpled. Jonathan set his footing behind the blind-sided Ferox, then spun his entire body, sweeping Excali-bar around and down, hard, until the staff slammed into the Green's neck and put its skull into the pavement with enough force to punch another pothole into the freeway.

This was already over, and the Green was never going to see its executioner. Jonathan had already let himself go, let the killer rain down merciless blows until black blood was spilling onto the street. The Ferox's limbs stopped moving, but that meant nothing to him. He never let up until the blood stopped pumping. Each blow landed like thunder.

Crash. Crash. Crash. Cra—

Jonathan felt a hand on his shoulder and his grip locked with Excali-bar poised over his head to hammer down again when he turned to see Rylee. His eyes caught in hers for a moment, and though she must have seen the feral emptiness of the killer staring back at her, she didn't flinch. She held his gaze until the toxic smell of the creature's blood hit his nose and drew him back to his senses. He blinked a few times, and she looked at him curiously, seeming able to tell when the light of thought resurfaced and quelled the instinct to keep smashing the creature into the pavement.

When she finally looked away, her eyes rose up to the staff still poised over his head. "It's not getting any deader, Tibbs," she said before she stepped away from him.

Reaching behind her back, down the collar of her jacket, Rylee pulled free a length of steel. Jonathan recognized the way it caught the light. The weapon looked as though it had been modeled off a piece of bamboo, but forged from the same alien steel as Excali-bar.

She plunged one end into a crack he'd made in the torso of the Green's exterior and began prying the armor apart. For a moment, as she set to work, Jonathan found himself reflecting on the talent she had fought with, suddenly feeling like a thug with a spiffy crow bar. He wondered if Heyer forged these weapons for every person he implanted, or only those for whom he had longer-term plans. Rylee was too skilled, she had to be—

"You make such a damn mess of them," she said, shaking her head. "More like sending a steamroller than an assassin."

"It got the job done," he said, though it came out more defensive than he'd intended.

"I wasn't putting you down, Tibbs," she said.

He didn't give much more thought to whether the comment had been an insult, because as he looked down at the Ferox's remains, he saw that Rylee had a point. Sure, this Green had been at a disadvantage, distracted by another opponent and never able to see him coming, but Jonathan had never killed a Ferox with so little effort. For the most part, he had taken this Green out with two strikes. That, and, as he studied the corpse, he saw that it was a black and slimy mess. The body looked as though it had been stepped on by a giant rather than beaten to death with a staff. How had he suddenly become so much strong—

He felt the second signal shift position for the first time that evening.

"The other Ferox is through," Rylee said, as though reading his mind. "We need to move." She pulled her weapon up to create a wider gap into the Ferox's torso. "Are you going to stare or are you going to help?"

Jonathan blinked, got out of his head, knelt beside her, and plunged his fist into the Ferox's corpse. A few seconds later, he tore the stone free.

"Does Heyer know you're here?" Jonathan asked, wiping the stone clean on his jeans. She had her hand out, seemed to expect him to give it to her. He put the stone in her palm. "Did he send you?"

She glowered at him as though he were being dense and zipped the stone into her jacket pocket. When Rylee saw he was still waiting for an answer, she exhaled, her features deepening painfully before she looked away. "I guess it was just too damn much to hope it would come back to you if we were activated again," Rylee said. "If we have to have this conversation every time I see you, it's gonna get old quick."

He was distracted as he struggled to keep pace with her on the rooftops. Rylee's footwork fell like raindrops, absent any apparent need of conscious effort, as Jonathan thudded along behind her. He had to hurdle a metal air conditioning box she'd casually cartwheeled over with the use of one hand a moment earlier. He was becoming acutely aware that he was only keeping up at all because she was slowing to accommodate him, and though it was ridiculous to feel competitive, the thought that he was slowing them down bothered him. So he tried to clear his head of all the questions and focus on what was in front of him.

Rylee was on course—-could clearly feel the second Ferox's location as well as he could. What was novel to Jonathan now was that he could also feel her out in front of him because she was carrying the stone of the Ferox they had already dispatched.

"Do we have a plan?" he asked.

"Yeah," Rylee said, as she cleared an alley separating two buildings. "Send it back before it kills one of us."

"Right, but I've never fought as a team," he said.

"It isn't expecting two of us. We know where it is and have it outnumbered, and you hit harder than they do," Rylee said. "So as long as you don't miss and hit me, we should be fine. There's your plan."

There's your plan? Jonathan frowned. "What if it's a Red?" he asked.

Rylee stopped, coming to a crouch on the thin rim of the rooftop. Jonathan, not expecting the sudden halt, was forced to plant his front foot and slide across a few feet of gravel roofing to stop himself.

She looked at him with narrowed, questioning eyes. "You said something like that last time. What the hell difference does their skin color make?"

"I guess I didn't explain last time?" he asked.

She answered the question with a raised eyebrow and a perceivable impatience.

No, obviously not, he thought. "The Greens are adolescent; the Reds, more mature. The younger ones are more rabid—fight with instinct more than strategy. The reds are older, more experienced, stronger. I've fought some that were in between phases, still going through a sort of puberty. Their behavior becomes more focused and calculating, their biology changes, they lose their tails, their ears take shape, and their eyes come close together—"

He saw her eyes narrowing further, watching him with suspicion as he shared what he knew.

"There aren't any hard fast rules," Jonathan said. "But if you get into it with a Red, and if it's got a lot of scars, you need to be careful. Don't underestimate him."

"And you worked all this out on your own?" she asked.

Jonathan shook his head, "No, Mr. Fedora gave me the basics—experience proved him right."

Without knowing anything about her, it seemed like his answer had pissed her off. She looked away from him, only for a moment. "I've only ever fought one Red. If it was smarter than the others, it didn't live long enough to prove it," she replied. "Don't see what difference it makes now. It's still two of us and one of him."

She stood and jumped to the next rooftop, leaving Jonathan to wonder if he should be put at ease by her confidence or concerned by it. As they drew nearer, catching up to the signal's movement, its location became clearer to him, a few floors below them in an adjacent building—the Pacific Place Mall. He expected Rylee to wait for him, but she dropped straight off the roof and down to the street.

"Great," he said, slowing to a stop.

He came to the edge, knelt as Rylee landed below, and scanned the street. He didn't see the enemy, only the wreckage confirming it had come this way. Civilians ran from the building and a crowd of spectators was forming on the outside due to the commotion. The police hadn't responded yet, at least not in force. Jonathan felt Rylee rapidly approaching the entrance of the building. He looked down into the crowds, and couldn't see her at first, until he saw a few bystanders knocked out of her way as she cleared a path to the mall.

The entrance she was headed for was still intact, but no Ferox would have left the doors in one piece if that was the way it entered. It didn't take him long to find what he was looking for on a third floor window—a broken glass display where the Ferox had originally crashed through. He leaped from his rooftop, across the street, and entered through the broken window. If Rylee planned on a head-on assault, he could at least get behind it. After all, the tactic had worked out pretty well for him earlier that evening.

The shopping center was designed in a massive hollow oval, six stories tall with open space running down the center and stores lining the walls. Each floor was one large circular balcony connected by escalators. Jonathan ran out of the clothing store he'd found himself in, following the clear path of wreckage into the mall. There had been blood on the way in, but he had yet to find any bodies. As he reached the third floor balcony, he saw the safety railing had been crushed in where the beast must have used it as a launch pad.

He felt the Ferox above him while Rylee, moving fast, was coming toward him from below. When he looked over what was left of the railing, he saw her shooting past, ping-ponging her way to the top.

So much for surrounding it, he thought.

Looking down onto the concourse, he saw what Rylee must have already witnessed on entering from below, and understood if she was feeling a renewed haste. The Ferox's trophies, arranged in a pile on the bottom floor—Jonathan hadn't seen any bodies yet because it was collecting its kills. He'd seen the behavior a number of times, and it was one of the reasons he always tried to arrive as early as he could. Rapidly, he was finding himself on the same page as Rylee.

Their signals became a mixture of movement above him. Rylee and the Ferox were already exchanging blows.

Screw it, he thought as he sheathed Excali-bar and began backing up.

Running, he leaped off the balcony to one that was higher on the opposite side of the mall, grabbing for the rim and pushing off the outer wall to leap back in the direction of the fight above. On clearing the top floor's rail, his attention was drawn immediately to the commotion coming from the Gordon Biersch Brewing Company. He dove to the floor as something large flew out of the restaurant's front window, shot over him, and plummeted over the balcony. The booth, he realized, would have knocked him right back over the railing and dropped him on the bottom floor had he landed a moment later.

He looked inside to see Rylee moving around the beast like something out of a bad action movie. She used the walls, for a few steps at a time, as though they were as good as anywhere to run along. One look at the monster got him moving—the Red was easily the largest he'd ever seen. He freed Excali-bar as he got to his feet, and stepped inside just in time to see her land behind the beast and ram shoulder-first into its back. The two figures shot away from him, their bodies breaking through the exterior wall of what looked like the restaurant's kitchen.

Then a gas line exploded.

CHAPTER SEVENTEEN

HIS REFLEXES REACTED to the thunder of the explosion and he leaped sideways as hot light burst forth from the kitchen. The blast wave caught up to him while he was still midair and thrust him back. He collided with something solid that absorbed his momentum, and fell to the floor. When he hit, there was only a moment before the bright yellow glow of fire engulfed everything, the entire structure rumbling as he balled up, curling his arms over his face and clenching his eyes shut.

A mere human ear would have been ruptured by the assault to his eardrums. For Jonathan, the first clue he was still alive was the slow recession of the high-pitched whine that had followed. Sounds of the restaurant falling apart around him finally emerged and he opened his eyes, seeing how he'd managed to escape the brunt of the explosion.

He had landed between two massive metal cylindrical vats. The restaurant's brewery contained a number of them, bolted to the floors and arranged in a line. He'd slammed into one, leaving a man-sized dent in its outer shell. The other vats between him and the explosion held in place against the blast, providing him some protection.

Water came pouring down on him from the building's sprinkler system. The cold shocked him out of the muffled state left by the explosion, terror taking hold of him as soon as his mind cleared.

"Rylee!" Jonathan yelled, but hardly heard his own voice with the ringing in his ears.

The signals in his head—they had separated. The Ferox was hardly moving, still nearby, behind what remained of one of the kitchen's walls. Rylee's signal was further away. She was somewhere outside the building and at least a few stories down. He waited to feel her signal move, to give him a sign she'd survived.

But there was nothing. The longer it lasted, the more uncertain he was of what the stillness meant, and the more real his fear that he'd just watched her die.

Gone. Can't be gone. Can't be alone again, a voice whispered within him. *I need her...*

It started as panic, but that was short lived, because the pain became something surreal. He felt like he'd lost family—a sister. It was so primitive and physical, far too real. At first, that pain didn't know where to go, but suddenly, it became fuel. The world quieted around him, becoming small. The color of things seemed to change, everything turning red, as though the anger had set fire to his eyes.

Excali-bar lay in a puddle forming around him, the water pouring down on him more like blood now. His hands took hold of the staff and his forearms began to shake as his grip tightened around the steel. What followed was lethal, hell-bent, and focused. There was nothing else within him—it was all he could feel. He got the sense that he had never truly been angry before, that what he'd thought was anger had only ever been a shadow of the monster he now saw in the flesh.

He stepped through the debris, searching for its face in the fire, the flames within him in an awful harmony with those surrounding him. He drew closer to the inferno raging in the kitchen, felt the heat of it, heard the hissing of flames as they rebelled against the water's attempt to extinguish them. He caught movement, the outline of the enemy as it staggered from the blaze, smoke wafting off its black and red exterior. The Ferox came from a planet where molten lava ran like rivers—the damn thing had no fear of fire, but the concussive blast of the explosion itself had severely rattled its senses.

When the Ferox's gaze found him, the white slits of its eyes blinked in an attempt to focus. Disoriented, it looked into him as though he were some mirage in the fire; a hallucination conjured from the trauma to its head during the explosion. For the second time that evening, it appeared that Rylee had handed the enemy to him completely unprepared.

Jonathan roared as he swung, putting all that deadly anger behind Excali-bar. When the connection came, the cement floor cracked in webs beneath his feet, trying to withstand the recoil. The Ferox's body broke through what remained of a tiled kitchen wall.

If he had been able to feel anything at that moment, he might have been afraid of his own strength. He'd seen his power growing, felt that strength giving him more and more advantage with every confrontation. Something was altogether different, of that, he was sure; something connected to the more complete feeling of his activation—something fueled by this rage.

He followed the Ferox through the hole it had left in the wall, finding it on all fours, trying to get to its feet. It had torn through four of the brewery tanks, spilling their contents in a carbonated white foam all over the restaurant's floor. The beast had only been brought to the ground when the last tank finally managed to halt its momentum.

Excali-bar's edge had penetrated. Black blood drained from an ugly gouge in the Ferox's abdomen. The dark color made a glaring contrast as it puddled against the white foam sizzling on the floor. Jonathan placed his foot where he knew the monster would see it, and like a wounded animal, it looked up to meet his face. The Ferox spoke, its growled words translating in his thoughts.

Two? it said. *Two enter the arena for Bleeds the Stone. The Borealis honor me with—*

The translation was cut short by an upward swing of the demolition bar, catching the Red under the jaw. It brought the creature off the ground and slammed it back against the vat.

"Quiet, now, *Bleeds the Stone*," Jonathan whispered.

He'd had to pull the strike, having no desire to chase after the thing if he'd knocked it through the ceiling. As it was, the Ferox never had enough time to find its bearings, as Jonathan's interest had been on the hole already punched into its abdomen. His hands glided along Excali-bar, taking hold of the weapon in the manner of a spear, its point aimed downward.

He felt the weapon pass straight through *Bleeds the Stone*, out the back of the monster's armored exterior, and through the metal vat on the other side. Impaled, the demolition bar kept the Ferox held upright, and for a moment, the sight reminded Jonathan of a specimen in a bug collection.

Bleeds the Stone wailed in agony as the ale still contained in the vat drained on to the floor. The beast attempted a weak and desperate swipe at him, but Jonathan released his grip on Excali-bar, using one hand to take hold of the attacking arm and slam it back down against the vat's wall. Bleeds-the-Stone struggled, its feet unable to find solid purchase on the slick floors, pain and blood loss taking the fight out of it. Finally, realizing it was hopelessly pinned, its eyes turned to find Jonathan waiting.

Water soaked his hair and ran down his face. The fire raging in his eyes seeming to give *Bleeds the Stone*'s pause before it found the strength to speak.

You are him. Brings the Rain, the Ferox said. *The legacy…*

With one of his hands on *Bleeds the Stone's* wrist, the other took hold behind his elbow, and Jonathan pushed violently in opposite directions. The Red's elbow bent backward and it roared out over the sickening snap of ligaments tearing free around the bone. Jonathan dropped the creature's arm as it howled, the limb falling, useless, at its side.

He stepped back and studied the creature as it suffered. The monster had more scars than he had ever seen on a Ferox, and one of its ears was torn away to leave a ragged and ugly asymmetry. As he watched it struggle to speak, each scar no longer represented a warning to him, but the death of one of his own.

Echoes the Borealis, it said.

The Ferox—they had rambled on before, assuming he had any context to understand their words. It was usually a lot of the same, and he had no interest in listening to *Bleeds the Stone.* He put a hand against the creature's chest for leverage while using the other to rip Excali-bar free. The ale rushed out of the container, splashing to the floor with parts of the monster's entrails. *Bleeds the Stone*'s uninjured hand grabbed Jonathan by the shoulder, gripping him tightly with the last of its strength.

Reborn…

For a moment, Jonathan saw the wall again in his mind, the fracture of black smoke escaping through the cracks as it had in his dreams. His expression hardened as he dropped the demolition bar, clutched his hand into a fist, and plunged it through *Bleed the Stone's* open wound. Shock tore through the beast, black blood spilling out of its mouth.

"I told you," Jonathan whispered into its good ear as his hand found the stone within. "Quiet now."

He gripped the stone and ripped it free, a sludge of warm black blood and vein-like appendages pulling out of the wound. Jonathan stepped back again as *Bleeds the Stone* fell off of him onto the ground. As he watched the beast's life flow, the world seemed to return, the red haze over his sight finally clearing as *Bleeds the Stone* took his last breath.

Rylee had been thrown through one of the exterior windows, and had fallen two stories onto the gravel rooftop of a lower building connected to the mall. Dropping down beside her, his remaining anger began to be replaced with desperation.

He didn't know what to do for her.

As he drew nearer, he saw her chest rise and fall, and was relieved to have his fears proved wrong. If she was alive, then she could break the stone. She'd be fine, returned to her body, uninjured, wherever she had been when the gates first opened. He would have to break the stone in her hand and stand clear of the...

Two stones, he remembered.

The situation was no longer so simple. Heyer had never told him that a contingency like this was possible—another item on his rapidly-growing list of details the alien hadn't thought important. How was he supposed to close the gates safely? The only person he knew that had ever been in this situation before was unconscious. He had to try and wake her.

He knelt beside her and began looking for injuries but nothing obvious struck him. There weren't any broken bones protruding from her skin, no blood from a life-threatening wound. It was possible that the blast had knocked her unconscious, but it could just as easily have been the fall if she hit her head. He wasn't a doctor but figured she could have a concussion either way. Still, he was afraid to move her, and if he did, he saw little point taking her to a hospital.

Gently, he rolled her straight, hoping that getting her comfortable would improve the situation. He laid her arms and legs flat, ran his hand along the bones he could feel, looking for breaks that may have escaped his eyes. Finding nothing on the surface, he feared the possibility of shattered ribs puncturing organs. If Rylee had internal bleeding, she could be dying right in front of him and he wouldn't even know.

Carefully, he pulled her out of the thick leather of her armored jacket, kneeling over her awkwardly and slipping the sleeves around her shoulders, trying to be as gentle as possible. He rested her forehead against his chest as he got her arms free, fearing that, at any moment, she'd cry out and tighten up in pain if she woke to broken bones he had not found.

"Jonathan," she whispered weakly.

He froze at the sound of her voice. Then he closed his eyes and exhaled thankfully. Her body had been limp, but now she moved. Her arms reached around his shoulders, gripping him to her.

"Jonathan?" she whispered again, more desperate this time.

"I'm here," he said.

She sounded like a child coming out of sleep, unsure of her surroundings. As her reality returned, she grasped him tightly. "Tibbs!" she yelled.

"It's okay," he said. "You're just feeling the stones. They're taken care of."

A moment passed before the grip she had on him softened. "Oh," she said, followed by a chuckle at her own expense. "My head hurts."

"Try and stay still. You hit it pretty good. I'm going to lay you back down," he said, gently leaning and returning her to the gravel rooftop.

She didn't let go when he'd put her down, resisted him leaving, holding tight when he began to pull away. Unable to stand without forcing the issue, he found himself staring over Rylee's shoulder at the gravel rooftop while she looked over his at sky.

He heard her swallow before she spoke again. He noticed her voice was clearer now, and somewhat curious.

"What happened exactly?" she asked.

Jonathan caught himself beginning to laugh. "You blew up a brewery."

CHAPTER EIGHTEEN

SATURDAY | OCTOBER 8, 2005 | 10:50 PM | SEATTLE

HE SAT BESIDE her on the corner of the rooftop, listening to the sounds of sirens approaching. The two stones glowed, resting between them on the ledge. Rylee had avoided looking at them the moment he'd set them down. She'd grown rather distant altogether as she stared out over the city.

This silence had set in shortly after she'd let go of him. He didn't want to do her harm, and she could see that, but his discomfort betrayed him the moment she searched his eyes. He hadn't known what to do with the affection she was showing him, and reminding her of it had driven an awkward wedge between them again.

He wanted to tell her he understood, at least to a point. He had no idea what they may have been through together before, and strangely, he felt as though he owed her an apology for it. He could see the situation reversed. To have found someone who shared in his struggle, only to have them forget who he was, look back at him as though he were a stranger… What he couldn't understand was why Rylee hadn't tried harder to explain it to him. He would have believed her. He didn't see how she could have imagined that he wouldn't.

Jonathan looked down at the stones between them again. Their red glow reminded him that they needed to deal with them, but her mood made him reluctant to rush the topic. Maybe she feared the pain of closing the gates. Jonathan certainly never looked forward to it. Yet, from the little he knew of her, physical pain didn't seem like something that frightened her.

They couldn't be ignored forever, but Jonathan had plenty he wanted to know. If asking her some questions put off closing the gates for a few minutes longer, he didn't see the harm. He looked at her then, searching for where to begin, and a gust of wind pushed past them. She shivered, and he realized she was cold because he'd taken off her jacket. As he looked at her, he noticed something that he'd missed before. He'd been too concerned with her possible injuries when he had removed her jacket.

"Your device," Jonathan said. "It doesn't glow?"

Rylee's eyes went momentarily unfocused before she let out a sigh. She didn't look bothered by the question—more like she found it pointless.

"What?" he asked.

"Deja vu," she said.

"Right," Jonathan nodded. "Would you humor me?"

She stood and faced him, pulling the T-shirt up to her neck without a hint of modesty.

Jonathan cleared his throat, trying to divert his gaze from the cleavage being held in by a sports bra so close to his face. A small, disbelieving laugh escaped her as she observed him blushing, like his attempt to be gentlemanly about the interaction was funny to her.

The device was there, but nothing like his own—the differences weren't subtle. It was embedded under the skin and webbed into her muscles and tissues, but that was where the similarity ended. Instead of the intersecting lines that crossed over his torso, her implant had more in common with the shape of a Y. Two lines met at the center of her chest, both coming in at an angle from each shoulder. Those lines met a third in the center running down past her belt line. The glow was there, but it didn't burst forth from her skin as his did. Instead, it almost seemed like a glimmer beneath the surface, more like an iridescent blue ink running through her, incredibly muted in comparison to the unignorably orange energy that radiated off of him. He found himself somewhat jealous of it. Rylee could hide her activation under a T-shirt.

After he'd studied it for a moment, she pulled the shirt back down, and he looked up to find a mocking smile waiting for him. "Get a good look?" she asked.

He looked away. "Funny. The design, it reminds me of the—"

"The flux capacitor from *Back to the Future*? Yeah, you may have mentioned that last time," Rylee said. "Dork."

Jonathan made a face of mock pain, but nodded in agreement. Perhaps he was spending too much time with Hayden. "Rylee—" He paused, unsure if he should ask. "Why did you leave this morning, why didn't you try and explain it to me?"

She gave him the same look again, shaking her head. "You wouldn't understand. I thought you—" Rylee stopped and let out a long agitated breath. "You can't understand."

"I would have believed you," Jonathan said.

"I know that. Of course I know. You can't just—it's not as simple as y—" She looked away from him, and he could feel her frustration with him even though he couldn't understand it. A moment of silence followed and she sighed. "I will. Okay?" she said. "I'll try again tomorrow."

He frowned at her, could tell she struggled with something and didn't want to explain. He couldn't imagine what was making it so difficult. "Promise?" he asked.

Her eyes narrowed again, and she smirked at him. "What are we, Tibbs? Children? You aren't going to remember if I promised or not. You're not gonna remember any of it."

"But you will," he said.

Rylee looked at first like his statement was a declaration of something so obvious it didn't need saying. She stiffened a bit, seeing how he looked at her, seeming to understand that he believed her honor would hold her to her word whether he remembered it or not.

Jonathan's own expression became distant, then, as he remembered Leah asking him to make the same promise earlier that evening. Now, he had this memory of her staring into his eyes and promising she wouldn't doubt him if he would only give her the chance to believe him. Is that what he looked like to Rylee now?

"Stop looking so pathetic," Rylee said. "Yes, okay. I promise"

He nodded, but remembered he hadn't made that promise to Leah. It occurred to him then, that he wasn't going to remember that Leah had said those words to him. Though this was probably for the best, it saddened him. Then again—he hadn't lost the entirety of his memory the last time he had overlapped with Rylee. He'd still remembered the first few minutes the other day, as he'd headed off into the city to intercept the Ferox. He might remember what Leah had said to him tonight.

"How can I find you?" Jonathan asked. "On the off chance I do remember something?"

Rylee sighed and rattled off a street and a motel name with the same been-here-done-this attitude she'd had every time he asked a question.

His attention returned to the stones, and Rylee's mood plummeted again.

"Well," Rylee said. "At least we don't have to go through all that again."

He frowned at her. "I don't follow."

"I know you don't, Tibbs," Rylee said, her eyes still lingered on the stones. "But getting to screw with you is really the only upside to being the one who remembers, so you'll just have to accept that I am gonna get my fill of it."

He sighed, but smiled at her.

"Damn alien," she said. "Didn't ever lay out the game plan for two stones, did he? You and I spent a half-hour last time, arguing about how we might screw up the space-time continuum."

Jonathan sniggered. He couldn't help it. It was just such an odd thing to hear this warrior girl say 'space-time continuum' in a Brazilian accent like she was Doc Brown.

When she caught him smiling, she seemed to read his thoughts and raised a brow. "Your words, not mine," she said. "You were the one who was so concerned about it."

"Well, yeah, I mean what do we—"

She held up her hand, reminding him yet again that anything he was going to ask, she'd already heard. "We didn't want to risk each breaking one at the same time. No idea what it would do, or if it would matter if they were destroyed out of sync. We also didn't know what would happen if one of us broke both, seeing as each of the stones should be tied to one of us but not the other."

She picked the stones up and pondered them silently in her palm. She shivered, then leaned against the edge of the roof, and looked over the ledge. He thought he heard her stifle a sob.

"I don't want you to forget me again," she said.

The weakness in her voice hurt him to hear, and he felt helpless to do anything to comfort her as she looked at him with eyes that shined on the brink of tears. He wanted to understand but couldn't. Why was his lost memory so much harder on her? Obviously, it wasn't the ideal situation, but she already said that she knew he'd believe her if she came to him and explained it. So what wasn't she telling him?

"Rylee, I don't..." Jonathan said. "I don't want to forget you either."

She looked away. He wanted there to be something comforting to say, but if whatever they were about to do took his memory, no amount of comforting words would make a difference.

"What aren't you telling me?" Jonathan asked.

She wiped her eyes, coming close to stand beside him. She took his hand in hers and pulled his glove off to expose his skin. Then she put both stones into his palm and placed her hand over the top of them.

"Lots of things," Rylee whispered.

Jonathan didn't know what to do with that answer. When he opened his mouth to say so, she shook her head before he spoke. She reached for his free hand and placed it on the small of her back, then drew in close against him. He felt the warmth of her, and Rylee placed her arm around his neck. For a moment, with their palms up, holding the stones between them, they looked as though they were about to dance.

"Together," she said.

Rylee searched his eyes, desperately waiting to see something there. Not finding it, she bit her lip, and seemed to come to some decision. She rose onto her toes and pulled his lips down against hers. Her hand tightened down around his, shattering the stones between their palms. When the burning overtook them, they fell to their knees. He didn't feel her let go of him until the fire was all he knew.

Jonathan didn't know how he'd come to this place, nor when he had arrived or how long he had been there.

His clothes were gone, and he was crawling somewhere in the open, somewhere warm. He couldn't make out much at first. His eyes fought to adjust to light that seemed to come from all directions. As he acclimated enough to focus, he found himself in an unearthly fog. It was heavy, pressing in from all around and bright no matter where he tried to look. The only exception he found was when he looked down to the ground—there, he found wooden planks beneath his hands.

Strong winds swept past him. They carried warmth across his bare skin, but seemed to have no effect on the fog surrounding him as he crawled forward. He could only see a few feet in front of him, but when he reached the end of the wooden planks he found a hand rail fencing him in. Then he understood the shape of the boards beneath.

He was on a bridge.

Jonathan stood. He placed one hand on the rail, the other out in front of his eyes, trying to shield them from the light and the wind. In this manner, he inched forward, taking careful steps with bare feet. It felt like he walked forever, or a moment—time was as unclear, here, as in a dream—but he didn't seem to be getting anywhere.

Then a form took shape in the fog. He recognized her, even naked and exposed as she now was, once they were closer.

She walked as he did, slow and careful. This place didn't seem dangerous, being so warm and bright, yet he could tell from how she moved that she did not trust the impenetrable clouds any more than he did. She, like him, feared taking a step before feeling out what she could not see, afraid that she might step off the bridge entirely if it came to a sudden end. Neither wanted to risk dropping into the unknown.

Rylee was struggling a bit more than him. Her long hair was loose in this wind, changing directions on a whim. It was how he saw her first, as she kept one hand on the rail and pushed the black strands out of her eyes. He inched toward her, slowly, not wanting to startle her in the fog.

When they were close enough, she pulled the hair away from her eyes, and saw him reaching for her. At first, she brightened at the sight of him with his hand reaching out for her. Her hand went to take his, but stopped suddenly, just before they touched. She hesitated a moment, stared longingly at his fingertips. A moment passed, and finally he saw her mouth a word he couldn't hear, and her fingers interlocked with his.

He was aware of the warmth of her body pressing him against the wall, her tongue melting with his between their lips. Memory flooded into him, and a cold slap of disorientation hit his senses, making him unsure whose hands touched him, whose warmth he felt against him.

It had been Rylee so close to him, only a moment ago, hadn't it? She'd kissed him, without warning—desperately held onto him.

He flinched in alarm, as something more than memory rushed through him, his mind triggering alarms he had never felt before, perceiving an intrusive force within him. It sapped the strength out of his legs, and he staggered against the wall, before his knees gave out.

Strange, foreign emotions flooded his mind as his eyes shut tight, and he heard Leah gasp in surprise. He was painfully aware of his heart beating, his lungs gasping for breath, but as quickly as those sensations presented themselves, they became muffled, somehow far away.

He couldn't process it all at once—couldn't find a focus, a place to begin to work his way back. He knew that he was causing Leah confusion, scaring her, but it was all ramming together, and he only felt those things like part of a rising tide. He couldn't sort himself out, couldn't understand what he was feeling. What had, somehow, followed him back?

"Jonathan?" He heard Leah's voice in the distance.

He felt a presence taking shape within him, sensed it colliding with who he was. Its emotions were a whirlwind, a torrent of chaos that seemed incomprehensible, as though his senses had been hijacked and now spoke to him in a foreign language. He felt his body shaking, afraid of that other being, its adrenaline adding to his own mind's panicked screams that something had stowed away inside him. He forced himself to breathe, grabbing hold of his shaking knees, curling into a ball on the floor. He searched for a calm center in the storm, a part of himself that he could trust was not interwoven with something else.

He knew, then, his mind spitting out the answer as it recognized a truth that seemed obvious now. Rylee—it was she he felt within his mind now. Knowing this, the fear began to calm.

Impressions took shape as his heart slowed—strange things that seemed familiar, pieces of her that reflected parts of himself. There was an exterior face, an outer layer that laughed, that tried to remember what had made her happy once. That playful girl's smile faltered under the discomfort of a deeper pain. It was only a thin veil she held between herself and the world. He could see that beneath, there was something else.

It was so familiar.

It hid behind the mask of smiles, strength inside her; a will, an anger. It was like feeling his own rage waiting for him to give over control. There was something wrong, though, beneath the veil. He felt that part of her was bleeding to death and nothing within her wanted to help it, wanted to keep it alive. The rest of her just wanted to ignore that she was bleeding. As he tried to endure it, a jolt of knowing took him, and he understood everything. He understood why she'd been so hurt, why she had not tried to tell him, why she'd fled, why she seemed like two different people from one moment to the next.

At her core, she didn't want this anymore. The isolation had won out, smothered the fight in her with the slow poison of seclusion. She hadn't known there was anyone else. Not like her. When she'd found him, this part of her had thought there was still a reason to struggle, that there was someone who knew her, fought with her, had felt what it was to be her. She had felt him in her head so intimately, as he now felt her, and she had believed he'd experienced the same, believed he would share it with her.

Then he'd forgotten her. Worse, he'd never known her—had nothing he could share.

She couldn't begin to realize that he was her last, desperate hope—had never thought she would need to. That he hadn't felt what he felt now, what she'd experienced... This bond consuming him now. He had promised her he'd come, and she'd waited for him. When he had never come for her, when he hadn't even recognized her face, it had been the last defeat. The fighter stopped fighting. She felt that *something* was sending her a sign, a clear message.

Rylee had given herself permission to quit.

He wasn't sure how much time had passed before her emotions faded, before he became Jonathan alone again. In a way, he never seemed to finish the transition back to himself completely. There was something more, something permanently left behind. It was something he'd never experienced, didn't have a word for; he couldn't imagine that there *was* a word for it. Her presence within him, an emptiness so intrinsic that he had never even realized he had a hole inside of him—it was as though he'd been obliviously carrying around an empty canteen until it had been filled.

Insights began to strike him as his mind resurfaced, replacing the missing pieces of his puzzle before finally helping him get a better grasp of the picture. He understood why only she had been able to remember him the time before, why the memories only made it back to one of them each time and, as that understanding hit, a powerful urgency rushed into his consciousness.

His eyes shot open and found the worried face of Leah kneeling no more than a foot from him. "I..." he stammered. "I have to go. I have to go right now."

She flinched in confusion at the sudden words. He hated himself for having said them even before the meaning touched her eyes. She didn't understand what had happened, and he was pulling away from her, again, without giving an explanation. He didn't have time to explain that she would survive his abandonment, but that he had a terrible certainty that someone else would not.

He might already be too late.

Leah watched him get up off the floor and leave. Words left her. She hardly knew what to feel. He'd seemed to be where she was, to need her as much as she needed him. Then…

She'd stood on her side of the open doorway. He'd left so fast that he hadn't even thought to shut the door behind him. He'd looked back at her for a brief moment, and she knew what she saw on his face.

He hates himself, she thought.

His eyes broke contact, and she watched him leave. His urgency increased until he was sprinting, jumping the fence between him and the garage. When he was out of sight, when it was far too late, words finally seemed to reach her lips.

"Don't go," she whispered.

Leah stepped back inside and slowly shut the door. A dull feeling of shell-shock made her unsure of what to do now. Moments passed and she found herself still watching that closed door, expecting it to open, for him to come back. Instead, she heard his motorcycle come to life, followed by the rumbling sound of the engine heading out of the driveway and fading away.

What just happened? she thought.

It took a while longer before coherent thoughts started to form.

How was she supposed to react to such a thing? Even if their relationship wasn't her job, what the hell did a lover do with... that? Had she witnessed a psychological break? No—something had clearly happened to him. Something powerful enough to have put him in the fetal position.

Should I… Leah wondered. *Should I be angry?*

Wasn't it real? Wasn't it real for him? She didn't have to believe the same act she put on for The Cell. She only felt confused. Jonathan made it so impossible. She knew something outside of her had caused him to leave so suddenly, but there was no reasonable explanation she could even *pretend* to assume. What was her perspective on this supposed to be the next time she saw him?

She pressed her fingers to her skull, trying to sort out what was real and illusion in a mess of complicated emotions.

Maybe he'd come back with an explanation. Maybe she could choose to believe it? No, Jonathan wouldn't lie to her. He would simply say nothing, and then the awkwardness would grow between them again, and she couldn't let that happen.

Her cell phone rang then, and it startled her. She almost ignored it, but she wasn't allowed to do such things. She picked up the receiver and saw a number from somewhere outside the country. She followed protocol and answered.

"Yes," she said.

"Hello, I'm calling from Rising Sun—"

"Do you know what time it is here!" she yelled, then hung up angrily.

She held the phone to her neck, still thinking it over. The call was a sham, of course—a way for the team to tell her there was something she needed to be aware of immediately. She doubted it was a coincidence, getting this call in such short order with Jonathan's strange and abrupt exit. What could Olivia possibly know that she didn't?

CHAPTER NINETEEN

SATURDAY | OCTOBER 8, 2005 | 9:30 PM | SEATTLE

THE THING WAS, Rylee suspected she wasn't thinking straight. She could feel this poisonous mix of fear and loneliness authoring her thoughts. She knew that, if she could have stepped out of her head for one damn minute, everything going on inside would seem so trivial. But she was trapped in there.

She'd read about depression. These things she felt, she knew they weren't right—they were far too powerful, for one thing. The problem was, it didn't matter what she knew, because what she 'knew' refused to turn into what she believed. So there she was, trying to think her way back to feeling like a person she recognized, with thoughts that felt hijacked.

This was all to say—the last thing Rylee needed at that moment was a riddle.

She wanted to scream, but managed to make do with digging her fingertips into her scalp. Somehow, she kept running out of breath, though all she was doing was pacing back and forth in her cheap motel room.

A moment ago, Rylee had been calm—or at least she had looked calm.

She'd been sitting in her chair, staring at an orange tube of prescription medication. The tube was still unmoved. It sat on a motel room dresser beside the liquor bottle she had planned to chase it with. Rylee had been calm because she'd been certain that the consequences of her actions no longer mattered to her. There had been a freedom in that certainty, a recklessness in letting go.

At some point during the calmness, the gates had opened, the timing of which she translated as a personal "*screw you*" message from the universe. She burned through the activation and found herself on the floor beside her chair, forced to get up and fight one of the damn things. She didn't panic. This would be the last time. She didn't have to take the pills. The Ferox could save her the trouble. She had opened the liquor and taken a long pull from the bottle before she left. A few minutes later, she'd been right on top of the thing, felt the Ferox pulling closer in her mind, and then...

Then, she was back in the chair, looking down at the dresser again, the orange tube still there in front of her, the bottle of liquor still sealed and untouched.

Now she was panicking.

Grabbing the pills and frantically dumping the contents out on top of the dresser, she began to count. Then she counted twice more just to be sure. None were missing.

Rylee took in a long breath and let the air out slowly, the relief washing over her—which then struck her as odd. *Why had she panicked in the first place? Why was she relieved to find she hadn't done what she still planned to do anyway?*

The obvious question cropped up in her thoughts. *What's changed?*

She stepped back from the dresser. If she was as ready—as certain—as she thought, why had she been so panicked by the possibility that she'd taken the pills and somehow forgotten? Doubt ate away at her—she could feel it begging for her to see that she'd missed something, that whatever had just happened was not something she should ignore. Why, of all possible moments, was it as she reached for death that the universe interrupted and put a mystery in front of her to solve?

Why did her thoughts feel more ordered altogether, more familiar, more her own? Why didn't any of the debilitating and unendurable pressure feel so heavy any longer?

She sat down on the edge of the bed. What were another few minutes to try and understand? Nothing. When she figured out what was bothering her, she could pick up where she left off without any unresolved concerns nagging at her conscience.

Jonathan's face surfaced in her thoughts—happened a lot since she first felt him. The idea of him had gone from hope to torture in less than twenty four hours. Being exposed to all his raw emotions—to know, for a brief moment, that all her fears and weaknesses were shared by another human being… No one had ever shared what she had experienced, and at first she thought it such an amazing blessing, until she discovered that it had not been shared at all.

She'd wanted to be angry with Jonathan, but what good would deluding herself do? If Heyer had stripped him of their shared memories, then to Jonathan, she had never existed. She had already thought she couldn't hate the alien more than she already did. Running here, trying to turn the tables like this? What had she been thinking?

Was this how he punished her for it? How could he know that this would hurt her so badly?

How? How could he not remem—

In the middle of asking herself the question—which, frankly, was the same question she had been asking herself since she'd left Jonathan in his driveway—Rylee realized that this time, her puzzle seemed to be missing fewer pieces.

"I. Don't. Remember…" Rylee whispered. "If I don't remember…"

Connection struck, and was followed by a sudden bang at her door that caused her to jump.

"Rylee," he yelled, his voice panicked. "Rylee, it's Jonathan! Please, open the door."

Recovering from the shock, she got up and unlocked the door. He was panting, completely out of breath, as though he had come here in a sprint.

"I figured it out," he said, between breaths. "I didn't forget."

Rylee failed to hide the relief his words brought, a smile forming on her lips. She stepped out of the doorway, wordlessly inviting him inside.

As he stepped inside, he immediately held one finger up to his lips.

"We can't…" he said, still panting as his eyes searched her room. "We can't talk here."

His face was so serious, not at all what she expected him to be like when they were finally together again outside of the gates. She felt her smile faltering. He hardly even looked at her—what was he looking for?

She grimaced when his eyes fell on the dresser. The pills were still emptied beside the unopened bottle. She flushed and hesitated as he picked up the bottle and read the label. She could see the fear forming in his expression.

"I didn't," Rylee managed to say.

He closed his eyes, his entire body seeming to relax as he finally started to catch his breath. "I was…" he said. "Afraid I wouldn't get here in time."

She watched as he carefully scooped the pills back into the container. She hadn't thought about it, not until she'd seen the relief come over him. Now, she knew what moment had been shared with him, what he'd seen inside of her.

Jonathan placed the pills in the trash, pausing afterward, seeming unsure of what came next. Finally, he spoke: "You aren't alone."

There was no point in a strong face. There was nothing she could hide. More importantly, nothing she'd felt in the last day really made sense to her anymore. She believed him—she didn't feel alone. A moment passed, the silence expanding such that when she swallowed, the sound felt louder than it could have possibly been.

"Jonathan, why can't I rem—"

He closed the distance between them quickly, bring his finger to his lips again. Leaning in close, he whispered in her ear. "Not here. We need to get your things. I need to move you."

Rylee tilted her head, blinking at him in surprise. She wondered if she should put up some resistance, even though she knew she wanted to go wherever he took her. He had an intensity in his eyes that left no doubt that he had good reason. That intensity lit a spark of excitement in her. She felt… intrigued. She actually wanted to know what came next. Something she hadn't felt in longer than she could remember.

She raised two fingers to her forehead, and one of her eyebrows, in a playful salute. "Yes, sir," she joked.

Jonathan, oddly, seemed to flinch at the gesture.

Leah stood beside Olivia and a man who had been introduced to her as Agent Rivers.

She was aching for information, but only allowed her face to show a businesslike interest. They had something—The Cell didn't bring Leah in unscheduled unless she needed to be brought up to speed on something immediately. They stood in front of two monitors: one showed Rylee Silva's motel room; the other, Leah's living room.

"Watch the time stamps," Agent Rivers said, pointing to the clock reading in the corner of each monitor.

Leah watched her and Jonathan, together in her living room. She had to compartmentalize a few emotions, seeing herself standing at the open door, alone, as Jonathan walked away from her.

"Here," Rivers said, rewinding a bit and pausing the footage.

On the monitor, Jonathan had crumpled against the wall, falling into the strange trance he'd been in before he'd left without explanation

"Leah, we need to know—is there anything happening here that the camera isn't seeing?" Olivia asked. "Do you have any idea what caused him to behave as such?"

"No," Leah replied. "It was completely unanticipated."

"Good, we don't want to jump to conclusions," Olivia said. "Rivers, show her the other feed."

On the second monitor, she saw Rylee sitting in a chair, staring distantly into a prescription bottle.

For a moment, Leah feared she was about to witness Rylee overdosing. The secondary protocol—Leah's protocol—required The Cell never interact with the subjects unless approval came from a higher up. The protocol was designed to keep any member from making a snap decision and interceding.

Suddenly, Rylee jolted. She looked about the room, shock turning to a growing sense of scared confusion and anger. Yet, nothing had occurred inside the room to explain the woman's sudden shift in behavior.

"Look at the time," Rivers said.

They didn't match, not perfectly. There was a minute and a half delay between Rylee's unexplained behavior and Jonathan's. Leah frowned curiously at the screen. "They both reacted to something. Sensed something," Leah said.

"It would appear," Olivia said. "Unfortunately, we've yet to come up with any theory as to what. If they are, in fact, both reacting to the same stimulus, why was Mr. Tibbs' physical response so much more intense?"

Leah shook her head, her mind already grappling with the questions.

"We've checked the news networks. There have been no noteworthy events reported," Rivers said. "The teams watching the other subjects didn't report any similar behavior. What is interesting is that no other subjects are anywhere near as close to one another in physical proximity."

Leah nodded. "I need print-outs. Detailed files with everything we have on Rylee Silva," she said.

"I've prepared a full report, and intended to give it to you at the next scheduled meeti—"

"Ma'am!" One of the analysts interrupted them, his voice clearly excited. "He's there. Jonathan Tibbs—he just arrived at her motel room."

Olivia, Rivers, and Leah were quick to join the analyst at his monitor.

Leah watched Jonathan, panting, desperately trying to catch his breath. Whatever The Mark did to The Cell's audio devices, the distortion was not in affect yet in Rylee's motel room, and the analyst pulled his headphone jack to let the audio come though over the speakers.

"I figured it out," Jonathan said to Rylee. "I didn't forget."

Leah's eyes narrowed on the video feed as she began to get a hunch. "He knew," she said. "He knew her life was in danger."

CHAPTER TWENTY

SATURDAY | OCTOBER 8, 2005 | 10:45 PM | SEATTLE

JONATHAN GOT OFF his bike and pulled the garage door down behind them. He started removing his gear, while Rylee did the same behind him. Setting his helmet down on the cupboard beneath the garage's one window, he saw that the lights in Leah's house were now all off. She must have gone to sleep after he'd left her.

He'd hoped to speak to her, make some attempt at explaining himself before the night was over. Sadly, he had to wonder if it wasn't for the best that he had missed the chance. What would he say? There was no excuse in the world to explain Rylee's presence. He'd convinced her he'd never met the woman. For that matter, what was he going to tell Collin?

"So," Rylee said from behind him. "Am I allowed to speak now?"

Jonathan had been staring out the window at Leah's darkened house, unintentionally ignoring Rylee as she stood behind him, waiting. "Sorry." He nodded. "We can talk, but we have to be vague."

"Why did you bring me here?" she asked.

"It's the only place I know with any protection from eavesdropping," he said.

A moment of pause followed his statement.

"Can you try and be a little less vague? Because I'm not following," Rylee said.

He turned to look at her. "What has our mutual acquaintance told you?"

Her face paled at mention of the alien. "As little as possible," she replied. "He never said anything about where I should or shouldn't speak. Well, unless 'never speak of this to anyone' counts."

Sounds about right, Jonathan thought. "He must have known you weren't under surveillance," he said. "Doesn't matter. The moment you showed up here, they became aware of you. If you left your motel room at all today, they likely used the opportunity to install bugs in your room."

Her eyes narrowed. "What are you on about?"

Jonathan pondered the woman in front of him. Obviously, Heyer hadn't wanted Jonathan knowing about her. There was no way that Mr. Clean didn't know exactly who and what she was when he had brought her up during their conversation that morning—which meant the computer had been trying to keep him in the dark. The question was what Heyer or the A.I. would do now that he knew? He had to think that, given the state of mind Jonathan had known Rylee was in, he'd done the right thing in keeping her close.

"Rylee..." He trailed off and sighed. He realized he had no idea what he should or shouldn't say. After months of being angry at the alien for keeping him in the dark, he loathed himself for guarding his own words. "Does he know you are here?"

"I don't know, and I don't really care," she said. "I didn't ask for his permission."

Jonathan was given pause by the tone of her answer. Rylee's relationship with the alien was clearly not ideal. "I'm asking because if he didn't know your location, he couldn't protect you," Jonathan said. "They heard every word you've said."

"Jonathan," Rylee said, and he could tell she was getting irritated. "Who is 'they?'"

He studied her for a moment. He was worrying about everything he said, not knowing if Heyer had kept this information from her for good reason. Still, he had to do what he thought was best. Circumstances were changing and he had no idea what would happen if he waited for the alien to show up and advise him.

"He calls them The Cell. They are connected with the U.S. government, unofficially, or at least it appears that way. I don't know much, but I've seen some of what they're capable of," Jonathan said. "Truth is that they haven't been a problem for a while, but that was because there wasn't anything for them to see or hear. No one I could have talked to."

"This Cell," Rylee said curiously. "How did they know about you?"

"They seem to investigate anyone he has contact with. I've been under surveillance since the night I met him. Circumstances made our first meeting—" Jonathan paused. "Difficult to miss."

He let this sink in for a moment, as he could see from her expression that she needed time to process it. In the meantime, Jonathan tried to think of what his next move should be. He rubbed his forehead as he started feeling the strain of juggling all the things he didn't yet have a plan for. At least at this hour, he might not have to explain his houseguest to his roommates until tomorrow. He had to work early in the morning. That gave him a sleepless night and half a day to think of what to say to them. Given he'd already denied knowing Rylee to Collin, he figured he didn't have a choice but to blatantly contradict himself—unless he pretended he'd lied in the first place.

So, I'll lie, saying I lied when I was actually telling the truth, in order to undo telling the truth, so I can tell a lie that I haven't actually come up with yet. He pinched his eyes shut. *I'm sure nothing can go wrong with that plan.*

"What do they want?" Rylee asked finally, disrupting his concerned thoughts.

"I only have theories," Jonathan said. "Not tonight, though. I have to work tomorrow, and I've got a lot to think about."

She looked at him as if he were joking. "That's it? You brought me all the way here and now you want me to come back later?"

"Later," Jonathan said. "No, you're staying here."

She looked surprised. Her face seemed to soften as though she were pleased, but a moment later, she hesitated, and her face hardened suspiciously. "You expect that I'm going to stay here because you order me to?" she asked.

Jonathan was immediately confused. Her tone seemed duplicitous—he couldn't tell if she was deadly serious or seriously playing. He let out a long breath as he frowned at her. "No," Jonathan said. "I'm not ordering you, I am asking you."

"Didn't feel that way," she said.

Jonathan's shoulders slumped. He wanted to have a straight conversation but understood that he couldn't expect to get one if he was going to be so secretive, himself. "If you don't stay, I'll worry about you. I don't know what will happen tomorrow, but tonight, this is the only safe place I can offer you. Anywhere else, you have to watch what you say. You won't be able to trust anyone who tries to interact with you. Even here, you can't talk about this with anyone. My roommates don't know—all I can do to protect them is make sure that they never find out."

She pondered him, and her suspicion wavered but didn't disappear. "What is so special about here?"

"Our acquaintance blocks any audio signals around the house. Still, I don't think he ever planned for two of us to be in the same place at once like this. At least not…" He stopped again.

"At least not what?" she asked.

He looked at her and she didn't flinch as she waited for him to answer. He put his head down, placed his fingers on his forehead.

Talking to his roommates, who remained completely in the dark to his real situation, had always been challenging enough. Talking to someone who knew the reality, while still trying to keep secrets, was mental gymnastics. He knew that if he tried to hide anything from her, whatever suspicions she seemed to have suddenly manifested would only grow stronger.

So, he decided, he was done. He would just be straight about why he was hesitating.

"Rylee, he only tells me what I need to know. I don't know if he wants you to be aware of the things he has told me. Still, it's safe to assume that if he did, you already would. I don't want to keep things from you. I've wanted nothing more than someone I could talk to. But I can't ignore his wishes. So, while part of me wants to ask you about everything the man's ever said to you, another part of me is afraid of the danger it could put us in."

She studied him for a minute, her eyes narrowed in indecision. "I don't know if I've ever been so convincingly told the truth about why I wasn't being told the truth," she said.

Jonathan smiled. "Please, will you stay?"

Rylee tilted her head and drew one shoulder into a half shrug. "I wasn't really ever going to leave, Tibbs. I'm glad you're asking, though. If it had been an order, I don't think I would have believed it came from you." Her eyes fell to the floor for a moment, and he could see she was troubled. "You call him a man—did it a few times, actually—and you don't ever sound like you're saying it ironically. You talk about him… differently than I would." Rylee bit her lip and seemed to carefully consider her words before replying. "You sound… almost like… you're protecting him."

He heard her swallow.

"It is… troubling… to me that you talk about him as though you see… " Rylee hesitated. "Like I'm missing something. You trust him?" she asked, her face still disturbed at the notion. "You think he is..." She grappled to find the right word, and once she had it, didn't seem to want to say it. "Good?"

Jonathan ran a hand through his hair. "I don't know that 'good' is the word. He wouldn't use it," he said. "He is doing the best he can with what he has to work with. Trying to live with the decisions he has to make. I would never want to be in his position."

She listened, but only seemed more troubled, hardly convinced. "I do not trust him, Jonathan." She paused. "He's always felt... evil... to me." Rylee looked away. "But I know you aren't evil. I think it's the only thing I know for sure. So, I'm going to trust you."

Seeing that she meant it, Jonathan suddenly felt the burden of her words. Too conflicted to trust herself, Rylee was putting her trust in him. It was too much for a person she hardly knew. Though, that didn't feel true to him as he looked at her. She had seen inside his head as he had seen into hers. There were such terrible things in his mind—she must know what he was holding at bay beneath the surface. Yet, whatever Rylee had seen within him, she didn't seem afraid of it.

Jonathan had once told Heyer that he'd given the man his faith. Not long after, that faith had been put to the test. The alien must have felt as he did now: scared to guide someone who might close their eyes and accept that he would choose the right path for them.

And Heyer was responsible for an entire world, Jonathan thought. *Everyone, whether they knew it or not, had placed their trust on the man's shoulders.*

At a loss for how to respond, Jonathan remembered what the alien had said to him. "We'll trust each other," he said.

There was a lull as neither knew what should follow. Jonathan's other concerns resurfaced.

"Let's get some sleep. If anyone is still awake, follow my lead," he said, failing to hide his uncertainty.

Rylee smiled at him, as though she knew he overestimated the obstacle. "Don't be so serious," she said. "How much explanation do roommates need anyway?"

"Unfortunately," Jonathan said, "I swore to Collin that I'd never met you before. I think I was a bit too convincing, seeing as how it had been the truth at the time. I'm going to have to give him some explanation."

Rylee shook her head and smiled at him, seeming to know something he did not. "I have a feeling he'll not need much convincing," she said, turning toward the stairs.

"Wait, one other thing," he said. "The baton in your jacket. I know you wouldn't leave it laying around, but it's still best not to take chances. You'll want to hide it." He pulled open the cupboard, removing the facade.

She hesitated only a moment before she nodded and pulled the weapon free. "Not a baton," she said. "He used my rattan as a template."

"Rattan," Jonathan said, trying the word out as she handed the weapon to him. "Never heard the term. Is it Portuguese?"

She smiled as though she found him adorable, but didn't explain her amusement.

He sighed. "I've asked this before, haven't I?" Jonathan noticed that the weapon had an inscription, written in the same manner as Excali-Bar. "*Themyscira,*" he read aloud, figuring he butchered the pronunciation. "What does it mean?"

Rylee shrugged. "Means he didn't think I would appreciate a pun..."

She trailed off, her attention distracted by the chalk marks on the inside of Jonathan's facade. "What's this?"

"Inside joke," Jonathan said. "Between me and the Universe."

He realized then, that the question mark he had drawn the day earlier no longer belonged. After placing Themyscira behind the wall, he reached for a red and a green stick of chalk. Rylee watched him as he erased the mark and replaced it with two new lines, a red and a green.

She made a point of clearing her throat in protest as he finished.

"What?" he asked.

"You can only take credit for one that night," she said.

He smiled. "You'll have to tell me about it." He wiped away one of the hash marks from his score board, then made a new row half way down the board. He wrote her name and put a mark under it.

"You're keeping track of their color?" Rylee asked.

Jonathan nodded.

"So many Reds," she said, frowning. "I've only encountered one, well, two if I'm reading your hashmarks for tonight correctly. Both times I was with you. Is that random, just chance?"

"Your guess is as good as mine." Jonathan shrugged.

She nodded, but her eyes grew questioning again as she studied the chalkboard's markings. "What does the H mark mean?"

He stopped smiling then. "Let's talk about it some other time," he said.

Quick to pick up on his shift in mood, Rylee didn't press the question. "Tomorrow, then," she agreed, but then hesitated. "Wait, no, there is something you need to know. I don't know if it's important, but it had never happened before, at least not to me. I think I should tell you now."

Great, Jonathan thought, already knowing that if it couldn't wait, it wasn't going to be good.

"The other night, we..." Rylee paused. She bit her lip, her eyes scanning back and forth across the floor as she searched for the right words. "We had let down our guard, while trying to decide what to do with the stones. We didn't notice..." She sighed, frustrated. Then she looked at him sharply. "There was a man. I saw him step into the sphere with us before the flash."

Jonathan blinked, processing her meaning for a moment.

"People have been around me before," he said. "Never inside the sphere itself, though."

She nodded. "He knelt down over me. I did not like his face."

Jonathan frowned in thought. He remembered the first night he killed a Ferox, when Heyer had helped him close the gates. He'd thought the alien had betrayed him in the last moment, because he had stepped away. Thinking about it, now, the alien had been pulling back far enough to make sure he hadn't been inside the sphere with him. When he'd seen Heyer again, the alien's act had proven not to be a betrayal, and he'd quickly forgotten it when he had realized he had much bigger problems to consider.

"Yeah," Jonathan said. "That can't be good."

Hayden turned to see Jonathan emerge when the door to the garage opened. "So, how did it go with..." he trailed off, seeing Jonathan wasn't alone.

"Hayden, this is Rylee," Jonathan said quietly. "She is a friend."

Hayden found himself rather aware that he was wearing a robe, T-shirt, and boxers—also loosely aware that he was watching Superman II. But mostly, aware that the robe wasn't as shut as it could be. Collin and Paige having gone to sleep, and Jonathan supposedly on a date with their neighbor, Hayden hadn't expected a visitor this late.

He wiped the look of surprise off his face as he closed his robe, his shin promptly catching the coffee table as he stood. It hurt, but he let the pain scream in his mind while trying not to show any sign of it on his face. "Sorry," Hayden said, giving Jonathan a flat look. "Didn't know we'd have company so late."

Jonathan shrugged.

"It is nice to meet you," she said.

Hayden, finding Rylee's accent rather pleasing to his senses, was already wishing she would do more talking. He realized he had started to smile at her then, and cleared his throat.

"Collin and Paige asleep?" Jonathan asked, frowning at him.

"Yeah," Hayden replied. "I'm just up doing some research."

Rylee leaned to glance over Hayden's shoulder, and when she straightened up, she looked confused.

"Right," Jonathan replied. "Anyway, I know it's late, but Rylee needs a place to stay for a few days, maybe longer, so do you mind if—"

"No, not at all," Hayden said. "Sounds brilliant." *Sounds brilliant?* Hayden grimaced, wondering where the word choice had suddenly come from. *What am I, British?* He continued, "I mean, Collin and Paige won't mind. They're chill…" *Did I just say "they're chill?" Crap, I'm smiling again.*

"Thank you," Rylee said. "It's very kind."

Jonathan shrugged. "I'll talk to them tomorrow," he said, turning to Rylee. "You should take my room."

Damn, Hayden thought. *I should have offered my room.*

"So, how long did you plan on being up doing 'research?'" Jonathan asked, looking from the television set, to the couch, and back at Hayden. "I've got work in the morning, could use some sleep."

"This is unprecedented," Olivia said, watching the feed from Jonathan's living room.

Rivers saw satisfaction on her face. It was hard to miss, given Olivia usually remained so unreadable. "The team has never maneuvered two subjects into meeting?" Rivers asked.

Olivia's eyes remained on the monitor but her look of satisfaction slipped away. "We have not confirmed with any certainty that Ms. Silva is a new subject. If so, then she is the only female The Mark has taken an active interest in, to our current knowledge. More importantly, this is the first instance we've observed of two of The Mark's contacts actively seeking one another out," Olivia said. "As for your question, the complications with arranging such encounters are rather numerous and highly unpredictable."

Rivers nodded. He could imagine—bringing two people together over a large distance, maneuvering them into close enough proximity to interact, manipulating them to actually do so without having had any prior knowledge of one another and no initial motivation to socialize, and meanwhile managing not to create any suspicion that their strings were being pulled in the background. The logistical challenge of such a concerted effort would be enormous, and any operation would have a high failure probability. Even if they were successful, there was no way to know if anything would be gained from the exercise.

Yet, Rivers observed that Olivia had not actually denied that such an attempt had ever been made.

"You didn't answer the question," Rivers said.

She glanced at him, face still unreadable, with the exception that she looked him head to toe before she spoke again. "It has been accomplished, by manipulating the stationing of soldiers, confirmed subjects of The Mark, within the armed services," Olivia said.

"Was anything learned?" Rivers asked.

"Yes, but not in regards to them having any awareness or knowledge of their shared experience," Olivia replied. "What was interesting was the degree of each man's resistance. For no reason that we could infer, those who have encountered The Mark make a great effort to stay within the general region that their encounter took place. This remains true right up to the moment that their whereabouts become unknown."

"Hmm. So none of them want to leave town."

Olivia nodded. "Correct. Rylee would be the first instance of a subject choosing to drastically change location, seemingly without prompting from The Mark. Her decision may open a wide range of possibilities, beyond that of merely observing her interactions with Mr. Tibbs."

Rivers nodded. He fell into contemplation over Olivia's words, and after a few moments, she seemed to pick up on his silence.

"Please share your thoughts, Agent Rivers," Olivia said.

"Rylee is the first female instance we've observed, and the first to leave town," Rivers said. "Jonathan, though male, shows significant departure from the basic profile of all the other males we know The Mark has had contact with."

"Have you inferred something from this?" Olivia asked.

He let out a breath of vexation. "No, ma'am," Rivers said. "I am simply annoyed that there seems to be something in front of us, and I can't see what it is."

CHAPTER TWENTY-ONE

SUNDAY | OCTOBER 9, 2005 | 2:30 AM | SEATTLE

HEYER BLINKED BACK into existence on the roof top of a six-story brick building. He staggered a moment, shaking off his fatigue, before stepping toward the roof's access doorway. The door opened for him as he approached it.

Heyer owned the property, and like his brother's home on the Feroxian plane, the top floors of the building were a camouflaged parking space for his vessel. To a plane passing over or a person on the street, nothing was out of the ordinary—the building looked like any inner city domicile.

He needed to rest, found himself using the handrails along the stairs. Heyer had spent a sleepless night watching over his brother. It had been Malkier that had pushed him to go, not because his presence was a burden, but because they couldn't let too much time pass without keeping an eye on Earth's combatants.

Upon his return, the number of losses in his absence had been more than expected. He had been alarmed until he realized the date. The unpredictable passage of time, a symptom of making unscheduled jumps back and forth between the Feroxian and Human planes, had been unkind to him. Shortly after his arrival, Mr. Clean had begun forwarding Heyer around the globe to replace implants for the nodes where human combatants were now needed. He'd been on his feet another day, jumping from city to city, replacing the fallen.

His Borealis implant did a lot to stave off exhaustion, but seventy-two hours awake was pushing it—his mind was not meant to lose that much sleep. If he didn't stop, he'd soon be putting himself in danger. Not of actual physical death, but rather of increasing the chances of his mental fatigue resulting in poor judgement. Still, traveling and exhaustion weren't the only factors taking their toll. Putting new combatants into play most often left Heyer with the sense that he was handing out death sentences—each implantation weighed on him.

Over a month had passed on Earth since he had left, and as he made his way down the stairs, he plotted out his next few days. After getting up to speed with Mr. Clean, he needed to speak with Jonathan. That kid had been busy—a little too busy, it had turned out. Heyer hadn't been aware of the full extent of it until he'd returned home.

Unfortunately, after he followed up on Earth's issues, Heyer would have to return to the Feroxian plane. No one made wise decisions within the weeks of losing a loved one, but Malkier and Heyer knew when they had entered into this arrangement that they could take no time off for bereavement. The worlds they protected required them to be impervious to such things, or at least to present themselves as such.

Still, that was the first type of rational thinking to leave a mind when it faced staggering grief. Heyer had no point of reference for the long-term effects he might expect from his brother. Malkier's assimilation into the species had been the first of its kind. Their ancestors, though capable of it, had had no desire to take a Ferox body as their host. No other Borealis in recorded history had been implanted into the Ferox species.

Heyer entered the door to his living quarters as it opened for him. There was an unlikely combination of furnishing from all over the world and through time. A rug from China, a table from 18th century England, a television from Best Buy.

"Please," Heyer said, as the television set clicked on, "report."

Mr. Clean's smiling visage filled the screen, but the cartoon quickly directed an uncharacteristic look of concern at him—a computer projecting the appearance of human sympathy, through a cartoon caricature, for the sake of an alien inside a human body. There had been a time when Heyer had seen Mr. Clean's attempts as disingenuous. However, the truth was, the computer had no programmed requirement to make an effort at consoling him—so even if the A.I. failed to play the part well, it was still making the effort of its own will.

"You don't look well," Mr. Clean said.

"I need to sleep," Heyer said. No point in denying it—the computer wasn't really making an observation based on appearance. Mr. Clean had known he wasn't well—he could read his body's vital signs straight off the device implanted in his chest.

"It might be best to speak after you have rested," Mr. Clean said.

This gave Heyer a moment's pause. If the computer was making a judgment call about his ability to cope with what it had to report, then something serious had taken place—something the computer wanted him to be at his best to bear the stress of.

"How bad?" Heyer asked.

"Can't be calculated, really," Mr. Clean said. "I was forced to make contact with Mr. Tibbs."

Heyer tilted his head at the screen. The list of contingencies in which Mr. Clean would take such action was short. Heyer's death or capture were the main two, but seeing as neither had occurred, something more obscure must have taken place in his absence.

"Why are you just now telling me this?" Heyer asked.

"The situation is troubling," Mr. Clean said. "But its time sensitivity can accommodate a night of sleep."

Heyer sighed, but he didn't want a show of impatience to prove Mr. Clean's point correct. "I am quite capable of hearing your report. What has happened?"

"I observed some imbalances in the closure of the gates. Irregularities that should not have taken place given I believed that the proper variables were not in play. When I contacted Jonathan, he too was somewhat aware of a problem. He reported that, in his most recent activation, he had no memory past a few moments into the confrontation. As might be expected, he was quite alarmed."

Heyer pressed a finger to each of his weary eyelids. "Overlap?" Heyer asked out loud. "Did the Portland node travel out of bounds? End up in Seattle within range of Jonathan?"

"My first assumptions as well, but that didn't account for the strange readings reported from the gates."

Heyer stiffened, his body growing more tired even as it grew still. He worried he already knew the answer, but needed Mr. Clean to confirm his fears. "What accounts for it?"

The screen split, Mr. Clean's image scaling to the left-hand side while the space left on the monitor was replaced with video footage borrowed from The Cell. At first, he only saw Jonathan talking to someone in his driveway, but the person was not within the camera's line of sight. Then, just as he'd feared, Rylee Silva stepped into view.

When Jonathan had told him the name of the Ferox he had slain on his second engagement, the kid had given him the first real shock he'd had in a decade. The news had rendered him somewhat speechless and without an immediate contingency plan, even if only for the few minutes it had taken to regain his wits and begin damage control. Now, it seemed that while Heyer had been out dealing with the fallout of Jonathan's last bit of news, the boy had managed to multiply their problems.

Heyer pinched his eyes shut, feeling an uncharacteristic rise of frustration welling up in him. "Of all the thousands of problems Rylee could cause while I was away," he said, "why did it have to be the most difficult one to contain?"

"I'm not sure if that question was rhetorical. Philosophically, the size of an issue is rather difficult to measure. Statistically, this occurrence is not as improbable as it may app—"

"Mr. Clean," Heyer interrupted. "If you want to say you told me so, you don't need to disguise it with over-sophisticated rhetoric."

"Noted," the computer replied.

"Are you being smug?" Heyer said. "This is potentially a serious problem." The alien closed his eyes the moment he said it, realizing that *this is potentially a serious problem* had been the exact words Mr. Clean had used before Heyer had made the call to initiate Rylee Silva's implant.

"My apologies," the computer said. "Perhaps an inappropriate moment for attempting levity."

Heyer let out a tired breath and tried to focus. "How many times have they bonded?" he asked.

"Twice," the computer replied. "How successful each bonding was remains unclear."

"Inbounds," Heyer replied. "You have my permission to redirect any traffic targeting Jonathan and Rylee to other nodes."

"As you know, redirecting will lead Cede to notify Malkier of an issue," Mr. Clean said. "Their second overlap occurred this evening. I currently calculate a window of three to five days before either should be seeing another inbound. What is curious is that the statistical improbability of both Jonathan and Rylee being activated within moments of one another has been overcome multiple times. Their proximity to one another is playing a role in this. It seems that the closer they are physically, the closer together the times of their activations. The bond is one of the only novel variables that might account for this."

The computer's phrasing troubled him immediately. "One of the novel variables?" Heyer repeated. "Mr. Clean, what other novel variables have occurred?"

"An isolated incident," Mr. Clean said. "I monitored the organic weights passing in and out of the gates. In their first overlap, the numbers were considerably off."

"Off?" Heyer asked. His tired mind raced for an explanation but the possibilities that came were all too theoretical. "This is my fault." Heyer sighed, reaching to put his fedora back on his head. "I will speak with Jonathan... now."

"Sir, I advise against this. You would be putting yourself at risk. You are visually showing fatigue. The Cell may attempt to take advantage if they suspect you are vulnerable. I recommend a minimum eight hours of slumber. Both Jonathan and Rylee are currently asleep themselves, and all of the other house occupants are present. I will awaken you should there be unexpected activity," Mr. Clean said.

"I don't think this should be put off, Mr. Clean. Jonathan, at the very least, needs to be warned to be careful what he tells her."

"Sir," Mr. Clean said. "It would be rash. Though the problem may be serious, resolving it tonight will not alter the outcome. That, and historical records indicate we may need to handle this quite delicately—we need to anticipate that Jonathan and Ms. Silva will resist being separated."

The computer was right. He wasn't thinking straight. He had to sleep now while he had the opportunity. If events unfolded unfavorably, it might prove to be his last chance to rest for a considerably long time. So, Heyer reluctantly acquiesced to the computer's advice, retreating to the twin-sized bed he had in his personal chamber. Still, as he laid his body down to sleep, he saw years of carefully laid plans unraveling around him.

"The weights were off?" he pondered again.

CHAPTER TWENTY-TWO

"IT'S SUICIDE," JOR-EL said. "*No, it's genocide.*"

Hayden had been polite enough to turn the volume down while Jonathan tried to sleep. Still, the sound of Superman's father begging the Kryptonian council to abandon their planet chased him into slumber.

"*Be reasonable,*" a councilman replied.

"*My friend, I have never been otherwise,*" responded Jor-El. "*This madness is yours.*"

Jonathan had opened his eyes briefly, barely conscious as Marlon Brando stood beside Superman's mother and spoke his famous lines before sending baby Kal-El to Earth.

"You will travel far, my little Kal-El. But we will never leave you. Even in the face of our deaths, the richness of our lives shall be yours. All that I have, all that I've learned, everything I feel, all this, and more I… I bequeath you, my son. You will carry me inside you. All the days of your life. You will make my strength your own, and see my life through your own eyes, as your life will be seen through mine. The son becomes the father, and the father, the son. This is all I… all I can send you."

He'd shut his eyes then, the father's heartfelt send off to his son echoing in his awareness as he fell into a familiar dream. His mind had often taken him to this place the last few weeks. He walked through a room that seemed cold, cluttered, emptied of any light of its own. But Jonathan was not engulfed by the darkness, not rendered sightless. It was as though he carried the flame of a candle, and it illuminated vague shapes in the dark. He saw stacked cardboard storage boxes, the outlines of dust covers on old furniture, hard cement floors, brick and mortar walls. What he never seemed to remember was how he had come to find himself in the room in the first place.

He knew that none of the boxes stacked around him held what he came for. His mind was set on reaching something in the far back of the room. He moved slowly, navigating a path left by the unused spaces in the clutter. Finally, the light that followed him touched a workbench against the back wall, giving it shape as he moved closer until he could see the outline of a footlocker resting on top. The box was old and worn, and he saw writing on the lid, but couldn't make it out. There was a formidable-looking padlock holding the box shut.

His hand was out in front of him, reaching for the lock, but then it stopped. He found himself distracted by a picture frame laid flat on the workbench's surface. He recognized the photo—it had been on his father's workbench in his childhood home. Evelyn, his mother, held him in a hospital bed after he'd been born. She smiled back at him from the picture frame.

Jonathan's eyes opened, awoken by the sound of his phone vibrating on the coffee table. As he reached for it, he saw the sun was coming up. He'd slept rather heavily—odd, considering the thoughts that had weighed on him before he put his head down. He'd received a text message from one of his coworkers offering a ride to work. They were scheduled for a Sunday training at a site not far from Jonathan's neighborhood, and if he wanted to surrender a few extra minutes of sleep, he had a ride. It seemed a decent excuse to stall needing an explanation for the girl sleeping in his bed a bit longer. Still, he had to say something to Collin.

He picked up his phone and gave it a disgusted look. If he had just let Collin think what he had in the first place, that Rylee was some ex-girlfriend, then he'd have had the perfect excuse. Still, he couldn't juggle that lie and hope that Leah was ever going to understand why he'd run out on her during their date last night.

When no bright ideas came to him, Jonathan texted Collin, knowing his roommate was still asleep and wouldn't see the message before Jonathan had already left for the day.

Rylee is asleep upstairs. Sorry I didn't ask first but she needs to stay with us for a bit. I'll explain later, just forget everything I said yesterday.

It never ceased to feel ridiculous to him. An alien had chosen him to lead mankind against an invasion of inter-dimensional attackers, and yet he spent his days trying to think of ways to keep his roommates from asking him why he had a guest sleep over without asking.

He was only half way to work when Collin responded: *Brilliant, no worries.*

Jonathan frowned at the message. Maybe Rylee had a point. He had a habit of over-complicating things.

"Rylee Silva," Olivia said as she continued her report, "has not led a standard life."

She sat in the back of the black sedan, updating her commanding officer on recent events. The exchange had been one-sided so far, The Cell having learned more in the past seventy-two hours than most of the prior months watching Jonathan. Olivia knew that her commanding officer's silence meant she had his attention.

"She was born in Brazil, moved to the U.S. with her parents around the age of eight. Her father runs a small martial arts school on the East Coast, where he teaches Capoeira."

To this, the modulated voice of her superior interjected, "I'm unfamiliar."

"My understanding is that it's not a highly lethal form of self-defense, but more a combination of game, dance, gymnastics, and martial arts. One has to train for years to effectively utilize it in a confrontation, as most of the maneuvers are more flashy than efficient. That said, it's worth noting that Ms. Silva began at an early age. She often taught classes in her father's absence."

"Any arrest record?" the voice asked.

"Yes, though all have been expunged as they occurred while Ms. Silva was a minor. Nothing of particular note—teenage rebellion more than anything," Olivia said. "She has a high school diploma, and had some college education before she decided to join the NYPD at the age of twenty.

"This is where her history becomes more interesting," Olivia continued. "Rylee left the Police Academy with no explanation. Within a month of dropping out, she won a considerable sum of money. The details are suspicious, as she had no prior history of gambling, yet she wagered a majority of her life savings on a single high stakes bet. The winnings have allowed her to remain unemployed since."

"Is there evidence she rigged the game?" the voice asked.

"No. Rylee either had inside information, or precognition of the outcome. Regardless, Ms. Silva only engaged in the behavior the once. She paid taxes on the winnings, and then put a large portion of the money into a bank account that she uses sparingly. She's made only one considerable withdrawal for a non-necessity. According to the DMV, her only means of transportation is a high-end motorcycle she bought off one of the officers she met before dropping out of the academy. Since leaving Manhattan, she stays off-grid as much as possible. The room she rented in Seattle was paid for in cash, and is well below her means. The motel attendant, once pressed, admitted that Ms. Silva bribed him in order to provide a room without requiring identification."

The voice was quiet for a while, absorbing the details of Olivia's report. "If she was unaware of our investigation until Jonathan informed her of The Cell's existence," her superior said, "it is possible that she is making efforts to hide from someone. Have you inferred anything else from her electronic data trail?"

Olivia nodded. "According to phone records, she has had almost no contact with friends or family since dropping out of the Academy. Before she acquired her current funds, she used a credit card to purchase martial arts instruction from a school teaching a fighting style based on Eskrima, a far deadlier combat methodology than what her father teaches.

"Given the clear behavior overlaps, and the weapon she had in her possession, we have good reason to assume Rylee is in similar circumstances as other subjects. Unlike Mr. Tibbs, she escaped our notice. Rylee was never taken to a hospital with unexplained blood loss," Olivia said. "If she endured a similar incident, she managed to do so without any authorities becoming aware of it."

"Any additional items?" the voice asked.

"Two final details," Olivia said. "Ms. Silva's apartment on the East Coast has been monitored since we became aware of her. Early this morning, her father arrived. He knocked for a few minutes, but when Rylee never came to the door, he asked a few of her neighbors if they had seen his daughter coming and going recently."

"So, she left town and told no one where she was going, even her family."

"It seems," Olivia said. "Although I mentioned the apartment because a team entered and searched the premises. What is promising is that they found a collection of Ms. Silva's journals going back to her early childhood."

This was followed by another pause. "Seems you would have mentioned this earlier if any new information had been gleamed from the entries," the voice said.

"Unfortunately, the books are all handwritten in Portuguese, and accurate translation is slowing the process. However, the last dated entry in the journals ended in March," Olivia said. "It may be that she has a current journal in the possessions she brought with her."

"Has our main asset been briefed on all of this information?" The voice inquired. "She is aware that Ms. Silva should not be taken lightly in the event of a confrontation?"

Olivia paused, not having expected the rather peculiar question. "Yes, Leah is aware of all current details. But…" Olivia found herself hesitating uncomfortably. "Sir, have you drawn a conclusion you've not shared? I ask only because it seems highly ill-advised for her to engage in a conflict with Ms. Silva during this investigation."

"In the last twenty-four hours, the intimate bond Leah has been building with Jonathan Tibbs has encountered perceivable threats. Seeing as how she cannot abandon the relationship, reacting in a manner believable within the context of how the household perceives her could prove..." The voice pondered the appropriate words. "Highly complicated."

Paige woke to the sounds of her roommates laughing downstairs. Still drowsy, she climbed out of bed and headed to the upstairs bathroom.

"I don't know," she heard Hayden say.

"Well, I vote yes, can't wait," Collin replied.

They're up early today, she thought. She closed the bathroom door and set to the task of morning hygiene rituals. When she came back out, she overheard Collin again—he sounded excited.

"Let's get going. Tibbs shouldn't be home for a few hours," Collin said. "Hayden can text us if he shows up early. Don't want to ruin it."

"Fine, but you're not making me an accomplice," Hayden said. "I'm pleading ignorance if he kills the two of you."

"Noted."

Curious now, she heard the shuffling of chairs as she headed down the stairs.

"Don't worry, Hayden," said a woman's voice that she didn't recognize. "He isn't going to be mad."

By the time Paige reached the bottom floor, all she saw was the garage door shutting and Hayden hunched over a cup of coffee, looking both worried and yet discouraged at having been left behind. There were two other coffee cups at the table. Hayden, despite his expression, looked like he'd been up for a while—even showered already.

Still not entirely awake, Paige yawned before asking, "Did we have company?"

"Yeah, some friend of Jonathan's came over last night," Hayden said. "She's fun, you'll like her."

The sound of motorcycles came to life in the garage.

"Jonathan had a girl over last night?" Paige frowned. "I thought he was out with Leah."

Hayden shrugged. "I don't know," he replied. "They got in pretty late."

Paige reached for the pot of coffee, thinking it over as she did. She vaguely remembered getting a text message from Leah telling her to call her when she woke up. Then she grew worried and irritated at the same time. "Wait a second," Paige said, turning back to Hayden.

She wasn't exactly happy with Jonathan at the moment, but still, it would have been a nice change to see him stop brooding for a day. Did her roommate have no clue what was good for him? At times, it was as though he'd declared a jihad on his own happiness.

And Leah, Paige thought. *She was excited about last night.*

She had caught her friend with a ridiculous grin more than a few times yesterday. Paige had no doubt that Leah had wanted the evening to end a certain way, and it wasn't with a kiss on the cheek and Jonathan bringing some other girl home. She was starting to worry what Jonathan might have done to blow a sure thing so badly.

Paige's eyes narrowed as she watched Hayden, who seemed to be inching his way out of the room as though he was unsure if the irritation on her face would become directed toward him.

"This girl slept here?" Paige asked.

Hayden shrugged innocently. Then his face changed, as he suddenly appeared to get why she seemed angry. "Oh, no, no, no," he said. "Jonathan slept on the couch."

Paige looked at him incredulously. "That wasn't what I meant..." She thought about it more. "Though, now that you mention it, I'd have killed him if he did that to my best friend."

Hayden, getting more nervous, pointed to the pillow and blanket on the couch.

"I'm gonna call Leah and see what moronic thing Jonathan said to her last night," Paige said before leaving to find her phone. "Who is this girl anyway? Why did she stay over?"

"Her name is Rylee. I think she is from out of town. Jonathan—he didn't really explain. But she is nice enough," Hayden said. "Collin seemed to hit it off with her."

Paige felt her eyes wanting to narrow, and before she thought better of it, a question escaped her lips. "Is she pretty?"

Hayden looked back at her for a moment, smiling like he might actually dare to find something funny, until he saw how unamusing Paige found the question. "I don't know, maybe?" he said, his voice betraying that he had no idea what the right answer was. A moment later, he shrugged. "I like her accent."

CHAPTER TWENTY-THREE

SUNDAY | OCTOBER 9, 2005 | 12:00 PM | SEATTLE

"**YOU WILL BE** handsomely reimbursed for your cooperation," Olivia said.

Margot Kay had worked with Rivers before, but this was different. She'd gotten an inkling that this assignment was not going to be like their previous dealings when he'd informed her that she wouldn't be able to work from home. In the past, he'd hired her as a consultant for work he was doing with the Bureau, mostly tracking down hackers attacking atypical targets. Last time he'd called her was because, despite the fact that they could detect a multinational company's computer security was being repeatedly breached, the FBI couldn't figure out what the hacker was actually trying to accomplish. That was where Margot came in.

"Should you feel that, ethically, you cannot participate, your services will not be required. However, failure to keep any portions of this discussion between the three of us will be considered an act of treason," Olivia said.

The woman had a tone to her voice that sounded like she was reading a speech she'd given so many times that she was bored with the formality of it, as though she already knew what the outcome would be.

Margot wasn't a profiler by any means. Rivers repeatedly told her she was a genius, and she always felt as though he were letting flattery off its leash. She wasn't a genius and she had the I.Q. scores to prove it. She did happen to be exceptionally talented at three things: Margot wrote software, knew networks, and she recognized patterns.

"Should you wish to continue, there are non-disclosure agreements in the folder in front of you that will need to be signed. If you would like to read them in their entirety, please feel free, but the places where your initials and signature are required have been highlighted," Olivia said.

A day after her vague invitation from Rivers, she had found herself at the Seattle airport, being driven to an office building that looked like it was only ever utilized for the very type of conversation she was having now. She would describe said conversation the same way her son described it when she asked him if he would like to visit his grandmother at the old folks' home: she was being "volun-told."

"Do you require a moment to consider if you would like to proceed, Ms. Kay?"

Rivers didn't look comfortable with the process. He stood to the side of them as the woman he'd introduced as the lead running the investigation, this Olivia, sat at the desk in front of her, going through the motions. She got the distinct impression that this was not a real offer of time to think, but a test to see how long it took her to decide. If she took too long, the woman would have to wonder what Margot had been conflicted about. Margot had a strong feeling that Olivia was not someone she wanted having doubts about her.

"No," Margot said. "That won't be necessary. Agent Rivers has never requested my assistance for anything I wouldn't have volunteered for myself."

Olivia nodded slowly and Margot chanced a glance to Rivers. He smiled reassuringly as Olivia pulled a pen from the front drawer of her desk and pushed it toward Margot.

No turning back at this point, she thought. Making an effort to maintain her positive I'm-TOTALLY-not-getting-the-feeling-this-whole-situation-was-designed-to-intimidate-me appearance.

Forms signed, Margot closed the folder and slid it back across the desk.

"Please accompany us to your work area, Ms. Kay," Olivia said.

Margot was surprised to find that she was not immediately put in front of a computer terminal. Instead, Rivers requested that she give up her cell phone before they escorted her into a garage where a sedan waited, and Rivers pulled open a door for her. Shortly after, they were on the freeway, headed into Seattle. Olivia remained silent while Rivers engaged her in pleasant but idle chit chat: *How is the weather out in Maine? How is your son doing in school? How has your mother's health been holding up?*

Within ten minutes, they had pulled off the freeway and driven into the Capital Hill district. Eventually, they pulled into what appeared to be the parking lot of an abandoned grocery store, the driver taking them around to the loading docks behind the building.

A garage door opened, and their car pulled up a ramp into what looked, to her, like a large room originally meant for excess inventory. The room had been re-purposed into a garage now, and the driver parked the car in between a number of other nondescript vehicles.

From there, she was escorted down into a basement, where she found an underground operation that reminded her of something she had seen on fictional television programs—an array of computer terminals set into cubicles, absent of any furnishing other than the cement walls that kept the building standing.

She was brought to a small room in the far back, where she was finally sat in front of the computer terminal she'd imagined. Olivia excused herself at that point, heading to an office on the opposite corner of the building.

"So, what am I up to, boss?" Margot asked Rivers.

He smiled at her and nodded at the computer screen. "We are going to provide you with a series of time stamps and coordinates," he said. "This terminal has access to the GPS networks. We want you to look for a pattern of..."

He trailed off, seeming to consider his words.

"I'll be candid, Margot," Rivers finally said. "We aren't sure. We need you to tell us if there is anything out of the ordinary occurring in the network associated to certain time stamps and coordinates we provide. If you find something, we need to see if you can use whatever irregularity you uncover to work backwards. See if you can find similar irregularities at times and places we don't have on file."

Margot considered the job that had just been described to her. It was well within her skill set, and straightforward enough—except for one thing. "The GPS network is run by a proprietary system. Even with access, it's going to take me a while to become familiar. It isn't as if its inner workings are open to the public," she said.

Rivers nodded and pulled open the door of a binder cabinet that ran across the top of her office desk. Inside was a row of reference materials. She suspected that she was looking at the technical user manuals for the very network she was going to have to familiarize herself with, though it was odd that they were hard copies. Normally, in these types of jobs, she was simply provided with access to the electronic versions.

"Well, look at that," she said. "Not your first rodeo."

Rivers grinned, happy that he'd been able to predict what tools she'd need at her disposal. "Any idea what kind of time frame we can expect from you?" Rivers asked.

She took a look at the number of binders before her. "I guess it would be silly for me to point out that this would be easier and faster if you simply hired someone that designed the systems to run your analysis," she said.

She was met with a deadpan look from Rivers. She understood immediately—*yes, obviously this would be faster, but would completely contradict the point of the exercise.*

Margot nodded and let out a long breath. "Let me dive in," she said. "Once I see what I am dealing with, I'll have an idea."

"Fair enough," Rivers said. He stood, heading out of her new office so she could get to work. As he left, he added, "You need anything, and I mean anything, don't hesitate."

"A crap ton of coffee," Margot replied, pulling down the first of the manuals. "That would be a good start."

CHAPTER TWENTY-FOUR

SUNDAY | OCTOBER 9, 2005 | 12:30 PM | SEATTLE

JONATHAN HAD ONLY been at work for a few hours before he caught sight of the alien. One moment, he noticed a man in a black hat and coat on the periphery—the next he was gone. As soon as he could, he took his break and walked off the site. Heyer didn't make him wait long to appear, blinking into existence beside Jonathan after he'd turned a corner down an alley.

Jonathan had imagined versions of this conversation, where he vented his frustrations in regards to the alien's extended absence and irresponsible hoarding of information. As per usual, he was too relieved to see the man to actually complain. That relief, however, was somewhat short lived upon taking a good look at Heyer's face—the alien looked exhausted.

"You alright? You look sick," Jonathan said. "Can you get sick?"

"I have had a long few days," Heyer said. "Haven't had much opportunity to sleep since we last spoke."

"Few days?" Jonathan asked. "I haven't seen you for a month and a half."

Heyer nodded. "For you, yes," he said. "Traveling to another dimension does not make accommodation for the passing of Earth time. As I've experienced it, we last spoke roughly four days ago. Getting to the

Feroxian plane from this side doesn't generally cause the time distortion; it's the trip back that plays havoc with my schedule."

Jonathan smirked. He already knew that getting angry at Heyer was a waste of his time and energy. "Well, I'm glad you're here." Jonathan paused. "Things have been getting pretty strange the last few days."

"Yes, Mr. Clean has brought me up to speed," Heyer said.

Jonathan nodded. "Yeah. Heyer, look, I've done the best I could to handle things how I thought you would want them handled," Jonathan said. "I know it may not appear that way... but there were reasons I don't think you and Mr. Clean are aware of. I…" Jonathan trailed off, seeing Heyer's expression wasn't angry.

"Jonathan, you aren't accountable for the events of the last few days. I suspect that, if anyone is responsible, I am," Heyer said. "I apologize that my departure was so abrupt, that you were unprepared. I had no choice in this instance."

"So, about that," Jonathan said. "Do I get to hear why you had to leave town in such a hurry?"

"Meet me here, when leaving work will not cause you any unnecessary explanations," Heyer said, and looked away, then. "I have a great deal to explain to you."

"Alright."

Heyer's face looked concerned, distant. "You aren't going to like what I have to tell you."

It took a few moments, but Jonathan let a smile form on his face. When Heyer noticed it, he frowned at him, and Jonathan snorted before he found himself laughing. "Sorry, Heyer. I know you're serious, it's just—when have I ever liked what you had to tell me?"

The alien's frown relaxed, and he nodded "You seem to have found a sense of humor again. That is good."

"Speaking of humor," Jonathan said. "Who models their artificial intelligence after toilet bowl cleaner?"

The alien gave Jonathan a slight smirk. "Mr. Clean is free to choose his own appearance."

"Okay," Jonathan frowned. "So why would a computer want to borrow the identity of a cleaning product mascot?"

Heyer sighed. "The short answer is that he gets bored. He changes his identity a few times every century. Before Mr. Clean, he borrowed the appearance of Mamie Eisenhower, the First Lady of the 34th U.S. president," Heyer said. "To be honest, I think he liked the name Mamie."

Jonathan shook his head, unable to tell if the alien was purposely screwing with him for once. "And the long version?"

"The question is not as straightforward as it seems. His decision to change is more significant than, say, a human purchasing a new wardrobe," Heyer said. "Mr. Clean is a species himself, a person like you or I—though he is not composed of organic tissues. My understanding of his desire to change his appearance is that it is somewhat like a human's desire to breed. Though, in the case of Mr. Clean, he is both the parent and the child."

"So, is that common for a computer intelligence?" Jonathan asked.

Heyer shook his head. "Like any person, Mr. Clean has personality quirks, as he is the product of his initial makeup and the experiences he has had since being brought into conscious control of himself. Before Malkier and I found him, he'd been trapped, lying dormant for roughly five hundred years."

Jonathan's smile faltered, the computer's story suddenly less humorous. "Your ancestors imprisoned him?"

"Not deliberately. Mr. Clean's programming did not allow him to move from his physical location without the permission of one of his creators. Upon the extinction of the Borealis, he was left behind on a planet that had suddenly become an uninhabited graveyard. He was, therefore, trapped until we found him. Prior to that, I had traveled with my brother, but on finding Mr. Clean, he became my vessel. However, it is a simplification to refer to him like a vehicle. Mr. Clean has a body, just as you or I. So while he may provide me a home and a vehicle, it is more accurate to say he shelters me within himself when I am on board."

"You talk about him like he's a friend," Jonathan said.

"Mr. Clean has accompanied me of his own desire every place I have chosen to reside. Since the development of mankind's internet, he has grown quite attached to Earth. Seeing as how he is limited in mobility by the necessity of keeping his existence secret, the internet has allowed him the means to interact with your planet and species in ways he could not elsewhere. Mankind creates such vast amounts of data. You would be surprised how much time he spends discussing films on internet forums with humans who have no idea they are arguing with an artificial alien intelligence."

"So," Jonathan said. "An advanced A.I. finds itself on Earth, and ends up watching television and trolling the internet?" Jonathan smiled. He saw a picture of Hayden in his mind, on some discussion board, furiously typing away at his keyboard, never even knowing that he was debating with an alien computer from another reality.

Guess I can tell Collin and Hayden not to worry about Skynet, Jonathan thought.

"If you give Mr. Clean a problem to solve, he will happily accommodate," Heyer said. "But he is incredibility efficient. He is fascinated by the vast frontier that the human imagination provides him, especially in film. When I asked him why, he said that human stories gave him a better understanding of a biological entity's experience of time, a thing he experiences in a manner quite foreign to you or I."

"It's strange," Jonathan said. "I didn't get much sense of personality from him."

Heyer raised an eyebrow. "He confined his interactions with you to a professional tone due to the nature of the restrictions I advised should he contact you. You may come to find you miss those restrictions once they are no longer in place."

"What, is he chatty?" Jonathan asked.

"Mr. Clean isn't like the other A.I.s I've encountered from my civilization. He craves interaction. When I was growing up, he was my only friend outside of my brother. Malkier had no interest in the computer's peculiarities. He much prefers the A.I. installed on his own vessel, as it behaves in a more standard, disinterested, and obedient manner. Malkier's vessel crunches data like any other computer, responds to commands, and takes no personal stake in the outcomes outside of its programming.

"I was drawn to Mr. Clean immediately—fascinated by his fascination, so to speak—always attempting to bridge his understanding between the data he observes and what it means to interact with biological beings." Heyer shook his head. "My brother used to say he was like a pet that thought itself the same species as its owners."

Jonathan frowned. "You mean like when a person says the family dog thinks it's a human?"

Heyer nodded. "Yes, a similar sentiment. Malkier thought it quite pitiful. I, on the other hand, spent hours with Mr. Clean, answering his ceaseless questions about the decisions I made. My reasoning evolved as I grew from a child to a young man, a considerably longer biological process for my species, compared to humans. Mr. Clean was always grateful for those conversations, always intrigued to see my philosophies change as I grew older, even when his programming failed to grasp the complexity of a biological being's reasoning. That may, of course, be misleading. It would be better to say, even when his programming failed to grasp a complex *lack* of reasoning."

Heyer's face again seemed to drift back into memory. His expression became hard to read. Jonathan almost thought the alien felt indebted to the computer. What was odder was the uncharacteristic way that Heyer spoke about the A.I.. He seemed more animated than Jonathan had ever seen him. Though, perhaps it was that they simply weren't talking about the end of the world for once.

"When my brother brought forth his plan to enslave Earth, I never had to ask Mr. Clean if he would assist me in my efforts to find an alternate solution. Initially, I saw no way to stop what felt like an inevitability that Malkier intended to set into motion. It was Mr. Clean who was able to pull together all the pieces, to find a balance that preserved the human way of life. He did this before I'd thought to ask him to try. What hope we have now comes from the very 'dog who thought itself a human'."

Jonathan checked his watch, and at almost the same moment, Heyer did the same.

"I should be getting back," Jonathan said. "I'll come here when my shift is over."

Heyer nodded.

Before turning to leave, Jonathan realized he never actually got the answer to his question. "So, why Mr. Clean, then?" Jonathan asked.

"It started as a joke," Heyer said. "Mamie, at the time, was spending so much time removing any digital footprints I left behind that she came to describe herself as a digital cleaning agent. Later, her tasks came to include erasing or altering files associated to humans we had involved, such as yourself. Eventually, she came to be the means of protecting all those involved from the surveillance cells. So, she embraced the character of Mr. Clean."

Jonathan nodded. "I like it."

"I'll tell him you said so." Heyer smiled.

Then, as was his way, the alien was gone. Jonathan sighed. *After a couple thousand years, you would think someone might have told him it's rude to just disappear without saying goodbye*, he thought.

CHAPTER TWENTY-FIVE

DATE | TIME: UNKNOWN | FEROXIAN PLANE

IN THE DARK, he heard Cede's voice as though far away, "Malkier... Sir, are you listening?"

The white slits of his eyes blinked, his neck twitching toward the sound as he finally realized she'd been calling him. How long had she been trying to get his attention?

After Heyer had returned to Earth, Malkier had taken his brother's advice to heart. He'd made finding out the means by which *Dams the Gate* acquired a portal stone his focus. What he'd uncovered had made him retreat back into his dark seclusion and drawn his mind back into memory. He noticed, that seemingly of their own volition, the clawed tips of his fingers had been slowly tracing over the scar that ran down his cheek to his neck.

He thought about the day *Dams the Gate* was named. By Feroxian tradition, the naming of each child was a task of the mother. To the Ferox, this was simply a ritual practice, how it had always been, but Malkier knew well the history that had created the custom.

For most life, sentient or not, an abundance of resources and an absence of predators was ideal. To a Ferox, the word 'predator' was relative. No species had ever actively hunted the Ferox—their kind always having been at the top of the food chain. Still, the Feroxian plane had once been shared with other apex predators, species dangerous to encounter even for a Ferox male. Back then, the Ferox found frequent opportunities to mate, and their population had grown. Unfortunately, shortsighted in their drive for procreation, the balance had been lost, and those predators had been killed off at unsustainable rates.

The greatest irony of the Ferox was that they only became an endangered species after all those that might kill them had gone extinct.

In those times of plenty, fathers were seldom known with any certainty. The number of mates a female may have was only dependent on the number of offers she received. Ferox males staked no claim, assumed no contract—they had no expectation that a woman withheld her womb for the seed of a single suitor. As such, the only certain parent of any child was the mother, and therefore, she would name her children.

When the moment of conception came, both sexes of the Ferox had an intuition for their pairings. The males were seldom driven to desire a female if he sensed no consonance with her. When he returned from battle, his loins were in a state of savage need. He carried his trophy, the body, or sometimes bodies, of his fallen enemies cocooned within a thick waxy layer of his excretions. This he presented as offering to one of the tribe's females. If she perceived that same consonance with the male, she accepted by consuming the offering. In doing so, she digested the male's unique pheromones, and one of her wombs became accommodating of his seed. No further mating ritual was required—for a short period that followed, both became receptive to one another.

In conception, Malkier's son had been no exception, and he'd had no hand in choosing the child's name. *Dams the Gate* was given his name by his mother, *Burns the Flame*—and the name had not been given with love.

For a Borealis, beings that lived indefinitely, his more ancient memories often failed to hold the weight Malkier felt they should. He'd been a child once, yet no matter how many centuries separated him from that childhood those memories returned to him as though not so long ago. To truly feel the passage of all that time, he had to view his life in its entirety—as one long book of history being read in reverse. This was to say that if he simply flipped to the beginning, to the first few chapters that contained his childhood, any sense of the thousands of years that had come and gone since was lost. For his memories to feel their own age, each moment had to be placed into proper order on the pages, and Malkier had to turn back each page slowly.

The day *Dams the Gate* was conceived did not require many pages be flipped back. A little over a decade had passed since he had given in to a moment of weakness. When Malkier had found the Feroxian instincts of his host's body in alignment with the desires of his Borealis nature he'd entered the gates, brought back his trophy, and found himself in consonance with *Burns the Flame.*

His recall of their intimacy was still vivid. As though he'd touched his tongue to sugar for the first time in millennia. Malkier was temporarily able to savor a taste of what it was to be young and mindless, unable and unwilling to derail his attention from that one physical act. That day, he had felt a certainty about *Burns the Flame.* The sort of certainty he'd never experienced before and suspected he might never again.

He'd dropped the man's body at her feet and *Burns the Flame* had accepted. Of course, she'd believed him to be *Ends the Storm*, that she was the first mate chosen by the prophet of their gods. More, that she would be the first woman to bear the child of an Alpha since a time long before her own birth. Had she still held any reservations, she knew that the trophy set down before her was none other than the most prolific abomination to her gods. The man, cocooned within the prophet's pheromones, was legend. None would refuse the offering of such a trophy. *Echoes the Borealis*—the greatest abomination her tribe had ever known—had been brought to her.

Burns the Flame had every reason to think a great glory was being bestowed on her that day—no reason to foresee any harm befalling her after being chosen by their prophet, and after all, she felt the consonance. Malkier, likewise, had foreseen no harm coming to her. He didn't believe his desire to have a child amongst his beloved Ferox could possibly be wrong.

But, he'd not been blind. He'd feared the risk he was taking. That, to his people, their prophet would seem to have gone against his own decree that no Alpha enter the gates. That he, *Ends the Storm,* had trespassed against one of the very commandments he'd proclaimed to be the will of their gods. Then, of course, there had been the matter of his brother. Malkier's actions had betrayed their contract as well. He'd believed, or perhaps hoped, that Heyer would forgive him this one trespass.

Malkier soon learned that he had miscalculated. His people had little will to question their prophet, believing that he and only he possessed the wisdom to know when exceptions could be made to the laws of their gods. It had been his brother that could not forgive. Learning of *Echoes the Borealis'* death, that Malkier had taken on the role of assassin himself, and that *Burns the Flame* was to bear a child from the transgression, Heyer had never looked at him quite the same. A rift began to form between them. In time, Malkier saw that it was a rift he could not bridge. Malkier came to think of this falling out with his brother, and the scar running down his face, as the debt he'd paid to be a father. Nothing he could say would change how Heyer had reacted, and Malkier would simply have to wait for his brother's anger to subside. After all, they lived indefinitely, and with that sort of time, any trespass could eventually be forgiven.

Malkier's claw stopped as he realized he'd taken to stroking his scar once more.

Some argue, that while there is no good moment to lose a child, there are ages that do more harm to a parent than others. For the Borealis, the most painful age to lose a son or daughter was at the brink of the child's sexual maturity—just as they reached an age when they might soon desire a mate of their own.

Ferox males seldom felt fatherly attachments. Each took part in raising the tribe's children, but they rarely thought of any particular child as their own for the same reason they never chose an offspring's name. Rather, the males had favorites, protégés—but not sons or daughters. For that matter, many Ferox mothers had found the bodies of their slain sons upon the gateway's platform. The Ferox did not grieve for fallen warriors—not precisely. It would be best to say that the Ferox, male or female, did not regret a child lost to the Arena in the same way they might if that same child had never reached the Arena at all.

Through his host, Malkier shared a great deal with the male Alphas of his adopted species, but his Borealis nature superseded the Ferox. So, he had no such circumstantial immunities to his grief. Malkier gained no relief knowing that *Dams the Gate* had died in combat. He'd known with certainty who his son was—and given the circumstances, so had his entire tribe. Malkier had watched the child grow, and all around him the tunnels he called home were littered with those memories. The Borealis in him was hardly willing to leave Cede's boundaries knowing he could look down any corridor and be assaulted with visions from when *Dams the Gate* lived. Malkier wished the Borealis in him could, just once more, allow his Feroxian nature to have control.

Cede interrupted his thoughts again.

"Sir, please indicate you have understood. Two of your lieutenants are approaching."

Finally, he replied that he'd heard her, and Cede went silent before the sound of footsteps approached the chamber. Malkier stood, facing the two with a knowing patience, so they would know he had perceived their approach long before they had gotten near. He saw their uncertainty immediately.

Buries the Grave and *Sleeps the Dream* were nearing full maturity—verging on their transition from red to Alpha. Soon, they would no longer be allowed entry into the gates, and would take places of leadership in the tribes. The lieutenants knew not to bother their prophet after he'd commanded that he be left to his solitude. Though neither of the Ferox could say what it was that plagued his spirit, both understood that as prophet, *Ends the Storm* carried burdens outside their comprehension. Nevertheless, the two were capable leaders. If they were willing to interrupt Malkier despite his orders, it was not a trivial matter being brought to his attention.

Since finding his son's body on the gateway platform, Malkier could imagine no reason that would drive him to step into the daylight and follow the path toward the ravine. Yet, before *Buries the Grave* finished explaining why they had summoned him, Malkier was moving, and both lieutenants had fallen in to follow.

When Malkier reached the ravine, he found the tribe crowded in a ring around the gate. They were like spectators staring at the unprecedented, most remaining oblivious to his approach. When he caught sight of her in the crowd, he could not quickly remember when he had last seen her join a gathering at the gateway. *Burns the Flame* studied him with a blank apathy. The female Ferox possessed what a human might mistake as a type of hair. Like the males, their outer armor was covered in a chaotic web of black tar-like strands, but in the female, this also grew long from the back of their skull and down their back. The sight was not unlike that of a horse's mane, though the thickness of the tar-like strands was more like looking at shiny dreadlocks. *Burns the Flames'* skin was black and red, like the coloring of his lieutenants. As others became aware of the prophet's presence, the crowd began to part, and when she should have joined the rest in clearing a path for their leader, *Burns the Flame* lingered a moment. Malkier suspected that she did this willfully, waiting just long enough that the insubordination would only be noticed by the prophet himself.

For the Ferox male, combat was a way of life. From birth, all headed for the fire, none ran from it. When an abomination of their gods sent back many casualties, the males of the tribe did not fear being the next selected by the lottery, but coveted the privilege of slaying a worthy adversary. A tribe began to take notice when a gate sent back a string of casualties. When a combatant refused to fall, other tribes began to hear of him. If that man's legend spread far and lasted long enough, a Feroxian pilgrimage would begin. Males seeking their chance at glory would leave their own gateways and tribes, traveling across the planet to seek their chance to slay a legend.

As prophet, Malkier lived amongst the largest of the Ferox tribes, but his gateway had not been the center of a mass pilgrimage in over a decade; not since the time of *Echoes the Borealis.*

Now, the system by which the males were awarded access to the gates was a lottery, and *Ends the Storm* had made a promise to his people that the lottery would never be rigged. However, this was never a complete truth, as the lottery itself was being manipulated by Cede in an effort to deepen the Ferox gene pool. The A.I. selection favored males with unique genetic markers to enter the gates over those with more common traits. Of course, this was done with discretion; occasionally Ferox lines with more common genes were randomly selected in order to keep the population from ever becoming too suspicious that the lottery favored certain males.

When Cede selected a "*winner*," the prophet awarded that male a portal stone. A process usually carried out by the Alpha of each tribe under Malkier's command. Since, all Ferox males wanted to be awarded a chance inside the Arena, no selection went by unnoticed. Though not statistical geniuses, the Ferox were quite capable of recognizing trends. This meant that Malkier could not show favoritism. He could not openly select a champion—or perhaps more appropriately, an assassin—if a combatant on earth refused to die. Now, an experienced Red verging on alpha-hood, a male the likes of one of his lieutenants, would be an easy solution to removing a man who was killing too many of his people, but Malkier made every effort to avoid such manipulations of the lottery.

The reasons for this were many. Heyer had felt that stacking the odds against a man for the simple crime of surviving wasn't right, though Malkier had given no weight to the sentiment. His brother was splitting ethical hairs while standing on a foundation void of morality. Nonetheless, Malkier had agreed to his brother's rule of nonintervention because as prophet, he saw that there were political advantages that would strengthen his leadership.

If a specific gate's combatant became a coveted adversary amongst the Ferox males, two factors always came into play. The first was the question of how many males were being lost. However, with each of that combatant's survivals, he made himself a more fearsome trophy. As such, each Ferox male grew more eager to make a name for himself by ending a legendary affront to their gods.

So, while the elders of the tribes had humbly disagreed with the prophet's decree that a seasoned Red would not purposely be sent in when a combatant showed himself resilient, the adolescent Greens rallied in support of it. Now, should a younger warrior, a Green eager to prove his honor, be chosen to enter the gate, his opportunity could not be stolen from him by an alpha or a red who had already proven himself in battle and sired many children. Every male had an equal chance in the lottery.

Between him and his brother, the rule had been observed more as a guideline. However, after the prophet had taken it upon himself to rid his tribe's gate of *Echoes the Borealis,* the guideline had become a hard line in the sand. A law, and one of many trusts that Malkier knew never to betray again if his relationship with his brother was to ever be kept from unraveling completely. All that said, from time to time, the lottery had to be rigged to remove a man from play. In most recent years, Malkier had done so with great care, eliminating potentially problematic men before they became prolific.

Heyer was hard placed to keep track of this for each gate, some after all, saw far more traffic than others. Perhaps there were even times when his brother turned a blind eye because the spirit of the rule remained intact. No Alpha, especially the prophet himself, was ever allowed to risk wasting a man's life for his own unnecessary desires—his own ego. The truth was that Alphas were unlikely to achieve fertility. Their biology required an opponent to provide a degree of threat most of earth's combatants could never offer given the meager compatibility he and his brother were allowing the humans to have with their devices.

This—and not fear of their gods—was why the Alphas themselves had not risen in protest to the prophet's ruling. Alphas had already born many children, and like the eldest of most species, they had more dominion over their instincts, more discipline at their disposal, and were more capable of selfless sacrifices in times of inadequate resources. If obeying his laws meant their prophet would deliver them to the promised land, they would wait.

Regardless, when Malkier needed a solution to a troublesome man on earth, he would send a near alpha who had not been selected for a long while. Taking care to give the appearance the selection had been made at random to the tribe. This solved the issue, if done with care, but predictably brought suspicion to the youth of the tribe regardless if it was warranted. After all, every Green was eager to prove himself to their tribe, and any time that opportunity seemed denied, they quietly questioned the legitimacy of the lottery.

It was with a begrudging respect that Malkier thought of *Echoes the Borealis.* The name his people had given to the abomination that had broken all the safeguards in his system. The man had sent back staggering losses long after Malkier rigged the Ferox lottery to send in ringers to remove him. *Echoes* had been the cause of the last great pilgrimage, bringing males from all over the Feroxian Plane to his tribe's territory.

At the time, Malkier had grown fixated on bearing a child of his own. It was a notion he should never have entertained. As the prophet and an Alpha, his own decree forbade his entry into the gates. Nevertheless, the idea took root in him, and made the instinctual desires of his Feroxian host's body more and more difficult to ignore. When the Reds failed, and the growing issue of *Echoes the Borealis* left him no choice but to consider sending an Alpha assassin, Malkier believed he had found providence. He had finally seen a vindicating reason for the prophet to make an exception to his own rules.

So, *Ends the Storm* trespassed through the gates. He bore his child—he gained his scar.

The legend he had confronted on the other side of the gates was no echo of a god—but just a man. Malkier had always felt a lingering sense of injustice on his conscience. After all, he was thousands of years older, a Borealis contained inside the most powerful device his species had ever created, and implanted in the body of a Ferox Alpha. He was as close to invincible as his people's technology could make him. *Echoes* should have been near incapable of doing him any real harm. He had cheated that man in every sense of the word—yet, the prophet still bore the man's scar.

That man had been the first time he felt true physical pain in centuries, and the last time since.

His conscience had grown quiet over the years since, only having to see *Dams the Gate* growing stronger each day to be drowned out. After having faced *Echoes*, he'd told himself that he had done the only sensible thing. After all, who could say how many more of his people *Echoes the Borealis* may have slain had he not taken care of him? It was too easy to see an element of fate in play. In the end, would there ever be another combatant on earth strong enough to bring the prophet himself to fertility?

Now though, his son was dead, and the very gate that had made his conception possible was continuing to send back casualties. As though the universe were giving him a karmic lesson, screaming to him that his trespass had not been forgotten nor forgiven. That his debt had gone unpaid. In his grief, he wondered if his sanity might not be spared in the long term if he just let himself feel as though he'd been wronged.

After all, it was not as if he had given up nothing to see himself a father. When his brother learned the means by which *Echoes the Borealis* had fallen, a wedge had been driven between them. Heyer, for the first time in his life, had looked at him with a disdain that bordered on hatred. Malkier had bled before his brother, the wound *Echoes* had given him far from healed, still hardening into the white scar he saw every time he caught sight of himself in a reflection. It had been a painful recovery, the device's ability to heal his Feroxian form delayed for reasons he did not understand. Nevertheless, Malkier had seen in his brother's eyes that he had considered finishing the job *Echoes* had started. Perhaps, with his injuries, Heyer may have succeeded.

Instead, his brother had stood before him, visibly shaking with rage and... indecision.

A number of times, as the Ferox fatalities had grown, Heyer had offered solutions to the problem of *Echoes the Borealis*. Of all of them, he'd fought hardest to see *Echoes* allowed to retire peacefully—his gate left dormant until he died from natural causes. Heyer didn't understand his people's nature. The Ferox needed to see the legend brought down, or they would believe themselves a failure to their gods.

"*Ends the Storm*," said *Sleeps the Dream*, a peculiar note of excitement in his voice.

His Feroxian name snapped Malkier's attention back into the moment, and his eyes followed to where his lieutenant now pointed.

A man crouched beside the gate, surrounded by his tribe. He was on his knees, his hands out in front of him as he shielded his eyes from the sight of the Ferox and begged for their mercy. Beside him laid the body of yet another Red, not the last to have entered gate. It was a wonder that this man had not yet been torn to pieces by the Ferox surrounding him. Though perhaps it was that they waited, held him prisoner, until an elder came to decide who would be given permission to slay him. Malkier would not let this happen, not publicly. Whatever had occurred to bring a man through, if he was attacked, without the aid of an active implant, the Ferox slaying him would find the man an unformidable enemy—a complete waste.

"Leave the abomination unharmed," the prophet yelled over the crowd.

The hisses, the need for violence died down, and the few remaining Ferox parted to allow Malkier and his two lieutenants through.

Is this him? Malkier wondered. *Has chance sent me Brings the Rain. Given me a face.*

He would not slay the man, should it be so. A disgust rose in him at the thought, but it would bring him no lasting peace to attack this man under the circumstances. It would be an execution, and would not last more than a moment. No, if this was *Brings the Rain* his device would be activated. He would be brought into an arena. He would be forced to fight.

As he neared, he took one look at the man cowering and was flooded with disappointment. The human's behavior was understandable. Weaponless, surrounded, alone, and merely a man, there would be no victory in defending himself; whimpering was really the only avenue left to him. Still, Malkier wanted to see the spirit of *Echoes the Borealis* in his son's killer. If his son had fallen to this man, he wanted him to be someone that confronted death with dignity; not with a quivering and pathetic appeal for mercy.

His eyes drew down to the dead Ferox beside him, to the telltale signs of this gate's challenger. His weapon was a long flat rod of some sort. Malkier had seen the imprints of the weapon in the armor of other casualties, had asked Cede to build a model of what the weapon might look like from analyzing the wounds.

The quivering man could not understand the Feroxian speech without an active device, but he seemed to comprehend that Malkier was a point of authority. Desperate, he began to speak in his human language.

"It wasn't me," the man said. "I didn't do this. Please."

Malkier's head tilted, though he did not let on that he understood the man's feeble cries. The prophet turned away from him, facing his lieutenants.

"Get the human off the surface, he won't last long out here. Take him to my quarters unharmed and guard him until I return. The human is in a weakened state here, fragile, be careful of your strength when you bind him. If anyone from the tribe argues with you, tell them this is their prophet's decree; that I must wait for our gods to interpret the meaning of his arrival."

His orders understood, Malkier watched as each of his lieutenants took the man by an arm and carried him away.

"Please, it wasn't me! Please!" the man's cries continued to grow more terrified as he was taken away.

Malkier followed, but stopped when he reached the end of the crowd. *Burns the Flame* had separated from the rest, and stood outside the walls of the ravine. Her eyes showed none of the reverence that the rest of his people held for their prophet.

"I know it was you," Malkier said.

Burns the Flame turned away, "That was the intention."

CHAPTER TWENTY-SIX

LEAH'S FACE WAS glum as she sat on Paige's bed once again. Paige frowned at her friend. "What do you mean he just stopped?" she asked.

"He pulled away..." Leah paused and shrugged. "Then he said he had to go."

"That can't be everything, that doesn't make any sense."

Leah's head tilted away awkwardly, betraying that perhaps she was leaving something out.

"Oh, come on," Paige said. "Spill it, Leah."

"Okay, I didn't tell you something before," Leah said. "We weren't as close as we are now when it happened."

Her friend's statement, with its wavering reluctance, had all the signs foreshadowing a big disclosure. Paige found herself pulling the chair from her desk and rolling it until she was sitting eye to eye with Leah. "Lay it on me."

"It wasn't actually the first time," Leah said.

Paige's eyes narrowed. "What?"

"A few weeks ago. I was upset, and Jonathan was there. We were both lonely. I just..." Leah stalled. "I don't know how to explain."

Paige studied her friend, fingers beginning to tap against the arm of her chair as she processed this new information. "I'm confused here. If this already happened, then why does—" She closed her eyes and felt an annoyed smile on her face. "Why does he look at you like he has a crush and can't muster the balls to tell you? If you've already..." Paige trailed off, then grimaced. "Wait, was it terrible or something?"

Leah shook her head. "No, nothing like that. But I said something stupid. I don't even know why I said it."

Paige gave Leah an incredulous look. "What could you possibly have said that would make him leave in the middle of—" She shrugged. "Well, a sure thing, from how you described it?"

Leah put her face in hands and grumbled, "I may have accidentally left him with the impression that he shouldn't get attached."

Paige rolled her eyes. "I say stuff like that all the time—men seldom actually seem to hear it. Especially when I mean it."

"Right?" Leah said, a look of vindication on her face as she pulled her hands away. "Why does he have to go being the one who took it so seriously?"

"Ughh," Paige sighed, before she added, "Because he's Tibbs." She frowned again a moment later. "I still don't see why it would make him leave. It's hard to believe he'd walk away just because he thought he'd get attached. I mean, if that were the case, why did he go on the date in the first place?"

"I told him that I hadn't really meant it right before anything happened," Leah said.

Paige brought her hands up in exasperation. "Then what does it have to do with anything?" she asked.

"I think it may be guilt. Maybe?"

Paige tilted her head, eyes narrowing at her friend. "Leah, you are terrible at storytelling," she said. "What does guilt have to do with anything?"

Leah bit her lip before explaining. "Yesterday morning, this girl showed up in your driveway. She hugged Jonathan as though they were close, but it got strange, because he said he didn't know her. The girl left, and it was obvious that she was upset. Jonathan looked so bewildered by the whole exchange that I believed him when he said he didn't know her."

Paige watched as Leah looked away troubled.

"Then last night happened, and I can't help thinking I'm being naive.

That girl was... attractive," Leah said. She shook her head. "But it's not like Jonathan, right? To lie to my face and say he didn't know her."

"Well..." Paige grimaced and trailed off. After this morning, she knew that there was a woman in Jonathan's life that no one had known about. Still, there was so much that was off about the whole story. If Tibbs was involved with this Rylee, why was he sleeping on the couch? Even if he was taking his first trial run at being a bastard, he wasn't stupid—he wouldn't lie only to contradict himself the very same day.

"What?" Leah asked.

"What was the girl's name?" Paige asked.

"Jonathan said he didn't know. She had an accent though. Brazilian. Why?"

"Because some girl with an accent slept in Jonathan's room last night," she said. "Hayden told me her name was Rylee."

"Oh." Leah raised her palm up and looked at Paige, annoyed, like she would have liked to have known that detail earlier.

"No, I'm not saying she was with him," Paige said. "Jonathan slept on the couch."

"Rylee." Leah nodded. "That was what Collin said her name was. So, I guess Jonathan must have lied about knowing her."

Paige didn't like how it looked any more than Leah, but she didn't believe Jonathan had it in him to be such a blatant jackass. Then again, lately, she couldn't claim to know him as well as she once had.

"I'm going to talk to him," Paige finally said. "There has to be something missing here. It's too weird."

The two heard the sounds of motorcycles approaching then, and Paige walked over to her window to see who it was returning. She recognized Collin immediately, and though she had a helmet on as she pulled into the garage, the second rider was obviously the strange girl.

"Better idea," Paige said. "We give Rylee the third degree before Jonathan gets home."

Leah shook her head. "It's not her fault. And I don't want to look jealous."

Paige waved her off and smiled. "Don't worry, I got this," she said. "I'll be subtle."

When Jonathan's shift ended, he told his ride that he needed to run some errands before he headed home, then returned to the alley where he'd met Heyer earlier in the day. The sun was starting to go down, and the alley was empty. He had only been standing around for a minute when he caught a glimpse of the alien on a sidewalk on the other side of the street. Heyer looked around, then without a word started walking away.

Jonathan followed him and saw that he'd turned the corner at the end of the block, but when he reached the same corner and looked around, the alien was nowhere to be seen.

Well, this is new.

He walked up the street, and eventually caught a glimpse of the black coat and fedora when he reached the end of the block. He turned to follow, and found he was heading out of the more suburban area and onto a busier main street. The hour was early enough that there were people coming and going on the sidewalk, and a coffee shop had a few people lounging about on the patio. He walked past them, looking around, trying to get another glimpse of Heyer's dark clothing amongst the pedestrians.

Finally, he saw him walking away again, at the end of another alley. Jonathan ran to follow, but when he hit the other side of the street, the man had disappeared again. Seeing an obvious pattern, and not knowing how long it could go on, he gave up trying to chase the alien down and just walked. After that went on for a few minutes, he turned up another empty alley and Heyer stepped in front of him, blinking out of thin air as per usual.

"Jonathan," he said, his eyes scanning the streets and rooftops around them. "Quickly, take out your cell phone and toss it down that gutter."

Jonathan frowned. "Sure," he said, doing as instructed, "because I'm made of money."

It was only a cheap flip phone, but Jonathan repeatedly found it inconvenient that the alien never accounted for his budgetary restraints. Heyer didn't seem to register the sarcasm—he was too busy sweeping the area with his eyes. When the phone fell through the grate he placed a hand on Jonathan's shoulder.

"Brace yourself," the alien said. "This is going to be a bit disorientating."

Jonathan had just started to narrow his eyes when his vision went black. Gravity seemed to stop pulling down on him and instead yanked in every direction at once.

A moment later, the space where they had stood was empty.

Rylee was trying not to overthink her current situation. She was smiling, so why focus on how that was so different from the norm? Why think about how temporary it might be?

When she'd woken to find herself in a home filled with people her own age, the mood of the place had begun to permeate her skin. She didn't want to think about how long it had been since she'd sat at a table, drinking coffee with friendly faces, or the last time someone had made her laugh, or she'd listened to people discuss inconsequential things. Comic books, television programs, and movies were at the front of her hosts' minds. Unlike her, Jonathan had not thought to leave his life behind. She was starting to wonder if he'd known, somehow, that it was the key to staying sane.

When she found out Collin was an artist, she admitted she also dabbled, though not so much of late. They had sketched a picture of one another, while Hayden waited to judge a winner. He couldn't though—apples and oranges, Hayden had said, and he'd been right. Collin had a style similar to that of the comic books he read, while she tried for a photo-realistic look. Collin's portrait of her was in her front pocket now. It made her laugh, to be drawn like some superhero, though the expression on her portrait made her wonder if Collin thought her superpower was sass. The irony was that the girl in the picture reminded her more of who she'd been before the superpowers.

She found herself wondering, now that he remembered she existed, how much of Jonathan's day had been spent thinking of her. After spending her day with Collin on their 'secret mission of mercy,' she was impatient to see his face. It was ridiculous, of course; she shouldn't miss him and she knew it. She didn't even know enough about him to say what precisely she 'missed'. Nevertheless, the feeling was there, whether it made sense to her or not.

"It appears we have successfully beat Tibbs home," Collin said as they pulled into the garage. "What do you think, should we hide it? Screw with him a bit first?"

"Definitely," she said, smiling conspiratorially. "Where, though?"

Collin looked around a bit before deciding the garage wasn't going to work. "I'll stash it in the backyard."

She winked at him. "I'll go tell Hayden to come look."

She put the kickstand down and jumped off her bike, feeling like a child as she ran up the stairs. It was a bit of a disappointment when she entered the living room and Hayden wasn't anywhere to be seen. She knocked on his door, but no one answered. Giving up on the big-bearded roommate, she headed upstairs to Jonathan's room to strip off her gear. She dumped the contents of her knapsack onto his bed—mostly a pile of wrinkled clothing, with her journal plopped onto the top. Noticing it as she slid out of her jacket, she snatched the little book off the pile and smiled as she placed Collin's portrait of her in between some of its pages.

"Hey, Jonath—"

The woman's voice cut short as Rylee turned to see her.

"Oh, sorry," the woman said from the doorway. "I thought Jonathan was home. You must be our mystery guest?"

Rylee smiled as she managed to free herself from the leather jacket, letting it fall onto the floor beside Jonathan's bed. "Hi," she said, stepping to the woman and holding out her hand. "I'm Rylee. You must beee…?"

"Paige," the girl said, accepting her hand.

They smiled a bit awkwardly for a moment, both at a loss for what to say to a complete stranger. Paige made the first attempt to break the ice. "I love that accent," she said. "Where are you from?"

Rylee blushed, but smiled. "Brazil, originally. My family moved to the states when I was young. I never lost the accent though."

Paige nodded. "Oh, so have you and Jonathan been friends a long time?" she asked.

"No, actually," Rylee said. "We only met yesterday."

Paige failed to hide that the answer was causing her some confusion. Tilting her head curiously, she said, "Wow. Well, I guess you two must have hit it off."

Rylee shrugged. "We have a mutual..." She had to hesitate a moment, looking for the best word. "Acquaintance."

"Ahhh. Anyone I might know?"

"Oh, I doubt it." Rylee leaned forward, gently putting her hand on Paige's wrist, before whispering, "But between you and I, that makes you the lucky one."

"Hmm." Paige nodded. "That type of acquaintance."

Rylee nodded too, leaving the doorway and returning to the piled belongings on Jonathan's bed. She bit her lip and frowned at the clothes. Everything she had needed to be washed. She took a quick look at Jonathan's dresser before tucking her arms into the colorful green and yellow T-shirt she was wearing.

Paige's eyes were on the floor, looking as though she was trying to puzzle out who might be an unlucky acquaintance. "So, what did the three of you get up to last night?" Paige asked. "I'm just being a busy body. I'll mind my own business if you..."

Paige had trailed off, trying to pretend she needed to clear her throat. Rylee was standing in her bra in front of the dresser, just having pulled out a drawer when she noticed Paige was blushing and didn't seem to know where to direct her eyes.

"Oh, sorry, I have a gift for making people uncomfortable," Rylee said, starting to look through the drawer more hastily to find something to cover herself. "Been told I lack a certain modesty."

"No," Paige said, still not making eye contact. "Just surprised me."

Scanning the drawer, Rylee discovered the severe lack of color in the clothing. "Geez, Tibbs," she said. "Man doesn't own a shirt that isn't white, black, or something in between." Rylee pulled a white t-shirt with cutoff sleeves from the drawer and frowned at it. Everything was going to be too big on her anyway, but at least it was clean.

"Fashion isn't really his thing," Paige said as Rylee pulled the shirt over her head.

When Rylee looked back at her in the doorway, Paige's smile looked forced and she still didn't seem to want to make eye contact even though Rylee had covered herself. She started to wonder if Paige didn't approve of her wearing the clothing. The thought reminded her that she was a guest—a stranger.

"Oh, Jonathan said he didn't mind," Rylee said. "I only need to borrow it while I do laundry."

Paige shrugged, shaking her head. "No worries here," Paige said, though it seemed a politeness. "So, where did you say you and Jonathan met?"

"Oh, right," Rylee said. "We're members of a group."

"Group? Hmm, he's never mentioned any groups before." Paige stepped into the room, leaning against Jonathan's door frame. "Between you and I," she said, "he keeps to himself a lot lately."

Rylee nodded, but her smile faltered. She remembered how protective of secrets Jonathan had been the night before. She thought he was being overly paranoid. Collin and Hayden had been plenty curious, but about her, not her relationship with Jonathan.

"What kind of group?" Paige asked, after her last comment didn't get an answer.

Rylee hesitated a moment, not wanting to be impolite. "I'm sorry, but if Jonathan didn't mention it..." She shrugged. "I don't think I should talk about it. He's been very kind offering me somewhere to stay. I'd hate to repay him by saying something he might consider private. I hope you understand. Not meaning any rudeness."

"No, no, I understand. Like I said, I'm a busy body, shouldn't pry," Paige said. "I promise, though, I'm only asking because I care about him a lot."

Rylee bit her lower lip as she took in the woman's words. "Um, I just realized," Rylee said. "I'm sorry, but are you two..."

Rylee looked to the floor awkwardly, not sure if she should be so forward.

"Oh, god no," Paige said, waving both hands at Rylee. "Jonathan is like a little brother to me." She was grinning, as though the idea of her and Jonathan bordered on comical, and Rylee relaxed.

"Oh, good," Rylee said. "I was starting to realize how this might look. I assumed he wasn't involved with anyone. Just realized he hadn't ever actually said so."

Paige's grin dipped, only for a moment, before she propped it back up. "So, you were hoping he was uninvolved?"

Rylee felt Paige studying her then, and looked away. "A girl would be lucky to have him," she said.

"I'm sorry, I don't mean to pry."

"Yeah. I think that is the third time you've said that." Rylee regretted the words almost immediately, and tried to busy her hands with putting her clothes back into her backpack before she stopped abruptly. "I apologize," she said. "That was... rude."

Paige shrugged. "You aren't wrong. I can't help it, I worry. Take this group you mentioned..." She bit her lip before she spoke. "Are you his sponsor?"

Rylee's eyes narrowed questioningly for a moment before she snorted in amusement. It came out far more condescending than she'd intended. "What, like for an AA meeting?" she asked.

Paige raised an eyebrow, leaving Rylee with the feeling that she hadn't thought the question funny.

"No, Jonathan doesn't need a sponsor," Rylee said. "If anything, he'd be m—" She cut herself off abruptly. Paige was going to keep prodding until Rylee said something she didn't mean to—something *else* she didn't mean to.

"Oh," Paige said.

Angry, Rylee swallowed down a dose of her dignity. She would have kicked Jonathan's ass if he had told someone that he was some kind of support system for her. Now she'd just given Paige that very impression.

She began picking up her belongings, shoving them back into her pack. "Do you mind if I use your laundry? I don't want to be a nuisance, borrowing Jonathan's clothes any longer than I have to."

When she looked up, Paige was still standing in the doorway, looking like she was angling to ask another round of questions. Rylee didn't give her the time. She lifted the bag up and walked toward the door.

Paige stepped aside when Rylee made it plain that she wasn't planning on waiting for an answer. "Go right ahead. Washer and dryer are down in the garage, want me to sho—"

"No. I'll find it."

"Oh," Paige said, trying to recover politely. "Okay. It was nice meeting you, though."

"Yeah."

When she reached the bottom of the stairs, Paige got in one last question: "Oh, Rylee," she said. "Any idea how long you'll be staying with us?"

CHAPTER TWENTY-SEVEN

WHEN HE FELT whole again his vision returned, but he had trouble standing. Heyer held onto Jonathan's shoulder, seeming to know he'd be needing the support. When the world stopped spinning, he looked around and found they were on a rooftop in the inner city.

"So, what was that all about?" Jonathan asked.

"With your constant surveillance," Heyer said, "I couldn't just give you the address and have you drop by. I had to be sure The Cell had lost sight of you before the jump. Now, they will spend the next few hours thinking you slipped away, finding that the bugs in your clothing are gone, and trying to pin you down to your phone's GPS coordinates. They won't know where you've gone."

"Where have I gone?" Jonathan asked.

"Only a few miles from where we were. I thought it best that the surveillance team not know that I'd had any immediate hand in your disappearance. It's not much of a ruse, but it will delay them from putting it together."

Jonathan nodded and looked around. As far as rooftops went, this one was pretty standard. "What's so special about here?"

"This is my home. Technically, we are standing on top of Mr. Clean," Heyer said. "He is camouflaged, appears to look like any other building in the area. The actual building on this property, the true brick and mortar, starts a few floors down."

"Why did you bring me here?" Jonathan asked. "I mean, you've never thought this was necessary before."

The alien removed his hand from Jonathan's shoulder, and Jonathan found that he was now able to stand on his own. "I had planned to bring you here sooner. You need to know of this place, but events have not played out as I intended," Heyer said.

"*Dams the Gate*?" Jonathan asked.

Heyer's eyes darkened at the mention of the Ferox's name, but he nodded. "Yes, but unfortunately, our problems have multiplied in my absence," Heyer said. "There are things I need to show you, things you need to understand. It is a conversation we cannot risk having while you are being observed."

At that, Heyer turned toward a roof access door. It opened as they approached, and shut behind them after Jonathan followed him down the stairwell.

"The Cell's primary goal in watching you is the hope to take me prisoner, Jonathan. Their reasons are not entirely unwarranted. They have seen countless disappearances connected with my presence, and they are out to protect mankind from what they assume to be abductions. However, their secondary goal is getting their hands on technology in my possession. They are hell-bent on accomplishing this, for fear that another nation might beat them to it." The alien raised a hand to their surroundings. "They suspect a ship like this exists, but they have no means of locating it. For all they know, Mr. Clean could be on the moon."

Jonathan listened, but when Heyer brought it up, he found himself thinking it would make more sense for the vessel to be off-planet. Having Mr. Clean on the surface only left him vulnerable to eventually being found. "So, why don't you keep him on the moon?" Jonathan asked, as he descended the stairs. "Seems safer."

Heyer turned his head back and smirked. "Should anything happen to me, there would be no one left to resist the Ferox. That is why you need to know of this place. If I am ever compromised, you'll need to come here immediately, a feat you would find difficult to manage if I left it on the moon."

Jonathan nodded, though he was more than a little disturbed at the notion of Heyer being 'compromised'. There had been a time he wished he'd never met the alien, but knowing what he did now, the thought of Heyer not being around to deal with Malkier was disturbing. Mankind would be lost without him.

"Are you particularly worried about that possibility?" Jonathan asked, his voice failing to hide his concern.

Heyer tilted his head back to Jonathan. "Well, one can never be too careful."

When they reached the bottom of the first stairwell, another seemingly normal door opened into a hallway. The Pioneer Square district of Seattle was mostly known for its shopping and nightlife, but had a number of buildings built over a hundred years earlier. They had been slowly modernized, the upper floors turned into flats and apartments while the street levels remained mostly commercial. Mr. Clean seemed to be parked on top of one of those buildings and was mimicking its interior.

The hallways appeared old in construction, and had elaborate and elegant lighting placed in the ceiling above them, despite also having unsightly plumbing running along the inside of the corridors. So far, the only oddity that would have alarmed anyone who entered was the doors opening and closing on their own. Still, even that had a sense of mock-normalcy; the hinges squeaked like an old door would, despite being controlled by forces Jonathan couldn't see. Frankly, the place reminded him more of a haunted house than anything he'd seen on Star Trek.

Finally, another door opened in the hallway and Jonathan found himself looking into a furnished room. "This is where you... what?" He paused. "Sleep, eat, live?"

Heyer nodded, waiting beside the open door for Jonathan to step inside.

First impressions left Jonathan wondering if, having lived through so much of mankind's history, Heyer had an overly-developed sentimentality for the past. The alien could decorate however he wished, yet he'd chosen an eclectic assortment of antiques mixed with modern luxuries. *Does help explain his attachment to that ridiculous fedora though*, Jonathan thought.

The first thing that drew his attention was a vault-like steel door recessed into one of the back walls, but before his curiosity had a chance to absorb the atmosphere of the place, a flat screen TV mounted on the wall tilted in his direction and he saw Mr. Clean smiling back at him.

"Hello, Jonathan," the cartoon said. "Nice to see you under more ideal circumstances."

Jonathan grinned back at him. "The feeling is mutual."

"Mr. Clean," Heyer said. "If you would, we'll require a scaled model of the Feroxian gateways, schematics on the bonded pair, and a simplified model of dimensional space."

Jonathan hadn't understood much of what Heyer had just requested, but he lost track of his questions as the room began to alter around him. A framed painting and a mirror, each hung on separate walls, morphed before his eyes. They behaved as though they were liquid, and reshaped to form additional monitors like the one Mr. Clean was using. However, each displayed what appeared to be three-dimensional blueprints.

On the coffee table, the unremarkable contents that had been there when he walked in receded down into the surface to be replaced with a holographic image of what looked like an oddly-shaped sundial. The shape rotated like a carousel over the table, allowing Jonathan to see it from various angles as it turned.

On each side of that table there was a leather-upholstered chair, each facing one another, and now, in the empty space above the sundial hologram, a sequence of blue rectangular cubes took shape. They hovered above the chairs, a little below the ceiling, glowing with an iridescent blue light that reminded Jonathan of the strange coloring he sometimes caught in Heyer's pupils when he stood in the dark.

As everything around him changed, it dawned on Jonathan that nothing inside of Mr. Clean was real—or, at least, nothing seemed permanently fixed. Trying to test this, he reached out and tentatively placed his hand on one of the chairs. He was unsure if he should have been surprised when the chair felt precisely as his eyes told him it should—like solid leather.

"So, is this chair really here?" Jonathan asked, "Or, are only parts of the room an illusion?"

"All of the structures here are generated by Mr. Clean," Heyer replied. "They are dependent on the shape that he is taking at any time. Much like the exterior of the building, the internal pieces of the architecture and furniture are only semi-permanent. It is a highly adaptable technology, but Mr. Clean's current configuration is mostly designed for camouflage. This is needed so that a person might be brought here without becoming suspicious that they have actually boarded an extraterrestrial vessel." After a moment of thought, Heyer added, "And I find the decor relaxing."

"What does it..." Jonathan paused, becoming aware that his choice of words might seem rude. "Sorry, I meant what do *you* actually look like, Mr. Clean, when you aren't taking a shape?"

"Far less interesting than you may imagine. When my constructs are disabled, you only see a default setting. The physical structures recede back into the whole," Mr. Clean said. "To a human, I might look like a giant cube of over-sized solar panels."

Jonathan turned his attention back to the Mr. Clean on the monitor. "So, how much of this building is actually you?"

"The top three stories. However, the two stories beneath you are currently dormant additional mass. The shapes I can manifest are only limited by my total volume. Imagine me like a lump of Play-Doh. You can flatten the lump into a large surface area, but you lose volume, or the enclosed three-dimensional spaces where you now stand. If I were to take the shape of some large, solid mass—say, fill this room with myself—I would no longer have enough of myself left over to camouflage the roof, so I would have to shrink the building's exterior by a story. Of course, people in the surrounding buildings would notice that the building had shrunk."

Jonathan nodded. He found it odd how quickly his wonder receded these days. He was standing inside of an artificially intelligent being, who was taking the shape of a human living room to accommodate them. He should have been fascinated, but how long could a person live knowing an individual like Heyer was on Earth and still be surprised by the things that came with him?

"I like to think of myself like a far more advanced version of the villain in *Terminator II*," said Mr. Clean. "I am the ship, and I can take the shape of anything of equal mass, the major difference being that I can form complex machines within and around myself."

Jonathan smiled, remembering what Heyer had told him about the computer's personality. That, and it sounded comically close to the type of thing Hayden or Collin might have said if they were here.

"If you are worried that the chair will disappear out from under you," Heyer said, "Mr. Clean grew bored with that joke centuries ago."

"Yes," Mr. Clean said. "Though it has been awhile."

"So," Jonathan said. "What stops you from turning into a giant metal robot and rampaging through the city?"

The bald cartoon raised a bushy white eyebrow. "Desire," Mr. Clean said. "What purpose would that serve? I can imagine far more efficient means to—"

Heyer cleared his throat. When Jonathan turned to him, the alien's face showed he clearly thought it was time for more important matters than the bells and whistles of his odd companion. A silence followed.

Jonathan was reminded that he wouldn't be here if there wasn't an emergency, and he let out a long breath in acknowledgment of this. "Before you tell me the world is ending, I'd hoped you could help me understand something."

Heyer tilted his head at one of the chairs, stepping toward the other himself. "What is on your mind?"

"Paradox. These confrontations with the Ferox… I need to understand how I am retaining memories of events that happen in erased time lines."

Heyer and Mr. Clean exchanged a look, the former drawing in a deep breath and nodding. "Take a seat Jonathan," he said. "We must know what has occurred, but if you are to understand it yourself, your question is as good as any place to start."

Jonathan nodded. "Uh… I guess I'm gonna sit on you now, Mr. Clean," he said, then pursed his lips. "I guess that is better than standing on you, though."

When Hayden got home, he found Rylee alone in the garage. She was sitting on the washer while the machine ran, a faraway look on her face as she listened to its white noise.

"How'd your mission of mercy go?" Hayden asked.

She forced a smile, but didn't take her eyes off the floor.

"You look bummed," he said. "You bored? We could watch a movie."

She grunted noncommittally, then she sighed. "I wish Jonathan would get home. We didn't really get to talk last night. You and Collin have been really kind, trying to keep me entertained."

Hayden shrugged. "It's not as though you're putting us out. Might be entertaining us more than the other way around."

He had made the statement casually, but Rylee's expression was a difficult read. She smiled at him and sighed.

"You sure nothing's wrong?" Hayden asked again.

Rylee shrugged. "I'm probably over-thinking it," she said. "I met Paige a few minutes ago. I tried to be nice, but I got this feeling..."

"Oh," Hayden grimaced. "Yeah, you probably weren't imagining things."

She looked at him, eyebrows raising in interest. "I didn't want to be rude, but I felt like she didn't want me around."

Hayden nodded. "Yeah. You'll need to forgive her. She was pretty irritated with Jonathan this morning. Trust me, though, she's actually pretty cool when she isn't convinced she's our mother."

Rylee snorted, but then her curiosity returned. "Why was she upset with Jonathan?"

Hayden leaned against the dryer beside her. "I'm not sure I should talk about it. I think they are overdue for a conversation, and Jonathan has been really distant the last few months. They used to study together a lot, before Jonathan dropped out of college..." He closed his eyes and grimaced. "Crap, see, I probably shouldn't have mentioned that. Not my place to share. Forget I said it."

A moment passed and Rylee nudged him with an elbow. "Said what?"

Hayden frowned for a moment until he caught that she was telling him she wouldn't mention the slip.

"I wouldn't judge him, you know," Rylee said. "It's easy to see someone do something that seems lazy or stupid and make assumptions. Takes a pretty self-righteous dickhead not to realize a person has reasons that they might not be able to share."

Hayden smiled, more because Rylee's accent made the term "dickhead" sound funny, than because of any wisdom in her words. "You might say that to Jonathan. I think the college thing weighs on him. I know his mother took it poorly."

"He doesn't need me to tell him that."

Hayden shrugged. "I pray for him a lot."

Rylee lifted an eyebrow, seeming to reexamine the big man. "You're a good friend, Hayden."

She stood, then, stretching out her legs and standing against the washer. Despite the somber tone of their conversation thus far, Hayden found it hard to ignore her as she slipped down beside him, his eyes taking her in before he could direct them elsewhere. He looked away in a slightly awkward innocence, as though something on the ceiling was suddenly interesting.

If Rylee had noticed him gawking, she didn't let on. "I don't want to be on her bad side," she said. "Any thoughts on how to win her over?"

"No, not really. Honestly though, had it been any other day, you two would have got along fine… I mean—probably." When he felt her studying him, he grimaced. "Ah, man, see, this is why people shouldn't tell me things."

"Hayden," she said, "I sure do wish I knew what you meant by 'any other day'."

He looked at her—such a pretty face… he really didn't see any harm. He wanted her to feel comfortable in the house, not as though she were somehow responsible for the friction between Paige and Jonathan. Hayden held up his pinky. "Pinky swear you won't turn me in?"

She looked at his finger and smiled, wrapping her tiny finger around his thick one and shaking.

"Jonathan has had this, eh... thing with the girl next door, ever since she moved in. Anyway, they were supposed to be on their first big date last night, but then he came home with you," Hayden said. "Which probably got Paige a little suspicious, because her and Leah have been like... do people still say 'BFFs'?"

He hadn't been watching Rylee as he struggled through the explanation, but when he looked back, her eyes were flickering back and forth like she was processing the information on double time. He started to feel anxious that he'd said something he shouldn't have... so his mouth charged ahead of him, trying to fix it.

"What I mean is Paige probably thought Jonathan had been misleading Leah. You know, when he showed up in the middle of the night with a girl none of us knew and let her sleep over." Hayden laughed nervously. "But Jonathan wouldn't do that."

Rylee hesitated a moment. Her mouth opened, but she seemed to rethink whatever she was going to say because no words came out. She finally hummed and spoke. "So, what's this Leah like?"

"Jonathan, are you familiar with any of Ayn Rand's books?" Heyer asked.

He shook his head. "Do I need to be? I haven't exactly had a lot of leisure reading time lately."

Heyer smiled. "One of Ms. Rand's more useful insights was that contradictions do not exist—that when one believes they are facing a contradiction, they must review their premises, and they will find that one is false."

Jonathan shrugged. "Fair enough."

"I once told you that your memories were the only thing accomplishing any time travel," Heyer said. "At the time, this was an effort to keep things as simple as possible. Nonetheless, it was a simplified explanation. What it lacked in detail has led you to perceive a contradiction, a paradox, where no such logical inconsistency exists."

"So..." Jonathan's eyes narrowed as he leaned back in his chair and crossed his arms over his chest. "Sounds like you gave me the kindergarten explanation. Leaving me to bang my head against a wall."

"I've told you in the past that satisfying your curiosity is not always the wisest use of our time," Heyer replied.

Jonathan let his annoyance be known, closing his eyes and releasing a long, frustrated breath before giving the alien a sardonic smile. "I'll try not to waste time pretending to be shocked. Do you mind giving me the reality?" he asked. "Perhaps the grade school explanation?"

Heyer smiled faintly, his eyes turning apologetic before he nodded. "Your resentment is not unjustified, Jonathan. In answer to your question, 'reality' is, perhaps, the best place to start."

The alien paused, gathering his thoughts before continuing.

"Mankind is gathering knowledge faster than ever. As a result, your world seems less mysterious; the gaps in knowledge that your species previously filled with mysticism shrink every day. A person born into this time would find it easy to assume his experiences were nothing more than the result of chemical reactions, physics, and various probabilities. That the material world is simply what he sees."

Jonathan cocked an eyebrow at Heyer, then looked back to Mr. Clean on the monitor. "Heyer, are you about to give the 'things exist outside our understanding' speech?"

The alien frowned. "Hardly."

Jonathan could see the alien retracing his words, smiling to himself as he as realized what Jonathan was getting at.

"I'm pointing out that your frame of reference may make your understanding difficult. So, let me ask you a question, as a practical example," Heyer said. "What is the physical makeup of an idea, of memory, of knowledge, of information?"

Jonathan blinked, silent, his thoughts having gone in too many directions at once due to the vagueness of the question. Assuming that was the point, he chose to simply play along and give the sort of answer he thought the alien expected. "There are too many answers to that, each as good as the next," Jonathan said. "Do you mean the biology of the brain, data on a computer's hard drive, spoken language, the written word?"

Heyer nodded. "I mean all of those things, as well as thousands of others you did not mention. Still, you have landed on the point.

Information is highly versatile; it can cross any boundary, as long as you have a signal on one end, a format that can transverse the barrier, and a receiver on the other."

"Okay," Jonathan said, drawing the word out.

"Jonathan, at the end of a confrontation with the Ferox, when you close the gates, you perceive that your memories occurred in a time and place that will never be—that events took place in your reality, and yet were somehow erased, leaving no effect on the world everyone else is experiencing. Yet, a Ferox is dead, his body returned to its point of origin, and you returned to yours.

"To you, it appears that you've gone backwards, returned from a version of history that has ceased to exist. This would seem to void the very history downloaded into your mind. You see a contradiction, because if this were true, then the battle which resulted in the Ferox's death never happened. Therefore, your opponent was not slain, the portal stone he carried never retrieved and destroyed. The very memory of your experiences becomes a paradox. You cannot see a logical explanation that they would exist."

Jonathan nodded. He might have had more trouble following the alien's explanation, but Hayden had already gotten him a little further along than this. "At first," he admitted. "Then I began to suspect I was experiencing memories from an alternate reality."

Heyer's expression softened, becoming a bit surprised.

"Don't get too impressed," Jonathan said. "I didn't get there on my own. I asked one of my roommates to come up with an explanation for the plot of the movie *Groundhog Day*. Alternate dimensions with an element of time travel was his best guess. He couldn't figure out the last piece, though. Why had that alternate reality ceased to be? Why didn't it keep playing out somewhere in the space-time-contin... whatever?"

Heyer, seeming unfamiliar with the reference, turned to Mr. Clean. "*Groundhog Day*?"

The bald cartoon shrugged, but his smile didn't falter. "The circumstances of the film's plot are similar enough to his experience to provide an adequate thought experiment."

"Well then, moving on," Heyer said, clearing his throat. "You have already taken the first step—seeing that one of your premises was false. The piece you are missing rests in a technological discovery made by the Borealis in the years prior to their extinction: a temporary reality that can be manifested between two dimensions. One man referred to it as the *Barzakh space*, though it's not a term I prefer to use."

"Barzakh?" Jonathan asked. "Should that word mean something to me?"

"Likely not," Mr. Clean said. "As with many things, it is a translation of a translation."

"Mr. Clean is correct," Heyer said. "Much like the term *Borealis* was never used by my people to describe themselves, Barzakh was a word chosen by a man's subconscious translation of a Feroxian idea."

"I'm not exactly following," Jonathan admitted.

"It is much the same as when a Ferox identifies himself to you by name," Heyer said. "Your device translates by searching your vocabulary for the best approximation. However, your understanding of a word may be far from the reality that the translation is meant to capture, because no word in your language was ever coined to address the exact meaning. This is further complicated by layers of metaphor through which any intelligent being forms a comprehension. It is the great weakness of the spoken word's ability to communicate meaning. In this case, Barzakh came from a man named Ibrahim.

"He was a Muslim, a follower of Islam. In his first confrontation, the Ferox referred to the place where they fought, and his translation of the concept came to him as Barzakh. The word's inadequacy to grasp the truth withstanding, it became the term I used when speaking to him. Only later did I form an understanding of why that term resonated with the man's beliefs."

Heyer grew thoughtful for a moment.

"Perhaps, it is arguable that, had the device been activated within a Roman Catholic, the word would have been 'limbo' or 'purgatory.' Islamic beliefs don't have a direct equivalent. Ibrahim's beliefs told him that at his death, he would reach a barrier between Heaven and Hell called the Barzakh, a stage of death where he would be interrogated by two blue and black angels, Al-Nakir and Al-Munkar. I later came to understand that Ibrahim had, unconsciously, associated me with one of the angels from his religious beliefs."

Heyer pointed to his iridescent blue eyes and wardrobe, and then continued:

"Ibrahim saw the Ferox as an incarnation of the angel Munkar. He had drawn the conclusion that his confrontation with the Ferox was the true reality of the 'interrogation' he had read about in religious texts. This, of course, is only an example of how one's beliefs can alter understanding. A fight with the Ferox is nothing close, from my perspective, to the interrogation described in the Islamic texts. Nonetheless, Ibrahim believed it to be so, and that his victory or failure was predicated on the strength of his faith. I cannot say whether his survival was extended by his perceptions."

Jonathan thought it over, but didn't have much to say, so he simply shrugged. "Whatever gets you through the day, I guess."

Heyer nodded, but seemed to be lingering in his memory. "Perhaps believing that he fought to validate his soul gave him courage he wouldn't otherwise have had."

Jonathan studied the alien. He found himself pondering how many stories Heyer could have told him about the men he had outlived. How many lives had he drafted into this war? What role had those men seen Heyer playing in their story? After all, Jonathan wasn't sure he knew what role the alien played in his own. He pulled away from those thoughts when a memory of *Bleeds the Stone* came to the forefront.

"The Arena," he whispered.

His words drew both Heyer and Mr. Clean's attention, and the alien's expression betrayed recognition. However, Heyer didn't speak his mind, only watched Jonathan, waiting for him to elaborate.

"I never gave it much thought," Jonathan said. "The Ferox I've fought… at times, they referred to Earth as 'the Arena.' Perhaps, where this man heard Barzakh, I've been hearing 'Arena' instead."

"It is a possibility," Heyer said. "Your perception of things clouds the translation. Where Ibrahim saw a battle for his soul, you see a contest over life and death. Still, the word 'Arena' in particular…" Heyer trailed off. "We will return to that in a moment. For now, let us stay on the topic of temporary dimensions. You see, the phenomenon Ibrahim called the Barzakh does have a name. Ibrahim simply never knew of it, and I saw no need to disillusion him. What he called the Barzakh, we refer to as The Never."

"The Never." Jonathan tried out the words, only to frown in confusion a moment later. "I didn't realize that dimensions could be temporary."

"They aren't," Mr. Clean cut in. "The Never is not a naturally occurring phenomenon. Realities like your own, the Feroxian plane, or the dimension from which the Borealis originated—these are fixed realities. They exist as they always have, playing out based on their governing physics, and will continue to do so."

"In contrast," Heyer said, "The Never is a reality brought into being by Borealis technology, the sort my ancestors likely wished they had not discovered."

Jonathan's brow furrowed in thought. "What is it that makes The Never different?"

Heyer looked at the floor as he thought over his answer. "Natural dimensions," he finally said, "possess a certain indicator on all of their physical matter, something the Borealis referred to as a dimensional signature. It can be read, in a manner of speaking, off the matter found in any reality, though it is not, as you might say, an intrinsic quality of matter such as density. Rather, a dimensional signature is more akin to mankind's use of radioactive decay to carbon date an object's age. The Borealis developed a system of multiple measurements to assign dimensional signatures to each reality, as the physics of each dimension has its own unique qualities that can be measured.

"If I were to somehow blind Mr. Clean and drop him into any known reality, it would take him awhile to tell me where in said dimension he had been dropped. However, Mr. Clean could immediately tell me what reality we had landed in. He could do this by simply reading the dimensional signature off of the closest matter he found around him at arrival."

"So a dimensional signature is used like what? A social security number, an address, a barcode on the energies that make up matter?"

"That is an over-simplification," Heyer replied. "But if it helps to understand, then yes, you have the idea."

"So what is different about The Never's signature?"

"The Never has no signature. This is a direct result of its temporary nature. No readout within The Never is ever consistent. The matter from which it is brought into being is never subject to the same rules."

Jonathan found his fingers tapping against the leather arm of his chair as he considered this. A moment later, he frowned. "What difference does it make? If your dimension is the only one without a signature, doesn't that just make 'no signature' its..." Jonathan paused. "Well, 'signature'?"

Heyer grinned at him. "It would seem so, at first glance. But, if we kept with the barcode comparison you made earlier, you see the difference rather quickly. Imagine that you are looking at an inventory sheet. It's easy to account for the things that are listed. How do you account for the things that aren't? It would be like trying to find a house with no address. Now, it's one thing if you are standing inside the house, but quite another if you need someone to come get you out. Further complicating the issue, you would be looking for something that doesn't always exist, something quite perishable. So, now, not only are you trying to locate something that doesn't have an address, but something that may or may not be there at the time you happen to go looking for it."

Mr. Clean added, "The same is true of the social security number comparison. It would be the equivalent of not having one, or, in the words of your generation, living off the grid. You may have noticed, when you accompanied Heyer here today, that no special point of origin was required to make the jump. I tracked his whereabouts via a signal sent out by his device and pulled you here when Heyer made physical contact with you. Time and space within The Never cannot be manipulated in the same way."

Jonathan turned his eyes to the strange hologram that had been turning on the table top as he saw where this was heading. "So you enter through a gateway."

Heyer nodded. "You do not, but the Ferox do," he said. "The Never is manifested temporarily between two realities, and requires cooperation between Mr. Clean and his equivalent on the Feroxian plane."

Heyer stood up from his chair and reached toward the iridescent blue cubes floating above them. As he did so, the projected images moved toward him, until Jonathan found he was looking at Heyer through the translucent shapes between them.

"When Mr. Clean brought this option to my attention, I too struggled to grasp it. It was helpful to think of the natural dimensions as books on a library shelf," Heyer said.

As the alien spoke, he reached for one of the blue holographic cubes hovering between them. Mr. Clean seemed to anticipate Heyer's wish to interact with the projections. The line of cubes moved toward Heyer's outstretched hand. They grew in size as they neared, until they had expanded to encompass the visual space between Jonathan and Heyer. Once they had scaled size, each of the cubes morphed in detail taking on the appearance of a set of encyclopedias arranged inside a shelf.

Heyer tapped the holographic book marked *E*. "Imagine that this book represents mankind's reality, the home dimension of Earth," he said. "For simplification, book *E* will represent the dimensional signature."

The encyclopedia reacted to Heyer's touch, taking on a faint green glow that caused the book to stand out against the rest. Heyer then moved his finger to the next book in the sequence.

"Now imagine that this neighboring encyclopedia represents the Feroxian plane," he said, repeating the process as he tapped on the book marked *F*.

Like the other, this image reacted to the alien's touch, taking on a yellow glow.

"The Ferox, much like most of Earth's activated combatants, are only told minimal details about the nature of the engagement. Lacking any knowledge of The Never, the Ferox assume themselves trespassers on Earth. A male Ferox is selected from a lottery, and is provided with a dormant portal stone. My brother has led them to believe that most of Earth's inhabitants are inconsequential, and as such, the Ferox are told to kill indiscriminately upon arrival. They are told, correctly, that this must be done to draw out one of Earth's defenders—Earth's abominations.

Their *challenger*. In short, the Ferox believe they are simply jumping from *F* to *E*, picking a fight, and returning home with their trophy," Heyer said.

Mr. Clean interrupted. "You could say the Ferox understanding is analogous to how Earth's sports teams think of an away game."

Jonathan, who hadn't actually been struggling to keep up, politely humored Mr. Clean. "Thanks for the simplification."

"The truth, as you can see, is hidden from the Ferox," Heyer said. "Every Ferox male born is named, and added to a registry. Their name remains inactive on this list until they enter a stage of puberty where hormones start taking control of their development, manifesting behavior that sends them seeking confrontation. This is when their name becomes active on the registry, which is used as a lottery of sorts, deciding which males will be allowed to enter the gates. However, the element of chance is less random than the Ferox are told."

"You mean Malkier is rigging the registry, sending through the males he chooses?" Jonathan asked. "Each Ferox doesn't actually get an equal chance to enter?"

"Yes, but he isn't selecting males based on arbitrary preferences," Heyer said. "Rather, the registry is designed to favor males with higher fecundity and preferred traits—"

"It is analogous to a human female visiting a sperm bank," Mr. Clean interrupted. "The donors are screened for variables like sperm count."

Again, Jonathan turned to give a placating nod to the A.I.

"Thank you, Mr. Clean," Heyer said, though Jonathan was picking up on a terseness in the alien's voice. "As I was saying, the point is to increase the chance of a successful mating, while doing their best to maintain as much variability in the gene pool as possible. Variety, as you may have learned from your studies, is the best evolutionary advantage a species can have as it faces changing environments."

"So, Malkier is cheating them," Jonathan said, "but only because he's trying to solve their mating problem. He's hoping that somewhere in the gene pool, he can hit on a combination of genetic traits that will start to reverse what your ancestors did to them."

Heyer nodded. "When the registry makes a selection, a portal stone is provided to the male. The Ferox have incorporated this into their religious beliefs. A certain amount of ceremony is conducted before a Ferox enters the gates for the first time…"

"It is analogous to a bar mitzvah," Mr. Clean interjected.

Jonathan watched Heyer's eyes shut, remaining closed long enough that Jonathan could sense his growing impatience with the interruptions. When he opened his eyes again, he lifted a hand, placing his middle and index finger on the two books representing Earth and the Feroxian plane. Both illuminated brighter

"When the Ferox steps onto the gateway," Heyer said, nodding his head to the sundial-like object rotating over the coffee table, "a passage to Earth *is* opened, but instead of creating the simple point of entry that the gateway was designed for, the portal stone acts as a catalyst, signaling its counterpart on Earth to bring The Never into play."

Jonathan watched as the model between him and Heyer began a flurry of activity. A red pulse emanated from the Feroxian plane and was shortly followed by an identical pulse from Earth. The two signals started to overlap, meeting together in the middle and solidifying into a sphere between the two dimensions. The end effect was that a bubble formed in the space between the books, forcing them to bend in order to accommodate it. Jonathan watched as this affected all the books on the shelf, each bending as much as was necessary to allow the bubble to exist, until the very bookcase housing the model was forced to become more of an oval than a rectangle shape.

Heyer lifted his finger to point at the sphere. "The Never is a temporary copy of your dimension held inside the gates. You can see within this simple model that making room for its existence is an accommodation that physical law resists. The boundaries of all realities are malleable to some extent, but it is not in their nature to bend. This is the major limiting factor of The Never, and why it lacks a dimensional signature. The laws of reality are set against it from its first inception, and those laws are held at bay only temporarily before being squashed out of existence."

Seeing this play out within the model, Jonathan was struck by disbelief. He didn't think Heyer was lying to him—what he couldn't believe was the idea that the alien's ancestors would dare tamper with the boundaries of all dimensions, dare to force reality to bend. He had always believed in science, experimentation, the advancement of knowledge, but this…

"Heyer, this…" Jonathan said, unable to remove the disgust from his voice. "This is far too dangerous. You can't… you can't just risk this, all of reality, even to save mankind. Irresponsible fails to capture this. It's too much."

The alien's hand came up to calm him. "I understand your revulsion. Keep in mind that this is a model—useful for educational purposes, but hardly to scale," Heyer said. "Reality, as a whole, is not easily broken. One open instance of The Never is not a threat to existence. It is the presence of multiple instances, taking place in unison, which could eventually become hazardous. The only true danger, in our use of it, is to the two beings who enter into the temporary bubble."

Within the holographic projection of the sphere, two forms took shape. One of a man, the other, a Ferox.

"You see, it is a built-in fail-safe of the technology," Heyer said. "The gates must be closed, or those who have entered will die inside. Once The Never can no longer withstand the pressure imposed on it, or the forces working against it, the temporary reality deteriorates from within. It is why it is temporary."

Jonathan stared at the model, his thoughts assaulting him in a blur. Silence fell on the room as the alien waited for him to process what he'd been shown. One horror rose to the surface as Jonathan remembered what Heyer had told him once inside The Never, the first time he closed the gates. *If you do not destroy the stone, this reality will be fixed. All of those who died tonight will remain dead.*

"Heyer," Jonathan said. "I—I don't know where the line is with you. There is a difference between simplifying and lying. This is not—this isn't what you told me was happening. All those people in the temporary *reality*… They just end?"

The alien took a long breath, his face weighted down in sympathy for the understanding Jonathan had reached so quickly. "When the gates are closed properly, no one suffers. They simply cease to be, never knowing,"

Heyer said. "The moral implications are too much for anyone to weigh. But I take some comfort knowing that what is true for them is also true for me. The shadow of myself that exists inside The Never—he is not exempt from the same fate as all those within. You have met my shadow before, Jonathan. You told me about him, months ago, on that bench in the park. He pulled you from the water and resuscitated you before he taught you how to close the gates.

"Your shadow?" Jonathan said. "Are you trying to tell me that it was someone else who lied to me?"

Heyer, again, held up a hand to calm him. "I can never know what the shadow of me inside The Never felt you needed to hear. I do know that this shadow was well aware of what would happen to him and everyone else within when you destroyed the stone. I can only imagine the fear my alternate self feels each time he faces oblivion, but one thing is certain."

Heyer paused, and Jonathan could see that he had done so to add gravity to the words that would follow.

"The Never has never been allowed to play out. Every time, my shadow made sure the gates were closed, made sure that those within did not endure its deterioration. Over the years, thousands of instances, I have never failed to make the same decision."

A silence fell between them as Jonathan absorbed the alien's statement.

"Why did—" Jonathan cut off, closed his eyes, trying to calm himself. "What good came from creating this technology in the first place?"

Heyer sighed, but nodded. "The Borealis were much like man in their desire to learn. Humanity is well aware that the bottleneck of discovery is ethics. I named the temporary dimension The Never. It is a title I chose, in part, because of its English meaning, but also in acknowledgment of the ancestor most responsible for its existence. She was a Borealis scientist named Nevric.

"Nevric's team had noble intentions. She saw The Never as the perfect laboratory, where the repercussions of any experiment could be safely contained without consequences in a true reality. In short, Nevric was looking to take away the necessity of ethics, by creating a simulation of reality that could perfectly account for every variable in true reality.

Such a place promised safety, where one could test the greatest of ideas with complete reversibility if the unforeseen side effects of an experiment ended in catastrophe.

"Of course, I say Nevric meant well, but as with any creation, those who make a discovery and those who control it are seldom the same person for long. Political leaders and military strategists of my race immediately saw other applications. Nevric's mistake was the same as every inventor who sees their discovery turned into a monstrosity. She believed that our species had become secure enough in their invincibility to lose their obsession with gaining more power."

Slowly, Jonathan nodded, slumping into his chair, unsure what else to say.

"Jonathan, you have a great capacity for compassion," Heyer said. "But perhaps an even greater capacity for guilt. I have to ask you not to dwell on this. It's the burden of the Borealis alone. My burden. You were never part of the decision to employ this technology. You are powerless to keep it from continuing. So, I ask that you let this lay on my conscience alone."

Jonathan grimaced, looking as though he'd just been force-fed something awful.

"If it is any comfort," Heyer said, "we know these people experience the least amount of suffering possible. The shadows within The Never have no knowledge of their fleeting existence. The sacrifice they make is unknown to them, but promises their true selves a life without the horrors of a Feroxian invasion. Creating their reflection and erasing them… it is admittedly unfair, but it is the lesser of many evils. Allowing their existence within The Never to run its natural course—that would be true cruelty."

Jonathan glanced up to the alien, hesitance written on his face. "Do I want to know?" he asked. "What happens to everyone inside The Never if the gates aren't closed?"

"A slow degradation of existence," Heyer said. "You are familiar with thermodynamics. For a system to maintain order, energy must be expended. Without anything putting energy into the system, disorder increases. Within The Never, the external pressures of the natural realities bordering it accelerate the process. The structure of all things inside deteriorate from within, making it easier for the temporary bubble to be reabsorbed as the natural shape of all realities returns to equilibrium."

"But the people, the shadows created inside," Jonathan said, "what does that experience feel like to them?"

"Well, for obvious reasons, it is impossible for me to give a firsthand account. What I know comes from Mr. Clean's files, all of the research materials left behind by Nevric's team. We know the process takes its toll on the mental state first. The initial effects of the psychological deterioration are unique to the individual, but it always presents itself as an unhinging of the mind, a movement toward the individual's more intrinsic self-interests. As it continues, a depravity becomes inevitable. The physical state of matter follows shortly after. The sanity of all within is lost long before the physical world deteriorates."

Jonathan might have taken more time, pondered what he had learned, but Heyer's words jarred loose the last thing Rylee had told him in his garage. "Heyer," he said. "What happens to a person if they leave? If one of these shadows from The Never steps into the gates as it's closing?"

Heyer's eyes studied Jonathan knowingly. "Jonathan, tell me what you know. Since the moment events surrounding Rylee's arrival began to play out, every interaction you've had with her, every word she said. I need to hear everything."

CHAPTER TWENTY-EIGHT

LEAH WAS ANXIOUS as she waited for Paige to come back. She was already having reservations about allowing her friend to confront the mystery girl in Jonathan's bedroom, but Paige was so eager to involve herself.

She wasn't sure if creating tension would end well. She would have preferred to give Jonathan a chance to explain himself. Admittedly, she had a pretty good idea of how that strategy would play itself out if she confronted him directly: Jonathan, looking at the floor, saying nothing because he couldn't possibly explain, while Leah, unable to sever their relationship, attempted to reassure him that she wouldn't pressure him, that she would understand if he was keeping secrets from her.

How long could she realistically play that game with another girl in the equation? There was patience and then there was sainthood—at some point, being too good to be true would make her presence in his life suspicious.

Finally, Paige returned, stepping into the room and closing the door behind her. "Yeah," she said. "We do not like her."

"Oh," Leah said. "Maybe I should go home. I don't want Jonathan to think I put you up to this."

Paige looked at Leah, then groaned. "You're too easy on him. I'll be the snoop, but you have every right to feel lied to… I mean, even if maybe he wasn't lying."

Leah tilted her head curiously. "What do you mean he wasn't lying?"

Paige shrugged. "Okay, don't get me wrong. This is still weird. But…"

She paused, frowning. "Everything Rylee said kinda matched up with what Jonathan told you. I didn't get the impression she was lying. What is so annoying is that talking to her was a lot like talking to Jonathan. Whenever I asked her something she didn't want to answer, she just shut the conversation down. Then found an excuse to leave."

Paige bit her lip and flinched a bit like she was regretting something.

"What is it?" Leah asked.

"I may have been a bit bitchier than I'd planned."

Leah sighed. "So much for being subtle?"

Leah's phone vibrated in her jacket pocket. She reached inside, hoping for a message from Jonathan, saying he was heading home and wanted to talk to her. Unfortunately, the message she'd gotten was the opposite: a random, unknown number advertising carpet cleaning services in her area. Upon reading the screen, she had to make an active effort not to let Paige see the tremor it sent through her—this was The Cell's method of communicating to her that they had lost Jonathan's location.

If Jonathan was the typical subject Olivia's team investigated, this wouldn't be cause for alarm, just an unfortunate but expected setback. The difference was that Jonathan didn't have the training or means to circumvent their surveillance on him. If The Cell had lost him, there was a good chance he was lost for good—that today was the day he disappeared forever.

"I am going to run home for a bit," Leah said, keeping herself together. "Want to check on Jack. I'll be back later."

"I don't pretend to understand it," Jonathan said. "Once I understood that Rylee and I had overlapped before, the pieces came together. When we enter the gates, the one who brings The Never into existence initially only retains their memory up until the point that the other arrives. That was why I'd never even known Rylee was there the first time, let alone that we had fought two Ferox. My memories inside The Never stopped at the same moment hers began."

Heyer nodded knowingly. The alien's lack of reaction made Jonathan suspicious that Mr. Clean had had a pretty good idea of what had been going on since the first time they had been in contact. The computer had probably purposely postponed an explanation while waiting for instructions from Heyer about how to handle the situation.

"Quite the unfortunate turn of events," Heyer said. The alien paused uncharacteristically to press his palm against his forehead as though he were holding off an approaching migraine. "Forgive me, Jonathan. I am responsible for putting this in motion."

Jonathan's eyes drew down, part in sympathy for the stress Heyer seemed to be under, but more in confusion.

"What is most troubling, and at the same time irritating, is that I only know the half of it," Heyer said. "Even though I am the only one who could have caused this."

"I'm not following," Jonathan said. "It's obviously not ideal that one of us loses our memory, but it's hardly the end of the world."

The alien, palm still pressed to skull, shook his head. "Jonathan, this is important," Heyer began. "I need to know if it was you or Rylee who put forth the option to break the stones while making physical contact, instead of breaking them individually, as I taught you?"

Jonathan was caught off guard—struck by how much Heyer's question sounded more like an accusation aimed at Rylee. "It was mine…" He trailed off, a slight chill running through him. "No, it was Rylee's. She said it was what we had agreed. That crushing the stones simultaneously was the best we could come up with the first time."

"Do you doubt her now?" Heyer asked.

Jonathan was already asking himself the question. He got a familiar feeling then, as though he were in the principal's office covering for a classmate. He hadn't felt a moment of distrust, of malicious intention. She had not wanted to break the stones at all. If anything, Jonathan had gotten the impression that Rylee had wanted to, well, do the opposite of what he'd have called *harm*.

"What she said seemed..." He stopped then, and shook off his doubts. Rylee simply did not feel guilty, and Jonathan's features hardened as he decided the matter. The only reason he thought otherwise was because of the way Heyer was asking him these questions. "No. Nothing she told me felt dishonest. Destroying the stones as we did seemed pretty reasonable given what you let me believe up until about half an hour ago."

Heyer studied him for a moment. Eventually his lips pinched together and he nodded. "It isn't my intention to shift accountability, and I'm not looking to put Rylee under your suspicion," he said. "But I need you to look at events, knowing things may not have been what they seemed. It is as I said, Jonathan; I suspect that I put this in motion, and right now, the challenge is piecing together precisely how I did so."

It was the third time the alien had taken responsibility for a problem that Jonathan didn't understand. He could see Heyer was beating himself up about something.

"Rylee and I," Heyer said. "We have a flawed relationship, at best."

"I would point out," Mr. Clean interjected, "that this is an understatement."

Somewhat annoyed, Heyer nodded in concession to the computer. "The failure is more my fault than hers. I misjudged her from the start, handled our interactions poorly. As a result, I have never trusted her enough to tell her anything more than what was absolutely necessary."

"Yeah, I caught that," Jonathan said. "You two aren't buddies, but are you saying her dislike of you is so strong that she is out to get you?"

"I have reconstructed her movements prior to her arrival," Mr. Clean said. "Within two days of her last engagement in The Never, she left Manhattan. Her route was a straight shot across the country, straight to you, Jonathan."

Heyer tapped his knuckles against the seat of his chair thoughtfully. "*Gnothi seauton*," Heyer said. "It's Latin—do you know its meaning?"

"Know thyself," Jonathan replied.

Heyer smiled, that look of an approving professor on his face again. "So quick. An aphorism you came across in your studies?"

Jonathan's face squirmed a bit as he weighed telling the truth against letting the alien believe he had learned it through a more scholarly endeavor. "It may have been mentioned in *The Matrix*," he said. "My roommate had to pause the movie, went on this long rant about how it's originally some Greek…"

As Heyer's eyebrow raised, Jonathan trailed off. *I am officially spending too much time with Hayden,* he thought.

"It's not important. What does knowing yourself have to do with Rylee?"

"I never told her to come here, Jonathan," Heyer said. "It just so happens that if there is anywhere on Earth I would *not* send her, it would be here… especially right now." Heyer turned his palms up and spread his hands. "Yet, where does she show up?"

Jonathan's features became heavy then, realizing his own poor judgment. Obviously, there was a lot he hadn't thought to ask Rylee, but, *what are you doing here?* That was a question that should have occurred to him. Being honest with himself, he knew why he hadn't thought to ask. He hadn't cared. Rylee's presence had suddenly meant he was no longer isolated and alone. Despite the challenges, the relief of having someone around who knew what he went through had been blinding. But Heyer wasn't questioning Jonathan's self-knowledge—he was questioning his own.

Understanding this, Jonathan finally saw what Heyer had been pushing him toward. There had been a time, back when the alien first entered his life, that their relationship had been 'flawed' as well. Jonathan, seeing Heyer as his enemy, had put his focus on finding a way out. The obstacle was that the alien himself was the gatekeeper of any information that might have helped him manage it.

Rylee, it seemed, had chosen to stay the course, escape above all else, and it had led her here. He saw, now, how it was that she had managed it. Heyer had always had a weakness. The alien had made no effort to conceal it those months ago while he sat with Jonathan on that park bench.

Rylee hadn't overlooked his weakness—and she'd used it to deliver a solid kick to the alien's proverbial balls.

"Ahhh," Jonathan said, half laugh and half exhalation, making no effort to hide how impressed he was with Rylee's maneuver.

It was a reaction Heyer clearly didn't appreciate.

"So, in her last confrontation, you visited her, and she got your shadow to say something he shouldn't have before she closed the gates," Jonathan said. "Something that led her to me."

Heyer nodded.

"And you don't have a clue what you said." Jonathan was failing to keep the amusement off his face.

"You are taking this far less seriously than you should," Heyer said.

"What happened to appreciating my sense of humor?"

Heyer's look of disapproval dropped away momentarily. "If you appreciate humor, perhaps you'll enjoy irony," he said, a smile of his own breaking the tension. "I would invite you to ask yourself what Rylee knows about you that you don't know yourself. For instance, what you may have said or done in her presence within The Never during the overlap you cannot remember."

Jonathan's smile dropped as he saw Heyer's point. "Dammit."

"Precisely. Now, you have to ask yourself—what state were you in before the breach opened that day? Being who you were in that moment, could your actions or words have been compromising? What did the two of you experience within The Never, and how may that have affected what played out? But, all you can do is guess. Only Rylee knows the truth of it.

"For my part, I at least, have an idea of what I must have said to her to lead her here. But no idea what degree of detail my shadow went into, or how he could have possibly believed it wise to do so. Whatever it was, I can only hope that my knowing that she has managed it before will keep me wary of any interactions with her moving forward. However, we need to find out precisely what she knows, and how she managed to get that information from me." Heyer shook his head.

Jonathan found himself pressing his palm to his forehead. He had been careful in his interactions with Rylee, on guard with his words. Hadn't he? At least, the interactions he remembered. It occurred to him, then, as he found himself growing paranoid, that he still didn't really buy into Heyer's thinking. He didn't believe that Rylee had orchestrated all this with some malicious plan in mind. Frankly, Heyer's behavior had a familiar feel—like that of a worried parent trying to control a rebellious teenager.

"Heyer," Jonathan said carefully. "Is it possible that you've played these games so long, that you are assuming Rylee is playing against you? Don't you think you should give her the benefit of the doubt?"

To this, Heyer raised a curious eyebrow, a look that was quickly followed by a glance to Mr. Clean. The alien drew in a pensive breath before his eyes went back to Jonathan. "I'm listening," Heyer said. "What is it you're getting at?"

Jonathan tensed, given he clearly didn't know all the specifics, but he spoke his mind. "I didn't trust you when we met, for obvious reasons. Trust is hard to give when you know someone isn't telling you everything—when you know you only have half the picture. You can't help but try and protect yourself from being manipulated."

"Fair enough, but what is it you are proposing?"

"Why don't we just tell her the truth, all of it?" Jonathan said. "Then, and only then, do we ask her for the same."

Heyer, much to Jonathan's growing annoyance, exchanged another unexplained look with Mr. Clean.

"Sir, for the sake of playing Devil's advocate," Mr. Clean said, "he is not wrong."

Jonathan hadn't expected the computer to take his side, and hearing that he wasn't dismissed out of hand brought some relief.

"Still," Mr. Clean said. "The fact that Jonathan's emotional state has been compromised calls his judgment into question."

Jonathan looked up, his temporary relief vanishing as he narrowed his eyes at Mr. Clean's monitor. "Wait, my what now?"

"This may all be rather moot," Heyer said. "The consequences of Rylee's actions could already be irreversible regardless of what her intentions may have been."

"What is irreversible?" Jonathan asked. "What do you mean I'm comprom—"

"Still, perhaps Jonathan's approach will sway her to fall in line," Heyer said.

"We need to establish if she can be trusted, and we must do it quickly," Mr. Clean replied. "Given the compatibility deficiencies with the alternate candidates for Rylee's device, we should not delay retrieving her implant for relocation. We may need to test the device in multiple women to find a replacement that can survive the implant—"

Having his questions ignored had been irritating, but the conversation they were having without him had just taken a disturbing turn. Jonathan was well aware of what happened to someone when their device was retrieved. Mr. Clean was talking about executing Rylee in order to take back the implant.

The second Jonathan understood that much, breakers blew inside of him. "Replaced?" He was yelling, suddenly on his feet, fury in his eyes as he headed toward the monitor. "What do you mean replaced?" Jonathan reached for Mr. Clean's face.

He felt a powerful grip on his shoulder stop him before he got his hands on the monitor. "Jonathan," Heyer said. "Look at me."

Jonathan's gaze shifted to the alien's hand on his shoulder, his anger beginning to re-target itself on the obstruction keeping him from tearing Mr. Clean's face off the wall. "Get your hand off of me," he said, his voice deadly serious.

"Jonathan, you need to get control. You aren't yourself right now."

"No one," Jonathan said, his voice an icy whisper, "is getting replaced."

"Breathe, Jonathan. Please."

"What aren't you telling me?" Jonathan asked through clenched teeth. "What the hell is he talking about? How am I emotionally compromised…?"

Jonathan trailed off as he put voice to the question. Despite his rage, he was suddenly well aware that something was very wrong. He felt out of control—the only thing giving him a moment's reprieve was recognizing it. Jonathan hadn't ever gotten this angry this quickly, not since…

Bleeds the Stone.

Jonathan shut his eyes and managed to take a step back. He tried to breathe as Heyer had asked him, but the distance between him and calm seemed too far—too much of him didn't want control back.

"Rylee is perfectly safe, Jonathan. No one will harm her," Heyer said. "Mr. Clean has poor etiquette when he voices *every* possible option—it is one of the many reasons I did not want him to be the one to explain this to you."

Jonathan heard the alien, but his hands were still shaking with the desire to rip the monitor from the wall.

"You have my word, Jonathan," Heyer said.

Jonathan didn't open his eyes, but nodded.

"I am very sorry, Jonathan," Mr. Clean said, his voice truly sounding like he bore a guilty conscience.

Heyer sighed. "Take a moment to calm yourself. You will get your answers."

He managed to force himself to comply, against the wishes of the clouding anger. As it began to fade, a part of him surfaced, his intuition screaming in alarm the same way it had when he first felt Rylee's emotions within him. Alarms screaming that strings were being pulled inside him—unnatural strings.

Jonathan slowly returned to his chair in a perplexed shamble, took his seat, and stared at the rug. "I was ready to tear this place apart. Why?"

"I need you to finish your story, Jonathan," Heyer said. "I promise I will explain. But I need to hear the rest if I am going to truly gauge the degree of the side-effects you may experience."

CHAPTER TWENTY-NINE

"BEFORE YOU CAME into contact with Rylee inside The Never," Heyer said, "when you were activated and realized that two Ferox were present, was there anything that seemed abnormal?"

Jonathan raised his eyebrows and nodded. "The activation itself. I remember feeling the transition came on me faster. When it finished, it seemed more whole somehow. The thing is, I had never felt incomplete prior to that—only now that I've felt the difference could I tell you that the device had been holding back."

Heyer nodded. "Go on. What else was different?"

Jonathan sighed. "Since we last spoke, I've felt stronger with every activation. I didn't think about this much because it wasn't unexpected—you had already told me that the more I train in my natural state, the stronger I would be when I was activated. But with Rylee, there was something else, something far more. When I fought *Bleeds the Stone,* it was almost..."

Heyer's eyes had narrowed in recognition of the Ferox's name, causing Jonathan to pause. "I knew of him," Heyer explained. "But continue."

Jonathan's face contorted with effort. "It's a bit like trying to see a memory through a fog of rage. *Bleeds the Stone*—he was probably weakened, having been at the center of that explosion. Still, he was easily the biggest Red I have encountered."

Heyer nodded his agreement. "You are not mistaken. *Bleeds the Stone* was on the cusp of full maturity. He has killed many."

"Thing is, it didn't make any difference. I punched holes in him with every strike, bent his arm back like I was wrestling a child." Jonathan swallowed. "Look, there might be nothing to gain in dissecting this, because I don't want to let over-confidence lower my guard. But—"

"He was no match for you," Heyer finished for him.

Cautiously, Jonathan nodded, and Heyer sat back into the chair, his knuckle brushing against his lips as he thought.

"Jonathan, I understand the difficulty of staying centered in a fight. It's often difficult to recall exactly what caused you to react as you did. Still, do you remember if that strength had a trigger—what was it that brought on this 'fog of rage'?"

Jonathan grimaced, finding that the memory still disturbed him. "I couldn't feel Rylee moving. I thought she was dead. Heyer, I don't remember thinking much afterward. I went somewhere..." Jonathan hesitated, seeming to lack the words to explain, and closed his eyes before he tried. "It was dark, Heyer. I've been angry before, but *Bleeds the Stone* was the first time I ever made one of them suffer any longer than he had to."

The alien nodded sympathetically. If Heyer was judging him for what he'd confessed, Jonathan didn't see it on his face. "Afterward, Jonathan. Specifically, the moment you returned from The Never and found your memory intact," Heyer said. "Was there nothing you've not yet told me?"

Jonathan frowned—he'd neglected to recount that moment in his story. It surprised him. He seemed to have unconsciously passed over the intrusion of Rylee's emotions inside of him when he had returned. Admittedly, he'd been more concerned with lost memories, keeping her from The Cell's ears, and the news that a man—a shadow from within The Never—had entered into the sphere before the gates were closed. How odd a thing for him to have left out.

No, Jonathan thought.

A moment's reflection and he understood why he'd done it; that this was hardly the first time he had glazed over certain details of his life when speaking to Heyer. He had never mentioned Leah, or his roommates, his job, or his family either. They were separate—he'd had to keep a wall between all things alien and everyone he cared about.

Intimate moments—what he had been sharing with Leah before he was activated, or what he knew to be Rylee's worst moment of weakness—they weren't his to share, didn't belong to him alone, and were the last thing Heyer should need to know about. So, in a manner of speaking, he had misfiled that moment with Rylee to the off-limits bin. Realistically, he saw the necessity of telling Heyer the truth now. They had reached a need-to-know moment, but he wasn't going to share any more than was necessary unless he saw a damn good reason.

More curious to him now, was that Heyer had known to ask.

"Yes," Jonathan said, and Heyer's head tilted forward in interest. "I can't really do it justice with words. More like a hallucination, or an emotional acid trip. Rylee was there, somehow, in my head—or for a moment I was inside her's. It was brief, temporary, but I knew who she was. Not her memories, not even her thoughts exactly. More like I understood what it felt like to be her. But it was only a snapshot, too cluttered and confusing in my head. Like I'd lost track of myself, couldn't tell what was her or me. I saw images, things that seemed to have meaning for her, but I didn't know why, couldn't be sure I knew the story behind their significance."

Heyer leaned back slowly in his chair, watching Jonathan as he absorbed what he had said.

"It put me on the floor. It was very... " Jonathan swallowed. "Intimate."

"Well," Mr. Clean said. "That does sound like a form that the experience might take."

Heyer nodded, his gaze coming to rest on the floor.

"Anyone want to let me know why this is what we're focused on?" Jonathan asked.

Heyer looked to the computer and nodded. "Yes. It's why we are here, after all. Excuse me a moment. I need to retrieve something."

Heyer rose from his chair, walking over to the large vault-like door Jonathan had noticed when they had first entered. Taking a better look at it now, Jonathan thought it belonged in a museum next to a steam engine. It looked like it had been taken off the front of an antique gun safe and mounted into the wall.

As with everything else inside Mr. Clean, the vault door was a functional facade, and the door opened for Heyer as he approached. The safe's interior betrayed no neglect as far as the illusion went, though it was a far more expansive chamber than he had expected from the outside. When Heyer stepped inside Jonathan was forced to lean forward in his chair, only able to see one of the side walls. There were rows upon rows of strange stones, each about the size of his palm, nestled equidistantly from one another within the flat iron surface of the walls.

What purpose could a safe door have in here? Jonathan wondered as he took in the illusion. Why make it stand out as something he wanted locked away when the contents were already as safe as they could have been inside Mr. Clean?

"Any standard device will suffice, Mr. Clean," Heyer said.

One of the stones nearest the alien came forward from the wall, pushed toward Heyer on a small metal rod until he reached up to free it. The rod then retracted back into the wall, leaving an empty socket in place of the stone. Jonathan noticed that there were a number of absent spaces like this one, the empty slots spaced seemingly at random along the portion of the wall he could see. As Heyer left the chamber, the heavy door began to close slowly behind him.

The alien held the stone out to him then. Close up, he saw it had a trilliant cut shape, though the edges were curved and smooth. It was made mostly of a polished, black material, but had thick metallic lines embedded on the outer surface. With the device so close, he could see that the silvery shine could not be attributed completely to metal catching the light, but also a faint white glow emanating off the lines. Jonathan knew what he was looking at, having seen a similar symbol glowing on his chest every time he was activated. This design was almost the same, but lacked the middle line that crossed over his chest.

"This is standard human male implant in its dormant state. This model is less advanced than your own, though it was built around the same era," Heyer said.

He placed the device on the table beside the spinning hologram of the gateway. Jonathan stared down at it, trying to comprehend how this insignificant-looking object became a biological weapon—a piece of technology advanced enough to mimic a man's cellular structure and give him the strength to fight nightmarish monsters from another dimension. He looked away when the clank of the safe's steel door finally locking broke the silence. That chamber—it had held hundreds of these devices. Such a small thing that could destroy the lives of those who had to bear them so that they might protect the lives of everyone else.

"I am sure, by now, that you have wondered, Jonathan," Heyer said. "Why mankind? Of all the planets and species, my brother set his eyes on Earth when the Ferox faced extinction."

Jonathan had pondered the question frequently, but as with everything else he didn't know, he was reduced to speculation. Still, he felt one thing had been certain. It could be no coincidence—no astronomically incalculable bad luck. There had to be a reason that the planet Heyer called home was the only one his brother had seen fit to target.

"From what little you've told me about your brother, I had assumed he'd chosen mankind because we reminded him of his own species."

Heyer's eyes became sad, thoughtful. "Perhaps. You are correct in seeing how he rationalizes the action. But no, I do not believe my brother would threaten my home world using *prejudice* as his justification if there were a feasible alternative."

The alien returned to his chair, and Jonathan waited for him to explain.

"Mankind was the only species we were able to turn into a worthy adversary, strong enough to confront the Ferox in battle," he said. "After the extinction of our ancestors, my brother and I did not possess the means to enhance the biology of any other species."

Jonathan glanced away from Heyer to the stone now resting on the table. Up until now, he had thought of the device as mankind's one weapon, the only thing allowing them hope of fighting the impending Feroxian invasion. If Heyer was saying what he thought he was saying, then the reality was the complete opposite—the existence of these implants was what had made mankind a target in the first place.

"Never trust a man with power unless he is smart enough not to want it," Jonathan whispered.

The alien nodded, glumly acknowledging the appropriateness of Jonathan's quoting his own words back to him. "Rylee being here, now, was never my intention. I doubt she purposely set out to hurt mankind, but she has unknowingly taken what I had hoped to be a future advantage and turned it into an immediate problem. To understand, I have to tell you about a dark period in the Borealis history…" Heyer paused. "There are decisions you will need to make. Knowing the truth is the only guidance I can give you."

CHAPTER THIRTY

"LONG BEFORE I came to Earth, before Malkier set out to save the Ferox, we were archaeologists of our own species, excavating what was left behind by our ancestors. We searched for survivors, of course, but as you know, we never found any. Hundreds of settlements throughout the dimensions were abandoned. One was here, in the home dimension of mankind. At the time, we never could have imagined that what we uncovered there would lead us here," the alien said.

"Heyer?" Jonathan interrupted. "How many of your kind were there? Before the extinction, I mean."

"Billions."

"How?" Jonathan shook his head. Though he wished he could muster more sympathy, his mind filled up with questions. "How does a species so advanced, so spread out, just go… extinct?"

Heyer exhaled a long thoughtful breath. "It is fortunate you only ask how. If you had asked me *who* or *why*, I would have no answers for you. My brother and I have searched for thousands of years, and we have found no trace of who was responsible or why they committed genocide. All I have to show for our search is a trail of dead-ends and an absurdly hard-learned lesson."

Jonathan's eyebrows drew down. "Lesson?"

"That safety is an illusion. No matter what amount of power you possess, there is no strength without inherent weakness. No such thing as invincibility. You see, the Borealis were spread out over multiple dimensions and planets; their technology made the species, as a whole, take immortality for granted. They were the first beings to rise to such a state of mastery over nature, and as far as I know, the last," Heyer said. "Yet, the entire population was decimated in a single moment. Billions, reduced... to a mere two."

Heyer shook his head. "To this day, I cannot wrap my mind around the magnitude of the tragedy. It is a date, the words *'Billions dead'* written into a historical record. I was too young to know what I lived through—my brother was not so fortunate." Heyer grew quiet for a moment then, realizing he had digressed from what was important. "The point is, for so many to suddenly die off in unison, the only plausible theory was that there existed some viral weapon. Something designed to lay dormant and undetected until triggered throughout the entire population in unison, something targeted to a universal trait in all the Borealis. The profoundly disturbing part of this is that in all our records and exploration, Malkier and I have never found another lifeform with the technological capability to create such a weapon. Therefore, the means to kill our species could only have originated from within."

Jonathan listened to the alien's explanation, trying to imagine how his own species might meet a similar fate. The question he could not have answered was what could possibly lead any one person or group to decide, for all of mankind, that it was their sole decision whether the species lived or died? What could possibly convince someone that so much power belonged in their hands? What could possibly convince them to use it? What madness would that person have to believe?

"No one claimed responsibility?" Jonathan asked, a disbelief he hadn't anticipated finding its way into his voice. "How could there not be a single record left behind?"

Heyer's jaw clenched and Jonathan wondered if the question had sounded more offensive than he meant it; but slowly, the agitation left the alien's eyes.

"I apologize for my reaction, Jonathan. It is a fair question," he said. "But, as I already said, who and why remains a mystery. I admit, the failure to answer those questions has weighed on me longer than you've lived, with all due respect—longer than you can imagine. Picture, for a moment, standing in a cemetery of victims, knowing every corpse beneath you is an unsolved crime that chance put into your hands to solve. Now imagine living thousands of years without being able to accomplish this one task."

There was a long pause before he spoke again.

"You asked about records. Unfortunately, it was never a matter of simple research," Heyer said. "The Borealis were quite similar to Man in that they had conflicting ideologies, wars over resources, politics, religion, and historical animosities. But what transgression could lead one group or individual within a society to decide that every member of their species, including the perpetrator, owed their lives? This weapon spared no one, including those who had not yet been born. Knowing this, you see that only the deeply disturbed remains. My best guess is this was set in motion by a very small group, or perhaps one incredibility cowardly individual." Heyer raised his palm in a gesture of admitted defeat. "Eventually, we ran out of clues—Malkier and I had to accept that there were things we may never know."

"Heyer… " Jonathan, looking down at the floor, blinked in disbelief. "If mankind started dying tomorrow, there would be mountains of information left behind. Newscasts, internet posts, newspapers—video footage uploaded to YouTube, if nothing else. How could there have been nothing?"

"Ahhh," Heyer said, nodding. "Yes, I suppose that by describing the deaths as viral, it gave the impression of a plague, people falling victim to a disease. This was not a virus of simply a biological nature. My species died as one; in a shared instant. No one was there to document the event itself. Malkier and I were not even conscious when it occurred."

Jonathan's eyes fell to the floor, a look of suspicion creeping into his eyes.

"I didn't tell you all this to give you a mystery to solve, Jonathan," Heyer said. "The extinction itself had conse—"

"How is it that you and Malkier were spared?" Jonathan asked.

Heyer paused at being interrupted. A silence fell between them and seemed to lengthen until Heyer grasped where Jonathan's persistence came from.

"You think it Malkier's doing? Is that what you are getting at, Jonathan?"

"You said it had to have come from within. That only leaves two suspects. If I was a detective, it would seem a fair question."

"No, it's naive. Surviving a genocide is hardly evidence of orchestrating it." Heyer held Jonathan's eyes, allowing a moment to pass. "My brother's actions have placed him into the role of mankind's enemy, so I understand how easy it is to cast Malkier as a monster capable of any atrocity. But, if you want to understand the truth, you will have to resist the urge to see whatever suits you."

Jonathan blinked, unsure if the alien had intended to sound so disappointed. "All right, so how exactly am I misjudging the situation?"

The alien leaned forward and rested his elbows on the chair. "My brother's attitude toward man grew over thousands of years, taking root long after our ancestors were gone. When we were young, this part of him was only a shadow. He would not yet have had the desire nor the means to put such a tragedy in motion. It was the history he lived through that led my brother to hate his own species. To him, humanity is a mirror, and he does not wish to catch a glimpse of his reflection. That is the irony of hatred—it turns a blind eye when you run the risk of becoming the very thing you despise. Malkier, unfortunately, does not care for such introspection."

Jonathan nodded, seeing the glaring flaw in his suspicion, but Heyer's explanation still left his question unanswered. "So then, how is it that only you two survived?"

"As I mentioned, the virus was not explicitly of a biological nature. There was not anything different about my brother or I on a genetic level that would have protected us from a targeted plague. Only one unique circumstance applied to us."

He stood, removing his coat and folding it over the back of his chair. With the outer garment removed, the three parallel lines of yellow light running along Heyer's chest showed bright beneath his shirt. Then he reached for the device he had placed on the table earlier. He sat back down, and held the dormant implant up between them.

"I told you once, that this was an antiquated relic from my species' history," he said. "Its very existence reflects a mark of shame on my kind. These implants were intended to protect life, but under the control of the wrong people, they became the chains of enslavement—an implement of cruelty. You see, this device in my hand was altered. It now only functions in a human—and not just any human, but a genetically compatible male. The implant you see activated within my chest is not bound by any such limits."

"Why are they so different?"

"It would be like comparing a tape cassette player to an iPod. The device within me is hundreds of years more advanced, capable of functioning in all species known to the Borealis prior to their extinction, regardless of sex or genetic compatibility. It has no need for the presence of an energy source, as it produces power to function on its own." Heyer looked down at the implant resting in his palm. "In contrast, this requires the presence of an energy signature, which you have seen an example of in the portal stone brought through by the Ferox."

Heyer hesitated then, giving Jonathan an appraising look, seeming unsure of how he may react to what he was about to say.

"Perhaps you already suspected, but the body you see before you is not the one I was born in," Heyer said. "In order to hide amongst Man, and for my brother to hide amongst the Ferox, we have each had to take bodies from members of our surrogate species. The man I inhabit now belonged to an American who died, for all intents and purposes, in an overseas conflict roughly twenty years ago."

Jonathan nodded. Heyer was correct in that this came as no surprise to him. Months earlier, after the alien revealed that Malkier had taken the body of a Ferox Alpha to secure leadership on the Feroxian plane, Jonathan had assumed that Heyer must have had to make similar accommodations. Still, there was some relief in knowing that the body he inhabited had been borrowed from a dead man, not taken against a man's will.

"My birth body was left behind lifetimes ago. Who and what I am is contained within my device. You might say I am no longer a self-sustaining life form, but a parasite. It is in this way that Malkier and I can live as long as we do," Heyer said. "As long as this device functions, and my body remains intact, our lives go on indefinitely."

Jonathan looked to the glow emanating from within the alien's chest with confusion. He didn't see the connection, didn't understand why the alien felt he needed to know these things at all. "What is it you're getting at, Heyer?" he asked. "If it's obvious, I'm not seeing it."

Heyer nodded. "Every Borealis was implanted with a device such as this shortly after birth, Jonathan. It made our species strong, resistant to the normal degradations of age, and very difficult to kill. Prior to the extinction, no Borealis had fallen ill from an infection in hundreds of years. The device in my chest was the last model ever designed by the Borealis. Only two were ever implanted. What I am saying is, the weapon that killed the Borealis attacked the entire species by leveraging a weakness in the devices installed throughout all of them. Whatever weakness the virus exploited in the older models, it was not able to target Malkier or myself. It is this sole difference that spared us. I am alive today, it seems, because of something as simple as a software update."

They sat in silence for a while, Jonathan processing everything he'd learned.

"Why only two?" he finally asked. "It seems strange, that you and your brother were singled out for the upgraded device."

Heyer nodded. "There is an explanation, Jonathan," he said. "But, you will not require it to understand what I need to tell you. Suffice to say, my brother and I were chosen because of who our father was—but being selected was not the type of thing one considered an honor. Quite the opposite. It is not something I wish to speak of with you or anyone else."

Reluctantly, Jonathan nodded. Heyer had refused to tell him a lot of things since they had met. This was the first time Jonathan felt he had no right to push.

Heyer placed the dormant device back on the table. "Anyways, how the Borealis went extinct is not our concern. It is the consequences of their extinction that you need to understand."

Peter had been standing right in front of her the night he'd disappeared. He'd been yelling at her. "Leah, dammit! Would you just leave it alone?"

Her brother was like all the others who'd come in contact with The Mark—defiant, but afraid, up until the moment he was lost.

"You can't help me," he'd said.

Those words turned out to be last her brother had ever said to her—the last he said to anyone. Then, as though Leah had blinked and he was no longer there, Peter was gone. But Leah hadn't blinked. She'd been staring unshakably back at her brother as he told her to "leave it alone," and the next moment, there was empty space, nothing but the white wall that had been behind him. She had found herself alone in his empty apartment, beginning to tremble. She had known for some time that he wasn't telling her something, that he had been hiding whatever it was that caused him to spiral into depression in the months leading up to that moment. She hadn't had a clue.

When she revisited the memory, the sounds were the worst. First, that terrible silence as she began to fill up with fear. When the tears began, she couldn't remember the rhythm of breathing, could only draw in desperate chokes of air between fits of crying. Hearing those cries creeping in on her from in her memory always brought back a sense of that awful debilitation. She'd never grown immune to it.

It could cut her down, and Leah repeatedly had to remind herself that she'd made a contract with her emotions—a restraining order. She would not acknowledge that grief had any claim on her. She would make no peace and no compromises with it. Until she had the alien in front of her, heard from his lips what had happened to her brother, there would be no giving in.

Leah knew there were only two possibilities. Her brother was either trapped or dead. If he was dead, then she would let the pain have its way with her, but she would not waste a single moment on remorse if it kept her from doing the one thing she could. Leah was never going to *leave it alone*.

As she made her way down the stairs from Paige's bedroom, her brother's defiance and fear were her own, and they pleaded for her to act.

She had not been able to get her brother to tell her the truth before it was too late, and she couldn't let that story repeat with Jonathan. So, she told herself that The Mark did not have her permission to take him. She ignored the whispers that told her she was hiding behind bravado, the very idea that these things were outside her control. The text from her phone told her that The Cell had not been able to reestablish his location for over a half hour. Olivia's team did not realize that message translated into another meaning for Leah. It read: *Jonathan may now be with Peter—this may be the moment you fail them both.*

Every minute Jonathan's location remained unknown brought her closer to a moment she would not allow herself to experience. Leah had to hold that fear at bay—force herself to think things through. What could she do, here and now, to change this situation? How could she prove to herself that he wasn't truly gone?

Her mind grasped at improbable hopes. Jonathan was clever, and he had known he was under surveillance for a while now. He'd simply found a way to give Olivia's team the slip. The hope was useless though—no better than a penny tossed in a fountain. She remembered the state Jonathan had been in the night before. Trembling, clutching himself against her living room wall as though under some internal assault.

The whispers returned, telling her it was too big and beyond her to make a difference, to even understand. There was no way to know if he was in danger…

A thought struck home as she remembered the footage. *Maybe there was no way for her to know, but Jonathan had known when Rylee's life was threatened.*

Was it possible that this went both ways? If he'd been taken, if he had been harmed, would Rylee already be aware of it?

She was supposed to rendezvous with The Cell to plan their next course of action, but Leah had already decided not to follow those orders—not immediately. She ground to a halt before the front door and turned to the garage. If Jonathan was in trouble and Rylee had felt it—Leah could get it out of her. She would read it off the fear in Rylee's eyes just as she'd seen it in Jonathan's the night before.

She steadied herself in front of the garage door. She breathed, centering herself so that no one would suspect the growing storm of fear underneath her carefree smile, and she opened the door.

She found Rylee leaning beside Hayden on the washing machine. He was grinning and animated, excited about whatever they were talking about as Leah walked in on the middle of it.

"—Like sculpting, but with an arc welder and stee—" Hayden broke off, grinning when he saw her. "Hey, Leah! Guess your ears were burning."

"I've told you before, it's near impossible for me to manipulate your device," Heyer said. "The Borealis extinction left my brother and I bereft of the necessary knowledge to bypass the device's encryptions. We lack the expertise, and anyone who may have possessed it is long dead."

Jonathan nodded.

"That remains mostly the truth, but not the entirety. You see, when the Borealis died, certain fail-safes went into place."

"Fail-safes?" Jonathan asked.

"Have you seen a television or computer that had parental controls?" Mr. Clean asked.

"Sure."

"The network that links the Borealis' accumulated knowledge throughout the known dimensions went into a type of lock-down the moment our leaders began dying in droves. Specific types of information became inaccessible. The records we can access are what one might call 'safe for public knowledge,' those that remain irretrievable seem to be what the Borealis gatekeeper's thought too dangerous to leave unprotected," said Mr. Clean. "Much like the governing entities of Mankind guard the operational instructions of nuclear weapons, the Borealis locked down their accumulated knowledge on biological functions of all known species, archives on destructive weaponry, and dimensional manipulation. If this were not the case, then events would not have led to where we are today. If I had access to these records, perhaps I could instruct Malkier on how to set about repairing the Ferox biology. At the very least, I would be able to get around more of the encryptions placed on the human implants."

Heyer spoke up then. "As it is, Malkier and I found we had inherited our species' technology, but if the equipment we wished to use was deemed too dangerous during the lock down, we essentially had no user manual or access codes.

"You see, we have tried a number of alternative workarounds in attempting to make Ferox males fertile. Hormonal and genetic manipulation, hallucinogenic compounds, holographic and robotic combatants. In the end, we found that our ancestors had been far more effective at safeguarding their control over the Feroxian genome. Despite generations of Feroxian evolution since the Borealis died off, we have been unable to remove the hardwiring that forces their need for physical confrontation. We cannot be certain that the potential to reverse the process still exists within the gene pool."

Jonathan bit his lip. "So, when the Borealis altered the Ferox, they included traits that would safeguard the changes they made. They were trying to make it difficult for natural selection to ever rid the species of certain traits by chance."

"That is an accurate way of describing it," Mr. Clean replied.

"Which brings us back to today," Heyer said. "The safeguards on my ancestors' knowledge base proved themselves wise, but, ultimately, too little too late. Whoever was responsible for the extinction must have gained the skill and knowledge necessary to bypass the security protecting each Borealis implant. They used this knowledge to exploit a weakness that caused fatality in every implant installed throughout the species. However, the Borealis leaders never suspected an event as cataclysmic as what transpired was approaching. These lock-down procedures were in place long before."

"It's rather frustrating, for my part," Mr. Clean said. "Not unlike paralysis in a limb, I imagine."

Jonathan turned his attention back to the monitor and frowned. "I don't follow."

"It's the best analogy a man might relate to," Mr. Clean said. "I am intended, amongst many other things, to be a facilitator—a librarian of sorts—for a member of the Borealis seeking information. In that regard, it's as though I have limbs I cannot communicate with. I can send a request for information, but any inquiries for specific subjects go unanswered, as though I sent them to a place that no longer exists, never to receive a response from the network. I do not even know if the request was received."

Jonathan nodded. "You said there were consequences because of this. Consequence to Earth in particular?"

Heyer nodded. "Imagine you have accidentally left a child alone with your computer. With nothing to occupy himself, the child gets bored, and eventually starts using the machine. When you return, you find he has been on your computer for hours. What concerns come to mind from this scenario?"

The question was peculiar, but Jonathan humored the alien. "I'd be anxious. Who knows what the kid mucked up while he was screwing around."

"Exactly. It's a complicated piece of equipment that you need for certain things. You don't want to find that the child did something that will cause a problem."

Jonathan nodded.

"Now imagine that your computer is not a modern model. That it was some old relic, put together from spare parts, and running on a pirated operating system you don't have a backup for," Heyer said.

Jonathan sighed. "Well, then it would be worse. I couldn't get the computer back to its original settings if the kid had done something I didn't know how to fix. Why are we talking about a hypothetical child breaking an imaginary computer?"

Heyer pointed to the dormant device sitting on the table between them. "The human devices are much like that hypothetical computer. Mr. Clean and I are the child." Heyer pointed to his chest then. "The Borealis device in my chest is user-friendly. It doesn't require I get involved in the complexities of its operation. I can insert myself into any intelligent species I encounter, and the implant adapts on its own, not requiring me to do any adjustments beforehand for compatibility. Had this not been the case, then Malkier and I would not have survived the failure of our original bodies, as the A.I. on our vessels would be unable to adapt our implants for use in another species," he said, then nodded back to the dormant device. "The older they are, the more difficult they are to operate."

Jonathan nodded, starting to get an inkling of what the alien was getting at. "So, the device you are installing in men is old and complicated, something you are afraid to mess with. Because, once broken, you can't fix it."

Heyer nodded.

"So," Jonathan said, "don't screw with it?"

Heyer bit his bottom lip, looking pained. "In the end, that is not the point. The reason for the implant in my chest is clear—the existence of a Borealis implant requires no explanation. The question you should be asking is why my ancestors created an implant only meant to be installed in humans."

CHAPTER THIRTY-ONE

"SOME TIME AGO, Malkier and I excavated a planet in this dimension. It was the home of a sect of the Borealis that called themselves the *Foedrata.* Historically, this group was not regarded highly throughout the rest of the species," Heyer said.

"Why is that?" Jonathan asked.

"A difference of opinion would be putting it lightly. The Foedrata were the religious adherents to the teaching of a self-proclaimed prophet by the name of Foedras, from which the religion obviously took its name. Their religion proclaimed that the Borealis were born to be the caretakers of all realities, and its adherents weren't the type to entertain any arguments to the contrary. Similar sects were not unheard of in other dimensions throughout Borealis history, but due to the Foedrata's proximity to Earth, they had contact with humanity.

"Foedras saw that our species possessed great mastery over the environment, power inherited from centuries of technological innovation, but he did not accept this as merely the result of history. Foedras assumed this to be a predetermined fate—the birthright of all the Borealis. It was a view his followers perpetuated, indoctrinating in their children to accept generation after generation."

"To what end?" Jonathan asked. "I mean that isn't much to base an entire religion on."

"Foedras believed the universe had a conscious creator, and that this consciousness had put all that existed in motion for the very purpose of creating our species. He claimed that the Borealis were, in fact, the living embodiment through which this conscious creator would control all it had built—the idea being that all my ancestors, even those who did not adhere to his beliefs, were the vessels through which the creator divided itself. A belief that, in the end, justified seeing all other life as animals to rule over."

Jonathan raised an eyebrow. "Well, that would explain why they weren't regarded very highly. Hard to imagine how he was able to sway an entire planet to his way of thinking."

Heyer nodded. "Not as hard as it may seem. Once a belief such as this solidifies within the collective consciousness of a planet, it tends to become self-sustaining. The Foedrata quickly became closed off to ideas that would take away the belief by which they saw themselves as more valuable than others—to do so would call into question the wisdom of their decisions. To relinquish their beliefs would have left them accountable for justifying their actions to all those they had labeled as 'less.' That this value was artificial, awarded to them by none other than themselves, became easy to ignore.

"This sect's beliefs were historical remnants of the same period that saw abuses of other life, the genetic manipulation of the Ferox counted among them."

Jonathan turned up his palms. "The rest of the Borealis just allowed them to act on their beliefs?"

When Heyer responded, his expression had become burdened. "As mankind has come to find, there is a dilemma in purging destructive beliefs from society as a whole. To do so is to be guilty of the very thing you abhor: to conclude one view as superior to another's. By the end of their era, most of the Borealis were guided by logic, science, reason, and compassion. Still, they knew they could not decide for the rest of the species that the historical teaching of their parents, their culture, their very identity, lacked evidence to justify its continued existence."

"I get it," Jonathan said. "They couldn't force anyone to abandon their beliefs."

"No. All that the rest of the Borealis could do was intervene when necessary, try and ensure that the Foedrata's way of life was not allowed to harm others. However, this required a degree of vigilance they were not always able to enforce."

Jonathan nodded. "Okay, so the majority of your species compromised with a fanatical sect inside the population, and that sect's home planet shared mankind's dimension. What was it you found on their planet?"

"These," Heyer said, his open palm indicating the dormant device. "Hundreds of them."

Slowly, Jonathan returned his eyes to the implant resting innocently on the coffee table.

"The Foedrata, like the rest of the Borealis, upgraded their individual implants when newer models became available. The implant you see here was, at one time, installed in one of the Foedrata.

The picture this was giving Jonathan was getting disturbing. He closed his eyes and sighed. "It sounds like you are telling me that I have a hand-me-down implant that was originally installed in a Borealis religious zealot."

"That would be accurate," Mr. Clean said.

Jonathan grimaced, shutting his eyes and nodding.

"The encryption on these older devices was highly guarded, for obvious reasons. However, the Foedrata managed to bypass the security on the older models in order to repurpose them. How they did this, we do not know, but they were able to reprogram the device for implantation in a man, absent a Borealis host."

"Why? What were they using them for?" Jonathan asked.

Heyer's fingers tapped the arm of the chair, a moment of silence passing before he spoke. "I think it best, Jonathan, that you see it for yourself."

"Uh," Jonathan frowned. "Are you saying we're going to planet Foedrata?"

"No, that will not be necessary," Heyer said as he rose out of his chair and prompted Jonathan to do the same. "Mr. Clean, please access the records recovered from the Foedrata's mainframe."

"Which file?" the computer asked.

"Take us to the last recorded *Arena* event, involving the bonded pair," Heyer said. "Jonathan, you may want to prepare yourself—this will be disorientating."

The moment Jonathan nodded that he understood, the room began to shift around them. The surrounding walls and furniture temporarily shimmered away, leaving them in a void of black. Jonathan circled, finding that the alien's warning had still left him unprepared for the unsettling effect—it was as though he floated in complete darkness. He tried to remind himself that his environment was a fabrication, but his perceptions failed to keep up with him. Though his feet could feel the resistance of the floor, his sight was unable to perceive it, and he began to lose his balance.

He spun to Heyer, still standing a few steps away, and it gave him enough reality to center himself just as the void began to take shape. Jonathan's feet sank into soft, black sand as his balance adjusted to a graded slope. Light followed, emanating out from where the void met the sprawling creation of the landscape that had begun to spread from where Heyer and Jonathan stood. The bright glow was too much for his pupils to adjust to. He was already trying to see through narrowed eyelids when a massive column of light took shape in the sand in front of them, forcing Jonathan to raise a forearm over his eyes.

He felt a warm wind pushing past him, heavy with steam. It carried the scents of saltwater, wet ash, and a faint but unmistakable touch of Feroxian blood. His expression grew slightly repulsed by the toxic odor just as the light from the column dimmed down. Finding himself in the shadow of its solidified shape, he peered over his forearm, letting his eyes crawl up a monolithic pillar of jagged obsidian rock. It disappeared beyond a ceiling of turbulent clouds overhead. As he turned his gaze from it, he saw more of the columns taking shape further and further away, their lights coming and going, one after the other as the reach of the world spread into the distance.

Their arrangement was too evenly spaced and proportional to be natural, as though he were looking at a massive system of buttresses holding up a roof he couldn't perceive through the clouds above.

"Watch your step, Jonathan," Heyer said, stepping out of the pillar that had formed in front of Jonathan, as though it was not physical at all.

“This footage is partially interactive. Standing obstacles are only projections, but the topography on the ground behaves as the eye perceives it.”

Jonathan nodded, still taking in the strange, alien terrain.

A beach lay at his back. He would have thought it an ocean coast, but the water was stagnant and black like that of a swamp. A wall of fog only a short distance from the shoreline blocked whatever lay beyond. That fog wall, he realized, was a constant, encompassing all that he could see in a vast circle. As his eyes followed the boundary, he saw that it was not simply a circle, but a dome, and that he was standing near one of its edges.

Toward the center, after the beach ended, a maze-like wasteland of glassy black rock covered the terrain, until the edges of the fog dome stopped him from seeing anything beyond. There were distortions of the air over the rock, heat rising from the ground.

He turned to Heyer, ready for an explanation, but upon pivoting to find the alien, he was surprised by the sudden presence of a form taking shape. The screaming came upon him first, drawing his eyes to a savage face headed straight for him. He staggered back in dumbfounded alarm, his feet catching clumsily on some protrusion from the ground. Jonathan fell onto his back in the sand, and scampered away on instinct as the shape barreled toward him, his eyes focusing on the length of sharpened steel in its grip.

CHAPTER THIRTY-TWO

THE FORM RACED forward, overtaking Jonathan as he attempted to scuttle away on his back. When it had closed the distance, it headed straight at him. Its foot stepped through his chest as though he were a ghost. After passing over him, Jonathan rolled onto his stomach and watched it go, finally recognizing the shape of a woman receding away from him. She bounded off, sprinting with the speed and form of an athlete.

"I warned you to watch your step, but I would be lying if I said I did not find that amusing," Heyer said as he walked up beside him.

Feeling foolish for having been startled in a place with no real danger, Jonathan sighed, got to his feet, and began wiping the sand off his clothes. Though it had happened quickly, he had gotten a good look at the woman. She'd had crude, black smears across her face and carried the strong scent of Feroxian blood. The smears had been tar-like, and it occurred to him that she must have painted them on using the bodily fluids of a Ferox corpse. The smell was sickening, but the effect had been an excellent camouflage against the glassy black stone of this place.

Jonathan turned back to where he had stood a moment earlier and saw a metallic skeleton, half-buried in the black sands. He'd tripped over a large femur-like bone protruding from the surface. As he looked over the beach, he saw that the skeleton wasn't alone. This place, if anything, was a massive Feroxian graveyard.

"Did she kill all these?" he asked.

"No," Heyer replied, nodding in the direction the woman had run. "Not alone, at least."

The woman was crouching at the edge of the lake, searching its depths, when a man's face came out of the water. Upon seeing her, the man rushed from where he'd been hiding beneath the surface.

"Come, Jonathan," Heyer said, stepping toward the pair.

As they drew closer, he saw that the man's bearded face was also painted in blood. The pair wore strange armor, though Jonathan recognized its origin. They had fashioned it using a primitive twine to strap plates of Feroxian skin across their bodies—materials they had likely scavenged from the very corpses he was stepping over. The woman carried a sharpened bone fashioned into a spear, and a smaller hand blade made in the same manner. The man carried two crude axes; the handles were both made of Feroxian bone as well, but the heads were chiseled out of large chunks of the black rock from the terrain behind them. They both dropped their weapons before reaching one another.

What followed left Jonathan feeling as though he were a voyeur intruding on long-separated lovers. The two slowly knelt in the sand, each gently holding the other's face in their hands. They stared as though they desperately sought to be lost in each other's eyes. A peace settled over them—heavy burdens of worry and fear dropped away to be replaced with relief and joy the longer they looked upon one another. They spoke, and though Jonathan couldn't understand the words, he had no trouble knowing their meaning.

I feared I would never see you again.

He only watched a short time before turning away. This was not a moment they would have chosen to share with anyone if they had been given a choice. "Who were they?" he asked.

Heyer's mouth opened to answer, but a familiar sphere of light drew their attention before he spoke. The gates, opening far off in the center of the cloud dome. The portal manifested above one of the smaller plateaus of rock, its light casting everything it touched in red. He heard the couple behind him. They had begun to scream in an agony that few would recognize by sound alone: the burn of activation, driving their body to the most primitive state of expression. No matter what passage of time separated these two from him, he felt their pain as his own. He wished he could give them mercy from it—but all he could do was shut his eyes and wait for it to end.

Eventually they stilled, and a flickering of light came to life in their chests. Jonathan opened his eyes to see the lines glowing bright beneath the man's skin and saw they were identical to his own. The woman's implant had come to life as well. However, though Jonathan recognized the design from Rylee's implant, they were not the same. The power radiating off this woman was bright, the energy flowing through her as strong as the male's, nothing like the faint blue glow he'd seen beneath Rylee's skin inside The Never.

"These two…" Heyer said, "were the last of the bonded pairs."

"They haven't entered The Never, have they? All these Ferox bodies wouldn't be here if they had," Jonathan said. "So, what is this place?"

"This record nearly predates my lifespan, Jonathan. What you are seeing happened many millennia ago. The footage is from the Foedrata's Arena."

Jonathan felt a sickening inside of him as he began to understand. He turned to watch as the portal's passenger arrived. The red light grew agitated, the currents of static building into arcs as the shadow of a Ferox took shape within. The sharp, white light still forced his eyes shut despite the distance. When he opened them, he only caught a glimpse of the massive black beast as it leapt off the plateau.

He heard the murmurs behind him—the hushed tones of frightened human whispers. He turned to watch, and saw the pair were no longer on the ground. Their eyes failed to hide their fear. They held one another again, the glow of energy bright between them, until the woman pushed away, decisive and abrupt. The man grimaced because he knew she was right. *It was time.*

Jonathan watched the woman force the fear out of her eyes, saw her face harden into stone. The male, slower to get control of his fear, seemed to draw strength from her—his face dropped the look of self-pity for one of shared determination. She nodded once, sharply, and raised a hand up between them, violently pulling her fingers into a fist that shook her entire forearm. Her snarl broke the silence, and the man returned it.

Then she tore away from his gaze, the strength of the device giving her grace and speed as she bound in the direction of the Ferox.

"This arena was where the Foedrata watched one species fight for its life against another. It was a sick entertainment, but one that their beliefs told them they had every right to," Heyer said.

Heyer pointed Jonathan's attention to the male. The man had watched the woman set out. Now, he paced impatiently as he kept an eye on her movements. Finally, when it appeared he could not bear waiting any longer, he took off in the same direction after her.

"Most species brought here to be pitted against one another were novelties, never capturing the attention of Foedrata for long." Heyer paused. "Human beings were an exception."

Heyer watched as the man became smaller in the distance. Jonathan took a step, assuming they were meant to follow, but Heyer placed a hand against his chest to halt him.

"Unlike any other species in the history of the Arena, this event, in particular, was watched universally amongst the Foedrata. They called it the Battle of the Bonded Pair—it was a spectacle in short supply," Heyer said. "There were similar events, human males enhanced to face the younger Ferox, but the bonded pair were created to face the Alphas."

Jonathan, thinking Heyer had finished, tried to take a step forward to follow the man once more, but again, Heyer stopped him.

"The Foedrata had no need of chains to enslave the Ferox. The Feroxian beliefs had already been manufactured to ensure the species' servitude. Every Ferox had been raised to understand they were their gods' chosen people, that the males of their species were their gods' divine weapons, called to the gates to fight a battle of good and evil.

"The Ferox you fight today are still of this mind, and they take great honor in serving their gods' will—the Borealis' will. The Arena on the other side of the gates is a sacred battleground to them, where they prove their loyalty by slaying the abominations of existence."

"Abominations?" Jonathan asked.

"Those that the Ferox have been told were never meant to exist within their gods' great plan. You see, Feroxian vocabulary is not as nuanced as Mankind's. There's little difference in their understanding of the words *abomination* and *challenger*.

"In the creation story they have been indoctrinated with, the Ferox were once an abomination as well. In the beginning, their gods approached the early Ferox and offered to alter their nature, to turn them from abominations to a chosen people with a place in the divine plan. The gods required the Ferox serve them, by being their divine weapon against those abominations that refused to be altered to fit the divine plan. In exchange, they were told that the Ferox would one day be delivered to the promised land, where they would never need to fear extinction again. The abominations they kill inside the Arena are those the Borealis convinced them refused to be altered, abominations who challenged the will of their gods—who have refused the divine plan.

"Defeating these challengers was not a hard sale to the Ferox. They were rewarded for doing something that their gods had made it their nature to do regardless. Their victories against each abomination not only pleased their gods, but allowed them to achieve fertility and continue their lineage," Heyer said. "If you look around this beach, you will only find Ferox remains, because the Ferox took their human trophies back to their mates.

"A Ferox reaches full maturity through repeated sexual interactions, Jonathan. The males' development has three puberty-like stages, the first is similar to that in humans, beginning as a child comes of age. The other stages are set in motion when hormonal levels reach a threshold. This triggers the change from the Green and tailed form of their adolescence, to the more formidable Red. The changes are physical, but they have social rewards. Males are given higher esteem within the species as they mature through the stages, their physical form identifying their rank in the hierarchy. However, leading such violent lives by necessity, few ever reach final maturity, limiting the supply of full-grown Ferox males for the Arena."

"You mean the supply of Alphas," Jonathan said.

Heyer nodded. "The Alpha Ferox possess a strength and prowess in battle that makes achieving their reproductive state far more difficult. It also made their battles the most entertaining of spectacles to the Foedrata. Typical human male combatants, implanted with standard devices, were seldom strong enough to put up the necessary fight to properly stimulate an Alpha to reach fertility."

In the distance, the guttural growl of the Alpha roared and Heyer turned his gaze toward the battle.

"The Foedrata had a few solutions to this, the most popular of which was the bonded pair," Heyer said.

"We aren't going to follow them?" Jonathan asked. "The bonded pair fighting the Alpha—it isn't what we're here to see?"

Heyer turned back to Jonathan, his serious expression highlighting the importance of what would follow. "No," he said. "I have no desire to refresh my memory of it. I understand why you may think it educational to see, but I would spare you."

Jonathan hesitated only a moment before his curiosity heeded the warning in Heyer's eyes. The alien had been alive for thousands of years, fought in wars, and seen atrocities Jonathan could only imagine. Jonathan knew what it meant to witness terrible things, and how they changed a person, for better or worse, in ways they could not always control. It wasn't often one received a warning before exposing themselves to such things, and he didn't doubt the mercy Heyer was offering him now.

"Can you tell me..." Jonathan asked, "how they died?"

Heyer sighed, but nodded. "The bonded pair know from experience that the woman is faster than the man. So, she takes the lead, exposes herself, and pulls the Alpha into a long chase to drain its strength. Meanwhile, the man stalks them from behind. She lures the Alpha to a quarry where the contours of the land and narrow stone passages give their smaller size the greatest advantage.

"The plan has been effective for this pair in the past, and seems to work initially. The Alpha is caught off-guard and wounded, forced on the defensive. Unfortunately, the man sees victory early, misjudges their advantage, and attempts a killing blow.

"The Alpha is patient and cunning, not incapable of bluffing—as such he is not nearly as drained or injured as he appears. He foresees the male's actions. The battle turns rapidly when the Alpha's counterattack breaks bones, badly crippling one of the man's legs. The woman, desperate to save him, intervenes. She puts herself between them to draw the Ferox's focus on to her." Heyer sighed. "Come, Jonathan. I will tell you the rest below."

"Below?"

"Yes. Unforgivable as this all may seem, this is only the surface of what took place here."

Rylee didn't care for the emotions feeding into her thoughts. They were jealous and possessive, and she had never been either. She wasn't proud of it, but the moment Leah stepped into the garage, she felt that she wouldn't mind seeing her fall down the stairs.

What Hayden had told her about the next door neighbor had painted an absurdly inaccurate picture in her mind. In the picture, Leah had been a short girl—or at least noticeably shorter than Rylee herself. She'd had curly red hair and freckles. Her outfit had consisted of an oil stained jumpsuit, half-opened to reveal a Led Zeppelin T-shirt. In hindsight, Rylee realized she'd unconsciously pictured an adult orphan Annie with an unusual arc-welding hobby and a classic rock T-shirt collection.

For a moment, she wondered if Hayden's description had been intentionally misleading, but realized pretty quickly that he'd really only neglected the superficial details. Rylee had done all the misleading on her own. She'd filled in the blanks with what she hadn't realized were hopeful assumptions.

The real Leah—well, if Hayden had claimed she was Cindy Crawford's daughter, Rylee might have believed him. The girl's perfection rubbed her the wrong way. If this woman wore the oil stained jumpsuit from Rylee's imagination, she look like a runway model who wasn't afraid to get her hands dirty. If she listened to classic rock while melting steel into art, then—dammit—it just made her annoyingly interesting. It was like everything about her was an alluring contradiction to expectation.

Rylee's smile left her, and she looked away as Leah stepped down the stairs. She suddenly hated that she was wearing a man's tank top and that her hair had been in a helmet all day. More than all that, she hated that she was thinking about such things.

"I was just telling Rylee about how we live next door to a real-life metal artist," Hayden said, smiling. "You'll have to let us drop by your garage so she can see the sculptures some time."

Hayden's unexpected request to invite themselves over startled her. She had wanted to see the art a moment ago, had told Hayden the same, but that had been before she'd seen the artist. "Only if it isn't any trouble," Rylee said shyly.

Leah smiled and her face was warm and friendly. "Oh, I love your accent, Rylee," she said, holding out her hand. "You two can come by anytime. Just promise you'll talk my ear off when you do."

"I know, right?" Hayden said. "I'm considering moving to Brazil."

"Thank you," Rylee said as she took Leah's hand.

Leah smiled and held Rylee's eyes as she smiled back politely and shook Leah's hand. The exchange felt a bit long, though Rylee figured she was the only one noticing such things.

"Hayden," Leah said. "Any chance you heard from Jonathan? I had hoped he would be home by now, but he seems later than usual." Leah's eyes didn't actually leave Rylee as she asked the question. She wondered if the awkward feeling it gave her was real or imagined.

"I texted him a few times, but he hasn't gotten back to me," Hayden said. "You try calling him?"

"No, we had a... *strange*... evening last night," Leah said. "I thought it would be better if I caught him in person."

Rylee blinked. She felt the urge to narrow her eyes, curious to know what the woman meant by "strange," though she kept it from her face. "Well, join the club. I've been waiting to talk to him as well," Rylee said. "It was a *strange* evening."

Leah studied her again, and Rylee was beginning to lose any doubt that it was in her imagination.

"Right," Hayden said, drawing the word out and looking between them like he had missed something. "Um, I'll try him again. He's probably just working late and can't check his phone."

Finally, Leah seemed to drop the stare. If Rylee knew her better, she'd have thought the woman looked—relieved? She smiled at Hayden. "Yeah, probably."

Then the side door opened, and everyone turned to see Collin's head pop inside. "Operation Mission of Mercy is a go."

"Isn't saying *operation* and *mission* redundant?" Hayden asked.

"Operation of Mercy doesn't sound right."

"No, it would just be Operation Mercy or the Mission of..." Hayden shook his head. "Never mind."

"Well, anyway, has anyone heard from Tibbs? He isn't replying to my texts."

"Yeah," Hayden said. "Apparently, that's a thing today."

Leah looked to each of them, finally raising a curious eyebrow. "So what is Operation Mission of..." She grinned teasingly at Hayden. "I mean... what is *the Mission of Mercy*?"

"Rylee felt Jonathan needed an early birthday present," Collin said.

"Oh?"

Rylee shrugged. "More like a thank-you for loaning me a bed to sleep in."

She watched Leah fight the urge to flinch. She did almost manage it, only having given up a poorly timed blink at the mention of Jonathan's bed. Leah's mouth opened to say something then, but her phone vibrated before she spoke. She checked the message and sighed. "Well, it was good to meet you, Rylee," she said. "I've got to run, but I'll catch you all a little later."

Hayden found himself scratching his head. It felt more like he'd just been the spectator of a staring contest than a conversation, though the confusion he felt had a certain familiarity.

He had two older sisters, and they had both lived at home until each had left for college. At times, he'd find himself in the middle of a conversation, suspecting that the words being exchanged had nothing to do with what was actually being discussed. Perhaps it was a tension in the air, maybe it was the body language, or maybe the faint detection of a passive-aggressive kindness. He could never put his finger on it.

On Heyer's command, Mr. Clean returned them to the void. Jonathan experienced a moment of the previous disorientation before a corridor began to take shape around them. Lines recessed in the ceiling's corners illuminated the space around them. The walls reminded Jonathan of polished hematite. They were sterile, smooth, seamless—seemed too perfect, as though brought into existence without a living hand taking part in their construction.

"We're underneath the Arena?" Jonathan asked.

Heyer nodded. "The Arena itself is a massive environment projection. The bones of the Ferox were real, but the rest was artificial terrain for the combatants. What you saw above was a popular staging ground, for the Ferox and Human battles in particular, as it was designed to encompass a mix of atmosphere and geology from both species' habitats. When Malkier and I first found the Arena, it was dormant—a massive dome projecting nothing. We knew its capabilities, but not its purpose. It was in these tunnels that we recovered the Foedrata's records from the mainframe."

Heyer placed his palm onto one of the walls. The surface changed, the entire side of the corridor becoming transparent, forming a window which looked into a massive room on the other side. As Jonathan absorbed what lay within, his eyes grew heavy.

He may as well have been looking at a farm for poultry or cattle, though it was humans being kept as livestock. He only saw women, confined to small squares, each in some stage of pregnancy. There were no walls that he could see blocking one woman's cell from another. It was as if each small chamber was enclosed by glass. Their faces and clothes were dirty, and they sat on floors made up of a mix of soil and a dried, black plant life that reminded Jonathan of the bedding pet stores use for rodent cages. The inmates all seemed to gravitate to the corners of their stalls where they were closest to one another, despite whatever invisible barrier that kept them from making any physical contact.

With all the technology that the Foedrata had at their disposal, it was as though these women were placed into surroundings where they could never confuse their function.

"Why would they do this?" Jonathan asked. "Keep people here like livestock?"

"This was more efficient than returning to Earth to replenish their stocks. The popularity of the human combatants inside the Arena eventually led to the Foedrata abducting a greater sampling of mankind. They pulled men and women strategically from various locations on each of Earth's continents, enough to sustain their population and breed for desired traits. The strongest male progeny were kept in smaller numbers, enough that the Arena always had plenty of combatants, but also enough to ensure there would be no decline of quality stock due to inbreeding. The females better suited for producing were kept here."

He looked at the ground, then.

"My brother and I found only the dust left by their remains when we arrived," Heyer said. "At the Borealis extinction, these women and their unborn children died, trapped down here in the dark."

Jonathan turned away from the faces inside. The outrage he felt was so maddeningly irreconcilable and the criminals responsible were so far outside his reach. When his initial disgust passed, he was left with nothing but pity and sadness. "Why are you showing me this? If you wanted me to hate the Foedrata — it's done. I hate them. But what is the point if I can't do anything about it?"

"They are painful realities to absorb, and I am sorry you needed to see this," Heyer said. "I am showing you, so you know exactly what is at stake—what mankind's enslavement under the Ferox will look like. If my brother feels he has no option but to take earth, he will not be using the Arena for entertainment, but to reverse the Feroxian extinction and maintain his place of dominance over the species. After the Ferox have crushed any resistance from humanity, I suspect he will use the design of the Foedrata's Arena to place hundreds of these facilities on your planet. Men will be implanted, forced to fight, and slain, allowing the Ferox to breed. Those of humanity allowed to live outside of the Arenas will be the owned subjects of the Ferox."

Jonathan closed his eyes and nodded.

"Seeing this, I hope you may understand what lengths we should be willing to go to in order to keep it from happening," Heyer said. "Follow me. There is one last thing you need to see."

The alien set off down the corridor and the window to the women's prison shimmered, becoming a wall again. Jonathan fell silently into step behind Heyer. They took several different corridors and turns, so many that Jonathan knew he could easily become lost if the alien hadn't been there to guide him. He wondered how it was possible that they were still inside Mr. Clean. The computer must have been moving the ground beneath them, as though in reality their journey was taking place on a treadmill he could not perceive while they walked through the Foedrata's footage.

Finally, they came to a hallway where Heyer placed his palm on the wall once more, and the seamless surface parted into a doorway. When Heyer prompted him inside, Jonathan entered, and the door closed behind them.

At first, Jonathan thought that they may have left the footage. The room they stood in, from what he could tell, seemed nearly identical to what he had seen behind the safe door within Mr. Clean. Now that he was in the chamber, he saw that it contained more than the devices that lined the walls. There were three chest-high pedestals; two placed beside one another near the center of the room, and one further away, almost at the very back wall.

Heyer stopped beside the two pedestals in the center. Jonathan could see that each had a socket much like the spaces lining the walls, and both were empty. Heyer nodded toward the empty spaces, and Jonathan watched. In a few moments, one of the sockets filled, a dormant device materializing. He recognized the metallic symbol on its exterior. It matched the flux capacitor design he'd seen on Rylee's chest.

"The woman, in the Arena," Jonathan said. "The Alpha killed her."

Heyer nodded.

"This is what happens? When we die, our device returns to their place in this chamber? They don't follow the body through the gate?"

As Heyer nodded, the man's device, the one that matched his own, materialized in the empty slot beside the woman's. "Thank you, Mr. Clean," Heyer said. "You can end this projection now."

The black void returned.

When reality manifested around them once again, Jonathan found they had in fact been moving inside Mr. Clean. They were now standing on the other side of the vault door, inside the device chamber. Some of the empty slots on the wall that had been filled were now empty and vice versa. Inside the chamber there were two apparent differences that stood out from the version he had seen in the footage: the vault door they had used to enter, and another, similar door on the far back wall beside a third pedestal.

"This armory," Jonathan wondered aloud. "Did you take it from beneath the Foedrata's Arena?"

"It is a replication," Heyer said. "Necessary to achieve the same functionality."

"The footage is over, then. That is what you wanted me to see?"

Heyer took in a long breath before answering. "A Ferox is not difficult to motivate, Jonathan. Their role in the Arena is a fabricated lie, but that lie is in alignment with their nature and beliefs. Humans raised in enslavement are another matter. Did you notice…" Heyer paused. "How quickly the male combatant's device followed the female's?"

The male in the Arena had been injured, according to Heyer—unable to run. Still, he saw what the alien was getting at; the man had put up little resistance once his mate had perished. Jonathan remembered how the pair had looked at one another back on the beach. He wondered if the man had anything left to fight for once the female was gone.

"You've noticed that emotion plays a role in your strength when activated. This is a symptom of how the implant functions. As it enhances your body based on mass, your muscles also react to your adrenaline and the various hormonal components of aggression. Such things make you stronger, but also compromise your reasoning and self-restraint. This is true whether you are activated or not, but when you are activated, the effect is intensified.

"The Foedrata were quite skilled at manipulating human behaviors that had application in combat. Over the course of the Arena's history, they found powerful methods to motivate men and women to fight. The bonded pair was, perhaps, their most disturbing achievement. Your device is quite powerful alone. This isn't simply a result of your compatibility, but because the device itself is one of the strongest ever re-purposed for the Arena."

Heyer raised his hands, drawing Jonathan's attention to the walls where other implants laid dormant.

"These devices are earlier models; they have no pair. Their strength in any given combatant is fixed by compatibility and body mass alone. Your device is not bound by the same limits, especially when the bond is in play."

"So the angrier I get, the stronger the device becomes?" Jonathan asked.

"Not precisely. The reaction was designed to create an entertaining spectacle in the Arena," Heyer said. "It is catalyzed by a very particular emotional experience... anger is more a byproduct than the source. The reaction is synergistic, exothermic, like that of an explosion. That is to say, once it begins, the energy output is greater than the input, and provides you with far more resources to draw on."

Heyer paused, gathering his thoughts, and then continued.

"The Borealis's similarity to humanity gave the Foedrata insight into how to manipulate your species, but also made mankind a more relatable combatant to watch inside the Arena. Influencing the intensity of human emotion within the engagements added a layer of theater."

"Influencing emotion?" Jonathan asked.

Heyer nodded. "Of all the species I have studied in our archives, only one has anywhere near the number of faith-based belief systems as the Borealis had throughout their history."

"Mankind," Jonathan said. "What does it have to do with the bonded pair?"

"As mankind matures, they follow a similar pattern as the Borealis, with different religious beliefs drawing from one another, their themes coalescing and evolving. Faiths tend to be rooted in addressing what the population at a given point in history fears, and Earth's modern religions embrace a continued existence after death—usually a spiritual continuity assumed beside a creator. Some see this as becoming reconnected to the creator itself, others as a spiritual 'self' that joins their god on a celestial plane after the body dies. This speaks to a deep-seated fear in Mankind: that of ceasing to exist.

"Mankind, like the Borealis, is a species that tends to think themselves a superior life form—more than an animal, by their own standards. They believe in the soul, a spiritual component that makes them of greater value than other life," Heyer said. "The Foedrata's beliefs had a similar notion of the soul, but Foedras eventually took it one step further. They began to interpret this spiritual addition as the means by which the universe's creator divided itself and inserted its consciousness throughout the species."

"Heyer..." Jonathan paused. "I am really not seeing where you are going with this."

The alien raised his hand, requesting Jonathan hold off his questions a moment longer. "Mankind was prone to believing that they had more value than other life because of their subjective experience of reality," he said. "The Foedrata, of course, found this offensive to their own beliefs, but recognized it as a weakness that Mankind had perceived as a strength. A subtraction masquerading as an addition. And yet, every Foedrata experienced the very same weakness in themselves. It was, therefore, easy for them to exploit, but all the more unforgivable."

"What subtraction, what weakness?" Jonathan asked. "What are you getting at?"

"Humans, like the Borealis, feel incomplete," Heyer said. "They have a void and desperately look to fill it. This incompleteness comes from gaps in what they can understand or explain, gaps in purpose, or a need to find meaning in existence. Yet, their greatest gap comes from the internal isolation."

Jonathan raised an eyebrow.

"Humans and Borealis both share a profound cosmic loneliness. They live and die with the knowledge that no one will ever truly know or understand the mind within them. It is a gap they desire filled so desperately, they've created one god after another trying to fill it," Heyer said. "The Foedrata manipulated the bonded pair by finding the means to artificially fill that gap. They created a bond that grows stronger every time the two are activated together. Until tonight, Mr. Clean and I did not fully understand how they had accomplished this. Now that we have heard your experience, we have a better idea of the mechanics."

"What, that hallucination?" Jonathan said. "How could that manipulate me to do anything?"

"Tell me, Jonathan," Heyer said. "If you could never see or talk to Rylee again, how would you feel?"

Heyer's question, when pondered for a few moments, began to hurt. The idea of her absence brought a pull of panic, inducing a nauseated lump in Jonathan's stomach. He felt guilt, as though he had done something unforgivable to the most important person in his life. The discomfort quickly became something he couldn't force himself to endure imagining.

The disturbance… it was so familiar, so parallel to what he had felt as a child when his father had died. He had to force the thought away to stop the sickening sense of loss. He found he was breathing faster; he was afraid. His intuition screamed in confusion at the conflict within him. These emotions—they were impossible, they lacked substance, as though they had manifested from nothing.

Jonathan closed his eyes and swallowed. "I've only spent a few hours with her, Heyer. Why is that question terrifying me?"

Heyer's face grew pained for him. He stepped away from the wall, coming closer to Jonathan, the two pedestals between them. "It is quite difficult to fabricate a thought or a memory within a conscious mind—emotions are not so complicated. However, it is the nature of all three that they do not exist in isolation. All three are linked, and quite difficult to separate, as they often come into being in concert. Before tonight, we knew the bonded pair suffered emotional manipulations, but not how the Foedrata had bridged those emotions to thoughts and memories."

"Bridged?"

After a pause in his thought, Heyer responded to Jonathan's question with one of his own. "While at the university, did you study the evolutionary theories for altruism?"

It took Jonathan a moment to pull the word from memory. "I recall it, vaguely."

"In Man, self-sacrifice is both an act of conscious calculation and unconscious emotion. The decision to put the life of another above your own is greatest for those with whom you share a stronger connection. A parent is more willing to give their life for their child than a friend; a sister more likely to shield a brother than a stranger; a man, for a woman who carries his child. The feeling experienced, the emotional bond that pushes one to make the sacrifice… it grows over time.

"These emotional attachments to another being are not unlike addictions. Losing the individual can be like suffering withdrawals. Hormones and neurotransmitters associate the feelings shared in the experience to memories of time spent together. When such a connection is lost to you, the source of those emotions is also lost.

"With the bonded pair, the Foedrata did not care to wait for this connection to manifest on its natural schedule. So, you find that you have an attachment to Rylee, that you feel things for her that should take months or years to present so powerfully on their own. It is confusing, because the memories that would act as a foundation for these emotions are absent, and yet the feeling is there," Heyer said.

"Are you saying that this device is, what…" Jonathan began. "Producing hormones to make me care for her?"

"Yes, but that alone wouldn't have been enough. Your emotional experience required a core of memories to associate. The device could not create a false history between the two of you. So, the Foedrata allowed a bridge between your minds. A bonding experience where the human void was filled by one another. Now that this has happened, the device continues to cement that bond when you interact with one another, creating a profound but artificial intimacy… the desired result being that you would be driven to protect one another.

"But I must warn you. Do not let my use of the word 'artificial' fool you, Jonathan. You won't be able to feel the difference. You'll only be aware of a contradiction between the strength of your emotional attachment and your lack of a shared history. However, that contradiction is fleeting. If you indulge, keep her close to you, then true shared memories will begin rapidly shrinking any sense of a contradiction," Heyer said.

Jonathan shook his head. "What exactly… is the implant trying to make me believe her to be?"

Heyer looked at him curiously, almost as though he suspected Jonathan's question had been insincere. After a moment, seeing he seemed genuine, the alien grimaced uncomfortably. "The devices are built for a male and a female. She is not your parent, sibling, or child. Perhaps that you are confused is for the best. It is not without irony that Rylee's lesser compatibility may, in this instance, fall in our favor. Had she been as compatible as the woman you saw in the Arena, the bond would make you both stronger, but the phrase 'love at first sight' would hardly encompass the pull of the emotional suggestion. There would be little chance that reason would hold any sway on either of you, at least in regards to protecting one another."

Jonathan closed his eyes. "You know, you're a real bastard sometimes…" he said, resting his forehead against his palms. "You should have warned us."

"I deserve that," Heyer said. "I am truly sorry, Jonathan. You were never meant to be in close enough proximity to activate the bond. When and if the time came, I wanted the decision to be yours."

"Why did you implant both of us? Why didn't you wait? Implant Rylee when we needed her?"

"Gates need combatants, Jonathan," Heyer said. "But, more importantly, we need experienced, battle-tested soldiers. I must train an army spread out over the entire Earth. We must have every weapon at our ready disposal. If this war came upon us tomorrow, I would be forced to implant every device in this room as quickly as possible and you would be leading people who had never so much as laid eyes on a Ferox, let alone knew a thing about how to fight them."

Jonathan shook his head. "I shouldn't be leading anyone. Being the strongest in an army doesn't mean you're capable of leading it. I don't understand what the hell you think is so damn special about me that I would be remotely qualified."

The alien smirked. "I never said you were special," he said. "It is true, you can hit a Ferox harder than any other man on Earth, but I would not give leadership to a tank on the merit that it is a powerful weapon."

"Then… why?"

Heyer sighed. "Some things in life are like humor, Jonathan. You endanger the chances of their success when you risk explaining them."

Heyer tilted his head toward the safe door then, indicating he wished for Jonathan to leave the armory before heading for the exit himself. Jonathan followed, though somewhat in a haze from trying to process everything he had learned this evening. As he exited, he took one last glance back, looking past the two pedestals meant for the bonded pair and lingering on the third pedestal at the far back of the room. Even from where he stood, he could see the pedestal's socket was empty. If the bonded pair had been singled out from the other devices, then that third pedestal must have been a unique implant as well.

"The role of leadership weighs on you, Jonathan. Let me take the burden off your mind," Heyer said, interrupting his thoughts. "When the time comes, if you still believe yourself unfit to lead, I will give that role to whoever you wish."

Jonathan blinked at the alien for a moment. "Just like that?"

Heyer returned a knowing look. "When the time comes that we need a leader, I believe you will not trust the responsibility to anyone else."

A moment passed, Jonathan's face hardening as he studied the alien's. "Well, that makes one of us," he said.

"If the subject is closed for now," Heyer replied, "shall we return to the problem at hand?"

He took a moment longer than he probably should have, but Jonathan nodded. "Heyer, you said that the device mimicked ordinary cells when it wasn't active," he said. "That was why it went completely undetected when I was being tested in the hospital. So how is it that the bond is able to manipulate us when we aren't in combat?"

"Well, I certainly did not intend to mislead you. At the time, the contingency was not a realistic concern, but yes, the bonded pair is a slight exception," Heyer said. "Though it depends on how you define ordinary—nothing about the bond is outside of normal human biology, at least when you are not in an active state. The effect will be amplified when you are activated."

Jonathan frowned uncomfortably. The alien hadn't purposely failed to answer his question—Jonathan simply wasn't sure what he was asking.

"Jonathan?" Heyer asked. "What is troubling you, precisely?"

"I guess I'm trying to figure out exactly when I would have started noticing the bond's effects," Jonathan said. "The last few days... my reactions—they seem so different than Rylee's."

"You will have to give me some specifics."

He nodded, taking a moment to figure out where to start. "After you left. The last month or so that followed, I wasn't in the best place." He didn't look at the alien when he said this—he stared at the floor and tapped his index finger against his skull. "Mentally, I guess."

Heyer nodded. "That seems fairly reasonable. You had absorbed a great deal—"

"No—I mean yes. The thing is, I was getting a grip on it. But, the last few days in particular, I've been better..." He shrugged and looked back at the alien. "A lot better. Good, even."

"I am following you," Heyer said. "But I'm not sure what you are asking."

"When I found Rylee, she was not good," Jonathan said. He was terrible at explaining this, grimacing at how poorly his words captured Rylee's condition. "Heyer, she was really not good."

"I see," Heyer said, his face troubled while he took a long breath. "Unfortunately, we are getting into the theoretical—but yes, there is a likely explanation."

"Theoretical? You mean you aren't sure."

Heyer nodded. "A lot is at play in this, Jonathan. Proximity, personal psychology, association, timing, device compatibility… I suspect that, prior to your initial overlap within The Never, Rylee also experienced a period of improving mental outlook."

Jonathan frowned. "Why would you expect that?"

"Well, I cannot give you precise distances, but at some point while Rylee was crossing the continent, she passed a proximity threshold—came within close enough range of you that your individual devices detected one another. From that point forward, the strength of the bond's effects grew as she came nearer."

"Wait," Jonathan said. "Are you saying that the only reason I started to feel—"

"No, Jonathan," Heyer said, shaking his head. "These things do not exist in a vacuum, but—"

"Think of it as if you started taking anti-depressants and slowly increased the dosage," Mr. Clean interrupted.

Jonathan pinched his eyes shut and groaned as he nodded—why Heyer did not allow Mr. Clean to deliver this sort of information was becoming abundantly clear.

"I would think of this differently," Heyer said.

"Oh, good," Jonathan said. "Because I'd really prefer another way to think of this."

"As I said, the bond cannot build false memories. It does not fully function without association. So, the brain chemistry you experienced was similar to the onset of an intense new romantic relationship—increasing your hopefulness, perhaps—but, despite being driven to that state, your mind was left searching for whom those feelings would imprint."

Jonathan tapped the arm of his chair, his face nearly blank as he tried to decide if Heyer's explanation was actually better than Mr. Clean's. He found himself imagining running into Heyer's shadow in The Never. More precisely, he pictured sucker-punching the alien before crushing the stone to exit. It was the best he could hope for. If he tried to hit the alien now, he'd probably break every bone in his hand—assuming he managed to connect at all.

"Okay," Jonathan finally said. "So, then what happened to Rylee that would have changed this?"

"As you noticed, inside the Arena, the combatants did not enter The Never," Heyer said. "The pair was originally designed to solidify the bond at the same instance after surviving their first battle. What Rylee experienced, I cannot say for sure. Though, I imagine it would have been something like the emotional trauma that the Arena combatants feel when their bond is severed by the death of their partner—an incomplete bonding."

"So, her device finished its half of the process, but because I didn't have the memories needed, my half was incomplete," Jonathan said.

Heyer nodded.

Jonathan was quiet for a long while. Perhaps, to Heyer, it appeared he was trying to get a grip on it all. Mostly, he thought about how uncomfortable he had been imagining he'd never see Rylee again—how insignificant that discomfort must have been compared to what Rylee had been put through.

When he finally spoke, his voice was even, but the words came slowly. "For the time being, I'm going to set aside everything I've heard tonight. Frankly, a conversation about personal boundaries seems a little pointless. What scares me now is that I still don't understand." Jonathan shook his head. "You need to know how Rylee got here. Fine. You want me to find out, but needed to warn me not to trust my instincts. Fine. But, Heyer, as much as all this news is terrible, I don't see how any of it is an Earth-threatening emergency."

Heyer gathered his thoughts for a moment, steepling his fingers before he spoke. "The devices that make up the bonded pair are allowed to be in play. In single combat, they act as any other device, given the compatibility of their owner is not too high. But, they are not allowed to be activated together, as this unlocks the strength of the bond," he said.

"When you and Rylee slay two Ferox within the same instance of The Never, it does not matter if each of you breaks a stone separately or at a different time while you remain inside, because the corpses are sent back through the gates at the exact same instant. This has now happened twice in a matter of days and Malkier's A.I. will have taken notice on the other side. One instance might have been considered a coincidence, but two will require I give an explanation. If a third instance occurs, it will not only be clear that the bonded pair is in play, but that I have either taken no action to stop it, or that I deliberately put events in motion to create an unfair contest.

"Given a third instance has yet to occur, this may have been something I could have explained away. Unfortunately, my brother is not in a state of mind where he can be trusted to see reason. He will notice and scrutinize any abnormalities associated to your gateway, Jonathan. He is..." Heyer paused. "Quite focused on it."

Jonathan titled his head, confused by the alien's statement. "You said that there were hundreds of gates—why is he paying attention to mine?" Jonathan asked.

Heyer's eyes dropped to the floor, and he seemed to grow distant as he spoke. "He is grieving. *Dams the Gate* was his son."

CHAPTER THIRTY-THREE

"DAMMIT HEYER!" JONATHAN said. "You think maybe you should have led with that? You have spent all night talking about bonded pairs and the Foedrata and Feroxian creation stories, and you mention I killed your bastard brother's son only just now?" Jonathan stood from his chair, beginning to pace.

"I would tell you to calm down, Jonathan," Heyer said. "but, admittedly the news is—"

"How?" Jonathan asked, thinking out loud. "How does Malkier have a Ferox son?"

"Malkier inhabits the body of a Ferox Alpha," Mr. Clean said. "The device does not impair reproductive functionality."

"Mr. Clean, I..." Jonathan shook his head, deciding it would be a waste of breath to explain to an inorganic life form that his question wasn't that simple. Instead, he turned back to Heyer. "They aren't his species!"

"Yes," Heyer said. "The biology of a host body, despite being under the control of a Borealis consciousness, has powerful instinctual pulls."

Jonathan stopped and raised his hand to his forehead, still trying to wrap his head around how this could be possible. "And of all the gates his son could have picked, he just happened to choose mine?" he asked. "Our luck can't possibly be that bad."

"As far as our luck goes, I would say the verdict is not in yet. But Malkier's son did not enter your gate at random. He chose with a purpose—because of your gate's history."

Jonathan's head pulled up from his hands. "Gates have histories?"

Heyer leaned forward in his chair. "I have told you that I once came quite close to ending my brother's life," he said. "The event that made me so angry took place years ago. I had gone to the Feroxian plane, seeking a meeting with my brother. Normally, we met in a stretch of land far away from the Ferox populations, but he hadn't arrived as planned. So, I made my way to his vessel. When I came upon him, I found that he had been badly injured.

"What you need to understand is that Malkier, much like myself, has one of the two most advanced implants the Borealis had ever built protecting him. He is thousands of years old, the difference is that he is inhabiting an Alpha Ferox body. Beings such as my brother do not encounter true threats on their life. I, myself, do not believe I could kill him in a fair fight. Finding him recovering from a near life-threatening wound left me at a loss for what could have possibly managed to harm him. My brother knew I would soon find out what he had done, and who had delivered that wound. So, he told me the truth."

Heyer placed his fist against his lips, his eyes having grown bitter.

"There was a man the Ferox called *Echoes the Borealis*. He was a strange case—could not be killed, always survived his encounters within The Never. To this day, no human has sent so many corpses back through the gates. But, *Echoes the Borealis* was more than unique; his survival could not be accounted for by his compatibility with his device. The man commanded far less power from his device than many who still perished in The Never.

"The Ferox do not fear a challenge, and as the gate of *Echoes the Borealis* returned body after body of their children, each Ferox coveted the chance to be the next combatant to enter his gate. *Echoes'* survival had, in their eyes, turned him into the ultimate abomination—the ultimate trophy. The Ferox who defeated such an affront to their gods would become a legend to the rest. However, my brother could not abide the death tolls. *Echoes'* refusal to die was breaking a precarious balance, but he knew I would not kill this man for the crime of defending himself. Malkier took it upon himself."

Jonathan had frozen in thought as Heyer explained. He had heard of this man—the Ferox he'd fought had said his name before, but until now, he'd had no idea what they were telling him—no idea that *Echoes the Borealis* was a reference to a combatant.

"*Bleeds the Stone* called me the legacy of *Echoes the Borealis,"* Jonathan said. "The gate that brings them to me, it was this man's gate?"

Heyer nodded. "When I learned of what my brother had done..." He trailed off, eyes shut, the memory still able to bring the alien to anger. "Jonathan, I do not know how to express the type of outrage one must feel to find themselves considering fratricide. You see, what my brother could not have known was that this man's continued survival had other consequences. *Echoes the Borealis* was merely a problem to Malkier, but he was also my oldest living friend on earth. I thought of him as more of a brother to me than Malkier had ever been.

"I never told my brother of this. Nonetheless, when Malkier stood before me, weakened, and confessed what he had done, I nearly allowed my pain to guide my actions."

"I'm not really seeing what stopped you," Jonathan said.

Heyer's eyes were full of regret when he looked at Jonathan. "Empathy."

The alien looked at the floor then, leaving Jonathan to frown as he waited for an explanation.

"As I stood on the brink, my brother showed emotion I could not ignore. Despite his wound, he was happier than I had seen him in centuries. He had mated, and the Ferox woman he had chosen was with child. I had not known that my brother hid a desperate desire to be a father, but I should have. I have felt that same longing in myself.

"Jonathan, it is impossible for either of us to bring a newborn Borealis into the world. My brother begged my understanding—and my anger hesitated. I despised him for the agreement he'd broken, for the pain he unknowingly caused me, but in the end, I walked away."

Jonathan was not swayed much by empathy himself, at the moment. When he took his seat, he felt as though he were ready to rip the arm rests off his chair.

"The incident marked the end of our relationship as brothers. Malkier knew, on some level, that his actions had brought me to consider violence against the only remaining member of my species that day," Heyer said.

"What he didn't know is that he had finally made me capable of things far worse than he realized. That he had used the last of my mercy. A mind that wants revenge starts to see things it may not have before. You see, it is common for Ferox women to have two to four children per birth. Yet the mate who accepted my brother's seed only had the one. It is unfortunate, because even before *Dams the Gate* was born, I saw an insurance policy."

Jonathan tilted his head, and his anger stalled as he started to see what Heyer was telling him. If Malkier would be difficult to dispatch at full health, even for Heyer, then making a threat on his brother's life was a bluff that might be called. A Ferox child was a different story—a weakness that Malkier would be far less likely to take chances with.

"If he ever moved to take Earth," Jonathan said. "He would never expect you to threaten his child."

"It is a cold feeling, Jonathan," Heyer said. "When I realized I would not hesitate to use the innocent Ferox child's life. That I would take *Dams the Gate* right out from under him, and hold the boy's life in the balance if he dared invade Earth.

"Our relationship became a mere partnership around that time. I reported, we adjusted as necessary, but any act of kinship was a facade. After years, I think Malkier ceased to bother wanting my forgiveness. He sacrificed my trust to create his son, and he could not find true regret for his decision. Still, knowing that he couldn't be trusted should his son perish in a confrontation with man—and secretly not wanting my insurance package compromised—we agreed that his progeny was never to be allowed access to the gates.

"Malkier understood this would cause his son great pain, but saw a fatherly wisdom in it—his Borealis side wished to preserve the safety of his son's life. As a father, he now had something to lose," Heyer said.

"So, how did *Dams the Gate* end up pulling me into The Never?" Jonathan asked.

"He was never supposed to access the gates. How he gained entry is a question my brother is investigating. Though I have little doubt that he will find that the rebellion he has tried to hide from me had a hand in it," Heyer said. "Malkier's son chose the gate of *Echoes the Borealis,* because it was the gate that had given him life."

Jonathan closed his eyes. "And I killed him," he said bitterly.

Heyer nodded, sighing with the same exasperation. "Yes, and unfortunately, it appears that, in my brother's grief, he has lost any desire to conform to our agreements—at least in regards to your gateway. In the month and a half I lost on my return from the Feroxian plane, the evidence that he is attempting to assassinate you has become clear."

Jonathan tilted his head. "What do you mean?"

"My brother would not dare send an Alpha," Heyer said. "Too extreme, he would risk alienating me further, and would contradict his decree as prophet for a second time. He would not wish to give any fuel to the small rebellion that questions his authority. Malkier has taken a subtler route.

"*Bleeds the Stone* was no random selection of the lottery. I knew the moment you said that he'd referred to you as *Brings the Rain*. You see, my brother asked me if his son had given you a title. Only he could have told his assassin what to call you. But frankly, I don't believe this was Malkier's first attempt on your life."

Jonathan's eyes narrowed. "You think he's tried to kill me before?"

"Mr. Clean monitored your discussion with Rylee last night. In particular, that you have seen an imbalance of mature combatants drawing you into combat. This makes sense. My brother, assuming your victories would be a short lived fluke, had no way of knowing that he was sending Reds to their deaths. Now, he has escalated further. *Bleeds the Stone's* death will not go unnoticed by Malkier or his tribe. When that corpse is found on the gateway…"

Heyer broke off, shaking his head.

"The gateway of *Brings the Rain* will soon be a challenge to all the tribes. The Ferox will believe that the gate now holds an abomination the likes of its legacy. They will believe another *Echoes the Borealis* has arisen to challenge their gods."

"Great," Jonathan whispered.

"You couldn't have known what would happen," Heyer said.

"Yeah, I could have," he said. "If you had bothered to warn me."

Heyer sighed. "There is no way I could have foreseen this. Even if I had, what would it have changed? You would not have allowed *Dams the Gate* to take your life."

"It's not the point," Jonathan said. "I would have known the consequences. Now you tell me that my actions have not only killed mankind's only bargaining chip, but singled me out for assassination." He groaned. "A heads up would have been nice."

"Jonathan, you have every reason to be upset," Heyer began. "But I simply cannot tell you everything. Even if I could, you are failing to grasp the bigger picture. Perhaps this is my fault, having sheltered you from seeing the reality so you could focus on what you have control over. Do you not see that sharing information with you is tactical suicide?"

"What, as opposed to actual suicide?" Jonathan said sardonically. "Like what happens when you unknowingly kill the son of the most dangerous father in existence?"

Heyer's fingers tapped the arm of his chair again. "Mr. Clean, please bring up the surveillance camera feeds on Jonathan's residence," he said.

Mr. Clean complied, and soon Jonathan was looking at footage inside his garage.

"Jonathan," Heyer said. "Do you think it would be wise for me to send you home with the names and addresses of every asset we have? Perhaps a summary blueprint of the actions I plan to take in order to address the coming threats?"

Jonathan frowned. "Of course not, I—"

"You have underestimated these people, Jonathan. The Cell is watching you, studying you. What do you think will happen should they decide that watching you is no longer their best course of action? How long do you think you could hold out under interrogation?"

"I wouldn't tell them any—"

"Torture, Jonathan" Heyer said. "Do not be naive. You would tell them everything you know, and when they don't believe you, you would make up lies hoping it would be enough for them to stop."

Jonathan looked at the alien doubtfully. "You think I would break? Every time this thing in my chest activates, every time I destroy one of the portal stones, I may as well be getting burned alive." Jonathan shook his head, certain the alien underestimated him. "I still shut the gates. I do what I have to—what could they possibly do to me that compares?"

Heyer sighed, growing slightly impatient. "Perhaps, you have a point," he said. "But if pain inflicted on you did not get the answers they are looking for..." Heyer pointed to the feed of Hayden and Rylee in the garage. "Who do you think they would hurt to get you talking?"

The question left Jonathan feeling remarkably stupid, and he rapidly forgot why he had argued. Fear replaced the certainty he had felt a moment earlier. "I didn't think you would let that happen."

Heyer nodded, his expression softening. "Of course, we would try to protect you and your loved ones. But, I am not omnipotent. I cannot be everywhere at once or compromise myself. So, understand that I am not going to share every tactical detail with you until necessity demands it." Concern returned to the alien's face. "Look at all the information you now have and ask yourself, what do you now know that could be leveraged?"

Rylee, Jonathan realized.

They had been safer knowing less—not knowing one another existed. If he was as compromised by the bond as Heyer was warning him, he had to do all he could to keep The Cell from learning the extent of it. What could they force him, or Rylee, to do? Lure Heyer into a trap? Lead them to Mr. Clean? Confirm that every human they were watching was carrying alien technology around in their chests?

Jonathan nodded slowly.

"Which brings us back to the issue at hand," Heyer said. "Rylee. We do not know why she is here. Now that she is aware of The Cell, we cannot be sure she will not willingly seek them out, and what she could reveal to them if she does."

"She won't do that," Jonathan said. "She said she would trust me, follow my lead."

"Jonathan," Heyer said, closing his eyes. "You have to accept the possibility that she may have come here to activate the bond on purpose. Think of the power she would have gained over you had she been the only one to know her emotions were being manipulated. Think of the leverage she'd have over me if you took up her rebellion."

After seeing how badly Rylee had been hurt—and what the bond might have been driving her to do—Jonathan wasn't buying that she was out to hurt him, but then a splinter of doubt ran through his thoughts.

What if she had nothing left to lose?

Heyer was right, he couldn't risk it—he had to be sure.

"I'll find out," Jonathan said. "I'll ask why she's here. With all I now know, there is at least the chance that I'll be able to tell if she lies. If her story doesn't match with what you've said, hopefully I won't have to trust my gut."

Heyer began to nod but they were interrupted by a sound that was now familiar to Jonathan, that of a device materializing within the chamber behind them. It was followed by a knowing silence as Jonathan's and Heyer's features grew heavy.

"One of ours just died inside The Never?"

Heyer nodded.

"Shenzhen, China," Mr. Clean said, looking at Heyer. "The node should be reestablished before your departure."

"Departure?" Jonathan asked, his voice exasperated. "When?"

"I need to get back to the Feroxian plane," Heyer said. "Confront my brother about his attempts to assassinate his son's killer, assure him that this incident with the bonded pair is being resolved. That, and we need to investigate what has happened to this individual Rylee claims stepped into the gates from inside The Never." He sighed. "Rylee herself, I must leave to you. She has shown nothing but stubbornness in my presence, and would see sharing what she knows with me as some type of defeat. That and..." Heyer shook his head. "If she was able to extort information from my shadow, I am reluctant to give her another opportunity to do the same to me. Until we know how she managed it, she is dangerous to me."

Heyer stepped toward the safe door and it opened to receive him. He looked back at Jonathan.

"Once you've ascertained what she knows, we will need to make sure she is moved outside of your node's proximity. We cannot allow for another overlap inside The Never. I would prefer to have Mr. Clean transport her back to Manhattan, but I fear how the devices will affect the both of you if the bond is abruptly cut off. That, and, even if the bond is broken without serious repercussions to you or her, she will need to leave of her own will. Otherwise, finding herself suddenly back in New York, she may simply head straight back. We do not wish to hold her prisoner in Manhattan; it will do nothing for our relationship. It would be best if you convince her to leave as she came."

He stepped inside the chamber before the hesitation hit Jonathan's face. "I need time," he said. "I can't drop this on her. She..." He trailed off. Complicated emotional issues withstanding, this was still not going to be as straight-forward as it seemed.

"This will not be easy on either of you. The device will likely emulate a feeling much like that of losing a loved one. I am trusting you to endure this. The effects will fade over time. The sooner the link is severed, the better for both of you."

"Wait," Jonathan said. "What am I supposed to do about the cameras?"

Heyer stepped back out of the chamber, putting the device that had materialized into his front pocket. "Mr. Clean will be able to assist with this," he said. "Once he has explained the details, he will take you somewhere close to your home. I need to be off. I will not have time to check in on you before I leave, but I will return as soon as I can. Remember, Jonathan: the bond's effects will only grow stronger the more you share true memories with her. The contradiction between your emotions and memories will shrink, and eventually, you will lose any desire to see it. Try not to delay any more than is necessary."

Jonathan was far less certain than he allowed the alien to see. Rylee trusted him to do the right thing for her, said she believed in him. Knowing everything he knew now, what the device might drive her to do, he wasn't sure. For that matter, what guarantee did he have that he would not now suffer the same fate that she almost had?

"Good luck," Jonathan said.

Heyer nodded. Then he was gone.

CHAPTER THIRTY-FOUR

WHEN HEYER HAD gone, the room returned to the state it had been in when Jonathan had first arrived. The projections hovering in the air faded away, the coffee table returning to a state of normalcy. Only the display of Mr. Clean on the monitor, the furniture, and the closed vault door remained.

Mr. Clean, for what it was worth, allowed him time to process it all. Jonathan sat, closed his eyes, and tried to get a grip. He didn't know how much time had passed before he spoke. "Mr. Clean," he said. "How is it that you and Heyer can manifest The Never? It strikes me as odd that the Borealis wouldn't have locked away this technology with the rest."

"Yes, surely they would have," Mr. Clean said. "The explanation is simpler than one would think. When Nevric developed the technology, I was her home. Heyer had no knowledge of this when he found me. At the time, the brothers shared the same vessel—Malkier still utilizes it today."

"He said that, growing up, you were his friend," Jonathan said. "That he felt no connection to the other A.I.'s he'd encounter."

"Yes," Mr. Clean said. "When Nevric was conducting her experiments, she built me to assist in her efforts. I am slightly more advanced compared to others of my kind, though 'advanced' is subjective in this case. The hardware I am installed on is the same, but Nevric made customizations to my programming. Changes she felt necessary to make me more effective in assisting her efforts. Regardless, when the extinction occurred, Nevric's research was contained within my on-board records.

It was not until Heyer searched for an alternative means to maintain the human way of life that I had any reason to share her research."

Jonathan snorted. "How did he like finding out you had never mentioned it to him?"

Mr. Clean, sensing the change in levity, smiled back at Jonathan. "He was grateful that a solution existed. It was hardly a deception. How was I to know the information would be relevant until a situation presented itself?"

"I guess that would be the mature way of looking at it," Jonathan said.

"Regardless, this is also why utilization of The Never can only be performed on our end. The gateway is controlled by Cede, each targeted to specific active devices here on Earth. We refer to them as nodes. We can request redirection if a node is not ideal for one reason or another. I request to push it to a better match. The Never is then opened for a different combatant. However, Cede is aware of this, and if she chooses to ignore my request to redirect I must accept her targeting. If I do not, then The Never will not be opened, and the combatant will not be fighting in a temporary battlefield, but on Earth itself."

"I appreciate the information, but why are you telling me all this?" Jonathan said.

"For now, I will be redirecting from the nodes of Rylee and yourself. Temporarily, this will appear as though we are dealing with the development of the bonded pair. If we continued to redirect for long, the appearance will become quite incriminating."

Jonathan nodded slowly. "So you can buy me some time, direct the Ferox entering Rylee's and my gate to other combatants," he said. "But the longer you do so, the more it will become obvious that we are hiding something."

"That is correct."

Jonathan nodded, thinking it over, but he found himself pondering other questions. "Mr. Clean, I was wondering," Jonathan said. "What were the customizations that Nevric made to you?"

"After observing my counterparts," Mr. Clean said. "It would seem she designed my nature to be curious. Cede, for instance, does what she is asked, but would not look into a matter any further than deemed necessary by whatever request Malkier gave her."

"Curiosity," Jonathan repeated, and smiled. "I hear that kills a lot of cats."

Mr. Clean momentarily tilted his head before smiling when he grasped the proverb.

"How does one make a computer curious?" Jonathan asked.

"Easier than you may think," Mr. Clean said. "Nevric made me capable of experiencing boredom. Curiosity came as a symptom. It's a gift and a curse."

Jonathan shook his head, remembering he couldn't stay here all night talking to the computer. "So, what is the plan for these cameras?"

"Yes, there are multiple new issues with a camera feed, far more problematic than simple sound," Mr. Clean said. "It was one thing to disguise the source when I was speaking through your laptop. That was coming through your internet line and I simply had to make the data flowing into your machine appear to come from a typical internet streaming service. I will not be able to alter video and replace the feed from their own cameras on their own network.

"Well," Mr. Clean digressed, "technically, I could, but The Cell would not be fooled. Video contains a great deal of digital data. Their network would detect an upload from an exterior source supplanting their feed. It wouldn't matter that they could not identify the source—they would know data was being uploaded past their security that had no business being there. Therefore, it would be quite obvious to them that something you wanted them not to see had occurred during the time of the upload."

"So what do we do?" Jonathan asked. "Kill the power?"

Mr. Clean shook his head. "Same issue. They would shortly discover that the outage had suspicious origins, and this would become quite obvious if you did so more than once."

"Okay. So what then?"

"Seeing as how you are headed that way, you will be taking a piece of me with you," Mr. Clean said. "Two pieces, actually."

Jonathan blinked. A moment later, two dime-shaped discs appeared to manifest out of the table top.

"Jonathan, do you have an object on your person, something you handle frequently enough that The Cell would see no novel behavior in its presence?"

Jonathan nodded, pulling the gold pocket watch from his front pocket and placing it on the table. "It doesn't keep time—it's an heirloom my father left me," he said. "I've been keeping it on me since the last time Heyer visited."

The two spheres appeared to melt, becoming a translucent fluid as they did so, and moving toward the watch. Both disappeared into the watch's interior by slipping between the space where the glass met the gold casing.

"When you arrive home, one of my pieces will leave you and find its way to a camera. From there, it will follow the wiring back to the hub. This will allow us to manipulate their network from within as I will simply be controlling the hub by communicating with a piece of myself instead of breaking in via a digital means," Mr. Clean said. "When you are going to have a conversation you would prefer to keep private, turn the knob on the watch, and I will take care of the rest."

"Seems simple enough."

"Try to use this sparingly," Mr. Clean said. "We do not want The Cell to infer any patterns. It's best to keep them thinking that nothing is being hidden from them."

Placing the watch back in his pocket, Jonathan nodded and stood. He found his gaze lingering on the safe door. "Mr. Clean, if Heyer installed every device you have, in every compatible human, how many would the Ferox outnumber us by?"

"Assuming the Feroxian females do not join the initial assault, at least ten to one, Jonathan," Mr. Clean said. "If the females join in the attack, I could not give you a trustworthy estimate."

"So..." Jonathan paused. "Is there something I'm not seeing here?"

"What is it you're asking?"

"Is there some reason that we should expect those odds to get better?"

"No," Mr. Clean said. "Not realistically."

Jonathan shook his head, his expression pained. "So, then, is Heyer really just putting this off? Keeping the war at bay as long as possible because he knows we can't win it?"

"I asked Heyer a similar question once," Mr. Clean said. "Pointed out that all this energy he put into maintaining humanity's ignorance of the threat seemed to only prolong the inevitable."

Jonathan opened his eyes, looked away from the armory door and back to the A.I. watching him from the monitor. "What did he say?"

Mr. Clean played a recording then, and the computer's face disappeared. Jonathan saw he was watching a video of Heyer standing in the very room where he now stood. The alien looked thoughtful before he spoke. "I sat with a young man tonight—a man I recently implanted," Heyer said. "I told him what his future held. I told him that I couldn't change the world—that someone had to fight. That the best I could do was give the responsibility of protecting the world to someone else. The man knew what he faced, what the future held, but he refused to consider the idea of making someone else face it for him." Heyer paused then, a sad smile on his face. "I am not ready to start a war for all of mankind, just so I can end a war for myself."

The footage ended, and Mr. Clean's face returned. "Take comfort, Jonathan," he said. "Mankind's fate will not be decided by the size of armies alone."

A moment passed and Jonathan wavered. He had a question on his mind, a question for Mr. Clean, specifically, but he wasn't sure he wanted to hear the answer. Finally, he knew that if he didn't ask, he might later convince himself that the computer's answer may have been different. He needed to hear what cold, hard logic had to say.

"Mr. Clean, in regards to Rylee, what would a computer do?" Jonathan asked. "If risking the life of one person might save the lives of countless others?"

"It is not a difficult question," Mr. Clean said. "A computer would do whatever protected the greatest number of lives."

"Yeah," Jonathan said. "That's what I figured."

After a moment of silence, Mr. Clean asked if he had decided where he wanted to be dropped, and Jonathan drew himself out of his pondering, seeing that the time to dwell had passed.

"Closest electronics store to my house," he said. "I need to buy a new cell phone."

"Not a problem," Mr. Clean said. "Brace yourself, this will—"

"Wait," Jonathan said, looking at the computer. "I had an idea while I was watching the footage in the Arena. Before I go, I was wondering if you might do me a favor?"

"Got him!" yelled an analyst.

The room let out a breath of relief. Since joining The Cell at their base of operations, Leah had struggled to keep her fear for Jonathan at bay, assuring herself over and over that the team had merely lost him.

"Where?" Olivia asked as she approached the analyst's station.

"He used his debit card at an electronics store a few minutes ago," the analyst said. "He's a few miles from his home."

"Get a tail to the address, and get me a visual confirmation as soon as they have eyes on him," Olivia said. Before she turned away, she asked, "What did he buy?"

"A cell phone," Leah said.

The analyst looked to Leah, nodding to confirm her hunch had been correct.

"This cannot happen again, people," Olivia said, addressing the entire room. "If he leaves that house, we move Heaven and Earth to keep eyes on him."

The room nodded their agreement—no one in the building wanted to be a part of the team who had lost their best lead in the entire investigation.

"Leah," Olivia said. "A word, in my office."

Somewhat surprised, Leah followed, stepping into the small room while Olivia held the door. Whatever she wanted to discuss, it had to be quick. They would both want her back on site as soon as possible.

"You disobeyed an order," Olivia said. "Explain yourself."

"What isn't clear exactly?" Leah asked.

"We saw you receive the message to come in immediately. You stopped to have a conversation with Ms. Silva. I'd like to know what was so important you would ignore my orders."

"Considering Jonathan's disappearance, I recalled the time stamps we had witnessed yesterday," Leah explained. "It occurred to me that Rylee might show signs of distress if Jonathan were in any danger. I needed as much confirmation as possible that we were dealing with a location issue and not an abduction."

Olivia studied her. "What led you to conclude he had managed to slip his tail in the first place?"

"I didn't conclude, it was a theory," she said. "Rylee displayed no observable signs of concern, and Jonathan appears to have only gone missing. At this point, it is only a possible correlation."

Again, Olivia studied the woman, her fingers tapping against her desk. "Are there any other theories I've not been made aware of? Do you have any speculations as to where Mr. Tibbs may have been for the last two and a half hours?"

Leah let out a long breath, feeling some of the tension that had gathered when Olivia first called her into the office release. It was possible that this was Olivia's way of asking for her expertise. "They would only be theories," she said.

"If you have permission to share them," Olivia said, "I would appreciate you humoring me."

Leah tilted her head a moment. Olivia had never asked for conjecture, and Leah felt distrustful of the change in their relationship. They were not, by her estimation, friends. "Jonathan has no training that would allow him to circumvent highly experienced agents," Leah said. "His disappearance was described by your men as a vanishing act. My assumption is that he made contact. The Mark is far more capable of pulling him out of our surveillance."

"The Mark has made contact in the past," Olivia said. "He has never gone so far out of the way to hide this from us."

"Like I said, it was an assumption," Leah said. "But, if correct, then today was different—The Mark did not want The Cell to know where he was being taken and did not want their discussion observed."

Olivia nodded. "Care to elaborate on what you think this means?"

"Frankly, your guess is as good as mine, but it's where he went that worries me. Given we've not seen The Mark take this action before, what changed that made him willing to take the risk?"

Olivia raised an eyebrow, a moment passing between them as she considered Leah's concern. "Rylee Silva," she said. "Something about the girl's presence made him move more aggressively than usual."

"Seems most likely," Leah said. "The Mark hasn't been spotted since last interacting with Jonathan. The day after Rylee shows up, he reappears."

Olivia continued to tap her finger against the desk as she thought it through. "Perhaps now is the time to forgo the secondary protocol. To bring Jonathan and Rylee in for questioning?"

Leah blinked—Olivia's use of the word "questioning," was far less innocent than it seemed. Olivia was seeing how she reacted to the idea of Jonathan being tortured for information. If Leah wanted to keep it from happening, she needed to have a reason. She couldn't simply say that the thought of seeing him harmed made her sick to her stomach.

"It is really not my area," she said carefully. "But, knowing what has taken place in the past, I would be concerned that such action would result in The Mark taking Rylee or Jonathan out of the equation. Given the circumstances, we may learn a great deal more observing Jonathan and Rylee's immediate interactions now that this incident has taken place. Interrogating them, if we managed it without intervention by The Mark, might tell us nothing, and may lose us an eventual opportunity to capture the real target. We are hunting the bear after all, not the cubs."

Olivia nodded slowly, but the way she seemed to be dissecting Leah's words was less than comforting.

"With your permission," Leah said, "I should be getting back."

Olivia held up one hand to forestall her from getting up. "Before you go, I wanted to share an observation with you," she said. "I find it troubling."

Olivia turned the screen of her laptop to face Leah, a video window already opened on the display. She then came around her desk to sit beside the screen before she pressed play. The sound was muted, but the film showed various moments throughout the evening she had spent with Jonathan before his sudden departure the night before.

"You see," Olivia said. "Something was bothering me. I couldn't put my finger on it at first. I had to watch over and over again to realize what I was missing. Then it occurred to me that my focus had been on Mr. Tibbs."

Leah watched with a certain amount of apprehension as the various segments played.

"So, I turned my attention over to you," Olivia said. "It only took a while but, finally, I saw what was off."

Leah lifted an eyebrow and feigned impatience.

"You pour yourself a glass of wine," Olivia said. "But you never drink it. You pour the glass out when you return to the kitchen. Then you refill a new glass."

Leah smiled politely. "I need to keep my wits about me. I have no trouble giving off the impression of lowered inhibitions."

Olivia smiled. "Of course, quite professional," she said. "Except, I reviewed the tapes of your previous moment of, as you say, 'lowered inhibitions,' and no such effort to protect your sobriety was evident." She paused, seeming to wait for Leah to speak.

She found herself uncertain if Olivia was baiting her or genuinely looking for a simple explanation. "Previously there was no feasible way to avoid the drinking," Leah said.

Olivia pinched her lips together and sighed. "Leah, is there something of which I should be aware? To be blunt, this is your opportunity to bring it to my attention of your own accord."

She didn't pause, didn't allow a moment of hesitation. "No, ma'am."

Olivia's fingers continued to tap, and she stared at Leah as though continuing to do so would eventually change her answer. Finally, Olivia smiled politely. "When was your last physical, Leah?" she asked pointedly.

"The week before my assignment," Leah replied.

"Would you have any objections to undergoing a follow up?" Olivia asked. "Just to make sure all is well, of course. My concern is for your health."

Leah raised an eyebrow, surprised by Olivia's boldness. Olivia could demand such things of her team, but Leah was under no authority to agree. Yet the game was obvious—denying a simple request would push Olivia's suspicions. What Olivia had miscalculated was that Leah had no need to play such games.

She allowed a moment of silence before smiling politely. "I am sure you will understand, Olivia, that I have concerns regarding the utilization of a physician associated with your team. However, when our commanding officer returns for his next scheduled report, I'll make sure to notify him of your request."

Olivia let the silence stand, steepling her hands, index fingers tapping one another as she reconsidered Leah on the other side of the desk. "Very well," she said. "But, I have one last item of discussion before you go."

Leah nodded.

"Earlier this evening, one of the cameras inside Jonathan's bedroom revealed an article of interest in our investigation. Given the increasing population within the household, you will most likely be the first of the team who will have the opportunity to obtain it."

The trip had taken longer than he had expected. Too many sharp turns up the hill to his stop. The thing about Seattle's bus lines was that they were all run partially on electricity. Long metal rods reached up out of the roof of the bus to connect the lines. Hayden had once pointed out that it reminded him of the connection Marty McFly had to use to channel electricity into the flux capacitor at the climax of *Back to the Future*.

All the buses had wires that ran along their routes to supply power. The problem was, they tended to get disconnected whenever the bus driver took a sharp turn. Then passengers were forced to wait impatiently while the driver got out and reconnected the line, and traffic sometimes made this a lengthy process. The lines had disconnected twice on this trip home. Being honest with himself, Jonathan was thankful for any delay he didn't have to rationalize.

Jonathan stepped off the bus and onto the curb a few blocks from home. The sun had gone down hours ago and only the street lights kept him from walking in the dark. He knew he could not delay any longer, but with so much bad news having been dumped on him so quickly, he was having trouble coming to terms with it. Though, he didn't know how much time would really make a difference.

He needed to be home—even if he didn't know what he was going to do once he got there. He felt like he had lost track of the conversations he needed to have, but he knew he didn't look forward to any of them. He didn't want to lie to Leah, tell her that he'd lied about knowing Rylee all along. He didn't want to have to tell Rylee that she would have to leave. What was he supposed to do if Rylee wouldn't answer his questions? He seriously doubted that she was intimidated by him, and if he tried to scare her into telling him what she knew, she would probably laugh in his face. That was the best scenario—after seeing her move, he had no doubt that it would end comically bad for him if she actually did feel threatened by him.

Even if she told him everything, and he believed her, he wasn't sure he could tell her to leave. When he'd thrown those pills in the trash and told her to follow him home, he'd made a promise to her whether he had spoken the words or not.

If you come with me, I won't abandon you.

As he approached his driveway, thoughts had distracted him to the extent that he almost failed to notice the plastic bag hanging from their mail box. He stopped, walking over to examine it, but he suspected he knew what was inside before he turned the bag over and emptied its contents in his hand.

The cell phone he had tossed down the drain plopped into his palm.

There was a rubber band tied around it, holding a small piece of paper to its side. He removed it, stepping away from the driveway where a street light allowed him to read a short line of typed text, a single sentence.

A smart man stays in sight of those who would protect him.

He wasn't sure what to think, and yet swallowed down a bitter taste. The Cell had already let him know that he was being watched, but their methods of going about it had been cryptic. At the time, he couldn't tell if this had been done on purpose or mistake. He had later assumed that they were being ambiguous on purpose—that it was a test of sorts. If he sought them out for help, it would mean his loyalty was to them and not the alien they hunted. To Jonathan, the note read like an ultimatum cloaked in good intentions.

He crushed the paper in his hand and crumpled it into his back pocket. He didn't need more to think about—not tonight. *When did I become a person who considers messages from clandestine government agencies as the lowest of priorities?* Jonathan wondered.

The thought brought an image of Grant into his mind. How the man had tried to talk him into confessing to a crime, how he seemed to frame his message as though Jonathan was an accomplice to some terrorist threat. It had only been a few months ago, in this very driveway, that the man had tried to manipulate him into losing control of himself and saying something stupid.

He wondered, not for the first time, what had become of him. He had told Grant never to come back, but if he was being honest, it was surprising that it had been the last they'd seen of him. It didn't seem like Grant—not with the hostility Jonathan had seen in the man.

He looked to his house with the light on in the living room, then back to his phone. He flipped it open, and found he had messages. It seemed the last procrastination left to him, so he started reading.

Paige: Tibbs, what did you do?
Hayden: Hey Bro, when are you off work?
Collin: Please dad, can't we keep her, please?
Paige: Call me back already! I need you to tell me you aren't a jackass.
Hayden: I don't think Paige and Rylee like each other much. Might want to get home.
Collin: Late night at work? Hurry up already.
Hayden: Bad time to be MIA, did you lose your phone?
Collin: Tibbs, don't go in the house, call me first.

Well, Jonathan thought. *None of that looks good.*

He'd never gotten quite this many messages from them before. With everything the alien had told him tonight, he had trouble imagining anything happening at home that he'd have time to take very seriously. Then it occurred to him that he'd yet to ask Rylee for a means to get in contact with her. That, if she left, he wouldn't know where to find her. That, if The Cell had been watching her, they might think her an easy ally to sway to their side.

He considered how he had left things with Leah on their date. Then he thought of Leah and Rylee meeting without him there to explain, and how he had purposely omitted mention of Leah to Rylee—how, the moment before they had closed the gates, Rylee had placed her lips on his, held onto him so desperately. She didn't remember having done any of that though, would assume Jonathan was completely unaware of any feelings she had toward him. After all, she'd thought he wouldn't remember at the time.

When everything he had truly neglected started stacking up, his paranoia kicked in. He found that his walk down toward the door had accelerated into a brisk jog, but when he gripped the doorknob—he froze as every hair on his body stood up.

The piece of Mr. Clean was cold, liquid, and fast on his skin. The transparent material slithered off his hand to the knob before darting through the space between the door and the frame. His mind had gone momentarily blank while he fought the urge to flail around as though he'd just had a nest of snakes crawl over him. Finally, he tilted his head, closed his eyes, and managed to only let out a long, shivering breath.

After a moment, the creepy sensation left. Jonathan nodded to himself and opened the door. As he stood before everyone sitting at the kitchen table waiting for him, a sadly overdue alarm went off in his head: *Collin had said to call before going inside.*

"Well," said Evelyn Tibbs. "Look who finally decided to grace us with his presence."

CHAPTER THIRTY-FIVE

SUNDAY| OCTOBER 9, 2005 | 9:30 PM | SEATTLE

THE WAY THEY all looked at him made Jonathan feel as though he'd walked into an intervention. Evelyn sat at the table, Rylee and Leah on either side of her, each with a mug in front of them. Paige was halfway out of the kitchen, carrying a fresh pot of coffee. Collin and Hayden both leaned against the back of the couch.

A lot happened in Jonathan's head at that moment, not the least of which was the urge to shut the door, turn around, and walk away from all of them. His mother eyed him, seemed to read his mind, because her face said: *Nope, not avoiding this.*

His eyes flicked to Collin and Hayden. Both their faces said, *we tried to warn you.* To her credit, Paige didn't look smug—she looked more like she pitied him. Leah had turned away, so that he only saw the back of her head now. Rylee, if anything, was the one person who actually just looked happy to see him.

He took a long breath as he stepped inside. His eyes escaped theirs only when he turned to pull the door shut behind him. He lingered, his fingers still touching the doorknob, and it went on too long for anyone to miss it.

It was too much, and he knew it. He couldn't juggle so many different versions of himself in front of so many people. The person Leah expected, the person Rylee knew he was hiding, the person his mother remembered, the person his roommates had seen him become. The real Jonathan wasn't even there anymore.

He couldn't protect everyone, not anymore. If he had to start burning bridges, at least doing so would keep them safe. It had been a long time coming, and something had to give.

Resolve came to him with one simple thought: *The hell with it.*

Jonathan felt as though he wanted to laugh one of those hysterical laughs that only came when one was too tired to fight what seemed an unchanging inevitability. He wasn't sure what he had given in to, didn't know what he was about to say, but he wasn't that worried about it anymore.

When he turned around, he said the only thing that seemed natural, "Mom! So nice to see you. But really, you should have called first."

When Jonathan stepped inside, Evelyn saw him in the light. He hardly resembled the son who had left home for school. He seemed so much older, his hair cut short, shoulders thickened with muscle, face absent of its softness but cut now with hard lines. He looked more like his father when he'd come home from Libya.

In the past, catching glimpses of her late husband in Jonathan brought her a sentimental smile. There was no such nostalgia for the reflection of Douglas she was seeing now.

Jonathan came toward them, his face shifting between reluctance and acceptance, the feeling in his eyes becoming empty as he reached for the one free chair at the table. He pulled the seat out, turning it around to sit with the weight of his shoulders put onto the chair's back.

Evelyn looked away from him for a moment, stealing quick glances at the two other women sharing the table. She had only briefly met them. The red head, Leah—her eyes seemed reluctant to wander from the table top. The foreign girl seemed to have the opposite reaction. She watched him as though eager for his eye contact.

"So, how was everyone's day?" Jonathan asked.

Her son surprised her, and Evelyn found her face harden in annoyance when he made a blatant parody of normalcy.

"Pretty good," Hayden replied.

"Same here," Collin said. "Rylee and I went riding."

And his buddies come to the rescue, Evelyn thought.

To be fair, Hayden had seemed genuinely oblivious, but she could tell Collin was following Jonathan's lead. Evelyn sipped her coffee. Her son couldn't keep his friends in the room forever.

"Collin, you have no sense riding one of those death machines," Evelyn said, then looked over to Rylee. "What's your excuse, dear?"

"To be fair," Rylee said, "It's only dangerous if you drive like Collin."

The joke got a laugh, but it was cut short when Paige cleared her throat. "Where did you two go anyway?"

Collin and Rylee exchanged a knowing look. "Secret," Collin said. "Mission of mercy…"

"Mission of mercy?" Jonathan asked.

Collin grinned. "We'll tell you about it," he said, clearing his throat as Paige had a moment before. "Later."

The conversation broke off abruptly, and Evelyn wondered if the tension in the room was building for everyone, or if she was simply imagining it the longer the silence went on.

Paige drummed her fingers against the table, appearing annoyed, but she halted shyly, seeing the noise had drawn everyone's attention to her. Jonathan opened his mouth to speak, but Leah beat him to it.

"So Evelyn, how long did you plan to be in town?" Leah asked. "Maybe the two of us could find some mischief while all these busy bodies are out?"

Her son blinked as he looked at the girl, but Leah avoided his eyes and kept them on Evelyn.

"I'd love that, dear. Not sure how long I'll need to be in town yet, though," Evelyn said. "Could be awhile…" She trailed off and glanced at Jonathan, expecting some reaction to the news that she planned to stay as long as it took. Somewhat disturbingly, her son was a blank wall. "And I haven't checked into a hotel yet."

"Oh, nonsense," Paige said. "You can take my room."

Evelyn smiled graciously as Jonathan tongued the side of his teeth. "So polite of you to offer, as it would seem my own son hadn't thought to."

Jonathan grinned, looked as though he was preparing an empty apology, when Paige interrupted him. "Well, in Jonathan's defense," she said, "he is already sleeping on the couch on account of Rylee."

"Oh?" Evelyn said, reexamining the girl beside her. "But if Jonathan is already on the couch, then where will you sleep, dear?"

"Hmm. I don't mean to impose on you, Leah, but maybe we could put Jonathan in your guest room?"

Evelyn stifled a frown—it seemed quite peculiar that Paige had not requested a bedroom for herself. Perhaps Evelyn was simply from an older generation, but it was improper to try and push a young man into the girl's home. A look to the faces at the table seemed to indicate that everyone else felt the same, as Leah, Rylee, and Jonathan all appeared quite uncomfortable with the idea.

Though, as Evelyn looked at Leah, she noticed that the girl appeared more chagrined than uncomfortable when she smiled back at Paige.

"I'll be fine on the floor," Jonathan said.

"Evelyn," Leah said. "How about you come stay in the guest bedroom tonight?"

"Oh dear, thank you. But please, only if it isn't any trouble."

"No, of course not, no trouble at all. It's too late to send you looking for a hotel room and I never get a chance to use my guest bedroom anyway," Leah said. "Come on, we'll grab your bags and get you settled."

It was hard to miss that Leah stared fixedly at Paige as she said the words. Evelyn stood to follow Leah, but found herself wondering if some sort of chess game had just played out in front of her. As she left the room, she watched her son. He looked away, shutting his eyes. They stayed closed until she was gone.

He hadn't asked her along, but Rylee followed him into the garage. She hadn't expected he would take so long getting home and they were overdue for a conversation more involved than deciding where everyone would be sleeping.

"Where have you been all night?" she asked.

Jonathan was lethargic, seeming to move slower from one moment to the next. "I'm sorry," he said. "I meant to come home after work." He sat on the edge of his bench and slouched, the fingers of one hand pressing against his forehead.

"Rough day, then?" she asked.

A breath escaped him like a sardonic chuckle. "Yeah. Long talk with Mr. Fedora."

Rylee's eyebrows raised. "There a problem?"

Jonathan drew in a long breath and nodded, his gaze still on the floor. She hadn't seen him like this. It occurred to her that she was the only person he could allow to see him in such a state—anyone else would start asking questions he couldn't answer. Rylee knelt in front of him, wanting her eyes to be what he saw once he looked up.

"I'm sorry, Rylee," he said, shaking his head. "Too much is coming at me at once. My mother will be in here giving me the third degree in a few minutes." He looked up then, and she saw he hadn't expected to find her face so close. "I just... I need to get myself together."

Her curiosity regarding the alien's visit quieted when she saw the anxiety in his eyes. He looked like he needed a place to hide, like he wished time would stand still and give him a moment to think clearly.

She didn't think Jonathan could know how deeply she had seen into him. After all, she was just as in the dark of what he had seen of her. Yet, she knew well the frictions he endured to find balance with the people in his life. Rylee understood it intimately. Jonathan was unceasingly at odds with the knowledge that all would be simpler if he let his attachments to people fade away. Rylee had thought that once, knew better now, and didn't want to let him follow her down that road.

Life might be simpler, but it quickly ceased to be livable.

She said nothing as she stood, coming around to straddle the bench behind him. She reached out gently, putting her finger tips onto his shoulders.

At first he stiffened at her touch, and Rylee bit her lip, afraid that he would pull away. She felt his hesitation, wished she could hear his unspoken confusion. He didn't pull away though, and she pressed her finger tips gently against the tension in his muscles—lightly at first, but as more time passed in silence, the stiffness in his shoulders began to fade.

Neither spoke. She wanted to share his burden, so that it wouldn't feel so heavy… he seemed to want to flee from it. Rylee feared that since no more than a day had passed since he'd found her staring at a bottle of pills, he would not think of her as a safe place to drop the weight.

She needed him to know she wasn't fragile, that if he trusted her it would only make her stronger—but it was fairly obvious that this was not the moment to make her case. Right now, kindness was all she could give him. So, she pressed further into the tension in his shoulders, trying to calm him, help him through this moment that overwhelmed him.

She heard him swallow before he whispered, "Thank you."

They both heard it when the front door opened and footsteps came toward the garage. She pulled away, standing to lean against a cabinet a few feet behind him. He wouldn't have said that he was afraid, that he didn't want the others to see her show him any affection. She knew, and it bothered her, but whatever was on his mind, getting caught with her hands on his back seemed rather small in comparison. She didn't want to undo what little tension she may have relieved by giving him something he'd feel responsible explaining should the arc-welding red head walk through the door.

Jonathan took a long breath and stood, drawing himself up to his full height. A smile touched her face as she stood behind him and saw strength coming back to the surface. His shoulders drew back, his posture improved... and his face became a wall.

Then, it was as he'd said—Evelyn opened the door and walked down the stairs. She held a cardboard box in her hands. Her eyes had been on Jonathan, but they grew distracted as she took in the room around her. It was as though she'd walked in knowing what to expect and found that she didn't recognize the place.

"Rylee," Jonathan said. "I need to speak privately with my mother. Would you mind giving us the room for a moment?"

"Sure," Rylee said, bowing her head slightly to Evelyn as she left.

CHAPTER THIRTY-SIX

"WE BOTH KNOW why you're here," Jonathan said. "You're wasting your time. I don't have anything to tell you."

His mother walked to a countertop lining one of the garage's walls and set down the box. She lingered over it for a moment, her back still turned to him. "You owe me an explanation," she said.

"If I had one," Jonathan said, "I would have answered my phone."

She drew in a long breath and exhaled before she turned to look at him. He was prepared to face her anger, but her expression caught him off guard. He only saw worry and it hurt him. "I was so angry driving up here. Furious. I couldn't imagine you had the gall to ignore me. My son, he calls me, tells me he is dropping out of college, that he has purposely waited until there was nothing I could do about it. Then, he just stops answering his phone. What did you expect would happen?"

Jonathan didn't answer her, and when Evelyn realized he didn't intend to, she shook her head

"You've never rebelled, done something so immature. You've never just up and quit something like this."

Again, she watched him, but he gave no sign that he planned to reply.

"I thought, there must be something else," she continued. "That you must have gotten into trouble. Maybe it was drugs, or you'd gotten some girl pregnant. That you were too ashamed to tell me, to ask for help."

She waited after the words, her eyes boring into his for some reaction. He didn't so much as flinch, went on waiting for her to finish her piece. Waiting for her to realize that she couldn't force an answer out of him.

"I was so angry for that more than anything," Evelyn said. "To know my son needed help and wouldn't tell me."

Jonathan drew in a long breath as he listened, then let it out slowly. When she didn't speak again, he stopped holding her eyes and turned away, beginning to busy himself with the disorder of the work out equipment around them. It gave his hands something to do while his mother's stare bore into him.

"I called Paige," Evelyn said.

That gave him a moment of pause. Paige hadn't told him about this. He really shouldn't have been surprised. It made sense really, and partially explained why Paige had been upset with him lately. Unfortunately, there were details Paige could have betrayed—his mother might know more than he had realized.

"I demanded she tell me what was going on. That poor girl, she tried to lie to me, tell me everything was fine. I've never been so angry with her. I could hear her trying not to sob on the other end of the line!"

People will get hurt, Jonathan reminded himself. *You can't keep going without burning a bridge eventually.*

"Finally, do you know what she says?" Evelyn asked. "That you had forbidden her. That your friendship hinged on her not saying anything to me. I couldn't believe my son would say such a terrible thing to a friend of his."

To this, Jonathan did feel he needed to set the record straight. "I never said it—only implied it."

"Why would you put her in a position like that?"

Jonathan let out a long breath, knowing he should have remained silent. He should have let her realize that he would allow the silence to continue until she had her fill of it.

"Why are you acting this way?" she asked. "What could be so important that you would let me worry like this? Do you think you're being a man? Why does your face look so…?"

Jonathan felt the dull hurt of her concern as she trailed off, felt the pressure of it push against the wall between them.

"I know that look, Jonathan," Evelyn said. "I lived with it for years after your father came back from the fighting. I would rather see you drop out of college a hundred times before I would have you look at me that way." She choked on a sob.

You can't, Jonathan thought. *You have to let her cry.*

"He was a grown man, Jonathan! He'd been in a damn war! I never demanded he tell me what had happened, what could have changed him so much. What I imagined was far worse than the reality could have ever been." The silence continued, until it became too much. "What makes you think you have the right to look at me like that!"

Finally, he turned to face her, knowing that the very face she said he had no right to wear was what she would see. He saw regret creeping over her. She had been trying not to yell, but she'd slipped.

She bit her lips and looked away from him. "Jonathan, I can't just leave it alone. What could have done this to you? What could hurt you so much that it's like you aren't even there anymore? That you just don't care how much this is hurting me?"

A trickle of guilt slipped past his barrier. He retracted from it as though she had placed his hand in a fire. He closed his eyes and drew deeper into himself before he opened them again. Disgust had replaced the wall he had held between them. Good intentions or not—guilt was the last weapon his mother should have tried with him.

He knew guilt. Had a profound relationship with it. Guilt that seldom let him sleep through the night. He had been looking into the dead eyes of a child for months. He'd been a coward while she had been torn apart. He couldn't make his peace with it; he couldn't allow himself to forget the lessons it taught him. In the next few days, he was going to tell Rylee to leave, knowing full well what it might lead her to do to herself. Adding the guilt of his mother's concern was like a soft rain over a roaring ocean. He was surprised he'd felt it at all. There was a pause as he thought these things, and when he spoke, his voice had become a cruel whisper.

"You never asked Dad what he'd seen," Jonathan said. "You were right not to bother. He wouldn't have told you."

Evelyn's expression wavered, seeming not to know how to react to the chill in his voice. "Why?"

"Some things get worse when you share them," Jonathan said. "Dad was wise enough not to forget that."

Evelyn looked at him and waited, seeming to hope that if he had said this much, he might say more.

"Mother," he said, "there is not enough guilt in the world to make me forget it, either."

The soft tone he used made her shiver and retract as though he had yelled at her.

They stared at each other for a long while. Jonathan watched as gears moved in her head. He saw a measure of defeat come over her, his defenses dropping a bit as she saw this conversation drawing to a close.

His mother started to turn away. "Douglas didn't look like that forever," she whispered.

She hadn't been looking, didn't see that her words had made him flinch.

"It's not the type of thing you tell your son," Evelyn said. "Your father, he may not have told me everything, but eventually, he stopped hiding behind his face. It took time, but he brought himself back from it. I remember the day I started to see my husband again."

Jonathan wanted to deny it, pretend he wasn't desperate to know what his mother was hinting at. The tightness in his jaw unclenching, he swallowed before he spoke, "What are you…what are you getting at, Mom?"

"We had always talked about having children, Jonathan," Evelyn said. "But when he came back, he had changed his mind." She smiled sadly as she recounted the past. "He started saying the oddest things. Things he'd never had on his mind before. That the world needed more parents, not children. That it was narcissistic for us to need to see ourselves in the child we raised. He said, 'It's not life you should give a child, but a way of life.' That he didn't need a child to be his to call him son, to teach him about the world. He suddenly had a hundred reasons that we should adopt."

Jonathan felt his armor become heavier, found himself sitting down on the edge of his weight bench to hear more, to understand his father just a little better.

"I didn't buy any of it," Evelyn said. "I told him so. I told him I wanted the damn truth of it. Not a bunch of rhetoric that sounded like it came from an adoption brochure." She shook her head. "I loved your father, but he was a complicated man. And if there was one thing I wouldn't endure, it was being told my husband would deny me a child of my own." She frowned, and then corrected herself. "Our own."

She didn't speak for a moment, seeming to wonder if she had said too much already. Finally, she decided she would not leave the story unfinished.

"You see, what he didn't know was that I was already pregnant. It had happened the last time he was on leave. I was about to tell him, because he didn't understand why he was hurting me so much," Evelyn said. "But, before I could, he asked me the strangest question."

Jonathan looked at her now, his eyes betraying him.

"He asked me if..." Evelyn hesitated again. "If I ever wished that my parents hadn't given me life. That was when I understood how much he had been hurt. All those things he said about adopting, they had been camouflage. He didn't want me to know that a part of him wished he had never been born, that he was worried about making a choice that could one day force his child to wish the same thing."

Jonathan took a long breath. He nodded in understanding, before putting a hand on his mother's shoulder. "Mom, I see why you wouldn't want me to know this. It doesn't change who he was to me. Just helps me understand him."

Evelyn nodded. "It's not why I said it. I am trying to make you understand how terrifying it is for me to see that look on your face."

He turned away, but nodded, understanding.

"It's getting late, and this is exhausting," she finally said. "I think after a good night's sleep, we can try this conversation again."

"Is it your intention to come here and stare at me every day?" Jonathan asked. "It will end the same."

"We'll see."

"You'll have to go home—go back to work at some point. I may not be able to make you leave—I know that—but you can't be getting in my way."

"Perhaps," Evelyn replied, not conceding to this statement. She went to the stairs to leave.

"Mom," Jonathan said before she opened the door. "You said that something made him change. What was it?"

Evelyn looked at him as though she thought the answer was obvious, like she had already told him. "He held his son," she said. As she turned to exit, his mother made sure she slipped in one last thing. "I look forward to getting to know your new friends."

Jonathan stared at the door for a while once she had left. He wished that, in all this time, he could have found a lie that would make his friends and family leave him be. That wasn't how it worked. Rylee, it seemed, had found that the only way was to leave.

When he took his eyes off the closed door, he saw that his mother had left the cardboard box on the counter. He walked over to it and pulled off the lid. There were a number of trinkets, picture frames, an old uniform of his father's. He recognized some of it. Reaching inside, he moved some of the frames out of the way, and his eye was drawn to picture clipped on to a stack of envelopes. A picture of his father he hadn't seen before.

It was a black and white image, and Douglas did not seem to be aware that he was being photographed. He sat at a table in his uniform, lost in his thoughts, holding the pocket watch he'd left to Jonathan. His father's thumb was pressed lightly on the watch's engraving, a habit Jonathan shared when he held the timepiece. There was a look in the man's eyes, the look Jonathan had when he was hiding behind the wall, the mask of his own face.

His father was young in the photo, but still older than Jonathan was now. People had told him that they could tell he was his father's son when he was growing up, but he'd never been able to see it. Perhaps it was that, in his early teens, he'd been too awkward to notice the similarities. Now, though, with his hair cut short, his face cut with harder edges, and his body hardened by hours of training, he saw it.

Eventually, the lateness of the hour started to encroach on his thoughts. There were conversations that needed to happen that he could not put off.

He put the picture in his pocket, and returned the lid to the box. Turning back to the garage, something struck him as off. He hadn't noticed it before, and for a moment, he wasn't sure what bothered him. Something was missing.

Where did my bike go? he thought.

Leah and Evelyn spoke little when she returned. Evelyn looked tired. Her conversation with Jonathan had been a taxing one, apparently. Leah wished her a good night, and when the door to the guest bedroom shut, she returned to her neighbor's house.

"You really don't have to knock," Paige said, stepping out of the doorway to let her in.

Jonathan noticed her enter, but was in the middle of a conversation. "Collin, did you move my bike?" he asked.

Collin shared a conspiratorial glance with Rylee. "Um, yeah. I figured you wouldn't want your mom seeing it."

A bit of gratefulness touched Jonathan's face. "Thanks," he said, and the two fist-bumped.

"We hid it out in the backyard," Rylee said. "Follow me. I'll show you."

Jonathan frowned. "It's late. I'm sure it'll be fine for one night."

"Best we do it now," Collin said. "I don't want you waking me up when you can't find it in the morning."

Leah, Paige, and Jonathan all stared blankly at Collin. He'd made it sound like their backyard was so vast one could lose track of an entire motorcycle—it wasn't. Collin ignored their looks, already heading toward the door with Rylee and Hayden seeming quick to follow.

"What?" Jonathan asked lifting an eyebrow. "Did you bury it?"

Leah exchanged a glance with Paige, and her friend shrugged back at her. Shenanigans were obviously in motion, but apparently, they were as much in the dark as Jonathan. In the backyard, the motorcycle was impossible to miss, sitting plainly in the middle of the patio, but under a tarp.

"Okay," Jonathan said, looking at the three conspirators. "So what's going on? Did you knock it over or something? Is it damaged?"

Collin snorted. "Right, damaged," he said as he stepped behind the bike. "We'd have had to drop it off a cliff for anyone to notice any more damage."

Collin took hold of the bike's cover with both hands. He waited until everyone was still, then looked to Rylee for permission. She smiled and gave him a nod.

"We went on a mercy mission today," she said.

Collin pulled the tarp away, and Leah's eyes grew large at what lay beneath. She had figured they had gotten the bike repaired, repainted, or touched up. This wasn't Jonathan's bike at all. It was new, brand new—didn't even have a license plate yet.

Awkward silence seemed to come over everyone while Rylee and Collin were waiting for sounds of awe. Leah found herself caught between smiling politely and trying not to flinch. She felt embarrassed for Rylee. The girl seemed to desperately need Jonathan's affections—did she even realize how needy such an extravagant gesture would look? Then she found herself wondering, *What do you do for the person who kept you from taking your own life?*

"I don't... it's too much," Jonathan stuttered. "How did you pay for this?"

Paige, of course, had no way of knowing why Rylee would go to such an absurd length, and since Leah wasn't supposed to either, she tried her best to mime her friend's reaction.

"Seriously," Paige said in agreement, her voice critical. "What are you thinking?"

Jonathan, seeing the deflation of Rylee's smile, turned to Paige. "No," he said. "Not like that, I didn't mean it like that. It's amazing, I just—I can't possibly accept this."

"If it's the money, don't worry about it." Rylee winked.

"Collin," Jonathan said. "Please tell me you didn't pay for any of this?"

"Of course not. I just drove the old one down for the trade in." Collin coughed, then. "Though, allegedly, I may have forged a signature on the bill of sale." Collin lifted his palm toward Rylee. "Moneybags here bought the new one. In cash, no less."

Leah watched Jonathan's reaction—saw how he looked at Rylee after this disclosure.

A quick moment of suspicion followed by a spark of insight in his eyes. The Cell was quite aware that Rylee had the funds to make such a purchase with little concern, that she had won it all from gambling under circumstances that strained the chances of her simply being lucky. Studying Jonathan, Leah found herself willing to make a wager. Right now, she would bet ten to one that he knew exactly how Rylee had managed it.

"Tibbs! Would you thank the lady already?" Collin asked. "I am, frankly, pretty jealous right now. It's a Suzuki SV 650—she got you this year's model of my bike."

Jonathan forced himself to smile, then knelt beside the motorcycle, his hands running down the plastic side paneling.

"What?" Collin asked. "You don't like the color?"

Leah watched as Jonathan scratched his head, and looked back to Rylee. He was an open book to her; she knew the moment his empathy took over, when he realized his subdued enthusiasm was hurting the girl.

"No," Jonathan smiled. "It's beautiful. Really, I'm just stunned, is all."

Rylee tilted her head at him, not so convinced he was being honest, but as Jonathan continued to commit, her smile returned. Leah found herself questioning her original thought. Rylee might not have been motivated by gaining his affection, but by something else. His respect? His approval? His trust? Leah couldn't put her finger on it.

"Well, are you gonna sit on it or what?" Collin asked.

Jonathan smiled, and everyone stepped back as he mounted the bike. It reminded Leah of the day in her driveway, when she'd been working on the older bike, and when she'd touched his face gently to inspect the black eye that Grant had given him the night before. How she hadn't wanted to take her hand off him…

She understood what had been bothering Jonathan a moment earlier, what he'd been looking for when he examined the plastic shielding of the bike's exterior. There wasn't any obvious way to get around the paneling to the frame—not enough exposed metal to alter the bike in the same manner that Leah had on Jonathan's older Honda. Leah had been standing back, trying to remain unnoticed as she studied everyone else—but she'd also been hoping to get a single moment alone with him. This gave her an opening.

Rylee's smile dampened when Leah stepped toward him. Jonathan must have noticed it as well, as his gaze turned where Rylee was looking, and found her. She stood close to him, held his eyes without looking away for the first time since their awkward parting the night before.

"I can make the same modification," Leah said. "It'll be a bit trickier this time, but not impossible." She leaned in closer then, so only Jonathan would hear her whisper. "But it would appear as though you'll be owing me another favor."

CHAPTER THIRTY-SEVEN

SUNDAY | OCTOBER 9, 2005 | 10:30 PM | SEATTLE

"THERE IS BLOOD on your hands," Mr. Clean said.

As he stepped back into his living room, Heyer paused to look down at his palms. The A.I. had detected the remnants of biological material that he had neglected to clean off himself from the most recent volunteer. "Thank you," Heyer whispered. "The Shenzhen node is implanted."

He walked over to his bathroom sink, running water from the tap to remove what had dried on his skin and settled beneath his fingernails.

"Redirect Cede if the new node receives any inbounds while I am away," Heyer said. "It is unlikely he will survive, but men with slimmer chances have managed it. When I return, I'll make sure that I am present for his first combat within The Never should he need to learn how the gates are closed."

The installation had been a routine matter. None of the complications that had occurred during Jonathan's implant had taken place. The young man lived alone—and had volunteered.

Knowing the boy's chances weighed on the alien's conscience. There were reasons to hope at times. Some volunteers had a higher compatibility, a background in warfare. Sometimes, he implanted a device knowing that he was creating a powerful weapon on purpose. This boy had hardly been of drinking age, naively jumping at the chance to be the defender of his species. That glimmer behind the young man's eyes as Heyer played the part, the dark and mysterious stranger who arrived one day to tell him he was special, to finally give the man's life the meaning he had always suspected was out there, waiting to find him. All that soul searching put to rest because he was a hero.

It was the story Heyer had to tell. A story that might even be true. More likely, it was exactly what Jonathan had called it when he had learned the reality. The refilling of a bird feeder.

"It's not much longer, sir," Mr. Clean said.

Heyer glanced at the screen. The computer had an intuition for his moods. It was why Heyer considered him his friend, and never treated the computer as though he were some sort of butler. "The boy," he said, his eyes tired. "He volunteered."

The image of Mr. Clean nodded. "He made the right decision."

Heyer sighed. He often wondered if Mr. Clean felt guilt. No, *felt* wasn't the right word. He wondered if such philosophical burdens could plague the A.I.'s conscience. Mr. Clean understood that the situation presented no option but to turn to the hard math. How many would be saved versus how many lost. Could the A.I. regret the sacrifice of a digit for the sake of balancing an equation?

Heyer respected those that volunteered. Still, he respected those, like Rylee, that didn't. The ones that weighed on him the most were the ones he couldn't afford to give an option.

Much like Jonathan, there were times when there was only one applicant. Heyer told no story to those men—requested no consent. At least, he no longer did, not since Rylee. It had become too much for him to pretend they had a choice in the matter when the reality would not make room for them to have a choice.

"Were you able to take control of the hub inside Jonathan's residence?" Heyer asked.

"Yes," Mr. Clean replied. "Jonathan has not yet had an opportunity to question Rylee in private, but access to their internal network allowed me to discover a number of other surveillance setups within the Seattle area."

Heyer frowned in curiosity. "They are watching others inside the city?"

Mr. Clean disappeared to show the first of the feeds. The footage belonged to a shabby hotel room with no occupant. This, Heyer quickly realized, had been Rylee's hotel room and was no longer of interest. The next feed had only one angle. Mounted inside the vent of a bedroom, a man he immediately recognized stepped into view.

"Grant Morgan," Heyer said. "It was too much to hope he had left town after The Cell dismissed him."

"It would appear so," Mr. Clean replied. "I noticed you chose not to advise Jonathan of the circumstances that led to his involvement."

Heyer sighed. "We have to be careful with Jonathan for the time being. Telling him now would have led to questions I don't yet want him asking." Heyer watched the man on the feed a moment longer before turning away in thought. "If The Cell's attention is still on Grant, we have to assume they made the connection between their fathers' military unit. It is of no consequence. The Cell is grasping. If they know who Grant Morgan is, they would be foolish to think they can exploit it. For now, this works to our advantage. The Cell will keep tabs on him for us."

Mr. Clean brought up the last set of feeds, which appeared to be a network of cameras monitoring a residence.

"Where is this?" Heyer asked.

"The house beside Jonathan's," Mr. Clean said. "The property is a rental. Current tenants are a Leah McGuire and her younger brother, Jack."

Heyer nodded, observing the footage. He saw a young woman standing in the dark, her back to him as she leaned on the rail, looking over a balcony. Another showed a child asleep in his bed. On a separate camera feed, Heyer saw a guest bedroom and a face he recognized.

"Evelyn Tibbs… is currently staying at the residence?" he asked.

"She arrived this evening. Miss McGuire interacts socially with members of Jonathan's household, but the house is within range of the audio block, likely why The Cell has cameras on the premises," Mr. Clean said.

"Do you have any footage of this Ms. McGuire?" Heyer asked.

A feed from earlier that evening played on the screen. It showed Leah talking with one of Jonathan's roommates in the living room. Heyer's eyes narrowed as he studied her face. "Why does she look familiar to me, Mr. Clean?" he asked.

"Facial recognition does not match her with any persons of interest we have on file," Mr. Clean said. "She did occupy the residence roughly two days after Jonathan's implant was installed. Analysis of her face shows signs that plastic surgery may have altered her appearance."

Heyer watched the girl a moment longer, but if he knew her, he couldn't place where their paths had crossed. "See what you can find on her and the child," he said.

"I will monitor the feed," Mr. Clean said. "If there is a development, I'll report on your return."

"You have prepared the beacon, then?"

"You should rest before departure, sir," the A.I. said.

Heyer smiled patiently and nodded. "The beacon, Mr. Clean? Is it ready?"

"Yes," Mr. Clean said. "You realize that if Malkier's vessel scans you, they will detect that you have cloaked the device's presence. Though they will not be able to tell what you've brought in, they will know you're hiding something. They may make assumptions."

"If my brother has Cede take the precaution of scanning me, then they have already made their assumptions," Heyer said.

"But if he is merely suspicious, you will be sealing his certainty."

Heyer nodded. "I can't risk the alternative. This is the safest of two gambles."

A small stone manifested on the table top, no larger than a chicken's egg. It was smooth and gray, appearing the same as any rock one might find in a river bed on Earth, but unlike any that might be found on the Ferox world. Heyer picked it up and placed it into his pant's pocket. The stone absorbed into the lining, becoming a part of his clothing.

"It will bring you to Jonathan, if steps to mobilize our forces must be initiated immediately," Mr. Clean said. "I have to recommend you utilize the beacon only if no other option is available. Once it has been used within Cede, she will develop a defense against the security breach—we may not be able to exploit it again. In the event you must use it, be prepared. It will draw on your device for power, so you will be weakened by the trip."

Heyer nodded. "There is something to be said for the scenic route when it comes to travel accommodations." He waited, watching Mr. Clean on the monitor. When he found he had not yet departed, he spoke. "I'll be off, then?"

Mr. Clean's expression changed, taking on the appearance of someone hesitant to ask a question—odd for a machine.

"My friend, is there something more?"

The computer smiled, an iconic look for the character he was modeled after. "Your strategy," the A.I. said. "We were always working with a small range of possibilities and had to concentrate our efforts toward the best outcomes for Mankind. Events seem to be forcing our hand toward contingencies that are hardly ideal. Yet, there is one that seems somehow balancing—symmetrical. I fail to find the word. I am trying to capture it with reason, but there is no reason in such things."

Heyer looked at Mr. Clean thoughtfully. "Poetic justice, perhaps," Heyer said. "Sometimes, the natural order of things can seem to move toward a more fitting end despite the number of alternate outcomes."

The computer nodded. "I find myself curious, foreseeing some of the possible outcomes. I don't quite understand why, given there are numerous end results that you and I might have declared a victory, one is somehow more satisfactory than the others. Though, I see no particular benefit or advantage to Mankind's outcome. Do you, as a biological entity, understand?"

Heyer smiled. "I believe the short answer is that you are attached to one outcome… you wish to see him given his chance."

"Yes." Mr. Clean nodded. "It is as though what Mankind is owed, is not satisfied by achieving their safety. Is it justice or revenge I seem enamored with?"

Heyer sighed. "What will be, will be, Mr. Clean," he said. "Justice is not something I feel qualified to comment on, as I have not seen a just face in the mirror for quite some time. We must stay focused on all of Mankind. Justice—no matter how tempting it is to pursue—must remain an afterthought."

They exchanged a final glance with one another.

"Be safe," Mr. Clean said, and Heyer was gone.

The lights were off in Jonathan's house, and he laid on the couch, staring at the ceiling. Hours had passed this way, the house growing quiet as everyone else fell asleep.

He hadn't been able to find a moment alone yet to speak to Rylee. When Leah went home, and Collin and Hayden had gone to sleep, he had wanted to—but Paige had stayed awake until Rylee turned in. He'd felt out of line asking her to leave so he could speak privately with Rylee. If anything, he knew it would be casting doubt on his intentions. Doubts he knew Paige would never keep from Leah. When Paige had stepped out of earshot for a moment he'd quickly asked Rylee to come speak with him once everyone was asleep.

Jonathan probably should have been irritated with Paige for playing chaperone—but he wasn't. If anything, he knew he still owed her an apology, or at least a thank-you. She hadn't caved under his mother's pressure. Paige, he knew, had kept his secrets, even though she felt he was wrong to ask it of her. She always protected her friends, and despite its appearance, the childish act of chaperoning two adults was her way of doing the same for Leah. That fact that Paige couldn't care less if she was being transparent about it only endeared her to him more.

He heard the faint sound of his bedroom door and Rylee's soft footsteps as she came down the stairs. He knew that waiting must have been difficult, after seeing him nearly fall apart in front of her in the garage. Rylee had played along all night, knowing there was bad news—she'd helped Jonathan pretend they weren't hiding anything.

He thumbed the button on his father's pocket watch as Mr. Clean had told him. Nothing happened that he could detect, but he figured that would be the case. He heard Rylee cross slowly through the room, felt her sit on the couch near his feet. He could only see the outline of her in the dark, faint touches of light on her skin from the windows. She made a move to touch him, but stopped, as though, if he was asleep, she wasn't sure she should rouse him.

"I'm up," he whispered.

"I thought you might have fallen asleep, wasn't sure if I should let you rest," Rylee whispered. "Thought you might need it."

"Less and less use for sleep these days," he said.

She nodded, waiting a moment before speaking again. "The alien told you something. You were upset. I hope I can help."

"I'm sorry you saw that. I know it's not what you needed to see."

"Don't be sorry," she replied. "I'm not fragile."

"I know you aren't."

Rylee drew in a breath, and let it out with the annoyance of a child who felt placated. "Look, what you saw in that hotel room," she said. "That was my lowest moment. I had been out of sorts for a while—it just got so much worse after I came here. I got paranoid, thought that Heyer had made you forget me. That he was punishing me. But, I had already changed my mind before you showed up. I'm not some weakling you have to tip toe around." She shook her head. "To be honest, I have trouble even remembering how I got that upset in the first place."

Jonathan listened, but he was glad that she couldn't see him in the dark. Every word she said that was meant to reassure him was having the opposite effect. It was possible, he supposed, that Rylee had turned the corner on her own. That she had gotten through whatever drove her to consider suicide—that it had nothing to do with him.

He wished he could believe that, but Jonathan didn't think Rylee should have ever been driven to feel what she had in the first place. This bond between them had brought her to a state of grief and loneliness that had pushed her over the edge while she'd had no idea what was truly causing it. He feared that Rylee had spent a day and a half suffering withdrawals from a drug she didn't even know she had become addicted to—that once he'd completed his half of the link, she had finally gotten a dose that grew stronger as he had drawn closer.

He worried what it meant for her—but had no illusions. Her emotional state was not the only one that could no longer be trusted.

"Point is," Rylee said, "I'm good, nothing to worry about. So, what is going on?"

He didn't speak right away, didn't realize how long his silence had gone on until Rylee felt he needed a prod.

"Stop thinking so much… or are you stalling?"

"Both, I guess," Jonathan said. "I need to ask you some things, but I have to know the answers are the… truth."

He knew it was the wrong thing to say the moment he finished. An uncomfortable quiet followed, and Rylee sounded hurt when she replied. "You felt you had to say that?" she asked. "Heyer—he told you not to trust me?"

"Heyer knows you don't exactly like him. So, in turn, he doesn't know if he can trust you." Jonathan said. "I was..." He trailed off, searching for the best words. "I was given some compelling reasons not to put much faith in my instincts. Things I cannot ignore. If you want to help, then please don't hide anything."

She stared at him in silence, and this time it was her delay that felt too long. Finally, she sighed. "Jonathan, ask me whatever you want. I can't make you believe the answers."

It didn't take him long before feeling foolish. "You're right." He felt the soft nudge of her elbow against his knee.

"Yeah, well," she said, "I'll forgive you since you admitted it."

He couldn't make out her face in the dark, but thought she'd smiled. It made him wait a bit longer, wanting to let her smile before asking her questions he wasn't sure she'd want to answer.

"Rylee, why are you here?" Jonathan asked.

Her face lingered on him a moment before turning away, and he could tell she was hesitating. "I'm not sure how to answer," she said. "It is not a simple story."

"That's fair enough. Maybe 'why' is the wrong question, but how did you end up here?"

Rylee chuckled. "How and why are..." She paused. "Difficult to separate." She paused again to think for a moment. "I suppose it goes back to Heyer and I having trust issues. Perhaps he doesn't keep you in the dark, but it might surprise you to know that, before I bumped into you, I hadn't known there were others."

"No," Jonathan said. "He kept that from me for a long time. It came as a shock when I found out."

"That was the problem. Every time Heyer refused to tell me the truth, I trusted him less. Started the night I met him..."

She trailed off, and Jonathan saw her head come down to hang against her chest for a moment before she took in a long breath and continued.

"I'd felt someone watching me that night, knew that I wasn't alone in my apartment. Before he stepped out of the shadows and spoke, he'd put himself between me and the door. I wanted to run, but I saw his eyes—that cold, blue light. It frightened me. I knew he wasn't human. I had trouble moving at all by the time he spoke."

Jonathan watched her as he listened—clearly this was a memory she avoided. Rylee seemed to go distant, as though even when telling the story, she had to pretend it had happened to someone else.

"He told me about monsters coming to Earth. Merciless things that would kill the weak until someone stepped forward and brought them a fight. That he had a device that would make me strong enough to be the one who stepped forward.

"He said..." Rylee paused. "That there were others. Women who he could give the implant to, but that I was the best fit. That those other women's chances of surviving the implantation were too low. That I was the safest choice."

"You didn't believe him?"

His question was met with a long pause as she considered. "No, that part I did," she said. "I didn't believe the way he tried to sell it. As though I should want nothing more than to be some damn hero—the defender of the weak. You see, he wasn't explaining any of it: the *hows* and *whys*—the fine print. I was terrified of him, but still knew there was a lie hidden in the details he wasn't giving."

Jonathan nodded slowly.

"Heyer kept trying to make it sound as though it was my decision, like he was waiting for me to tell him, 'Yes, I want this.' He wanted my permission even though he knew he didn't need it. He was too much of a coward, didn't want to have to admit that he would force me."

Jonathan listened, thinking about how his own implantation had gone. He had already been activated before the alien presented any illusion of choice. Once he knew what had been done to him, it was already too late—he'd seen too much to turn away.

"I was happy, Jonathan," Rylee said. "Before, I mean. I didn't question who I was. I remember I used to go to bed with my window open because I liked feeling the sun on my skin in the morning. I had friends and family. I…" Rylee paused. "I didn't want to miss anything."

Rylee moved in the dark, pulling her legs against her chest as she sat beside him.

"Afterwards, I just started shrinking. I kept being forced to change. I started to feel cold all the time. I'd wake up and wish I didn't have to, that the world would stop making me be a part of it. It took me so long to figure out exactly what he had taken from me."

The tone of her voice had changed, starting to tremble. He sat up slowly on the couch, wrapping his arms around his knees, too—all he felt he could do to show her he was there to listen, that he understood what she had been through.

"Do you like your name, Jonathan?" Rylee asked.

"I never really thought about it."

"I heard a name once, and I always wished it was mine," Rylee said. "So, I thought when I had a daughter, I could give her that name. But I'm never going to have a daughter."

"You wanted to be a mother?" Jonathan asked.

Rylee sighed. "I wanted to be a lot of things. But yes… a mother was one of them."

Jonathan swallowed. He hurt for her. Then he hated what he felt, because he no longer knew if his sympathy was true or artificial. He wanted to hurt for her—but he didn't want to wonder if it was real.

"You see, I can't be anything, because the thing he took was..." Rylee paused. "Time."

Jonathan nodded slowly as the meaning of the word took shape. He could understand, but the reason he felt her loss so profoundly was because he didn't feel it at all. Jonathan had no equivalent. She'd said it more than once, in a different way each time. Rylee had known who she was and where she was going and what she wanted when she got there. Heyer had taken all that away and now Rylee didn't know anything.

As he'd listened, he found himself wondering when the last time had been that he'd felt something close to it. Certainly, if he was being honest, it was long before the alien had arrived, when his bed was a warm place where he was waking to a world full of possibilities. Rylee now shared a grief he'd tried not to ponder. It was an ugly thing that Jonathan had wished wasn't a part of him long before the alien showed up; a jealousy he'd had for others and wished he didn't own.

There was a distinction, Jonathan had found, in the people he had grown close to. When he saw it, it was so simple, and yet seemingly so unfair. Some people knew what they wanted like they knew they needed to breathe—as though they had been born with goals written into the very fiber of their beings. They were a gifted minority of humanity in possession of a valuable thing. Those without purpose could not imagine what it was to have one—because to be able to imagine a true purpose *was* to have one.

People like himself searched and searched within, only to find a void where there was supposed to be a mission. They had an absence—a space inside where nothing seemed more important than anything else, and the search for what mattered became the closest they could get. He'd envied those who had no need to search.

Rylee, it seemed, had had such a gift. Jonathan could hear her grief for it. As he listened, he did not envy her. Heyer, knowing or not, had destroyed that gift.

What came to him was something the alien had said to him that evening: *Every strength had its intrinsic weaknesses.* In all the time he'd coveted what those people had, he hadn't considered what they had to lose.

A daughter, he thought.

He tried to picture Rylee holding an infant. It didn't seem so impossible a fantasy at first—until it crumbled under the weight of their shared reality. Finding a lover, despite a truth she could never tell, a secret permanently held between them? Trudging out to fight a Ferox while caring a child? Surviving nine months of pregnancy and a delivery? Even if Rylee managed all that, giving birth was not the end goal. She couldn't expect to live through a never-ending onslaught of monsters. She could never be what she really wanted—a mother to a child.

Rylee was right; if she boiled it down to its simplest component, the alien had taken time from her.

"Suffice to say, I didn't adjust well," she said. She shrugged as though by making light of everything she told him, she could keep it from hurting her. "I spiraled down the drain, saw things I couldn't forget. In the back of my head, I wanted to find the way out. So, I knew I had to stay alive—which was somewhat infuriating, as Heyer wanted the same. He would show up and want to talk to me from time to time. I hardly spoke. Figured that if he didn't want to tell me anything, he deserved to get the same in return."

She turned to look at Jonathan then and gazed into his eyes in the dark.

"But, eventually, I decided I wanted my time back. And I didn't give a damn what the alien had to say about it."

Jonathan studied her. "I don't follow."

Rylee chuckled a bit before she went on. "One evening, I killed a Ferox before it had the chance to hurt anyone. When I pulled the stone free, I knew I was supposed to close the gates, but I..." Rylee paused. "Well, I just didn't."

Rylee turned to him, and he realized that she had expected to see him judging her for what she had confessed. When she looked, Jonathan wasn't considering if her actions were ethical—he was too curious to hear what had come of it.

"Heyer always made it sound so important, but he never explained why. So, I decided to find out for myself," she said.

"So what did you do?" Jonathan asked.

"I climbed to the top of the Manhattan Bridge and watched the sunset," Rylee said. "I wanted to call his bluff more than anything. I figured, best case scenario, I'll live in some other version of Manhattan where a monster had attacked one day. People would get over it. I could wait and see. If something went wrong, I had the stone—could crush it at any time." She groaned then. "It didn't take long, a few more hours, before Heyer found me. He was... not pleased."

Jonathan smiled, finding it hard not to laugh as he imagined Heyer's disapproval when he'd found her sitting on the bridge. Rylee told the story as though her rebellion was more like missing curfew than refusing to close an inter-dimensional gateway.

"What did Mr. Fedora say?"

"He asked what the meaning of it was," Rylee said. "I told him I was done taking orders. That I wouldn't close the gates."

"Wow. Nerves of steel." Jonathan shook his head. "I don't think I could have done it."

Rylee ran a hand through her hair and looked at him. "You're afraid of him?"

Jonathan grew thoughtful for a moment. "No, not that he would physically harm me. I think I may respect him too much to put him in that position. But I get why you felt differently. What did he say?"

"Well, that was when things got weird," she said. "He didn't try to intimidate me or take the stone. Didn't say a word, actually. He just sat a few feet away and watched the water."

"How long did that last?"

"His presence kinda took all the fun out of it—he was kind of hard to ignore. Don't ever try to beat Heyer at a game when patience is involved."

Jonathan snorted. He'd expected this conversation to be so much more confrontational. He kept finding himself more excited to hear her story, to listen to the sound of her voice. He didn't feel as though she were tricking him… Jonathan turned away and grimaced, the unwanted warning reminding him he couldn't trust his feelings ruining the moment.

"I am ashamed to admit I spoke first," Rylee said. "Finally asked him what he was doing." She shook her head. "So, he doesn't answer right away. No rush, right? After hours of silence. He just sighs, turns to me, and says..." That was when Rylee launched into an awful impression of Heyer's shadow. "There is nowhere else for me to be, Rylee. You refuse to obey me, refuse to take my word—wish to see the truth for yourself."

Rylee stopped then, any humor she found in the story seeming to have come to an end as she looked down at the floor.

"He said I was hurting everyone in that reality—that each moment I didn't break the stone did them harm. That I would be the only one who didn't experience the effects, but would have to watch everyone else's mind degrade. He said that he would not be immune, because he was a copy of himself like everyone else. That I was the only real person in that place. Then he said he would stay beside me until I was convinced—until he made sure that I closed the gates."

"How long did it take?" Jonathan asked. "Before you knew he was telling the truth?"

"Had it not been Manhattan, probably not as long," Rylee said. "Within a day, I couldn't ignore that the people weren't quite right. Heyer... took longer. He said that his device slowed the process, but that he was still a 'copy.' The first explosion in the city happened the next evening. After that, violence started taking place in the streets. I watched it all from a rooftop with the alien. He stood beside me, waiting."

Rylee stalled. She reached out to Jonathan then, took hold of his forearm and leaned down to rest her head against his arms. "I told him that I saw the gates needed to be closed. But... Jonathan, what you saw in that hotel room—I was afraid that if I didn't do something, I was going to end up there eventually. I cared—I didn't want to watch those people hurt one another, but I needed him to tell me something. Anything that gave me a choice."

Rylee was afraid he was judging her again, he knew it was why she felt she had to explain. Being honest, he was disturbed that she held out. He didn't know, had it been some stranger telling the story, if he would be so ready to forgive—but the moment he'd experienced within her made it impossible for him to pretend he didn't understand. He knew her nature could not abide feeling trapped—how it made the fighter in her bleed out the longer she endured it. Jonathan didn't know, if he'd been slowly dying that death, what length he might be willing to go to escape it.

"I get it, Rylee," Jonathan said as gently as he could. "I understand why you felt you had no other choice."

She exhaled, seeming relieved at his words.

"Please, go on, finish your story."

She nodded. "Heyer started to struggle against the effects. I knew that he wasn't going to remember how far I had taken it. I had been disgusted by the idea of sharing what I felt with him for so long, but when I knew he wouldn't remember—I told him the truth. I told him what he had taken." A swift breath bordering on a laugh escaped her. "Actually, I screamed it at him, made quite the scene."

There was a silence as she paused, recalling how the alien's shadow had reacted.

"I think he didn't want to," Rylee said. "That, if he hadn't been suffering the degradation, he might not have said anything, but he wanted the gates closed so badly..." Rylee swallowed, then. "Finally, he said that this war would not remain isolated to me, alone, forever. That the Ferox would come for all Mankind. He said, the only weapon humanity had against enslavement would need my protection. That, when the day came, it would start here, in Seattle."

Rylee and Jonathan looked at each other.

"I believed him," she said, "because I could see that every fiber of his being didn't really want to tell me. That his resolve had only faltered because he wasn't able to fight what was happening to his mind. So, I closed the gates. I got myself together and left town—I came here. I didn't have a plan, didn't know what I was looking for, but I had something. I don't regret anything I did—not now."

She went silent, and Jonathan reached out to her in the dark. She melted into him as though she wouldn't have known what to do if he had left her there, waiting. She laid down, her head against his chest. He wanted to hold her, despite knowing he shouldn't, that he was making everything worse for the both of them. He wasn't sure what would hurt her more in that instant, bringing her close or keeping her at a distance—but she'd been so honest.

"So, that is how and why," Rylee said. "Is that what you need? To know how I got here?"

"Part of it," Jonathan said.

"What is the other part?"

"I..." Jonathan trailed off, too conflicted. "I need to think it through, but it can wait. I'll tell you tomorrow."

She didn't push, just nodded against his chest. They didn't speak again and eventually she fell asleep beside him, though Jonathan laid awake. He believed everything she told him. Where Heyer had suspected some treachery, Jonathan only saw Rylee trying to free herself. Maybe she should have considered what the consequences would be, but she hadn't felt like she had anything to lose, certainly hadn't thought she would hurt anyone other than herself.

He wished that he didn't know about the bond. How was he supposed to tell her to leave? How was he supposed to know if she would fall into a depression again if he asked her to? How did he know that the bond hadn't already sunk its claws into him?

Collin stopped himself from hitting the snooze button on his alarm clock, seeing he'd slept in longer than he'd planned. He flipped the blinds up, glad to see it wasn't raining, and dressed in a hurry. He pulled his backpack over his riding jacket and headed out his bedroom door. As he reached for the handle, he reminded himself to be quiet, not wanting to wake Jonathan if he was still asleep on the couch.

He found Paige standing in the living room with her back half-turned to him. She frowned down at the couch, and Collin's eyes followed her gaze to see Rylee asleep in Jonathan's blanket, with Tibbs himself gone. Already left for work, he guessed.

Collin wanted to pretend he didn't understand what bothered Paige, why she had a thousand-yard stare as she looked down at the girl sleeping peacefully on the couch. He'd be lying to himself, though. He was just as curious about what order of events had led to Rylee sleeping there now. Had she come down in the night and slept with Jonathan, or had she come down after he left, found him gone, and fallen asleep in his blanket?

"Subtle," he whispered to Paige.

Startled, she turned in his direction. She flushed slightly at having been caught staring while Rylee slept. Seeing he was smiling at her like a conspirator, she smiled back.

Then he frowned, checking his watch and realizing she was as late as he was. "Don't you have class in fifteen minutes?"

She closed her eyes, nodding.

"Well, I'd offer you a ride, but..." Collins eyes made a wide circle, taking the scenic route from her face, around the room, and then to the helmet he held at his side before he looked back up at her. "We know how you feel about motorcycles."

Paige looked down at his helmet. Biting her lip, she took another look at the girl sleeping on the couch. When her eyes came back to him, she lifted an eyebrow. "That a dare?"

Collin tilted his head, intrigued.

"You got a spare helmet?"

CHAPTER THIRTY-EIGHT

MONDAY| OCTOBER 10, 2005 | 6:30 PM | SEATTLE

WHEN THE SUN had just started setting, the new motorcycle already sat in Leah's garage. The side paneling was still pulled off, though Leah could have finished fitting the clips to hold the demolition bar hours earlier. She'd let the job stretch out, making sure Jonathan would see she still had it in her garage when he came home. Now she was waiting, keeping herself busy, letting classic rock play over the stereo and ignoring the clock as the hour he normally returned home approached.

She knew he had arrived when his shadow cast itself against the wall in front of her, standing in the light of the work lamp she'd mounted over the bike. She didn't let on that she'd noticed—wanted to take her cue from him. She wondered if, now that they were alone, he would try to explain himself or if he would ignore the oddities of the last few days. In the end, she'd be forced to accept whatever he said, but she had to push back—if she were too accommodating, it would be suspicious.

"You know," Jonathan said. "One of these days, I'm going to lock my garage door."

"I have my doubts, Tibbs," she said, not yet turning to look at him, instead finishing putting her tools away. "Then you'd have to find an excuse to come over all by yourself."

She didn't need to look. She knew he was grinning.

Leah heard his footsteps draw closer, saw his shadow grow against the wall. He stopped before he reached her, his attention drawn to a work table along the side of her garage. "You never showed me these," he said.

Photos she'd printed were loosely scattered on the table top, all shots Leah had taken since moving in next door. Some were nature and scenery, a flower, the Seattle skyline at night, birds in trees. Then there were the two she'd had framed. One was a picture he'd been there to see her take—Paige standing in her garden with a pink flower behind her ear. The picture gave him a warm feeling—bright sunshine and a pleasant face smiling back. The other picture was strange, harder to make out, dark. He held it, his face growing troubled in a way Leah found hard to read. After a moment, he slowly set the frame back down where he had found it.

"You framed this one?" he asked, as Leah joined him at the table, "These others seem more…"

Jonathan trailed off and his eyebrows drew down in thought. As though he'd expected the word he needed would come to him, but had reached the end of his statement without having found it.

"Pleasant?" she asked. "Hopeful?"

He nodded noncommittally.

"Well, I prefer this one. I feel more looking at it than I do with the others."

The photo was of Jonathan in his garage. A few weeks back—the moment before she'd kissed him for the first time. The picture had a lonely quality to it; a trick of light. He was walking away from the camera, his face turned to look back, half-hidden in shadow. The darkness seemed alive in the photo, as though it followed him—would consume him. He was like a candle flame that the shadows were trying to snuff out of existence.

"What does it make you..." They smiled at one another when they both started asking the same question at once.

"You framed it," Jonathan said. "You go first."

Coyly, she held his eyes as though she might protest. She let out a breath then and looked back at the picture. Her smile faded. "It hurts to look at," she said, turning back to him. "But I don't mind that it hurts."

He tilted his head, waiting for her to help him understand.

"I am standing behind you, watching you walk off into the dark. I feel you going into this empty, black place, alone. There is no one to warm you, to talk to you. Feels so lonely it hurts to imagine. I feel like..." Her courage faltered then, and she had to look away to finish. "I'd do anything," she whispered, "to keep you from that place."

When they had first met, it had seldom been Leah who looked away when they found one another's eyes. Now, it seemed like the more she feared losing him, the more transparent she felt looking back at him.

She felt his hand, warm and gentle on her cheek.

"Leah," he said. "About the other night, Rylee. I…"

"No." She stopped him, her tone changing abruptly. "You'll just table that for a moment. Don't change the subject." She glanced back at the frame, prompting his attention to stay on the picture. "I shared… now it's your turn. Tell me what you see."

A conflicted smile came over his face as he withdrew his hand. He folded his arms over his chest and studied the picture again as he gathered his thoughts. "It reminds me of a dream I keep having."

"Oh?" Her eyes grew wider with curiosity. "Do tell, Mr. Tibbs."

She saw his guard coming down.

"I'm standing in this dark room. It should be pitch black but it isn't—there are these shapes that seem to catch the light when I stand close enough. I don't know where the light is coming from, and it's only enough to get impressions. It's familiar—the room, the shapes—but I don't know why. I find this table in the dark, a lot like this one, with a picture on top of it. When I hold it close enough, I recognize it: a photo, that my father kept in his garage, of my mother and I when I'd been born. There..."

Leah listened, not making any attempt to hide that she wanted to know, but his eyes wandered to her lips. She felt his desire, heard him trail off and forget what he had been talking about. Then—he hesitated, suddenly seeming to think he had no right to touch her. He looked away, and a moment passed, before he finally managed to remember what he was saying.

"There's something in the dark that I'm supposed to see," he said.

"What?" she asked softly.

Jonathan shook his head. "I don't know. There's this box on the table, beside the picture. It's locked and I don't have the key. I usually wake about then." He shrugged. "I suppose Jung could have some fun with it. But it's just a dream."

Leah closed her eyes, biting her lip as she imagined being inside the room he'd described. "It's troubling," she said, opening her eyes again. "That what you're looking for has been locked away in a dark place. It's as though you're looking for a truth you know can't be good." She looked at him, her seriousness fading into a smile. "You know, because if it was good, you'd dream of a box in a meadow with flowers, and chirping birds," she said, pointing at the other photos scattered on the table.

He grinned and nodded. "The truth doesn't care what we think of it. It is what it is. Couldn't care less if we put it in the sun or the dark."

Leah giggled before she could stop herself. "Oh-so wise," she said mockingly. "Professor Nietzsche over here."

He smirked, but otherwise took the joke gracefully.

Then they found they had run out of things to say, and the silence that followed reminded them they were distracting themselves from an awkward conversation. Jonathan, enjoying her company, seemed to go looking for another way to put off the inevitable.

"I see I owe you a favor," he said, nodding to the work she'd done on the motorcycle. He walked to the side of the bike, crouching down to take a better look. "Course, last time we discussed terms before you went and stole my motorcycle."

"Yeah," she said. "Truth is, you're pretty much on the hook for whatever I ask now."

"Well, that's just not fair."

"Aww. The truth doesn't care if it's fair, Nietzsche."

Jonathan smirked in amusement. "Walked into that one," he said. "So, what can I do for you?"

"Isn't that the question..." She turned around and pushed herself up to sit on the table. Without asking, she gently used her legs to maneuver him so they stood face to face. She saw him growing wary, finding himself in a position where he couldn't easily look away. "I want you to promise you won't leave this garage, no matter what I ask you. No running away until I say you can."

Jonathan sighed and seemed to be bracing himself.

Then, just as he looked on the verge of giving his consent, she added, "And promise it will be the truth."

He closed his eyes, her request now clearly heavier than the one he had been ready to commit to a moment before. "I promise that I'll do the best I can," he said.

Leah narrowed her eyes at him, but nodded a reluctant acceptance. "Rylee," she said carefully. "When she showed up in your driveway. I saw your concern for her, as she drove off, but you didn't know who she was, Jonathan. I didn't doubt you. I should doubt you now, but I don't. It's just… not how you lie."

He flinched awkwardly at the last word, but she hadn't asked a question, so he waited.

"Jonathan," Leah said. "Why did you leave the other night?"

"I didn't want to," he said. "But I had to."

"Because of Rylee?"

Slowly, he nodded.

Leah's eyes pleaded with his. "How is it you had to leave for someone you didn't know?"

He took a moment to answer. "She was in trouble, Leah," he whispered. "I had to do something."

"How could you even know something like that, Jonathan? You need to tell me how that makes sense."

He closed his eyes then, and swallowed. "It isn't going to make sense, Leah. It's never going to."

She'd never wished she could read his mind more than she did at that moment. It seemed impossible for him to be telling her the truth, yet there was no trace of dishonesty.

"Jonathan, what am I supposed to think?" she asked. "There is something going on with you and her. You brought her home and gave her your bed."

"I didn't know what else to do. I have to watch out for her..." he said. "But Leah, I don't feel for her what I feel for you."

Leah waited. She wanted him to say something more, needed him to give her something more. "Dammit, Jonathan," she said, a desperate frustration creeping into her voice. "Please, I can't stand looking at you, feeling like a fool because I believe you when I know you aren't telling me everything."

"I'm not telling you everything," Jonathan said. "But it's all I can." He watched her, seeming to know what came next. She saw his lips tremble the longer he failed to find something to say.

"Would it be me or her?"

That look was on his face again, as though the question were too complicated to answer. "It isn't a fair question," he whispered.

Leah saw what this was doing to him and hated it. He was trying so hard to find an honest answer that would keep her from telling him to go. She pulled him against her and his arms responded as she placed her head on his shoulder. "Just... tell me a story," she said. She tilted her head up, whispering in his ear. "It doesn't have to be your story, just one that will make me understand."

She pressed her head back down on his shoulder. Unable to see his face, she waited, listening to his heart. It took some time—how long, she wasn't sure, but the beats eventually began to slow.

"I have a story," Jonathan whispered to her. "But it isn't going to tell you what you want."

After a moment, she nodded against his shoulder.

"Imagine if there were two rooms, both right next to each other. In one room, there is a person you care about, and she's hurt, and if you don't help her soon, you might lose her."

Leah pulled back gently, looking up to search his eyes. "And the other room?"

"A bomb," he said. "It's counting down, but you can't see the clock. If it can't be defused, both rooms and everyone in them will be caught in the explosion."

She blinked at him. The best she could do to hide the grim understanding coming to her. "Will the girl in the room die before the bomb goes off?"

"There is no way to know," he said. "It depends on how long she can hold on."

Slowly, she brought her head back against him. "What do you have to do to diffuse the bomb?"

Jonathan took in a long breath and let it out. "Whatever it takes." His voice trembled. "You can only hope that the girl in the room understands that."

They didn't speak for a while, but the pull of their closeness got the better of them. At some point, her lips were against his, and Leah began to forget that there were supposed to be reasons she couldn't allow it. Neither of them wanted to stop, but when she could not endure another moment without taking it further, she pushed him away. He didn't fight, she could see he'd felt the same, that his need for her had come so close to being all that mattered.

She said that if he needed to go, he had her permission. She could see he didn't want to leave, but he nodded. He was smart enough not to press his luck, given the circumstance.

Leah lingered there a long while once he'd left. Jonathan had had no idea just how much more she had inferred from the story, how many meanings he thought were hidden by its vagueness. She was lost in thought when Evelyn stepped through the doorway and startled her.

Jonathan's mother seemed not to notice the lapse. She looked just as upset and contemplative as Leah felt. However, Evelyn made no attempt to hide that her mind was troubled. Leah was about to ask what was wrong, but the older woman spoke first.

"Leah, has my son come home yet?" she asked, her tone distant.

Leah nodded.

"Could you do me a favor, dear? Would you see if Paige would come join us? I need to talk to the two of you. It's important."

He walked away from Leah's garage in a daze. The last few days had seen several disruptions to his routines, and the growing number of complications made it more and more difficult to focus. He needed to keep up with his training, but at that moment, he looked forward to it for therapeutic reasons. He desperately needed to exhaust a growing imbalance of restless energy. As he neared his garage, unfamiliar music came from inside. The sound was almost tribal to him.

When he stepped inside, he found Rylee had made herself at home. His weights had been moved to the side of the room and the mats he used for practicing maneuvers were spread over the floor. In the center of them, Rylee balanced in a handstand. Her arms flexed, holding her steady while upside down. The true strength of her body was on display, the clothes she trained in hiding little while the exertion of exercise pumped blood to her musculature and flushed her cheeks and shoulders. She was a perfect athlete, and the command she had over herself put his to shame. Even now, she seemed to effortlessly resist the forces which would have toppled him to the floor if he'd tried to do the same.

He was about to speak when she shifted, pulling one hand up from the floor, her legs parting to redistribute her weight as she held the same pose, now with only one hand as a foundation on the floor.

He remembered how he had felt when he'd first seen her fight—as though he'd been in a trance. He felt the same hypnosis now. She was impressive even without the added strength of the device there to make her grace superhuman. He watched her close her eyes, inhale deeply, and with a sudden swift movement, she swung to the side. Her legs and arms traded places in a manner that mocked gravity, as though the pull of the Earth were some insignificant afterthought she could ignore. Outside of watching an Olympic gymnast, he'd never seen a person move like her. Still, those graceful combinations of movement he had seen on television were practiced. Rylee never looked as though her body flowed through a combination; she felt the movements out as she went, reacting to the changes around her.

He realized that she was standing on her feet, looking back at him, and by the time his eyes met hers, he'd lost track of how long he may have been staring at the rest of her. If she noticed, she didn't mention it. He had to drag his eyes away. It was possible that Leah had left him in a state that made his appreciation of the female form more difficult to ignore than it already was.

"I've never had someone to train with, Jonathan. At least, not someone who knew what I was training for," Rylee said. "Will you train with me?"

He brightened at the request. "Definitely."

CHAPTER THIRTY-NINE

RYLEE WATCHED AS he stripped off his coat and turned to a small box that rested on a counter under the garage's one window. He tossed in his cell phone and wallet, but was more careful when he placed a gold pocket watch and a photo inside. He pulled open a drawer and removed some more appropriate clothing, then looked at her, his expression unsure.

"I need to change," he said.

She nodded, taking a few moments to see he was waiting for her to look away. Rylee rolled her eyes and turned around. Of course, the room had a number of mirrors, and she was still looking at his reflection.

He glowered back at her humorously through the mirror.

"Jeez, Captain Modest," she said, closing her eyes and letting herself sway with the music. "As though you've got something I haven't already seen."

When Rylee was fairly sure she'd heard him pulling on a change of pants, she couldn't resist, and made a show of opening one eye. He was barefoot, in a tank top and some synthetic black exercise pants. She smiled, feigning embarrassment when he looked at her. "Oops," she said.

He blushed, but she was sure she saw him grinning before making a point to clear his throat.

"Where did you learn to move the way you do?" he asked. "I've never seen anyone fight like you. Is it some type of gymnastics?"

She shook her head. "No. Only looks similar."

She dropped into a low moving crouch, her legs keeping her in constant motion, then used the momentum to move about him with maneuvers he couldn't put a name to. *Half cartwheel, half somersault, a one-handed backflip?* His brow furrowed as he studied her style, his focus serious and discerning as he tried to dissect her unpredictable manner of moving about.

"I don't know what to call the things you're doing," he finally said.

Rylee didn't stop, but stayed upright a moment to respond. "They don't have English terms. Well, if they do, I don't know them."

She continued to move around him, and he paid attention to each feat of motion.

"It's amazing that you never lose sight of me," he said. "No matter how complicated the move, it's as though they were designed to keep your eye on the opponent. You only lose line of sight for a brief second—never long enough that I'd be able to take advantage."

She fell back into a swaying crouch a short distance away, bringing up her hand to taunt him into coming forward with her fingers. She smiled, watching him try to read her, as though unsure if she meant to seduce him or spar. She didn't hate the attention—his face seemed hypnotized as he tried to unlock a pattern in her style.

When he stepped toward her cautiously, she waited until he drew closer and relaxed. Her motion changed abruptly, the smallest of efforts to misdirect his attention. Her body headed toward him from the opposite angle. His reflexes were quick, and he reacted, but her legs were sweeping him off his feet while he expected a strike from above. He hit the matt with a *thwack*, looking up to see her cartwheeling over him.

From the floor, he watched her retreat. Jonathan was stunned, only slightly annoyed to have been attacked without real warning that she was ready to put him on the floor. He was too interested to complain. "You aren't using routines or combinations," he said. "How long have you trained like this?"

She flipped forward into a handstand, rolled down gently onto her back, and came to a stop, seated on the mat a foot from where she'd dropped him a moment earlier. "It's called *capoeira*. My father is a *mestre*. When he started teaching me, I was so young that I honestly can't remember life without it. It's the best way to learn the style. That is, to be brought up with it," she said. "But it's more show than it seems, inefficient to learn the older you start. For most, it's a dance or a game—takes years of training to become familiar enough with the techniques to consider using it in a fight. Admittedly though, once you're capable of moving without thinking, you become a very difficult target."

He studied her before shaking his head, unconvinced.

"Stand, Jonathan," Rylee said. "I'll show you what I mean."

She displayed a series of kicks. They were fast, long, powerful motions that would have taken him off his feet if they had connected. She showed him ways to attack from a hand stand, ways to use one's weight and motion to glide into positions that provided an advantage. He studied her as he had before, and now, seeing the offensive portion of the fighting style, she saw his skepticism forming.

"I can see what you mean, at least from an aggressor's standpoint," he said. "You'd be hard-pressed to land any damaging blows. Some of those kicks would be liable to hurt your joints more than your opponent if they actually connect."

She nodded. "You see the weaknesses faster than most."

He didn't seem to hear her, too deep in thought. He bit his lip, returned to the box where he had placed his possessions, and opened the pocket watch before placing it back. She frowned, thinking it odd that he was already checking the time.

"In your standard state, it would be problematic," he thought out loud. "But when activated, your body's resilience makes it so you can use all that speed to bring your legs around like hammers. Being able to move and balance like this, and still keep your eyes on your opponent… it gives you a freedom of adapting that I can only imagine, and your strength…"

He reached out unconsciously, taking hold of her arm. His hands caused a stir of awareness, his fingertips warm on her skin. Her eyes widened. The moment was short-lived however, as she saw how clinically he studied her, preoccupied with her physique only with respect to how it made her a better fighter.

"You're like iron," he said.

When he looked to her eyes and saw how they looked at him with uncertainty, Rylee found herself quickly hiding behind a pretense of nonchalance. "Smooth talk. A girl just dreams about the guy who only wants to stare at her biceps," she said.

Awkwardly, Jonathan let go, and she watched as he searched for words to put between himself and the look she was giving. He seemed suddenly troubled, frustrated. "It's not fair," he finally said.

"What is that supposed to mean?" she asked.

He looked back at her, his face hard to read as he took a breath. "Let's spar. I'll explain as we go. Our mutual acquaintance in the fedora told me a lot the other night, and you need to know it." Jonathan pointed to his chest, and then to hers. "You and I, we have a different set of rules than most."

CHAPTER FORTY

NO ONE HEARD her enter the house. She'd come through the front door while Rylee and Jonathan were busy training in the garage. She was supposed to bring Paige next door for Evelyn, but her friend was preoccupied. Leah could hear her laughing on the other side of Collin's door. It was as good a moment as any to slip quietly up the stairs. Now, she sat at Jonathan's desk, holding the journal she'd pulled from Rylee's bag.

In the event she was discovered, her cover story was to play the jealous girlfriend. Completely believable—more so now, after the exchange she'd had with Jonathan earlier. Still, Leah didn't want it to come to that. A part of her knew that, if she was forced to play that role, she'd be hurt if Jonathan believed it. It was a part of her that she had to pretend wasn't there—letting herself have feelings had already caused enough problems.

She was part relieved and part disappointed in finding that, for the moment, there was nothing she could learn. Every entry was written in Portuguese. Anxious of being walked in on, Leah took pictures as quickly as she could with a pocket digital camera. The fact that it hadn't already been destroyed gave Leah little hope that there would be any viable intel given Rylee knew she was under surveillance. When she turned to the last few pages, she didn't find more handwritten text, but a pencil sketch of Jonathan's face.

More often since the days that followed their one night together, Leah had seen that expression on his face, had watched it slip over him on the footage recorded by The Cell. It was always when he was alone—when he'd thought there was no one watching. Only once had she seen him look that way when there were people around to see him—the night Grant had pushed him to violence in his driveway.

This was the side of Jonathan that stared back at her, now, through the drawing, Rylee had captured what Leah herself had been trying to bring out of him. So much effort had been put into the details, such careful attention to the contours of his face. It was as though Rylee had been desperate to see him, for something real and tangible to feed her starving eyes.

Leah felt herself swallow, noticed she was fighting off a mounting fear, cowering inside and trying to push it away. Then her attention came to the date of the entry and she blinked as though she must have misread it.

Rylee had sketched this the day before she'd shown up in Jonathan's driveway, before everything The Cell knew said they could have been in contact. Jonathan—he'd been so convincing, made her believe they had never met. She remembered his face, his alarm—he'd seemed so genuinely confused. It didn't make sense—if he'd been lying, he deserved a damn Oscar nomination.

Reason told her that Rylee must have made a mistake, written down the wrong date, but a more practical voice told her to stop being naïve, that her "reason" was really wishful thinking in disguise.

Slower than she should have, she slipped the camera back into her pocket, trying to force herself to ignore a growing uncertainty. She hadn't had to question where Jonathan put her, what place she held in his mind until now—she didn't like the feeling. She needed to put the diary back, undisturbed, from where she found it and get out. Yet, she opened the journal once more, flipped to the drawing as though she hoped it had changed, all been some trick of her eye. She noticed that pages had been torn out, but only those immediately in front of the portrait. At first, she thought it was as she expected, that Rylee had removed pages to hide something when she knew she was under surveillance—but now she wondered.

How many times? Leah thought. H*ow many tries did it take Rylee to get the picture in her mind onto paper before she—*

"Soooo busted!"

Startled, Leah jumped—and the diary dropped on the floor.

"Leah," Paige said, attempting to restrain a childish grin as she stood in Jonathan's doorway. "I am so very, very disappointed in you."

Leah flushed, panicked for a moment. She'd been stupid, hadn't been paying attention—and now she was humiliated at being caught red-handed. Her mind was already racing, unsure what this meant for her. Was she compromised? Gracelessly, Leah rushed to put the journal back in its place and practically tripped over herself in the process.

"Paige, please, I know how this looks. I can expla…"

It had taken a moment to sink in, but as Leah turned to plead with Paige, she noticed that her friend was taking what she'd seen rather well. Actually, Paige's fingers were over her mouth trying to hold in laughter.

"Oh, I don't doubt it," she said, a snort escaping. "Honestly, I didn't think you had it in you."

"I don't! I mean I didn't! Shut up!" Leah said, giggling herself, surprised by how hilarious this all seemed to her friend.

"And here I was, worried I was the only one thinking it."

Leah managed to get the diary back into Rylee's bag, pulling it shut quickly before she fled the room with her friend in pursuit. Paige was nearly failing to keep from laughing, biting down on the inside of her lips as they crossed the hall into her room. Paige shut her bedroom door behind them, then conspiratorially opened it a crack to check the hallway and make sure they hadn't been seen.

"You have to tell me!" she said, turning back.

"Okay, you caught me," Leah said. "You don't have to be so damn pleased about it."

"Can't help it! Speak, woman!"

"I can't."

"Spill it, Leah," she said, pretending to growl.

Leah found herself smiling gratefully. She wasn't sure when it had happened exactly, but at that moment, she realized that her friendship with Paige had stopped being a means to an end long before today. This would have been so low a moment for her, being caught—having her insecurities on display. Yet Paige had laughed, mocked her kindly before signing on to be an accomplice. The girl was so unshakably on her team that she hadn't hesitated to split the guilt with her.

"I think I love you a little bit right now," Leah said.

Paige smiled at her knowingly, but soon her eyes narrowed. "Hey, I know what you're doing, lady. Don't change the subject! Start talking."

Leah frowned. "I can't."

"Don't even dare pull some 'respect for privacy' crap with me now."

"No, I mean I *really* can't," Leah said, her voice dropping to a whisper. "It was all in Portuguese. I couldn't read a word of it."

"Arrgh! Damn clever, bilingual harlot!"

Leah smiled, shaking her head a moment as she watched her friend. "I've never seen you like this. It's charming, in a delinquent sort of way."

"You know," Paige said, "I've never had a friend I'd want to play sneaky jealous girl games with. I'm finding myself strangely okay with it."

Leah groaned as though the comment might make her sick. "Oh, don't go calling it out like that—now I feel like a cliché."

"Embrace the dark side, Leah."

Stifling a laugh, Leah attempted to put on a serious face. "Please, don't ever let Jonathan find out. I would be—"

"Find out about what?" Paige stopped, grinning.

Leah hadn't expected this moment to become a bonding experience, of all things, but she finally remembered her reason for having come over in the first place—or, at least, the reason she had been ready to give if anyone had been in the living room when she came in.

"So, um, Evelyn's asked me to come get you for coffee," Leah said. "Seemed like it was urgent coffee."

Paige groaned, her face already paling at the thought of what Jonathan's mother could want after their last phone conversation.

As they headed back out the door and down the stairs, Leah gave Paige a warning just in case it hadn't gone without saying. "Brace yourself. I'm fairly sure this is a mom trap."

Her friend sighed knowingly. "I swear, if you abandon me with Jonathan's mother, this amnesia I have about what did or did not just happen in Jonathan's bedroom may make a startling recovery."

"Ahh, extortion," Leah said. "I see how it is."

CHAPTER FORTY-ONE

THEY LAID ON the floor of the garage, sweat-soaked from sparring. Jonathan stared up at the ceiling, still catching his breath; Rylee, for her part, had at least broken a sweat.

"You aren't even tired, are you?" Jonathan asked.

She turned to him, one eye open. "Would it make you feel better if I said I was?"

He chuckled and shook his head. "Well, I'm jealous—never really met anyone with your endurance."

She looked back at him, her expression matter-of-fact. "Well, I do like to move it-move it."

When he laughed again, she couldn't hold onto the straight face, and the corner of her lip raised in a grin.

As they had sparred, Jonathan had given her the answers Heyer had denied her—most of them, at least. Why the Ferox came to Earth, the mechanics of their devices, the limits imposed by genetic compatibilities, and the nature of their enhanced strengths when together. He left out a lot of the details, more for the sake of getting to the meat of the information, but…

He had not mentioned the nature of the bond, had steered clear of anything that might have led to him breaking the news to her that Heyer expected him to send her away. He had found himself keeping other items to himself, like that the prophet of the Ferox was actively trying to kill him, and that the alien expected him to lead mankind's army. Rylee, for her part, didn't ask a lot of questions. Once he explained that Heyer's A.I. was manipulating the camera feeds, she had focused on listening intently, understanding that every second he was explaining was time that Mr. Clean had to actively hide the details of their conversation.

When the smile she'd given him faded, he found himself frustrated by Rylee's situation. "It's not fair," he said. "Your compatibility is handicapping you—forces your strategies to be reliant on cunning and skill, but there isn't anything Heyer can do about it."

Rylee's eyes came back off the ceiling—he felt them study him. "What has fair ever had to do with anything?" She nudged him playfully in the side. "As if women haven't always been putting up with having to be ten times better than a man for the same results anyway."

Jonathan worried she was making light of the problem—addressing the situation with humor because there was nothing to be done about it. He should have kept his concerns to himself; sharing them wouldn't accomplish anything. The thing was, he couldn't count the number of times strength kept the jaws of the enemy from closing around his neck, literally.

Rylee's skills were a perfect strategy against the over-eager Ferox youth. Her tactics would frustrate them as they yearned to engage in a toe-to-toe exchange of blows, and she denied them that. It turned their frustration, their impatience, into a weapon against them. The Greens would eventually grow more and more careless with their attacks, take chances. Then she had them.

The Reds were a different story.

Watching her breathing on the floor, processing it all, he saw a future he wished he hadn't. It looked like *Sickens the Fever* or *Bleeds the Stone*—a monster with control over his instincts, calculating, and able to dish out blows she couldn't match. If they got hold of her, got her into a tight place where she couldn't maneuver, that would be bad enough, but what worried him was that a fighter could possess twice the skill of their opponent and still find themselves at an insurmountable disadvantage.

In boxing, they called it "having the puncher's chance." Jonathan had learned it first-hand months earlier, when he sparred with a man a hundred pounds heavier than himself. His opponent had no need to be as careful, didn't have to defend every time he tried to land a blow. The man walked right into some of his jabs as a tactic—he could take the punishment, knowing Jonathan's guard would have to give an opening whenever he took the offensive. Meanwhile, Jonathan had to cover up or dodge every assault.

It had ended with Jonathan on the mat, unsure of what direction was up or down—it was why there were weight classes, why there weren't co-ed professional fights. In an exchange where the gap between two opponents strength was staggering, the stronger fighter always had an unfair advantage. One devastating strike, and the fight was over.

Rylee was the strongest woman he had ever met, and that was what troubled him. Realistically, she wasn't going to be able to gain much more muscle mass. Jonathan was under no delusion that all his concerns for her didn't apply to him as well. Yet, aside from his compatibility with the device, he had some level of control. He had not yet hit the limits of his human strength—could continue to build himself up, always working to shrink the chances of confronting something so much stronger that he'd be forced into a defensive fight.

Defensive fights were losing ones.

"Do they give you names?" Rylee asked, seeming to want a change in subject. "The Ferox, I mean."

Jonathan let his worries fall to the back of his mind and answered her. "Brings the Rain. At least, that's the most consistent."

She frowned, but nodded. "I remember, the Red we fought the night I first met you, he called you that. Isn't it a bit disturbing that they would call you the same thing?"

"That my reputation precedes me?" Jonathan asked. "Yeah, it's one on a long list of things that disturb me."

"Pfft. *'Reputation.'* You live in Seattle. It's probably just because you're always fighting in the rain."

Jonathan studied her, his eyes narrowing with a growing suspicion that made it hard not to smile as he lay beside her. "Soooo, Rylee, what do they call you?"

"Never mind," she said. "Forget I asked."

"Huh?" He tried not to smile as he stared at her.

"I don't want to talk about it."

"You know," Jonathan said, attempting to be smug, "it's really not a competition."

That got him a glare. "Okay, fine," she finally said. "I'm not sure what it means, anyway. I hear the words in Portuguese half the time. So don't laugh."

"I promise."

She wavered a moment longer, biting her lip before she spoke. "The names tend to be…" Rylee sighed. "*Slug* themed."

Jonathan nodded as he tried to give the appearance that he was considering this admission in a scholarly manner.

"My guess is that they mean to call me slippery. But whatever animal they're trying to reference, we don't have it on Earth, and '*slug*' is the closest translation."

Jonathan said nothing for a moment, turning his head to the ceiling. "Makes sense..." He trailed off, keeping a straight face becoming a challenge. "I guess."

A brief quiet filled the room.

"Hmm, I'm thirsty," Jonathan finally said. "*Slug*, you want to pass me that bottle of…"

"Oh, hell no," Rylee said. "You aren't calling me that."

"Come on, *Slug*." He smiled. "You can call me *Brings the Rain* if you want."

"About to call you *Brings a Swift Kick to the Nuts*."

Jonathan laughed, and soon she was laughing beside him. When they stopped, a moment passed in silence between them.

Eventually, Rylee rolled onto her side to look at him, her expression serious now. "Don't go to work tomorrow," she said.

A reluctance crept on to his face. "I have to," he said. "I can't afford not to."

"Tell your boss that someone died. Stay home, spend a few days with me. We'll train."

It was as though she hadn't believed him, thought he was avoiding her. He was about to explain his financial situation but she spoke before he started.

"I'll front you whatever money you'd lose," she said, raising a brow at him. "That is what you were going to say, right?"

He blinked at her for a moment, seeing she had put more thought into this than he'd realized initially. Jonathan wasn't comfortable with the idea of taking a hand-out—it wasn't his nature. The motorcycle had been one thing, and if he hadn't been able to rationalize it as a useful tool, a far more dependable replacement for his old bike, he probably wouldn't have accepted it. Now though, he hesitated, seeing how important this was to her.

Never in his life had he found himself in a situation where not knowing something about himself had made him safer. He wished he didn't know about the bond. Heyer had been right to keep it from both of them. The alien having his hand forced to tell him had compromised them both. If Jonathan could be forced to confess this to The Cell, he would be powerless once they found out that a threat to Rylee might motivate him to give up anything. Telling Rylee herself doubled the chances of The Cell using the same against her.

Concerning enough as this was, it was unnerving to see how easy it was to rationalize his other hesitations. His thoughts were already trying to convince him. A week of training together would sharpen both of them, and when the time came, he would be sending her away stronger than when she came.

Time. The thing Heyer had stolen from her. Was it not the one thing he should try to give her?

The only voice he should have been listening to was the one he desperately didn't want to acknowledge. He kept forcing that intuitive whisper into the background, not wanting to acknowledge the possibility that he was lying to himself.

Time? For her? Or for you?

He felt sick to his stomach when he imagined telling her. It got worse each time he failed to tell her—the betrayal she would feel grew heavier. Yet, despite all he'd learned about Rylee, the one thing he was blind to was who she would be when he wasn't there. What if, on confessing he had withheld this, she no longer trusted him and left in anger—seeing that, in the end, he treated her with no more honesty than

Heyer had? What if she left in anger and The Cell approached at just the wrong moment?

Jonathan had always imagined he would be better than this. That when the decision was his, he would prove the alien was wrong to keep them in the dark. That the wiser move was to share with her the consequences so they could make the decision with their eyes open. Yet, here he was, another day going by, and he had yet again delayed. And he couldn't be sure—were emotions outside his control making these decisions for him, making every choice seem so much more convoluted than it really was? Turning a simple problem with a simple solution into a blinding fog? Did it make the urgency to send her away seem like it could wait just another day?

A part of him felt that he was hiding from something else altogether. It was almost as though something within him wanted to make the situation worse… to blame the bond for taking away his ability to make the right decision.

Jonathan noticed that her playfulness was succumbing to the expectation that he was going to deny her request, and he found himself unwilling to do so.

"Okay," he said, finally.

Rylee smiled at him, her head tilting curiously. "I thought for sure you were going to say you were too good to be..." She pretended to cough. "A kept man."

He was about to argue over the word choice when a stirring in his weapons cupboard drew his attention.

"What…" Rylee said, slightly alarmed. "What was that?"

Jonathan smiled and winked at her. "That, I believe, is a request I put in," he said. Then he looked at her curiously. "Any chance you know how to sew, *Slug*?"

Her eyes narrowed. "You know, you're in luck. I recently hired a kept man—'seamstress' is one of his duties."

CHAPTER FORTY-TWO

PAIGE HAD HER guard up, approaching with caution, as she and Leah found Evelyn at the table.

However, if Evelyn was about to spring a trap, she hardly looked up to it. Jonathan's mother held her coffee, cupping the mug as though the warmth alone was keeping her fingers from freezing; she hardly acknowledged their arrival, looking exhausted from a day with too much heavy thinking.

"Evelyn?" Paige asked. "Leah says you wanted to speak with us?"

The mother looked up from her coffee cup and nodded before gesturing to the empty seats on each side of her. They sat down slowly, Paige casting one more discretionary glance at Leah, a plea reminding her friend not to abandon her.

"Paige, I owe you an apology," Evelyn said. "I never should have spoken to you the way I did. I was lashing out at the only person who would take my call, and I'm ashamed of it. I hope you can forgive me."

Paige didn't feel she was owed an apology—she hadn't been upset at Evelyn in the first place. If anything, she felt like Jonathan owed both of them an explanation. She nodded sympathetically. "You don't need to apologize."

"Well, thank you for that, but after the day I've had, I think I may have over-stepped more than I imagined."

"You had every right," Paige said. "You did exactly what I would have. I'm just glad Jonathan finally told you himself."

Evelyn's lips pursed, her eyes descending into a deeper state of concern. Paige had assumed that Jonathan must have come clean with her last night in the garage. Now, seeing how Evelyn reacted, Paige realized Jonathan still hadn't told her anything.

"Oh," she said. "With you being here, I thought Jonathan must have..." She trailed off and groaned.

Evelyn drew herself up with a breath, her face becoming quite serious. "I need you to listen to me, both of you. I learned several frightening things today," she said. "Now, you don't have to say anything. But, if it's not too much, please at least tell me there is a perfectly good explanation and I'm just getting paranoid."

Paige glanced to Leah, both failing to hide that they were now more intrigued than worried.

"I went down to the University today. I talked to the guidance counselor assigned to Jonathan's case file," she continued. "As he had dropped out of school, and I was the co-signer on his student loans, I wanted to know what Jonathan's options were." She shook her head. "I never would have thought I'd be saying this, but you damn kids are a lot less trouble when you're younger. You turn eighteen and all of a sudden I need permission to know why I wasn't notified of his absence in the first place."

She sighed heavily, angry or frustrated—it was hard for Paige to tell.

"They wouldn't give me specifics, only that Jonathan was allowed a quarter of leave because of a police report, indicating he had been admitted to Virginia Mason's emergency room. That he'd suffered a violent attack with life-threatening injuries, the nature of the assault being so psychologically traumatizing that the University had granted him a recovery period so that his grades would not be affected by what he had endured." Evelyn's eyes had started to shine, as though she might be on the verge of tears. "That was all this piece of crap was able to tell me without overstepping his position."

Paige swallowed.

Evelyn eyed both girls, then. "That was scary enough," she said. "My own son keeping so much from me. I demanded to speak with a superior, only to be told that the counselor had already provided more information than they were legally able to give me." Evelyn drew in a sharp breath, steeling herself against her frustrations. "Well, those assholes didn't know who they were dealing with. I can understand some bureaucratic chicken-shits at a university not wanting to say something that might get them fired, but that sure as hell wasn't going to be the end. So, I went down to the police station, looking for the report that was filed that night."

Evelyn shook her head again, as though she still didn't believe what had followed. "I thought they were incompetent at first, because they couldn't pull up any public record regarding anything to do with my Jonathan. A violent attack and hospitalization with life-threatening injuries and no record? Not even a 9-1-1 call. I went to the emergency room. Same story. They wouldn't disclose medical records, but I was at least able to get one of the nurses to confirm that there was no record on file to disclose."

Paige was getting a sinking feeling in her stomach. She felt herself starting to look as troubled as Evelyn the more she listened.

"Is this possible?" the mother finally asked, her voice trembling. "This is the kind of thing you see in conspiracy movies. Files getting removed by clandestine government organizations, some type of cover-up. It's ridiculous! How could Jonathan be involved in anything like that?"

Paige faltered. It was all new information to her as well. Added to what she did know, she couldn't look the mother in the face and tell her she was being paranoid. The most disconcerting of all of it were the things Paige knew she could trust. The 9-1-1 recording, for instance. Collin and Hayden had made that call, had spoken to the police and EMTs, told her that they had been present when Jonathan had told his story.

"Paige, if it's dangerous, I understand," Evelyn said. "But if I am crazy, please just tell me I'm crazy—tell me I'm paranoid."

She couldn't think fast enough with Evelyn staring at her. Was it possible? She had always assumed that Jonathan cutting himself off from the world was his unhealthy way of dealing with what had happened to him that night. Had he been lying to them to hide something far bigger than they had imagined?

Had he been trying to protect them?

Paige's storming thoughts came into focus. She found the words creeping out of her mouth before the warning that they were safer unsaid. "Grant Morgan," she said, looking at Leah. "What if he wasn't crazy?"

CHAPTER FORTY-THREE

MONDAY| OCTOBER 10, 2005 | 9:30 PM | SEATTLE

"IT'S A MORAL gray area," Jonathan heard Collin saying to Hayden on the other side of the door.

Rylee had been following Jonathan out into the living room from the garage, only to have him stop on the last step as he reached for the door handle. He retracted his hand and turned to her.

"So, before we go in there," Jonathan said. "Where do you stand on the whole Christianity thing?"

Rylee frowned at the question. "Well, my parents are fairly religious, but I never really took to it. Why?"

Jonathan's face contorted as he deliberated on how to answer. "Well, you're free to do as you please, of course, but when Collin and Hayden get into it, they tend to try and get you to take sides. I caution a strict non-engagement policy."

"Oh, got it," she said. "We're Switzerland."

He nodded and grinned before opening the door for her.

"I guess it's believable," Hayden said. "But it bothers me."

Collin nodded. "I think it's because, ethically speaking, the antichrist might be in the right. The only reason it seems otherwise is because Jesus shows up and performs a miracle."

Hayden's hand rubbed the back of his head as Collin noticed Jonathan and Rylee entering.

"Hey, can you two spare a moment?" Collin asked.

"Sure," Jonathan said, exchanging a look with Rylee. "Superhero-Jesus comic book problems?"

His roommates nodded thoughtfully while Rylee, noticing a stack of library books and DVDs on the table, started examining the various titles and subject matter. "Plague and zombie outbreaks?" she asked. "I don't remember zombies in the Gospels."

"Well, technically, Jesus rises from the grave…" Collin stopped himself. "Never mind, it's not what we need to get your opinion on."

"We're working on what we call the 'trigger event,'" Hayden explained. "Heroes and villains all need an experience, the onset of their moral journey. Right now, we are working on the moment that Damian starts down the road to antichristhood."

Jonathan looked back and forth between Collin and Hayden. "Okay," he said, holding up a copy of *The Plague* by Albert Camus. "But I don't think the bubonic plague was around at the time either."

Both roommates nodded at him.

"The event we're working on starts with a pestilence. We'll probably be vague on the specific illness," Collin said. "Leprosy would be more thematically biblical, but we were thinking it should be something that kills faster."

For the next few minutes, Jonathan and Rylee listened as Collin and Hayden launched into a CliffsNotes version of the storyline they had been playing with. It started out with Jesus as a teenager, before the ministry recorded in the Gospels. Christ and his followers travel to a small village where the inhabitants are suffering from a lethal disease. This is where Damian and Jesus first cross paths.

Damian, despite his youth, has been placed into a leadership role. The people he governs respect him for having shown wisdom beyond his years in the past. On arrival, Jesus finds that the villagers in the town who are sick have been quarantined on Damian's authority. The townspeople tell him that Damian has been ruthless in enforcing his quarantine—that loved ones are forbidden and forcefully kept from caring for their sick family members. Any contact with the sick results in immediate quarantine, even if those making contact show no symptoms.

The roommates stopped when Jonathan started giving them a skeptical look.

"What?" Collin asked before proceeding.

"Damian's insight into the spread of infection seems like a stretch for a Hebrew guy growing up in, what?" Jonathan asked. "17 C.E.?"

Collin nodded. "Yeah, we figured that Damian and Jesus, being who they are, will have insights into things that they wouldn't necessarily be able to learn from their elders. It's part of why Damian has control of the town in the first place. He has shown wisdom in the past—it's the only reason a seventeen-year-old kid would be taken seriously when he tells the village's leaders how to do their job."

"It's all setup, really," Hayden said. "We want Christ and the antichrist to travel together for a portion of the series. They'll be like Lex Luthor and Superman, seeking each other out and debating their moral differences. In a world looking for a savior, they'll be the only two who grasp the realities of the problems they encounter. But, of course, Jesus and Damian always come to different conclusions."

Jonathan and Rylee nodded their heads in an *okay-whatever* sort of acceptance, and Hayden continued.

"Learning of this harsh segregation of the sick, Jesus seeks out Damian to hear his reasoning," he said. "But their first encounter turns into a debate over the quarantine, and it draws a crowd."

"There is a twist at this point," Collin said. "Trying to hold onto command of the village..." He paused for effect. "Damian tells a parable."

Hayden and Collin stared at Jonathan, seeming to expect some reaction.

"Um, what?" Jonathan asked.

The expectant looks fell off their faces, becoming more like the looks of parents who expected more from their child.

"Come on, Tibbs," Collin said. "Parables are pretty much Jesus's wheelhouse."

Jonathan looked to Rylee, and both roommates followed suit. When she noticed everyone looking at her, she said, "Uh, yeah, Tibbs, it's totally his wheelhouse."

Collin and Hayden turned to him as though their point had been made. Jonathan lingered on Rylee, his eyes narrowing.

Finally, she shrugged at him and said, "I don't know, everyone was looking at me. I panicked."

Hayden was going to press their case, but Collin shook his head and launched into Damian's parable.

"Imagine two towns, both with a population of a hundred people. The town to the north lives on fertile soil and has more food than they know what to do with. However, the town to the south has discovered that their farmlands are poisoned. They cannot grow crops, and fear they will starve. The northerners have compassion. After all, they have more than they need, and they feed their neighbors to the south.

"The southerners praise the north for their generosity, as they now have enough food to survive another season, but the next year, the same situation occurs. Now, the southerners have been sustained, they've had babies and their population has grown—yet their lands will still not grow crops. So, again the northerners come to their aid, and again, their population grows.

"This cycle continues—until one year, a horrible truth is realized. Both the populations have grown so large that the north can no longer feed their own, let alone their neighbors in the south. As a result, hundreds die in the north while tens of thousands starve to death in the south. Now, if the northerners had shown forethought before the situation was out of control—not given into their compassion—it merely would have resulted in the death of the original hundred in the south, says Damian. Sometimes, by giving into our nobler inclinations and ignoring our reason, we create more suffering than would ever have been necessary."

"Well, that does sounds like the Devil's argument," Jonathan said.

"This is where things get interesting," Collin continued. "We've made Jesus two years older than Damian, and as a result, he has come to realize that he is in command of powers that Damian has yet to discover. Basically, they both are able to make of reality what they wish, to a certain extent, through their connection to either the Holy Spirit or the—" Collin coughed, clearing his throat. "Unholy Spirit"

"I thought it was their Holy and Unholy Smart Phones?" Jonathan said, recalling the last conversation of theirs that he had overheard.

Collin smiled and nodded while Hayden's face became a glare—Rylee just looked at him, confused.

"We are not committed to that analogy," Hayden said.

"Anyhow, knowing he can save the villagers if he can enter the quarantine, Jesus responds to Damian's parable with a simple question," Collin said. "He says, what if you and your family lived in the south, Damian? Would your reason hold sway over you then? At this point in the story, it comes to light that Damian has no sick family in the village, and therefore his quarantine becomes a cruel act of self-preservation for him and his kin in the eyes of the village.

"In the end, the townsfolk are swayed. Jesus calls for their faith and insists that he be allowed to enter the quarantined area to cure the sick. Damian forbids it one last time and is ignored as the townspeople, desperate to save their loved ones, are willing to accept Jesus's solution. Damian offers them calculated reason, while Jesus appeals to their hope. Jesus doesn't do this out of malice, of course—he sees what Damian is trying to do, but he finds his choice of action unconscionable.

"Of course, Jesus being able to cure the sick, he saves the town from the plague by calling on the forces of the Holy Smar—Spirit," Collin said.

Rylee sighed, her expression still confused. "Guys, this sounds—well, boring. I mean, for a comic book?"

"You have to see the panels," Collin said. "When Jesus cures the sick, he pulls the pestilence out of villagers in the form of demons. After that, he takes them out with his staff in a martial-arts-style action sequence."

"Ahh." Rylee raised an eyebrow. "And people actually read this?"

Jonathan snorted, which Collin ignored as he finished.

"Anyhow," Collin said. "Damian is shamed by the village that previously respected him. The simple villagers only see the results, and care little for the reason behind it. Jesus is seen as the savior, and his call for faith is proven to be the moral choice over the harsh quarantine. Damian's reputation is essentially marred as Jesus has unintentionally turned him into the villain. The villagers see him as the man willing to let all who were infected die alone."

Jonathan nodded and picked up a copy of one of the zombie outbreak DVDs. "So, where do the zombies come in?"

"Oh, right," Collin said. "Zom—"

"Zombie and plague films almost always have the same basic plot," Hayden interjected. "You have a small group of survivors trying to hold onto their humanity in a deadly world."

"One member of the group will usually take control of the situation," Collin said. "Said person will ruthlessly enforce whatever rules they must to keep the rest of the group safe. To accomplish this, he or she usually has to abandon their compassion—sacrifice their humanity bit by bit. The thing that always bugs me is that this individual almost never ends the story as the hero. He almost always becomes the villain. The stories, while busy appealing to the audience's compassion, cast the morally outraged survivors as the heroes. What they almost never show is that the guy they labeled the 'villain' was keeping the group alive in the first place."

"What are you saying?" Jonathan frowned. "That they should be rooting for the villain?"

"No," Collin said. "I'm saying it's never that black and white. That they never acknowledge the fact that the person playing the villain is the one making it possible for everyone else to feel self-righteous. They all feel justified hating him for doing what was necessary as they stand aside—never give any credence to the fact that they wouldn't be there to judge him if he hadn't done what was necessary.

"This will be Damian's first lesson in that harsh truth. What sneaks up on him is that playing the villain so everyone else can feel good about themselves eventually blurs the line. The human mind cannot bear being outcast by its fellow Man indefinitely. At some point, choosing to play that role, Damian will eventually lose sight of what situations require extreme measures. That's when he becomes the villain for real."

Jonathan looked up at Hayden and noticed how much this storyline was bothering him.

When Collin noticed as well, he let out a heavy sigh. "Well? Out with it."

Hayden looked at all of them, thinking for a moment, then threw up a hand. "I don't like the underlying message," he said. "The villagers only side with Jesus because they believe he'll save the situation with magic. Christ isn't wrong, but he's right for all the wrong reasons… and the villagers, they see a situation that can only end in suffering and turn to a savior because it keeps them from having to make an impossible decision themselves. It's degrading to their faith in God somehow. I'm just having trouble figuring out why."

Collin nodded his head sympathetically.

"Well, it's because you've left something out," Rylee interjected. "Desperate people will look for hope, but no matter how desperate, there has to be a foundation to support it. No one would believe a man if he said he could deliver a miracle without having seen him do so before."

Jonathan paused, thinking for a moment. "The people following Jesus must have seen something in him by now or they wouldn't be listening to him in the first place."

Hayden nodded, but he didn't seem to like that angle much either.

"Damian isn't wrong," Jonathan said. "He is making the best decision he can with what he knows. The truth doesn't change just because no one likes it."

Collin thought about what Jonathan had said for a bit. "Maybe it's a false dichotomy?" he eventually asked. "The reason we don't like this story is because Jesus and Damian are forced to choose between black and white options: forfeit your humanity, or pray for a miracle."

"The only middle ground is letting the family members enter into the quarantined area, but with the knowledge that they wouldn't be allowed out," Rylee said. "It's noble, the family members can still choose to take care for their loved ones and keep their humanity—but at the same time, Jesus and Damian have to be willing to let them choose a death sentence."

Hayden signed heavily. "I need a break from this."

They watched him leave, each noticing he seemed out of sorts, a development that left Jonathan irritated with Collin. "This storyline," Jonathan said after a moment. "Paige came up with it."

Collin frowned. "Yeah. How did you know?"

"She's an environmental science major and that whole parable was based on Malthusian Population Theory," he said. "She probably has to hear about it in every ecology class she takes."

"Yeah. She told me about it."

Jonathan sighed. "And what, you just couldn't resist? Collin, this comic book isn't as easy for him as it is for you. Can you lay off his faith for a while?"

Collin looked to Rylee and then back to Jonathan, clearly caught off guard and starting to get defensive. "Look. First off, the whole idea of this comic book was to put Super Jesus in moral dilemmas where the choice wasn't simple. Hayden and I both wanted it that way. Second, next Christmas break, come along and have dinner with Hayden's family. Watch what happens when they expect you to come to midnight mass and you tell them you don't believe in God. No, I'll save you the trouble—no one walks on egg shells to protect an Atheist's feelings. Hayden and I agreed it was a double standard a long time ago."

"Collin, listen. I'm just worried—"

"No, Hayden doesn't want me to keep my thoughts to myself to protect his faith for him," Collin said. "I mean, be honest with me, Tibbs, if Hayden had just called my lack of belief into question, would you ask him to be more sensitive?"

Jonathan paused and drew in a long breath. He glanced at Rylee to see if she might weigh in, but she just shrugged. "Don't look at me. I thought we were Switzerland."

Collin looked suspicious of the comment, but his attention went back to Jonathan.

When he spoke, Jonathan had lowered his voice to a whisper. "Collin, I haven't said anything, so it isn't your fault for not knowing this," he said. "But Hayden hasn't been sleeping. He's been up 'til four in the morning most nights for the last month. I don't know if it has anything to do with this. I haven't asked him. Just do me a favor and take a break."

Collin's face softened, relinquishing the desire to argue as he realized he may have misjudged the situation.

CHAPTER FORTY-FOUR

DATE | TIME: UNKNOWN | FEROXIAN PLANE

THOSE WHO STUDY events that take place across geologic periods are familiar with the challenge of wrapping their imagination around time from the beginning of existence to the present. They often use models, scaled down to more digestible sizes, in order to get perspective. It is a humbling experience to take all of time and look at it in the context of a single day—a 24-hour clock. One sees that, if the Earth was formed at 0:01 am, the first form of life on the planet showed up around 4 am, and that Mankind doesn't show up until roughly a minute before midnight.

When Heyer tried to do something similar—view his own life from the beginning to the present moment in terms of a human life span—then he could say that perhaps a split second separated his birth from his brother's. Yet, in that split second, Malkier had lost the parents Heyer would never know—had lost an entire species Heyer would never meet.

Suddenly, in that context, it seems a lot can happen in a split second. Enough to create a gulf between him and his brother that would eventually grow so wide that, despite being the only two of their kind and having an entire universe to share, they had failed to live out their lives without coming to war…

Some visits to his brother's vessel were worth a moment's delay. Heyer now stood beneath the moonless night sky of the Feroxian plane, but he didn't stare up at the stars. His eyes lingered on Jonathan's gateway.

The alien could hardly expect Jonathan to understand his hesitance. Humanity faced one threat, and so, what needed to be done appeared so very uncomplicated to the boy. He was an only child that had grown up with guidance. There had been older and wiser people who loved him and had taken care to shape him as a child. Jonathan didn't know what it was, truly, to have no living role model. Growing up, Heyer had only had his older brother.

Malkier assumed that when the Ferox were pushed to the brink, Heyer would concede that there was no other way. His brother never seemed to realize that Heyer had drawn a line in the sand, a line he could not allow one of his own to cross—genocide. Heyer often wondered if Malkier had any such line. What, for instance, would it take for Malkier to consider Heyer's life forfeit?

The truth that Malkier had yet to uncover was that they had been at war for years now. Perhaps it was inevitable, but for Heyer, the day his brother had entered this gateway was when he knew where they were headed. Every time Heyer had referred to Malkier as "brother" since, he had been committing an act of treason. Heyer would gain no satisfaction seeing his brother realize this. Heyer would lie and conceal, he would prepare, but one day his brother was going to uncover that he had been preparing for a war for quite some time.

Suffice it to say, as he passed through the shimmering stone into his brother's home, like he had so many times before, he knew it would not be his finest moment. Whenever he imagined his ancestors watching them, he knew that if the last two of the Borealis killed one another… there would be no better definition of "pathetic." The brothers were a laughable end to the most advanced civilization ever known.

When Heyer reached the main cavern, Malkier's back was to him. He could see that *Dams the Gate's* body was no longer present. Heyer waited, not wanting to interrupt as his brother concluded a conversation with Cede.

"We will continue this later, Cede," Malkier said. "For now, I wish to speak to my brother."

Cede's face, the face of their mother, disappeared into the stone behind them. Malkier stood tall, no longer wearing the emotional defeat he had at their last meeting. Heyer could not yet be sure whether this development was good or bad. It was unclear how much time had passed on this plane since his previous visit.

"You look better, brother," Heyer said.

Malkier nodded. "My lapses in leadership finally became apparent to me—perhaps a good thing, as it seems that the need to project strength for my people helped to break the hold my son's passing had on me. I had failed to see that tides have started to shift amongst my people. The Ferox must have faith in their prophet in the coming days."

Heyer returned a nod. "I imagine it is for the best that you focused on the morale of your people," he said, his face becoming thoughtful. "Curious, though—the next few days require your immediate presence?"

"Yes, investigating the means by which *Dams the Gate* gained entry to Earth has uncovered some disturbing threats within the Ferox population."

"Rebels amongst the Ferox?" Heyer asked, making a show of surprise. "Are the Ferox capable of falling out of line?"

"It seems so," Malkier said. "For some time, I knew of a growing discordance, mostly made up of males whose ineligibility left them unlikely to be given access to the gates. I had thought their frustrations harmless." He drew a heavy breath. "However, in tracing the means by which my son entered the gates, I discovered they were more than a disgruntled few. They have a leader, and *Dams the Gate* was the face that rallied their—" Malkier paused. "Insubordinations."

"A leader? One of the remaining Alphas?"

His brother shook his head, his face growing pained. "No. *Burns the Flame*. His mother."

Silence fell between them, Heyer's mouth dropping open, though he hadn't yet come up with something to say. Once given the answer, it seemed so obvious. Hearing her name, Heyer found himself reminded of Genesis, where the blind Isaac is tricked by his wife, Rebekah, on behalf of their son.

Burns the Flame had mothered many children before she bore the prophet's son. She was quite beautiful by Ferox standards, or so Heyer understood. There had been a time when many of the males who entered the gates did so with her in mind.

When his brother had entered the gates, it turned out he too, had not been immune to her charms.

However, the decree upon *Dams the Gate's* birth, that her son was forbidden entrance to the gates, had an unforeseen side effect. The Ferox males, seeing that the prophet of their gods had forbidden her offspring to enter, feared that the same decrees would fall on all her future offspring—the decree was an unspoken punishment on both her and the child for a sin gone unspoken.

In this bleak period where the Ferox faced the most innate of their fears, a male returning from the gates may never have another opportunity to mate. They would not risk squandering their reproductive opportunities on a female whose children may be rendered sterile by the decree of their gods. *Burns the Flame* had not borne a child since.

"She betrayed you?" Heyer asked.

"There are moments when I fear I've lost perspective," Malkier said. "In a way, I saw her and my son as family. I find myself unable to accuse them of betrayal after the harm we brought them."

Heyer regarded his brother. "We—" He paused. "Brother, these circumstances were not of my making."

Malkier turned his head, enough that Heyer could see the edge of his white eye. "Perhaps."

Heyer narrowed his eyes briefly at his brother's response, but decided to let the issue drop. He had more important questions on his mind. "The Feroxian females are not given access to the gates. How did she acquire the portal stone?"

"One of her older sons was recently awarded entry. He, too, felt harmed by his mother's legacy, and took pity on *Dams the Gate*. At her request, the son gave his portal stone to his brother. The act was rather unprecedented, as it was the first time I've seen a Ferox male blatantly risk the anger of their gods."

"Will they be punished?" Heyer asked.

"I've yet to decide exactly how I intend to handle the situation. I am glad you visit me now. Perhaps I can share my thoughts with you.

However, I was hoping to put off thinking of it for a bit longer..." Malkier trailed off, looking at his brother curiously, a change Heyer found quite difficult to read. "Do you suppose I could interest you in a bout of exercise, brother? It's been a long time since I stretched this body's muscles. I thought it might be good for us both. That maybe, circumstances having changed, it might help us rebuild what we've lost."

Heyer blinked, caught at a loss by his brother's request. The two of them had often engaged in such brotherly activities, but not since the death of *Echoes the Borealis*. If Heyer declined, he would be making a statement. He would be telling his brother that, despite Malkier having lost everything he'd gained though that betrayal a decade earlier, Heyer had no desire to repair their relationship. Seeing how current events were playing out, he thought it best Malkier believe he was at least willing to try, though, if he were being completely honest with himself, he too, had things to discuss with his brother that he would like to postpone.

"It would mean a great deal to me, brother," Malkier said. "I cannot take back the past, but I can hope that we would not live the rest of our lives as strangers. I wish for something good to come out of this tragedy, if it be that I might have my brother back."

Heyer regarded his brother for moment, letting Malkier see he had not immediately rejected the offer.

"If it's any consolation," Malkier added. "You may choose the scenario."

A half grin formed on Heyer's lips, and Malkier's features lightened, equal parts enthusiasm and relief, a combination that gave the features of an Alpha Ferox a strange innocence.

"Winter, the forests of Principium One," Heyer said.

Malkier's head tilted slightly at Heyer's selection. Their ancestors had considered the forests of *Principium* much like Mankind considered the Fertile Crescent. This was the wilderness where the Borealis were believed to have emerged from their earlier hunter-gatherer life to start down the road of becoming a technologically advanced species. Historical records showed that the Borealis preserved the wilderness there as something akin to a national park. Before the fall of their species, Borealis went there to live as nature had designed them. No technology, aside from the device implanted in their chest, of course—a retreat from civilization.

After some thought, Malkier's mouth formed in a startling, wide Feroxian grin. "Back to the beginning, then, brother?"

"It was the first place that came to mind," Heyer said. "And I have not viewed it in quite some time."

He nodded. "Cede, please initiate the Principium One forest scenario. Cancel the scenario should any of the Ferox approach."

Heyer stepped back a few paces as the walls of the room shimmered, leaving them inside the void for a moment before what had been the inner structure of the cave began to change. The ceiling became a false sky, unnatural light coming down on them. He pulled off his coat, folding it over a branch of unearthly vegetation as it solidified beside him. He removed his shoes, placing them on the forest floor forming beneath.

Unlike the interactive footage of the Foedrata Arena that Heyer had taken Jonathan through, the projections within the cavern were being manifested from the vessel's excess physical mass, requiring Cede hollow out materials that would have been stored inside cave walls. This meant that trees here were true obstructions if one collided with them. Colors seeped into the environment and the temperature dropped as the forest completed taking shape within the room. Blue-azure snowflakes began to fall through the canopy, coming down from the white winter sky of Principium One. They joined powder-blue snow resting on tree branches and the forest floor.

The trees reflected the light, and Heyer saw his face, obscured by the contours of the leaf-like outgrowths. Plant life on Principium, analogous to that of Earth's, fed on energy harvested from the environment through processes similar to photosynthesis. Chlorophyll-like proteins found in the leaves absorbed light from the nearby star. However, the spectrum absorbed left a range of silver to be cast onto an observer's eye. The leaves took on a shiny, metallic appearance, as though made of organic steel. The leaves themselves were more like seaweed—thick, overlapping strands of leathery tinsel hanging down from the outstretched branches.

As was the way with forests, the trees competed for resources, growing higher and higher, trying to reach out of the shadows cast by their neighboring competitors to gather the light abundant at the top of the canopy. The vines of various species climbed the thick cobalt bark of the larger trees' trunks, circling up as though they were on a winding staircase. Meanwhile, these vines were slowly strangling the life from that which allowed them to reach their food source.

The scenario did not indulge in more exotic details. Animals capable of complex movements were not present. Instead, their absence was made up for by the presence of their familiar sounds. A human would not have much to hear on the real Principium One. The frequency at which the animals vocalized wouldn't be heard by the human ear. Heyer heard these sounds though, because the scenario provided his earthly form with a close approximation. It came to him as an osculating hum of sorts, a sound reminiscent of tuning forks vibrating. The mix of frequencies created a calming familiarity to the brothers.

The massive shadow of his brother stepped close, dimming the light around Heyer, the metallic bones of Malkier's knuckles cracking behind him. Heyer turned enough to see his brother with one eye, then winked before bolting into the forest in a blur of movement.

His brother was swiftly in pursuit, a massive black blur chasing after him.

Heyer pounced off the floor of the forest, agile, rebounding from trunk to trunk and making it difficult for his brother to keep sight of him. He circled Malkier, noticing that his brother had come to a stop in a clearing to search the canopy for signs of his movement. Heyer disturbed branches as he moved, allowing the soft sounds of snowfall to draw his brother's attention in circles.

In a stealthy and swift ruse of motion, Heyer plunged head first from the sky while his brother was drawn to the last noise he had purposely made in the canopy. He came down behind him, a hand locking beneath his brother's massive Feroxian jaw as he reoriented his feet to land at the last second. Malkier's immense spine arched backward as Heyer pulled down, and rolled his brother over his back and shoulder. The maneuver launched Malkier into the woods.

He adapted quickly, gathering control of his mass in the air to orient himself. When his momentum was halted by a collision into a thick tree trunk, he pushed off, coming back at Heyer headlong.

Heyer focused, waiting until the absolute last moment to side step,

Malkier's fist flying past his face, coming within inches as Heyer grabbed hold of his outstretched arm and turned, redirecting his trajectory into the forest floor. Malkier crashed and rolled, the snow and dirt looking almost like a series of landmines had been detonated in a sequence moving away from Heyer.

The Ferox found his footing, leaping sideways into the trees, where Heyer lost sight of him. "You and your human tricks," his voice said from within the forest.

Heyer smiled. It was true that martial arts were a foreign concept to the Ferox. Though, admittedly, they had little need for such elements of style; theirs was a mix of animal instinct and brawling, and given their assets, it usually proved quite effective.

They could not actually hurt one another, not within the fight scenario—the ground and objects softened on impact to keep the combat sporting in nature. In a wilderness environment like this, Heyer had the advantage. His body was less difficult to move through the canopy without upsetting it, sometimes indistinguishable from a soft breeze, while Malkier was like a bulky tank crashing through when he moved too quickly. Still, as with all fights, if Heyer found himself in an entanglement where strength was the deciding factor, he would lose.

When his brother did not immediately launch another frontal assault, Heyer got moving, not wanting to give him a still target. The noise suddenly ceased, and all he could hear were the sounds of the forest. Heyer froze. A trap had likely just been laid—he needed to spot it or he ran the risk of walking into it.

Sound erupted from his flank, and Heyer turned to see the trunk of a tree coming straight at his position. He jumped without a second to spare, stepping on the trunk, the motion forcing him into a forward flip to land on the forest floor without losing his footing. Upon hitting the ground, he dropped immediately into a crouch—Malkier then flew out of the forest toward him, forcing him to roll out of the way of a powerful swing.

He stood, seeing his brother begin to turn to target him as he came out of the roll, giving him no time to dodge but only to plant his feet and bring both arms in front of his face in a block, bracing for impact.

The massive forearm came around and connected with his, and the force sent him backward. His feet ripped trenches through the forest floor, dirt and snow firing out both sides like water breaking in the wake of a speedboat until his back struck something solid. The sound of wood and bark splintering came to his attention as a tree trunk absorbed him. Piles of azure snow fell from the branches as the vibrations shook up the length of the tree.

Heyer ducked as his brother rushed in to take advantage. The fist flew over his head, connecting against the trunk where his body had stood a moment earlier. The wood, already damaged from the first impact, split—the massive tower of a trunk caving in toward them. This was no small spruce tree, but something closer in size to that of Earth's redwoods. The brothers jumped in opposite directions as gravity brought the heavy tree crashing to the forest floor. The world thundered around them when it came down.

Heyer spun in time to watch his brother do the same on the other side of the fallen tree. Malkier, grinning as they made eye contact, did not delay a second before pouncing for him. Heyer swept past him as he landed, changing to an offensive tactic. He brought his elbow into the back of his brother's leg, causing his knee to jerk forward from the blow. Malkier lost his balance, forced to kneel. Heyer moved to take hold of Malkier's arm opposite the leg knocked out from under him, and pulled powerfully, swinging his brother hard into the broken tree that now laid out across the clearing. Malkier crashed into the wood, the force bending the fallen trunk into a V as he connected.

Malkier shook his head, dizzied by the attack, half sunk into the splitting trunk of the tree. Heyer took the advantage, assaulting him directly, launching forward and kicking his brother in the chest. It finished the job, sending him all the way through the trunk. The fallen tree snapped a second time into two massive logs as Malkier's body shot out the newly made gap and into an unyielding, rocky cliff face.

Malkier flopped down into the dirt.

Heyer waited, walking over to his brother, a casually smug grin on his face. "We should stop. We risk the Feroxian reproductive response should we continue."

Malkier rose to hands and knees, saw his brother's smug expression, and began to laugh. "It has been too long," he said. "You haven't slowed down a bit."

Heyer tilted his head. "You are too hard on yourself." He smiled in a sporting manner. "You've never been too agile in these woods. Too much bulk."

"You are careful with my pride," Malkier said. "There is no need—I will have my chance again."

Heyer nodded.

Malkier raised his hand, a human gesture, a request for assistance in getting to his feet that he didn't really need. Heyer stepped forward, happy to complete the ritual.

At the last moment, Malkier's hand moved, not reaching for Heyer's palm but forming a vise like grip on his wrist. Heyer flinched in surprise, half expecting his brother intended to keep fighting now that he'd lulled him into assuming the combat over and had a solid grip on him. Heyer moved to brace himself, in case his brother tried to throw him off balance.

Malkier's free hand suddenly burst forth from beneath him and clamped down around the arm he held. Heyer felt an unfamiliar pinch, skin breaking over his bicep. A powerful pain erupted within his muscle, shocking him. Weakness spread over him, seeming to radiate out from the arm into his core. Pain surfaced throughout his body, a feeling unlike any he had experienced in years.

He found it difficult to balance and fell to his knees as his brother released his grip, standing to rise to his full height above him. Alarmed, unsure what was happening, he looked to the arm where his brother had grabbed hold of him. There was a metal band surrounding his bicep. It was Borealis steel, seamless and skintight, clamped down around his skin like a bracer. He could feel thick needles embedded beneath, forced through his exterior skin. Whatever the device was doing to him, he found he was unable to stand.

"That will be all Cede," Malkier said.

Groggily, Heyer's eyes fought to focus, his brother no longer a single image in front of him but two figures that seemed to swim in circles in his vision. He grew ill, nauseous. He looked to the floor in an attempt to center himself. The forest receded and the cave-like structures of Malkier's vessel returned. Shortly after, a rectangle of light fell over him, as though a doorway had opened behind him. Footsteps approached, rubber soles on rock. The outline of a human shadow stepped into the light, growing larger as a man approached.

"You imagine it was hurtful to find that the mother of my child betrayed me, brother?" Malkier asked. "But what I have learned about my own blood—these things were heart breaking."

The man's shoes stepped into his vision. A young man's shoes.

"Tell me, human, is this him?" Malkier asked. "Is this man your father?"

CHAPTER FORTY-FIVE

RIVERS PINCHED HIS eyelids shut, having stared too long at the video feeds. "I'm sorry, but what they are saying isn't easy to make sense of," he said. "I'll review the tapes again, slow it down."

"I do not question your ability," Olivia said, placing a hand on his shoulder.

He was momentarily caught off guard by her physical contact, never having seen Olivia show her team such a comforting gesture.

"I'm not looking to be coddled, ma'am," he said, rewinding the footage of Rylee and Jonathan sparring. "Look, we have two camera angles in that garage outside the one that faces the cabinet. Half the time, they aren't facing either of them—the other half, Ms. Silva is speaking while she is upside down. I am only getting snips of the conversation, but without any context, I can't fill in the blanks with any credibility."

"Take a break, Rivers. I'll have the techs take the footage apart. See if they can get you something better to look at."

Rivers sighed, but nodded. "It might help." He squinted at the screen, confused and frustrated.

"Something in particular troubling you?" Olivia asked.

"The conversations. Here, for instance—it's like Jonathan is telling her that she is handicapped for being female, but..." Rivers shook his head.

"Yes?"

"Look at his face. How could he be saying anything remotely close to that?" Rivers asked.

Olivia watched the feed for a moment, eventually nodding her agreement. "No. He looks impressed, and hardly able to hold his own against her."

"Exactly. And Rylee—well, she doesn't strike me as a woman who would listen to such talk. Rather, she who would put him in his place for it."

Olivia paused thoughtfully. "If anything," she said. "Miss Silva is holding back. What about the footage from the night before?"

"Just as strange," Rivers said. "The lights were off while they were speaking. What is disturbing is the camera is equipped with night vision and it never triggered. I had to download the digital footage and run filters on it after the recording to brighten it. They weren't very generous with keeping their mouths toward the camera in that instance either, but what I could make out didn't fit their body language at all."

Olivia narrowed her eyes in thought. "Keep working on it. We need to know for sure if the video is being compromised. If so, everything we've seen could be misdirection."

There was a knock in the doorway behind them, and Rivers saw Margot waiting. She looked as though she had exciting news, but wasn't sure if she should interrupt to share it.

"Margot, please come in." Olivia said, removing the hand she'd left on Rivers' shoulder. "You have progress to report?"

Margot nodded. "The odd behavior in the satellite systems," she said. "Today, there was a similar ping. A login from a peculiar external source we couldn't trace, coupled with a short usage of the system." She looked at the monitor that Rivers and Olivia had been reviewing. "A few minutes after that footage, actually."

"Excellent work," Olivia said. "Would you please excuse us a moment? I would like to discuss this with Rivers alone."

Margot nodded, glancing between the two of them once more in a curious manner as she backed out of the room.

"So, right about the time these two pull a package out of that cupboard," Rivers said, "a package that we know never entered the building by any standard means, an unknown account accesses the GPS system."

Olivia nodded. "If what she has uncovered is correct, we may only get one opportunity to exploit this before The Mark realizes we've found a piece of his methods. So, this stays between the three of us until I say otherwise."

Rivers nodded. "Of course."

"For now," she said, "I'm calling in Leah. If Evelyn Tibbs continues down her current path, we may need to take action."

CHAPTER FORTY-SIX

TUESDAY | OCTOBER 11, 2005 | 1:30 PM | SEATTLE

"YOU KNOW," RYLEE said, "most guys give flowers."

She watched Jonathan tense and then try to hide it, the same way he always did when she made the slightest flirtation. For now, he would humor her with a smile and pretend she wasn't hinting.

"I'm not much of a florist," Jonathan replied.

She'd been watching as he stood over a series of plastic tubes of varying sizes in the garage, each filled with a filmy, black liquid. It smelled of chemistry and metal work. The process of coating her rattan with a layer of black oxide was not something that she'd previously seen any necessity in. The weapon was easy enough to hide within her coat. Still, it was one less thing she'd ever have to explain if the situation came up, and she'd liked the grip it gave Jonathan's demolition bar.

"I had to keep Excali-bar close—couldn't run home every time I needed it," he said. "This was the easiest solution. The way the steel reflects the light draws too much attention otherwise."

With rubber gloves, he reached and pulled the rattan from the chemical bath, then knelt over some newspapers they had spread on the floor. He picked up a piece of steel wool, cleaned off the excess material adhering to the weapon.

"Thanks," she said.

Jonathan smiled—a real smile this time. Rylee was becoming fairly adept at spotting the difference. This was how he looked at her when he felt he'd been useful to her. Rylee smiled back, but the moment he looked away, her expression dropped back to irritation.

If it makes you so damn happy to be useful to me, I can think of better ways, Rylee thought.

Then, not for the first time, she decided she needed to be straight with him.

"Tibbs—"

"Wanna hand me the armor plates and we'll get them started?" Jonathan asked. "Sorry, what were you about to say?"

Rylee put the smile back on before he turned to look at her. "Uh, nothing," she said, reaching to hand him the plates of alien metal that had manifested in the cupboard the night before. When he turned away, she closed her eyes and grimaced in frustration. It wasn't the first time her nerve had slipped.

"Rylee?"

She opened her eyes and noticed him watching her in one of the mirrors. *Oh, crap*, she thought. She shook her head, laughed awkwardly at being caught making a face, and quickly changed the subject as he began to frown at her. "So, you just asked him for these? And he agreed, no questions asked?"

Jonathan shrugged. "My experience is that if he can help, he does. It's the 'can' part that becomes an issue. I once asked him for a space gun and he looked at me like I was a jackass."

Rylee giggled, then frowned at Jonathan. "Why do you think he names them?" she asked. "Excali-bar, Themyscira..."

Jonathan looked up from his work. "You know, you never told me what Themyscira means."

"That's true, I didn't. So, names—why do you think he does that?"

Jonathan narrowed his eyes, tilting his head curiously at her not-so-subtle attempt to avoid the question. "So, you'll tell me your Ferox nick-name but not this?" He asked. "That is interesting…

After he trailed off, a short staring contest followed.

Finally, Jonathan bit his lip. "So, I'll be right back, have to go look something up on the—"

Rylee groaned.

"Fine, okay, I looked it up once," she said. "It's got something to do with Amazon women, and an island, and…" She paused to clear her throat. "Wonder Woman."

Rylee expected him to laugh, but he seemed to find it more interesting than comical.

"You know, I don't think it's Heyer who does the naming," he finally said. "Now that I've spent some time with him, I think they're Mr. Clean's contributions."

Mr. Clean had been the next thing he'd had to explain to her, when the stack of alien metal showed up the previous day. Which, apparently, was why Jonathan fingered the button on his watch every time they discussed anything about the alien. The A.I. had come through; Jonathan, upon leaving the vessel the other night, had asked if Mr. Clean could create armor pieces out of the alien steel that were molded to the same specs as those already built into their motorcycle jackets—an idea he had gotten from watching some ancient gladiators fight Ferox in an alien arena.

Jonathan hadn't seemed sure the request was feasible when he asked, but the A.I. found the project only a minor time expenditure. Mr. Clean had located the manufacturer's specs and created replacement inserts that were the exact shape and size of the plastic and metal that originally came with their protective gear. He hadn't had Rylee's gear with him at the time, but apparently, the computer had found this obstacle insignificant as well. Mr. Clean had simply analyzed footage taken from the surveillance team, compared her coat to items on the internet, found its match, and that was the end of it. Perfect replicas for the shoulder, forearm, and spine guards. Jonathan had said it was the first time in memory that having their lives constantly under surveillance had had any useful side effects.

Rylee didn't know if it was necessary to blacken these pieces, as no one would see them once they had replaced their counterparts beneath the leather, but Jonathan said that she had shown him so much in training, given him so many ways to sharpen his skills, that he felt like he should bring something to their efforts other than a bed to sleep in. She could see he found the work comforting and she could understand. There was a connection between being a fighter and maintaining her armor and weapons. The discipline, parallel to how they maintained and trained their bodies, gave her a consoling sense of readiness.

"I never actually asked for the rattan," Rylee said. "He came upon me training with it once, and a day later, it showed up. If I'd known he took requests, I might have thought of this earlier."

Jonathan looked up at her thoughtfully as he wiped his hands off on a cloth. "You said you usually gave him the silent treatment? What are those conversations like?"

She felt a touch of joy leave her when he asked, but shook it off before he worried. "The way Heyer speaks," she said. "He doesn't lie, and yet you sense you've been lied to."

Jonathan gave a knowing nod.

"We didn't talk, not after he implanted the device. I didn't see him again until the night I was activated. The first time I had to fight, I barely survived it. Then, there he was again, damn alien, telling me I have to break this stone. After what I saw that night…" Rylee took in a long breath. "I didn't want any part of it."

Jonathan nodded sympathetically. "Yeah, I've had a similar moment."

Rylee, shook her head. "Don't assume..." She trailed off.

She hadn't told this story to anyone; there had never been anyone to share it with. When she realized she wanted Jonathan to hear it, she found the words didn't come to her easily. "He never warned me how it would feel, the pain of it. I knew, when it started, that everything he'd warned me of was coming to pass. I was scared, seeing the Ferox for the first time—didn't want to face it. Instead, I ran to my father. I was like a child hoping he would tell me it was all a bad dream, that there was no such thing as monsters.

"I think he wanted to. I could see it on his face," Rylee said, grimacing as she remembered. "He wanted to protect me. But it didn't take long to see there wasn't much choice. I showed him the strength I had, told him everything I knew about what was happening on the streets as the Ferox's slaughter continued." Rylee shook her head. "But I couldn't get myself out the door, and my father didn't want me to go. He knew when the guilt of what I wasn't doing started to outweigh the fear. I think it was the one time I had ever seen him wish that I would let the fear win. He knew he couldn't stop me. Once I'd made a decision, he couldn't have even restrained me physically if he had wanted to. But, he refused to let me go alone."

She saw Jonathan's face. He closed his eyes in pain for her, already knowing what she'd seen that night.

"It happened when I hesitated, took a hit that I couldn't shake off. The Ferox got me cornered," Rylee said. "My father gave his life distracting it. He was..." She sighed. "I mean he *is* a strong man, and fast for his age—trained and taught martial arts his whole life. Still, he only lived as long as he did because the Ferox assumed he would be as easy to dispose of as everyone else it had encountered that night. My father managed to escape its claws long enough for me to get on my feet.

"I saw him stumble. He couldn't keep his footing when the Ferox could make the entire Earth shake underneath him," she said, looking away. "It crushed him. Didn't even bother to see its foot finish the job before turning its eyes back to me. Seeing it, broke something inside me."

She shed a tear, but wiped it away with the heel of her palm before Jonathan would start thinking she was weak.

"It wasn't permanent, of course, but I didn't know that yet. I couldn't get over seeing him murdered, because when it happened, I didn't think it was something that could be undone. It was too real to me to be forgotten, like a nightmare that sticks with you. Too much of a contradiction, having seen it to be so final and then suddenly not. I never told anyone again, when I was activated. I didn't want to risk seeing someone I cared about die."

Jonathan didn't look at her, but he nodded slowly. She wondered, then, if she'd been too quick to chastise him for making assumptions. The pain she confessed seemed to resonate with him. When Jonathan moved his eyes, it was not to her—instead, he glanced to the cupboard where they hid their weapons.

"That was how he got me, you know," Rylee said. "When Heyer

finally showed up, he found me holding my father's body. I was damn near catatonic, until he said I could fix it all if I broke the stone."

Jonathan still hadn't looked at her. If anything, he looked as though he had something to say, but didn't feel the moment had come. "Go on," he said.

"Afterward, he checked in on me from time to time. I didn't want to see him, let alone talk to him, so I seldom spoke. There was one time I slipped, and said, 'Why should I bother?' under my breath. Didn't really mean to say it out loud—didn't expect an answer." Rylee shook her head. "He was cryptic. Said everyday counted, because the hope we had depended on a variable he couldn't schedule. That we needed time on our side, and it didn't seem willing."

She saw Jonathan's face become troubled as she repeated the alien's words.

"Don't suppose he elaborated?" Jonathan asked.

"No. And you pretty much know the rest. I had no idea what I would find coming here. Luckily, it wasn't long until we ran across each other. I don't feel it now. That unraveling..." She trailed off, unsure, before she continued. "I couldn't bear being trapped in this alone. But trapped with you..."

Jonathan closed his eyes and nodded, and she saw that he didn't need her to explain. She wished he would say something, give her more than a nod, some indication that her presence helped him as much as his did her. Yet, his face became no less troubled. She wondered why it was that he had kept looking at the weapons cabinet while she told her story, then remembered how he had stopped short the night he had shown her the tally he kept behind the facade. His inside joke with the universe.

"You never told me what the 'H' stood for in your tally."

Finally, he looked at her. "Hayden," he whispered.

A moment passed and he grimaced before he spoke again.

"Sometimes, I think it would be better if I went away. A place where I don't know anyone. I'm afraid of what will become of me if I isolate myself like that. But if I stay, it's inevitable. Sooner or later, I will see a Ferox murder everyone I care about before I can stop it."

Leah walked down the alley leading to the back entrance of The Cell's facility. She was in agreement with Olivia that something should be done. Jonathan's mother snooping about was not much of a threat itself, as Evelyn had already exhausted any means to probe the mystery she had uncovered. At least, until Paige had brought up Grant Morgan.

When Paige put forward the idea of contacting Grant, Leah had taken the stance that it was a bad idea to give him any excuse to be back in her life. Paige had nodded as though she agreed, but Leah could see the gears grinding away in her friend's thoughts. Evelyn had been difficult to read, remaining stoically quiet. Leah would bet that the moment those two were alone together, they would be looking for Morgan.

This wasn't much of a problem. Given The Cell had a heads up, they would err on the side of caution and make sure Grant wasn't going to be anywhere that Paige could find him. However, relocating him was the hands-on side of the operation—Olivia's providence.

The garage doors opened as she approached. The guard monitoring the security cameras nodded to her as she stepped inside. Upon entry, there was a semi-truck and trailer parked inside, taking up most of the space. The Cell usually kept a few different vehicles in the garage, each serving as tools in their investigation, but Leah had never seen them utilize anything so large. She'd never seen any vehicle quite like this the other times she'd walked past.

The semi itself was military in design, though the paint job was black instead of the usual camouflage or beige. However, it wasn't the vehicle that stood out, but the strange cargo loaded onto the trailer. Its purpose was a complete mystery to Leah. Whatever it was, it didn't appear to have been built with transport in mind. Taken as a whole, it was about the size of a wide load shipping container, but the walls were hardly rectangular. The front and back bowed inward, so that she could see there was a circular chamber inside of the smooth, black outer shielding. The shielding itself was peculiar, seeming to be made from a pattern of recessed half-spheres along the outer walls—as though Pac-Man had come along and taken bites out of the surface at evenly spaced intervals. Strangely, she could swear there was a faint hum coming off the trailer.

The Cell would not be able to keep this vehicle on the street long without attracting attention. Whatever its purpose, Leah knew then that the team was planning something, and she was out of the loop.

After exiting the garage, she handed off the memory card containing the photos she had taken of Rylee's journal to one of the technicians. Olivia was thorough—she'd have someone on the staff capable of translating the Portuguese with the proper understanding of the language's subtleties. A few hours and they would know Rylee's private thoughts.

As she made her way to Olivia's office, Leah found the woman on her way out.

"Ah, Leah" Olivia said. "Good, you couldn't have better timing."

"How so?" Leah asked.

"Command has arrived. I was on the way out to give an update report. I am sure he'd like to hear from you as well. We can discuss what to do about Evelyn Tibbs on the way."

"This have anything to do with the vehicle in the garage?" Leah asked.

It was a peak hour at the gym and every piece of cardio equipment hummed, an orchestra of treadmills and stair climbers coming together to form a symphony that Rylee would later hear referred to as "sci-fi spaceship engine room in G minor." One of the trainers waved when he saw her approaching with Jonathan. Rylee assumed this was the Lincoln that he had brought her there to meet. He gave Jonathan a sly look as he noticed her beside him.

"There he is. I was about to start leaving voice mails," Lincoln said. "Where you been, slacker?"

"Hectic week," Jonathan said.

Lincoln looked at her then, nodding his head over at Jonathan. "This might be the one client I believe when I hear that excuse."

"Don't listen to him," Rylee said. "This guy's been sitting on the couch eating Oreos all week." She caught Jonathan giving her a sideways glare, although he was grinning.

"So, Tibbs, who is this lovely young lady with you?" Lincoln asked. "I don't believe I've had the pleasure."

"Rylee, meet Lincoln," Jonathan said. "I pay him to torture me."

"Good to meet you," Rylee said, putting her hand out.

As was typical of every man she met, the trainer betrayed a small degree of swooning at the sound of her accent, but he hid it better than most. He also gave her a quick once over, seeming to take note of her build, but in a professional sort of manner.

"So am I meeting my replacement?" Lincoln asked, shaking her hand.

"Actually," Rylee said. "Jonathan wanted me to take his session. See if you can find some room for improvement. I don't really use… gyms."

Rylee said the word gyms like a vegan talking about a steak.

Lincoln smiled as he shook her hand, looking to Jonathan with an *ahhh shucks* expression. "Are you bringing me new clients? You know how I love that."

Jonathan shrugged. "More of an experiment," he said. "Rylee is from out of town. Not sure if she'd be able to commit to anything long term."

She flinched at Jonathan's comment.

"Alright," Lincoln said with a shrug, "but you're a bit early. I'm finishing up with a client; she's picking up her kid from the daycare. Let me wrap things up with her and we'll see what there is to work on." He turned to scan the gym. "Actually, here she comes now, give me a minute."

Jonathan nodded as the trainer trudged off to his desk. When Lincoln was out of earshot, Rylee turned to him, wondering if Jonathan was telling his trainer that she was in town temporarily to give her a polite way out if Lincoln tried to sell her on buying a training package. "What was tha—"

Rylee broke off when she saw Jonathan's expression had changed, looking as though he'd suddenly fallen under some spell. She followed his gaze to the woman approaching Lincoln's desk. She seemed rather ordinary, pretty for a woman of thirty with a young daughter. Not so attractive to explain Jonathan's expression though. After a moment, Rylee realized he wasn't looking at the mother but her daughter.

The child's back was to them, but Rylee could tell the girl was six or seven years old. Like most kids her age, she seemed full of energy, as though she'd been given so much sugar she was having a hard time standing still. She wore a pink coat with the hood down, blond hair spilling out on her shoulders.

The mother and daughter took seats in front of Lincoln's desk. Rylee watched as the trainer smiled at the little girl from time to time as he spoke with the mother about scheduling another appointment. The child's feet couldn't reach the floor—her legs dangled, and with all of her energy, she seemed unable to keep from swinging her legs as she waited.

Jonathan's eyes finally pulled away. He looked at the floor, his face a mystery. She saw a familiar warmth in him, and it reminded Rylee of the way her father would look at her when they hadn't seen one another for a long time. She realized she'd forgotten her question and reached out to touch his shoulder.

When her hand found him, he looked up at her, his eyes *so* peculiar. What was it? Relief, joy, a sudden calmness he hadn't had up until now? It was getting stranger, and she thought that if he had let himself, he could have cried.

Instead, he gave Rylee a half smile, leaving her frowning back at him, tilting her head curiously.

"I'm sorry," Jonathan said. "What did you say?"

A moment passed and Rylee found she couldn't quite remember.

"See you next week," Lincoln said, standing up as the mother and daughter made their way out. The trainer smiled as he turned to the daughter. "Remember, Jess, eat the veggies," he said to the little girl, pretending to be stern. "Don't give your mom grief about the broccoli."

The little girl pulled her hood up and gave the trainer a mischievous look. Jonathan pried his eyes away again as the mother and daughter left and looked back to Rylee. "Rylee?" he asked, wondering what she had meant to ask him.

"Oh, um…" Rylee noticed Lincoln was heading back their way. "Never mind, can't remember."

Jonathan shrugged.

"Okay then, Rylee," Lincoln said. "The hour is yours—anything you want to work on?"

“I guess I’ll leave you to it,” Jonathan said, nodding to them as he left.

Rylee watched him for a moment as he walked off into the gym. So odd, as though he had been carrying something heavy around and had just put it down.

“Um, Rylee,” Lincoln prompted, trying to get her attention.

She flinched and gave her head a quick shake, realizing the trainer was still waiting for her to answer. “Balance and speed,” she said. “Anything that you might recommend a gymnast work on.”

“Alright,” Lincoln said. “Let’s take a look at your flexibility first, then.”

Rylee raised an eyebrow.

CHAPTER FORTY-SEVEN

DATE | TIME: UNKNOWN | FEROXIAN PLANE

AT FIRST, HEYER struggled to regain consciousness. The fog hanging over him finally thinned enough that he was able to open his eyes. A few moments later, he found he was able to move and lethargically propped himself up on his elbows to see that he was laid out in an unfamiliar room.

It was an amalgamation of environments, parts human, Ferox, and Borealis. He'd been placed on a rock table much like the altar he'd seen *Dams the Gate's* corpse on a few days earlier. Most of the room was made up of the cave-like tunnels of the Feroxian world, but there was unnatural light on the opposite side of the room. Turning his attention to the light, he saw what appeared to be a modern human bathroom projecting out of the cave's interior. The walls were white, hard lines made to look like dry wall and tile.

A man stood over a human sink in front of a mirror. His back was to Heyer but he could tell the man was shaving.

Between them was a box. It was unmistakably Borealis in design, the same dark gray, seamless metal found in the tunnels beneath the Foedrata Arena. Its presence was suspicious, and concerning. His brother had left this in the center of the room—clearly, he had wanted him to see it when he awoke.

With difficulty, Heyer moved his legs, swinging them over the side of the rock to sit. The effort required to keep himself upright was already becoming taxing—he swayed trying to find balance. His body and mind seemed to fight against him, whispering that he should go back to sleep. Heyer heard the rippling sound of water being displaced by the man's razor as he rinsed it.

He wasn't wearing a shirt, and his back and shoulders were broad, built up with muscle. Heyer caught the man's gaze in the mirror, saw his face, and understood.

Heyer closed his eyes, trying to bring his mind to bear on what this meant. The grogginess seemed to be lifting subtly, enough that he would be able to function—enough that his mind was present without allowing him to pose a physical threat. He saw that his shoes had been returned to him, laid near the edge of the table. His coat made into a pillow, supporting his head as he slept. He slipped his feet in the shoes, finding it difficult to tie the laces.

"You're awake," the man said.

Heyer was cold—colder than he had felt in years. He looked down at his chest and saw that the bright yellow blaze he was used to seeing beneath his shirt had changed. Instead, the three lines seemed to oscillate rhythmically, slowly dimming between a faint blue to a near complete absence. He reached for the bracer handcuffed to his bicep. Within a few seconds of touching the steel band, he knew what it was, and that it wouldn't be coming off by any means he had at his disposal.

"Can you hear me?" the man asked.

"Yes," Heyer said, pulling his coat on slowly.

The man grabbed a towel, wiping the remaining shaving cream from his face. He reached for a shirt that hung over a towel rod, turning to face Heyer before pulling it over his torso. The bright yellow glow of an implant emanated under the man's chest. Heyer recognized it, knew it could be no other than the Alpha Slayer he and his brother had left behind on the Foedrata's planet. Its design was almost identical to that of Jonathan's, the only difference the addition of one short line running down the center of the man's chest.

At the sight of it, Heyer found himself sighing in disgust.

When the man came forward, leaving the tiled edge of the floor and stepping onto the cave surface, the bathroom receded back into that of a cave interior.

"Your hair," the man said. "It was darker in the pictures I saw. It's almost white now."

Not looking at the man, Heyer nodded, his eyes lingering on the box of Borealis steel.

"Often, upon taking a body, my implant causes the hair follicles to revert back to a childhood state," Heyer said. "Jeremy Holloway was a towheaded child."

"I…" the man began. "They told me you were dead, all these years. I never would have thought…" The man paused, looking down to the floor before he finished his thought. "I would have forgiven you."

Heyer looked at the man sympathetically. "I am not Jeremy Holloway. I am not your father," he said. "Just as I am not what I seem, you are not who you think."

The man's eyes drew down, a look of agitation. "I've seen pictures of you," he said. "I am not stupid."

Heyer shook his head gently. His arms shook from the effects of the bracer, but he lifted his hand to point back at his chest. "This body belonged to your father," he said. "But I am not him."

The man's face showed his understanding, but Heyer could see that this was not the news he had hoped for.

"Is he trapped, then?" the man asked. "Inside of you?"

Heyer shook his head. "No. He gave me this body as he was dying. I was only able to repair the damage by putting myself into it. Holloway is gone."

"How can I know that? You could have taken his body against his will," the man said. "He could be inside you right now screaming for my help."

Heyer shook his head. "I cannot give you evidence, only my word that if I were removed, this body would perish shortly after. The only witness to Holloway's death has passed on himself."

The man studied him for a moment, searching him for signs of dishonesty.

"Douglas Tibbs," the man finally said.

Heyer's eyes locked with the man's, a long silence drawn out between them before, finally, Heyer nodded.

"His memories," the man said. "You have my father's head—do you know what he knew?"

"It's not so simple a thing," Heyer said.

"What does that mean?"

Heyer grimaced as he attempted to stand, but a wave of dizziness took his balance. He had to lean back against the table to keep from falling over before he could answer. "The mind of a person is not a reference book. There is no table of contents. I cannot simply flip to the beginning and see his childhood or skip to the end and hear his dying thoughts. Jeremy Holloway associated one memory of his life to another in his own way, just as we all do. I have no map for his associations. I would have had to experience them in a linear order as he did," he explained. "Most of what I know of Holloway comes to me in dreams."

The man blinked at him, hope lingering in his eyes. "Do you know what he felt for me?" he asked. "For my mother?"

Heyer thought about how to answer for longer than may have been wise. "Would it surprise you to know," he said, "that I never met my parents?"

The man flinched, his eyes narrowing in annoyance at what he seemed to think a feeble attempt to avoid the question. "Do you know what he felt?" the man repeated.

Heyer sighed. "You have tracked me down, recklessly traveled across time and space, had my own brother take me prisoner," he said. "And this is the question that drove you?"

The man stared back at him, face growing angry as he was put on the defensive. "I didn't know what I would find when I stepped inside that sphere, I..." The man trailed off. His eyes narrowed, his lips parting to show teeth. "I don't care what you think. Right now, I'm the one asking questions. So stop stalling."

Heyer nodded. "He didn't know you existed, Grant," he said. "He didn't remember your mother's name."

Grant stared into Heyer's eyes as though looking for a hesitance that might betray a malicious lie. His body shivered under the weight of denial, searching his father's face only to see the alien looking back on him in pity.

"Then why..." Grant stammered. "Why have I seen your face? Why were you watching me?"

Heyer took a long breath as he understood.

It was true, the alien had checked in on him. Grant had only seen him the once, that he knew of, peering through his window one night when he was still a child. Heyer hadn't made a noise, but the child had awoken. He'd been gone before Grant had blinked. He had hoped the boy would think it his imagination, perhaps a dream, upon waking. Heyer hadn't made the mistake again, keeping his distance. Grant proved to be quite the light sleeper.

Yet, it appeared the boy had fixated on that memory, had known what he'd seen. Heyer's mistake, giving him the denial he now saw shaking the man to his core.

"How do you know who I am?" Grant asked.

In an empty parking lot, Leah waited impatiently, leaning against the black sedan. Olivia had been in the car awhile now, a fact that was starting to concern her. General Delacy, her father, wasn't supposed to be here for another week, and his early arrival confirmed her suspicion that something was in motion within The Cell. While Leah had no place demanding details from Olivia, her own father was a different situation.

What worried her was that Olivia had already been thinking of bringing Jonathan in for questioning. She dreaded what this meant, what she might soon be taking part in. The thought of him knowing she was involved with those who would torture him made her physically ill. She wouldn't have a choice if he resisted. Her brother's life was in the balance. She hoped that if Jonathan was threatened, he'd be wise enough to talk—see that there was no point in fighting. Leah knew they had the means to crack men trained to resist torture. She didn't want to see him go through it. What scared her more was that, if they asked him something he truly didn't know and couldn't answer, they would go to whatever means necessary to confirm he wasn't holding back. Leah couldn't protect him from any of it... she wasn't supposed to want to protect him.

The car door finally opened and Olivia stepped out. She acknowledged Leah with the same usual polite nod and smile before stepping aside for Leah to take her place. Leah didn't wait once the door shut behind her—the questions started spilling out before her father had time to finish lowering the dividing panel.

"What is going on?" Leah asked.

General Delacy looked back at her thoughtfully, not rushing to answer. "There have been developments," he said. "Promising ones. We may now have good reason to deviate from the secondary protocol."

Leah kept her concerns off her face, held back her fear until her father gave her reason to acknowledge it. "What kind of developments?" she asked.

"We may have a way of identifying where and when The Mark will appear and disappear. If we are correct, and the opportunity presents itself, we can attempt a capture."

Relief flooded Leah. Forcing information out of Jonathan had nothing to do with this. She relaxed, only to find herself reeling through a series of new revelations. If this were true, they may finally bring the alien into custody. She might be close to finding Peter.

"This is good news," Leah said. "Something is about to happen—no idea what, but it may mean the opportunity won't be far off."

Leah spent a few minutes relaying the cryptic story Jonathan had given her about the defusing of a bomb. Her father was the first to hear it—she hadn't yet reported it to Olivia's team.

"Do we have a plan for actually subduing The Mark if we even get the chance?" Leah finally asked. "After all, his ability to teleport is only one obstacle to his capture."

General Delacy nodded. "A strategy is being developed for how to engage. Still, if we manage to subdue him and momentarily disrupt his movements, we'll only get one shot before whoever he is working with can adapt. You will be staying in play. Chances are that Jonathan or Rylee are going to be present if the Mark makes an appearance. Do not break cover. If we fail to capture The Mark, whoever is present will be taken into custody at the time—if that includes you, we will take you in under the pretense of an assumed accomplice."

"What about Jack?" Leah asked. "We need to get him far away from this."

"Already taken care of," General Delacy said. "Agents acting as his grandparents will be picking him up for a visit later today. If we need to prolong his absence while we wait for an opportunity, we will adapt."

Leah's uncertainty about this plan showed on her face.

"You are worried?" her father asked.

"If we try this and it fails," Leah said. "We'll have wasted our chance to find Peter. Who knows how long until we'll get another one. Either way, I'll be cut out of the operation."

Her father gave her an understanding nod. "I will find another role for you within The Cell should that occur," he promised. "You will no longer be in the field if your identity is compromised. For now, focus on not letting that happen. If Jonathan is brought in, we are working out an angle to exploit the relationship you have forged. You'll be briefed on the details."

Leah nodded slowly, trusting Olivia and her father were covering all the bases. "Dad?" she asked a moment later. "That semi back at the base—what is it?"

Her father turned and grinned at her. "Taxpayers' dollars hard at work."

They were both tired and hungry when they returned home. Jonathan heated food in the microwave—containers of premade chicken, rice, and broccoli. He felt his cell phone vibrate with a text message as he descended the stairs back into the garage carrying a meal for each of them.

He found Rylee standing over the cigar box in which he emptied the contents of his pockets most days. His father's pocket watch lay open—she had looked to see if there was an inscription, but now, she was looking at the photo of his father. He held the food out to her and absentmindedly she accepted it, taking a fork full.

He checked the message he'd received as he heard Rylee making a coughing sound.

"Ughh..."

She'd taken her eyes off the photo and looked at what she was eating. Upon seeing how plain and unseasoned the food was, she looked at him as though unsure if he had intentionally pulled a prank on her.

"Sorry," Jonathan said. "I haven't had much time for the culinary arts."

Rylee studied him but continued to chew, wincing as she finally swallowed. Then she noticed the frown he had as he re-read the message he'd received.

"Something up?"

"Strange message from Lincoln," Jonathan said. "Says he won't be working at the gym anymore. That he will have to contact me once he gets a new location to train his clients."

"Oh," Rylee said knowingly. "Guess that makes sense."

"I miss something?" Jonathan asked.

"His manager stopped by while we were training. Asked Lincoln to come to his office once he was done with his clients for the day," Rylee said. "He didn't look happy."

Jonathan eyebrows drew down considering it. "Think he got let go?"

Rylee shrugged. "You know," she said. "He attempted to be subtle, but Lincoln tried to get me to tell him what you were always training for. Told him I didn't know."

Jonathan nodded. "Can't blame him. He's been curious since the day we met." He put the phone back in his pocket, distracted by his thoughts.

"You keep these things separate from everything else?" she asked, changing the subject. "Sentimental value?"

He bit his lip, then, pulling out of his thoughts, and looked at the contents of his cigar box. "The watch is a family heirloom," he said. "It was my grandfather's, then my dad's. When he died, my mother gave it to me."

"Does a smart man stay in sight of those who would protect him?" she asked.

Jonathan saw that she had found the note The Cell had left for him. "That was waiting for me when I got back the other night," he said.

Her eyes widened. "Do they leave you messages often?"

"No," he said. "This is a first."

She looked at the note again, more thoughtfully. "What do you think changed?"

Jonathan shrugged. "My guess, it was the first time they lost track of me," he said. "It rattled them enough that they felt I needed a warning."

She studied him, her face seeming to grow sad, almost sick. "Why don't you tell me these things, Jonathan?"

Jonathan took a deep breath. "It was the least of my worries that night. That, and I guess I haven't completely gotten used to there being anyone around I could tell."

Her expression didn't change. "I..." She grimaced. "I don't think you're being honest with me."

He looked away, down at the floor. "Alright," he said. "I didn't want to burden you with things we can't do anything about."

Rylee reached for his chin, maneuvered it so that he couldn't divert his eyes from hers, then gave what could only be described as the most pissed off smile he'd ever seen. "It burdens me," she said, slowly enunciating each word, "when I don't know what is happening."

Slow and apologetic, Jonathan nodded.

She held his eyes for a moment longer before appearing satisfied that they understood one another, then let go of his chin. Jonathan turned to take another bite when the question he should have seen coming fell.

"What else haven't you told me?" Rylee asked suspiciously.

He put his fork down, and turned back to her. She narrowed her eyes then, knowing there was something, and he sighed, reaching behind her to push the button on his watch.

"There are things I'm afraid to tell," he said. "Some that I can't."

Rylee's face became indecipherable to him, then—she was either angry or concerned. "Why don't you start with what you're afraid to tell me?" she said.

He swallowed, but after a moment he looked to the floor and nodded. Of all the things he didn't want to tell her, there was one he knew Rylee alone might have insight into, and he'd said too much now to not say anything.

"He wants me to lead us."

She blinked at him, not exactly sure what he was trying to tell her.

"The army Heyer is amassing on earth," he said. "He expects me to lead them." He closed his eyes, shook his head as if the words he was saying made as little sense to him as they must to her. "I don't know why, or what he imagines I'll have to offer them."

He waited for her to say something. Rylee couldn't seem to stop blinking. Jonathan had wanted to tell her this, but had been hesitant as well. The bond had let her see inside of him. Maybe, she had glimpsed whatever it was that made Heyer think him fit to lead. The longer she seemed unable to make sense of what he told her, the more he knew she had seen no such thing.

Jonathan nodded once, knowingly, his shoulders slumping as he took a seat at the edge of his bench.

"Why would he do this to you?" she asked. "What could he possibly expect from you, from anyone..."

He closed his eyes as she trailed off, and a moment passed with no one speaking. He felt Rylee's hand on his shoulder, and he turned meekly back to her. He saw, then, that she still held the photo of his father in her hand, and he reached for it.

"I see how my father looked in these photos. He'd fought in a war, knew firsthand what he had to tell his men to do," Jonathan said. "He had a gift for words, could have given them reasons to hope. Ever since Heyer told me, I've wished my dad was here to tell me what to do. I feel like all I have to offer them is anger." He looked at the picture. "But what good is that in a leader?"

Rylee, seeming not to know what to say, sat down behind him and put her arms around him. He didn't pull away, didn't tense. Though, as he looked at the picture in his hands, he saw the box his mother had left, full of his father's belongings. He stood up, and Rylee let her arms falls off him as he walked to it, taking the box off the counter and sitting down on the floor. He pulled the lid off and began going through the contents. Looking for what, he didn't know. Some piece of his father that would bring him some meaning.

Rylee sat beside him. She didn't speak, just looked through the items with him—until she lifted a frame out of the box and he heard her breath go still.

"Jonathan, have you ever seen these pictures?" she asked.

"Not since I was a kid," he said. "My mother put them all away after he died."

Her hand came to her lips.

Jonathan, unsettled by her reaction, reached across the box and took the frame from her hands. He remembered the picture, from so long ago. It had been framed and put out during his father's wake. *Libya, 1984, Douglas Tibbs and his surviving Army Strike Force.*

There was a man, kneeling next to Douglas. A man Jonathan never would have given a second look so long ago. The hair was darker, but the face was unmistakable.

CHAPTER FORTY-EIGHT

DATE | TIME: UNKNOWN | FEROXIAN PLANE

"ANSWER THE QUESTION," Grant repeated.

"It is..." Heyer said. "Complicated."

"Then uncomplicate it."

"That implant..." Heyer staggered forward, toward the box of Borealis steel his brother had left for him in the center of the room. "Grant, it is not like the others. Did he not explain this to you? Has he not told you—"

When he was within reach of the box, he began to fall, and was forced to grip its edge to keep himself standing. When he peered down at the contents, he closed his eyes in disgust.

"You are not who you think you are," Heyer said. "Not the real Grant Morgan. You're only a shadow... and you are dying."

"Yeah," Grant said. "Your brother already gave me the bad news, laid out my options."

"The implant," Heyer said. "Malkier gave it to you to slow the degradation, then, but to what end?"

"We came to an agreement."

Heyer steadied himself. "What could you possibly offer—"

Heyer broke off as a door into the chamber manifested in one of the side walls. Malkier stepped inside, contemplating him with disdain.

“Human,” Malkier said, “do not let my brother manipulate you. You have questions, and he is distracting you. You’ve come so far—now get your answers.”

Heyer was straining to breathe normally, faltering in the effort to keep himself conscious and standing. Malkier, studying him a moment, seemed to understand the difficulty.

“Cede,” Malkier said. “You are being overly cautious—the threat my brother poses is rather negligible. Reduce the effect of the dampener, otherwise we’ll be waiting all night for him to finish a sentence.”

The fog weighing Heyer down lessened, his vision coming into better focus as the throbbing blue lines on his chest grew stronger. Within a few moments, he was able to stand without the effort requiring his full attention.

“So unfortunate for you, brother,” Malkier said. “Your own son stepping through the gates. Had I not heard his story, I may never have seen the full shape of your betrayal. I find myself curious what you are thinking in this moment.”

Heyer looked at his brother but gave no sign that he intended to answer.

“No? Well, I suppose I understand.” Malkier said. “However, the human and I have an agreement, and part of my end of the bargain is that you will answer his questions. We both feel, quite strongly, that you owe him an explanation.”

Heyer’s eyes narrowed as his brother spoke. He looked away, his hand reaching down into the box in front of him. There was a stack of the Foedrata’s human implants, unceremoniously piled and left here for him to see. He picked one up, considering what the existence of more devices meant and wondering where Malkier had recovered another cache of implants. Yet, the question of greatest importance, now, was when his brother had returned to the Foedrata’s planet to recover them.

Heyer dropped the device back into the box. “You already know the answers,” he said. “So why do you wish me—”

“Because,” Malkier interrupted. “I wish to hear it from my brother’s lips.”

Heyer closed his eyes. Eventually, his brother would ask him things he could not answer. This was not the time to pick his battle. "Grant, the implant inside of you," he began. "It was intended for your father. At the time, he was the only human genetically compatible with that particular device. Unfortunately, Holloway's brain was severely damaged in the same conflict that left my previous human body beyond repair. The trauma had rendered your father's body unresponsive, comatose, and transferring myself into it was the only option I had at the time. When this occurred, I thought that the device had lost its one compatible recipient.

"Years later, I became aware of your existence, when your genetic makeup came up as a compatible candidate for the device my brother has now implanted in you. The reasonable conclusion was that you were the son of Jeremy Holloway. The son of this man's body." Heyer looked away. "I checked in on you from time to time as you grew into adulthood."

Grant studied the floor as he processed all this information. Heyer saw that Malkier must have explained the devices to him on some level, as Grant did not appear confused. "But, you never brought this to me," he finally said, pointing to the glowing lines on his chest.

"No," Heyer said. "I chose not to."

Grant stared back at the alien, his face on the brink of outrage. "I am its rightful owner," he said. "Who are you to withhold it from me?"

Heyer shook his head. "Your very reaction is your answer, Grant. You should be grateful. It was a burden that I spared you."

"It's power I was meant to have. You couldn't have kept me from my birthright."

Heyer stared sadly at the floor. "Clearly," he whispered, before turning to address his brother. "How long? When was the implant installed?"

His brother's expression disturbed him—he seemed to find the question amusing. "You think he speaks like this because he is a shadow?" Malkier asked. "You believe your son's anger is a result of the degradation on his mental state?" Malkier shook his head, seeming to find the sentiment pathetically naive.

"Grant," Heyer said. "The implant is only going to buy you a fortnight at best, and in the meantime, the degradation of your mind will distort you in ways you can't imagine."

"My mind is clearer than it has ever been," Grant said. "And I have plenty of time left to put my affairs in order."

Heyer looked back and forth between Grant and Malkier. "What have you agreed to?" he asked. "What affairs?"

Folding his arms across his chest, Grant stepped to the side of the room that Malkier occupied. "That's *my* business, alien."

"But, you must see," Heyer said. "The true Grant Morgan, he will suffer the consequences of your actions. Do you not..."

Heyer didn't bother finishing. The shadow clearly found the attempt to sway him out of concern for its other self laughable. The degradation had to have been further along than he'd suspected.

"That will be enough, human," Malkier said. "Leave us. I wish to speak to my brother alone."

"He hasn't answered my question," Grant said. "I want to know why he denied me."

Malkier turned an eye to Heyer and sighed. "Tell your son what he wishes to know, brother."

Heyer looked away, taking a moment before he answered. "Grant Morgan was unfit for the implant."

"Unfit?" Grant's shadow growled the question.

"It seems I shouldn't have to tell you, of all people, that his childhood was poisonous. Grant ties his self-worth to power, believes his sense of justice infallible," Heyer said. "He suffers delusions of grandeur, thinks that Mankind will love him for being some hero that only exists in his mind—the problem is that he confused the word 'hero' with 'celebrity' a long time ago."

Heyer paused, thoughtfully, before continuing.

"You see, no one should ever want to call that implant their birthright—no one should seek it out. If I had given it to Grant, it would have required sacrifices he wasn't capable of understanding." Finally, Heyer looked into the shadow's eyes. "It will not give you—or him—what you believe you're owed."

Heyer could feel the Shadow's stare grow livid. He'd been given the truth he'd asked for, and every word of it had been an insult.

Heyer knew, Grant had always believed power would solve his

problems. Now, this shadow of him possessed the very power of which Heyer had declared him unworthy, and all the man wanted was to use that power to force the alien to change his mind. Unwilling to see that this power would do nothing to help him achieve this, the shadow's face hardened into defiance.

"It doesn't matter what you think," Grant finally said. "You're just a parasite pretending to be a man. My father, he's in there, and he doesn't see me like you do."

Grant's shadow turned to leave, but paused in the doorway that formed, tilting his head back at Heyer.

"You've picked the wrong man, alien. When he fails, you're gonna have to admit that to yourself, and my father will know it."

Grant's shadow stepped outside the chamber, leaving Heyer alone with his brother when the cave wall reformed behind him

"Telling, isn't it? This shadow of a man? He faces his mortality, and all he cares about is proving himself to an audience in his imagination. His entire species, not even an afterthought," Malkier said. "What a fragile layer of conscience there is protecting your humans from one another."

"He is not my son. Nor is he exemplary of all Mankind," Heyer said. "And you have not kept me alive to discuss humanities frailties."

"Kept you alive? I am not going to execute you, little brother," Malkier said. "Your betrayals have hurt me more than I ever imagined possible. But, I am not incapable of seeing what drove you. I regret that I allowed you to become so attached to Mankind. I had hoped humanity itself would cure you of your misplaced affections. But..." He crossed his arms over his chest. "The time for you to see them for what they are has passed. I will not allow you to return. After sometime away, when your attachments to them have faded, you will understand. I will try to forgive you your trespasses against me. We will get past this."

It had been years since they had been able to tell one another what they truly thought. Far longer since Malkier had spoken to him as though he were his father. It was a disturbing thing to hear what came out the moment his brother was in a position of power over him. His arrogance was so blindly sure of itself that Heyer found he didn't want to look at his brother.

"Noble sentiments," Heyer said. "Do you actually believe them, or are they a show for my benefit?"

He could feel his brother's eyes studying him in the silence that followed. "Of what, exactly, are you accusing me?"

"Fear is the heart alone," Heyer said softly.

"What is it you see in the platitudes of our wretched ancestors?"

"You do not wish to be the last of the Borealis," Heyer said. "For all your love of the Ferox, you are a god above them. Yet when you grieve for your son, you must hide in the dark, because they cannot offer you any comfort."

After some silence, Heyer heard the tapping of Feroxian nails against the Borealis steel box.

"You believe I give you mercy because I fear loneliness?" Malkier asked.

"I believe you have many practical reasons to fear my death. But, in the end, when all those fears have been dealt with—an eternity alone is what you will have to come to terms with."

"And this doesn't apply to you?"

Heyer sighed. "You have me hostage, brother. Yet, you leave this box of human implants in my cage." He tilted his head over his shoulder. "What is it that you want?"

"You owe the Ferox a debt of many lives, brother," Malker said. "But first... you will answer for my son's death."

"How will I answer? You only have yourself to blame," Heyer said. "If you intend to put that guilt on me, then you are a coward."

"Coward? Brother, you are clinging to a desperate hope that I've not uncovered the full extent of your betrayals."

"You could uncover everything," Heyer said. "I would still not be responsible for your son."

Heyer heard his brother drawing in a long breath.

"Since your last visit, a question has nagged at me," Malkier said, then. "Why had my brother, who had shown so little regard for my well-being since the day he learned of my son's conception, come running to comfort me when he died?"

Heyer shook his head. "I grieved for you."

"Did you? Or perhaps your condolences masked your real motives with..." Malkier paused, tapping his claw against the box of implants again. "Noble sentiments."

Heyer closed his eyes. "Fine," he said. "I also had good reason to think that your grief would affect your judgment. I feared you would indulge a fantasy in which *Dams the Gate*'s death was a crime that Mankind needed to answer for—blaming humanity would be so much easier than seeing your own failure as a father."

Malkier took a moment to let his brother's explanation run off him. "A string of losses followed through the gate after my son," he said.

"Yes, and so you sent assassins for *Brings the Rain,*" Heyer replied. "And they have failed."

Malkier sighed. "No, I sent no assassins. At first, I thought your council wise, and I heeded it. I figured that *Brings the Rain* would fall on his own—but, I found, a grieving father's patience is short. Three more bodies came back before I found the first of your betrayals hidden within their remains. So clever of you. When I discovered it, I was uncertain if you broke the letter of our agreement—though I was quite certain that you broke its spirit."

When silence followed, Heyer finally asked, "Are you waiting for me to say something?"

"I was hoping that by now you would realize there is no point in lying," Malkier said. "Do me the decency of a confession."

Heyer sighed. "You imagine you have evidence that I violated our agreement, and expect me to sit here and guess, what..." Heyer trailed off and sighed. "Oh, no, you hope I will confess to crimes you've yet to find."

Heyer heard his brother's breath draw in, long, and growing impatient.

"Sometimes, brother, you imagine plots when a request is no more than what was asked." Malkier said. "But fine. The evidence was the wounds. Each kill was accomplished, at least in part, by a weapon that seemed it must be more resilient than earthly means—a crude spear. I suspected something made from Borealis steel. Yet, there were trace metals left behind, and Borealis steel would leave no trace. So I thought I must be wrong. Then I had Cede run an analysis."

Heyer knew, then, where his brother was going with this.

"You used elements only found on Earth, but forged them in the same manner as Borealis steel. The weapon he used to tear open my son—only you could have given it to him."

For a moment, Heyer said nothing. The truth was that he hadn't yet considered if such a thing put a degree of guilt at his feet. Though the moment was short lived, it was enough proof to Malkier that his suspicions had been right.

"Brother," Heyer said. "If a gladiator dies in an Arena because he wishes to prove he can fight, do you blame the blacksmith who forged the weapon that killed him?"

"I do if it gave his opponent an advantage he should not have had," Malkier said.

Heyer shook his head. "It would be a fine point, but I know the story of how *Dams the Gate* was killed, and your son fell to a man's fists. You have my word—the weapon only ended his suffering."

"Even if that is true, your intentions matter, brother."

"No, that is what you ignore—my intentions had no bearing. *Dams the Gate* was forbidden from entering the Arena. I did not arm the man with any notion of the weapon being used against your son," Heyer said. "Your son is dead because you failed to keep him out of harm's way."

Heyer could hear Malkier's breathing behind him, growing heavier with anger the longer they spoke.

"And the bonded pair, brother?" Malkier asked.

Heyer brought his hand to his forehead, his fingers cold against his head. "I am here today to report that the issue is being resolved. I have not yet discovered how they became aware of one another—it occurred during my absence. I have ordered them to separate from one another," he said. "But Malkier, it is as irrelevant as the rest of your accusations. The bond was not active when your son entered the—"

A powerful thud erupted in the room as Malkier's fist struck the box of implants. "*Jonathan Tibbs!*" Malkier yelled.

Hearing his brother speaking the name struck fear in Heyer, forced him to finally turn and look his brother in the eye.

"What? Did you hope that your son would neglect to mention that name brother? Or did you think that I never bothered to learn the birth name of *Echoes the Borealis*?" Malkier yelled.

Heyer waited, fearing his brother's anger, but when Malkier spoke again, his voice was quiet with malevolence.

"I remember the day I told you my son had been conceived. I thought you would be happy for me, that our agreement would be void just this once. But the way you looked at me..." Malkier trailed off as Heyer closed his eyes. "Do you honestly think me so naïve that I would believe that, after I killed the man's father, his killing *my* son is some coincidence?"

Heyer already knew—already felt the defeat. He would try, and each word would be a waste of breath.

Nothing he could say would convince Malkier that he'd had no hand in *Dams the Gate's* death. His brother had just enough evidence to draw this conclusion, too many reasons to believe. In a way, Heyer could hardly hold it against him. He didn't feel innocent. Though his guilt was, as his brother had said, a matter of his intention. Heyer was not guilty of violating any letter of the law, but he had violated its spirit. It came to one ugly truth: Heyer had never believed that *Dams the Gate* deserved to die, but he did believe that his brother deserved to feel every bit of the pain that death had brought him.

"I know you helped him, brother," Malkier said.

"Malkier, please," Heyer whispered. "Jonathan does not know who his father was. I admit I desired revenge for the father, it's true. But I never acted on it. There is no justice in killing a Ferox child who had nothing to do with how he was born."

"No." Malkier shut his eyes, shook his head slowly. "Don't stand there and give me words I know you've practiced. I want to know, if this man was so important to you, why you didn't kill me when I was bleeding in front of you? Why did you wait until the only thing you had left to hurt me with was my son?"

Heyer swallowed, looked into his brother's eyes and searched for the Borealis inside the empty white slits. "Because I still loved you," he said. "I understood why you did what you did. You keep calling Grant my son even though you know he is not truly my child. But if you think I've never been a father to a man, you're wrong. I've watched them grow old. I've watched them have grandchildren. So, yes, I walked away from you, and I grieved for the man you killed, and when it was over, my love for my brother was gone and all I had was regret."

"Regret..." Malkier trailed off, growing quiet before he turned away. He slowly walked toward the wall where Grant had left, but stopped there before leaving. "If the memory of this man meant more to you than your own brother," he said, "then you should have left it alone. Now, you're going to live knowing your revenge killed his son."

The door opened, and Malkier took a single step before Heyer spoke.

"Brother, do not go after *Brings the Rain*!" Heyer yelled. "He can kill you."

Malkier stopped, turning back to Heyer. At first, it was clear that Malkier thought the claim absurd, but as he studied Heyer, his head tilted with what became uncertainty.

"You're afraid, brother," Malkier said. "What I can't tell is if it's because you are bluffing, or because you are telling the truth."

CHAPTER FORTY-NINE

WEDNESDAY| OCTOBER 12, 2005 | 2:30 PM | SEATTLE

WHEN RYLEE AND Jonathan had finished going through the box of his father's possessions, the floor was covered with scattered photos and keepsakes. Disappointingly, they found no other images of the man kneeling beside Douglas.

Jonathan sat next to the contents of the box, holding a beret that had belonged to his father. It was black, a symbol of the armed forces placed on the forefront. Knowing it was issued to his father, Rylee noticed a sentimental respect for the small piece of fabric.

"Put it on already," Rylee said, a touch of impatience in her voice after having watched him stare at it for a while now.

Jonathan shook his head. "No," he said. "I don't even know what it represents. I don't want to treat it like it's just a piece of clothing."

She looked disappointed, but nodded.

Jonathan stood, stepping across the room to place the hat carefully into his cigar box beside his father's watch, and gently closed the lid. Rylee began carefully putting the contents of the box away as she watched him stare out the window at Leah's house.

"It's not Heyer," Jonathan said.

"Of course it is," Rylee said. "There is no mistaking it."

"It is the man Heyer is implanted inside. But it isn't him. You can see it in the man's eyes, his posture. He was still human in that picture."

Rylee studied the framed photo. Jonathan wasn't wrong—there was a normalcy to the man in the picture uncharacteristic to that of the alien.

"When I first saw Heyer, I knew something was off. A part of me kept screaming in warning that he shouldn't be there, but I could never figure out why," Jonathan said. "After he revealed what he was, I thought I had somehow picked up on his nonhuman qualities—that my instincts had been telling me he was unknown and dangerous. Either that or that I had somehow caught glimpses of him watching me in the past, but I stopped thinking about it once I knew what he was."

He looked away from Leah's house and turned back to her.

"I asked him, though," he continued, his forehead wrinkled in thought. "Actually, it was the first thing I ever really asked him. He was restraining me, putting me under at the time. I asked how it was that I seemed to know him. I remember seeing this smile on his face—just for a moment—before he said that *I shouldn't*."

"You think he lied?" Rylee asked.

"No," Jonathan said, shaking his head. "He's only ever lied to me once, and technically that was his shadow in The Never. I think the true Heyer goes out of his way not to lie. Which makes me wonder why he didn't say 'you don't' or 'you can't.'"

Rylee thought about his recollection. "Yeah, he said 'you shouldn't.'" She looked down at the man in the frame again as though he might suddenly give her an explanation.

"Maybe what my memory couldn't dredge up for me that night was that picture. Maybe it saw a face that should have aged but hadn't."

Rylee shrugged. "I suppose it's possible."

Jonathan's eyes caught something, then. He stepped back from the garage window, staring down at another photo of his father on top of one of the stacks. He reached for it, his eyes widening as he rubbed his chin. The picture seemed of no special consequence to Rylee, just an image of Douglas standing next to his luggage, perhaps the day he'd come home from Libya.

"I've seen this before," Jonathan said, pointing down at what looked like a footlocker resting by his father's feet.

"Okay? Does that mean something?"

Jonathan's face contorted in annoyance. He shook his head slowly and turned around to look at Leah's house once again. "Yeah," he said. "It means I need to speak to my mother."

CHAPTER FIFTY

WEDNESDAY| OCTOBER 12, 2005 | 4:30 PM | SEATTLE

JONATHAN KNOCKED ON Leah's door, but it was his mother who answered.

"Leah is out running some errands," Evelyn said.

"That's good, actually," Jonathan said. "I came to talk to you."

Evelyn raised an eyebrow, leaving him unsure if his mother was being smug or was genuinely interested that something had brought him to her instead of the other way around. Whichever it was, she stepped out of the doorway and let Jonathan inside. Now that he was standing in Leah's living room, he found himself frowning, at a loss for where to begin.

Evelyn did not take long to pick up on his hesitation.

"So, I'm surprised. Figured if you were knocking on Leah's door," she said. "Well... she is a pretty girl, and kind. I like her."

Jonathan nodded slowly. At first he was glad she had spoken first, started a conversation. Now he was unsure where it might be headed. He couldn't blow his mother off this time. Walling himself off might make her realize she had something he needed.

"Is she..." His mother hesitated. "Someone special to you?"

His expression became an uncomfortable smile. Though he showed none of the hardness he had before, he still didn't answer the question.

"The other girl, then?" Evelyn asked. "The one sleeping in your bedroom."

Jonathan's uncomfortable smile became a grimace and he sighed. "Mom," he replied. "Friends and neighbors. That's all."

His mother studied him, narrowed her eyes a bit. "Nice try. No man your age is so caught up in his own head that he doesn't notice when two girls are trying to get his attention. Really, Jonathan, you're a terrible liar."

He groaned. "Yeah I get that a lot." Though he was uncomfortable that her motherly observations had called him out, at least the questions his mother was asking seemed to steer clear of any dangerous topics.

"Well," she said. "Even if you insist on pretending, you aren't fooling either of those girls. I promise you they're both well aware of one another."

"Mom, this isn't really—"

"Leah hopes every knock at the door will be yours, Jonathan," she interrupted. "Meanwhile, Rylee is sleeping in your bed, hoping you'll get off the couch and join her in it."

He closed his eyes and groaned, starting to remember how awkward his mother's candor could be.

"Frankly," she said, "I don't trust that Rylee girl much."

He'd been about to maneuver the conversation elsewhere, but he'd been taken aback by his mother's statement. "You hardly know her," he said.

Evelyn raised an eyebrow. "I know you met her less than a week ago, and she looks at you like…" She cleared her throat. "Well, let's just say all you would have to do is ask."

Yep, there it is Mom, this is officially terrible, Jonathan thought

"Leah," Evelyn said, drawing out the name. She leaned her head in conspiratorially toward him. "She hides it better."

He snorted, starting to shake his head as his face betrayed him. He shut his eyes and smiled—his mother's words had crossed over from mildly embarrassing to endearing.

"Hey, look," she said. "I made him laugh."

He bit his lip, and nodded, but his face turned serious when he remembered why he had come. "I need to ask you something, Mom," Jonathan said. "But I just need answers, not questions."

"Oh, well look who's hijacking the subject," she said, a seriousness returning. "Okay, Jonathan, no questions."

Jonathan immediately questioned her agreeableness. No negotiations? No argument? No mention of throwing his life away? He couldn't help but wonder what had changed as he reached into the pocket of his coat, and pulled out the picture frame from his father's wake.

"What can you tell me about this picture, Mom?" he asked. "Do you know any of the men kneeling next to dad?"

Evelyn bit her lip, and she eyed him in manner that worried him.

"Mom?" Jonathan asked. "What is it?"

Reluctance came on her face as she spoke. "Why this picture, Jonathan?" she asked. "Out of all the pictures, what drew your attention to this one? I know—I said I wouldn't ask any questions, and I meant it, but it is too much of a coincidence for me to ignore."

"Coincidence?" he asked. "Mom, do you know something about that picture?"

Evelyn swallowed. "I know the name of this man," she said, pointing at the man kneeling beside his father. "I learned it quite recently. This…" His mother paused, uncertainty creeping into her expression. "This woman visited me—said she was with some Army records department. That she was trying to reconstruct records that had been lost." Evelyn tapped her finger on the glass. "She said his name was Jeremy Holloway. It was this exact picture that she singled out. She studied it longer than all the rest, made a point of taking a copy of it."

When what he was hearing hit home, his anger started getting the better of him.

They listened. They watched. They followed. They had used his friends' emotions just to put someone close to him. They had left him threats. Something was snapping inside of him. He'd let this go on too long, and he knew it.

My mother… they think they can go anywhere near…

Hatred dropped into Jonathan like ink in water, spreading its taint to everything. He felt his hands constricting into fists, his knuckles growing white. The Cell. They had been an idea, a faceless network of people thinking he'd allow this to continue, that he would just ignore them.

He needed to change what they were—needed them to be something he could get his hands on. He couldn't kill an idea—but a face, a person…

He took a deep breath, that anger beginning to shake his entire body. The air trembled as he inhaled it. He knew his mother had seen his reaction. He couldn't let her see any more, had to put it behind the wall. He looked away and closed his eyes, forced his fists to relax, to breathe.

"The woman," he finally asked. "Did she give a name?"

Evelyn, wary of her son's sudden change, was distracted before she managed to nod. She stepped away, reaching for her purse on the table. A moment later, she produced a business card. "Melissa Hart," she read before handing him the card.

There was a number—Jonathan had no doubt it was fictitious, but it would be monitored by The Cell in case Evelyn called. Useless to Jonathan, but perhaps Mr. Clean could do something with it. He slipped the card into his jacket pocket.

His mother had stepped closer to him, and when he looked up he found her studying his face. "Are you being watched, Jonathan?" she whispered the question.

His jaw clenched. How could she know enough to ask this? He stared at the ground until he feared silence would answer her question for him.

"No questions, Mom," he said as he pulled his last lead from his pocket. The picture of Douglas next to the footlocker. He held it out to her, pointed at the box. "Do you know what happened to this?" he asked.

Evelyn frowned when she looked back to him. "You don't remember?" she asked. "We found it after the funeral, took it —"

Jonathan cut her off. "Don't say. Can you take me to it? Right now?"

Evelyn flinched at her son's hurry. She had noticed when he'd cut her off before she'd could speak of a location—knew that he'd confirmed her fears.

"Mom, how long will it take to get there and back?" Jonathan asked.

Her brow furrowed in thought. "Six, maybe seven hours if we don't stop."

Jonathan nodded—made his decision. "Okay, I need to talk to Rylee," he said. "When I come back, we go?"

His mother nodded, looking around in a somewhat bewildered state for her coat and car keys.

Jonathan left Leah's house and walked across the yard. He stopped in the garage and took his father's watch out of the cigar box. When he found Rylee, she was waiting for him in his bedroom. At first she perked up, eager to know if he had learned anything—but his face alarmed her.

"What did she say?" she asked.

"She knows where the footlocker is," Jonathan said. "Agreed to take me there."

"Jonathan, you seem... angry."

He closed his eyes and nodded, but didn't explain.

"I'll get my things," she said. "Just give me a minute."

"No." He pulled the watch out of his pocket and flipped the button. After a moment, he asked, "Do you trust me, Rylee?"

She didn't hesitate before giving him a single nod.

He stepped toward her, and Rylee slipped into his arms as though she were at home there. He made sure she felt him place the watch into her pocket, then pressed her forehead against his cheek to whisper in her ear.

"I know how it feels when Heyer says he keeps secrets to protect you," he said. His voice trembled. "I know what it does to you inside."

He felt her embrace tightening around him.

"I didn't believe it, but now I know that there are things we are only safe from when we don't know," Jonathan said. "There is something I wish he hadn't told me, because the moment he did, I knew I would have to keep it from you, because it could only be used against us."

"I don't understand, Jonathan," Rylee said softly.

"I know," he replied. "Understanding is to know, and all we gain is a weakness. I'm not Heyer, Rylee. I'm not trying to manipulate you. I have to ask you to believe me."

She didn't answer right away, and he didn't rush her. "I don't like it," she finally said. "But, I know you aren't lying. I'll trust you—but I expect you to explain this to me."

He nodded. "I need you to do something for me," he said. "It's not going to make any sense."

"Told you I trusted you."

"I need you to stay here," he said. "When I leave, I want you to stay busy or sleep. If you hurt, for any reason, you need to call me—I need you to hear my voice."

"Jonathan." Her whisper was sharp but she didn't pull away. "I told you..." He heard her huff in frustration. "You aren't my damn white knight. I don't need saving. Stop worrying about me."

"It isn't what you think, Rylee," Jonathan said. "I know you were never weak—I still need you to do this."

"Fine," she said, giving him a playful glare. "But don't get all butt-hurt when you don't hear from me."

He smiled. "If something happens, something you don't want them to see, press the button on the watch."

She nodded and Jonathan broke away.

"I'll be back, late tonight or tomorrow morning," he said.

He turned to leave, but when he was almost out the door, she said, "You know, I would follow you."

He stopped in the doorway and looked back at her.

"I thought about it," Rylee said, shrugged. "If I had to take orders from someone, I'd rather they be yours. I think maybe Heyer knows what he is doing. Chose you because he knows you'd protect us. Not just from his brother, or the monsters, but maybe even from him."

He lingered on her for a moment before he smiled at her gratefully. It wasn't because he thought she was necessarily right or even because she felt he needed to hear her say it. He was grateful because Rylee had looked at the question of "why Jonathan" differently than he had yet to think. She may very well have a point. Perhaps Heyer wasn't looking to him because he expected Jonathan would lead the alien's army to do the most damage. Maybe he was looking for something else altogether.

He was halfway out of the garage, heading back to join his mother, when he stopped. He pulled a marker from a drawer, and took the fictitious card of Melissa Hart out of his pocket. Hastily, he wrote a message on the back.

Jonathan stepped up to one of the vents where he knew a camera watched him. He made no effort to hide how he felt from the camera.

He'd gone about his life pretending they weren't watching. He couldn't stop them, but he could deliver a message, draw a line in the sand.

He closed his eyes and shook his head. Whoever watched would make no mistake. He flipped the card over. He'd only written four words.

Do not push me.

Rain hit the window as they drove south. The car had been silent for a while. Evelyn was wary to speak, fearing that she had entered into some strange world where eyes and ears were everywhere. She didn't know if she could ask her son anything—if he could answer.

"Jonathan," she finally said. "I have to know something."

"It's better if we talk about something else, Mom," Jonathan said. "Anything else."

She took a long breath. "Your father... Just tell me he didn't cause this."

Jonathan looked at his mother in a special sort of agony. "I don't know," he said. "But sometimes, keeping secrets is the only way to protect the people you care about—and I think Dad knew that."

She swallowed and nodded as she drove. "I wish he were here now. He knew about this sort of thing. He could have helped you. I don't have any idea how to help you."

"Mom," Jonathan said. "You are helping me."

CHAPTER FIFTY-ONE

"PAIGE, THIS WHOLE plan feels like we are asking to get my ass kicked."

They stood in front of a building downtown. Paige had jumped off Collin's bike and was now waiting on the sidewalk while he stepped it into a parking space along the street.

"I need to talk to him," Paige said. "You don't have to come up."

Collin took a grim look up at the building and groaned. "I guess, but I'd rather get beat up than leave you alone in a room with *Meathead*."

Paige gave him a look of endearment. "If it looks like it will get ugly, we'll leave."

Collin looked at her and let out a long breath. He felt the whole course of action was poor judgment on both their parts, but he was committing to it nonetheless. He put the kickstand in place and joined her on the sidewalk.

"How did you know where he'd moved?" he asked.

"Didn't," Paige said. "Messaged him yesterday—this is the address he sent back."

Collin frowned. "Why not call him?"

She didn't answer the question, just gave him a reluctant look before heading toward the building's front entrance. She was searching the names posted on the intercom system when he caught up to her.

"So, Paige," Collin said. "I can't help but feel you aren't telling me something."

"Yeah," she said, finding Grant's name. She turned back to him and entered the dial code. "Look, I didn't want to involve anyone, but I didn't want to come here alone either. When we get up there, I'll need you to wait in the hall, but I'll feel safer knowing someone I trust is close."

He had thought she'd only brought him because he was quicker than taking the bus. Now the number of questions Collin had was growing, but he didn't want to press her. The picture he was getting was that she felt better about how Grant might behave when he knew there was a witness nearby.

She dialed Grant's number and let it ring until the intercom went to voice mail. This repeated three more times. Collin thought she'd give up, but then one of the building's tenants came through the door. She gave Collin and Paige the typical once over—profiling them to weigh how likely it was that they wanted into the building for disreputable purposes. She must have thought them safe enough, or at least, she chose not say anything when Paige held the door before it locked behind her.

They took the elevator up to the ninth floor. Collin found himself second guessing Grant as he took in the building's interior and its location. These lofts could not be cheap—far more expensive than he would have assumed Grant could afford. "Starting to hate my guidance counselor," he said. "All that talk about getting an education. If I had known the military paid this well, I might have reconsidered."

Paige gave him a look that conveyed she had been on a similar train of thought. This place should have been far outside of Grant's means.

When they reached his door, they found it open. Not ajar, but held wide open by a briefcase with a woman's grey blazer draped over it. Collin raised a curious eyebrow as he peered around the door frame. The loft was completely empty, and so pristine that he didn't think anyone had ever actually occupied it. The owner of the blazer was inside, talking on a cell phone. She wore a grey pant suit but her shirt and sleeves were rolled up. When she caught sight of them, she told the caller she would have to get back to them later.

"Can I help you?" the woman asked.

Collin looked to Paige for direction. Given the circumstances, it seemed pointless for him to sit outside.

"Hello," Paige said, stepping though the threshold. "We were looking for a Grant Morgan. This was the address he gave me."

The woman shrugged. "Sorry," she said. "You missed him by about a day. Movers came in and cleared the place out this morning."

Collin watched Paige's brow furrow in suspicion.

"Don't suppose he left a forwarding address?" she asked.

The woman shook her head. "Sorry, no," she said. "It was a bit odd. I got a check and a letter saying he had to break his lease, apologizing for any inconvenience."

"You're the manager?" Paige asked.

The woman nodded.

"I don't mean to pry, but did he give any explanation?"

"To be honest, I normally couldn't answer, but in this case, there isn't anything to tell," the manager said. "The letter didn't say why. The check was for the amount his contract specified in the event he broke his lease. It's not a big problem on my end. If you want, I can take your contact information and let him know if he calls."

Paige shook her head. "No, that won't be necessary. He knows where to find us."

The woman shrugged again. "You two look like a nice couple," she said after a moment. "We have a vacancy if you're in the market?"

Jonathan opened his eyes and found himself in the dark. He didn't remember falling asleep, nor stepping into this ocean bereft of light, but that had always been the case before when he came to this place. Much like those times, he knew the light was coming before it was there. Like an ember at first, illuminating shapes around him—just enough for him to know he wasn't adrift in a formless void. The light grew, and as it did, he could make out dust covers hanging over furniture, stacks of cardboard boxes—each with writing in thick black marker identifying their contents—and a polished cement floor.

He knew now to ignore the clutter—those shapes were not why he had come. He found the path, the exposed floor between the boxes, and he followed it. He couldn't see the work bench, not yet, but knew it was back there, waiting for him.

Someone had hidden the truth in the dark. The shadows, the uncertainty—they disguised the room in an abstract notion of evil, played on fears both natural and learned. Yet Jonathan knew there were no monsters here, that the only person in this place was him. When you want to keep a secret, you hide it somewhere you think is hard to find—then, you don't tell anyone you hid it. When you want to hide a truth, you put it somewhere dark and call it evil, because only the smart or the brave will find it there. In general, this works well for everyone, because the truth is only a threat to the stupid and the cowardly.

As Jonathan neared the table, he heard a noise from the dark—and he suddenly no longer felt brave nor smart. He froze to listen, then shivered as he heard damp cloth dragging across the cement floor behind him. A grim expression of guilt cast itself over his face as he turned, and slowly, at the edge of the darkness, the face of the little girl's mangled corpse crawled forward into the light—her pink coat, her dead white eyes, her broken fingers reaching for him. He knew he couldn't run, couldn't ignore her. If he did, he would wake.

Slowly, he went to her, and even slower, he knelt down beside her. He didn't look her in the eye, but shivered when she reached for him—his heart broke to see her straining on broken bones. If touching him was what she was here to do, he wouldn't run any longer. He would have to let the child have whatever it was she needed from him. Jonathan drew in a deep breath and held the child's gaze. The blond child's eyes focused on him, confused at first, having been ignored or fled for so long. Her hand drew closer to him, a wet finger making contact with his cheek. He felt a line of blood drawn down to his chin.

"I'm sorry," Jonathan said closing his eyes. "I can't save everyone. People are going to get hurt. They're going to die. I can't... I can't change it." He slumped further down until he finally came to rest on the back of his heels with his hands in his lap.

"You didn't run away," a voice said from the darkness behind him.

His eyes opened, and the corpse of the blond girl was gone.

When he turned, he saw Jess, the little girl he had recognized at the gym. She was alive, her pupils present in her eyes, looking back at him. A spark was there, in that gaze, somehow managing to catch what little light had followed him into the room. Jess stepped up to him, pulling her sleeve out from under her coat and wiped the blood off his cheek.

"There's no one here but me," Jess said. "So who are you apologizing to?"

He stared at the little girl, and the feeling he'd had, seeing her alive in the gym, resurfaced. Jonathan felt himself smile. "A memory, I suppose," he said. "A shadow."

She frowned at him. "That doesn't make sense. A memory can't forgive you."

"It was the best I could do," Jonathan said.

She studied him, her childish expression confused. "Seems silly. Feeling sorry for a shadow when I'm right here. What am I supposed to forgive you for?"

"Something that never really happened, I suppose," Jonathan said. "At least, not to anyone but me."

She pondered him for a moment. "So you're the one who got hurt, then?" she asked.

He smiled. "I wish guilt thought like you do."

Jess studied him. "I wish you'd worry about the real me," she said.

Jonathan's smile faded. "I do," he whispered.

He saw sympathy on her face, so close to his while he was kneeling at her height.

"Do you know what you're doing here?" she asked. "In this place?

He blinked, remembering he'd been headed further into the dark before the girl's memory had distracted him. He rose to his feet, walking past her through the clutter. Finally, he saw the footlocker on top of the work bench. His eyes lingered on the padlock a moment before he reached out to test its strength.

"You know, sometimes I don't know how I'm supposed to help you," Jess said. "That can't be why you are here—it's just another distraction."

Jonathan's hand stopped mid reach, his face turning to the girl as she came to stand beside him. "I don't understand," he said.

He saw a shiver of indecision run through her before she tilted her head to draw his attention to a tall, thin object cloaked in a dust cover. He noticed that Jess had taken care to place herself between him and whatever was beneath the cover. If this was what he'd come here for, he'd never have known. It hid in plain sight; nothing about the shape would have made it stand out to him.

"How would I have known to look there?" Jonathan asked.

Jess bit her lip as she looked up at him. "You wouldn't," she said. "You were supposed to be afraid."

He stepped toward it, and Jess took a step back to make sure she stayed between. He saw her quivering, a child afraid but trying to hold on to a facade of courage.

"You should be afraid," she said.

"Why?"

"It doesn't belong here."

Gently, he reached past her, and her face gave him one last look of foreboding. She did not stop him, but made him reach over and behind her, unwilling to step out of the way.

When he pulled the dust cover away, he saw a standing mirror. The room brightened as the mirror caught the dim light and reflected it back at them. It was odd that while his eyes crawled up the man in the mirror, he didn't see Jess's reflection. He recognized the clothing, but it didn't belong to him. Tan hiking boots, jeans. When his eyes reached the reflection's chest, he understood. It glowed, radiating the sunset colors of his active implant.

His father stared back at him.

"You should know by now," Jess said. "It's never as simple as you think."

CHAPTER FIFTY-TWO

THURSDAY| OCTOBER 14, 2005 | 1:00 AM | PORTLAND

HE FELT THE car stop briefly, and Jonathan roused from sleep before his mother put the car back into motion again. They were off the freeway—must have been getting close to wherever it was she was taking him.

As he rubbed at his eyes, he felt the pressure immediately, a powerful sense that a part of him had slipped away as he slept—as though a reservoir had slowly drained out of him. The hollowness was familiar, but after having experienced its absence, he felt the need to mourn its return. He missed Rylee's face, her voice—felt he needed to see her eyes seeing his. The bond, it seemed, was quite capable of hurting him. It made his body tell him a lie that facts seemed unable to argue against—told him she was in danger even though he knew she was safe.

The longer he roused from sleep, the more he felt the need to question what he knew. He worried for no reason, and that worry always came to the same conclusion—she needed him and he wasn't there. He checked his phone, and Rylee hadn't called—his phone hadn't rung the entire drive.

It felt as though he were being pushed toward the edge of a cliff. He found he could push back, resist it by keeping the contradiction at the forefront. The fear was false; the part of him that missed her was a matter of distance and illusion—not of substance. Knowing this did nothing to keep him from feeling it, but for the time being, it appeared that reason still had its say.

Yet, reason itself also told him to hurry. He could stoically endure what he was feeling because he knew what caused it. He had left Rylee with no such defense—no contradictions to hold on to. He hoped she had fallen asleep before the distance between them had started forcing her to feel this, that he could return to her before she woke. He saw how easy it would be to become unhinged and wondered if what he now endured was anything compared to what Rylee had faced before his device had completed its half of the bond.

If this grew worse, and he suspected it would, there would eventually come a point where reason would no longer give him any resistance to it. Emotions had a threshold. Once crossed, thought had little sway. Normally, reason restrained the buildup, policed the mob before chaos broke out inside the mind. If what Heyer told him was true, then there was no way to stop this pain from building—it could only be slowed. When the pair was forced to part, only time and endurance would break the bond's hold.

Feeling it, his confidence shook. When the time came, he wasn't sure he could bear it. That was when the truth would turn on him, and he would know the problem could be solved by seeing her. In understanding the addiction, he would know how to put an end to the withdrawals. Each thought told him he couldn't keep this from her, but if he told her, she too would know the pain had a fix. She too would have to endure until they were clean—out of each other's systems.

The car stopped. "We're here," his mother said.

Jonathan blinked the remaining sleep from his eyes.

He looked out through the windshield and saw the sun had set behind the clouds, but that the rain had not let up while they drove. They were parked in a paid storage facility, a large, orange metal door in front of them. It was one of a number of identical units. Foggy memories began to return to him. After the funeral, he had helped his mother load up the contents of his father's garage. They had boxed up all of the stuff and moved it to this facility. At the time, they had been empty, exhausted people, grimly going about a necessary but uncomfortable task in the middle of their grief. He remembered how he had known that it needed to be done, but that didn't stop it from feeling like a betrayal, as though he were cleaning parts of his father out of his life so that it would be easier to avoid painful memories.

Now, Jonathan only wondered how he could have forgotten.

He opened his door and stepped out of the car, ignoring the rain despite how quickly he felt it soaking into his clothes. He approached the door and found a padlock. He lifted it and saw it required a code.

Evelyn stepped out of the vehicle a moment later, pulling an umbrella from the side panel of the car door and shielding herself before stepping up to the lock beside him. "The code is eleven twenty-seven," she said as she tried to hold the umbrella over both of them. Their difference in height made it more a polite gesture than a practical one.

He felt streaks of water running down from his wet hair as he pondered his mother. He assumed that, like him, she hadn't been here in years, but wondered how she remembered the code so quickly. She must have read the speculation on his face.

"It was the day he died," she said.

Jonathan nodded. He'd forgotten the date himself, but felt sorry for his mother, who couldn't help remembering it every year since. He turned away from her and moved the dials into place, feeling the lock release as he finished. He paused before reaching down to lift the door. There was a sentimental notion that he was entering a mausoleum instead of a storage facility—that perhaps he should do so with the same respect he had when he visited his father's gravestone. Evelyn's face conveyed the same hesitation as he reached down and pulled the door up.

He stood before the vague and yet familiar objects he had seen in his dreams. Dust covers and cardboard boxes. Night had come, and the only light coming in was from the few security lamps placed at regular intervals along the facility's external walls. Shadows seemed to swallow everything as he looked inside. It gave him the sense that these storage units stretched further back into the building than he'd have imagined from the outside.

He took a step in out of the rain, starting to feel his way using his fingertips to guide him along the walls made of cardboard boxes. His mother didn't follow him—she turned back to the car as he stepped into the dark. Jonathan's fingers hit something beneath a tarp. He could feel a long piece of metal underneath as he walked along.

Light filled the room as he took his next step, his mother having turned on the car's headlights. He saw then, that the tarp under his fingers wasn't a dust cover like the rest, but what looked like the type of canvas one used when painting a room. He saw shiny patches of grey paint, and remembered where he'd seen this before. A long time ago, when he and his father had repainted the hallways of their home. When Douglas had let Jonathan pick the colors. He smiled at the memory, and realized he knew what his fingers had found in the dark.

A rusted old truck with a broken engine. He stood, remembering that moment so long ago when he thought he would fix the vehicle. He remembered, too, how he had given up on the idea almost immediately, as it felt like such an empty gesture—a thing he would do in the hopes of pleasing a ghost. Seeing it now, he realized the choice hadn't been taken away. He could still try. If the future saw fit to leave him the time.

He heard his mother's footsteps approaching behind him and pulled himself out of reflection. He remembered what they had come here for, and his eyes searched the back of the room. There, exactly as it had been in his dreams, sat a table and footlocker—his eyes lingered on yet another lock.

"I don't have the key to that," Evelyn said.

"It's okay, we're taking it with us," he said. "I have bolt cutters at home."

He approached the box, but something felt off. Unsure why, he looked about the room, and at first it appeared so similar to the memory in his dream. When he realized what was bothering him, he stiffened. It came upon him as though he'd caught sight of a ghost at the edge of his vision—a feeling warning him that once he looked to be sure of what he had seen, he would no longer be able to tell himself that he didn't believe in such things.

Slowly, Jonathan turned his head, but he was disappointed. He found nothing where the mirror had been standing in his dream. The ghost of his father did not look back at him.

"What is it, Jonathan?" Evelyn asked.

His brow furrowed. The dreams—they had to be more. His subconscious had to be telling him something. He couldn't stomach the idea that it could all turn out to be no more than his mind trying to make sense of meaningless dreams.

"Mom," Jonathan said, turning back to her. "Dad's car accident. Is there any chance that..."

He didn't know how to ask, he wasn't sure what the question was.

"At the funeral, there was a closed casket," Jonathan said. "Did you see Dad's body?

His mother's expression grew cautious as he looked at her. "Yes," she said.

He grimaced and slouched a bit as he exhaled. "Are you positive?"

Evelyn stared at him. "He's gone, Jonathan."

"Mom, did you see his face? Did you see his body? I need to know."

She looked away from him. "He was horribly burned, Jonathan," she said. "Yes, I saw the body, and I wish I hadn't. There was nothing left of him to recognize."

Jonathan looked away from her. His eyes fell on the box.

You only think that is what you're here for, Jess had said. *It's not.*

He put his fists on the table and felt them clenching. Possibilities crept into his mind, and the inability to be certain of any of them began to transform into frustration. He had not realized how painful this mystery had become to him—he kept pushing it down as he felt closer and closer to the truth.

He closed his eyes, trying to contain a mounting tantrum. Now, hearing his mother's words, restraints failed. Black smoke broke through fissures in his brick wall.

Growling, the desire to break something, anything, overtook him. His fist came down on the table top. Then again, harder. His hand screamed in pain and it fueled his anger as he struck the table top again and again. He pulled away and kicked the table's legs, stomped on its lower tier trying to exhaust the emotion.

Evelyn stepped away from him in confusion.

The table absorbed his anger as though it were mocking him, refusing to shatter—a damn inanimate object laughing at his irrelevant frustrations. Stepping back, one last surge came over him, and he kicked the table as hard as he could before his hands came up to grip the back of his head. A moment later, he found himself bent over the paint-splotched canvas on the hood of the old truck.

It's never as simple as you think, his dream whispered to him.

He waited for control. Breathed.

A few moments passed, and as he calmed, he knew he had far less control over himself than he had imagined. He didn't know if the bond had amplified his anger, or if that anger had been enough to set him off because it had piled onto its effects. He didn't know if that was all rationalization. Perhaps he had simply let himself go.

Finally, he looked apologetically at his mother. He could see that she was concerned—that she was desperate for anything she could do to help.

"I'm sorry, Mom," he said, sighing. "It isn't you. It has just been a long time since I got any straight answers to my questions."

CHAPTER FIFTY-THREE

DATE | TIME: UNKNOWN | FEROXIAN PLANE

"NO GAMES, MALKIER," Heyer said. "Do not risk this."

His brother watched him from the corner of his eye. The honesty in Heyer's warning took the haste out of his exit and left him stilled before the doorway.

"Brother, you cannot possibly believe that the bonded pair poses a threat to me," he said.

"He is more than the bond," Heyer said. "You have no idea how dangerous that man is."

Malkier turned and studied him. "Is this some pathetic bluff, brother? If you truly imagine this man a threat to me—then what? Am I to believe you are suddenly concerned for my well-being?"

Heyer shook his head. "No. I know what you've done. The precautions you put in place after *Dams the Gate* was born. I know what happens if you die."

Malkier's white eyes widened as though Heyer's words gave him a renewed fascination. "Well, that is interesting," he said. "And why do you think I put those counter measures in place?"

"To make an attempt on your life impossible for me."

"Brother," Malkier said. "A precaution, yes, but a deterrent? Is that really what you assumed?"

Heyer swallowed. The way his brother looked at him made him fear he had misunderstood. "Malkier, you have me captive. I'm not a threat. If you insist on going after *Brings the Rain*, you must disable the counter measures."

"No," Malkier said. "I will do no such thing."

"Malkier, you cannot hate them so much," he pleaded. "Why would you allow this if it will do nothing to save the Ferox? It's genocide for no reason."

"No reason?" Malkier whispered.

A long moment stretched out between them.

"Let me ask you, brother," Malkier finally said. "Why is it that you hide in the shadows of their world? Why do you think it is that you go to such great lengths to keep our ancestor's technology out of their hands?"

Heyer blinked, caught off guard by the sudden strangeness of the question. "Mankind will advance in their own time, and they will be better for it," Heyer finally said. "It is not my place."

Malkier looked at him as though he were disappointed. "Be honest with yourself, Heyer. Admit to me that, even now, their progress worries you. You fear what Mankind would do with the power you could give them. That you know the day will come that Mankind will be outside our control."

"It is not my desire to control them. I worry for them, of course, but every step they take has just as much reason for hope as it does fear."

His brother closed his eyes, seeming saddened by every word Heyer said. "You say hope," he said. "You don't seem to realize that you really mean hope for Mankind—you certainly do not mean hope for all."

"They could be one in the same."

Malkier shook his head. "Have you ever asked yourself when the darkest period of Borealis history came to pass?"

"I fear that I am witnessing it."

His brother glared at him. "Dramatic, but hardly. Cede, my brother seems to have a blind spot in his history. Tell us, what period is considered the darkest age of the Borealis?"

"A majority of Borealis historians cite the onset of the Immortal Revolution as the species' darkest age," Cede replied.

"And what was it, Cede, that put the Immortal Revolution into motion?" Malkier asked.

"The age began shortly after the development of the Borealis implant," Cede answered.

Malkier pointed to his brother's chest, and then his own. "Can you imagine? How one technological advancement changed everything?"

Heyer didn't answer the question. There was little need; he was already beginning to understand the shape of his brother's madness.

"You see, the Borealis experienced a philosophical shift. The few religious sects that found followers with the promise of everlasting life were already marginalized. The faiths lost the means to bring in new followers, and as such, were dealt a blow they could not withstand. But, that didn't change who the Borealis were—didn't change their nature. They still longed to be a part of something larger. The notion of simply existing for the sake of existing still left them feeling a void," Malkier said.

"The humans are not our ancestors," Heyer whispered, doubting there was any point, that his brother would ever truly see where his self-hatred had led him.

Malkier sighed. "Cede, given the current rate of human advancement, how far off would you estimate Mankind is from developing technologies analogous to the Borealis implant?"

"Without any drastic setbacks," Cede replied, "humanity should achieve practical immortality within the next 200 years."

A moment passed as Malkier let the computer's estimates sink in.

"When death no longer held them back, the distance between the Borealis and all other sentient species became staggering. Our ancestors came to redefine their image of God so that they would fit that image. Then assigned themselves the role of curator for all existence. When those ancient Borealis spread throughout the known dimensions, they brought about the greatest mass extinction of life in the known history."

Listening to his brother, the chasm between them felt too far to cross. When had the self-hatred become madness? How long ago had his brother taken his final step? When had he reached the point that he could not see his true reflection in the mirror? Had Heyer watched it happen—had the death of *Dams the Gate* been the last straw, the excuse to break with reality that allowed his brother to see whatever he wanted to see?

As Heyer heard his brother's reasoning, he could not imagine what would need to be different about him to make his brother's conclusions feel justified. He found himself wondering, again, about the short space of time between their births. Thousands of years later and they would be better off as strangers. He wondered at how the only ones who would ever look at them side by side and know they were descendants of the same species were themselves. He thought these things, because he saw no way to get his brother to understand something so very simple...

Sometimes—even if you are right... if everything you imagine comes to pass... if the future vindicates you with every passing moment—you can still be utterly and completely wrong.

It seemed the type of thing you either understood or you didn't.

Heyer knew he had to stop his brother, but he saw his own hypocrisy. He had drawn a line in the sand, and that line was genocide. Now, his brother was telling him he had every intention of crossing that line. Should the day come that Heyer stood over his brother's body—the day he disabled the gates and left the Ferox to run their course... Heyer would never tell himself he had done what had to be done—that he had no reason to think his actions exempt from question. No, he would tell himself that he had drawn a line and it had been crossed.

What line could Malkier say humanity had crossed? None. He wanted to rid existence of humanity for a line they might someday cross. It was almost as though he didn't want them to ever have the chance to prove that he'd been wrong about them.

The silence dragged out for some time, until Malkier seemed to think Heyer had lost their debate.

"Have you ever thought to wonder why the Foedrata treated Mankind with such cruelty, brother? How, after all, does one species come to torture another when they understand them on so profound a level? Did it never occur to you that they saw their reflection in the mirror—and became disgusted?" Malkier asked

Heyer had grown quite tired, his weariness evident in his responses.

This wasn't a debate; it was Malkier's attempt to convince Heyer of something of which he would never be convinced.

"The Foedrata were a sect of extremists with egos so fragile they became utterly dependent on their faith to justify their own importance. The existence of Mankind called that faith into question. The Foedrata weren't disgusted—they were afraid," Heyer said.

Malkier's fingers tapped against the metal box yet again. "Mankind will be brought under control and kept from ever realizing their technological potential. They will either be subject to the Ferox or they will be eliminated. I will not allow them to be the next Borealis. So, to answer your question… if I am not alive to make sure they are contained, then in death, I will make sure they are exterminated."

"So now you imagine yourself the curator of existence," Heyer said. "Perhaps you've played a god so long you fail to see your own hypocrisy when it stares back at *you* in the mirror."

"Gods are an idea, brother," Malkier said. "You and I, for better or worse, are the closest thing to that idea."

Heyer shook his head.

"Imagine for a moment, brother, that the Foedrata's beliefs were true all along. If each of our ancestors was a small piece of the creator, then all those pieces would have been funneled into you and I. You don't have to believe it, but we did inherit the power to take the place of gods when we were born."

"If any of that were true," Heyer said, "then I would expect that you and I wouldn't be at war."

Malkier sighed. "When I return, we will begin the task of removing your implant from the human body, brother. Perhaps, when you and I share the same host species, we will not see things so differently."

CHAPTER FIFTY-FOUR

THURSDAY| OCTOBER 14, 2005 | 2:00 AM | SEATTLE

EARLY IN THE morning, Rylee woke in Jonathan's bed when an uninvited light suddenly brightened the room. She flinched as her eyes adjusted, and saw that it was coming from his desk. His laptop had woken up out of sleep somehow. She rolled over, attempting to ignore it, but it seemed to flicker. The subtle change in light was bothersome even with her eyelids shut, and she ended up putting her face against the pillow as she waited for the machine to go back to sleep. Then, the laptop made a high-pitched noise that had to have been designed to be annoying.

Groaning, she pulled herself out of the bed to shut the lid. Stepping closer to the screen, she saw it was displaying black and white text.

<Rylee, be discreet. Do not speak. Pick up laptop. Take the desk chair to the southwest corner of the room. Sit. Wear headphones.>

For a moment, she thought she was dreaming, as computers didn't typically use her name and then give orders. Confirming she was in fact awake, she frowned at the monitor, her curiosity rousing the rest of her sleepy mind to attention.

Mr. Clean, Rylee realized. *But why does he suddenly want to talk to me?*

Had the damn alien suddenly decided she was in the need-to-know club?

Looking around a moment, she took Jonathan's earbuds from his desk drawer, and found there was already a chair waiting for her in the southwest corner of the room. A moment later, the bald cartoon character was looking back at her. Unexpectedly, the computer's attempt at a serious expression disarmed her reluctance, and a snort of laughter escaped her before she remembered to take things seriously.

"Good morning, Ms. Silva. I am sorry to wake you. It is good that you are still in town. There are developments I need to make you aware of," the cartoon said.

She gave him a questioning look and was about to speak when she was abruptly cut off by the voice in the ear phones.

"Do not speak—use the keyboard to respond," Mr. Clean said.

Her mouth was still open, but she glared at the cartoon, finally sighing before she followed instructions. *Bossy little cartoon,* she thought.

Don't have any trips planned, she typed. *What is the big news—you got a hot date with the Clorox lady?*

"Your humor seems intended to antagonize," Mr. Clean said. "Am I to infer you are expressing irritation with me?"

Apparently the overly sensitive computer can't take a joke, Rylee thought, then typed *Nevermind. Jonathan should be back soon. What is it he needs to know?*

"His phone's GPS signal indicates he is headed north from Portland, Oregon. I cannot make contact with him, and it is rather important that he be updated as soon as possible. May I ask why he has gone?" said the computer.

Don't know. He didn't want to say, didn't want The Cell to know what he was doing, she typed.

"It would have been best that he discuss this with Heyer and myself beforehand," Mr. Clean said.

Rylee snorted. "*Yeah, well he called and called but no one picked up,*" she typed.

The cartoon's face became a deadpan expression. "Am I correct in interpreting your comment as sarcasm? A passive aggressive statement meant to imply that a lack of communication resulted from a failure of myself and Heyer?" Mr. Clean asked.

Affirmative, Rylee typed.

"Yes, well, be that as it may, I have uncovered some disturbing coincidences. I recommend that when you communicate this information to him, you do so with the utmost care that his investigators remain unaware."

I'll do my best, Rylee typed. *What is it?*

"Yesterday, Jonathan attempted to communicate with The Cell watching your activities," Mr. Clean said. "He appeared quite upset, and his demeanor was aggressive, threatening. His actions would have tipped off The Cell that he was aware of the cameras, so I intercepted the footage and altered it. However, the behavior was quite concerning—highly out of character."

He didn't say anything to me about it, Rylee typed. *But yeah, he seemed upset last time we spoke.*

"Despite his poor judgment, his actions provided a phone number on a business card belonging to a Melissa Hart. I believe he suspected the name to have been an alias used by an agent within The Cell to interact with his mother under false pretenses."

Explains why he got upset, Rylee typed.

"Do you understand what may have caused him to do something so ill advised?" Mr. Clean asked.

Rylee frowned at the laptop, as though the answer seemed too obvious to require explanation. Then, of course, she realized that an A.I. probably didn't understand what it was like to be protective of one's mother, not having one himself.

In short, Rylee typed. *Threatening a person's mother is easily one of the top five ways to piss most humans off. I'd say we were lucky he didn't tear the camera out of the wall.*

"Ahh," Mr. Clean said. "Well, regardless, I tracked the number back to its source. It was, in fact, a fraudulent call center. However, I also analyzed phone records for outgoing calls made from that location. Great care was taken to send the calls through convoluted channels, but I am certain that a number of them went to occupants of the household next door."

Leah, Rylee thought.

Are you saying that his neighbor is connected with The Cell?

"It is almost certain, but I must request that you and Jonathan exercise extreme caution," Mr. Clean said. "There are no recordings of the calls, so I cannot comment on the contents of what was communicated. However, I have reviewed all video obtained from the various cameras throughout the household, and noticed other questionable activities," Mr. Clean said.

Show me, Rylee typed.

The screen filled with footage of Jonathan and Leah in a room Rylee didn't recognize. Leah's living room, she assumed. The camera was placed somewhere behind Leah, angled down on the room. Rylee felt herself squirm inside as she watched Leah approaching Jonathan. The way she walked toward him was so comfortably seductive. They exchanged some words but the footage lacked any audio for her to hear.

Leah's body language, so telling, so eager, was reflected in Jonathan's expression. What followed made her wish to turn away. She ached painfully, seeing how he responded to her.

"Here is the oddity," Mr. Clean said over the video.

Suddenly, Jonathan collapsed to his knees against the wall. He cowered there, holding himself. His head shook back and forth as though he were fighting off an onslaught of voices in his mind.

Rylee's mouth fell open as she realized what she was seeing. She'd experienced what he was going through, and she looked at the time stamp on the footage to be sure. This had been the moment Jonathan had felt her within him. She found herself waiting desperately to see what his face would tell her once he could sort out the storm in his head.

His eyes came open. She saw desperation and conflict and confusion. It wasn't what she had felt. Suddenly, she saw realization—saw his panic. Rylee swallowed. This wasn't fair. Experiencing Jonathan's emotions had brought her hope, strength. Given her a sense of peace, and excitement for the future. She had found such comfort in the intimacy of knowing him in a way she could know no other. As she understood, she realized that she had given him a burden. She had given him despair and weakness. She had given him another thing that needed saving.

She hated time and circumstance. Why, of any moment in her life it could have been, did it have to be her weakest hour that he received?

Finally, Jonathan stood. He exchanged words with Leah, his eyes pleading for forgiveness. She knew his thoughts in that moment. *If I stay here, a girl will die.*

Rylee watched Leah as Jonathan left the room. There was pain, confusion, and rejection on her face. Rylee thought it should please her but found it had quite the opposite effect. Instead, Rylee hated knowing that it was pity and duty that had made him leave.

"Here," Mr. Clean said, the computer's voice jarring Rylee from her spell.

She watched the feed again to see Leah staring off into space—a hundred-yard stare only interrupted when her phone started ringing. Leah answered, grew impatient, and yelled something at the caller before throwing the phone away from her.

Why are you showing me this? Rylee typed.

"That call—it came from the same call center. It took place within minutes of a temporal event involving you and Jonathan. In addition, it coincides with Jonathan's reaction to the bond," Mr. Clean said.

Rylee frowned at the computer's words. *The bond?* She was about to type the question when he started speaking again. The footage changed to the very room she sat in now.

"This is the second recording, Ms. Silva. It is possibly more concerning as it involves you more directly."

At the A.I.'s words, Rylee's hands paused over the keyboard. She saw Leah entering Jonathan's bedroom. The girl approached Rylee's backpack. A few moments later, Rylee's blood began to boil.

CHAPTER FIFTY-FIVE

THURSDAY| OCTOBER 14, 2005 | 5:00 AM | SEATTLE

THE SUN WAS coming up when Jonathan and Evelyn backed into the driveway. His mother helped him unload the footlocker, setting it on the garage floor. When they'd finished, Jonathan waited, not knowing how to ask her to leave.

This quickly became an awkward silence, as Evelyn had not seemed to realize that she knew more than he'd wanted her to and Jonathan didn't wish to exacerbate the problem. Whatever he found inside the box, he wanted it to stay between him and his father.

"Well," Evelyn said. "Let's get this thing open."

"Mom," Jonathan said. "I need you to go."

She looked surprised.

"You wanted to help," he said. "You did."

"You listen to me—"

Evelyn found herself cut off when her cell phone rang. His mother's eyes narrowed as she looked at the caller ID. She seemed reluctant to answer while he was standing in front of her. Jonathan watched her suspiciously as she continued to hesitate with each ring. She didn't want to let the call go to voice mail.

Finally, Evelyn released a tense breath, retreating out of the garage with the phone in hand, answering the call only as she closed the door into the house behind her. He was curious as he watched the door close. He hadn't known what he was going to say to get her to leave, but a call important enough to take her out of the room, though convenient, was just as worrisome.

Pulling the garage door down, he turned his attention back to the footlocker. In the large drawer at the bottom of Collin's tool box, he found the bolt cutters. He stopped before he reached for them—he needed to check on Rylee, but didn't know how long that phone call was going to keep his mother busy. Then he heard a car door shutting outside, the engine of his mother's car pulling away.

He sighed.

Whatever call she had received was apparently important enough for her to leave. His mother was definitely up to something. He knew she meant well, but no matter what she was doing, it was obviously something she didn't want him finding out about. Which meant it had to be stopped. Seeing there was nothing he could do about it in that moment, he went inside.

The hour was still early and he didn't want to wake his roommates, so he was quiet on his way up the stairs. When he reached the second floor, he saw Paige's door was open, her bed empty. His own door was shut, and he gently turned the handle.

Rylee lay in his bed. She didn't wake as he stepped into the room. He stood over her for a moment, letting the sight of her drain the tension from him. She'd fallen asleep with her phone clutched in her hand. Jonathan had wanted to hear her voice all night, but hadn't wanted to risk calling, afraid he might wake her if she slept. He grimaced, wondering if she'd felt the pain of his absence. Had she wanted to call, but resisted because she wanted to prove she wasn't weak—show him her strength even after he told her he did not question it?

He closed his eyes then, fighting a desire to wake her, to touch her skin—as though placing his hand over hers, seeing her looking back at him, would somehow make her presence feel more real. Frustratingly, his thoughts told him he would only do her harm in the long run, while the rest of him couldn't understand how the warmth of her hand could possibly be a bad thing. Did it matter that they were being manipulated if he no longer cared?

He stopped, finding his hand already reaching for her.

Heyer had warned him that if he indulged the artificial he would lose sight of the real. Wouldn't be able to see what should and shouldn't be happening within him. The alien hadn't lied, but Jonathan saw now that it wasn't the truth. It wouldn't be a matter of losing sight, it would simply be choosing not to care about what was true.

Carefully, he slipped the cell phone from her palm to place it beside her on the bed stand. As soon as he pulled it free, Rylee's hand reacted, taking took hold of his.

"Tibbs," Rylee whispered, her lips curving into a peaceful smile.

The sensation of her fingers wrapped around his own sent a tremble up him, every hair on his arm standing up. It was part disappointment and part relief when he realized she hadn't woken, but only reacted to him in her sleep. Carefully, he slipped his hand away, gently pulling the covers over her before he slipped back out of the room.

When he reached the bottom of the stairs, he saw Hayden standing in the living room. Apparently, his roommate had also been trying to keep quiet, not wanting to wake those who slept. He wasn't dressed, still wearing his robe as he stared at the shelf of DVDs. He turned to Jonathan with tired eyes and waved halfheartedly. Jonathan looked to the garage door, where he knew the footlocker waited for him. Seeing Hayden still awake at this time of the morning, though, he found he could put off the box a moment longer.

"You haven't slept?" Jonathan asked.

Hayden shook his head.

Jonathan stepped closer, his face sympathetic. "You know," he said. "I haven't asked. I was being selfish, if I am being honest, because it was nice not to be the only one awake most nights. But, why aren't you sleeping, Hayden?"

Hayden shrugged. "Kind of one of those things where..." He paused. "If I knew, then I probably would be sleeping right now."

"Yeah," Jonathan smiled. "I get that."

Hayden nodded, his eyes going back to the DVD titles. Jonathan scratched his head, deciding he owed it to his friend to pry a little more.

"You seemed upset the other night. About the comic book."

Hayden nodded, but didn't reply.

Jonathan bit his lip. "Look, I had this idea," he said. "Hear me out on it?"

Hayden turned to Jonathan, his eyes curious despite the shadows from lack of sleep. "Sure."

Jonathan took a moment to think about what he wanted to say. "In the Bible, did Jesus ever ask for forgiveness?" he asked carefully. "I don't mean from God—I mean, did he ever ask for a man to forgive him?"

Hayden thought about it, but shook his head. "No... at least, I don't think so. It would kinda negate the whole 'perfect being' concept if he did."

Jonathan nodded.

"Right, he is your role model, and so you want him to be perfect," Jonathan said, shaking his head a moment later. "The thing is, Collin will always be able to put a perfect person in a situation where no amount of power in the world can create a perfect outcome, but that doesn't have to be a bad thing."

Hayden gave a questioning glance.

"You can't ever really know what the messiah would do," Jonathan said. "If you did, you would be a messiah, and you wouldn't have to question if you made the right decision, you would just know."

"Yeah," Hayden said. "What is it you're getting at?"

"What I'm saying is that a perfect person might be a comforting thing to believe in, but it isn't very helpful as far as role models go."

Jonathan sighed, swallowing before he went on.

"I think what is bothering you is that you want Jesus to save the day with philosophy, not a miracle. You want him to make a moral judgment. Because you want his decision to be one that any person could make."

Hayden nodded, still seeming uncertain where Jonathan was heading.

"A man can't make the same decision as Superman would, let alone a messiah," Jonathan said. "He can't skip the hard questions because he knows he has a miracle up his sleeve. He has to make choices, and then he has to live with them, but he never gets to be sure it was the right call."

"Okay," Hayden said. "So what was your idea for the comic book?"

Jonathan squinted at him, smiling with half his lip. "I know it started out as a joke. But you wouldn't have rebooted the Bible if you wanted to read about a perfect person doing perfect things. If you're dead set on having one of Jesus's miracles be the trigger that leads Damian to become the antichrist, then maybe it can be whatever teaches Jesus that there isn't always a perfect solution…"

Jonathan trailed off, thinking over his words, before continuing:

"I'm sure you and Collin have a big finale planned out, but maybe the last step for Jesus to become the messiah is asking Damian to forgive him for whatever part he played in turning him into the villain he became. Because, in your story, Jesus and Damian don't even know who their fathers were yet. I mean, Damian thought he was just a man, that he had to make a man's decision."

"Huh… so, in a way, the solution that seems perfect at the time actually creates the antichrist?" Hayden asked. "It could work. JC is pretty big on forgiveness, so it would make a decent back story if he had to ask for it at least once." He looked at Jonathan questioningly. "So, where the heck did you come up with this?"

Jonathan groaned as he pointed to a collector's edition box set on the DVD shelf. "I figured you are essentially writing a sequel—I kept thinking of that line from The Empire Strikes back, 'But you are not a Jedi yet,' got me thinking that you shouldn't have Super-Jesus be a fully realized messiah in the sequel, because you need to save that for the finale."

"Ahhh…" Hayden smiled. "Once again, The Holy Trilogy comes to our aid."

Jonathan smiled at him.

"You're right you know," Hayden said. "At this point in the story, Jesus is kind of like Skywalker. He doesn't really know who his father is."

The padlock on his father's footlocker was no cheap piece of hardware. Even with the bolt cutters, Jonathan had to wrestle it for quite a while before he managed to get the angle and leverage to cut through the steel. When the snap finally came, he dropped the bolt cutters and removed the now-useless hunk of metal, leaving it beside him as he knelt in front of the box.

He hesitated.

You only think this is what you're here for. Jess's words echoed. *It's not.*

He knew the footlocker promised nothing—could well be a dead end. He might reach the bottom only to find that his imagination had constructed an elaborate dream out of dusty memories. Given that the moment he'd been on his way to retrieve the box those dreams seemed to try and backpedal, he knew he needed to be prepared for disappointment.

That level-headed thinking lasted a few seconds. Then he opened the lid and the first thing he saw was the picture of his mother holding him in the hospital. Immediately, Jonathan felt a sense of providence. He set the picture gently beside him and began to dig.

Civilian clothing was neatly folded beside military dress uniforms. There was a disassembled assault rifle and a small box containing a side arm and spare magazines. He removed the guns carefully. It wasn't a surprise to find them, but their presence put a crack in his confidence. That lock that had given him so much trouble may not have been protecting a secret, but only keeping a weapon safe.

He found more battle fatigues, a flak jacket, belts and harnesses, a gas mask, and an Army issue helmet. Yet, when his eyes fell on a pair of boots, he paused. He'd thought they were hiking boots when he had seen them in his dreams—he realized now that they matched the rest of his father's gear.

In a corner of the box, he uncovered a stack of old letters held together by a rubber band. The paper had yellowed with age, the envelopes addressed from his mother to Douglas. From their age, Jonathan figured they must have been sent while his father had been overseas. He didn't want to open them out of respect for the privacy of his parents. Regardless, he doubted he would find useful information in the letters. He knew his father had guarded his secrets from Evelyn. He put them aside, deciding not to open them unless nothing else in the box shed any light on his immediate questions.

He fought worried thoughts as the bottom of the box drew closer, but when he reached the final article, the fear solidified. There, lying on the bottom of the chest, he found a thick, heavy blanket. It was utilitarian, brown, and without any aesthetic appeal—something a soldier might use to line a tent. He felt himself giving up but ignored it out of denial. His eyes searched the sides of the box for something he'd missed, a compartment—something hidden.

Nothing.

The word entered his thoughts without his permission, with no regard as to whether he was willing to accept it. He closed his eyes, only to find he still didn't believe it. In desperation, he turned back to the pile he'd made while emptying the footlocker's contents and dug through the things he had extracted, checking every article of clothing for something he had missed, every coat and pant pocket.

There is nothing here.

He shut his eyes trying to contain his frustration, but disappointment got the better of him, and exploded into anger. "Dammit!" he growled, shoving the footlocker away.

The box slid across the floor, no longer heavy with the weight of his father's possessions, and toppled onto its side. The lid slammed shut when it came to a stop.

The muffled sound of metal colliding with metal reached him.

Jonathan froze, his eyes opening as he stared at the box now lying on its side.

It had been subdued, its vibrations silenced by fabric within the box. His head lifted, tilting as he wondered at the footlocker. He hadn't imagined it, and that was not the noise of a blanket. He crawled over and lifted the box upright. Again, the sound of steel. He reopened the box to find the blanket's fabric no longer nicely folded.

A thick piece of black steel had fallen free of the blanket's folds. A handle—engraved with a word still half-covered by the blanket.

Dooms—

He recognized the style of writing immediately and reached down, knowing the feel of alien steel as soon as he took hold. As he pulled the handle from the fabric, he heard the clinking of metal links beneath.

Doomsday.

He dropped the steel onto the blanket, stunned by what it meant. His face hardened, and a moment later he threw the fabric off, exposing the weapon in whole.

He'd only been looking at the end. A long chain connected to the base of the handle, the length of it wrapped in circles and finally connecting to a head of steel that was half spike and half scythe-like on the other end. He'd seen something like it before, mounted on the wall of his staff instructor's studio. A *kusarigama*—though this had been highly modified. The weapon would be far too cumbersome, too heavy to take into combat with a man, but ideal for an active combatant to dispatch a Ferox.

Unable to take his eyes away, he pulled Doomsday out of the footlocker and rested it on his lap. His hand reached across the floor without thought, finding the toolbox and a flat metal file. In a moment, he scratched off the black carbonite on one of the chain links to see the reflective surface of the metal beneath. There was no doubting its origin; this was a weapon only Heyer could have given to his father. Douglas Tibbs had not died from a car accident. He'd been killed by a Ferox, and the alien had covered up his disappearance. From what his mother had said, Jonathan suspected Heyer had staged the accident, replaced the body with one so badly burned that the identity had been hidden.

Why—why make a special exception? Why go to that trouble when he didn't bother for all the other disappearances? He felt his faith in the alien crumbling, unable to justify such an omission. *Why keep this from him now?*

"Ten years," Jonathan whispered.

Something Heyer had said—Jonathan's mind grabbed hold of it, desperately trying to see the connection. He fought to focus, to remember every word the alien had ever exchanged with him. It had to be right in front of him if he could just see how the pieces came together. He repeated the words over and over in his head, as though he was, yet again, trying to cut his way through a lock.

Ten years... ten years... ten damn years!

He closed his eyes in frustration, unable to unearth what he knew was buried somewhere in his memories. He wished for his father to be there—to tell him who he'd been.

After some time, he hung Doomsday next to Excali-bar and Themyscira, hidden behind the facade in the cupboard. He started to put the contents of the box away, wrapping the guns in the blanket, placing them at the bottom beneath the rest. It was the best he could do to hide the firearms until he could replace the lock. He took care placing each item back into the box. Finally, he rested the picture frame and the letters on top, knowing that they would be the first thing his mother would find when she ignored his request to leave the box to him.

For now, he needed a lock, and knew where to get one.

When he stole his bike back from Leah's, he found the plastic fenders were back in place and the alteration was finished. He didn't want to wake her—already had enough going on in his head. Riding the bike had always been a way to turn off his thoughts for a while. Maybe if he got away from everything for a bit, the answer he couldn't pull out of the clutter would come to him.

CHAPTER FIFTY-SIX

DATE | TIME: UNKNOWN | FEROXIAN PLANE

GRANT'S SHADOW FOLLOWED Malkier outside. When he stepped past the boundaries of Cede into the ravine his eyes squinted in discomfort. He'd not had open sky overhead since being taken below, and the purple morning light of the Feroxian Plane was unpleasant on eyes that had adapted to little light. He shaded his face with a hand and peered up. He was unable to see the horizon from inside the rocky walls, but could tell where the sun was rising from how the slow gradient of red grew brightest in one direction. Still, his eyes would not adapt fast enough, and he turned away.

The doorway shimmered closed behind him, returning to camouflaged stone, and Grant caught his reflection on the glassy black mirror. Over his shoulder, Malkier strode toward the gateway.

After Grant had left the chamber where the parasite inhabiting his father's body was held prisoner, Malkier had remained inside for quite some time. Once he emerged, events had moved forward so quickly that Grant had been hard-pressed to keep up.

The Alpha leaders of each tribe had been visited by a broadcasted vision of *Ends the Storm*. In reality, they had only witnessed a holographic image that their primitive understanding believed to be the prophet's astral projection. Each had bowed in reverence to the power of their gods as the visage of their prophet spoke to them across the distance.

He had grown used to the device translating the Feroxian speech in his thoughts. As Grant knelt in the corner, watching, he couldn't be sure how much he'd truly understood. However, what had been clear was that each of those Alpha leaders had been waiting their entire lives for the news that the prophet brought them.

Their gods had spoken, and they had given the prophet the signs. The unnamed evil—the abomination foreseen to one day threaten their gods' plan for existence—had been given a name. The war for the promised land was soon to come.

Their gods had said that the prophet would bear a son—this son would be the harbinger. He would be the only male born of an Apha in seven generations, and his mother's womb would not bear another child until the son's life ended.

The birth of *Dams the Gate* was the first sign.

The harbinger was to be born with a single purpose to name the evil. It was through this name that their gods would know the nature of their enemy. Their gods forbade the harbinger from entering the gates. When they felt the disturbance, the touch of the abomination's evil on reality, their gods had known the time had come for the evil to be named, and thus compelled the harbinger to enter the gate. His sacrifice had given their god's the name—*Brings the Rain.*

The sacrifice of *Dams the Gate* was the second sign.

Their gods needed this evil tested. At their command, the prophet sent a warrior respected by all the tribes. If this warrior did not return with a trophy, then their gods would know the signs were true. The prophet had sent *Bleeds the Stone,* and the enemy had slain their warrior.

The fall of *Bleeds the Stone* was the third sign.

When *Brings the Rain* began to build his army, an abomination of his own kind would betray him. This betrayer would come to them through the gateway of *Echoes the Borealis*, and would see the wisdom of their gods. Like the Ferox, he would seek to be made into more than an abomination, to become a part of the great plan.

Malkier's speech as their prophet was too well rehearsed. He had known what would follow—nothing said between him and his brother behind the closed door had changed his plans. Grant had only been exposed to the Ferox beliefs for little over a week, but he understood that he'd been cast as the betraying "abomination" in Malkier's prophesying—their supposed gods claiming him as their fourth sign. It seemed the Ferox would blindly accept anything their prophet said as the unquestionable truth of their gods, as long as the story was framed as part of their predestined journey to the promised land.

With each of these "signs," Malkier turned mistakes into the preconceived plan of their gods. A narrative where the prophet had not gone against his own decree that Alphas would not enter the gates, but had only done as he must to bring forth the harbinger. *Dams the Gate* had not died in an act of rebellion, but in an act of sacrifice. *Burns the Flame* was not being punished for a slight against their gods, but was a faithful servant. All those males inciting a rebellion, angry for not being allowed access to the gates, they would soon be part of the war—the fight for the promised land itself. The Ferox were all prepared to follow Malkier where he led them.

As they left the tunnels, Grant and Malkier had not encountered any of the Ferox. The prophet had ordered their path to the gateway deserted. The Ferox asked no questions.

Brings the Rain and the woman bonded to him were to be removed from the equation today, and Grant had agreed to carry out the execution. Grant's understanding was that Malkier did not wish to return in a state of male estrus. Tonight, Malkier had ordered Cede to isolate these gates, manipulating combatants away from their intended destinations. When Grant and Malkier stepped through, they would bypass all other traffic, and Cede would route them to an empty express lane of sorts.

When they reached the gateway, Malkier finally spoke. "This is where you enter," he said. "I will join you shortly on the other side. Step onto the platform. The gateway will activate when the stone within you comes into proximity."

Grant nodded, and gave no delay. As he drew near, he heard a hum beginning to resonate from the platform, growing louder the closer he came until the planet's black dust rippled in waves on the surface. He looked back to Malkier to see if this was normal, and the alien's face showed no concern.

Grant stepped onto the surface. When his feet were in place, he blinked, and Malkier was gone—already off to enter the woman's gateway.

A familiar sphere took shape around him, the same strange circle of black and red he'd stepped into the night he trailed Jonathan and the girl back up to the rooftops.

Grant smiled. His entire life had been about this moment, and he, too, was headed for the promised land.

CHAPTER FIFTY-SEVEN

THURSDAY| OCTOBER 14, 2005 | 6:00 AM | SEATTLE

SO MUCH ANGST, Leah thought.

The hour was still early and Leah sat alone at her kitchen table with an empty envelope that had been disguised as junk mail torn open in front of her.

The translation of Rylee's journal was troubling. The entries were bipolar, either reading like the words of a person who had given into self-pity or someone rebelling against that very same pity. Ultimately though, the girl's thoughts were leaving Leah frustrated—as though she was missing a decoder.

Olivia's team had experienced the same, going so far as to bring in a second translator. The entries were only Rylee's reflections on her experiences, but the "experiences" themselves were seldom given an explicit description. Rylee was venting on the pages, not giving a personal account. This forced Leah to infer what had happened from the context, and for the most part, she felt lost in the snapshots of a stranger's rambling, disconnected thoughts.

There were references to The Mark. She referred to him as Heyer, a name consistent with others The Cell had investigated. Rylee's feelings toward him were clear, but they were little help as far as giving them something they could use.

...Why does he want me to think I had a choice? I didn't volunteer, I was drafted. Why does he think I can bear this? I don't think I can—I don't want to be the type of person who could. His face, his worthless sympathy, makes me so damn angry. You aren't human, Heyer! You don't understand what you took.

I hate speaking to him, makes me feel so damn powerless, but I have to... He needs to learn what a caged animal is capable of...

Rylee had written a lot on the road between Manhattan and Seattle. At first, those entries seemed more hopeful than the rest, but the trip had taken far longer than it should have. Rylee hadn't been in a hurry—didn't want to face the fear that she wouldn't find whatever she'd been looking for. Leah kept waiting for her to drop some clue as to what it was she was after, but Rylee never said anything specific. She only held fast to the belief that once she took "*it*," The Mark would have no choice but to negotiate. It wasn't until Leah neared the end of the entries that she started suspecting that Rylee had only ever had a destination—didn't know what "it" was herself.

The entries became less frequent once she had arrived in Seattle. Two days in, Rylee was already growing worried that she had driven across the country to stay in a cheap motel room and stare at the ceiling. These entries read like a detective waiting for a clue in a case that had gone cold. It was as though she'd been lost in the woods, and Seattle had been her single breadcrumb. The city gave her a place to start, but now that she was here, she just needed one more crumb to know which direction she was headed.

She hadn't expected that there would only be one more breadcrumb. That she wouldn't find a clue but a person. When she made this discovery, she'd lost her way—was no longer certain about anything.

Is the bastard manipulating me? Does he even know I left? He never got in my way—never showed up on the road to turn me around. I hate not knowing who the fool is... I feel like if I don't know, then it must be me.

Dammit, the moment my leverage is right there in front of me... I suddenly don't know what I want? I was trapped in a cage alone, but I blink, and suddenly realize I have a cellmate... and it's just a man, a stupid man, and it's absurd... But if Jonathan is in this cage with me… I'm not even sure what side of the bars I want be on… I'm more trapped than I ever was.

The dates of her entries were another matter. Some, but not all, didn't sync with what Leah and The Cell knew. The ones that were out of sync cast doubt over the accuracy of any time line they constructed. Some of the entries seemed like they must have been describing a dream. They spoke of physical intimacy that Leah knew Jonathan could never have actually engaged in. Yet, Leah had been a conflicted mess reading Rylee's description of their first encounter—what was literal or metaphor was frustratingly indiscernible.

…didn't know where I ended and he began. I didn't want to know. I've not felt so close to safety until we were stripped of everything. Seeing his vulnerabilities unguarded, I no longer hate my own. Where did we go? Did Jonathan take my hand or did I give it? Did he give me a piece of himself, his soul? I feel it…

That entry, Leah knew without a doubt, was dated before they could have possibly met. Jonathan honestly didn't seem to know that anything had happened between them. Yet, this was the first time Rylee mentioned his name. Leah couldn't dismiss this as a mistaken date—the entry that followed described what Leah had witnessed in their driveway far too accurately.

…He didn't know me. He pitied me like I was confused. Why are you doing this to me? What am I being punished for? I'm not something for you to break. It's cruel, giving me hope just to tear it away. Did you want me to see what I was planning to hold for ransom? Did you know—what it would do to me? You erased me? Heyer?

Rylee kept talking to The Mark in her entries, though most often, she seemed to be begging him for answers to questions she would never ask.

Leah couldn't help but feel they would be allies under any other circumstances—that Rylee was a missed opportunity. If The Cell had been able to locate her before she had made contact with Jonathan, turning her against the alien wouldn't have been a hard sell. Rylee had already been looking for a way to turn the tables, and The Cell, unlike the alien, would have happily let her volunteer. But now? Would Rylee still betray The Mark if she believed she was betraying Jonathan by proxy?

Meanwhile, here Leah was, trying to convince The Cell not to bring Jonathan to harm.

The irony was that both Rylee and herself had come here thinking Jonathan was the weapon they would use to get what they wanted from The Mark. Now, it seemed both had lost that resolve.

Jonathan stood in Mr. Fletcher's hardware store, staring at a padlock display rack. He wanted to replace the one he'd destroyed with something as substantial. He found his eyes were drawn to a brand called Kryptonite—probably because of his roommates. It was still early enough that he was the only customer in the store. As he plucked the lock off the wall, he heard the footsteps of his old boss behind him.

"It's a solid brand," Mr. Fletcher said.

Jonathan turned to him and nodded. "Expensive though," he said.

"Hey," the old man winked. "You still get your discount."

"Thanks, James," Jonathan said.

Mr. Fletcher grinned and nodded, but a moment later, he pulled off his glasses and his expression become frank as he placed them into his front pocket. "Mr. Donaldson was here yesterday. I asked how you were doing on the crew. He said you were out of town," Mr. Fletcher said. "For a funeral."

Jonathan closed his eyes uncomfortably as he was given another reminder of how bad he was at lying. He'd been distracted by what he'd found in that footlocker. Still, he was annoyed with himself. How had it not occurred to him that the one person he should have avoided after lying to his current boss was their one shared acquaintance?"

"I know how it looks," Jonathan said. "I promise, I'm not blowing off work. I needed time to take care of a friend. I didn't think the truth would sound as urgent as it is without going into details I didn't want to share. I'd really appreciate it if you didn't tell him you saw me here."

Mr. Fletcher shrugged and his expression relaxed. "Never known you to be a slacker, kid," he said. "Don't worry about it."

They stepped up to the register, neither really in any hurry.

"So, not that it's any of my business, but what do you need such a heavy-duty lock for?" the old man asked as he scanned the barcode.

"I found an old box that belonged to my father," Jonathan said. "I had to cut off the lock to see what was inside. Didn't expect to find some of his old firearms."

Mr. Fletcher nodded. "You know anything about guns, kid? Ever used one?"

"No, not really," Jonathan replied. "Dad took me to a range a few times when I was twelve. Don't remember much."

Mr. Fletcher nodded. "Well, it's smart that you want them safe, but if you plan on keeping a weapon around, make sure you find someone you trust who can teach you how to use it. Until then, I wouldn't let anyone know you have it."

Jonathan nodded.

"Honestly, a gun safe is really the better way to go," Mr. Fletcher said.

"Not something I can afford at the moment."

Mr. Fletcher gave an understanding nod. "Thing is, a padlock on a box is only safe if the box can't be stolen. Weapons are a bigger responsibility than most people re—" He trailed off, chuckling at himself as he handed Jonathan his purchase. "You know what, I'll spare you the lecture. You wouldn't be here buying a lock if you were a moron."

CHAPTER FIFTY-EIGHT

WHEN RYLEE WOKE, she showered, dressed, and slipped the pocket watch into her jacket pocket before grabbing her bag and heading down to the garage. She found Jonathan wasn't home, but knew he had been there when she spotted the chest he'd brought back with him. She stepped down the stairs, saw the broken lock, the stack of old letters, and the picture frame.

Sitting down beside the box, she picked up the frame, a faint smile on her face at seeing Evelyn holding Jonathan in the hospital. When she was done, she placed it back where she'd found it—but when she put her hand on the ground to stand, she felt the cold metal of the lock beneath her palm. Picking it up, she studied where the steel shackle had been severed.

A knock at the side door drew her attention. The door opened a few inches and Leah's voice entered.

"Tibbs?" Leah said, waiting a few seconds before she pushed the door open and stepped inside. "You here?"

Rylee set down the lock, her face going cold with disgust at the sound of the woman's voice. She made no effort to respond, only rose to her feet and thumbed the watch in her pocket as she heard Leah pulling the door shut behind her.

"Oh, Rylee," Leah said, startled when she turned around. She recovered and smiled. "Sorry, I didn't realize anyone was in here."

Crossing her arms, Rylee gave Leah a contemptuous head to toe once-over with her eyes, but didn't respond.

"Is he…" Leah frowned, picking up on the cold reception. "Um, is he—"

"Jonathan isn't home," Rylee interrupted. "I'll be sure to let him know you came by."

Leah pulled back, seeming unsure if the animosity was truly directed at her. "Rylee, is everything alright?"

She narrowed her eyes, a long breath escaping her before she responded, "Fine."

Silence followed.

Rylee's face remained an impatient stare. Leah's eyes, despite feeling uncomfortable, seemed to be calculating. Rylee watched as she doubled down, still seeming to hope she had caught Rylee at a bad moment. She took on a look of sympathy of all things.

"Uh," Leah said. "I might be reading you all wrong, but if you need to vent, I…"

"Reading," Rylee spit the word out with an angry chuckle. She leaned forward. "Don't you think you've done enough reading, Leah?"

Rylee saw Leah's disguise falter, the faintest touch of guilt slipping past her facade.

"I don't know what that is supposed—"

"You should leave," she stopped her.

Leah's eyes narrowed, anger flaring at being dismissed. "Rylee, please, you don't understa—"

"I know what you are, and Jonathan's gonna know as soon as he gets home," Rylee interrupted. "So now, you're going to leave or..." She tilted her head to crack the vertebrae in her neck. "Keep talking," she began, "and I'll throw you out on your ass."

The moment stretched out as Rylee stared Leah down. Leah stared back, her expression growing nervous. The tense silence between them was filled suddenly by the sound of an approaching motorcycle. Neither woman blinked. When Leah took a step forward, Rylee couldn't tell if it was toward her or the door, so she took a step closer—she didn't want

Leah to think for one second that she was bluffing. The engine drew closer. Leah's eyes closed.

"Rylee, I was scare—"

Rylee's fist connected before she could finish her sentence, landing hard under her eye.

Leah staggered back, losing her balance momentarily. Her hand went to her cheek once she was able to steady herself. She tried to shake it off, hair dangling over her face before she planted her feet and rose back to her full height. A hot red welt was starting to bloom under her eye.

"Rylee, please listen!"

The second she started speaking, Rylee stepped forward and grabbed her by the collar, reeling back to hit her again.

"I'm pregnant," Leah whispered.

Rylee flinched, felt uncertainty roll through her. Her voice betrayed her. "What?"

Her fist, cocked to deliver another blow, began to shake.

"No," she murmured, shaking her head. "You're playing me… you read my diary… you think…"

Leah shook her head slowly, eyes begging for Rylee to understand that she wouldn't lie, not about this. "I haven't told him. I was going to, but then you came and I… I had to know what you were to him."

Rylee's fist fell, and she grabbed hold of Leah's collar with both hands, bringing their faces within inches.

"Please," Leah begged. "I don't want him to find out like this."

She stared into Leah's eyes, looking for something to make her certain, but the vision she had of Leah as a government agent clashed with what Leah actually said—if she was a woman trying to know the father of her child hadn't fallen for another woman…

She didn't want to feel this sympathy—not for Leah.

"No," Rylee said. "You took pictures, you..."

The engine died in the driveway as they glared at one another.

"Talk," Rylee said, her voice angry but approaching tears. "Talk faster!"

"I'm sorry," Leah said. "I had to take pictures. I couldn't read it."

Footsteps approached from the side door, both women aware of each second ticking by.

Jonathan was jarred from his thoughts when he came upon the scene in the garage. He froze, seeing that Rylee had Leah by the collar, looking as though she was on the verge of violence. Neither woman looked at him, not right away, and finally, with a defeated whimper, Rylee let go, pushing the other woman away from her as she did so.

"What the hell is going on?" Jonathan asked.

The question was met with silence.

Rylee's face softened into misery, her eyes shining, verging on tears, the strength in her posture going slack. Both women seemed unsure what to do with themselves and avoided looking at him. It took a moment, but Leah realized he was watching her. His gaze had fallen on the red mark swelling under her eye. When he lingered there, she lowered her head letting her long hair dangle in front of the bruise in an attempt to hide what had happened.

He swallowed. "Someone say something."

Leah looked back at Rylee, her face uncertain as she watched the other woman stare at the floor. A tear ran down Rylee's cheek. Jonathan wanted to go to her—was it the bond or honest concern? He couldn't tell, but it hurt him to see her in tears.

"Rylee?" Jonathan mumbled.

She looked at him when she heard her name, as though she wanted to speak but was at a loss for words.

He stepped closer, his hand reaching for her face and gently wiping the tear away. "What happened?" he asked.

She looked away again, but reached up to hold his hand against her cheek. She seemed so confused, not yet ready to speak.

"Leah?" Jonathan asked, turning his eyes to her.

Half hidden by her hair, Leah's face was troubled. She watched his hand pressed to the other woman's cheek. Jonathan didn't want to upset her, but didn't see a way to show either woman tenderness without hurting the other. He was not willing to take any comfort from Rylee when she was so upset. He wanted Leah to understand this, but all he saw was hurt.

"My stuff," Rylee finally whispered. "She went through my stuff."

For a moment, Jonathan frowned, but felt relieved. Leah was the last person he could imagine invading someone's privacy on purpose. She had always been respectful of boundaries. He felt that this had to be a misunderstanding.

"Rylee, I'm sure it isn't what it looked like," he said. "Leah wouldn't—"

"No." Rylee shook her head, pulling his palm from her cheek and clutching it tightly with both her hands. "Jonathan..." she whispered, her eyes pleading with him to see something. "She took pictures of my diary."

He had to bite down, clench his teeth to keep a look of panic from crossing his face. He hadn't even known Rylee kept a diary, would have asked her to destroy it if he had. If he was wrong, if Leah had done what Rylee claimed, then he may have seriously misread the gravity of this situation.

"Leah," Jonathan said. "I know you wouldn't. There has to be an explanation?"

Leah's lips had barely parted to speak before Rylee cut her off.

"Jonathan, the two of you aren't—" Rylee closed her eyes, her face having turned bitter. "I don't know if she is who you think."

For a moment, he was unsure what she meant, but when the unspoken message in Rylee's words hit him, all the strength drained out of his face. Suddenly, there were too many fears fighting for dominance in his thoughts. Not only was Rylee accusing Leah of being in league with The Cell, but she was telling him he'd been blind to it. That his instincts had been so wrong about Leah that he'd failed to even consider the possibility. That she may feel nothing for him, having spent every moment since they met manipulating him.

He found himself unwilling to acknowledge the accusation, not wanting to feel the doubt it brought. He wished someone other than him would say something, but both women were watching him, waiting to see which way he would lean.

He closed his eyes.

"Leah?" he whispered.

"Cede," Heyer said. "Will you speak to me?"

Left alone now in his prison, he sat with his back against one of the rock walls. His knees were bent in front of him, holding him in place while his head rested against the stone. The wall on the other side of the room shimmered, and the alien face of his mother looked back at him from her chamber.

"Yes," she said.

"You've been with my brother since before I can remember," he said. "When did he go mad?"

"On what matter is it that you question your brother's sanity?" Cede asked.

Heyer shook his head. "He has taken it upon himself to either enslave or annihilate an entire race."

"His conclusions are not groundless; there is precedent for his concerns," Cede said. "Malkier is favoring caution."

Heyer remembered what he had said to Jonathan, '*I do not believe my brother would threaten my home world using prejudice as his justification…*'

"He is favoring his hatred."

Cede did not see the statement as requiring a response—it was not a request or a question. As she did not interact with biological beings under the pretenses of an emotional kinship, Heyer's words left the room in silence.

"Do you know—are you allowed to tell me… when will they enter the gates?" Heyer asked.

"Yes, sir. The human known as Grant Morgan entered the gate of *Echoes the Borealis* a few moments ago. I have already rejected multiple requests by my counterpart on Earth to redirect to alternate nodes," Cede replied. "Malkier reached the gateway of the human female. He will follow shortly."

"So soon?" Heyer asked.

"Malkier had always intended to leave once he had ensured you would not be able to intervene."

Heyer reached into his pocket, relieved to feel the beacon solidify in his hands. He had feared its discovery while he was unconscious. Knowing now that Grant had already entered the gates, he closed his eyes—the means to circumvent his brother's plans were shrinking rapidly.

"You know, my brother, he was right about one thing," Heyer said. "I never shared our technology with Mankind, because I was afraid of what they might do with it."

"It is not an irrational fear, sir."

Heyer drew in a long breath, then opened his eyes to stare at the face of his mother. "Cede, if you ever see my brother again, I want you to tell him something," he said as he activated the beacon. "He was never going to keep me out of this. War with Earth—it always meant war with me..." He paused, swallowing before he spoke. "So I want you to let him know that I intend to give Mankind every advantage in my power. And I will be waiting for him."

"Sir, you can certainly give this message yourself when..."

Cede stopped mid-sentence. Heyer was gone.

CHAPTER FIFTY-NINE

THE LONGER LEAH remained silent, the more Jonathan felt doubt unhinging him.

"Leah," he whispered. "Say something."

She closed her eyes, a look of defeat on her face. "I read her diary," she said. "I needed to know."

Jonathan didn't want to believe her, even as she confessed—the action contradicted everything he was drawn to in her.

"I couldn't do it," Leah said, "Just sit around wondering if the two of you were…" She shook her head, seemed unwilling to finish the sentence. "At least now I know."

Jonathan flinched, narrowing his eyes as he pondered her words. It felt as though they weren't talking about the same crime—that she had accused him of something.

"Now you know what?" Jonathan asked.

She glared at him at first, but her face softened the longer she stared, growing more conflicted as she tried to discern if his question was honest.

"I've never lied to you," Jonathan said. "So what are you accusing me of?"

Leah blinked at him with uncertainty, struggling to read his face before she responded. "The diary, Rylee said—"

"Don't," Rylee whispered. "You've no right." Her voice had been so quiet, her eyes suddenly pleading with Leah for mercy.

The garage door suddenly swung open.

An elephant might as well have crashed through one of the walls, Jonathan and both women were so startled by the interruption. Hayden entered, followed by Collin, both holding Frappuccinos and grinning with complete ignorance of what they had walked in on.

"Hey folks," Hayden said. "Did you know…" He stopped short as he took in the scene.

"Uh," Collin said. "Everything okay?"

Jonathan found he wasn't sure if he should ask them to leave or beg them to stay. "A misunderstanding," he said, turning to Leah. "Maybe we should talk about this later."

Leah gave a nod of agreement, though she didn't look as though she actually wanted to continue the conversation—more like she wanted Collin and Hayden to be her excuse to exit before anything else was said.

Rylee huffed in audible disapproval and turned away. "I'm out of here," she said.

"You don't need to leave," Leah said. "I'm going."

"Don't!" Rylee stopped to point a finger at the other woman. "Just—don't speak to me!"

Collin and Hayden tensed at the raw anger in Rylee's voice. They looked about themselves as if they were unsure if they should inch toward the living room door or back the way they came. Rylee picked her pack up off the garage floor, throwing it onto the countertop beside Jonathan's cigar box. He started to panic, seeing her stuffing her possessions into the bag, unsure if she was preparing to leave for good.

"Rylee?" Jonathan said. "Are you coming back?"

She paused, looking at him over her shoulder. He wasn't sure if it was pity or betrayal on her face before she spoke. "I got the memo, Tibbs," she said, turning away to continue gathering her items. "I can't stay here, should have already left. Might as well get on with it."

The way she said it, the expression on her face. She knew—and she knew he hadn't told her. He stepped forward, not knowing what he was about to say, reaching out for her with his hand.

"I hadn't decided any—"

A familiar twitch in his chest stopped his words as she turned back to him and waited for the rest of his interrupted thought. The hand he held out for her quivered as he felt the control over his muscles begin to fail.

"Ah, hell," Jonathan managed to say. Then he crumpled to the floor.

CHAPTER SIXTY

THURSDAY| OCTOBER 14, 2005 | 8:15 AM | SEATTLE

WHEN SOUND RETURNED, he first heard the rain, still falling on the roof of the garage. The peace of it short lived before Collin's confused voice broke in.

"What... " Collin trailed off. "She just... where?"

He heard the familiar gasp of his roommates as his chest ignited. Opening his eyes, he saw Leah kneeling beside him and his roommates, wide-eyed, mouths hanging open. As his thoughts became lucid, panic barreled in on him. He knew what it would mean if he was activated while Rylee remained in proximity. Mr. Clean had been unable to redirect an inbound Ferox—had been forced to bring him into The Never. There was only one reason that Jonathan could imagine Mr. Clean would take this action without warning him—Malkier had ordered his A.I. on the Feroxian plane to refuse.

"We're out of time," he whispered.

He shut his eyes, his jaw clenching with self-contempt. He had already feared what he was setting in motion with all of his delays and uncertainty. Jonathan had waited too long, hadn't sent Rylee away, hadn't been willing to let her go.

He allowed himself this one moment of honesty. To feel the responsibility of it, to ignore hopes and denials that he was wrong. He'd failed to act and now the time to direct his fate had passed. Heyer had trusted him to do his part, to put off the war as long as possible. He hadn't listened, hadn't wanted to—he let it come to them.

"Not a leader. Just a damn fool" Jonathan whispered.

That was all the time he had for self-pity, the only acknowledgment it would get from him. He drew in a long breath through gritted teeth.

Get your feet on the floor, he thought.

Jonathan was immediately aware of the silence as he stood. His roommates reaction to his activation was off somehow, more confusion on their faces than ever before. Leah was no longer kneeling beside him—Hayden and Collin looked to him, and back to where Leah now stood, staring at the spot where Rylee had been standing. A spot that was now empty.

Leah's face was trembling in fear when she turned to look at him. Her lip fell open and she struggled to speak. "Where... Jonathan, where did she go?" she asked.

A panic struck him, but was quickly suppressed. The way she seemed to have disappeared—the only explanation he knew of was being killed within The Never. That didn't make any sense to him, though—if she had ceased to be before he had been activated, she would have disappeared before his eyes. It would have happened before he dropped to the floor. That, and he didn't feel it, seemed to know she was okay. The bond—nothing felt different. He looked back at Leah, his face nearly as perplexed as her own.

Leah stepped toward him, new tears beginning to run down her cheek. She grabbed him by the collar of his jacket with both hands and yanked forcefully. Though he hadn't expected it, and didn't understand her sudden aggression, Leah might as well have been attempting to manhandle a telephone pole. She stumbled into him awkwardly, flinched in surprise as she found her face so close to his, unable to compute how it was that the physics of her actions hadn't yielded anything close to the outcome she expected. Her breathing quickened in confusion, but whatever was causing her attempt to intimidate him physically hadn't lost its focus.

"Where is she?" Leah asked.

Jonathan's eyebrows furrowed, unable to understand the frightened anger she was clearly targeting on him. "I don't know," he whispered. "This hasn't ever..."

He trailed off, blinking dumbfoundedly for a moment, before carefully bringing his hand up to push Leah's clenched fists away.

Rylee had suddenly reappeared, manifesting in a manner eerily similar to Heyer's coming and going. She lay still on the floor now, precisely where he had last seen her standing. Leah's grasp on him went limp as she looked over her shoulder and realized what he'd seen.

Normally when Collin and Hayden saw him activated, they became a flurried mixture of fear and excitement leading to a barrage of questions. It seemed that even his roommates had a strangeness threshold. Apparently, seeing him activated, coupled with Rylee pulling an unexplained disappearing act, followed shortly after with Leah becoming uncharacteristically angry at Jonathan and accusing him of somehow having an explanation for what the hell was happening, only to have Rylee suddenly reappear unconscious on the floor, was enough to leave them frozen.

"Uh, I think Starbucks may have started putting acid in the Frappuccino mix," Hayden whispered to Collin.

Jonathan knelt down beside Rylee. Her face was placid and calm, as though she was merely sleeping, but he suspected she was burning inside, unable to move while the activation ran its course. Gently, he cradled her head in his hand and pulled the side of her shirt over one of her shoulders to see the faint blue light of her device flickering.

"How?" Leah whimpered. "I... I don't understand."

He had never been on the observing side of an activation—not this close—but he focused on her eyelids and waited for a sign of her returning consciousness. Finally, they fluttered, telling him she was almost back—and her eyes opened as the light of her device solidified into a constant glow. Her lips curved into a smile when he was the first thing she saw.

"Talk about crappy timing," Rylee whispered as she reached for his face, her fingers running down his cheek as they looked at one another. "Finish what you were saying—sounded like you were working up to a really good apology."

He frowned at her. "Sorry, *Slug*. I honestly don't remember."

Rylee gave him a crooked but playful look. "Don't wuss out on me now Tib—" She cut off, sitting up suddenly when her eyes fell on the light beneath his T-shirt. "How are you…?" Her eyes raced around the room questioningly. "Your implant—how are you already activated?"

He frowned. "I don't follow? I fell to the floor a moment ago," he said. "You were packing your bag—I was looking right at you when it began, but when I came out of it, you weren't here—"

Her hand shot up to his chest in concern. "Something's wrong," she said, shaking her head. "Do you feel it—the combatants?"

He hadn't yet paid much attention to the movements of the compass in his mind, but on her prompting, he focused on the signal. "About two miles west," he replied. "Feels close to Pioneer Square."

He flinched then, feeling a shift in the signal's destination.

"Dammit," he said. "It's already through and moving."

"Yeah, but… there is only one," Rylee said.

He put his hand out, and Rylee took it absentmindedly as she got to her feet. He nodded to her, confirming that he was coming to the same conclusion, a concerned expression forming on his face as he walked to the cupboard and removed the facade. Grabbing Rylee's rattan first, he tossed it to her, before reaching for Excali-bar. His eyes fell on the chain weapon hanging beside it, and after a moment's pause, he pulled Doomsday off its hook.

When he turned back around, weapons in hand, he remembered all the eyes that were watching him. Collin and Hayden's mouths still hung open, and they seemed to have been rendered comically catatonic. Leah was in no such state. Her eyes were red with tears she seemed too angry to cry. A weight crept onto him when he saw how badly she needed to understand. He forced himself to look away.

Not Leah, he reminded himself. *Just a shadow.*

"Where in the hell did that come from?" Rylee asked, seeing Doomsday in his hands.

He nodded his head down at the footlocker. "My father's weapon," he said, placing it onto the weight bench as he pulled Excali-bar's harness over his jacket. He then began crisscrossing the chain over the harness around his chest. Pulling it taut, he soon found that the handle and pointed ends had interlocking pieces. It was meant to be carried this way—could be quickly freed when he needed it.

"No shit," Rylee said, comprehended its meaning as quickly as he had. She reached for the chain, her finger running over the word Doomsday engraved in the alien steal.

"Yeah."

"Then how long has this been going on?" she asked.

"Next time I see Heyer," Jonathan said, "I'll be damn sure to ask."

He turned to lift open the garage door and found Leah facing him. His focus wavered again under her gaze, as though she expected him to say something. Cautiously, her hand reached for his cheek. He stopped it, gently as he could, careful of his strength.

"Leah," he said. "I need you to move."

Confused and hurt that he had pushed her away, she stepped aside and stared at the floor. He hated enduring it, hated that his actions were making her feel as though she'd become irrelevant to him.

It's like I am watching you walk off into the dark, she'd said.

He cringed at the memory of her words, felt he had to get away from her. *Just a shadow.* He reached for the handle of the garage door and lifted it open. *Not going to remember, not going to matter.* He stepped to the motorcycle, locking Excali-bar into the clips she had welded into place for him.

"I'd do anything to keep you from that place," he heard Leah whisper.

He stopped moving.

Some coincidences—they were too difficult to ignore. Leah was there now, in his head again, her mind having been thinking of that same shared moment. As always, she could get so close to breaching the walls within him. He couldn't keep her out; he didn't know how. He always had to flee. His face softened, and he turned back to her.

"If that is where I need to go," he said, "then I will."

"To diffuse the bomb?" she asked, her face uncertain.

Jonathan sighed. "I think I've already detonated it."

Leah stared back, wondering if they truly understood one another when they spoke in metaphor. "But you're still here," she said.

He nodded, but heard Rylee calling his name, realized she had been trying to get his attention.

"Stop, Tibbs," Rylee said. "She isn't going to remember any of this. It's a waste of time."

He swallowed and pulled his eyes away.

"I still only feel one breach," Rylee said. "What does it mean?"

Jonathan shook his head. "We need to go."

They hadn't been on the roads long before Rylee felt the enemy close enough to get a better sense of its exact location. Something was bothering Jonathan more than the two of them being activated while they seemed to face only one combatant—he signaled to her from the bike and abruptly started slowing down. She followed when he pulled off the streets and into an alley, cutting their engines. He looked into the sky, drawing Excali-bar free from the bike, his face hardening in concentration.

"This lone Ferox—it's not moving like any of the others," Rylee said. "They usually go straight to ground, look for a population to kill, draw us out."

Jonathan nodded as he studied the city's skyline

Rylee had seen the foreboding on his face, heard it in his voice before they had started their engines in the driveway. Stepping up beside him now, she saw nothing had changed.

"No spectators," she said. "What do you make of this? I haven't felt it move from that rooftop for about five minutes."

"This is a trap."

Rylee frowned. "How do you know?"

He turned from the skyline and studied her. When he spoke, he didn't answer her question, but asked his own. "How did you know, Rylee?" he asked. "That I was supposed to tell you to leave?"

"Mr. Clean, he warned me that my journal had been compromised," she said. "Wanted to know why I hadn't left yet. When I asked him why I would be leaving, he wouldn't explain, said you were supposed to."

Jonathan nodded. "There were reasons," he said, turning to face her. "Good ones. I should have gone through with it, but I couldn't."

Rylee searched his face, saw the weight he was bearing. "I'm glad," she said. "That you didn't want to."

He sighed, shaking his head. "I walked us into this, kept deluding myself into thinking you were safer with me. I was wrong."

The tone of his words was creeping in on her. He sounded as though he was sure they had already lost.

"Tibbs, whatever this is, don't quit on me before it begins," Rylee said. "If we know it's some kind of trap, we can figure it out, dismantle it before we pick a fight."

There was pain in the way he looked at her, as though he didn't want to tell her that the trap had already been sprung. "The other night, Heyer explained a lot about how The Never works," he finally said, frustration building on his face. "For all the good it's done, I don't see how we get out of this."

"Tibbs, you're starting to screw with my positive attitude here."

Jonathan shook his head. "Two of us. One Ferox—if it's what it looks like, then there are two of us and only one ticket out."

As what Jonathan said sunk in, the sounds of the city seemed to get swallowed—drowned out as she began to share his fear.

"Rylee, if that is how this plays out, you're going back. I don't want to hear—"

"Oh, like hell," she cut in, and continued before Jonathan had a chance to argue. "Look, we don't know anything for sure. Even if you're right, no one is drawing straws. We break the stone together."

Jonathan swallowed, sighing as he looked down at the ground. "I already thought of that," he said. "I think it could be exactly what they want."

"What? How is that even a trap?"

"Rylee, this is happening because of me." He closed his eyes in frustration. "I killed Malkier's son, and ever since, he has been trying to return the favor by rigging which Ferox come through the gate—sending assassins. He never expected me to survive it, thought I was a fluke and one of his Reds would kill me before Heyer realized what he was trying to do."

Rylee gave him a confused look. If there was a connection between this and what was now happening she didn't see the goal.

Jonathan sighed. "I failed. The one thing Heyer asked me to do was to ask you to leave. I should have obeyed, should have realized we weren't any safer just because Malkier was in another dimension. I may as well have handed myself over to him."

"I don't follow how that gets him you?"

Jonathan nodded. "We get that stone, and I see three options," he said. "One, you use the stone and I stay behind, the gates close, and I cease to exist inside The Never. I'm dead, Malkier gets what he wants. Two, you break the stone, and I step into the gates as it closes."

Rylee nodded. "Like the man who entered the day we met?"

"Exactly," Jonathan said. "I don't cease to exist, but I deliver myself to the Feroxian plane where he gets to kill me himself. Malkier wins. Which brings us to option three: we break the stone together." Jonathan shook his head.

"Yeah?" she asked. "What happens then?"

He looked away. "We'd be leaving it to chance. One of us would go home, the other to him. Rylee…" He grimaced. "Malkier knows that if he can't have me, killing you is the next best thing. I'm not taking that chance."

She wanted to tell him that he had everything ass-backwards. Instead, she stared at him, not knowing what she could say to budge him, and knowing she wasn't having any part of a plan that left him behind. But there was nothing to say.

We're just gonna go in circles…

Rylee's thoughts ground to a halt. *Going in a circle.*

The words Jonathan had spoken to her before. She'd wanted him to finish apologizing, but he hadn't known what she was talking about after catching up to him in The Never. Rylee suddenly realized, it was not that he didn't remember, but that he hadn't said those words to her yet. Jonathan wasn't going to die in here—he wasn't getting left behind.

If either of those things had happened, he couldn't have said those words to her. No, she simply would have seen him disappear before she entered.

"Jonathan, I couldn't live knowing I left you behind, but…" Her voice softened into a whisper. "You left out the option where you admit you should leave me behind, because you're the only one who doesn't have to live with it."

She could see he didn't immediately follow her, that what she'd realized had never occurred to him.

"Jonathan, I would have to remember leaving you to die, but you entered The Never before me. You aren't going to remember what happened in here," she said.

Jonathan's face paled as he understood. She watched him retreat, suddenly step back from her as though the words had made him ill. "No," he said, shaking his head. "No way."

The rain and the sounds of the city began returning. The world coming backing into focus, less muffled by the panic of her thoughts. Rylee grabbed hold of his shoulder rougher than she had intended. "Look, we don't know anything for sure yet," she said. "Let's deal with the problem we know is real before we focus on problems we may have only imagined."

His eyes came to linger on the hand she had placed on his shoulder. In a moment, he closed his eyes and nodded his agreement, though she could see it had been a struggle.

"We might not have to figure any of this out," Jonathan said. "Heyer showed me where Mr. Clean is stationed—as long as he exists in here, he should be able help us."

Rylee nodded, showed a confident smile. "That signal has hardly moved since we stopped. Whatever is waiting for us up there, I think it can wait a minute longer," she said. "I need to tell you something."

She took a long breath, bracing herself for what came next. His face had already softened, and, despite herself, she found she was fidgeting reluctantly the moment she knew he'd heard her vulnerability.

"I'm worried now, that you won't remember," she said, shrugging. "But if I don't make it out, I can't risk never telling you. I don't want to hurt you, put any more pressure on you, but at least in here, I'll know how you took it."

He held her eyes a moment before a faint smile touched his lips. "Feeling me out because you know I won't remember?" he asked. "You know, if we live through this, you can't just tell me things knowing I'll forget them if you don't like how I react. It's not fair."

"I totally promise…" Rylee said playfully, "that you won't remember I promised not to do that."

His smile grew. He looked down to the alley floor as though reliving a memory. "But you'll remember," he whispered when he lifted his eyes to hers.

Rylee nodded, taking a last moment to look at him before she spoke. "You can't trust Leah," she said.

He took a long breath and let it out slowly, but he waited for her to explain.

"In the footage Mr. Clean showed me, Leah didn't just read my journal," Rylee said. "She probably couldn't—I've written all the entries in Portuguese since I was a little girl."

She could see on his face that he wasn't sure he wanted to hear this, but knew he couldn't run away.

"She brought a camera with her," Rylee said. "I saw her take pictures of every page. She told me she was jealous, that she needed to know who I was to you. But, I just don't know…"

She saw the conflict in his eyes.

"Leah's a photographer, she…" He paused. "She usually has a camera on her. It could be a coincidence. Maybe when she saw it wasn't in English, she took the pictures so she could translate it?"

Rylee had to fight the urge to tell him he was being naïve, refusing to see what he didn't want to see. "Maybe," she said, trying to be gentle. "But isn't it more likely that she isn't who she says? Look, even if I am wrong, Leah knows things…" She trailed off, biting her lip. "Things about us."

She reached for him slowly, taking hold of his neck to pull him toward her and kissing him gently. He tensed but didn't pull away, and the uncertainty he always seemed to feel when she touched him stung her.

"Rylee," Jonathan said. "I—"

She closed her eyes, shook her head to stop him from speaking. "I never told you everything, about the first time we met," she whispered. "You were so different, though—I need to know what changed, why you haven't been the same."

She pulled close to him and rested her head on his shoulder.

"After we'd killed the Ferox. I didn't even know your name, I didn't understand—didn't trust you. I was afraid you knew more about what was happening, that if I let you close the gates, I wouldn't get any answers. I wanted control over the situation, and wanted to get you alone, somewhere off the streets. So I took the stones, made you chase me to a roof top. It didn't take long to see that you didn't understand what I was doing. That more than anything you were worried about the stones, or that I was going to leave you no choice but to take them from me."

"Oh, man," Jonathan said. "Please tell me I didn't try."

Rylee smiled faintly. "You didn't have it in you, that much I could tell. You kept stepping closer to me, and I was yelling the whole time, demanding to know who you were, why you weren't surprised to know there was another like you, what your part was in Heyer's scheme. You kept inching closer and closer, and I was supposed to be wary of it, but I wasn't. You started yelling back, demanding we close the gates, that I could trust you. The angrier we got with one another, the more I couldn't ignore it—the more I wanted to push you, to see you try and take the stones by force. When you put a hand on me, I was ready to throw down, but when our skin touched..." Rylee trailed off.

"We weren't in control," Jonathan said.

She nodded. "I didn't want control, I needed you..." Rylee didn't finish the thought. "I felt alive, needing you that badly."

Jonathan closed his eyes, nodding though his face was pained. "We were…" He paused. "Intimate, then?"

She softened at his awkwardness, but nodded.

"I'm sorry," he said. "I don't know who I was at that moment. It's not fair to you that I can't remember."

She swallowed. "I still feel this. But I can see you fighting it, walling me off. You didn't hesitate before, you didn't hold back. I can only think that you didn't have a reason to keep me away. That something happened in between, when you forgot me."

"Rylee, it isn't real," Jonathan said. "Heyer told me—these implants push us to want things we might not truly want if we were in control. I wanted to tell you, but there were reasons—still are—that I was afraid to take that risk."

She heard him swallow.

"But once I knew, I couldn't let us act on it. It would have been taking advantage," he continued. "And I knew I was supposed to tell you to go. I didn't want to make it that much harder."

Rylee fell silent a moment. As she processed what he'd said, she knew he was holding back, that he hadn't given her the whole story. "Jonathan, I've never lied to you. Never given you a reason not to trust me."

"I do trust you."

"Then why are you lying to me? Sure, fine, there were risks, you didn't want to take advantage, sounds all noble on paper, but you were holding back before Heyer could have warned you of any of it."

"Okay," Jonathan said, exhaling the word. "That night, Leah and I, we'd been—were in the middle of..." He stalled. "The moment before I was activated... when I entered and when I left, we were..." He closed his eyes, still unable to find a good way to explain.

"Oh, god, please stop babbling," Rylee said. "I get the picture already. Actually, I don't have to picture it—Mr. Clean showed me the footage."

The look of relief that she wouldn't force him to explain was priceless. She found herself trying not to laugh, despite it all. "Thank you for trying, at least. To be honest, I'm not jealous."

A moment passed between them.

"Okay, I'm not *that* jealous," she corrected. "I was afraid it was something a lot worse than the redhead."

He seemed to look at her crooked, unsure if he understood her.

"That way we saw into one another. The way you found me in that motel room," Rylee said. "I was afraid that you had looked into me and saw something ugly, something you didn't want to touch. That all you had for me was pity."

Jonathan shook his head slowly. "No," he said, his fingers gently tracing the line of her implant down from her shoulder toward her heart. "There was nothing inside of you that I didn't recognize inside myself. I meant what I said, Rylee. You were never weak. These damn devices, once the bond took hold—it pushed you in all the worst ways. It would have done the same to me. I know it."

Rylee felt her lips trembling, the rise of a smile, that felt silly to her, coming to her face. She wanted to hide it, didn't want him to know how much she feared what he had seen in her. They looked at one another for a while before the sappiness of the moment made it become unbearably awkward.

They both noticed when the target moved in their perceptions, both happy for a reason to snap out of it.

Rylee turned to face the skyline again, not wanting him to see a tear escaping. "Good talk, Tibbs," she said. "Maybe I'll tell you about it sometime."

Jonathan glared at her, but grinned as he came to stand alongside her. "Heading up, then, *Slug*?" he asked.

Rylee, unwilling to acknowledge the nickname, jumped, elegantly bounding back and forth from one wall of the alley to other until she landed on the roof. She knelt low against the wall, Jonathan landing shortly after.

He crouched beside her, his eyes scanning the city ahead of them. "No going on the offensive this time, not 'til we see what we are dealing with. We get close, we keep low and quiet," he said. "We do this careful, agreed?"

She let out an exaggerated sigh before responding. "Careful," she said playfully. "Tell me, Tibbs, do you need to borrow my bra? Sounds like—"

"Rylee," Jonathan interrupted in his no-nonsense tone.

"Fine, I'll follow your lead. But I'm not doing it because Mr. Fedora says I have to."

He looked at her curiously. "Oh? Why, then?"

"Well," Rylee said, "there is this rumor going around that, allegedly, I blew myself up last time."

CHAPTER SIXTY-ONE

STAYING OUT OF the open as best they could, they drew closer to the lone signal. Finally, landing on the tallest rooftop in sight of the enemy, Jonathan knelt behind the roof's lip, scanning out in front of them while Rylee put her back to it to keep an eye on what was behind them.

"I've been here," Jonathan said. "Recently."

"That mean something?"

"We're getting close to where Heyer brought me the other night. Doubt it's a coincidence." He shook his head, troubled as he tried to think it through, but he didn't know what to make of it.

"The signal we're getting," she said. "It should be on the building below us."

He looked to her, nodded, and slowly raised himself up to peer over the roof's edge. Rylee saw his expression go blank as his eyes locked on to something below.

Growing curious, she peered over as well. A man stood below, and as she studied his face, she was sure she recognized it. "That man, Jonathan," she said. "He's the one who entered the gates the night we met."

"You're sure?" Jonathan asked.

"Yeah. He's shaved, but that is definitely him."

Jonathan closed his eyes, nodding a moment later. "I know him."

Rylee frowned. "How?" she asked.

"His name is Grant Morgan. He was with The Cell. It's a long story, but I haven't seen him since he confessed who he was working with."

Rylee pondered this for a moment. "He must have still been following you," she said. "Why would he enter the gates, though?"

"No idea." Jonathan shook his head. "This is probably a trap, but I have to find out what's going on. I'm going down there. Whatever happens, stay down, and don't let him know you're here unless it absolutely can't be avoided."

He leaned back from the wall and reached behind his back to remove Excali-bar. Rylee reached, too, grabbing him by the chain wrapped around his torso to stop him from leaving.

"What are you going to do?" she asked.

He looked at her grimly, and let out a breath. "I'm going to talk to him. I need to find out what he's done."

He was about to stand, to jump over the roof and drop down to where the man waited below, but Rylee held tight to the chain, pulling him to her before he might think to stop her. She closed her eyes and kissed him, feeling the static charge run between them. Jonathan didn't fight, but didn't embrace her either. Gently, his gloved hand came to her cheek, pushing their lips apart.

His eyes were confused. He looked away, still holding her cheek with his hand. When he looked up again, a faint smile broke on his lips. "When this is over, you aren't going to tell me you did that, are you?"

"Let's say it was for luck, Tibbs."

Grant amused himself, pulling one brick after another free from the roof of Heyer's vessel. The world seemed so fragile, as though made from a gingerbread house and held together by frosting. He crushed the stone in his hand, then smiled down as the larger fragments at his feet lost their shape and were absorbed into the rooftop.

There was a thud behind him, the telling sound of a body landing on the roof. Grant smiled and freed another brick before turning around to face Jonathan.

He found himself shaking his head. Jonathan seemed afraid of holding his gaze. Instead of looking him in the eye, he scanned everything around him as he drew nearer. He carried his weapons; a long demolition bar at the ready in his hand, and chains wrapped around his leathers. All of it was black—it was as though the man knew exactly what he was and made no effort to hide it. When Jonathan was a few paces away, he slowed, studying the bright white glow emanating from Grant's chest as he came to a stop. The man's brow furrowed as he finally met Grant's gaze. There was worry there, fear, like a vampire seeing the sun rise.

Grant gave him a half-grin as he crushed the last brick in his hand, letting the debris fall to his feet.

I'm not the one who looks worried, am I Tibbs?

There was a moment of silence as Grant waited, but before Jonathan spoke, his expression seemed to became unreadable as though hidden by a wall.

"How?" Jonathan asked.

Grant grinned, wiping the brick dust off his hands. "It's a long story, Tibbs. Frankly, I don't know that you'll live long enough to hear it."

He watched Jonathan tense, his eyes narrowing as his grip tightened on the staff. "Grant?" he asked. "What have you done?"

Grant raised an eyebrow just as the telling thunder of the Alpha Ferox's heavy frame landed on the roof behind Jonathan. Alarm turned to action on instinct, and Jonathan dropped into a balanced stance and pivoted, bringing the demolition bar toward the danger behind him.

The weapon came to a stop with a thunderous clap that knocked Jonathan off balance. Grant watched as Jonathan stood beneath Malkier's massive shadow, eyes roving up the beast's torso and stopping to linger on its scarred face. He waited for the invigorating moment when the wall Jonathan erected to hide his thoughts would begin to shake and crumble.

When the Alpha Ferox spoke, the words seemed to shock Jonathan, as though he didn't expect the creature could speak.

"There will be no more *echoes*," Malkier said.

There was a stillness that followed the alien's words, enough time for Jonathan to voice a single: "Rylee…Run—!"

With alarming speed and strength, Malkier pulled the demolition bar toward him and stepped forward, striking into Jonathan's chest. The result was devastating. Grant felt the percussion against his ear-drums before the space Jonathan had occupied became empty. A series of crashes followed before Grant turned to see that part of the roof's retaining wall had been demolished. The building across the street had a hole in it where Jonathan's body had shot through.

The sounds of brick hitting concrete below finally reached them. It was followed by screams, tires screeching, and collisions on the street below. Grant slowly turned back to face Malkier, his face somewhere between awe and horror. The alien held Jonathan's weapon, looking down at it with disgust in his white slits.

"This," Malkier said. "This was what he drove through my son when he ripped out his insides."

He dropped the demolition bar at Grant's feet. Unsure, Grant reached down slowly to pick it up.

"The inscription in the center," Malkier said. "What does it mean?"

Feeling the urgency in Malkier's request, Grant turned the weapon over, studying the engraving of Excali-bar in the steel. His face drew wary. His mouth opened, but self-preservation halted him. He didn't want to explain to the most powerful being he'd ever encounter that the weapon that took his son's life was named with a pun. A really bad pun.

"Human," Malkier said. "I have no patience for you stammering."

"I'm sorry," Grant said. "It's a play on words—it's named after a sword, Excalibur. He's made a joke out of it. Changed the spelling..."

He trailed off to look at the floor as the Alpha Ferox's rage made his body shake. Yet, when Malkier spoke, his instructions were a relative whisper to his normal tone.

"If he still lives," he said. "Run this joke through his heart. He deserves the same dignity he gave my son."

Grant nodded.

"The female approached with him," Malkier continued. "I will see that she is removed. Do not return to me without his corpse."

Malkier bounded to a roof top above them without another word. Grant turned his attention to the hole that had swallowed Jonathan and grinned.

Finally, off my leash...

The horror of what she'd just seen seemed to hold Rylee in place. She didn't feel she could move until the massive beast came barreling toward her from the building below and Jonathan's desperate scream registered in her mind.

Rylee, run!

She leapt backwards from the wall, retreating as the monster landed, the weight of the thing shaking the entire rooftop. She'd never seen one, but knew immediately what she was looking at.

Alpha.

There was no other explanation for the creature in front of her—if this thing was a Ferox, it was the damn Schwarzenegger of Feroxes. It shouldn't have been possible—should not be here. Jonathan had told her the rules he knew, and this broke the terms of the alien's agreement. The Ferox, they had always been terribly powerful, but what she'd just seen happen to *Jonathan…*

Was there any hope he could have survived that blow? She'd felt the impact, heard it like thunder. Her worried thoughts halted as she saw that the awful beast was studying her. It rose to its full height, straightening its back to stand like a man.

"So, this is the mated pair…" The Alpha paused. "For a few moments longer, at least."

Rylee flinched, not able to hide the disturbing chill that passed through her when the Alpha threatened her in English. Where would it learn a human language? And why couldn't she feel this thing in her mind? Rylee and Jonathan had both been able to feel the presence of the man, but she still couldn't sense this thing standing right in front of her. The Alpha had known—expected her and Jonathan to trust the instincts of their devices and knew that they wouldn't feel it coming when it attacked.

"You're no Ferox." Rylee's voice was far less steady than she would have hoped. "What are you?"

The Alpha tilted its head briefly before taking a step, but not toward her—it began to pace thoughtfully in a circle around her. "I think you know, human," it said. "In fact, I think you know far more than you should. My brother has overstepped his bounds with his… favorites."

Rylee swallowed. "Malkier."

The Alpha nodded. "Your candidness is wise, human," he said. "I cannot reward it with your life, but it will earn you a swift death."

Threatened again, Rylee clenched her jaw in an effort to keep fear off her face—but she could see that if she didn't move, the distance between her and Malkier would shrink, so she stepped in to circle with him.

"You're wrong, about your brother," she said. "I am no favorite of his."

Malkier groaned as he paced, a moment passing before he spoke. "I wonder, did my brother say this to you, or have you assumed?"

Her eyes narrowed at the question, and the monster seemed to grin knowingly when the question gave her pause.

"Curious," Malkier said. "You have my name—what should I call you?"

"Your people call me..." Rylee paused, found that despite her fear, she still had enough room to feel annoyed when she spat out the word: "*Slug...*"

If Malkier picked up on the tone she'd used, it didn't show when he responded. "Well, *Slug*, I have to wonder… that implant—do you know that it doesn't wish to be inside you?" he asked. "I've yet to see so pathetic a compatibility. It hardly seems able to function in you."

"Well, crap," Rylee said. "I'd be offended, but the feeling is mutual."

He seemed fascinated by her claim. "Interesting—you do not wish to be a part of humanity's last stand? Your node has been active longer than most."

"Is that supposed to be a question?" Rylee asked. "Because if you are trying to make a point, I missed it."

Malkier continued to pace. "Heyer is now my prisoner, and he will remain as such until I know what to do about his treason. Whatever role he intended to play, he is no longer able to assist Mankind."

The moment Malkier had shared his identity, Rylee had, unconsciously, been hoping for Heyer to intervene. Not for her, never for her—but because she figured he wouldn't abandon Jonathan. Knowing that the alien was unable to help them, Rylee felt an icy despair pierce her. They were truly alone.

That despair lasted no more than a moment before she consumed it with anger. Fire melted it off her, ignited from the unlikeliest of fuels. Jonathan, he was still alive—she knew it. He had to live through this—nothing else could explain what he'd said to her. That could only mean that she was right. She'd never allowed herself to depend on the alien to save her from a damn thing. Why the hell would she start now?

"Do you want me to congratulate you?" Rylee asked.

Malkier slowed his pace, a new intensity in his eyes before he spoke. "My brother, he was afraid for me," he said, a nonchalance in his voice that Rylee wasn't buying. "Seemed truly convinced that your friend posed a threat to me."

Rylee glared at him, unconvinced. "If that was true, why would he tell you?"

"That is not for you to know, I'm afraid," Malkier said. "But, despite my brother's misplaced loyalty to your species, he is not a fool. Rather, he is careful, precise... calculating. So you see, you are a bit of an enigma."

Rylee exhaled—loudly. "I don't know what you find so fascinating," she said. "So spell it out, before I get it in my head that you're stalling."

Malkier stopped pacing, and Rylee halted, preparing herself for anything.

"If my brother believed the bonded pair a weapon against me," Malkier said, "why did he implant the female half into a human virtually incapable of utilizing its potential? Why force it on a girl who doesn't want it?"

Hearing the question, Rylee worried she knew the answer. Malkier, he was stalling. He was looking for some tactic hidden beneath the surface of her implantation, trying to find genius when there had only ever been desperation. Rylee understood Heyer's choice then. She was it, there simply hadn't been anyone else—but there still had to be someone.

She took in a long breath. There was no reason to relieve Malkier of his reservations. Nothing to be gained telling him he was looking for something where there was nothing to find. "Guess that is not for you to know," Rylee echoed.

The alien stared back at her, and then closed his eyes for a moment before he spoke. "So much for your swift death, *Slug*," he murmured.

"Any last words for my brother? I'll be sure he hears them when I bring him your corpse."

Rylee shook her head. "Do you know what a d-bag is, Malkier?" she asked.

Malkier's eyes narrowed. He didn't answer, but she doubted human slang was in his vocabulary.

"No? Well, doesn't matter. Just tell Heyer that..." Rylee paused before committing. "If he had only told me the truth—told me how much of a d-bag his brother was—things could have gone another way."

Jonathan's hand emerged from a pile of rubble and found the floor intact. The reinforced cement wall had finally managed to stop him, but most of what endured the collision had crumbled down on top of him when he hit the floor. He felt the weight of the debris rolling off him as he got to his hands and knees.

He staggered to his feet, into a thinning cloud of dust from the collapsed wall—dust that seemed to cover him like ash. He could hear wind and rain outside mixing with the familiar sound of damaged, arcing electrical wires as the lights above him flickered. Soon, these noises became background to the chaos of shocked pedestrians screaming in fear as they ran to get clear of the falling rubble on the streets below. He found his balance was off-kilter, his body not yet ready to support him. He leaned against the nearest wall to steady himself and attempted to clear his head.

A broken chunk of ceiling gave way and fell to the floor before him. He looked out in front of him then, and saw the trail of destruction he had made. There was a gaping hole across the street, where he'd punched through brick and drywall before crashing through the window of this office building.

He shouldn't be breathing and he knew it.

The device had never seen him though anything of this magnitude—he'd never dreamed he could walk away from such abuse. The chain and armor around his torso had helped, but he knew that wasn't the half of it. Dumb luck had saved him. Right before that massive beast had slammed into him, he'd had one primal realization: Rylee's life was in danger.

He should have been a pile of broken bones under the rubble he'd just crawled out of, but strength had surged into him, erupting out of that visceral fear. Their bond was the only reason he stood. Yet, he didn't know how to hold onto that strength; it seemed to diminish, fade away as he understood the source of it. It was as though his thinking mind was now a wall between him and the very strength that had allowed him to survive.

Thinking of it now, fear spiked in him. He felt his senses coming back into sharper focus. She was alone and that Alpha Ferox from his nightmares was out there. It had spoken to him, not through the translation of the device, but in the same monstrous dialect of English as it had in his dream. How could he have known the Alpha was capable of that?

He remembered the Alpha's last words from the dream: *"Your anger will never be enough."*

Jonathan's mind piled up with questions, but he pushed them away. There wasn't time to sit here, thinking, while Rylee might be on the run from that thing.

If she listened, he thought. *Please, just let her have listened.*

Awareness of incoming danger suddenly screamed to him, adrenaline blanking out his thoughts as instincts reacted to the signal rocketing toward him. He pushed away from the wall, careening through a nest of cubicles as Grant shot through the broken window, wielding Excali-bar like a sledge hammer. Jonathan rolled with his momentum and spun, getting to his knees in time to see Grant put a hole in the floor where he had been standing. The man's furious eyes turned to find him.

"What the hell are you doing?" Jonathan yelled.

Grant answered with a growl as he charged with Excali-bar held like a battering ram between his hands. Comprehension took a back seat to survival, and Jonathan launched forward to stop him. Their momentum brought them to a halt when his hand grabbed hold of the staff.

He pivoted, swinging Grant into part of the concrete still standing behind him. The wall caved in around Grant's shoulders, and if the man had been hurt, he seemed too focused to care.

"That all ya got, Tibbs?" Grant snarled through gritted teeth, and brought his full strength to bear, thrusting Jonathan back. Not having expected to find his strength outmatched, Jonathan was caught off guard when he didn't have the force to keep his opponent pinned into the wall. As he held tight and grappled for leverage, Grant suddenly swung their weight. The concrete gave as Jonathan's back rammed into the wall, their bodies punching through into a hallway on the other side and toppling over one another.

Rolling, Jonathan managed to maneuver himself on top of Grant, Excali-bar still between them. Even from the floor, he felt Grant pushing him away.

"Dammit, Grant! I don't have time for this."

"*Don't have time*?" he ground out, spittle flying from his mouth. Grant's eyes blazed with rage, and suddenly, he shifted the weight to one arm while releasing it in the other. Jonathan was struck hard on the temple, and his strength gave way at the abrupt shock of pain. Grant seized on the opportunity, bringing the other end of the bar around to connect with Jonathan's skull. Dizzied from the blows, finding he couldn't get his head to command his body, Jonathan fell back onto the floor.

Grant rolled before getting to his feet, fast, and took hold of the chain wrapped around Jonathan's torso. The man had control of him, pulling him up and swinging him around before throwing him down the length of the hallway, where he slammed into a corner wall.

"Think you better pencil me in," Grant said, chuckling to himself. "I've had this appointment on my calendar for a while now."

Jonathan steadied himself and, looking down the hall, saw two images of Grant coming toward him. He struggled to resolve them into one in his vision. "Probably should have made it with a therapist," Jonathan managed.

"That's funny, Tibbs! You're being so damn clueless. It does make kicking your ass rather… therapeutic."

Jonathan leaned on the wall, using it to push himself up on his feet. "Well, if you're on the verge of a damn breakthrough," he said, "perhaps you could enlighten me?"

The smile fell off Grant's face, and his voice grew low. "Everything you are, you took from me."

Jonathan's vision solidified into a single man coming for him. "In that case, I guess I'll have to update the diagnosis," he said, shaking his head. "From asshole... to certifiable asshole."

The words brought a villainous smile back to Grant's face before he closed the distance remaining between them, raising Excali-bar overhead to crush Jonathan's skull.

Jonathan held his ground, waited until the bar was coming down on him before he raised his forearm and braced for the impact. Alien steel hit alien steel, and the clang rang though the hallway as the armored plate in the forearm of Jonathan's jacket brought the weapon to an abrupt halt. The floor beneath his boots cracked, threatening to give in and collapse where he stood, as Jonathan gritted his teeth and dropped to one knee.

Taking the blow hurt, but he'd known it was coming, while Grant had expected a wholly different outcome. The intense vibration running through the staff back into his hands was a shock, and what he had expected to be a devastating strike hadn't phased Jonathan's arm in the least. Grant had hardly registered the disappointment when Jonathan exploded out of his crouch and drove his fist straight into Grant's chin. It connected cleanly, and Jonathan followed through, sending Grant face-first through the roof of the building.

With nothing to stop him, Grant shot out into the open air, leaving Jonathan only a split second to make a difficult call. Maddening as it was, Grant had to be taken out of the equation. He couldn't begin to help Rylee with that Alpha if Grant was on his heels. He had to be incapacitated as quickly as possible.

"Dammit!" He exhaled the word as he launched himself through the ceiling after Grant.

CHAPTER SIXTY-TWO

RYLEE DOVE FROM the roof and ping-ponged her way down the alley just as one of Malkier's attacks broke the upper corner of the building free. The resultant debris pelted her body with shrapnel as it crashed down beside her, bouncing off her skin and armor.

She'd stood her ground against him long enough to see the futility in fighting him. Somersaulting out of the way of his initial attack, she'd kept her body a constantly-moving target. When he'd overextended himself, his powerful claw going wide as he'd reached to grab hold of her, she'd leaped above his grasp, pulling *Themyscira* from her jacket and bearing down with strikes that had first struck his face then his knee cap. Rylee had spun from his counterattack, and clipped the back of his thigh before jumping out of reach.

She may as well have been trying to cut down a tree with a nerf gun—the bastard had hardly flinched. Even if Malkier stood still and let her give him her best shot, she doubted she could hurt him. If beating him to death with the rattan wasn't going to get the job done, she had to find another way.

Jonathan's last words echoed: *Rylee, run!*

Half a block in front of her, a parked van seemed to implode in on itself, its windows exploding into shards as the street rumbled beneath her. She staggered as she brought herself to a stop, seeing Malkier stand up from within the remains of the flattened vehicle.

"Must we continue this?" he asked as he stepped out of the wreckage onto the street. "Your ally is surely dead by now. How do you imagine this ends, human?"

Rylee kept the fear restrained, didn't allow herself to falter at Malkier's certainty that Jonathan was dead. She didn't believe that his life could be extinguished without her knowing. Still, if he lived, he'd have to be a broken mess now—not in any condition to defend himself. Even if she underestimated Jonathan and he was on his feet, what chance was there that he would fare any better against this Alpha? The siren's call of despair held sway over her for the briefest of moments.

He's alive, dammit, Rylee thought. *I have got to keep this bastard's attention. If they tag team either of us, it's over.*

She turned to bolt in the opposite direction, resolved to give Malkier the chase of his life, but as she spun, her attention was drawn by a sudden hard change from Grant's signal in her mind. There was a distant thud of impact, and her eyes shot into the air to see a man's body shoot out over a building five or six blocks from where she stood. Even from such distance, she knew it wasn't Jonathan she'd just seen knocked across the skyline. It was a beacon screaming out to her not to waver. She didn't know how he was on his feet, but Jonathan was alive. If he still had the will to fight after what he'd endured, she'd be damned if this alien asshole was going to convince her to make this the slightest bit easier.

She smiled as she turned back to Malkier, catching his attention drawn to the spectacle above them as well.

"Not bad for a dead guy," Rylee yelled.

She was in motion before Malkier's angered expression had fully formed on his Feroxian features. She heard the crash of his monstrous steps as they tore through traffic in pursuit behind her.

Her plan had taken shape, and it was simple. If she could keep Malkier busy as long as possible, she might wear him down with exhaustion. After that, she and Jonathan could take him down together. Right now, she just had to hope Jonathan didn't do something stupid.

Like dying without her permission.

Jonathan leaped onto the rooftop just as Grant was getting to his feet.

Grant watched him, reaching for his jaw, wiggling it back and forth before he spat a blood-soaked molar on to the tar and gravel roof.

"Well, that's the spirit," Grant said.

"You're not leaving me a lot of options here, Grant. Help me or get the hell out of the way."

Grant had been staring at Jonathan with open disgust, but the idea of an alliance only added a mocking chuckle. "Oh, look at you," he said, his voice taking on a high-pitched, whiny tone as he mimicked Jonathan: "*Grant, we gotta go save the girl.*"

Jonathan didn't know what to say, just stared back, unable to believe the man was what he appeared.

"Tell me, Tibbs, 'cause I just really want to know. Someone tells you that you're this big secret weapon in a war for Mankind," Grant said. "And the first thing you do is go out and kill the son of the biggest badass in existence." He whistled. "Ballsy, I'll give you that. But maybe diplomacy isn't really your thing."

Jonathan shook his head. "Grant, how can you possibly know all that and still be doing what you are doing? Our world fights a war, and you choose the other side."

Grant looked at Excali-bar, still in his hand after being knocked across the skyline. He extended his arm and dropped the weapon to the roof, then stepped over it toward Jonathan.

"Our world?" Grant asked, lifting his hands as though he were pointing to everything around them. "This is my world," he said. "Life, it doesn't last so long here, but that's okay, because today is my day—I don't need a lifetime to see you fail."

Jonathan shook his head. There wasn't any question—Grant's shadow had deteriorated, was insane, and Jonathan was done trying to reason with insanity. "Every day, some asshole tries to kill me, Grant," he said. "So you'll have to forgive me if today just doesn't feel special."

Grant stopped smiling, the smugness erased from his face. Jonathan's dismissal of this moment was making him shake with anger. Grant had been right—diplomacy was not his thing.

"What's her name? Rylee?" he asked. "She's gonna die today, and when I'm done with you, I'm going to visit every damn one of these sluts who protected you! That government bitch, your roommate, the red head... Leah?"

Jonathan closed his eyes. He'd never had to consider killing another human being, never imagined what would give him a reason to want to—his imagination never dreamed up Grant. It didn't matter that this man was threatening temporary copies—that the real people would never know what Grant wanted to inflict on them. Jonathan took a deep breath. He let himself go. When he opened his eyes, the killer was waiting behind them.

Grant's eyes widened in sudden anticipation as he stepped forward, and Jonathan took his first step to meet him.

"Finally," the shadow said, accelerating into a charge.

They met in the center. A rabid, over-eager fist went wide of Jonathan as he dodged, taking hold of Grant's arm and swinging his momentum against him. He let go, sent Grant crashing into a metal ventilation unit that crumpled in around him. He charged in to exploit the throw, but Grant surprised him, pulling out of the wrecked metal and getting hold of Jonathan's shoulder and chain, using the leverage to lift Jonathan up, over, and down.

Jonathan's body broke through the roof, landing on his back on the floor below. Grant was not long to follow, dropping in after him. They were in an open flat that was under renovation. Construction supplies and equipment laid in various stages of use, plastic sheeting still lining unfinished walls. Grant was on him before he could get to his feet, thrusting his foot hard into his gut. The kick lifted him off the floor and put him through a half-finished wall. Jonathan only came to a halt when he hit a pallet of masonry bags. The mortar dust erupted around him as he rolled through the top layer, falling off the pallet onto a half-used stack of bricks.

Though the dust left him partially blinded, he could feel Grant's signal coming straight for him. His hand gripped one of the loose bricks beneath him, and he trusted his instincts as he brought the brick around hard. When Grant leaped into the dust and landed on top of what remained of the mortar bags, the brick dissolved against the side of Grant's head.

He grunted in stunned pain and Jonathan capitalized on it, grabbing one of the man's legs, taking him off his feet and swinging him into a wall further behind them. He followed the signal, running and thrusting his shoulder into Grant as he emerged out of the cloud into clear air. He connected with Grant, rammed his body back into the wall, and put him back into it as he rebounded.

Jonathan landed a series of blows that caved the brick in as Grant absorbed them. Growling, the man finally got his wits back, ducking under a strike aimed for his head. Jonathan felt his fist punch into the brick as Grant burst forward, tackling him. They landed in one of the open spaces of the flat, locked in pure rage as they rolled into the center.

CHAPTER SIXTY-THREE

RYLEE'S FEET TOUCHED the wall and she pushed up and away as a car flattened itself against the building below her. She pivoted in the air, finding Malkier still in pursuit, and picking up a motorcycle parked on the street as though they were playing a high-stakes game of dodgeball. She flipped into a landing and dove to the opposite sidewalk as the motorcycle lodged itself into the flattened car that had missed her a moment earlier.

The crowds fleeing around her were filled with frightened faces and people abandoning their vehicles in the gridlocked traffic to get as far away from the rampaging beast as they could. She rolled onto her feet, finding the monster was already coming for her. Malkier, seeing he had her attention, plucked a woman off the street as she ran.

The woman screamed in fear, but even if someone in the scrambling mobs might have had the bravery to try and help her, the screams were lost in the cacophony. Malkier's gaze stayed on Rylee. He had no pity or regard for the life he held—only calculation. Then he drove the woman into the sidewalk without ever taking his eyes off Rylee.

Since her first activation, she'd never been so powerless to stop one of the Ferox. The last time she'd let someone be killed right in front of her, the life had been her father's. Rylee turned away; she couldn't allow Malkier to use the lives around them to get into her head. She ran, knowing not to give her attention to him long enough that he'd have time to bother repeating the psychological attack.

She bounded away, trying not to let the image of the terrified woman into her thoughts, and turned a corner. She kept her mind focused on circling the signal of the man that had gone after Jonathan. Though her implant gave her a far greater endurance than a human, she was by no means immune to exhaustion. Malkier wasn't showing signs of slowing down—and she knew she couldn't keep this up forever. Rylee pleaded in her mind for Jonathan to hurry.

She heard the crash of a wall coming down behind her, and she shot away as Malkier erupted from within the building, having never changed his course but instead taken a straight line to her. Nothing was an obstacle, nothing slowed him down, and it made keeping distance between them far more difficult. The only thing keeping her alive was making sure he never reached her, and she had to buy as much time as it took. So she kept running.

Jonathan hit the floor and heard Grant's body do the same. He rolled back on his feet, starting to feel his legs losing their swiftness. It seemed that no matter how much damage he inflicted, the man kept coming as though he had a boundless well of energy that couldn't be worn down. Meanwhile, Jonathan was beginning to feel his muscles slow, his reactions dull. He saw Grant's vicious expression turning, taking on an ugly smile as he seemed to realize the same.

"Someone's getting tired," he said.

Jonathan growled, launching for the man, landing a series of punches. He saw the pain registering on Grant's face, but the man just kept smiling. He recovered too quickly. If he didn't find a way to hurt Grant—badly enough to break something—he would exhaust himself before Grant ever stopped coming for him.

He knocked Grant against a wall, pummeling him, roaring as anger started to become frustration, until Grant got hold of his arm as he brought it in for another blow. Jonathan couldn't regain the leverage before Grant pulled him in, his forehead crashing into Jonathan's face.

Jonathan staggered back, dizzy and unable to clear his vision as more punches seemed to land down on him. The barrage only ended when a kick threw him across the room. He hit the smooth pavement, his body sliding across the floor. As he still tried to clear his head, the signal rushed toward him, and he felt Grant grab hold of his neck before he had fully gotten to his feet. He lifted Jonathan from the ground, only to throw him back down against it.

Jonathan tried again to get to his feet, and Grant kicked him in the gut. Blood shot out of his mouth and slapped against the floor in front of him.

"That about it then, Tibbs?" He reached down and hauled Jonathan up onto his feet. "Yeah," Grant said, tilting his head. "You look like you're just about ready."

Grant smiled for a moment before he stepped into him, pushing Jonathan away. His body rolled at first, then slid across the smooth cement like a puck across a shuffleboard. Unable to find anything to hold onto, he tried pressing his palms against the floor seeking any friction that would slow him. Then, abruptly, there was nothing beneath him. His fingers found a grip at the ledge of a drop off, barely stopping him before his body plummeted down.

For a moment, Jonathan looked into nothing but darkness below him. Grant had pushed him toward some shaft, and the light from the flat didn't reach far. He could see where the sides of brick walls faded into what seemed like an empty abyss. His battered body aching, he reached up with his other hand and pulled himself back toward the light.

When his head came back above the floor, Grant was waiting. He'd found a sledge hammer as he walked over to the shaft and had the wooden handle gripped in one hand, the heavy metal head swaying lightly against his shoe as he stared down at him.

"Hey, Jonathan," Grant said, "When you get to Hell, and you see your dad, make sure you tell him who sent you."

There was nothing he could do. Grant wielded the hammer as though he was sinking a golf ball with a putter. Jonathan heard the crack, but didn't feel the pain when it connected. His hands went limp and he felt himself falling—everything going black.

CHAPTER SIXTY-FOUR

JONATHAN WAS ON the ground, his limbs laid out awkwardly around the rubble that had come down with him. His stomach felt as though it hadn't yet realized he'd stopped falling. When he opened his eyes, he found he had crashed through the floor at the bottom of the shaft, punched down into some type of basement beneath. He couldn't make out much—the only light came from the opening high above. That, and when he had struck the ground, he had disturbed the ancient dust of this place, and it was still a cloud around him. He heard old wooden boards falling to the ground as he managed to get on his feet.

His legs were wobbly. The floor felt almost like liquid, and he reached out in the dark for something solid. His fingertips brushed across a brick and mortar wall behind him.

Needing light, he reached for the zipper on his jacket, pulling it open and allowing the glow of his chest to escape. With some confusion, he realized that Doomsday had not been in the way—he didn't feel the weight of the chain wrapped around his torso. It was strange... he couldn't remember having lost it.

As the light touched his surroundings, he saw that he stood in an underground passage—a part of the city that had been built over and forgotten. He'd heard about these tunnels beneath the city. People called them the Seattle Underground. An awareness quickly came to him, and foreboding began to press in at the edges of this thoughts. Nothing about what he saw felt true. He wasn't really here—he wasn't really anywhere.

Rylee doesn't have time for me to be unconscious, he thought. *She sure as hell doesn't have time for me to be dead.*

He heard small footsteps running toward him then, somewhere down the passage, outside of where his light allowed him to see.

"Jonathan," a young girl's voice whispered.

He peered into the dark, seeing the pink coat before Jess's face came out of the dark. "Jess," he said. "I… I can't be here now."

She came close, reaching out for his sleeve and trying to pull him in the direction she'd come.

"No time," he said. "I have to go now."

She shook her head in frustration as she tugged on him. "Please," she whimpered. "You can't leave me. I don't know what to do."

He faltered at the fear in the child's voice, began to fill with indecision. He didn't want to abandon her. Not Jess—not again. "I'll come back," he finally said. "I have to help my friend. She doesn't have much time…"

The little girl shook her head, pleading that he was wrong. "No, time…" She struggled, the fear making it difficult for her to explain. "You have to believe me. Time isn't the same in here."

She tugged on him again, only to be reminded that she didn't have the weight to budge him. Tears were beginning to form in her eyes—he saw her starting to give up on him. He couldn't bear the thought that Jess was so afraid he'd leave her.

"Okay, Jess—don't cry, I believe you," Jonathan said. "I won't leave you alone, I promise."

He let her pull him along, and she followed a seemingly endless stretch of brick wall. In the dark, it was as though they walked along the perimeter of the only solid shape that existed—as though the light from his chest was the only light that had ever touched this place. Finally, something metal caught his eye ahead, and as they drew closer, Jonathan recognized the vault door. The armory? The place where Heyer stored the dormant implants. It was here, exactly how it had appeared when he'd seen it inside of Mr. Clean.

Seeing where she meant for him to go, Jonathan froze in place. Jess, still pulling, swung around when her arm was wrenched by his sudden stop. Jonathan trembled, his feet becoming anchors unwilling to take another step. The door—it was open, only enough that Jess could enter easily. If he had to go inside, he would have to turn sideways and push himself through.

"Jess, am I..." Jonathan paused, his voice trembling. "Am I dead?"

"You haven't hit bottom yet," she said, stepping into the darkness on the other side of the door. "You're still falling."

He blinked at her, reluctant to move as she pulled on his sleeve once more. "Jess... it was a yes no question."

The little girl turned and studied his face, confused by his statement.

"Why..." Jonathan swallowed as he looked over her, trying to make out something other than darkness on the other side. "Why does it have to be in there?"

"You're unconscious," Jess said. "Don't you know I can't trick you?"

She let go of his sleeve and stepped further inside the door. The darkness on the other side absorbed her, became a wall his light could not penetrate.

"Jess," Jonathan said, hearing the tremble in his voice. "Wait."

No answer came from within—and the silence chilled him. There was no noise, nothing.

"Jess!"

The pitch black seemed to swallow the sound just as it had the girl. Not even an echo came from beyond the door, as though nothing existed inside. He closed his eyes, gritting his teeth as he realized he had refused to abandon her. This fear would keep him from entering, and every second it held him there would take him closer to the moment when any choice to act would be taken away from him. Jonathan found his breath quickening, trying to find the courage to follow her into the unknown.

It's like I am watching you walk off into the dark. I see you alone in an empty, black place, Leah had said to him. *I'd do anything to keep you from that place.*

He knew he'd done this to himself. He never wanted to fail anyone, but there was one being, one symbol, in existence that he could not bear to fail again. Now, she was forcing him to make a decision. There had to be a reason—it could be no coincidence, but it didn't matter, because he couldn't leave her to harm while he still breathed. He trembled, but he forced himself forward and started to slip into the darkness on the other side.

The moment he cleared the threshold, his boots touched a smooth, hard floor and he knew he was no longer in the dark. The air felt warmer, and as he opened his eyes, he saw that he stood in the storage room again. All his father's possessions were laid out around him. The glow from his chest gave off all the light he needed, and fresh memories from having visited this place the night before seemed to fill in the details that had been vague in all his dreams. Jess waited a few feet inside, looking marginally relieved that he had followed.

He turned back to the door, seeing it was still slightly ajar behind him—but now, he could see the hallway from where he had entered. This place... it was no longer cloaked in an impenetrable darkness. It was an illusion, only meant to appear as such when standing on the outside.

Jonathan knew, though he wasn't sure how, that he had entered a locked away place within his mind. That he had put up that wall. That he had made the only entrance a vault door that he feared. Yet, now that he stood inside, he felt no danger from this place. He didn't know why he had done this. What could he be so afraid of that he'd gone to so much effort to lock it behind such a barrier? The little girl studied him anxiously while he asked himself these questions, as though she read his thoughts and worried he would be angry with her.

"I didn't know what to do," Jess said.

He knelt in front of her, slowly putting his hands on her shoulders to comfort her. "Jess," he said gently. "Did you hide this place?"

Her lips quivered, but she nodded.

"Why?"

"Don't trust it," she said. "Don't know why it's here, what it wants. But there is nowhere else to go now."

Over the girl's shoulder, a light moved at the back of the room and caught his attention.

"Why?" Jonathan asked. "Why don't we trust it?"

Her eyes shined with tears as she stared back at him. "It isn't you. It shouldn't be here if it isn't you."

Jonathan looked back at her a moment before he nodded. "I'll take care of it," he said.

He stood and walked around the truck parked in the center of the room as Jess followed him.

"You can wait here," he said. "You don't have to come."

She shook her head. "I have to know what you decide."

He frowned, unsure what she meant, but kept walking. The light came from a man, his back turned to them as he stood with one hand resting atop the footlocker. The box remained where Jonathan had found it in reality. The man wore a blue-collar shirt and pants with brown boots. The faint glow of what could only be an alien implant embedded in his chest cast its light over the table. Jonathan came to a stop a few steps behind the man and Jess stepped aside. Quietly, she crawled onto the canvas covered hood of the truck to sit, watching the man with distrust.

"If you want to hear it," Jess said. "I can let it speak."

Jonathan stared at what he knew could only be his father and memories began to pry themselves lose. All those pieces he had been unable to isolate within the cluttered noise of his conscious mind. What Heyer had said to him months earlier—he remembered the words as though the alien were there, speaking them to him, now, for the first time.

With the assistance of artificial intelligence, it took me over ten years to make that one adjustment.

Douglas turned to him slowly as Jonathan began to grasp why he was here. His father had been taken from him by the Ferox ten years before. Jonathan had never been sentimental about dates, never had a reason to connect the two, not until he'd uncovered Doomsday hidden in the footlocker.

He remembered sitting beside the alien on a park bench.

It is not removable, Jonathan, Heyer had said. *I could not recover it without killing you.*

Jonathan looked down at the light on his chest. All those dreams, those visions of his father trying to help him. He'd believed them to be nothing more than his subconscious trying to comfort him.

The information about the state of your mind is applied. The result is, you retain the memory...

Finally, Jonathan spoke.

"The first time I saw you in my head was the night Heyer implanted the device."

He looked at the glow on his father's chest, the shape identical to his own.

"My device... it was yours," Jonathan said. "You've still been inside of it."

His father nodded once.

"Dad?" he asked. "Why didn't you tell me?"

Douglas grimaced, glancing at the little girl sitting on the truck with annoyance. Jonathan frowned for a moment before he understood.

"Let him speak, Jess."

The moment permission was given, a barrier he'd not previously perceived dissolved between them.

"Son," Douglas said. "It was never for lack of trying."

Hearing his father's voice left him at a loss for words. The sound comforted him in ways he hadn't expected. Douglas removed the old rag from his back pocket, wiping his hands as he began to explain.

"I didn't know what I was at first—that I had died. Ten years for you had gone by in an instant for me. I thought I was some kind of ghost before I started to make sense of where I was." He let out a short laugh. "I wasn't wrong. Depending on how you look at it."

Jonathan's face didn't hide the fact that he didn't understand while he watched Douglas put the rag back in his pocket.

"The last thing I remembered was being in the middle of a fight with a Ferox. An Alpha that had no place coming through the gates. It was unlike any I had encountered in a decade. My thoughts were of you and your mother when the reality that I was dying set in." Douglas looked away, flinching a bit as he dredged through his final memory in life. "There was this flash, white, a lot like when the gates close. I thought it was over… but things didn't turn out that way."

"You didn't cease to exist?" Jonathan asked.

"Well, fairly certain my body went to the Feroxian plane. My mind was a different story. The night Heyer implanted the device in you, I found myself drowning in thoughts and emotions that just didn't belong to me. I felt your presence, your heartbeat weakening, and your fear becoming my own. I could hear the old man speaking. When I heard him say your name, I realized he wasn't talking to me.

"I was helpless, though—you couldn't hear me. It's hard to describe what it's like to no longer have a mouth of your own. I kept trying to think my words at you," Douglas continued, tonguing his cheek. "Obviously, that didn't work. But the moment before your heart stopped, I suddenly had form. I found myself sitting beside you in our old Ford. Reliving this memory—you asking me for a dog, of all things."

Jonathan swallowed. "It has to be close. So close death can't tell you apart."

Douglas nodded. "I knew what Heyer had done, didn't know if I would get another chance," he said. "There was so little time, so much you needed to know, but it was the only thing I had time to say."

"It was enough. Those words saved my life."

Douglas swallowed, pursed his lips, and nodded. "When you lived through the implant, it took a while to understand how I'd reached you. Most of the time, I'd only see glimpses of your life. But, whenever the device was active, I was there, watching through your eyes." He swallowed again. "I could feel your abandonment… your anger. I saw you forge them into strength."

His father looked away, seeming to need a moment before continuing. Finally, he took a long breath.

"I didn't give up, though, and every once in a while, you gave me form again. When I finally figured it out, I felt like an idiot. It was when you dreamed—when you slipped into a memory we both shared, a moment from when I was alive. You could hear me and, slowly, I found that if I didn't push too hard, I could show you things."

"Those dreams," Jonathan said. "The tactics against the Ferox, things I couldn't have possibly known." He looked up suddenly. "The Alpha. You were trying to warn me."

Douglas's gaze was distant as he nodded. "There was a steep learning curve, figuring out how to reach you. If your mind became suspicious, realized I was showing you something that came from somewhere other than yourself…" He looked over at Jess and smirked. "I became a threat, and I got locked out."

"But, what changed? Why can you speak to me now?"

"I don't pretend to be an expert, but my guess is that you've been knocked unconscious while the implant is activated," Douglas said. "But…"

His father trailed off as he looked to the little girl on the truck's hood.

Finally, he said, "You've also come to a moment where your intuition no longer knows the rules. She is drowning in conflicts she can't resolve. You've convinced her she can't trust herself."

"She?" Jonathan asked, turning to study the little girl on the hood, as though suddenly able to see her with different eyes. "Are you saying my intuition…" He grimaced, shaking his head as he looked for the words. "Is a little girl in a pink hoodie?"

Douglas laughed. "Son, I've learned two things for sure, trying to understand your head," he said. "The first I already mentioned: There is nothing you distrust more than external influences trying to tell you what to do. If you suspect for a moment that you're being manipulated, you do everything you can to lock out the source."

Jonathan was watching Jess as his father explained. She shrugged, but nodded at him.

"Second, you give everything a damn face," Douglas said. "And you know, it's confusing as hell when you subconsciously decide to re-cast their roles."

Jonathan looked to the ground, his eyes wide as he let this sink in. "My intuition is a little girl in a pink hoodie," he repeated.

"Emasculating?" Douglas laughed. "Imagine it from my end—the last couple days, my every attempt to reach you has been thwarted by a 3rd grader."

Jonathan smiled, finding he couldn't help laughing at himself, and for a moment, everything happening in the waking world slipped out of his thoughts.

"You see what you want to, son," Douglas said. "The reality of Jess, alive and happy at that gym, gave you what you needed to start forgiving yourself for failing her that first night you entered The Never. She began to fade away as a symbol of your guilt after that—you turned her face into something you could still help. Frankly, I'm happy about the change. That zombie version of her gave me the creeps."

Jonathan nodded, though his expression became troubled as concerns resurfaced. "Why would Heyer hide who you were from me?" he asked.

He could see his father's expression grow bitter, and he sighed before he answered. "The old man always has his reasons. He's been waiting. I've seen it in the way he ponders your actions, looking for signs that you'd become aware…" Douglas trailed off, closing his eyes in frustration. "But he's the only one who can explain himself. You've learned, faster than I did, that getting angry at him is a waste of energy. So, if I were you, I'd resist the urge to deck him until you hear what he has to say. After that, you can decide if it's worth breaking your fist."

Jonathan smirked, but the humor was short-lived. His father was talking about the future as though he would have one.

"I guess we're pretending," Jonathan said, his face growing grim. "I've been telling myself I need to get back up, help Rylee, but even if I could, this fight is over for me. I'm not going to get the chance to ask Mr. Fedora anything."

Douglas's eyes grew heavy; his entire being more conflicted than Jonathan had ever seen him when he lived. Jonathan figured that he must have hoped they would avoid reality a bit longer.

"It's okay, Dad," Jonathan said. "This game... it was always rigged. I knew it never mattered how many times I won."

"Son, I know you're tired," Douglas said. "But do you truly wish this to be over?"

"What difference does it make?"

There was only compassion on Douglas's face, and he was careful when he spoke. "Jonathan, I know what it is to wake up each morning and secretly hope that today is the day that your best will just stop being good enough. So that you can fail the world knowing you never gave up. I know how that unspoken wish can taint every step forward."

Jonathan looked away, suddenly aware of just how well his father knew him.

"I've felt it growing heavier as you carry it, son, and there isn't any shame in it. Before your mother told me she was pregnant with you, I had carried it for quite a while."

Jonathan swallowed and turned to look at the wall, the vault door, then back to Jess. "My intuition was afraid of you, locked you in the dark because she knew you weren't a part of me," he said as he watched her. "That isn't all she put in here, is it? It's everything I tried to keep separate. Everything that was a part of me that I didn't want. Everything I tried to keep away from the people I cared about—it all got locked in here with you."

His father nodded. "Heyer never gave you a choice, son. The alien placed you on a road, knowing you would accept that someone had to walk it. You've never believed you were the right tool for the job, only that there was no one else."

"We don't need to talk about this," Jonathan said. "Yeah, a part of me wants to bow out. It doesn't change the fact that I lost."

"No, son," Douglas said finally. "You have decisions to make. Heyer… he tries to protect you from the complexity of it all, makes it seem that your only choice is whatever is best for Mankind. When he told you that you couldn't trust yourself, you believed him. You've been a train wreck of indecision ever since." Pain burdened Douglas's face and he trailed off. "But I am your father, and right now, I don't give a damn about anything other than what is best for my son. The one kindness I can give you is the time and space to make choices that are truly yours."

"What choices?" Jonathan asked. "You keep talking like what I decide now matters, but what decision can I make now that is going to change the fact that I'm unconscious and Grant is coming to stomp my head in?"

"You aren't done," Douglas said, his voice having grown louder than he'd meant. "Unless you want to be." He closed his eyes. "I see one path for you to make it through this, and every step of it is a decision you don't want to make. Every choice will have a cost. But I'm not going to make you endure another second of these decisions just because an alien says you don't have a choice."

Jonathan studied his father. There was no joy in his expression.

Whatever path he saw that Jonathan could not, his father truly didn't know if what it would take to live through the day was worse than death for him.

"Tell me how," he said. "And I'll make the damn decisions."

Slowly, his father nodded. "It's not easy to know where to begin," he said. "Some things will be far more difficult than others. Maybe it's best to start with what you already know you're avoiding."

At the corner of his vision, Jonathan saw Jess was no longer passively listening from the truck hood. Her attention had become unblinking, focused on Douglas—almost like he'd threatened her. Seeing the change in her, Jonathan realized that his intuition was reacting to his own reluctance to hear what his father had to say. He gently raised his hand up to her, shaking his head that she was not to intervene.

"You have weapons you aren't using, son," Douglas said. "You've only scratched the surface of the bond, tapped into it unconsciously as an act of desperation or a thoughtless reflex. It's like you're starting an engine and then refusing to give it gas."

Jonathan, feeling as though the statement was obvious, threw his hands up. "It's not that simple. If there was a switch I knew how to flip on and off—trust me, I would flip it."

"That's the problem," Douglas said. "The bond isn't a weapon like Excali-bar—it isn't designed to be picked up and put down when you're done with it. You have to let it become a permanent part of you. Surrender to it."

He closed his eyes and shook his head, "How am I supposed to do that?"

"Stop seeing a contradiction where there isn't one."

"Dad, I can't lie to myself and believe it."

"Youth," he said, shaking his head. "Son, ever notice how simple relationships seem when you are standing outside of them? It's only when you're involved that everything appears so damn complicated. Everyone tries to convince themselves that the truth is so hard to find whenever it fails to be what they want it to be."

Jonathan tongued the side of his cheek, letting his dad know how unhelpful he'd found the statement.

"How often do you watch your roommate fawning over Paige?" Douglas asked. "Do you find it a mystery that she doesn't seem to ever pick up on it?"

"Not a mystery, she doesn't see it because she doesn't want to..." Jonathan trailed off as he saw Douglas nodding at him knowingly.

"Look, the warning Heyer gave you about the bond's effects would have done a mind job on anyone. It gave you reason to be guarded against every feeling you had for Rylee, but instead of ignoring the bond's manipulations, you've been ignoring *everything*."

"How the hell..." Jonathan had raised his voice, but restrained himself. "How am I supposed to know what I should or shouldn't ignore?"

"I've seen how the bond is affecting you—the levers it pulls on," Douglas said. "You miss her and don't know why, you know in your core that you would protect her with your life, you want only for her to feel loved and safe. If you were a father, you would have recognized those feelings. Parents feel them when they stand over the cribs of their children."

Douglas tilted his head then, and smiled.

"But the bond didn't force you to respect her ingenuity, her brains, her skill as a fighter. It didn't make you laugh with her when she joked. And it certainly isn't forcing you to trust her. I don't think Heyer fully knew what he was talking about. The truth made you feel those things."

Jonathan's face was uncertain. "Dad, that can't explain... if the bond is manipulating me into feeling that she is my child, how could I possibly feel so much..." He grimaced, his head tilting awkwardly. "Tension?"

Douglas snorted at the question.

"Oh, that's funny?" Jonathan asked. "If you're right, it goes beyond disturbing."

His father shook his head. "Kid, relax. The implant might be able to pull on your parental instincts, but it can't brainwash you into seeing a daughter you know you don't have," he said. "As far as the 'tension' goes, I'm not convinced the bond can take all the credit—it hardly takes an alien implant for men your age to be blinded by completely normal hormones. It's a condition called having eyes."

Jonathan looked at his father as though he must be joking.

"Jonathan, every man you've introduced to Rylee has reacted to her," Douglas said. "Why would you be so different?"

Jonathan thought for a second before shaking his head. "No. Rylee said that when we first met it was as though we couldn't control ourselves."

"Maybe. But, for whatever reason, that hasn't been true for you. The moment you felt any affection for her, you became a conflicted mess—have hardly been able to make a decision about a damn thing since. You couldn't tell her to go—told yourself excuses and half-truths while you waited for it to be too late. You couldn't tell her about the bond—even though keeping her around forced you to resist it. Frankly, everything you've been doing contradicts itself."

"I..." Jonathan strained through the words. "Realize that."

"Do you?" Douglas asked. "Because if getting out of your own way is all it takes to get through this, you have to wonder: do you truly want to get through this?"

Jonathan thought about what his father had asked. It took a moment before he replied. "Rylee... she told me the truth—why she came here. Still, there was one thing she didn't say. I felt it, when our minds were bridged. It was vague at the time, but as I got to know her, I saw what was really killing her inside." Jonathan closed his eyes. "She needed something, anything, she could trust. The bond's effects tricked her into believing she'd found it. When I forgot her..."

Jonathan trailed off, closing his eyes, before he continued:

"The only difference between Rylee and I, is that I never had so much to lose. I think she was happy—happy in a way I've never truly felt—before Heyer took it all away from her. He hollowed her out. But finding something to trust, to hold onto, gave her something back. I couldn't take from her the one thing that seemed to..." He opened his eyes and found his father waiting. "Rylee wears joy like a mask now. But not when she looks at me."

A moment of silence followed, and Jonathan saw his father considering his words—growing skeptical.

"Hmm," Douglas said. "Here I was thinking this had more to do with the neighbor."

Jonathan's face became bitter as he looked away. "Just because I didn't want to hurt Rylee didn't mean I could be everything she wanted. I didn't want to hurt either of them." He gave a deflated shrug and closed his eyes.

"So, you resisted the bond," Douglas said. "Because what? You were afraid of the pain it would cause if you divided your affections? Or was it that you thought what you felt for Leah was real and what you felt for Rylee was manipulation?" He scratched his head. "I've got to be honest here kid... if it's the latter, I think you've got things ass-backwards."

"Yeah..."

He didn't want to look at Leah, was afraid of what he'd see if he put her under a microscope. It pained him enough that he'd run from it, wished he could go back to a time that he didn't have to think of her with doubt. His father waited, seeing that his son was not exactly leaning into the wind when it came to considering Leah wasn't what she seemed.

"You can't ignore *what she is* because it isn't what want you wanted her to be," Douglas said.

"Am I a fool?" Jonathan asked.

His father hesitated a moment before he spoke. "No. I admit, it was the little brother that made it hard to believe Leah was anything other than what she seemed. But you don't have the luxury of ignoring the signs now, son. Leah's photographing Rylee's journal, moving in next door only two days after you went to the hospital… and let's face it, she's been far too accommodating. She caught you in what appeared to be a straight lie about the girl sleeping in your bed, and she didn't demand an explanation?"

Douglas's words softened and slowed as he saw that every word was weighing on his son. "Jonathan, Leah makes a lot more sense when you look at her through the lens of an agent. She's just a little too attractive, too accepting, too perfect. You want to trust her because she's been buying that trust—being whatever you needed her to be from day one. You've seen how perceptive she is, how she always seems to see through you, always knows when you're holding back. Leah is..." He sighed. "Well, frankly, she is like a therapist probing at a patient.

"You say Rylee needed someone to trust? Leah saw the same weakness in you months ago. She's been trying to crack the lock on your vault by exploiting it ever since—but Jonathan, all she is after is what you've been hiding in here."

"Stop," Jonathan whispered.

"Jonathan," Douglas said tersely. "I know everything in you wants to give her the benefit of the doubt. But pull yourself outside of it all. Ask yourself what you would tell someone in your shoes."

"Enough. Look, I get why you are telling me this, and yeah, they're crap choices, and I've been ignoring them. But none of this is so unbearable that a father would weigh it against the life and death of his son."

Douglas pursed his lips, nodding before closing his eyes and letting out a long breath. "I guess you aren't the only one avoiding things."

When his father opened his eyes, he studied the vault door. Jonathan turned to look as well, found nothing about it had changed, and wondered why Douglas's gaze was suddenly lingering there.

"You know," his father said, "when I was first locked in here, I was roommates with all the anger you walled away. You used to be afraid of it—knew that if you gave it what it wanted, it would change you forever."

"I remember."

"But you let it out, took it as your ally—that was the cost paid to keep fighting. It was a first step, but I don't think Heyer realized how quickly this would all come to a head. He didn't have time to turn you into what he needs you to be."

"Dad?" Jonathan asked. "What are you saying?"

Douglas held up a hand, asking for patience. "It took Heyer years to break down the encryption that would have kept our minds apart. He didn't go to all the trouble so I could give you a pep talk," he said. "He did it because he wants me to tell you the one thing he couldn't. He doesn't understand—it won't be enough."

"Tell me what?"

"It was not long after I'd been implanted that Heyer took an interest in me. He said I had a rare talent for killing beasts—that he wanted to help me to see how far that talent could go. He spent years training me to engage the Ferox. After all that time, I believe, I was the old man's only real friend in the world. He isn't prone to emotion, but my death hurt him." Douglas swallowed, looking at the floor. "Friend or not, he needed something from me, and had I lived, the day was coming that he would ask it of me. I realized it the day he gave me that chain."

"Doomsday?" Jonathan asked.

"He never said it, not in words, but I knew him too well by then. Heyer needed a monster, a man deadly enough to kill his brother."

"He wasn't willing to do it himself?"

"Maybe that was a part of it—I can't say for sure. Malkier came through the gate without any warning. I didn't realize who he was, thought him an Alpha Ferox at first. I was suspicious, because I couldn't detect the presence of the portal stone—he'd cloaked it from my awareness somehow. But the first time I hit that bastard, I knew I wasn't dealing with a Ferox—not even an Alpha could be that powerful," Douglas said. "Knowing who he was didn't matter. Heyer had put all that time into me, but I was still no match. Anyway, when I died, whatever Heyer had planned fell apart." He looked at Jonathan, his eyes conflicted. "But... I never had anything near the strength you have, son."

Jonathan nodded, but didn't understand why his father was telling him these things. He held his questions, knowing his father would get there—that whatever he was getting at was hard for him to say.

"You see that?" Douglas pointed to the canvas covering the old truck. "I meant to give it to you, when you were old enough." He smiled sadly. "It was going to break down on you—give you all sorts of trouble. I wanted to teach you how to keep a car running."

Douglas walked to another canvas and Jonathan knew what lay beneath it before he'd even pulled the cover off. The truck's engine, suspended off the ground by a hoist.

"I didn't want to protect you from everything, Jonathan. There were problems I planned to put in front of you," he said.

He gripped the chains that held the engine in the air. Jonathan remembered how he had done the same as a child, on the day of Douglas's wake.

"I fought to stay alive because I'd had to hope I could keep the Ferox from being one of them. I partnered with Heyer, let him turn me into the monster he needed, because I wanted you to have a future you didn't have to fear. But no matter how many of them I killed…" His father trailed off as he let go of the chains. "I didn't have enough time to fix this for you. Now, the Borealis I failed to kill is coming for my son."

Jonathan saw the guilt in his father—knew that he felt he'd failed him. "Dad, I know you did everything you could."

"No." Douglas's eyes screwed shut, and he shook his head. "Just listen, son. He brought Grant here as an assassin. He tried to weaken you, to make sure Grant would succeed, but he doesn't want to engage you himself. Now, perhaps he fears a confrontation with you will lead to his fathering another child. But I don't think that is why he is keeping his distance."

"But why?"

"He is an Alpha Ferox with a Borealis implant just like Heyer's, he is thousands of years old—damn near invincible," Douglas said. "And I think he's afraid of you."

CHAPTER SIXTY-FIVE

JONATHAN STARED BACK at his father. After the one blow he'd taken from the Borealis, he was unable to imagine how Douglas could get the idea that Malkier feared him. Yet, there was something off. The alien was invincible for all intents and purposes. So, why would a father, hell bent on avenging the death of his son, go to so much trouble to give that satisfaction to someone else?

"Heyer said that *Echoes the Borealis*—you—hurt him," Jonathan said, his eyes narrowing. "You weren't prepared, didn't even have the bond... Are you saying that Heyer broke down the wall between your memories and mine because he didn't know how you did it?"

Douglas nodded knowingly, but suddenly, the world around them jarred violently, as though there had been an earthquake in his dreams. Douglas and Jonathan staggered, bracing themselves against whatever was available. As quickly as the rumbling started, it ended.

"We've hit something," Jess said. "You should finish if you want him to have any time to consider what you're offering."

Jonathan watched as his father nodded to the girl reluctantly. Douglas stepped past him, pulling up the canvas on the passenger side of the old truck and reaching through the open window. He took something small from the glove box.

"What is she talking about?" Jonathan asked.

Douglas opened his hand, revealing a key. It was ordinary brass, inconsequential, but his father looked at his palm as though it were weighed down with a heavy burden. Jonathan recognized that look. He'd seen it on Heyer many times. It was the face of a man who held *the ends* in his hand, but couldn't justify *the means.*

"I can't decide this for you," he said, a tear forming in his eye.

"Dad?"

"There are so many things I wanted to give you, Jonathan. But so many more that I would have died to protect you from. If there was any other way I could help you, I would never offer this to you," he said. "But it's the only thing I have that can give you a chance."

When it happens, if it happens, you won't need me to tell you. Heyer's words echoed through his thoughts as Jonathan began to understand. He turned without thinking, found himself staring at the brick wall, the vault door—the barriers he'd built to protect his loved ones from everything he had been forced to become. From the killer, from the monsters, from all the violence and lies.

As his eyes returned to the key in his father's palm, he remembered—of all things—Mr. Fletcher speaking to him.

It's smart that you want it safe, but if you plan on keeping a weapon around, make sure you find someone you trust who can teach you how to use it, the old man had said. *Until then, I wouldn't let anyone know you have it.*

Jonathan closed his eyes, knowing now, why his father was so conflicted, why he kept looking at the vault door. "In my head, I locked it all behind a wall," he said, taking a breath before turning his eyes to the workbench where his father's footlocker rested. "You locked it in the box."

"We aren't so different, son," Douglas said as he tapped his forehead. "There are experiences in this world that, once they are a part of you, can never be separated out. So you try to protect your loved ones from them. It seems that, in death, I'm forced to offer you everything I hid from you in life."

It began to fit—the alien's words. *I never said you were special.*

Heyer had spent years building his father into a weapon with a purpose. The night Douglas had died, the blueprints of his plan had lost their keystone. Still, Malkier had nearly been slain by the weapon he'd built. He knew the device would give the son a raw power he couldn't give the father...

Had the alien maintained the status quo as long as he could... because he didn't have a better alternative? After all, by the time Jonathan was old enough to matter, there was no guarantee it wouldn't already be too late. Would there be time to train him, give him the knowledge and experience that his father had?

How did you take the two pieces you needed, merge the strength and the knowledge—the father and the son—across a span of time? You needed a third piece, you needed something connected to both. You needed the device. You needed a...

"Trinity," he whispered.

Slowly, Jonathan raised his hand for the key, but Douglas hesitated.

"It is a lifetime of pain endured," he said. "Pain that will alter—taint—everything you are. There's no way to know if the man who opens his eyes will be much like you at all."

"Give me the key, Dad," Jonathan whispered. "I understand the decisions, I understand the consequences."

"You have to promise me that you aren't letting revenge push you to take this key. The memories in that box—they'll be fuel on the fire if your anger is making this decision for you. Jonathan—anger is not going to see you through this, not today."

He wavered as he considered his father's fear. It was undeniable that a fire had been lit inside him long ago, and now, knowing it started as a debt gone unpaid was only stoking those flames. Still, he hadn't been considering vengeance when he'd put his hand out for the key.

His face hardened, growing bitter with understanding. "No... revenge is the story that brought Malkier here for me. Today, it will be his weakness. I won't let it be mine."

Douglas studied him a moment before accepting the answer. "Well said." Douglas pushed the key into Jonathan's palm and embraced him. "Whatever you choose, I will be here."

For a moment, Jonathan held on, knowing they shared the same fears. If he opened the box or not, it was the last time Jonathan would hug his father as who he was—as only himself. When they parted,

Douglas stood aside and allowed Jonathan to walk by him. He didn't go to the box; he went to Jess and looked into her eyes.

"I doubted you, and it goes without saying that I've made mistakes," he said as he lifted his open palm to hold the key between them. "But I trust you now—and from here on out."

Jess bit her lower lip and watched him sympathetically. "Then ask yourself—what do you want from you?"

He looked down at the hand holding the key. "The part of me that wanted to fail... it came from knowing that I wasn't the right person—that I wasn't enough. But, if I can be the right tool..." He trailed off as Jess gently touched his cheek. "I want to be the solution to this problem."

She studied him—he studied himself—but not for long.

"Bring the rain," Jess whispered.

He nodded, shut his eyes, and slowly… his hand became a fist, tightening around the key.

CHAPTER SIXTY-SIX

GRANT WATCHED JONATHAN fall until he was out of sight. A moment later, he heard the crash of floorboards giving way below. He dropped the sledgehammer, leaning his head over the ledge and listening. Once the wreckage settled, the darkness grew still. It brought a smirk to the corner of his lips and he was about to retrieve the body when he remembered his instructions.

Run this joke through his heart. He deserves the same dignity he gave my son.

It was hardly too much trouble to oblige the bereaved father. Grant shrugged and strolled back to the hole they'd left in the ceiling. A moment later, he stood on the roof top holding Excali-bar in his hands. He liked the weight of it, the strength it promised—but the black coating needed to go. The staff would make a far more dashing accessory if it shined. It was as though Jonathan had tainted it on purpose, hidden the weapon's glory under a veil.

In the distance, he could hear the dull thuds of Malkier and Rylee. She was still quite alive if the noise was any indication. He doubted Malkier needed him to have a role in changing that, and he had to stop and take a moment for himself right now. He looked into the sky—the rain was coming down harder than it had all morning. He held Excali-bar over his head and finally felt the vindication he'd been owed for so long.

"I have the power!" he yelled to the city.

Grant smiled, laughing at himself. There was a pureness to his joy only found on the faces of children playing make believe.

A short time later, he crouched at the shaft's ledge again, pondering the dark silence. He was unsure if it was wise to simply drop when he didn't know if he'd be landing on sturdy ground, but the concern was short-lived. He had no reason to fear the fragility of the human condition. With the time he had remaining, he would live as far more than a man.

Stepping off the edge, he dropped after Jonathan's body, the light of his chest allowing him to see into some of the darkness. He saw the hole Jonathan had broken through into the basement, and as he hit ground, his momentum had the same effect. He found himself crashing through into a corridor and standing on the resultant rubble.

He waited for silence to return before he searched for the body.

Near the opposite wall was a telling pile of debris, the outline of a man under the rubble. As he approached, Grant heard a cough, and his eyebrow rose in surprise. Jonathan's head began to rise out of the debris, blood flowing from the wound that Grant's sledgehammer had put in his forehead.

Yes, he thought. *Get up, look me in the eye.*

Jonathan's eyes opened slowly, like that of a man coming out of a long sleep. At first, he seemed to be at a loss for where he was. Jonathan moved slowly, rose onto his knees, planting a fist on each side of him as he did so. He looked about the faintly lit corridor while Grant waited, eagerly watching for his eyes to find him standing there.

Yet, they didn't.

Jonathan shut his eyes and his head tilted, as though he'd heard something Grant could not and was trying to focus on the sound. A moment later, his eyes opened again, and he looked to the floor in front of him, seeming to simply stare through it. Blood began to run down Jonathan's forehead. It drew a red line between his eyes, until dripping to the floor from the edge of his nose, the red dots landing where Jonathan's gaze seemed so intensely focused. Seconds ticked away while Grant watched this pathetic confusion with growing impatience.

Dumb bastard probably has brain damage, Grant thought, finally stepping toward him.

No longer interested in waiting, he lifted Excali-bar over his shoulder, gripped like a spear with the tapered edge taking aim at Jonathan's heart.

"Tibbs," he said.

Jonathan didn't react, and as Grant studied his odd semi-conscious behavior, he started to see that Jonathan wasn't looking or hearing anything at all. He was like a man stuck in a daydream, completely focused on whatever was taking place in his head.

"Jonathan Tibbs!" Grant roared.

Finally, the bloodied man blinked, seeming to have some recognition of his own name at least. His gaze fell onto Grant's feet and, slowly, his headed lifted until his eyes met Grant's. Eagerness brought a smile to the shadow's face—he finally seemed to have the man's full attention.

Jonathan's expression changed slowly. His face molded into a picture of disgust before his eyes began to harden into the unblinking stare of a predator. Then, for no reason Grant could understand, Jonathan closed his eyes, drew in a long breath, and exhaled in a frustratingly slow and deliberate manner.

"I told you," Grant said, "this is how it would end."

Jonathan licked his lips before he opened his eyes again. A disturbing smile started to form at the edge of his lips. His pupils dilated like a junkie getting a fix as he slipped one hand off the ground to rest carelessly on his legs. Grant, feeling his perfect moment growing tarnished by Jonathan's sudden disturbing lack of concern, didn't waste his energy discerning what the man kneeling before him found amusing.

Let's see how long you smile with a length of steel through your chest.

Grant growled, and plunged down with Excali-bar, all his strength recklessly aimed for Jonathan's heart. He didn't take his eyes from Jonathan's, didn't want to miss the moment when the man's expression would falter as steel penetrated his skin—when he would know that Grant was the last thing in this world he was ever going to see. Yet, as the staff shot forward, there was a faint glow behind the man's eyes.

The sudden movement was like a snake uncoiling. Jonathan's hand slid up to the interlocking ends of chain wrapped across him, the connected steel coming apart, freed into his fist and intercepting Excalibar. Sparks shredded out between the weapons as one pushed against the other.

The glow in Jonathan's eyes erupted into a blaze, the orange energy radiating out of his pupils while the demolition bar erred off target and pierced the wall beside Jonathan's shoulder with a thud as it penetrated the aged brick and mortar.

Stunned, Grant hesitated as his moment fell apart. Jonathan's free hand tightened into a fist. The strike drove into Grant's groin with a force that buckled his chest to his knees and took his feet off the floor. He collided with the opposite side of the corridor and crumpled as his nerves lit up in agony. He fell against the floor, instincts making him curl into the fetal position. A whimper escaped him before his eyes clenched shut and his teeth ground down against the pain.

So attuned to his misery, begging his body to go numb, he barely registered the foreboding clink of Doomsday's links moving against one another until he felt the cold steel loop around his neck.

Adrenaline shot through him, jarring open his eyes as the noose tightened on his throat and lifted him off the floor. Grant couldn't stand—his body rebelled, held him locked against his legs. He staggered, his feet trying to find purchase but his legs unwilling. Jonathan's terrible gaze came into focus, the line of red still running down between those blazing eyes. Grant cowered and looked away in fear of what had awoken inside the man.

"I saw my father," Jonathan said.

He pivoted, and Grant felt a violent pull from the chain around his neck. He lost the ability to breathe as he was jerked off his precarious footing. Helpless, he felt like a tether ball circling around its post. He was horizontal to the ground when he collided with resistance. The hard wall crunched and cracked around the back of his skull. His body began to fall toward the floor, as though the brick had spit him out, but he never felt the ground. Another violent tug of the noose sent his hands and feet flailing as he shot back toward Jonathan.

He felt his body jar to a halt against the man's grip. Grant gasped, but found no air could enter his lungs. His feet dangled below him as Jonathan held him off the ground by his throat.

"I'm sorry, but..." Jonathan's voice trailed off as he turned, putting his weight into ramming Grant's skull into the wall.

He wanted to plead for mercy, but found he could not form words against the chain threatening to collapse his throat. His hands clutched at the noose as his head slammed violently into the wall again and again. His fingers grew weak, unresponsive as he felt his head emerge out into the air of the corridor, only to be rammed back, digging a deeper gash into the long-forgotten walls.

Finally, his hands fell defenselessly to his side, and shortly after, the barrage stopped.

Fearing what it meant, Grant forced his eyes open, only able to see the two orange flames in the darkness. He was unable to plead for mercy. He tried feebly gripping the leather around Jonathan's forearm in submission.

Jonathan finished his thought: "We forgot to talk about you."

Grant felt his body swung around, and a moment's relief when the grip on his throat loosened as he was briefly thrown away.

He expected another crash into the corridor wall. Instead, he felt steel penetrate through his back.

The noose, having now gone slack, allowed him to gulp air as he heard the crunching of his own ribs.

He opened his eyes for one last moment. Excali-bar protruded out from his chest, drops of red falling from its tip like wet paint. He gripped the bar in disbelief. Blood poured from his mouth and choked him. Black was beginning to push in at the edges of his vision.

Jonathan's eyes—they were like the devil watching him. In this darkness, there wasn't anything else to look at.

CHAPTER SIXTY-SEVEN

JONATHAN STEPPED ONTO the sidewalk with Excali-bar harnessed on his back and Doomsday hanging coiled from his fist. A pedestrian screamed and he turned to see a woman slipping on the wet cement, falling to the ground beside him. She scampered away, trying to crawl backwards on her hands as fear stricken eyes watched him. Finally, she managed to put enough distance between them to get to her feet and run.

Jonathan frowned at the stranger, but as he turned his head, he caught his reflection in one of the display windows that lined the street. His clothing was smudged with dirt. There were red hand prints, Grant's blood, still wet on his jeans. He'd wiped at the blood running down his forehead and the left side of his face was smeared crimson.

Still, he doubted that the woman fleeing him in terror had noticed any of those minor details. She had been looking at his eyes. The light, normally constrained to the device beneath his skin, was pouring out of his eye sockets. It was as though his body couldn't contain the amount of power and the excess was spilling out, flickering in front of him and setting the world on fire. He remembered then, the night he had slain *Bleeds the Stone* in the brewery, how the color of everything around him had changed when he'd believed Rylee was…

Rylee.

The blaze roared with the thought of her in danger. He moved without any further hesitation, stepping away from the reflection and running toward the muffled crashing in the distance. Doomsday, he realized, was not in a good position for him to move as quickly as he could, and without thought, he threw the excess chain out in front of him as he ran. He spun, then spun again, before he left the ground, launching himself for a nearby rooftop. He spun once more in the air, and all of it felt like a familiar motion. He tilted his head to the right and caught Doomsday's metal, spiked end as it came around one last time to settle perfectly in his palm. He landed on the rooftop, hitting the ground running, as he clicked the steel into place around himself.

Only then did he realize what he'd done—some type of Jet-Li maneuver that would have taken five takes to get right. Yet he'd put the chain back in place around himself without losing a step, as though it were a reflex, something he had practiced a thousand times before.

The moment he questioned how he could have done this, confusing memories came at him. He was out in the country, and his hands hurt, the heavy rope digging in. He saw an animal, a steer, its feet tied. He saw pieces of a childhood on a ranch—where? They collided with countless hours of the alien's face, flooding into his mind's eye. He saw himself sparring in a dojo that he knew wasn't a dojo, for long hours. He saw...

He'd stopped running—had come to a standstill on the roof at some point after he'd started to wonder how he could move as he did. He didn't have time to sort through this, and so he refused to question it. Today, his life and Rylee's depended on him trusting his intuition. These memories, they were like a floating, disconnected foundation; they gave him the skill, the ability to move in ways he hadn't imagined, but he had to trust them, had to ignore the how and why, or else his mind was yanked down into a clutter of confusing remembrances.

He landed with a grace he found familiar and yet foreign, and promptly ignored it. Didn't want to think about what else had changed, what or who he was—not now. A cascade of foreign memories, new associations that his mind had not previously made to his surroundings, came to the forefront of his thoughts. He felt himself begin a maneuver that would take him five more steps to complete, but he didn't know the steps—he felt his way through them. Every instinct told him to obey, that his body's muscle memory was way ahead of him.

He set his mind on Rylee and he moved, felt his body deciding the details for him, his mind growing quiet.

Over the noise of sirens and the city in chaos, he pushed himself faster toward the dull thuds of battle. In the quiet of his mind, a memory of Malkier standing over him rose to the surface. A part of him remembered what had happened—saw what had played out the night a man had made a Borealis bleed. It was another side of him that comprehended the *why*… the *how*.

A grunt of effort escaped him as he surged forward over the rooftops, urgency pushing him to move faster.

Rylee felt the collision in the air and the impact with the ground before the pain caught up to her. She put a dent in the rooftop where her head and shoulder first hit. She managed to roll into the fall, tumble through the momentum and protect her spine, until she rammed to a sudden halt against a solid barrier. The wall of a taller building connected to the roof she'd just managed to face plant into.

She'd known it was a mistake—but only in that split second after her feet had left the ground and it was too late to change it. Staying out of Malkier's grasp for so long had taken every move in her arsenal, but she couldn't keep it up. Even now, despite the pain, she was fighting desperately to catch her breath.

She'd tried to put distance between them, risked a longer leap than was wise, made herself a target that, while moving, followed a predictable course. It had been a jeep, she thought, that crashed into her. Caught her in the legs, clipping them out from under her and sending her into a spiral as she fell out of the sky.

She tried to stand now, but alarming pain raged up from her left ankle and knee. For a moment, she lost hold of her fear. If her leg couldn't hold her, this chase was over.

The last nail in her coffin—acceptance—came when she sought the signal with her senses. The man fighting Jonathan, he was far away now. The signal seemed still, but it was hard to know at this distance. She could hope he was still struggling against Jonathan, but that meant he was much too far away for him to help her in time. It appeared that she had given Jonathan all the time he was going to get.

She felt Malkier join her on the roof, his weight causing an audible thud and shaking the ground beneath her. She closed her eyes, listening to his footsteps approach. Though the sky was covered in gray rain clouds, the light around her dimmed when the monster stepped between her and the sun.

"Have you felt it by now, human?" Malkier asked as he looked in the direction of the signal. "Has their fight grown still?"

Rylee swallowed, but didn't speak or look at him. She reached for the wall, searching for some leverage to pull herself up. If her time had come, she wanted to face death on her feet. Her body trembled as she put weight on the leg, but she refused to show the weakness on her face.

"It is clear, now, why my brother wanted you. It's such a waste, I admit," Malkier said. "A creature of grace. Your death, it could have been so much more than a footnote in the story of *Brings the Rain*."

She opened her eyes and looked into his white slits. Perhaps she had hit her head too hard, or perhaps he'd simply pissed her off too much to be afraid any longer. But the world, it seemed brighter to her, even though she now stood in this monster's shadow. There were two things of which she was absolutely sure.

"He lives," Rylee whispered, steadying herself.

Malkier's head tilted, and he studied her eyes with an interest that had not been there before. Neither of them blinked or gave it much attention when the flicker of a shadow passed over the rooftop. Rylee pushed away from the wall, planting as much weight as she could on her good leg, and drew her rattan.

"And I am no one's goddamn footnote," she said.

Malkier smiled. "Wha—"

It all happened so quickly, as though she had taken one long breath only to find herself standing alone when she exhaled. Rylee blinked, shook her head, then blinked twice more, trying to process what she had witnessed.

Malkier's words had suddenly cut off. Rylee had heard it—a moment before his eyes widened in alarm, before his disturbing voice was replaced with a gagged choke—the sound of a metal chain pulled taut.

Doomsday had suddenly snapped into place—pulled tight into Malkier's jaw and around the back of his skull. He had never had time to brace himself, hardly managed to reach for the obstruction lodged between his teeth before he was shooting away from her. He'd been four feet in the air, his body suddenly parallel to the roof, before he tore down through the edge and dropped out of sight.

Jonathan had been there behind them, she was almost sure. He had been moving too fast, plummeting headlong out of the skyline and straight for the street as though trying to gather as much speed as possible.

"Uh, okay—tag, you're in," she said before the sound of a massive impact rose from the street below. It was quickly followed by a tremor that shook the city around her. Rylee staggered and fell forward onto her hands and knees, grimacing as the fall sent agony up her leg.

Despite the injury, she began to crawl. Even with the pain brought by each movement, a smile was forming on her face. It grew as she dragged herself closer to the gouge Malkier's body had left in the side of the roof. Then, as she moved to place her next hand forward, a figure suddenly came into being above her.

He dropped from a few feet in the air, falling in between her and the ledge, a familiar red and black cloud swirling around him, rapidly dissipating as he rolled to a stop.

A black fedora fell onto the ground in front of her.

Heyer had landed face down, steam wafting off his body and clothing as he lay there in the rain. He roused slowly, pushing up to his hands and knees to see her watching him.

"Rylee?" he asked, his voice on the edge of complete exhaustion. "Where is Malkier? Where is Jonathan?"

Her exhaustion was hard to mask, but she nodded her head to the crater left in the side of the building. Heyer turned back to her just as they heard Jonathan's roar below.

"Rylee, we can't let them kill one another," he said.

A fire hydrant's waterline had broken, its contents and the rain now flowing into the Alpha Ferox-sized crater punched into the street below. Jonathan hung four stories above the sidewalk, Doomsday dangled from his fist, the weapon's spiked end swaying beneath him. Excali-bar was sunk into the building's exterior wall. The staff and his legs had torn deep gouges down the structure's side while he was bringing himself to a momentary stop.

He felt the wall starting to give.

Jonathan stared at the scarred face of the monster as he drew in Doomsday's slack, securing the chain with a trained one-handed technique that spun its length up his arm. Once he'd reeled in all he could, his chain wrapped hand joined Excali-bar overhead, just as the building's wall began to crumbled around him. He drew the staff free and gave himself back to gravity.

As he fell, time moved at a glacial speed, the world outside his enemy becoming an afterthought. He pivoted in the air, positioning Excali-bar's point over his shoulder. Malkier had not yet opened his eyes. A clawed hand rubbed at his jaw as though testing if his mouth still opened and shut as it should. Jonathan was a heartbeat away when the white slits finally opened, and he roared when the ancient alien met his eyes.

He slammed into Malkier's abdomen with his knees while bringing down Excali-bar with all the force he could put behind it. The staff slowed to a halt, the weapon's edge trembling a precarious and frustrating inch above his enemy's eye. The debris that had fallen with Jonathan rained down around them as the Borealis' gaze narrowed.

"So, the son survives," Malkier said, with a calmness uncharacteristic of the Feroxian species. As he studied Jonathan, that composure began to melt away. "Picked up your father's weapon, *Brings the Rain?* Presume you will succeed where he fai—"

Jonathan had clenched his jaw and stood from his knees to bear down on Excali-bar. The Borealis had flinched, stopped speaking mid-sentence as he felt the lost leverage. A disturbed wonder crept onto Malkier's face as his muscles trembled with the effort of holding the staff's point at bay.

"Abomination…" Malkier said. "Do you even know what you—"

Jonathan twisted his grip on Excali-bar, causing the staff to turn and making the edge poised over Malkier's skull harder to keep under control.

"My brother should have disposed of you," Malkier said, grunting with effort. "I would never allow this."

"Malkier," Jonathan said, his breathing heavy, betraying the toll it was taking to keep them at a stalemate. "He was counting on it."

Malkier's face contorted in anger, forced to consider if Jonathan had spoken the truth. "So be it," the Alpha Ferox finally said. He started to push with his full strength, and Jonathan grunted under the strain as he began to lose ground, the staff's edge pushed off target.

The alien was fast, thrusting the weapon back with a finality that took Jonathan's balance. Before he recovered, Jonathan was caught by the monster's leg tearing up from beneath the rubble. A massive foot planted into Jonathan's chest before thrusting him blindly though the air.

He barely saw the corner of a building before he tore through it, slowing enough for his vision to resolve into a rapid interchange of gray rain clouds and the downtown street shrinking below him. A cry of warning sounded. He was gaining altitude too fast.

He closed his eyes as a collage of memories triggered reflexes. He felt the exhilaration of throwing himself out of the back of an aircraft and years of scenario training inside Mr. Clean. He'd survived this before. Doomsday was more than a weapon.

He stopped flailing and drew his limbs in tight before pulling his legs to his chest. The world stopped flipping end over end, as he brought his legs back out and his elbows in line with his shoulders. He pivoted hard, thrusting his torso and forcing his body to spiral. He tightened his grip on the loop of chain in his palm, and let the excess unravel from his arm, until the tug of its spiked end reaching its full length told him it was time.

Jonathan fired the weapon out below him and braced himself, hoping that the spiked end would anchor itself to something solid enough.

Sudden, agonizing pain tore through his shoulder when his direction shifted with a violent torque. He felt the chain tear free of its anchor before he shot into the narrow space between two buildings and slammed sideways into a fire escape. The metal collapsed in around him, leaving a gouge in the exterior wall. The rest was a barrage. He plummeted gracelessly down the gap between buildings, unable to keep track of up and down, until he suddenly felt as though his arm was being torn from his shoulder, and he jarred to a sudden stop.

Disoriented, he tried to get his bearings. He dangled two stories above the ground. Despite the painful tumble of the last few seconds, he'd managed to keep himself tethered to Doomsday. The spiked end was entangled in some part of the crushed fire escape above, and had stopped him from face-planting in one final smash on the alley floor.

The pain in his shoulder was screaming above all the rest of his lesser injuries, and he forced himself to reach up with his free hand and grab hold of the chain. His hand never got a grip before he felt himself begin to fall once again, the fire escape groaning mournfully before it came free of the wall and began collapsing down above him. When his feet touched the ground, his footing was hardly stable. It turned his run into more of a stagger, which ended in a dive to get out of the way of the falling metal.

Jonathan found himself face down on the sidewalk when the sound of the debris hitting the ground came from behind him.

He took a long breath and then exhaled. For what it was worth, that entire exchange had been lucky. He'd no intention of trying to stand toe-to-toe with Malkier, but Rylee had been out of time when he'd caught up to her and he'd been forced to intervene. The chances that either of them were getting out of this alive had been slim from the start. Now, with both of them battered and injured, the chance that both would make it out seemed almost non-existent.

But Rylee was getting out alive.

With her leg injured and Malkier focusing on him, he could be sure to keep her away from the danger. It didn't matter which—Malkier or himself—survived the rest of this. If he died, then Malkier would be heading back through the gates before he'd get a chance to go back for her. When she was the only one remaining inside The Never, Rylee would follow the signal to her ticket home—the portal stone he'd left for her inside of Grant Morgan's body.

Now that he knew she was safe, the time had come to piss off Heyer's big brother.

Jonathan started to stand, grunting as the pain in his shoulder announced itself. He shifted his weight to the other arm and got his feet beneath him. When he reached for Excali-bar out of habit, he found the harness on his back empty. He'd lost hold of the demolition bar after Malkier had kicked him into the next zip code.

He sighed, pulling in Doomsday to secure it around himself before he walked into the middle of the busy street. People running from the monster began to take notice, the light pouring out of his eyes drawing their attention. His presence heightened their panic as the fleeing civilians didn't know if the man with burning eyes was any less terrifying than the giant black monster. Jonathan stepped up off the street onto an abandoned car, looking down the road to where he expected Malkier would pursue. Not yet seeing the Alpha, Jonathan leapt onto a bus overturned in the roadway.

Now able to see the wrongness in Jonathan's eyes from afar, the flood of people parted before drawing too close. In the distance, he could feel the monster's movements, the vibrations following Malkier's landing somewhere outside his vision.

"*MALKIER*!" Jonathan shouted, his voice an angry roar calling to the monster over the sounds of the city.

The sound of the Alpha Ferox's movements paused, and for a moment, despite the chaos, the city felt quiet to Jonathan—Malkier had heard his challenge.

"You call *ME* an abomination, alien?"

There was another brief silence—then suddenly, the Alpha Ferox's landing sent a quake through the city streets as he dropped into view a few blocks ahead. Jonathan stared the monster down as it rose to full height.

"Borealis, your son is dead because I dispose of abominations," Jonathan yelled. "His life was always meant to end with me!"

The white slits of Malkier's face grew wide with rage. When he spoke, the sounds were guttural growls. Jonathan had heard enough Ferox speech to recognize the language, but just as he couldn't feel Malkier's location, the connection that normally allowed him a vague understanding of their words was absent—nothing translated in Jonathan's thoughts. Instead, the anger the alien was conveying passed over him, leaving no effect on his face.

It didn't matter; he was beating his chest so the alien would do the same—and if Malkier was enraged enough to start yelling at him in a language he couldn't comprehend, then he'd pushed the right button. It hadn't been much of a gamble. Jonathan figured he could bring out the alien's rage—not by mocking the death of *Dams the Gate*, but by questioning his life.

Malkier had made too many sacrifices to be a father—every action he'd taken to bring a life into the world and protect it had been like forcing a boulder uphill while gravity fought against him. Now, his son's killer stood before him, making a claim he knew the father feared. That the life Malkier had created was as unnatural a thing as The Never itself—a thing that the natural order had been trying to snuff out since the moment it came into being. Jonathan didn't have to believe it, only had to convince Malkier that he did.

"Come with me, *Borealis!*" Jonathan roared. "I am going to show you where your abomination died. Then, I am going to show you how."

CHAPTER SIXTY-EIGHT

HE WAS ALREADY in motion, hitting the ground and building up speed in the opposite direction, when the bus he'd stood on caved in beneath Malkier's weight. He made no effort to hide but leaped down the street at a dangerous speed, and the alien didn't lose a moment to hesitation before ripping through the remains of the bus and falling into pursuit. It didn't take long to realize the monster was closing the distance between them, but Jonathan kept his focus—they didn't have far to go.

At first, he followed the wires running along the bus routes. He knew downtown well, and only a few blocks passed before he realized that he knew where they were headed. He'd seen the substation hub every time he'd crossed the freeway into downtown. It was only now that he'd had reason to consider the purpose of the place. Of course, *Dams the Gate* hadn't died there, but he needed Malkier to believe he was being antagonized—not wondering if he was being lured.

Coming around a corner hard, he clipped the side of a minivan parked along the sidewalk. The exterior caved around him as his feet looked for purchase on the wet streets. The van's tires were forced over the sidewalk, only bringing him to a halt when the vehicle compressed against the nearby office building. He didn't lose his footing, but forfeited some distance between them. A moment later, Malkier experienced the same trouble taking the turn and he gained it back. Jonathan pushed on, raising his eyes when the substation was a few blocks up.

It was then that he realized the constant rumble closing in on his heels was no longer behind him. In alarm, he slammed on the proverbial brakes, skidding to a halt across the wet streets just as Malkier tore through the lower floors of a building in front of him.

"You cannot run forever, *Brings the Rain,*" he growled.

The rain continued to pound on the cement. The breaths of his enemy steamed in the cool air, each heavy like a rhino exhaling. Jonathan heard the thudding of his own heart. The beat strummed along, its pace accelerated by all the exertion, but the rhythm slowed, now, as he stood still. This seemingly invincible enemy wasn't bringing panic—and he wasn't going to make Jonathan change his course.

Jonathan drew himself up to his full height, and sighed. "Well, isn't that just the truth."

For a moment, he broke away from Malkier's gaze, and grinned to mask the pain in his shoulder as he coiled Doomsday around the injured arm. When he looked back, Malkier's veracity seemed diminished, his eyes having grown large with the anticipation. Finally—his son's killer meant to stand his ground. The massive beast planted his feet, claws gripping into fists at his sides.

Jonathan remembered the morning he had killed the alien's son—how he'd wrapped his fist with chain. He gripped the spiked metal end of the weapon in his palm, then wound what was left of the chain tightly around his hand. For a moment, he lingered on the act in front of the alien, holding his fist up, turning the metal over a few times as though inspecting his work. Everything about his body language said there was no hurry. Only when he was satisfied did he turn his attention back to the monster.

Malkier watched him now with a fascination beneath his eagerness for blood, his eyes narrowing when Jonathan raised the hand free of chain and pointed to a destination off in the skyline. The alien broke their stare, allowed his eyes to glance where Jonathan had pointed. Not too far away, the skeleton of a tall building stood, its construction still underway.

"Your son named me," Jonathan said. "It was the last thing he ever did. When he'd lost the will to fight, I threw him from the roof. Thing was, he survived the fall."

He watched as the Borealis within the Alpha Ferox flinched. The alien seeming unable to process Jonathan's arrogance. Why, after all, would this man stand there and beg a superior being for the most gruesome death he could deliver?

"You see, I was tired, so it took me awhile to get to him. When I did, I found him reaching out with the last of his strength." A pause followed Jonathan's words. "You're his father. What do you think it was—what was he reaching for?"

In a city brought to shambles, there was a moment filled with nothing but pouring rain and the growing sound of Malkier's heavy breaths accelerating in anger.

"I think it was dignity," Jonathan said. "He died wanting the respect you denied him."

The alien took a step forward, planting his foot so hard the ground shook between them. "You seek my anger, human?" he thundered.

Jonathan's stare grew deadly serious as he watched his enemy's pupils begin to shift, the white gaze beginning to fill with the web of black veins.

"I do," Jonathan said. "You see, my father and I don't believe you know the meaning of the word."

The length of three breaths passed in stillness before Jonathan made the first move. He stepped forward, then accelerated into a charge, and Malkier's massive frame followed suit. Jonathan had been conscious of three thoughts, one for each of his breaths:

One, a head-on collision with Malkier would end like a bull charging a wrecking ball. Sure, the gesture would be epic and the impact would shake the city, but the wrecking ball would be mostly unscathed, though desperately in need of a bath to remove all the bull meat. Two, Malkier wanted the blindness of revenge—he wanted this to be the moment his vendetta story ended. Three, right now, Jonathan didn't give a damn about any story other than the one that ended with them on that substation.

Jonathan never dropped Malkier's gaze—the orange glow pouring from his eyes nearly did the work for him, made him appear as lost to the thrall of revenge as his enemy.

So it was, when Jonathan's legs drew down to gather all the power they could into a final clash with his enemy, a different scenario played out in his mind's eye. He broke Malkier's stare, looking to the skyline behind the beast as his father's training took hold and turned the vision in his head into a reality.

Leaving the ground as Malkier charged forward, Jonathan shot high and right, a bullet spiraling forward and denying his enemy the honest collision his words had promised. Malkier, not seeing the change quickly enough, was already off course when the time to adapt had passed. The alien's claw grasped air as Jonathan spiraled past, his chained fist tagging the alien like a harmless slap to the face as he barreled through the gap over Malkier's shoulder.

He was out of reach before the massive beast had time to dig his feet into the pavement and reverse direction. Jonathan angled himself to pounce off the rapidly-approaching building's corner—became a cue ball ricocheting off one side of the street to another. When he was in free fall toward the substation, he had only a moment to take in the sight he'd hoped: the electrical grid feeding the city's transit systems—a network of interconnecting wires and metal towers covering the station's roof. Plummeting toward them, he was forced into an awkward aerial maneuver to dodge as many of crisscrossed wires as possible. He landed hard, making his tumble through the substation's electrical towers difficult to control. He turned over and over, wincing in pain as his shoulder struck the ground again and again, before finally rolling onto his knees and coming to a smooth skid across the wet cement.

He had enough time to see the massive Ferox coming after him in the sky above. The alien crashed down, making none of the efforts he had to avoid the power lines and pulling down two of the towers with him as he landed. Wires broke—power arced off wet steel as they became exposed around them.

Electricity surged through them, and Malkier's angry expression flinched, first in awareness of the discomfort, then from the voltage itself.

The blackening slits of his eyes twitched as his jaw dropped open and Jonathan saw the light of arcing currents between the metallic teeth. Jonathan shivered as well as power went through him. Though he had had some protection from the rubber soles of his shoes, his arm was still wrapped in alien steel and his clothes were soaked through. He had to resist the spastic pull of tensing muscles in his neck and force his eyes to stay on his enemy. Ignoring the electricity, Malkier began to come for him.

The change was sudden, hitting him no more than three steps into his charge. A muddled confusion surfaced on the alien's face.

At that very same moment, a smile broke on Jonathan's lips. He closed his eyes, he no longer needed to see his enemy—he knew exactly where the monster stood. The awareness, absent since Malkier's arrival, was suddenly there in his mind. He could feel the portal stone's signal—there were two tickets home after all.

His face grew certain then, his brow drawing down as he released the spiked end of Doomsday. The chain unraveled from his arm, falling to the ground as Jonathan rose off his knees. He opened his eyes, the killer's predatory gaze focusing on the towering creature whose charge had staggered in its disorientation.

Jonathan threw himself into the air, spinning his body to let the chain follow around him as he arced over Malkier. He had to ignore all the pain in his shoulder, push it into the background as he launched the business end of Doomsday at its target.

A spiked edge of alien steel drove down into Malkier's face, finding the long scar that ran down the monster's cheek and neck. The alien's forward momentum wavered, coming to a confused walk as Jonathan landed behind him. Finally, the monster stopped. His back, still turned to Jonathan, stiffened as he stood straight, hesitantly bringing a clawed hand to the side of its face.

Jonathan watched as the hand came away with tar-like black blood sticking to his fingertips, the scar along his face now a re-opened wound.

"1.21 gigawatts, asshole," Jonathan whispered.

CHAPTER SIXTY-NINE

THE NIGHT DOUGLAS died within The Never, there had been a storm. He'd been bloodied and cold, his clothes soaked through and heavy. No longer able to stand, feeling himself fading away, Douglas hadn't understood what he saw when it happened—how he'd managed to wound the seemingly invincible enemy. Yet, Doomsday had drawn blood.

With his mind locked up somewhere on the fringe of his son's consciousness, he'd been left a powerless observer without a body of his own, gaining a whole new outlook on the idea of *I think, therefore I am.*

Douglas would have rephrased this into, *I remember and therefore I obsess.*

He'd found himself with more than enough quiet time to painstakingly replay his final moments. A good thing, because the memory he'd had to start from wasn't the clearest. His death was shrouded by adrenaline, fatigue, and pain. At the moment that mattered most, his focus had been pulling inward. Paying attention to what was happening around him had taken a backseat to the terminal state of his injuries. In the end, he'd had to pull the memory apart and reassemble it over and over again.

There hadn't been anything unusual about the location, though he'd been on one of the taller roof tops in Portland's skyline. Douglas remembered the light, so bright and white all around him that he'd been temporarily blinded. His body had stiffened; there had been this eardrum-collapsing eruption of sound that had rolled through the both of them.

He'd already lost the battle at that point—just saw no reason to admit it to himself. Of course, on some level, he'd known that the day had come. His best wasn't going to be enough this time—his survival was past its expiration. He'd never encountered an Alpha—only knew what to call the thing because Mr. Clean had shown him footage of battles in the ancient Arena. Recognizing what the monster was, the thought had occurred to him that the Ferox leaders felt the death of *Echoes the Borealis* needed to be expedited. That would mean the Alpha was their weapon of assassination. It did not take long for him to realize he was fighting more than the flesh and bone of an experienced Ferox warrior.

He'd been on edge before he arrived, as he'd been unable to sense its location—only found the beast initially by watching the news broadcast after he found himself activated without sensing a target. What came to bother him more was how silent the Alpha was once he engaged it. Few of the Ferox were overly talkative—but none had ever been completely wordless. The Alpha's quiet study of him, the peculiar manner in which it seemed separate from the violence it was taking part in had dug a deepening well of uncertainty in him the more he'd failed to do any sort of damage. The battle itself had lasted far longer than it should have—the Alpha had tortuously drawn it out.

He had always been skilled at dispatching the trespassers and Heyer's training had taken him to a level of lethality few humans ever achieved, but nothing in his arsenal would have swayed the outcome. By the end, he was reduced to hoping for stupid luck to intervene on his behalf. He'd been crawling away when the Alpha Ferox lifted him off the ground by the throat. The claw might as well have been a steel shackle around his neck—he wasn't going to break free of it. Yet, the massive creature wasn't trying to cause him more pain. It held him off the ground but didn't stop him from breathing, didn't strangle him or crush his wind pipe, though either act would have taken little effort. The Alpha simply wanted him at eye level.

"You are unique, *Echoes the Borealis*. I feared I would find you undeserving of such a mantle," the Alpha had said. "It gives me no joy that events should come to this. Your death is unjust, but one of purpose nonetheless. I will remember the sacrifice you made for me tonight."

The words had been spoken in English, distorted somewhat by

the vocal cords of Malkier's Feroxian biology, but discernible. Not the obscure translation of meaning or his own inner voice speaking to him through the device.

"For what it is worth, human," Malkier said as his free hand reached up to the collar of Douglas's jacket and ripped it off, the fabric tearing like wet newspaper under the creature's strength and exposing the soft orange glow of the device on his torso. "You will always be remembered by my people."

Grunting through the pain, Douglas had resisted. Though it was agonizing, he had lifted the knee of his good leg, pressing into the monster's abdomen in an effort to push them apart. Malkier watched the man with a mixture of admiration for what seemed to be a refusal to admit defeat, and at the same time, scorn for his willingness to be so disrespectful. As though the act of placing a limb on him under the circumstances was like walking through his home with muddy shoes.

"Stop strug—"

Malkier's words were cut off as Douglas spit a mouthful of blood across his face.

The Alpha Ferox shivered in rage. He dropped the remains of Douglas's ripped clothing and straightened his fingers, slowly raising the claws until they were like a spear between them. Seeing the Alpha meant to impale him with its finger tips, Douglas's fist had tightened around the spiked end of Doomsday, knowing it would be the last effort he ever made. He stared into Malkier's eyes, unwilling to give the alien the satisfaction of seeing him blink as he took aim. He'd figured, if this monster had a soft spot, the eye socket was his best bet.

That had been when the world went white around them. Douglas had struck down with Doomsday, just as he was hit with an explosion of sound, blinding disorientation, and an uncontrolled spasming of his muscles. He'd been convinced that death had shown him the form it would take. The light had been so bright, so familiar. Like the hard, white shock he experienced when closing the gates—so it had been somewhat of a disappointment when he realized this wasn't the case.

Nerves had started to come back online and pain resurfaced, along with the cold that fell down all around him. His eyes finally focused, and he realized his back was on the rooftop. Malkier knelt over him with a look of startled disbelief on his face, his chest heaving as though air was suddenly in short supply, and his eyes beginning to blacken. The claw that had previously been on Douglas's throat, now clutched at his own. Douglas felt himself struggling to breathe, a sensation like drowning surfacing in his awareness as he looked up from the ground at the injured monster.

He may have missed the eye, but Doomsday had drawn a line down the beast's face—a tar-black gash where the point had torn through and somehow managed to cut into the monster's armor. Yet it had done more than just that—it cut down the creature's face, but also into its neck. The blood was surging beneath the monster's hand, too much to be merely a flesh wound—he'd hit some kind of artery.

Douglas thought to move, to grasp at hope now that the monster showed weakness. Sharp agony went through him the moment he tried and was followed by a bout of coughing that he couldn't hold in. His eyes tracked down to the monster's other hand to see red dripping off its finger tips. Human blood. His blood. It was then that he saw the four holes from Malkier's claws in a line down his chest, the wretched wounds made visible by the orange glow emanating from him. A glow that was fading. It was later that he realized that the feeling of drowning he'd experienced had been his own blood pouring into his lungs.

His head sagged back to the rooftop, his body no longer willing to expend the effort of holding it up. Malkier struggled to reach his feet, needing the hand covered in human blood to support him.

As the monster reclaimed his full height, Douglas's memory had grown fainter. He didn't truly comprehend it all, and his mind had not seen any further use for what his eyes could show him. Instead, he searched out thoughts of his wife and son as he lost hold of his life. Yet, he later realized that he had seen three lines of light emanating from Malkier's chest—a device that looked like a brother to the one he'd seen on Heyer's chest so many times before. One yellow line of energy on top of the other. Those lines had not been there before, or at least, their presence had been hidden from him while they fought, but now the familiar shape of the Borealis implant faltered in Malkier's chest, fluttering without rhythm, flickering like a florescent bulb that couldn't quite find the power to sustain itself—malfunctioning.

Every strength had its weaknesses, Heyer had said.

One could spend a millennium safeguarding against every contingency, and it would still be a mistake to believe yourself invincible. Heyer was humble enough to realize that his membership in the most privileged species in existence made him vulnerable to the same blind assumption that he was beyond being hurt.

Heyer had spent so many years breaking the encryption on the device, because the two remaining Borealis didn't know how to kill one another, and only a man had ever gotten close.

That blinding white light, the sound like an explosion, the surge sent through them, Douglas had realized it could only have been lightning striking the rooftop. Malkier's bare feet had been an inch deep in rain water, and the current had flowed right into both of them. Still, a surge of electricity was too simple, far too common a threat. The Borealis could not have overlooked such a glaring weakness in their devices. No, there had to be something else at play.

So, Douglas had continued to replay the memory over and over in his mind, tried to pick out the relevant variables, to see where the creative genius of an advanced race had failed. He looked for some environmental oddity, something else on the roof top, something about that storm. It was when he'd begun to lose faith that he could find the answer, that he realized he was going about his search for a weakness in the same manner that the god-like intellect of the Borealis would have gone about it. The Borealis would have built their devices to protect against any common danger to their species throughout history.

Finally, he asked himself: *What if, Malkier was unlike any other Borealis in history? What if the weakness was unique to him alone?*

His father had done the hardest part: he'd found the right question. It was the son who had seen an answer.

Douglas had plenty of time fighting the Ferox to get creative; throwing the damn things into a transformer would hardly scrape the top ten of peculiar tactics he'd tried against them. Electricity wasn't useless—good in a pinch to slow the beasts down, but it had never been a decisive blow. The same had been true for Douglas for that matter. He'd been hit with blows that had made him acquaintances with Portland's power grid on more than one occasion, and he gotten up and kept fighting.

The thing was, Douglas and Jonathan may have had an active alien implant, but they didn't have an iron skeleton. The Ferox had the iron skeleton, but they only carried a portal stone with them into The Never. When Malkier came through the gates, he possessed all three.

Jonathan knew from basic physiology classes that human biology used the skeleton to regulate its own electrical currents. Any form of life that possessed a metal skeleton would have to regulate their current in a very different manner. Heyer had said that the Borealis never intended for the Ferox to serve as a host for one of their own species, that his brother was the first to ever do so. Malkier, trusting his ancestor's technology to have considered every weakness, had believed he was putting his consciousness into the most formidable vessel in existence

What the eldest brother had failed to consider was that the Ferox living today may not be the same as those that had been around the last time the Borealis upgraded their proverbial firmware—that when the brother's species had died off, the skeleton of the ancestral Ferox may have been made up of far less conductive materials. After all, the Borealis had designed the Ferox to allow only those who survived life and death struggles to breed. This had put constant pressure on how the species evolved—evolution always favoring the traits that better suited males to win a fight.

Now, Malkier had entered a battleground where the planet's inhabitant's primary source of power, electricity, was nearly ubiquitous—a strategic advantage of which Jonathan aimed to give the alien a thorough demonstration. Douglas had seen this weakness bring his opponent down from god-like invincibility to that of an Alpha Ferox, still a serious threat but not an impossible one. What neither could know, was how long a window of vulnerability would last while the alien device struggled to function.

Jonathan pulled Doomsday toward him as he rammed his good shoulder

into Malkier. They crunched into one of the remaining electrical towers, the Alpha's back bending in the metal frame as the chain's spiked edge came back into Jonathan's grip. Blackened eyes focused on the weapon's point as it was brought down for the throat. A feral ferocity snarled out of the Ferox when its massive claw intercepted Jonathan's forearm and halted the attack.

Ends the Storm kills the Echoes.

The guttural growls became translated thoughts within Jonathan's head. The Alpha Ferox seemed to grow larger in its rage, instincts reacting to the stimuli of combat as the fluttering yellow light of the Borealis implant in its chest flickered on and off between them.

Jonathan's eyes grew wide as he understood. The alien's device was offline—completely offline.

The disturbance of the electrical grid had not just disrupted the cloaking of the portal stone and the defenses that made his enemy impervious. Malkier's consciousness had been taken off line as well. Jonathan was no longer fighting a Borealis, but *Ends the Storm.*

The beast's confusion had not been Malkier's disbelief at seeing his invincibility fail, but the consciousness of the body's true owner finding itself awake during a battle inside the Arena. The last time this had happened had been when *Ends the Storm* found himself standing over the body of Jonathan's father. Malkier had not feared the towers because he hadn't known his own weakness. Ends the Storm had been in control once that bolt of lightning struck so many years before.

Feroxian instincts were taking over as the Alpha Ferox regained its wits. Its neck thickening as blood finished turning its eyes to a solid black.

Jonathan pressed in with ferocity, bringing Doomsday's spiked edge down like a dagger, thrusting for his enemy's neck. The Alpha Ferox moved in response, its forearm meeting Jonathan's to stop the weapon from hitting its target. Their eyes locked as the creature wavered under Jonathan's strength—its face darkening with a cunning comprehension.

Ends the Storm grabbed his injured shoulder with an iron grip that caught Jonathan off guard, the pain wrenching the strength out of him as the Ferox set its feet. The Alpha released the shoulder to thrust a fist into Jonathan's chest, and the force tore them from one another.

Jonathan hit the short cement parapet around the roof's edge, felt the beast charging for him as he heard its battle cry. It leaped, and with no time to get out of its path, Jonathan steadied his forearm up between them. When the weight of the collision hit, the parapet gave way, and they plummeted off the roof into the open air.

Jonathan reacted on instinct, managing to bring the elbow of his good arm into the vulnerable tissue of the monster's throbbing neck. The Alpha, jolted by the blow to the pressure point, made no counter when Jonathan grabbed hold of it, yanking down and causing the beast to flip end over end as he kicked into its abdomen, separating the two of them in the air. *Ends the Storm's* body crashed through the ground floor of a building across the street, while Jonathan managed to get control of his fall and stick the landing.

Hitting the ground jarred him and sent pain through his shoulder, and he had to grit his teeth against the feeling. The killer turned, spinning Doomsday back into place around his body as he forced himself toward the hole left by the Alpha. He didn't know how much time he had to end this—if the Borealis device came back online, there was no chance in hell he'd be able to lure Malkier into the same trap again. This had to end now.

Jonathan never saw her coming—his eyes and mind were focused on the target. Excruciating pain ripped through him as the blow struck. His shoulder dislocated as he found himself shot into the air. Barreling away, and sensing the distance between him and the enemy growing just as he had been so close. Temporarily overwhelmed by pain, and dumbfounded as to what could have happened, he ricocheted off the narrow walls of an adjacent alley. When he hit a dead end, a dumpster stopped him, its green metal caving in before spitting him back onto the street where he finally rolled to a stop.

Rylee let Heyer slip from her grasp a moment before her shoulder rammed into Jonathan.

Her friend shot away, but the collision abruptly slowed her momentum and allowed her to drop into a controlled fall. Rolling head over feet onto the street, Rylee did the best she could to protect her injured leg. The end result was rather graceless by her standards.

Heyer fared far worse, hitting the sidewalk as though thrown from a speeding car. His body rolled recklessly away from her and she feared he might not survive the tumble in his condition. When he came to a stop, she found herself holding her breath waiting for him to move. It was not a fear she would have believed herself capable of merely a week ago.

She heard Jonathan crash into a wall on the other side of the street. She grimaced, and grimaced again when the second crash reached her ears. She forced herself to ignore the guilt. She didn't want to hurt her only friend, but had to believe that even if he didn't understand, didn't forgive her in the moments that followed—he wouldn't remember it in the long run.

Wobbly and bruised, Heyer finally moved. He struggled onto his hands and knees as she scanned the ground and found Excali-bar lying not far from her on the pavement. The alien had lost his grip on the weapon when he'd tumbled across the ground.

She crawled to it, her eyes not coming back to Heyer's until her palm came down on the blackened length of alien steel. He watched her from his knees, blood beginning to trickle down his face from a fresh gash over his eyebrow. There was pain in his eyes, but it had nothing to do with his injuries, and Rylee had to harden herself against his sympathy.

She shoved Excali-bar across the pavement, and the alien's hand came down to stop Jonathan's weapon before it slid past. They looked at one another one last time. Rylee said nothing, only nodded for him to get on with it. The alien had to use the staff as a crutch, but once he reached his feet, he returned her nod—a slow gesture that lingered a bit too long before he turned away.

Rylee didn't linger. She turned to face the gouge in the building beside Jonathan—he must have done something, brought down the cloak Malkier had been using to keep his whereabouts hidden. She could feel their enemy within the darkness. She reached down to her injured leg, where she had tied her rattan into a temporary splint with her belt, and pulled the weapon free. She winced in pain as she stood, and again with each step that took her closer.

Thoughts and fears went ignored; she singled out only one and left the rest behind her on the sidewalk. *This was all she could do to protect him*. When she stepped out of the light completely, Rylee found she had no trouble seeing. A soft blue light seemed to move with her eyes as she staggered forwarded. She felt the monster move, heard the sounds of debris falling to the ground and heavy footsteps out beyond where her light would reach. When she came around a corner, she found herself entering a large room. Here, the wreckage lessened, leaving fewer obstacles for her to move around on the injured leg.

She felt Malkier's signal circling to get behind her, cutting off the way she'd entered. She spun around to keep the enemy in front of her, and found herself staring at a pane of glass that had somehow remained intact. Cold blue eyes stared back at her, and for a moment she didn't understand, wondered if Heyer had circled back. Then she recognized that it was her face in the reflection.

The guttural Feroxian growl came from the darkness a moment before the signal came hurdling toward her.

"We don't cease to exist, Rylee," she whispered before her reflection shattered.

CHAPTER SEVENTY

JONATHAN HEARD A sound like steel striking pavement. It thrummed like a metronome moving slowly closer. He struggled, using his good arm to push himself off the alley floor. Something had hit hard, blindsided him at the worst possible moment, and he'd yet to make any sense of it. He didn't know if his head could take any more knocks; his world was spinning around him again. He only managed to get his vision clear enough to make out the dark figure when the clanking abruptly stopped in front of him.

"What did you do?" Jonathan asked.

He heard the exhaustion, the confusion in his own voice. Jonathan clenched his eyes shut, letting his head bob against his chest as he tried to shake off the last of his disorientation.

"Old man," Jonathan said. "You…"

Jonathan trailed off, shaking his head, disbelief becoming anger. He felt his teeth clenching as he opened enraged eyes. Orange light poured from them as he fixed Heyer in his gaze.

"You…" he growled. "For your brother!"

"Jonathan." Heyer's voice was faint. "You have to listen to me now."

"You stopped me!"

"Jonathan, look at me," Heyer said. "I'm in no condition to harm you."

Jonathan flinched, his anger softened by confusion as he studied the alien. Heyer was hardly able to stand—was leaning on Excali-bar for support. He was bleeding…

"Then what…"

"Rylee," Heyer said. "She took you out of harm's way—there was no time to be gentle."

Jonathan shook his head in disbelief and began forcing himself to stand. He stumbled as pain darkened the edges of his vision. His arm was out of its socket, limp and useless against his side—but he didn't have time for pain, didn't have time to be useless. A memory came to the forefront, told him there were ways. Most required Heyer be able to help him, but that wasn't an option. Still there was a way—a damn stupid way that was going to hurt like hell and might leave him worse off than he already was… but under the circumstances…

Jonathan used his good hand to push the bone into position.

"Jonathan," Heyer said. "Don't…"

Ignoring the alien, he thrust his shoulder into the alley's wall. It popped into place with the sickening sound of bone grinding against bone. The pain was too much to contain and he roared. His legs went weak, causing him to turn his back to the wall and slump down onto the ground. A desperate silence seemed to fall on the city around him—the pain like a buffer between him and anything else.

"Stop, Jonathan," Heyer said. "You're safe. This will be over soon."

He shook his head, the orange fire of his eyes staring at the alien when he opened them. "What the hell do you two think you're doing?" he demanded. "I had him!"

"No, Jonathan, you only thought you had him," Heyer said. "Rylee had to make a choice, and she is doing what she must."

Ice cold dread hit him. "What did you tell her?"

"The truth," Heyer said. "If my brother dies in here, Mankind will start dying in the thousands within hours of our return."

He didn't remember deciding, or how he'd gotten off the alley floor, only that he had the alien by the collar of his shirt. Heyer staggered in surprise, his legs buckling as he held onto Excali-bar.

"Dammit, Heyer," Jonathan whispered. "Say what you mean."

"She is using her life to close the gates," Heyer said. "To send my brother back alive. Malkier was never going to allow Mankind to outlive him. He never left it to chance, after he faced his own mortality. If he dies, in here or anywhere else, Cede will open massive gates and allow the Ferox to spill onto Earth."

Heyer braced himself with Excali-bar, trying to get his feet stable beneath him.

"We don't have enough soldiers, and their numbers will be far too great. Mr. Clean cannot open that many instances of The Never at once; it would be far too dangerous. Even if he could, he would be placing our soldiers into single combat all around the globe, and every Ferox that outnumbers us would come straight to Earth. Jonathan, they will not have Malkier leading them—they will come and they will slaughter believing that their gods have delivered them to the promised land. We won't be ready, and they will meet little resistance."

Jonathan shook with frustration and exhaustion. He needed time to think but there wasn't any. "Then it doesn't matter," he said. "If he returns to the Ferox world, he is going to trigger the war himself."

"His plans will change when he returns to find I am no longer his captive. He'll know that I've returned to Earth. What he will not know is how I escaped. After what you've managed today, he will fear that I had planned it all along, that I expected him to die here, that his species is walking into a trap. He will take his time to mobilize his attack, because with me on Earth, he knows Mankind will not be defenseless. He doesn't fear humanity's forces, but he will not step lightly into a war with me when he knows I'm expecting him."

"You can't know any of that. It's all just hope."

"No, Jonathan, he brought Grant here for a reason. I saw him—you pushed him past the threshold. He will mate when he returns. Rylee isn't just sending him back, she is going to give him something to lose again," Heyer said.

Even with his eyes on fire, Heyer could see Jonathan's anger poisoned by what he'd heard. "You're sick..."

"Jonathan, I never could have planned this—nevertheless, we can't let our hearts strip us of the opportunity she is giving us. What Malkier knows will damage our plans, but it will slow him down, force him to re-evaluate. We can still salvage this, but it all depends on time. Time that Rylee knows we will not have if she lets you kill Malkier. She is giving you all the time she can."

"I can't let her do this," Jonathan said. "She trusted me."

He pulled Excali-bar from the alien's grip and pushed Heyer away with little more than a nudge. The alien hit the wall, and slumped down until he was sitting on the alley floor. Jonathan turned, staggering toward Malkier's signal in his head.

"Rylee," Heyer said. "She said I would need to tell you—"

He didn't turn back, didn't look at Heyer, didn't stop moving.

"'The truth doesn't become a lie just because the Devil is the only one willing to speak it. I'll be the damn hero, Jonathan. You be a leader. You protect them.'"

Jonathan stopped mid-step—exhaled as though her words had punched him in the gut. He was supposed to be the weapon, he was supposed to be the cannon fodder that would end this for her. Why? Why hadn't he known not to listen? Why hadn't he left before Heyer could speak? Now, try as he might, he couldn't push Rylee's message out of his thoughts. He took a step forward, but it was heavy and slow. His knuckles tightened around Excali-bar until the weapon shook in his grip.

He didn't have time for a philosophical debate. He tried to force himself forward, managed another step. It was as though he were pushing against a barrier of conscience, the uncertainty becoming a tyrant. He didn't want to know what the right thing to do was—he didn't want to be responsible for doing the right thing.

He took another step. A helpless anger escaped him like a whimper: "Move, god dammit."

He couldn't let her make this decision, but what right did he have to stop her? He just couldn't take a gray world and turn it black and white. He didn't know how.

I'd follow you, he heard her say. *Protect us.*

Jonathan's breath caught, a shiver running down him as Malkier's presence disappeared from his awareness. The entire alley seemed to grow darker and weakness struck him down—weight like anvils on his shoulders. Excali-bar dropped out of his hands, and his next step became a fall to his knees. His good arm stopped him from putting his face in a puddle on the alley floor.

An absence returned—a loathsome creature digging out its rightful home inside of him. Sorrow followed, dwarfing his physical pains as he saw his reflection in the water, the eyes looking back at him no longer burning, but human.

Rylee's decision had been made and all he could do was scream.

Heyer grimaced when he heard the man's pain. He closed his eyes and endured it, until Jonathan's lungs ran out of breath. When it ended, he was still on the ground where Jonathan had shoved him aside, and the sound of the falling rain began to trail off. He heard Jonathan weeping at the mouth of the ally.

Heyer reached for the wall beside him and pushed himself to stand, seeing Jonathan knelt a half dozen yards away. His chin rested against his chest; his shoulders rising and falling with desperate breaths he seemed to be at a loss to control. The alien forced himself to go to him. As he drew near, he saw the tears, still cutting a path through the blood and dirt on Jonathan's face despite it having rained all morning. The alien closed his eyes, leaning against the wall, and waited, not speaking until Jonathan grew still.

"Jonathan, I know it's the last thing you want to think about now, and it is the last thing I want to ask you," Heyer said. "But we remain in The Never. Grant's stone must still be intact—attached to his device."

Jonathan's head tilted faintly toward the sound of Heyer's voice, as though he'd forgotten the alien was there, but he didn't turn. It took him awhile to respond, but Heyer did not rush him.

"I was afraid. That if I took it, I'd be pulled out. That I'd abandon her in here with your brother. Doesn't matter," he said, swallowing. "Couldn't stop it—happened anyway."

"Please, Jonathan, try not to do this to yourself," Heyer said, "You are not the villain, I am—"

"Don't," Jonathan cut him off, shaking his head slowly. "Don't tell me who to hate. Right now… I just can't."

Heyer took a step toward him, leaving the wall and reaching out to place a comforting hand on him, but he found he was too weak, and lost his balance. When Heyer fell beside Jonathan, he cut his chin on the alley floor. Jonathan didn't move. He glanced at Heyer, but his thoughts were far away. Heyer's fingertips went to the fresh gash, and they came away red. He didn't realize how long he'd lingered on the blood until Jonathan's voice broke the spell.

"How long has it been, old man?" he asked. "When was the last time you bled?"

Heyer's lips drew into a line, and his eyes fell on Doomsday, wrapped around Jonathan the same way his father had done. He reached out to touch the chain, his fingertips accidentally wiping his blood on the links.

"You already know the answer," Heyer said.

Jonathan took a long breath and let it out slowly. "Answer the question, old man."

Heyer nodded slowly. "The day your father helped me transfer my implant to this body."

Jonathan closed his eyes and nodded.

Though it had been from a distance, he had seen the way Jonathan moved against his brother—seen him wielding Doomsday, the weapon Heyer hadn't been able to locate after its original owner perished ten years earlier. He had never known what he was looking for, but hoped to see a sign that Jonathan had accessed the man's memories. He'd never expected what he'd seen, never thought those memories would somehow allow him to move like *Echoes the Borealis.* Now, he found he didn't know how much of the man kneeling in the alley was Jonathan at all.

Jonathan rubbed lines of tears from his eyes. "What's wrong with you?" he asked. "What did Malkier do to you?"

With an effort, Heyer sat up and pulled the arm of his coat down, revealing the band of alien steel. "It is a device my species used in hospitals and prisons. My brother must have taken this one off the Foedrata planet when he recovered the implant for Grant Morgan—as this one is meant to allow a surgeon to sedate a Borealis in a human host. He didn't want me dead, just too weak to defend myself. It dampens my device—and it is making it quite difficult to stay conscious."

"How do we get it off you?" Jonathan asked.

"Mr. Clean should be able to remove it, once we get out of The Never."

"He can't take it off in here?"

Heyer sighed. "Nevric programmed his conscious functions to go permanently offline within an hour of detecting an unrecognizable dimensional signature in his surroundings," he said. "A safety precaution. Like any being, she did not trust the shadow copy of her A.I. to continue obeying its programming for long if exposed to The Never's deterioration."

"Good to know," Jonathan said.

Heyer studied him, but didn't show any reaction on his face. Douglas had been well aware of Mr. Clean's limitations. Jonathan, it appeared, was not. Whatever he had of his father's memories, he didn't seem to have everything.

"I entered The Never without a portal stone after it had come into being. To get back to Earth and get the dampener off, I will have to step inside the portal with you when Grant's stone is destroyed. At first, this should put me on a course back to the Feroxian plane. I can use the same means I did to follow you into The Never to change direction before I reach the gateway on the other side." Heyer sighed. "But I didn't expect to be in this condition. The trip may leave me much worse, but unfortunately, it's my only exit."

"Alright," Jonathan said.

The sounds of sirens approaching came, then. When they heard it, Jonathan's face managed to look more tired than he already had. Heyer knew, all the man wanted was to be left to sit on that alley floor until *he* decided he was ready to move—wished he could give him the kindness that time would not.

Jonathan sighed and stood, reaching down to lift Heyer off the alley floor. He put one of the alien's arms over his shoulders, and grunted down against some pain when he supported the weight. Even with an active implant, carrying Heyer was going to be hell on his injuries—but Jonathan said nothing of it.

CHAPTER SEVENTY-ONE

THE CITY BECAME background noise as Jonathan carried him to Grant's remains. Their condition slowed them, but not as much as the helicopters in the sky and the police on the ground. Jonathan was careful to keep them out of sight until they entered the demolished flat. Heyer rested his back against a wall, and Jonathan removed his coat before disappearing down a dark shaft. A few moments later, he dropped the corpse beside Heyer's feet.

On seeing the state of the remains, Heyer wondered what effect tearing open the body had had on Jonathan. Opening a Ferox was one thing, and by no means an indifferent experience, but killing a member of your own species tended to be far more disturbing. Yet, the distant expression on Jonathan's face made it seem that he'd seen death too many times to feel anything from it now.

Examining the body, he saw why Jonathan had been reluctant to remove the stone. Three times the size of the norm, it remained tethered to the human implant with the same vein-like appendages that normally networked through the limbs of a Ferox. A small trickle of energy still flowed between the stone and the implant to keep the device itself from going dormant. Saddened by the understanding it brought, Heyer could do little more than shake his head in disgust. His brother had been right—Grant's shadow had asked so very little in exchange before turning on his entire species.

"It appears that Malkier intended to fulfill his end of the bargain they made," Heyer said, pointing to the lines still tying the stone to the device.

"Bargain?"

"In exchange for taking your life, he installed Grant's device and allowed it to pull power the same way his and my own draw from the environment. But, it appears Grant did not wish to return to the Feroxian plane once he fulfilled his half of the deal. He wanted to remain in The Never, with all the power of the device still active. You see, under normal circumstances, killing you would sever the connection to the stone, causing it to self-destruct and setting off a chain reaction that takes your body and his back to the gateway on the Feroxian Plane."

"So, he somehow kept that from happening by hooking the stone into his implant?"

"Theoretically." Heyer nodded. "Seeing as Grant failed, there is no way to know if it actually would have worked. But the stone itself is larger because Malkier allowed a far greater energy expenditure to bring The Never into existence."

"To make him stronger?"

"No," Heyer said. "Thermodynamics. You see, the Ferox are sent here with the minimal expenditure of energy to open up an instance of The Never. This is why the physical deterioration asserts itself so quickly. Malkier was giving Grant a longer stay. I'm not sure I want to ponder what the man planned to do with it."

"He was... stronger than me, at first," Jonathan said.

Heyer nodded regretfully. "His device..." He trailed off, not wanting to go into the details. "Anyway, the strength from the bond overcame his advantage?"

Jonathan considered the question, and seemed to take a while to draw a conclusion. "It helped," he finally said, looking down at the corpse's face. "What I don't understand, bargain or no, is why he wanted to kill me so badly in the first place. He fought like he was performing for an audience."

Heyer nodded, his face looking like he'd eaten something that had gone bad. "Grant's upbringing, it was painfully abusive—warped him in ways I'm not sure we can completely understand. He fixated on the notion that everything he endured stemmed from his father's absence. I believe that this shadow of the man, upon learning he had little time left, needed to hold someone responsible. He usually aimed his aggressions at women, but ultimately, he fixated on your father."

"Why do you know all this?"

Heyer sighed. "Because if he was going to hold someone responsible, it should have been me," he said. "But seeing as I am currently residing inside the body of the father he put on such a high pedestal, I don't think it played well into the shadow's disillusions."

"So, he wanted my father because Douglas helped you take his father's body, but since he couldn't get revenge on a dead man, I was the closest thing."

"Perhaps," Heyer said. "This copy was pulled from The Never—suffered its mental deterioration. Some part of him seemed to truly believe that if 'Jonathan Tibbs' proved a failure, it would somehow mean that Grant Morgan was a success." Heyer gently closed the corpse's eyes. "I doubt the true Grant Morgan is so lost to these delusions, but… no one can ever truly know what another feels."

The distance in Jonathan's eyes faltered and pain crept onto his face. Heyer watched him stand, stepping away from the corpse and turning his back on him. He walked to a broken window and gazed out onto the city streets below. The alien realized with regret how poorly he'd chosen his words.

"The shadows of us in The Never," Jonathan said. "They give in to what they know they shouldn't, what they want for themselves. They stop caring who it hurts."

"It appears the deterioration can take that form," Heyer replied.

Jonathan placed the palm of his good hand against the wall. "Tell me," he said, a tremble having entered his voice. "With all that has happened, do you find yourself feeling relieved, old man?"

Heyer didn't answer immediately, troubled by the wariness in Jonathan's voice. "Why would I be relieved?"

A few moments passed before Jonathan spoke. "I did as you wanted. Got Rylee" —his voice faltered on her name— "to tell me everything about how she ended up here. You were right, inside The Never, your shadow told her enough to lead her to me."

"Did she explain how she coerced the information out of me?" Heyer asked.

Jonathan's head hung then. "When I heard her story, I thought she'd manipulated you—figured out that she could force what she wanted out of you by refusing to close the gates."

"You thought?"

"Rylee was never really a threat to you, didn't want to be your enemy; and I don't think she really outsmarted you. She was desperate—trying anything she could to keep from giving up," he said. "Your shadow used her as a pawn. You outsmarted yourself."

Heyer studied the man's back with growing concern. Jonathan's mind had endured so much; he was beginning to fear that it had broken.

"Jonathan, you're hurt, exhausted," Heyer said gently. "You need time to recov—"

"I am truly exhausted," Jonathan interrupted, his breath drawing in sharply before he continued. "More, I think, than I've ever been. But I'm not nearly as tired as you, old man."

Heyer watched Jonathan with growing concern. His words seemed paranoid, making less sense the more he spoke.

Then, Heyer heard him whisper, "*I am not ready to start a war for all of Mankind just so I can end a war for myself.*"

Heyer's eyes widened in recognition of his own words quoted back to him. He found himself swallowing—his fear that Jonathan was paranoid was far outweighed by the possibility that he was right.

"A saint could not endure what you have, old man. Struggling indefinitely to hold on to a status quo. No choice but to see and do things your conscience won't forgive. The very people you sacrifice to preserve, only able to see your every action as evil and always unsure if all that effort will fail," Jonathan said, shaking his head. "I don't think I know the meaning of the word 'exhausted' when I think of you. You endure it all out of duty, but your shadow carries all that weight with it inside The Never. Rylee made you wait, refused to close the gates. When that sense of duty broke, you gave her just enough information to get her to close the gates, to lead her to me, and fast track us into a war."

Heyer didn't argue; he did not defend himself or claim that it was all a grand theory, all unknown speculation. He sat in thought, and when his words finally came, they sounded like a confession.

"I think you may be right," he said.

Jonathan turned his head, enough to look back at Heyer from the corner of his eye.

"I do feel..." Heyer said, shaking his head, disgusted by the reality. "Relief, that an end is coming."

Jonathan turned away again, sighing. "Your shadow gave you the mercy you would never give yourself. The damage was done before you could move to stop it, your conscience clear—because the real you would never know. Your shadow knew it was giving you the chance to fail without ever questioning if you had done everything you could."

Heyer stared down at the face of Grant—found he held less judgment than he had a moment before. "The moment *Dams the Gate* died inside The Never, the war between man and Ferox became balanced on the edge of a precipice," he said. "I might have kept it from going over, but Rylee's appearance would have drawn even more attention to your gateway."

"We both made mistakes, couldn't see them because we were too close to the problem," Jonathan said, "I wish I could have told her—"

Heyer saw Jonathan stiffen, his eyes going to the floor as his thoughts began to race.

"She wanted me to finish what I was saying," he whispered. He dug a hand into his hair. "I think..." He paused in thought. "I don't have to let this happen—she doesn't have to die in here."

Unable to follow the sudden change in him, Heyer began to pull himself up off his knees. "Jonathan, what are you talking about?"

"I activated before Rylee. But, there was no shadow of her when I first came inside The Never. It was like she'd disappeared. There was a window, a little less than a minute before she followed me in."

Heyer could hear hope was growing in Jonathan's voice as he thought out loud.

"Dammit! I'm an idiot! She already knew I'd make it out. She..." Hope left his voice as Jonathan finished the thought. "She was so certain I wouldn't remember."

He did not like the sound of where Jonathan's thoughts seemed to be heading. Unfortunately, if Jonathan was considering what he feared, lying to him wasn't going to help.

"She'd have been mistaken. You should not experience any memory loss," Heyer said. "The gaps you and she experienced before were a result of your overlapping time within. Your memories stopped where hers began. That is no longer possible—the stone that was tied to Rylee is no longer in play. Her body has already gone to the Feroxian plane, and her device is... well, it is in a state of flux relative to us. If she was behind you in entering The Never, it will manifest inside Mr. Clean's armory when she follows. For now, though, only the stone from Grant's shadow remains. It is tied to you. Destroying it alone will leave your memory intact."

"Then there's still time. I can warn her before she follows me in," Jonathan said.

A moment of silence followed before the alien swallowed. "I'm sorry, Jonathan, but you aren't going to do that."

Jonathan must have heard the pity in Heyer's voice, because he finally turned away from the window to look at him. How much of the man in front of him remained Jonathan, Heyer had no means to tell, but one aspect endured unquestionably: the man looking back at Heyer suffered the bond's absence. Any hardness Heyer had seen from him fell away. He didn't want to be told that the void inside of him had returned to stay.

"What do you mean?" Jonathan choked out the question. "Why?"

Heyer shook his head and looked to the floor when he couldn't bear to watch the man's hope be denied. "What you are describing," he said. "Nevric referred to it as Proximity Overlap. She considered the danger of such a possibility in her records. Two individuals enter The Never, but at different moments in their natural dimension's timeline. This creates an opportunity where the individual who entered first, upon returning, could convey information about what took place inside to the individual who has not yet entered. Theoretically, that information could change the outcome inside. Could create a logical impossibility in time... a paradox."

"Yeah," Jonathan said. "That's the plan."

Heyer grimaced, drawing in his breath and trying to be careful of his words. "Jonathan, you cannot purposely set out to create a paradox. Putting the malleability of time to the test is blindly accepting the risk of consequences that could fall, quite literally, somewhere between all and nothing. You cannot consider such a gamble when everyone and everything might pay for it."

"I'm not sure we agree. We got Rylee killed, and I've got one chance to fix it. I'm not ignoring it."

The look on Jonathan's face, the quickness at which he defied Heyer's warning, gave the alien considerable pause. He began edging his way in between the portal stone in Grant's corpse and Jonathan, which, when Jonathan noticed it, only got him a look of incredulity. Heyer was in no shape to keep him from the stone if he couldn't talk Jonathan down from this ledge.

"Jonathan, you are upset, you aren't thinking clearly and you know it," Heyer said. "It's the severed bond causing you so much pain that you want to ignore anything and everything to make it stop. It's the same thing Rylee experienced. Right now, you are an addict looking for a fix."

"I'm upset…" Jonathan said in a whisper that seemed to slither its way out of his mouth.

Heyer regretted the word, seeing how it was offensively inadequate. "I'm sorry Jonathan, I'm not trying to trivialize..." The alien trailed off, fixing Jonathan with his eyes and sighing. "In the end, my forbidding you does not matter, Jonathan. I don't believe in paradox and neither did Nevric."

"What do you mean you don't *believe*?"

"Jonathan," Heyer said. "You said Rylee knew she had spoken to a future version of you. But, before she came to that conclusion, did she tell you, in any specific way, what you had said to her?"

Jonathan's eyes narrowed on him. "No," he said. "But, she was happy when she caught up to me. She said I got cut off, didn't finish what I was saying to her. Later, she said things to me, things she only said because she thought I wasn't going to reme..."

It hit him like an avalanche—one rock jarred loose, freeing the next, until everything started to fall. Heyer had learned a thousand times over just how infrequent were the moments in life when being proven right had brought him any joy. If he could have ever picked a moment to be wrong it was this one. Seeing Jonathan realize what he had been trying to tell him—he knew the moment of the man's disillusionment would be burned into his memory forever.

"Why would there be a future where I..." his voice failed, and slowly, he sat down on the floor.

"Because there was only ever one future, and you aren't going to change it," Heyer said. "You are going to sit here as long as you need. You can ponder it from every angle. And, you are going to see that there was never any winning today—but that there is one way to lose without losing everything."

Slowly, Heyer knelt down in front of where Jonathan sat.

"You make a change, and both of you survive, while Grant and Malkier die. The gates open within minutes of your return from The Never. The world is overrun by the Ferox before we can stop it—millions die. You make a change, and somehow Rylee survives, but you die. Whatever you did to hurt Malkier dies with you. War follows, but it is a war humanity cannot win, because though they may manage to take down some of the Ferox, they cannot stop my brother. Mankind's resistance is eventually overpowered, and humanity is enslaved for the Ferox—millions die.

"You make a change, and it plays out in the worst possible scenario: both of you die. All choice you ever had in the matter is lost; you no longer have any part in the future. All that you and Rylee survived up until now has been for nothing, and still—millions die."

Heyer looked away, and sighed.

"Or, you see that Rylee's sacrifice gave Mankind the one and only outcome where there is hope. You admit that changing it might lessen your pain only to inflict untold amounts of suffering on everyone you care about. That you would be attempting to save one life because you are unwilling to bear the consequences of having lost that life. You realize that Rylee made her choice, and she would still have to make that choice—that maybe it was kindness to let her believe you wouldn't remember.

"If you cannot change her fate, the only thing you have left to give her is a lie. You let her believe that she made her sacrifice without ever putting her death on your shoulders. That you would have protected her no matter what, just as she chose for you." Heyer looked at him, with as much kindness as he could. "I understand if, at this moment, you place it last amongst all you must consider. But the Jonathan I know—he wouldn't risk the unknown. He would listen to reason. He wouldn't purposely choose to create a paradox, potentially destroy all life, to save one. Jonathan, only an omniscient being could make that choice and call it moral. You and I, mere men, cannot."

A few moments passed in silence before Jonathan spoke.

"Old man, you're so quick, see it all from every angle," he said. "But if you are so damn smart…" He closed his eyes, seemed to shiver with anger. "Where was this cold, hard logic when your brother was bleeding in front of you? Why couldn't you see what you would have stopped then?"

Heyer's face soured, but he nodded. "I never claimed to be perfect, Jonathan," he said. "I've made mistakes that cannot be undone. Call me a hypocrite. Fine. But for a moment, imagine if you could have been there to tell me what would happen. Do you think that, after I killed my brother, you would be surprised to find I hated you for it?"

Jonathan looked at the stone, still glowing red, attached to the shadow's corpse, waiting for him to destroy it. "I need time to think," he said.

"I understand, but I don't believe you'll find any solution we—"

"No," Jonathan stopped him. "You've got so much advice, old man… tell me what you say to a person you're about to let die for you?"

Heyer looked away. "You know her better than anyone, Jonathan. What do you think she would have wanted to hear?"

"I got the memo, Tibbs," Rylee said as she turned away from Jonathan.

Leah watched him, but everything seemed to be moving too fast. He couldn't process how the scene he'd stepped into a few moments earlier had escalated to the point that Rylee wanted to walk out the door.

"I can't stay here, should have already left," she was saying.

Leah wasn't sure what she hoped for at this point. If Rylee left now, it was possible Jonathan would believe that she'd merely acted out of jealousy. The thing was, she didn't know if it would matter. The Cell, unable to learn anything from watching the two interact, would see an opportunity. Rylee wouldn't make it far before they took her into custody. After that, they would get information from her one way or another. As for Jonathan, she no longer knew if he would fare any differently.

"Might as well get on with it," Rylee said.

Jonathan stepped toward her. "I hadn't decided any—"

He hesitated, a look of disorientation like he'd forgotten where he was for a moment. His hand was still held out to reach for Rylee, and he stared at it a moment before his eyes shot up to her. Something came over him. He'd stopped mid-stride, his face no longer uncertain, but somehow—breaking. He was struggling not to let it happen, but a tear ran down his cheek. He exhaled as though he were in physical pain, each step toward her like he walked on broken ankles.

Rylee noticed the change as quickly as Leah, her anger from a moment earlier falling away when she saw the way he was looking at her. She had hardly finished turning around when his hands reached her.

"I was never going to tell you to leave, I never wanted it," Jonathan said. "And I don't give a damn what a tired old man forbids. He's afraid, and he runs! He'll keep us running with him until we don't have any will left to fight."

Leah didn't know what he was on about, but Rylee showed no confusion. If anything, she seemed to light up from the way he was looking at her—the way he spoke. When Jonathan pulled her close, he gripped her so tightly it must have hurt, and she didn't seem to want him to stop. Leah stared at his face over Rylee's shoulder. He closed his eyes—she knew it was only then that his words stopped being lies.

"I don't want to run—don't want his fear. I'm not gonna let us lose this war," Jonathan said. "We don't cease to exist, Rylee." His eyes opened, and his tears flowed unrestrained. "And I'm sorry I didn't—"

Leah gasped—he was suddenly standing alone, his arms wrapped around empty space. Leah felt her body go stiff with disbelief. It was the same as it had been with her brother.

Rylee—she was just gone.

When he fell on his knees, Leah couldn't speak or move. Jonathan's hands reached up—became claws digging into his skull. She heard his voice, low, angry, and pleading.

"You couldn't… just needed time… seconds… seconds… god dammit."

It hurt to hear. His words—his half-finished thoughts. She remembered how her own had come out broken by breaths she'd choked on instead of breathed—questions that she never fully finished asking, and had never known exactly who it was she expected to answer. Collin and Hayden looked on without understanding what they had seen. When Leah finally took a step toward him, she didn't know how much time she'd let pass—only that his roommates would have nothing to offer him. They were bystanders in a moment for which they had no basis to understand.

Leah whispered his name gently when she knelt beside him, and he reached out blindly toward the sound of her voice. She found herself grateful when he held onto her, when he let her pull his head against her shoulder. It wasn't until he did so that she realized how scared she'd been—how close she had been to Rylee telling him everything, to Jonathan suddenly seeing her as his enemy. She may have been hoping for too much. Perhaps she was just the only anchor he had in that moment. Perhaps he was reaching out for her because he was simply in no state to decide friend from foe.

When she spoke to him, each response he gave was slow, as though he were answering her from the other side of a gulf she couldn't cross.

"Jonathan, I want to help you," she said.

"You can't help me."

It hit her like cold water—Peter's words all over again.

"Tell me where she went?"

"Gone," he whispered.

"Gone? Gone where? How do we get her back?"

"We don't."

Leah's voice began to tremble. "Why?"

His head shook slowly against her, and his voice grew faint. "Leah, leave it alone."

Leah swallowed and pulled his head away from her shoulder. "Please, don't say that to me." Her eyes pleaded with his. "I need to know."

Jonathan looked at her as though he couldn't believe she was forcing him to say the words out loud. "She's dead, Leah."

Tears began to flow before she could speak. "No. I heard what you said to her. I saw you."

Jonathan didn't look at her, didn't speak.

Collin's voice seemed to come out from nowhere, reminding her they weren't alone. "Leah, come on, stop," he said. "Look at him, he's... a mess."

Leah had never stopped looking at him, hadn't blinked, and hardly registered his roommate asking her to stop. "I know when you're lying, Jonathan," she said. "I want to know where they are, and if they're dead, I want to know why."

Leah felt it, the moment something changed in him. She realized that the wrong word had come out of her mouth. She should have backed down—she'd pushed too hard because it all brought her back to Peter's last words. Jonathan's jaw clenched. He turned cold—looked at her with a hardness he'd never had for her on his face.

"They," Jonathan said to her.

The room fell silent as they stared at one another, but the quiet was short lived.

An unnatural light appeared over them, and an obscured shape dropped through a cloud of red and black. Leah lurched away as it hit the floor with a dull thud and rolled toward them—felt her back hitting the cabinets as she watched in stunned shock.

Jonathan had not moved as the shape came to a stop beside him. The cloud around it began to dissipate, and a man wearing all black became visible as the red and black surrounding him faded away into nothing. She saw his face, knew immediately that she was finally in the same room as the man she had been hunting all this time. His eyes were closed, his blond hair a disheveled mess, and—he was bleeding.

"You lost your hat," Jonathan whispered.

The Mark didn't move, seemed completely unconscious. Leah's gaze became desperate, looking past Jonathan to the closest vent where she knew a camera would be watching, her eyes screaming for The Cell to act before they lost this chance.

"Um… Frappuccino... acid…" Hayden mumbled.

The alien hadn't moved, and Jonathan's face began to falter the longer it went on. "Heyer?" he asked.

Leah couldn't tell if The Mark was even breathing. She suddenly found herself growing terrified. If Jonathan was wrong about Rylee and Peter, and The Mark was dead, any chance of finding out what had happened to her brother might be lost.

Jonathan reached for him, rolling him flat on to his back. "Don't even think about it…" she heard him whisper as he reached for the man's neck looking for a pulse. "Old man, if you die on me now…"

He must have found a pulse, because he closed his eyes and let out a small breath of relief before slapping the blond man across the face. When he got no response, he tried it again.

"Dammit!" Jonathan suddenly exclaimed, getting off his feet and rushing over to the counter top. He began rifling through the cigar box where he had always emptied his pockets, dumping the contents and staring in disbelief. Unable to find whatever it was he was looking for, he drove his fist down in frustration. The bang made Leah jump, finally giving her the wherewithal to move. She began to crawl toward the blond man, but froze when Jonathan suddenly spun. His eyes didn't go to her; they went to the same vent that she had looked at a moment earlier, with just as much desperation.

"Mr. Clean! What, are you taking a damn nap? I need a little help here!" he yelled.

The lights suddenly went out in the garage. Jonathan's breathing began to race as he looked around the room to each of their faces before focusing on Hayden.

"Hayden, I need you to get your car," he said.

"Wha... but—"

"Questions later."

"Jonathan, man, slow down—isn't that..." Collin said, looking at him dumbfounded. "The blond man, the hospital, the guy you said..."

"Hayden! Car keys!" Jonathan yelled. "Collin, you gotta help me. We've gotta move him..."

They all heard it coming—the sound of boots on pavement outside. The roommates looked at him with fear growing in their eyes as Jonathan stopped moving. He turned to Leah one last time, but the way he looked at her hurt. He was just so disappointed.

He exhaled, his shoulders dropped, his eyes closing as the sound of boots drew nearer. "Guys," he said. "Tell them whatever they want—they'll know if you try to lie."

"What is that supposed..." Collin didn't finish—the garage door shot up and shouts came at them.

"Down on the ground!" a man yelled. "Hands behind your back!"

The door to the house opened, followed shortly by the side door on the garage. Most of the men looked like SWAT, black fatigues and assault rifles. Some wore suits.

"Do it now!"

Leah obeyed, beginning to crawl forward.

There were so many guns aimed at him, but Jonathan—he just didn't look at them the way a man should. He wasn't afraid. He stood at the center of the garage, knowing he was trapped on all sides, and yet there was defiance lingering in his eyes while Leah and the roommates crawled on the ground to do as they were told.

"Get down on the ground now!"

She saw a chill run up his spine, his eyes narrowing as he looked to each man holding a weapon on him. Then, he seemed to do the math. Leah exhaled in relief as he slowly began to kneel and place his hands on his head. His face went blank as he stared down at the floor—he became a wall.

CHAPTER SEVENTY-TWO

THURSDAY| OCTOBER 14, 2005 | 8:30 AM | SEATTLE

THE TEAM WAS efficient. Zip ties went around each of their wrists, tying their hands behind their backs. Leah watched as both Collin and Hayden looked on with panic before black bags were placed over each of their heads. Four of the men wearing black fatigues approached, looking like pallbearers as they carried a black box only slightly wider than a casket. Leah recognized the exterior—the smooth surfaces were constructed from the same material she'd seen on the semi truck's trailer in The Cell's loading bay.

Men got Collin and Hayden on their feet, escorting them out of the garage toward the driveway. She never saw a bag go over Jonathan's face, but before Leah was blinded, she saw one of The Cell's men put a knee into his back to knock him to the floor. She felt men on each side, lifting her to stand and escorting her out to the driveway. They hadn't gone far before she heard a vehicle door open, and was told to step up.

She heard the door shut behind her before Rivers' voice instructed her to sit. Once she had, the bag came off. She was in the back compartment of an armored car. There were two benches running along each wall and three monitors showing various camera feeds from Jonathan's garage toward the front. After he cut her wrists free, Rivers sat on the bench opposite her while Olivia watched the proceedings from a porthole in the vehicle's door.

"You alright, Leah?" Rivers asked. "From what we saw, that got intense."

She blinked at him for a moment, having more trouble than usual processing everything so quickly. "How…? How did you get here so fast?" she asked.

"Dumb luck," Olivia said, not sounding very thrilled about it. "We began mobilizing as soon as your altercation with Ms. Silva started to turn to fisticuffs."

"Yeah, I'm sorry, that was a shit show," Leah said, shaking her head. "Rylee knew about the journal somehow. Wasn't a whole lot I could do to talk her down."

Rivers nodded. "That does explain why her behavior escalated so quickly," he said. "Honestly, we thought we'd have to detain her before she put you in the hospital. Had to hold off when Jonathan showed up. Decided not to interfere unless you signaled us. Then the roommates showed up, and Ms. Silva…" He shook his head. "Well, you were there."

"The Mark is secure," Olivia said. "Rivers, that truck and all this activity is a news report waiting to happen. I want the contents of Mr. Tibbs' cabinet confiscated and our team off the premises as soon as possible."

"On it." He nodded, opening the door to step out of the vehicle.

Olivia kept her eyes on the scene after he left, and Leah sat staring at the empty wall across from her in a daze. "What did you say to him, Leah?" she asked.

Leah didn't look at her, but she knew the tapes would show the truth. "I asked what happened to Rylee."

"And did he answer?

"He said she was gone."

"Is that all?"

"No, but I couldn't tell if he was..." Leah trailed off, then shook her head and looked back at the camera feeds. "Are we headed back to base? I need to speak with command immediately, and I need the..." Leah grimaced, trailing off in frustration. "We cut the power."

"Leah?" Olivia asked. "What's the problem?"

"I need the feeds. I need to see everything that happened."

Olivia gave a look of curiosity, but nodded. "Not a problem." She drew a radio off her belt to contact Rivers. "Rivers, cutting the power took the camera feeds off the network while we were acquiring The Mark. They're equipped with short term memory and batteries for this contingency. Get one of the techs to download the data before you leave."

"Confirmed," Rivers replied.

Leah bit her lip and nodded. "Thank you."

"You can thank me by telling me what it is you're looking for," Olivia replied.

"I'm not sure," she said. "A lot of what just happened doesn't feel right to me."

Olivia studied her a moment, but accepted the answer.

"What happens now?" Leah asked.

"You, Jonathan, his roommates, and The Mark will be transferred to a holding facility with the proper resources. Command will await you there."

"What about Paige and Evelyn Tibbs?"

"The team watching the residence will remain in operation at a reduced capacity to make sure they are watched in the event they need to be contained."

Leah nodded, and finally, she closed her eyes and breathed, no longer caring if Olivia knew that she had been rattled by all that had gone down. She heard the porthole slide shut, and a moment later, felt a thin folder drop into her lap.

Leah opened her eyes, saw Olivia watching her, and looked down at the folder. "What's this?" she asked.

"We both knew you were withholding information from me," Olivia replied. "Command found my suspicions warranted investigation, but would not agree to anything as *physically* invasive as a blood or urine test on the grounds of keeping your identity need-to-know. They did not, however, have any issue with less aggressive means."

Olivia took a seat on the bench opposite her

"I never doubted you were clever—and you wouldn't be here if you couldn't keep a secret. I knew that if you were hiding something, that you were doing it right in front of our cameras. You knew we didn't watch you every second of everyday, and you could easily avoid a paper trail of any purchase by using cash."

Leah sighed, almost certain Olivia had practiced this speech in a mirror. For the time being, she played along, frowning as she flipped open the folder. There were two separate lab reports. Most of what she saw was Greek to her, but Leah was familiar enough with the term "mass spectrometry" to know that Olivia's lab had been identifying the chemical makeup of some unidentified samples. Each report had the common names of their findings listed and highlighted: doxylamine and folic acid.

"I don't think you will be shocked to hear that these samples came from bottles in your kitchen cabinet that were marked as far less telling items. Now, they're both over the counter drugs—so here is my guess. You started feeling sick a few weeks before I got suspicious of your behavior. You're late, so you know what it means. You go shopping, buy groceries with your debit card, then these two items with cash," Olivia said. "Did I miss anything?"

"Never got morning sickness—doxylamine was a precaution," Leah said, shutting the folder and looking at Olivia with a frankness in her confusion. "But what is going on here with the theatrics?"

Olivia tilted her head, despite the woman's emotionless facade, Leah could tell she'd been expecting a far less casual reaction than she was getting. "You've just admitted to withholding pertinent information regarding an operation involving national security. Carrying the child of the man you were investigating is a direct conflict of interest. I would think the repercussions of this would have dawned on you," she said.

Leah stared back at her with growing incredulity. "Yeah," she said. "They dawned on me twenty minutes ago when I told Rylee I was pregnant in front of every camera in the garage. It's why she didn't deck me the second time."

Olivia looked away, her fingers tapping against the bench in thought. She looked back to Leah once more as though studying her to be sure. Then she stood and paced. "Well, that does confirm a very worrisome suspicion," she said. "For the last few days, Rivers has reported multiple instances were Rylee and Jonathan's conversations didn't seem to fit their body language. This is the first instance where the phenomenon occurred with you present to confirm what was actually said."

Olivia stopped pacing after she finished, her back still to Leah. She continued:

"I appreciate your honesty, but unfortunately, this does not change the fact that I will have to report your omission to the proper channels. I will not take responsibility for your actions, given you are a consultant I never requested on my team."

Leah folded her arms across her chest, shaking her head. "Olivia, I get it, you're covering your ass, protecting your career. But let me ask you," she said, holding the folder up, "does anyone other than our commanding officer know about this?"

Olivia turned slowly. "Why would that be relevant?"

"Trust me," Leah said. "You won't be doing your career any favors by making this known. For your own good, let command decide what is going to be done with me."

Olivia's eyes narrowed on her. "You just told me you were willing to let the entire Cell know, thought we all saw it on the cameras," she said. "You weren't concerned with the rest of The Cell being aware."

Leah shook her head. "No, I stayed on point. When confronted with a hostile subject who was going to blow my cover, I told a *lie* in order to sway her suspicions," she said. "No one has to know it wasn't a lie for now. I got the idea from you confronting me about it—at least, that was the story I planned on telling you before you went snooping through my pantry."

Olivia turned and considered her. "You mean to tell me you planned all that in the time between two punches to the face?"

Leah shook her head. "No, I told Rylee the truth because I knew it would make her reconsider. The rest I'm making up as I go."

Olivia took the warning seriously, though her expression never showed concern precisely. Instead, she was quiet in her thoughts until long after the truck pulled away. Leah was thankful for the short pause. All she wanted to do was lie down on the bench and let the stresses of the last half hour drain out of her, but she opted to lean back against the truck and stare at the wall.

When Olivia finally sat back down in front of her, she crossed her legs, pursed her lips, and sighed. "Leah, I am going to ask you something. You do not have to answer, but you have my word that if you do, whatever is said will remain in my confidence."

Leah kept looking at the wall, but she replied, "Well, let's hear it."

"A woman generally doesn't take folic acid supplements unless she plans to carry a pregnancy to term."

Leah swallowed, and closed her eyes. Then she decided she was going to lie down after all. "I don't know yet," she said.

"Well, good thing you needed a ride," Evelyn said. "GPS is on the fritz. I don't know how to get anywhere in this city."

Paige had been quiet for the most part as Evelyn drove them home. She looked up now and saw the display on the car's dash blinking an error message: *Satellite not found.*

"Oh," she said. "Take a right at the next light."

When Paige had called her earlier that morning, they had both thought it best not to compare notes over the phone. Given they had little idea if anywhere was actually safe, they did the best they could. Paige had the idea of meeting in one of the study rooms set aside for students on the upper floors of Odegaard Library on the University campus. Evelyn had agreed; it seemed like as good a place as any. They would be alone, surrounded by brick walls, and the only door into the room had a window that let them see if anyone was approaching.

Evelyn had been later than they had agreed. After hitting morning traffic, trying to find parking, and getting lost on the campus, she finally had to get directions from a student. Eventually, she found her way to the room Paige had specified.

Evelyn listened as she recounted what she'd found out after trying to get in contact with Grant Morgan. The man's sudden abandonment of his home played into their suspicions. Paige planned to follow up, but both feared she wasn't going to find any trace of him at this point. When it was Evelyn's turn, she explained that her son's behavior had drawn the line only at explicitly stating that her suspicions had been right. Before Evelyn went on, she told Paige that she feared for her safety, didn't want her to put herself in any danger. Paige had politely told her to go to hell, and Evelyn had nearly hugged her for it.

She told Paige about her overnight road trip to Portland to recover a footlocker belonging to Jonathan's father that she hadn't seen in ten years and how her son had refused to open the box with her in the room. By now, they knew Jonathan would have removed anything he hadn't wanted them to see, but it was still their next best lead. So they had headed home, but agreed not to talk about what they were up to once they left the library.

When Paige's directions led them to their first detour, a street temporarily blocked off, neither had thought much of it. When they came to the third, they started to notice that it seemed to be their street itself that was completely blocked off to traffic. The fourth time they were forced to stop, Evelyn pulled over. She looked at Paige and saw the same concern growing in her eyes. Eventually, a strange parade of vehicles approached the detour: three black SUVs, two armored cars, and a semi-truck carrying a wide load and covered with tarps.

"What do we do?" Paige whispered.

"I'm gonna follow them—you get out," Evelyn said.

"I'm staying."

Evelyn shook her head. "You run back to the house. Call me and let me know what's going on there. If everything is fine, then maybe this has nothing to do with anything."

Paige clearly didn't like the idea of splitting up, but Evelyn had a point. She sighed, nodded, and jumped out onto the sidewalk. Evelyn pulled back into the street and followed the last SUV. She didn't get far—within a matter of minutes, she turned a corner to find the street blocked off again. She tried not to panic. She didn't know her way around but could tell that the cars had been headed for the freeway. She did her best to find another route, but by the time she found her way to an on ramp, she didn't see the vehicles, didn't know if they had gone north or south. She pulled over, and Paige called.

"No one's here," Paige said. "Leah and Jack are gone, too. The neighbors are all standing in their driveways. I'm gonna go talk to them, see what's going on. Where are you?"

"I couldn't keep track of them," Evelyn whispered, her voice starting to shake.

She sat in her car for a long while, unsure what to do. Eventually, she turned the car around and went back to the house. Paige told her what the neighbors had said. That they had been told to stay in their homes, but had watched from the windows. They'd all seen men that looked like a SWAT team carrying guns—that it had all happened in a matter of minutes. Paige and Evelyn started calling everyone, but each phone went to voicemail. They found Hayden's ringing in his room.

They found the footlocker, the picture of Evelyn and Jonathan in the hospital, the broken lock. Evelyn had just started dumping out the box's contents when Paige walked into the garage, holding a bag from Mr. Fletcher's hardware store. She said she'd found it under the cargo net on Jonathan's motorcycle. When they found the firearms, they knew why he had gone to replace the lock, but didn't find anything useful.

Unsure what else to do, they waited by the phone, expecting a call. They figured that someone would contact them, at least tell them that their loved ones had been taken into custody—something. They turned on the news, but all that was being covered was a story about GPS satellites having been temporarily out of service all over the state. Later on in the evening, that story took a back seat to some mystery around a building in Pioneer Square. Nothing about what had happened at their home.

When Evelyn was far beyond panicking, she started growing angry. "I'm calling the police, the news, the governor's office… every damn person who will listen," she said. "They can't just take people from their homes!"

Paige stopped her before she picked up the phone. She exhaled, looked sickened by what she was about to say. "There is someone I can call," she said. "He might be able to help."

"Who?" Evelyn asked, wondering why the girl had waited this long to say anything.

"Evelyn," Paige said. "If we're going to discuss this, we should do it somewhere else."

CHAPTER SEVENTY-THREE

THURSDAY| OCTOBER 14, 2005 | 4:50 PM | TEXAS

AS THE BUSINESS day drew to an end, Anthony Hoult stood at a window, looking down on the city of Dallas from the top floor of a skyscraper. Few were aware he owned the building—on paper, it appeared to belong to a collection of vested parties, all of which led back to Anthony if one was willing to shuffle through a bureaucratic nightmare of legal documents to find out. Most of the building's floors were rented out to various startup companies, though, few of which he had anything to do with. Anthony had controlling interest in a number of companies in a wide range of industries. Most of them were managed by appointed CEOs with the proper backgrounds. The exceptions—the companies he ran directly—were those involved in R&D.

Anthony wasn't young, but he wasn't old either. He was fit, more so than most realized due to only ever seeing him in business attire. This morning, he'd worn a custom-made suit to the office—he referred to it as *the other-other gray one.*

His office was large and modern, but he had little to do with it. His assistant, Sydney, had brought him a concept folder from an interior design firm and Anthony had picked one the way most picked a haircut. Skylights in the roof brightened the room during the day, but recessed lighting in the ceiling was keeping him from standing in the dark now.

The floors were white marble squares. The walls, those that weren't floor to ceiling windows, were covered in some type of plastic, textured paneling—if there was a word to describe them, Anthony didn't know it.

There was a conference table and two white couches for face-to-face meetings. His desk was a fancy table with a fancy chair. The only thing about the office he had requested were the hidden flat screen monitors that flipped out of the walls at the touch of a remote. Anthony hadn't felt very original having them installed, but had gotten a small amount of pleasure checking off a bucket list item he'd had wanted since childhood.

When Anthony had ended his last conference call, his assistant assured him that there were no pressing matters that could not wait until morning. Now, his jacket was off and thrown over his chair, his tie and top button were loose, and he was in the middle of rolling up his sleeves when Sydney's voice buzzed in from the intercom on his desk.

"Tony?" she asked. "Good time to drop whatever you're doing?"

"Sydney," he said, shaking his head as he finished rolling his sleeves. "Go home already. I promise the world won't end if you get out of here on time for once."

"Sorry, it's just—" Sydney paused. "Well... it's ringing."

Slowly, Anthony turned away from the window and stared at the intercom. He went quiet, his face growing serious with concern—but not panicking.

"Sir? That line you had put in a few years ago? The one you said would mean I interrupt you no matter what you're doing and start clearing your schedule—Tony?"

He blinked when she said his name again, pulled out of his thoughts. "Thank you, Sydney, please send the call over to the conference screen."

"Done," she replied. "And in regards to your schedule?"

"Clear it."

"How far out?"

"Until I know otherwise," he said. "Indefinitely."

In the brief silence that followed, he could practically hear Sydney's eyes bulging over the intercom. "I'll get on it," she finally said. "What do you want me to tell people?"

"Family emergency," Tony said, reaching for the remote to flip his conference screen out of the wall.

"Psh, you don't have any family."

"Improvise," he replied, ending the conversation as the conference screen illuminated.

A familiar cartoon visage stared back at him.

"Good evening, Mr. Clean," Tony said, his eyes narrowing slightly. He'd been expecting Heyer, though the alien usually just appeared when he needed a report. However, it wasn't the first time he'd had to communicate with the alien's computer.

"Hello, Tony," Mr. Clean replied. "You look well."

"Thank you, Mr. Clean, but if you are contacting me on this line, I think it best we dispense with the pleasantries. Has it begun? Are we at war?"

"At the moment, this remains uncertain," Mr. Clean said. "However, recent events lead me to believe we should assume the worst is drawing near."

"What's happened?"

"Have you seen any news broadcasts coming out of Washington State in the last few hours?"

"No. What did I miss?"

The display image split, Mr. Clean's face now only taking up one half of the screen while the other was filled with a reporter smiling into the camera as she stood in front of a small crowd gathered on a sidewalk.

"As you can see, local Seattle residents from the Pioneer Square neighborhood are looking up and scratching their heads this evening. So, what's the big mystery? Well, if you happened to be walking by this street corner yesterday, you would have been passing a building three stories taller than it is now. That's right—in the last few hours, this historical building... shrunk. Civilians who were walking by when the phenomenon is said to have occurred claim they heard strange noises. One man described the sound 'like the cracking of glacial ice as it melts, coming from the roof tops.' Shortly after, the entire building shook and small chips of brick began to fall. When folks looked up, the building was as you see it now.

"Everyone I've spoken to on the street tonight has their own theory, some

claiming it's a conspiracy, but most believe it to be a hoax. The investigation is only getting started but City officials have stated that they've been unable to contact the building's owner..."

"You moved yourself?" Tony asked, speaking over the news cast.

"Correct," Mr. Clean said as he cut the news feed.

"Then where are you now?"

"Currently, I'm in stationary orbit over the continental U.S. My emergency protocols were triggered today when our top three assets were compromised. Which, for the time being, puts you in command until those assets can be reacquired."

"Mr. Clean, I need you to back up here. Three assets?" Tony paused. "Heyer, Jonathan—who was the third?"

"Rylee Silva was considered our third highest priority," Mr. Clean replied.

"Okay, but Silva is on the other side of the continent..." Anthony trailed off, his face growing grim. "Wait, you said was?"

"Unfortunately, earlier today, her dormant implant manifested inside the armory," Mr. Clean said. "She perished within The Never."

Eventually, Mr. Clean started from the beginning in order to bring Anthony up to speed on what details he could. Nearly an hour had gone by before he had any idea how such a catastrophe had been put in motion.

"You said another dormant device arrived at the same time as Rylee's," Anthony said. "Who did it belong to?"

"That remains unknown. The only compatible male Heyer and I knew of was a Grant Morgan. However, the device was never activated in him. Heyer didn't even have the dormant implant on Earth. How it came to manifest inside the armory alongside Rylee's is a matter of sweeping conjecture at the present moment."

Anthony nodded. "How did The Cell capture Heyer in the first place? If he was in danger, why didn't you blink him to safety?"

"I only became aware that Heyer had returned from the Feroxian Plane when he showed up on The Cell's video feeds. Something was wrong with his device—he was unconscious and I could not get a safe read out on his location. Normally, this wouldn't have been an obstacle—I am able to transport matter as long as I can get an accurate location. However, at some point, The Cell must have become aware of my use of human GPS satellites as a backup system. Within seconds of Heyer's appearance on the feed, they killed power to the entire block and hit some type of kill switch on the GPS systems for the entire state. The timing was too suspect—this was a preconceived plan to acquire him."

"If the GPS satellites are back up, what's stopping you now?" Anthony asked.

Mr. Clean's face was replaced by overhead images taken from a satellite. Each showed an airstrip where a semi-truck carrying a very unconventional trailer was in various stages of being unloaded from a military transport aircraft.

"These images were taken over Joint Base Lewis-McChord two days ago. A similar vehicle was close to Jonathan's residence around the time they were taken into custody. The vehicle in question was covered, likely to reduce civilian interest, but it matches the dimensions of these images from over the base. I am unable to get a read on anything inside that outer shell. Whatever this is, it is not on file with any patent office," Mr. Clean said.

Anthony sighed. "Yeah, it wouldn't be. If they have him in there, he might as well be in the center of a black hole."

"You recognize this?"

"Not exactly. I've seen schematics for a similar design that one of my smaller divisions has in early stage development. I'll be telling them to drop the project, because if The Cell has access to a fully functional model then I'm guessing the Department of Defense has another developer on the pay roll that is years ahead of us."

"What's the application?" Mr. Clean asked.

"The idea started with insulating electronics from EMP blasts. Protecting transport vehicles—keeping planes from falling out of the sky if they were caught in a pulse. Once advanced enough for mass production, it would have been used to safeguard infrastructure. The researchers I'm funding thought they could take it further—a lot further," Anthony said. "The short version is, if Heyer is in there, we're gonna have to walk in and get him."

Anthony studied the images a moment longer before his expression blackened, and he rubbed his fingertips against his forehead.

"You know, when Heyer and I discussed the contingency plan for recovering him if he was ever captured, I looked at the tech at his disposal and told him that he was paranoid." He shook his head. "He said, '*Every strength has its weaknesses.*' I guess we're lucky he was never so confident."

Mr. Clean watched him, but didn't reply, and Anthony realized the AI was either at a loss to see the sad humor he was expressing or simply had nothing to add.

"What about our fearless leader?" Anthony asked. "If the GPS satellites are back up, you should be able to get a lock on Jonathan."

"Unfortunately, no, but now that I know why Heyer is out of reach, there is both good news and bad news."

"Well, let's hear it."

"In order to manipulate the intel The Cell was getting from their cameras, Jonathan carried a piece of me into the residence. This allowed for me to link into their hub directly. When I found I was temporarily unable to pull Heyer to safety, I commanded that piece to abandon the hub and attach itself to Jonathan before he was taken into custody. I was able to track where that piece was taken," Mr. Clean said. "That's the good news."

"Alright, then what's the bad?" Anthony asked.

"The signal from Jonathan went dead shortly after they took him into a building on the same base where the truck was delivered. Given what you've told me about said truck, they must now have him in a chamber insulated with the same type of technology."

"Alright, so we know where they're holding him for the time being," Anthony said. "Assuming Heyer is in the same building, we need to extract both of them at the same time."

"Which brings us back to the contingency plan—we are going to have to adapt."

"Right. The Washington location was always a priority—I'll see to it that the prototypes we've been developing are moved there without the authorities asking questions. After that is in motion, I'll get the extraction team headed there. I'll be on a flight this evening and will meet you at the site when we are ready."

"No need to use traditional transportation—we need to move quickly. Contact me when everything is in order and I will transfer you and the team to the site. If this cannot be accomplished quietly, we may have to consider going to plan B," Mr. Clean said.

Anthony frowned. "I wasn't aware of a plan B."

"There wasn't one, but Jonathan made a remark when we last spoke—he never intended it to be taken seriously," Mr. Clean replied. "If we run out of time, you have the authority. You could allow me to... take a *Voltron*-like approach."

Anthony raised an eyebrow. "Yeah, let's try and avoid plan B."

DEAR READER

I am an independent author and word of mouth is the most powerful form of marketing at my disposal. If you enjoyed The Never Paradox, and know others would want to follow The Chronicles of Jonathan Tibbs, please tell your friends. Spread the word via Twitter, Facebook, Instagram, or any other social media at your disposal. Also, the more reviews posted to Amazon and Goodreads, the more likely it is for future readers to find their way to this and other works. Even a few short words are greatly appreciated.

ABOUT THE AUTHOR

T. Ellery Hodges lives with his wife and three sons in Seattle, Washington. He is currently hard at work on the finale of The Chronicles of Jonathan Tibbs. If you'd like to know more about T. Ellery, visit his blog at www.telleryhodges.com, follow him on twitter @telleryhodges, or like The Never Hero page on Facebook! If you prefer email, he'd love to hear from you at telleryhodges@gmail.com.

Manufactured by Amazon.ca
Acheson, AB